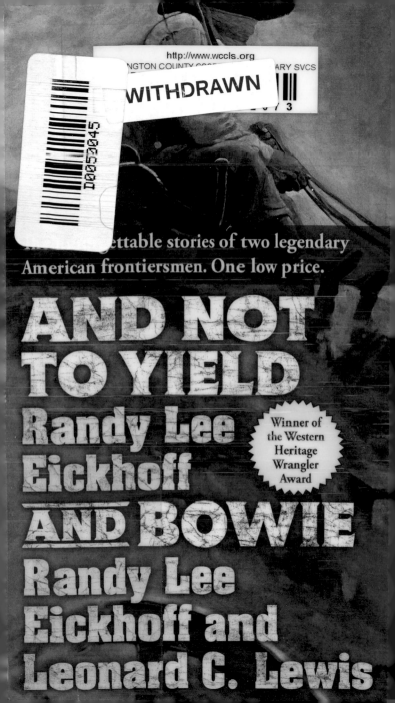

...ettable stories of two legendary American frontiersmen. One low price.

AND NOT TO YIELD

Randy Lee Eickhoff

Winner of the Western Heritage Wrangler Award

AND BOWIE

Randy Lee Eickhoff and Leonard C. Lewis

$9.99
($13.99 CAN)

US $9.99 / CAN $13.99

ISBN 978-0-7653-8363-1

9 780765 383631

5 0 9 9 9

Praise for *And Not to Yield*

"An epic novel of an epic life . . . Robust, rich, and vigorous, *And Not to Yield* is a thorough pleasure."
—Ralph Peters, *New York Times* bestselling author
of *Valley of the Shadow*

"A good portrait of an age and a place as well as of a man, briskly narrated and engaging." —*Kirkus Reviews*

"[A] majestic epic." —Richard S. Wheeler,
Spur Award–winning author of *Anything Goes*

Praise for *Bowie*

"[A] masterful, realistic retelling of the Jim Bowie legend... grand and compelling." —*Kirkus Reviews*

"A magnificent achievement of fact supporting fiction to re-create a story in words that cannot fail to bring tears to the eyes and a lump to the throat . . . A stunning novel."
—*Amarillo Globe-News*

"An interesting blend of fact, lore, and legend combined to create a verbal picture of Bowie as he might have been, perhaps even as he was, told by those who knew him."
—*Ocala Star-Banner*

"The authors cleverly show both sides of Jim Bowie, the hero and the villain, certainly no common man and no saint, bu................ *rs Weekly*

Books By Randy Lee Eickhoff

NOVELS

The Fourth Horseman

Bowie (with Leonard C. Lewis)

A Hand to Execute

The Gombeen Man

Fallon's Wake

Return to Ithaca

Then Came Christmas

And Not to Yield

THE ULSTER CYCLE

The Raid

The Feast

The Sorrows

The Destruction of the Inn

He Stands Alone

The Red Branch Tales

*The Odyssey: A Modern Translation of
Homer's Classic Tale*

NONFICTION

Exiled

AND NOT to YIELD

Randy Lee Eickhoff

| AND |

BOWIE

Randy Lee Eickhoff and Leonard C. Lewis

FORGE®

A Tom Doherty Associates Book / New York

AND NOT TO YIELD AND BOWIE

A Forge Book
Published by Tom Doherty Associates, LLC
175 Fifth Avenue
New York, NY 10010

www.tor-forge.com

33614057662073

Forge® is a registered trademark of Tom Doherty Associates, LLC.

ISBN 978-0-7653-8363-1

Our books may be purchased in bulk for promotional, educational, or business use. Please contact your local bookseller or the Macmillan Corporate and Premium Sales Department at 1-800-221-7945, extension 5442, or by e-mail at MacmillanSpecialMarkets@macmillan.com.

First Edition: July 2016

Printed in the United States of America

0 9 8 7 6 5 4 3 2 1

Contents

AND NOT to YIELD

for Raelene

Acknowledgments

I would like to thank the Deadwood Public Library, for helping with research for this book, and Leon Metz, who generously gave me free access to his wonderful library.

I owe a great debt to Barbara Wild, the copy editor, whose careful work on the manuscript kept many errors from the reader.

Sing to me, Calliope, Muse of Epic Poetry, and tell me the story of the man whose own wisdom and trickery wounded him and caused him to languish far from the loving arms of his wife. Sing to me the story of that wanderer who sacked Troy and sundered her heaven-built wall only to be forced to roam uncharted seas and visit strange lands where he faced many trials. Sing to me his adventures among nations of all manners, minds, and fashions. Sing to me of a man, abandoned by the gods . . .

—Homer's *Odyssey*
translated by Randy Lee Eickhoff

S'il faut choisir un crucifié, la foule sauve toujours Barabbas.
If it has to choose who is to be crucified,
the crowd will always save Barabbas.

—Jean Cocteau
Le Rappel à l'ordre

More are men's ends marked than their lives before:
The setting sun, and music at the close,
As the last taste of sweets, is sweetest last,
Writ in remembrance more than things long past.

—*Richard II* II.i.11–14

A brittle glory shineth in this face:
As brittle as the glory is the face.

—*Richard II* IV.i.287–288

PART ONE

Youth

Of arms and the man I sing

CHAPTER 1

"*ONCE UPON a time a long, long time ago, a good knight loped gently over the plain on his faithful horse, and this good knight felt badly in his heart because he had a terrible deed to face. . . .*"

Papa told me that story. I was five. He told me many stories. His face always smiled. His face was always tired.

The knight came over the green fields. He went into a forest. Everything was dark and scary. He was looking for the Green Knight. The Green Knight had let him chop off his head. It rolled on the floor of King Arthur's castle like a bright green and hairy ball. But the Green Knight picked up his head. He got on his green horse.

"*'I'll be waiting for you to come to me in a year and a day for your return blow,' the Green Knight said, and he galloped away. Now Sir Gawain, for that was the good knight's name, had to let the Green Knight chop his head off. . . .*"

Here is the house. It is white and red. Papa says red is more dura . . . dura . . . lasts longer.

The trees in the grove are green and brown.

The road is dusty. When the buggies and wagons go by, the dust hangs in the air. I cough.

Papa and Mama and me and Oliver and Lorenzo and Horace live there. There was another Lorenzo. He died. Papa said that the name hadn't been used up. That's why Lorenzo is Lorenzo.

Rock of ages, cleft for me;
Let me hide, myself in thee.

He sang me to sleep with that song.

"Sleep time, little Jim," he said. "Close your eyes. Nod your little head."

And I pretended to close my eyes.

Then I came awake.

Mama made biscuits for breakfast. I poured syrup on them. The syrup came from Papa's store on the first floor of the Green Mountain House. I used to watch the men play dominoes. They sat by the stove in the winter and they played dominoes.

I liked the store.

Then Papa got sick and lost it.

We went on a trip and Papa got a farm in a bunch of trees and Lorenzo teased me and hid among them and I couldn't find him and then Celinda was born and Lydia was born and

Lor, Lor, my pretty little Pink,
Lor, Lor I say,

We had a hidden cellar where Negroes used to hide when the bad men came looking for them. It was filled with hay so they could sleep on it.

"Your Uncle Aaron was at Bunker Hill when the British attacked. And there they stood, brave men holding their fire until Israel Putnam shouted out, 'Don't fire until you see the whites of their eyes!' And Aaron held his fire, kneeling there as the Redcoats marched up the hill . . ."

Old Dan Tucker was a fine ol' man,
Washed his face in a frying pan,
Combed his hair with a wagon wheel,
Died with a toothache in his heel.

CHAPTER 2

WE WERE hiding in the branches of the trees near the dirt road leading down to Homer. Horace and me. We had been there since noon. Mr. Dewey came by in his wagon. Horace shot one of the horses in the butt with his slingshot. He hit that gray mare solid with a buckeye. She gave this high whinny and took off like Ma's cat the day she stumbled and poured hot water over it. We laughed at Old Man Dewey. He sat up there on his buckboard seat. He pulled back on the reins for all he was worth and shouted, "Whoa! Consarn you! Whoa!" And other words that we didn't expect a deacon to be shouting. That buckboard went racing lickety-split down the road. Horace and I near fell out of the tree, laughing as we did at the way Old Man Dewey bounced around in his seat.

"Jim!"

"Uh-oh," Horace said. He shoved his slingshot in my hands, shinnied down that chestnut tree, and hightailed it toward the barn as fast as he could run, which was pretty fast, 'cause he always won the races at school when Mr. Deasy made us run them on the last day of school when our parents would come to see what we had learned and—

"James Butler Hickok!"

I peeked out from the branches and saw Pa coming hard down the lane from the house toward the road. I sighed, wedged Horace's slingshot between two branches, and climbed down.

"Yes, Pa?" I asked as he came up.

His eyes were wrathy and he had tiny white lines around his mouth. His forehead shone with sweat. His butternut shirt had dark sweat patches under his arms and on his chest. He held on to the tree for a moment, breathing deeply.

"You all right, Pa?" I asked. He had been sickly again lately and Oliver and Lorenzo were doing most of the farm work.

Pa gulped for air and waved his hand at me. I stood by quietly. The sun was warm on my shoulders and meadowlarks were singing in the field over the split-rail fence behind me. I watched a gray squirrel scamper across the ground with a buckeye in its mouth. It saw me and raced up the tree Pa was leaning against.

"Did . . . you shoot . . . Mr. Dewey's horse . . . with a slingshot?"

I frowned. "No, sir," I said. I didn't add that it was Horace who shot the horse. I didn't want to wake snakes. Horace was almost three years older than me and could hit like a mule could kick. I was no fool.

Pa stared hard at me for a second. "Mr. Dewey says he saw you in the tree just after his horse was hit. He was almost thrown from his wagon. Now, why would he invent a story like that, Jim?"

"I don't know, sir," I said. I tried to look away from Pa. But his eyes pulled mine back like magnets did nails.

He nodded slowly. "All right, Jim. I believe you." And just at that moment, that damn squirrel bounced on the branch holding Horace's slingshot and it fell like a divining rod right at Pa's feet.

He looked down at it a moment. Then he looked back at me. I could see the disappointment in his eyes.

"Pa—"

He turned and walked away from me. He trudged down the dusty lane toward the house, his shoulders bowed as if he carried the whole world upon them. I sighed and picked up the slingshot. I looked up at the barn and saw Horace peeking out the door, laughing. I shook my head and grabbed the slingshot by the Y and held it up so he could watch while I pulled the two arms apart.

"Hey!" he shouted, and came running down toward me. His face looked grim. I threw the slingshot in the middle of the road and took off running for the grove. I glanced once over my shoulder. I saw his grim face. I ran faster into the shade of the grove. I ran toward the middle, then hid behind a tree, lying flat on the ground, watching.

Horace ran into the small clearing, then paused, trotting uncertainly around in a circle. But he couldn't find me. He stopped and put his hands on his hips, yelling, "All right, Jim! I know you're around here! You might as well come out and take your lickin', 'cause when I find you I'm gonna beat the crap outta you!"

He had big hands. I crept backward until I was another tree line back. Then I got to my feet and slipped back out of the grove. I ran back to the house. I went into the house. My shoes rattled on the puncheon floor. Ma was making molasses cookies.

"Can I have one?" I asked.

Ma gave me a hard look. "What's this I hear about you shooting horses with your slingshot?"

I sighed and shook my head. "Didn't," I mumbled. But I knew she wouldn't believe me, either. She was nice, but she had a hard look in her eyes that hurt when she turned it on you.

"Then who did?"

I looked up at her. Her eyes were looking hard at me and I looked away and hoped she couldn't see Horace at the back of my mind.

"Don't know," I mumbled again.

She sighed. "James Butler Hickok, you stand up straight now. Hear?"

I straightened my shoulders and looked up at her hairline.

"Now, who shot Mr. Dewey's horse?"

I swallowed and shook my head.

"It wasn't you, was it?"

I shook my head again.

She sighed again. "I didn't think so. It was Horace, wasn't it?"

I shrugged.

"All right." I looked at her eyes. They were softer now. A tiny smile hovered around her lips. She nodded at the table. "You can have one cookie. *One!*" she emphasized as I reached for it. I studied them carefully, then picked the biggest one I could find.

"Thanks, Ma!" I shouted, and ran back outside.

Right into Horace.

"So. You squealed on me, didja?" he snarled. He looked at the cookie in my hand. "Gimme that!"

He snatched it from me.

"Give it back!" I said hotly.

He sneered and took a bite. "What you gonna do about it?"

"I'll . . . I'll—"

"You won't do nothing," he scoffed. He crammed the rest of the cookie in his mouth.

A sudden madness came down upon me. I slugged him in the stomach. A look of surprise came over his face as the breath *whooshed!* from him in a mouthful of cookie crumbs. He bent forward at the waist, trying to suck air back in. He got cookie crumbs as well and gagged. I hauled off and smacked him again on the nose. Blood smeared itself over his cheek. Tears came to his eyes. I took a deep breath and came into him, windmilling my arms, not paying attention to where my fists landed, just feeling a savage pleasure when they did.

"Momma! Momma!" he cried. He tried to push me away. But it was useless. A strange happiness came over me. His hand grabbed my face. I bit his thumb. He howled.

Something grabbed me from behind. I turned and started hitting again. Pa stepped back in surprise. His boot caught the threshold and he stumbled backward and sat down hard on the floor. *Whomp!* He stared, startled, at me.

I was breathing hard and turned back to Horace, but he was down on all fours in the dirt, bawling, blood spotting the dirt beneath him.

"What in the world?"

I looked back over my shoulder at Ma standing in the doorway, looking from Pa to Horace to me and back to Pa.

"He—" I started to say, then clamped my mouth tight.

Ma looked down and saw the half-chewed cookie in the dust and nodded slowly. "Horace, you should be ashamed of yourself!"

He lifted a tearstained face. "He hit me when I wasn't looking!" he cried. "Unfair!"

"You were too looking!" I said hotly.

"Liar! I wasn't!"

"Well, you're looking now!" I shouted, and stepped forward and smacked him again as he started standing. He fell backward. I jumped on top of him and began to pummel him as hard as I could hit.

"That's enough, boys!" Ma said.

I looked up at her just as Pa pulled himself up off the floor and came out. His hand grabbed the back of my collar and pulled me off Horace. I stumbled, trying to get my balance, when Pa released me, and fell into the dirt. I looked up at him. His face was furious. Behind his head, a gray-white cloud floated over the sun. I watched a hawk swing low under the cloud and fold its wings as it dived down toward the field.

"Go to your room!" Pa said.

I rose, dusted my pants off, and walked into the house to my room. I closed the door and sat on my bed. Dimly I

heard Pa giving Horace a tongue-lashing and knew I would
be next. I lay down and pulled a book out from under my
pillow. I glanced at the title: *The Last of the Mohicans.* I
found my place where I had put the hickory leaf and began
to read. I had to work to make my way through some of the
sentences, but it was worth the trouble.

> "Softly, softly," said the scout, extending his long rifle
> in front of the eager Heyward; "we now know our work,
> but the beauty of the trail must not be deformed. A step
> too soon may give us hours of trouble . . ."

It would be nice to be reading this on the braided hearth
rug over the patterned oilcloth covering the floor in front of
the fire with the wind howling outside, I thought. I shivered
as the thought came close to me. Lorenzo read the Bible aloud
once like that. The story of David and Goliath. Pa sat on his
deacon's bench. He nodded and listened quietly as Lorenzo
read. Pa didn't have to look at the word to correct Lorenzo
when he made a mistake. Ma sat in her slat-backed rocker. It
had ivy painted along the back. She had a lard oil lamp on a
small spool-turned table beside her so she could see to sew.

I guess that served Horace rightly for taking my cookie.
But Ma looked mighty mad. Horace had it coming. Why,
back last spring Horace had thumped me in the school yard
when I wouldn't let him use my shooter after he had lost all
his marbles to Ben Allison. That wasn't right, 'cause I knew
Horace would lose mine, too. We were studying about the
Revolutionary War then and that was when Mr. Deasy had
told us about James Fenimore Cooper and his books and—

I heard Pa's boots thump on the puncheon floor and hastily
slid the book under my pillow. I had my hands clasped behind my head when he opened the door and came in.

"Jim, do you know what you've done?" he demanded.

"Yes, Pa," I said. I kept my eyes on the ceiling.

"Look at me," he said sternly.

I looked at him, then watched his lips as they puckered and bent, pushing the words out.

"We cannot have you boys fighting amongst yourselves. Remember what the Good Book says: 'Whosoever smiteth you upon the left cheek turn to him also thy right.'"

"Yes, Pa," I said automatically. Pa was always quoting the Bible. He had a lot of that crammed up in his head, although sometimes he got to where he was confused and couldn't remember it. Pa had wanted to be a preacher and was studying to be a Presbyterian minister at Middlebury College back in Vermont. It was there that he met Ma. Her father had been with Ethan Allen's Green Mountain Boys in the Revolutionary War. But then a typhoid fever epidemic came along and Pa caught it while nursing the sick and then near died from brain fever. Sometimes he remembered everything; then sometimes it all went away from him and he would wander around with this vacant look in his eyes for days. But this wasn't one of them days.

"Remember that he who troubleth his own house shall inherit the wind," Pa said. "He who fights with his brethren by his brethren will he be slain and his body will roll in the dust and dogs will lap his blood. Absalom! Absalom!"

He closed his eyes and struck himself in the chest softly with his fist.

"You all right, Pa?" I asked.

He stood still for a moment, then opened his eyes and looked down at me. His eyes looked glazed and I waited to see if he would remember where he was and what he was doing, but then a look of puzzlement came into them and he frowned.

Ma's voice called from the kitchen, "William? Will you come here?"

Pa half-turned toward the door, then looked down at me and frowned again.

"William?"

Her voice sounded a little higher.

He turned and left, blundering into the doorjamb with his left shoulder.

CHAPTER 3

I HEARD the voices on the playground.

"Your pa's an ijjeet!" Rody taunted. His big yellow teeth grinned down at me. His breath smelled like onions. He laughed and poked me in the chest with his fist. "He walks around like this!" He walled his eyes and puffed out his cheeks and stomped stiff-legged around me. The others giggled. Horace told him to quit it because Mr. Deasy was looking.

Rody stopped and turned to Horace, jeering, "And we know why you know that, Ho-race!" He made his name sound like *whores*. "You spend enough time smooching his butt." He puckered up and made kissing noises. The others laughed nervously.

The word sounded bad the way he said it. Sarah McLaughlin had once kissed me on a dare and the kiss sounded like that: *smooch*. Only softer and nicer. *Smooch* was a strange word. It could sound pretty or it could sound ugly. When Rody said it, it sounded ugly and Horace's face turned red clear up into his hair. His hands curled into fists, but he turned and walked away from Rody.

"Smoochsmoochsmooch," Rody called, mocking him. He made that kissing sound with his lips.

"The Hickoks," someone said scornfully behind me.

I turned and stared into Dotje's pimply face. His big buck teeth had ridges on them and looked green. He smirked.

"Ain't a backbone among 'em," he said. He poked me in the chest with his dirty finger. "You a kisser, too? Do you kiss your mama before you go to bed?"

"Yes," I answered.

"Hey, everyone! He says he kisses his mama every night before he goes to bed."

Everyone turned to look at me. Someone sniggered, and then everyone laughed. I felt my face grow warm.

"I do not!" I said.

"Oh. Hey, everyone, he says he don't kiss his mama every night before he goes to bed!"

They all laughed and he laughed and stuck his finger in his nose, digging.

I glanced at the door to the classroom, but Mr. Deasy had gone back inside. I looked back at Dotje, then hauled off and smacked him. His finger rammed into his nose. He cried out and jerked his finger away. Blood gushed from his nose. I smacked him again for good measure. He fell to the ground, bawling. Blood dripped onto the ground, a curious red against the brown dust.

CHAPTER 4

I FELT warm and rose from the bed and walked on tiptoes to the door and peeked out. Pa was sitting in his slat-backed rocker and Ma had wrung out a cloth and was laying it across his forehead, saying, "There, there, William. Deep breaths. That's right: deep breaths."

Pa obeyed, taking long, slow deep breaths, although I could see in his face that he didn't know why he was doing that. "Polly," he said. He frowned. His face looked white and cool but pinched. He was trying hard to get the answer to what he couldn't remember. He looked up at the mantel over the fireplace where daguerreotypes of my grandmas and grandpas sat. He shook his head. He glanced at me and shook his head. I could see he didn't recognize me. I turned away and went back to my room and picked up the book again.

One moccasin is so much like another, it is probable there is some mistake.

"Jim! Wash up and come to supper, now!" Ma's voice cut through the words and I marked my place in the book and rose and went out. I stepped to the basin and ewer next to the deacon's bench beside the door. I splashed some water into the basin and scrubbed my hands hard with a bar of gray soap that felt like it had grit in it.

"Cleanliness is next to godliness," Pa said. His eyes twinkled as he rubbed my hands pink with the towel. "Always remember that, James. Cleanliness is next to godliness. You can't have one without the other."

I dried my hands on the damp towel and turned to the room. Horace was already at the table, glowering at me. Lorenzo sat across from him. He gave me a half smile as I sat next to him. He poked me in the ribs with his finger and I squirmed away from him.

"Cut it out," I mumbled. Pa gave me a puzzled look from his place at the table.

"This is supper time," Ma said sharply. "You boys straighten up! We've had enough of your gamboling around this day. We'll have some peace now. Understand?"

I glanced once at her blue-gray eyes and nodded quickly.

"Yes, ma'am," I said. Lorenzo and Horace were quick to come on the tail of my words. We had been tomfooling enough for the day, she seemed to say. I had heard that tone of voice enough to know that all issues were hereby settled by the grace of God and Ma's firm hand, which could raise a welt on a person's dignity with the help of a willow switch she kept standing in the corner by the fireplace as a silent reminder for one to mend one's ways before they got a chance to be unmended.

I glanced down at the table. The tablecloth was clean and white and pressed. The small brown crock holding the milk for the table stood near Pa's hand. A pattypan holding biscuits stood next to it. A bowl filled with Boston baked beans in thick molasses was in the middle of the table next to a platter of chicken fixin's.

Ma took her place at the end of the table and sighed deeply. She held out her hands. Horace took one. I took the other and Lorenzo took mine. He held out his other hand. Pa took it gingerly. His eyebrows twitched. My sister Celinda shook her curls and cocked her head at him. He smiled and took her tiny hand in his. Lydia laughed and smashed a spoon on the small table in front of her chair next to Ma's right hand.

"William?" she said. Pa looked at her. "The blessing?" she said. He frowned, trying to remember. A soft sigh escaped her lips. She glanced at Horace.

"All right, Horace. Give us the blessing."

He pouted and glared at me.

"Horace," she said again, a bit more sharply.

He bowed his head and mumbled, "Thou hast again remembered us, O Lord, and we would not forget thee. Bless this food, we pray, and help us to serve thee well."

"And?" Ma prompted.

I watched him glance from the corners of his eyes at Ma. His eyes shifted over to mine and he heaved a deep sigh.

"And forgive us our transgressions and let us forgive others as we would have them forgive us. Amen." He rushed the last and glared at me as I worked hard to keep from laughing.

"Amen," the rest of us echoed.

Ma straightened and handed Lydia a piece of biscuit soaked in honey. Lydia squealed and began smearing her face with it.

Lorenzo took the brown crock and filled Pa's glass with milk, then his. He handed the crock to me. I poured my glass full and handed the crock on to Ma. I took a sip, tasting a hint of cream behind the milk.

Briefly I see Lorenzo crouching by our patient cow at daybreak in the barn after bringing her in from the lush green pasture next to the orchard, his fingers tugging at her dugs in an old and secret ritual of the morning world.

Pa took the glass in his hand, looking at it questioningly. He sipped it. His face brightened. "A miracle!" he said. He beamed as he looked around the table at us. "If we all live on good drink as this, why, we won't have a rotten tooth in our heads and our stomachs will know great comfort! Eh, what do you say, Polly?"

"Of course, William," she answered. She glanced at Horace. "Straighten up and stop looking daggers at James. You received nothing more than you asked for and now it is over and done with. No more." She glanced warningly at me.

"Yes, ma'am," I mumbled. I grabbed a biscuit and stuffed it in my mouth to prevent myself from having to say more. I looked boldly across at Horace. His eyes met mine, furious for the moment. Then they wavered and slipped away, glanced back, then away again. He bent his head, studying his plate as he ate silently.

CHAPTER 5

"YOU ARE named after the great Roman poet and lawyer Horace," Papa said. He smiled at Horace. *"Ira furor brevis est."*

"What's that?" Horace asked.

"'Anger is a short madness,'" Papa said. "It would do you well to remember that."

"And me, Papa?" I asked. "Who am I named after?"

He smiled. "Why, you are named after King James who gave us the new Bible."

I looked at Horace. "You're named after an old poet. I'm a king."

Horace pouted. "I wanna be a king, too!" His lower lip trembled as if he was going to burst into tears.

"And me, Papa?" Lorenzo asked eagerly.

"You, Lorenzo, are named after a man who saved a woman's soul by bringing her to our Lord Jesus Christ!"

Lorenzo's face fell. I grinned at him.

"I'm still the king!" I crowed.

"And Oliver? What about Oliver, Papa?" Lorenzo asked.

"Oliver? Why, Oliver is named after the man who brought true Christianity to England and threw the evil people who pretended to love God out. He was a great man. A truly great man."

"Tell me where I was born," I said importantly.

"No, tell *me,*" Horace said.

"I'm the king," I said. "I go first."

Horace pouted.

Papa smiled. He had a nice smile when he smiled that way. "Horace, you were born when we lived at Union Center. James, you were born in Homer."

"Who was Homer, Papa?" I looked importantly at Horace. Anyone could be born at a Union Center. There wasn't anything special about that name. But Homer?

"Homer was a great, great poet," Papa said. "He wrote the *Iliad* and the *Odyssey*. Stories about great heroes." He closed his eyes.

> " 'Sing to me the story of that wanderer who
>   sacked Troy
> and sundered her heaven-built wall only to be
>   forced
> to roam uncharted seas and visit strange lands
> where he faced many trials.
> Sing to me his adventures—' "

And I sat, openmouthed, listening to the adventures of a man whose name was that of my birthplace. Even Horace and the others listened, and great envious looks were cast my way by Horace because no such legends came from a place called Union Center.

CHAPTER 6

ON SUNDAYS, Pa loaded us all into the wagon and we made the journey down Little Vermillion Creek to the Presbyterian church. We passed the McLaughlin farmhouse and I watched eagerly to see if Sarah or Josephine would be standing at the half door to wave at us as we drove by in the buggy. Pa would give me the whip so I could wave it at them. Sarah was a sweet one, but Josephine had a strange look in her eye whenever she was around me and she would stand real close to me so I could breathe the vanilla that she put behind each ear and on her neck. I would sniff real hard and suddenly I would get this hungry feeling in my stomach that would leave me so weak that all the cookies in the world wouldn't fill it.

Nahum Gould would see us coming and limp around in a state until Pa pulled the team to a halt and handed Ma down to one of us.

"William! William!" Gould would exclaim. (He always addressed Pa with both names—"William! William!"—as if he was having a hard time making Pa understand that he wanted to talk to him.) Gould would come to our wagon, swinging his game foot around in a half circle and giving a little hop. He had lost part of that foot when he had stopped to clear a stone from his plow and something startled the team (a snake was usually given as the cause) and the team bolted, dragging the plow blade over Gould's foot, cutting it in half. There was a sternness about him that disturbed a lot of people, but he was always kind toward us. I just think the others weren't willing to look beneath the Quaker name to the man himself before gouging his name. This was usually done by someone wanting to be the biggest toad in the puddle, who would put warts on another to make himself look more important to others.

"Nahum," Pa would say calmly. Then he would step down and Gould would grab Pa's arm just above his black-coated elbow and draw him aside, whispering urgently to him. We weren't supposed to know what the urgency was about, but we all did. Gould was a rabid Abolitionist and belonged to the Quaker church across the road. He would keep Pa until our church bell rang and Pa gently excused himself to join the rest of us standing by the door waiting for him.

I didn't care much for our church, a white clapboard affair with a steeple and bell. The church stood on a small knoll, surrounded by locust trees and tall elms, above Tomahawk

Creek not far from a wooden bridge that seemed to always have a pall of perpetual gloom thrown over it. In the fall, the whitewashed walls shone like ideal Christian purity in the morning sun. But there didn't seem to be much Christianity practiced there other than lip service to the deity and memorized prayers that one could mutter absentmindedly upon command. There always seemed to be a night-musty smell to it like old men. Reverend Robert Cowley did his best to bore the young boys there. He started each service the same way:

"O Lord, open our minds, we pray, that we might receive thy noble wisdom. Hasten, O Lord, to guide us through these terrible times that we might do thy bidding and carry thy message to those who need it most."

That was about as far as any of us got in the service except for the times when our mothers would elbow us up to join in a hymn or two when Reverend Cowley ran out of steam and decided he needed a minute or two rest to gather his thoughts in order to purge us more of our sins, real and imagined. We set off on our own journeys until we came to the familiar end:

"Come down into our hearts, O Lord, we beseech thee. Drive away from us all the snares of the enemy and may thy holy angels dwell among us to keep us safe in peace and may thy blessing be always upon us, O Lord. This we pray in thy name. Amen."

And then there would be a mad scramble for the door despite our mothers' heavy sighs. But only Mrs. Beaufoy took exception at our mass exodus from the altar of the Lord.

"You boys are setting down the long road to hell and damnation!" she complained loudly once when Horace accidentally stepped on her corns.

That caused all of us to laugh when we got outside, for

every boy in the county (and some of the girls as well) knew
about the collection of drawings her husband, Philip, kept
hidden in the tack room in the barn. When he stood up to
do the reading in church *"Visit, we beseech thee, O Lord,
our homes and drive away from them all sin . . ."* why, we
kids would stuff our fingers in our mouths to keep from
laughing. Petey Sweeney got the giggles once and stuffed
his fingers so far in his throat that he gagged and vomited
in the pew. We all left church early that day to keep from
getting the bug that Petey's mother swore he had. We all met
later down at the swimming hole at Tomahawk Creek to discuss this windfall. We thought that we could make this a
regular thing. But no one wanted to follow Petey's example, so that ended that.

CHAPTER 7

I LIKED the Fall, the best 'cause that was when there
would be this smoky smell to the air, sharp and cold: rainy
and wintery and leaves burning and the corduroy of our
churchgoing clothes. The woods that Tomahawk Creek cut
through would be full of color and turkeys and squirrels
were plentiful for hunting. I didn't have a gun. But I had a
good slingshot that let me stun a few squirrels and once a
turkey, but when I ran up to throttle him or cut his throat
with my barlow knife he suddenly came awake and took a
chunk out of my arm. Gobbling angrily, he chased me
through the woods, jabbing at my backside. I came out
of the woods howling and running for all I was worth. That
turkey should have stayed in the woods. But I guess I had

really made him angry. He chased me all the way to the house. Pa heard me howling and came running from the barn. He had been splitting wood and still had the ax in his hand. He stopped, wide-eyed at the turkey chasing me around and around Ma's clothesline post. Then Pa caught the turkey up by his neck and quickly upended him. The turkey gobbled angrily. His wings thrashed and beat at Pa's chest.

"What on earth?" Ma said. She came to the door and I ran to her and buried my face in her apron, bawling. "What's going on?"

"I reckon Jim's brought us dinner," Pa said somberly. He held the turkey up. "Looks like a nice one." He smiled down at me. "Good job, Jim." He took the turkey around behind the house. The turkey gobbled and suddenly there was a squawk and a loud *clunk!* and then the turkey didn't gobble anymore. Ma smiled down at me. She smoothed my hair back.

"Well, Jim, I guess you've earned a cookie for this day's work," she said. She took me into the house and gave me a molasses cookie and a glass of buttermilk.

Ever green summer keeps changing to autumn. . . .

At Christmas, there would be lanterns in the windows as we drove by for early service, rumbling over the wooden bridge in the wagon, listening to the echo of the wheels off the wooden planks and wishing we were back home instead of making the trip to hear Reverend Cowley tell us the story of Christmas one more time. It wasn't so bad going back home or stopping at homes along the way to sample early baking. I remember the ropes of green branches and the holly and ivy that had been wound around the pier glass and holly and ivy, green and red, looped around nails tapped

around doors and windows. Christmas was a good time of
the year. That was the year I got a fiddle for Christmas and
Pa showed me how to finger it a bit and then arranged for
Dan Tucker to teach me what he couldn't teach me.

CHAPTER 8

D IMLY I dreamed footsteps creaking on the floorboards of my bedroom and was already fighting awake
through black night to the dim light of a lantern when
Father called softly, "Jim, boy, wake up."

I rose on my elbows, blinking in the lantern light. Over
against the wall, Lorenzo turned restlessly on his side to
face the wall away from the light, grumbling in his sleep.
Soft shadows danced on the rough-hewn wood walls where
our clothes hung on nails to keep crickets out of them. I
yawned.

"Yes, Father?" I said. I knuckled the sleep from my eyes
and yawned again, tasting the thick night in my mouth. I
shivered as the blanket slipped down from my naked chest
to gather at my waist.

"I need your help, Jim," Father said quietly. He glanced
over at Lorenzo, indecision working on his worried face. He
looked pale and drawn in the yellow light, but then Father
always looked pale and drawn, thanks to the typhoid fever he
caught while helping nurse the sick when he and Mother
were visiting North Hero on the shores of Lake Champlain
in Vermont shortly after they were married. Father had been
a seminary student, studying for the Presbyterian ministry
at Middlebury College, but after he came down with typhoid
fever his mind was never quite the same again. He had

gotten better—or so Mother said—since we came to Illinois, but there were times when he lapsed into a bewildered confusion. When that happened, we just had to go along with him to keep him out of trouble until he came out of his fog. On his good days, he could still split a chalk line with an ax even though he looked tall and stringy.

"Leave him be, Father. I'll help you," I whispered, throwing the covers off and swinging my legs off my bunk to the floor. I stood, moving my feet gingerly to keep from sliding a sliver into my foot. I didn't want Mother digging around in the bottom of my foot with one of her needles to get the sliver out. The last time that happened, I hurt for a week.

Father frowned for a moment, then nodded. He waited while I pulled on my pants and shirt and heavy woolen socks. I picked up my boots and nodded at the door. Father turned and I followed him out into the kitchen. I pulled a chair from the table and sat, working my boots on, tucking my pants into the tops. The kitchen was still warm from the banked fire in the small cast-iron stove. I could smell the yeast in the bread dough rising beneath a clean dish towel in the heavy stoneware bowl. Mother always set the dough before going to bed so she could bake fresh in the morning.

"What's wrong?" I asked, rising and settling my feet in my boots. I worked the left one around a bit to ease it. The boots were new and stiff and pinched painfully just above my instep where I had a small bump growing on each foot. Doc Simpson said that was because I had worn boots too small when I was growing, so my feet never filled out with the rest of me.

"We have to go over to Nahum Gould's place," Father whispered. He raised his thumb and forefinger and massaged his eyes, the bridge of his nose.

"Now?" I asked. "It's still dark out. Nobody'll be up."

"Sh. Not so loud," he whispered. He glanced at the closed

door that led to his and Mother's room. "I don't want to wake your mother. She'll only worry."

My stomach felt queer as I stared at him. "Why would she think that? And why are we going over to Nahum's place this time of night?"

"One of Nahum's boys rode over and asked if we could collect some Negroes from their place. Some bounty hunters came through Wedron yesterday afternoon looking for some runaways. Nahum's afraid that someone might have seen them being brought over to his place. His boy rode on up the line to Bill Dewey's place to warn him. We're to collect the Negroes and bring them back here, then take them on up to Dewey's place in a couple of days."

I frowned and shook my head as I crossed to the door and slipped my canvas jacket off its peg. I took down my hat and set it firmly in place, pulling the brim down to my ears. I flinched as it rubbed across the sunburn on my forehead, and took it off. I had been hoeing weeds all day without a hat and was paying the price. I glanced in the small mirror, looking at the red on my nose, the freckles standing out. The sun had brought out red glints in my auburn hair. I resettled the hat gingerly and looked at Father, fidgeting in the middle of the room, shuffling back and forth from one foot to the other.

"What's wrong?" I asked.

He blinked, then looked away, troubled. "I think we should take Lorenzo, too. Oliver has to cut back trees in the morning so he should sleep."

"Let him sleep, Father," I said gently. "He was up at four this morning, plowing."

Father's lips narrowed into a thin line, his face setting stubbornly. "I think Lorenzo should come. We might need him."

"All right, Father," I said resignedly. "You wake him. I'll go hitch the team."

He nodded and turned back to the bedroom. I opened the door and stepped outside into the cold fall air. I shivered as the cold struck my exposed face, making me feel cold even though I was well bundled in my flannel shirt and jacket. I pulled a pair of gloves from my pocket and slipped them on. My breath appeared as tiny clouds of mist.

"Frost on the pumpkin come morning," I muttered as I walked across the yard to the barn. Then I remembered it *was* morning as I touched the iron hasp covered with a light sprinkle of frost. I slid the door open and walked inside, pausing to feel for the lantern beside the door. I lit it and carried it down to the end of the barn where the wagon harness hung on the wall. The horses watched me as I passed their stalls, their hooves moving on their straw bedding.

"It's going to be a cold one," I said to them as I came down the line. I slipped the harness over them, fitted the bits, then walked them out of the barn and backed them into place. Sam grumbled as I hooked the traces. "I know," I said soothingly. "I don't want to be up, either."

I climbed into the wagon and drove the short distance up to the house. Father came out with a sleepy Lorenzo beside him. They climbed into the wagon and I clucked to the horses and pulled out into our lane leading down to the dirt road and turned south, heading down to Gould's place.

"Damned inconsiderate—" Lorenzo began.

"Don't take the Lord's name in vain," Father said mildly, interrupting him.

"Sorry," Lorenzo mumbled, and huddled on the floor of the wagon, bracing his back against the seat. "This couldn't wait until morning?"

"No," Father said. "Best we get them moved under darkness."

Lorenzo sighed and fell silent, but I could feel his resentment at being shaken awake in the wee hours. Or maybe it was mine. Father had been moving Negroes up through our place as a stop on the Underground Railway for the past three years, but recently it had become very risky. More and more bounty hunters were out on the road with blank warrants that allowed them to seize any Negroes on suspicion and take them to the nearest authority until proper ownership could be established. But "the nearest authority" was vaguely defined and most bounty hunters would simply seize any Negroes they found off a private property and take them back down across the Mason-Dixon Line and put them back on the market. Some farmers down south would hire bounty hunters to find runaways when they didn't have any, paying a dollar a pound for any Negroes brought to them, claiming ownership. It was a way of getting fresh slaves cheaply.

We drove past the McLaughlin farm and I turned to watch the black windows, half-hoping the creaking of our wagon in the frosty night would rouse the McLaughlins and I would see a light come on in one of the windows and the figure of Sarah slip behind the curtain. But the only thing that stirred was their rooster, who crowed indignantly at being awakened as we passed. I sighed, my breath puffing gently out in front of me in a small cloud. I glanced down at Lorenzo, grinning up at me, reading my mind. I shook my head and his grin grew wider. As Father patiently held the reins on the horses, I turned back to the front and watched the black limbs of the trees, still half-covered with fall leaves of gold and brown, stretching out over the white ribbon of road stretching in front of us. The brush along the roadside seemed dark and threatening in the white moonlight. No sign of life flickered near us outside of strange night sounds that seemed like the chirp of crickets and the whirring of locusts in the trees. But crickets and locusts would not have been out at that time of year, and I shivered, wondering what the sounds I thought I was hearing were. The guttural twang of a bullfrog rolled up from beneath the wooden bridge over Tomahawk Creek as we rumbled across the worn planks and past the church, its white sides glowing ghostly in the pale light.

It was a night made for ghosts and goblins and suddenly I imagined the night growing darker and darker and the stars colder and colder. We rounded a bend in the road and saw the twisted limbs of a sycamore that had served as a hanging tree a few years back for Cage Harpe—who passed himself off as a second or third cousin to Wiley and Micajah Harpe, the two brothers who butchered about thirty men before they were killed. But no one paid much attention to Harpe's claim until he tried to rape Dolly Beaufoy (there was some question there, as quite a few boys and men had sampled Dolly's charms) in the grove and was caught by her cousin who was looking for a stray cow at the time. The cousin locked Harpe in the corn bin and went to get the sheriff, but his brothers took Harpe from the bin and hanged him before the sheriff could get back. The sycamore always seemed dead after that. Even when sparse green leaves dotted its dark limbs. I watched uneasily as we came closer and closer to it, then breathed a silent sigh of relief as we passed by safely without hearing Harpe moaning.

Lorenzo heaved a quiet sigh of relief behind me. I grinned and glanced over my shoulder at him. He shook his head and burrowed deeper into his heavy coat. Father cleared his throat beside me. I looked at him, sitting easily beside me, quietly contemplating the moving haunches of the horses in front of us.

"Ghosts and goblins and witches won't harm you unless you let them," he said quietly. He smiled gently. "That is a promise we are given in Psalms, Jim. 'Thou shalt not be afraid for the terror by night; nor the arrow that flieth by day.' Set your mind at ease. What we do is right and for that we won't be harmed." His eyes turned toward me. "We are told that, too."

"Yes," I wanted to say. *"Yes. I know. But do those who*

want to harm us know that as well? The Good Book pro-
vides comfort to those who don't have a good right cross.
Or a pistol." But I didn't voice my words. Father took a dim
view of those taking the teachings lightly. I heard Lorenzo
moving uneasily behind me and knew that he shared my
thoughts. Hadn't Dotje's father one night when he was riding home from the Green Mountain come across Harpe? At
least, Henry claimed that when Father found him blundering along the road on foot, stinking of whiskey and his pants
stained from where he had soiled them.

"Where's your horse, Henry?" Pa asked.

Henry squinted, trying to focus upon Pa's face, weaving
back and forth from his place in the road. "I tell you, William,
he was after me. As certain as that tree bears apples"—he
pointed to the hickory tree—"he was after me. It was hor-
rible. His tongue hanging out all black and his eyes bulg-
ing out and I could smell the earth of the grave around
him and he was mumbling and howling and—"

"Who, Henry? Who stole your horse?"

Henry swallowed and glanced wild-eyed around him,
then leaned forward, saying, "It was Cage Harpe, as I stand
and breathe, William. Cage Harpe. I tried to run away, but
my horse threw me"—I nearly chuckled at that, for I knew
Henry's mare was nearly toothless and the best one could
whip her to was a shambling trot—"and then he was on me
leaning over me and I smelled his stinking breath," and Pa
leaned back here from Henry's own stench as he started
to gabble, "andthenhegrabbedmeandshookmeandhiseyes-
wereallbloodshotand—"

The horses turned into Nahum's lane and I shook the
memory away as Father guided the horses up to the barn
door. Nahum was waiting and threw the doors open and we
drove inside. He swung the doors shut and stood nervously
around, wringing his hands as we climbed down, stiff from
the cold ride over.

"William, William, thank God you've arrived!"

"Don't have a conniption fit, Nahum," Father said soothingly. "We're here. Now what's the problem?"

Nahum took a deep breath, trying to calm himself. His eyes were bright with anxiety and angry righteousness. "A couple of bounty hunters were in Homer yesterday—"

"There are always bounty hunters in Homer," Father said mildly. "Since when has that bothered you?"

Nahum sighed and wiped his hands across his eyes. He suddenly looked tired and old. His beard was a gray stubble against the soft flesh of his cheeks and jowls. His fingers trembled as he tugged at his lower lip. "I've had words with Hiram Jenkins. You know this, of course, William."

Father nodded. Everyone in the county had heard about how Jenkins had taken a shipment of grain from Nahum and then tried to short him on bushel measure. Nahum had a warrant served on Jenkins, who settled out of court to keep a black mark off his business. But people still found out about Jenkins and his business practices and began to take their business to a mild-mannered Quaker in Utica.

"All right, Nahum," Father said.

"It's just that I'm afraid—"

"Don't worry about it, Nahum," Father said. "We're here now. We might as well take them back with us. How many are there?"

Relief showed on Nahum's face. He sighed deeply and turned to limp to the back of the barn. He had a false room built in the back there by the corn crib. He had finished picking a couple of days before, and dry leaves hung like pieces of parchment between the slats. The door was hidden by bales of straw on a dead roller. He took a hay hook and tugged the bales aside. The door was still barely visible. He took the hook, placed it in a small hole, and turned it. The door swung open. A man and a woman looked out at us, silent, waiting, their black faces shiny with expectation. The man held a small girl on his lap. Her eyes were big with fright. The man wore a stained butternut shirt and canvas pants. The young girl was in a soiled blue-white checked dress. The woman wore a black dress. She was pretty; her negroid features softened her café au lait skin.

"It's all right," Nahum said soothingly. "These are the Hickoks. They will take you on to their place."

"Ah thought we'd stay heah for a couple of days," the man said suspiciously. He held the young girl away from us.

"Yes," Nahum said. "That was the plan. But something has come up. It will be safer to move you earlier than we thought."

The woman nodded and looked at the man. "You know we have no choice. Now don't be pigheaded and let's go. Trust in God, Jethro. Trust in God." She smiled down at the little girl. "Now don't you worry, Sarah. Y'papa won' let nuthin' happen to you."

"A family?" Father asked.

"No, suh," the woman said. "This man is Jethro." She nodded at him. "His master sold his wife downriver. The girl was to go to Alabama. But—"

"Ain't no man got no right to break up a family," Jethro said angrily. "Jus' 'cause we niggers don' mean we ain't family."

"Yes," Father said. "And your wife?"

The man's face fell. Tears filled his eyes with hopelessness. "Ah hope she can join us. We tryin' to ge' to Chicago. Her sister lives there."

"Can you help Momma?" the little girl asked. Her eyes were as big as liquid brown pennies in her thin face.

"We'll try," Father said. He looked at the woman. "And you?"

"Ah'm Hannah," she said. She smiled, suddenly shy. "Ah came 'long to help." Her face clouded. "But it time Ah was leavin'." She looked at me and Lorenzo significantly. Then she looked back at Father. "But Ah don' think this is the time for that."

Father nodded. He turned to Nahum. "We'll trouble you for a couple of blankets, Nahum. And some straw to spread over them. I'll have Horace bring the blankets back in a couple of days."

"No need," Nahum said. "Clara's almost finished quilting new ones. Keep them. I think you'll have more than enough need for them before this is all over."

Father nodded. "Thank you," he said politely. He turned back to the Negroes. "Get ready."

"We's ready," Hannah said. The man nodded and picked up a flour sack in one huge hand. He rose, balancing the young girl on his hip, holding the flour sack in the other. Father glanced at Hannah. She smiled faintly and held her hands open. "All Ah have y' is seein'."

Father turned to Lorenzo. "Get a fork and spread some straw over the bottom of the wagon." He turned to me. "Go up to the house with Nahum and get some blankets to put over the straw and over our friends here. Then help Lorenzo cover them with more straw."

"Yes, Father," I said.

I slipped out of the barn with Nahum while Lorenzo began spreading straw over the bed of the wagon.

"Best to use the back door, I think," Nahum said lowly. I followed him as we made our way carefully through his garden. The pumpkins glowed like large orange balls in the cold white moonlight. I waited by the door while Nahum went inside the house to gather the blankets. I looked around uneasily, feeling the night pressing in hard upon me, shivering slightly against the cold. The door opened and Nahum handed an armful of blankets to me, then disappeared, returning with a small box filled with glass jars.

"Clara put up some jam," he said. He smiled half-apologetically. "We were planning on bringing it over, but"—he grimaced and looked down at his foot—"I've been feeling gimpy lately. You might as well take it with you now." I took the jam. I knew he was feeling awkward about putting us out this way and was trying to make up a little for calling us out on such a cold night. We always had at least a day's notice before a group of Negroes was brought to us even though they would usually be brought in the dead of night. We had never had to go and collect them before.

"It's all right, sir," I said politely. "We don't really mind. And thank you for the jam. Mother will appreciate your thoughtfulness."

He cleared his throat and looked away as he patted me clumsily upon my shoulder. "You're a good boy, James," he said gruffly.

I followed him back through the garden and to the barn. Lorenzo had spread the straw evenly over the bed of the wagon. I climbed into the wagon and spread the blankets around on the straw and climbed down. Jethro placed the young girl in the wagon, then helped Hannah into the bed. They lay down and I covered them with the extra blankets while Lorenzo started pitching the straw over them to cover the blankets.

"That really won't keep anyone from looking in your wagon if they want to, William," Nahum said.

Father shrugged. "I guess we'll have to cross that stream when we come to it. I don't know what else to do on short notice."

Suddenly I remembered the pumpkins. "Father, I have an idea if Mr. Gould will go along with it."

They turned to look at me questioningly. "What is it, Jim?" Father asked.

I faced Nahum. "I couldn't help but notice that you have a good pumpkin crop," I said. Nahum frowned, nodding. "Well, I expect they're about ready for market." He nodded again, impatiently. "I reckon we could haul them there for you, if you like, couldn't we, Father? After all, we already got the straw bed prepared, so they won't bruise."

Father and Nahum stared at me; then Father laughed gently. "Why, yes. It would be the neighborly thing to do." He turned to Nahum. "In fact, we *will* take them on into Lowell or Homer for you, if you wish. That way, you would only have to make one trip yourself with your corn."

A light dawned in Nahum's eyes. His eyebrows rose and he looked at me respectfully. "You've got a good head on your shoulders, James." He nodded and said, "William, I don't expect you to take those pumpkins on in for nothing. I'll be willing to pay."

Father shook his head. "There'll come a time when I may need your help, Nahum. Let it ride until then."

"I don't like being obligated," Nahum began, but Father interrupted.

"This isn't the time to be debating, Nahum. Dawn's coming and it would be best if we were on the road by then."

Nahum opened his mouth to protest, then changed his mind. "Of course, of course, William. You are, as usual, right. All right. Pull around to the side and we'll load those pumpkins on top of the straw." His face began to gleam with excitement. He laughed and rubbed his hands together gleefully. "I'd like to see Jenkins's face if this ever gets out."

"We'd better hope that it doesn't," Father said dryly. "We're still breaking the law." He coughed suddenly and grabbed the wagon side for support. He took a deep breath, forcing himself to be calm.

"Father—" I began, but he smiled wanly at me.

"I'm all right, Jim. You and Lorenzo pull the wagon around to the patch and begin loading those pumpkins. Gently. Remember we have people beneath the load."

Hannah's muffled voice came from beneath the straw. "We 'preciate that, suh. They's 'nough load heah now."

I couldn't help but smile admiringly at her stoicism. I

climbed into the wagon and took the reins, clucking gently to the horses as Lorenzo slid the doors open. I guided the team around to the side and reined in next to the garden. We loaded the pumpkins swiftly, piling them gently upon Hannah and Jethro and his daughter, then carefully stacking the pumpkins along the sides to give an illusion of a full wagon.

"We'll meet you in town tomorrow afternoon, Nahum," Father said as he climbed onto the seat beside me. Lorenzo stepped carefully in over the tailgate and settled down in one corner. He huddled deep into his coat.

"I don't know why I always get the tail end," he complained.

"You'll be warmer there," I said. "At least you're out of the wind."

"Ah'll trade places if'n y'want to," Hannah said.

We laughed and Father took the reins, clucking to the team. We pulled out of Nahum's lane and turned back toward our farm. "All right," Father said softly. "We're on the road, now, so no more talking until we get home."

False dawn began to appear in the east with soft streaks of pink and purple. The breeze began to pick up as we neared Tomahawk Creek. I shivered as its frosty fingers felt their way down the collar of my coat. I glanced back at Lorenzo, muffled to his eyes with his coat, arms wrapped around him and hands tucked under his armpits as he huddled for warmth. I rubbed my nose upon the sleeve of my coat.

Father laughed softly. "I'll bet they're a lot warmer than we are despite being beneath those pumpkins," he said. He cocked an eyebrow as he regarded me. "Sometimes I think the good Lord is always working to help man out in his time of difficulty. Man just can't see the good for all the suffering around him. Now, you take Hannah and Jethro and Sarah back there." He raised his head, indicating the wagon bed. "God has seen to make them warm despite their misery."

But I was cold enough that I didn't want to see the lesson behind his words. "God didn't pitch that hay into the wagon, Father. And God sure didn't put them pumpkins over them to hide 'em."

" 'Those' pumpkins, Jim," he admonished gently. "A person who lets his words get away without care is one who will be hurt by them." He sighed. "And as for God—" He paused, leaning his head back to look at the tops of the trees as we moved slowly down the road. "It's all a matter of your point of view. If you think you are miserable, then you are and always will be. But if you look at the small things that God gives you for comfort, you might be surprised how happy you are. Jethro and Hannah and that little Sarah are forced to flee and to live in hidden places. But they are free," he said quietly and firmly. "And they are warm and fed and have each other. There are a lot of people in this world who are not."

"But—" I started to object, then fell silent as two men rode out of a small stand of willows, blocking the team.

Father reined in and straightened in his seat. He gathered the reins through the fingers of his left hand, straightening the back of the reins with his right, holding them beside him. The men were bearded and filthy. One of them rode up to Father's side of the wagon. "Morning. You appear to be out early." He glanced into the back of the wagon. He gestured at the pumpkins. "A good crop, it looks like."

"God's been good with his yield," Father said quietly, but I recognized the iron behind his words. I had heard it enough whenever I got into mischief. I half-turned to watch the other as he rode up to my side.

"What you looking at, boy?" he asked gruffly. His eyes were hard and gummy.

"Nothing," I said, meeting his stare.

"Something, I think," he said harshly.

"No," I answered recklessly. A thrill began singing its way through me. "Believe me. I'm looking at nothing."

A dull flush began to creep up from under his grimy collar as my taunt finally crept through the muddle in his mind.

"Be quiet, Jim," Father said.

"Better listen to your pa, boy," the leader said. "We don't need no lip from a weanling."

"Oh?" I raised my eyebrows. "Then who do you need it from?"

The leader stared hard at me, his lips thinning into a hard, straight line. "I think we should take a look in that wagon," he said. "It's too early, I'm thinking, for any farmer to be taking crops to town at this hour."

"Not when he has to make more than one trip and a full day ahead of him," Father said calmly.

"Uh-huh. And pigs might fly, but I gotta see one before I believe it," the leader said. He looked over our heads at the man who was trying to stare me down. "Get down, Clem, and make certain that's only straw under them punkins."

Clem started to swing down from his saddle, but Father suddenly whipped the slack reins across the face of the leader's horse. "Yaaah!" he yelled.

Instinctively I threw my arms up and shouted, and Clem's horse reared and lunged, away from me, sending Clem spinning head over heels into the ditch beside the road.

"Goddamnit!" he roared, and yelped with pain.

"Sumbitch!" the leader hollered as his horse began to buck and plunge.

Father slapped the rumps of our team with the reins. They lurched forward. He slackened the reins, slapping them again over the horses' backsides, and they lifted into a gallop.

"Stop! Stop! Goddamnit, I'm ordering you to stop!" the leader shouted, but Dad ignored him and leaned forward, urging the team into a faster gallop. I glanced back at Lorenzo, clinging white-faced to the sides of the wagon to keep from tumbling over the tailgate. An angry bee whizzed by; then I heard a sharp *pop!* and realized the man in the ditch was shooting at us.

"Get down!" Father said sharply. His arm hit me like an iron bar in the chest. I tumbled backward on top of the pumpkins. I heard Hannah yelp beneath me and the pumpkins as I sprawled over them.

Several shots sounded; then Father slid the wagon around a curve and rumbled over the wooden bridge. "Hold on!" he yelled. I raised my head, watching as he pulled hard on the reins, turning the team sharply into a small trace running through a grove of oaks along the side of the creek. The horses high-stepped awkwardly to keep from falling as they worked against the bits in their mouths, but Father straightened the team and wagon and pulled them to a halt behind a willow stand by the creek.

"Father!" I exclaimed, but he shushed me with a wave of his hand. I turned to look behind us as I heard horses galloping over the wooden planks of the bridge. But the men didn't turn into the small side road and galloped on toward Wedron, the sound of their passing slowly disappearing.

Father clucked to the team and guided them carefully through the oak grove until we caught the Utica road. Then he worked his way back to our farm, following the back roads and trails that only the farmers knew.

The sun stood halfway to noon by the time we turned into the lane leading up to the home place. Father drove around to the back of the house and reined in. The team stopped and hung their heads, their lathered sides heaving for breath. Father slumped suddenly in the seat, the reins going slack in his hands.

"Father!" I said, alarmed, and climbed back over the seat. I grabbed his shoulders, but he waved me away, his face white, drained.

"Get the others in the cellar," he said. "Be quick about it!"

The door opened and Mother stepped outside. Alarmed, she stepped forward to the side of the wagon to help Father down. He took her arm and stepped down. He stumbled and would have fallen had she not slipped her shoulder under his arm. He tried to smile.

"We have guests," he said faintly. "In the wagon. Under the pumpkins."

She took in the situation at a glance, then turned and called, "Horace! Oliver! Come quickly!"

My brothers appeared to her call, Oliver shoving a slice of bread into his mouth and chewing vigorously. She pointed at Lorenzo climbing stiffly out of the back of the wagon.

"Unload those pumpkins!" she commanded. I started toward the back of the wagon, but she stopped me, saying, "Jim, you leave them to that! Come and help me with your father."

"Yes, ma'am," I said. I stepped forward and took Father's other arm. Together Mother and I helped him into the house and to their bedroom. He fell heavily upon the mattress. The springs of the old iron bed squeaked in protest. Mother rolled him to his side and started to tug off his boots. She glanced up at me. Her ringlets hung over her angular face.

"All right, Jim," she said quietly. "I can take it from here. You help your brothers. How many did you bring back?"

"Three," I answered. "A man and his daughter and a woman."

Her eyebrows rose as she gave a hard tug and pulled one boot off. She dropped it on the floor and started tugging on his other boot. "The man and the woman aren't married?"

"No, ma'am," I said.

"Uh-huh," she grunted as she gave a hard yank on Father's foot. "I guess you'd better put the man in the cellar and the woman and the young girl in Oliver's room up in the attic. He can move in with you and Lorenzo for a while."

"I don't think the girl will want to be separated from her father," I said. Mother eyed me appraisingly. I shook my head and continued. "She seems to cling to him. Her mother was sold down the river and I think she's afraid of losing her father, too, now."

"What do you suggest?"

"I'd say put the father and the girl together in the cellar. It's warm and dry down there and it won't be long before we move them over to Panton's Mills. A day or two at the most."

"That soon?" I nodded. She frowned. "All right. What happened?"

I grinned and shook my head. "You know, don't you? Nahum said that he's afraid that Hiram Jenkins may have associated him with the Underground. If Nahum's right, it won't take much for someone to connect Dad and us with it, too. Everybody knows Father's a deacon close to Nahum's church." I shrugged. "I think we'd better act as if we know somebody knows about us."

Mother gave a tiny smile. "You're thinking now, Jim. Good. Put the man and the little girl in the cellar together. But be certain there's plenty of blankets and a couple of lanterns down there. Little girls are easily afraid of the dark. Put the woman—what's her name?"

"Hannah," I replied.

"Hannah, then, in Oliver's room up in the attic. Tell Oliver to go over to Panton's Mills and tell Mr. Panton that he needs to stay over there and pretend that he's working for him. That'll free up a room. Mr. Panton will go along with that. Besides," she added dryly, "he'll have a bit of free labor."

"Yes, ma'am," I said.

"We'll say that we took Hannah on to help me take care of your father," she said. She glanced at Father lying half-awake on the bed. "May be that I'll need her, too," she muttered half to herself. "If anyone asks, we'll say that your grandfather sent her out here."

And so Hannah became a part of the family. She stayed with us long after the others left and when still others came through to stay a few nights with us. When I came down with a sore throat and my tonsils swelled to the size of hazelnuts (*"Lord, child! Ah don't see how y'can breathe!"*) she brought honeyed tea to me and played checkers when I tired of reading Washington Irving's *The Sketch Book of Geoffrey Crayon, Gent.* Sometimes she would sing the simple songs that I could saw out of my fiddle. Sometimes she would just sit quietly with me. And I would know that she was there and that was enough.

CHAPTER 9

"**J**IM! TIME to get up!"

Mother's voice came strongly through the door to our bedroom. I pulled myself up from a nightmare and glanced over at Lorenzo, but his bed was empty. I frowned and rolled my head to look out the window at pale sunlight shining brightly through the muslin curtains. How had I slept so late? My bed felt hot. My face was damp. I felt slimy and cold. I swung my legs over the side of the bed and sat up. I felt dizzy. I reached down and got my stockings. I pulled them on. They felt rough on my feet. A bead of sweat rolled down my nose. My mouth was dry.

"Mother!" I called. My voice sounded like a crow cawing. "Mother!"

But it was Hannah who opened the door and came in.

"What's the matter wit' y', boy?" she said. She put her hand on my forehead. It felt cool and I grabbed it and held it. "Here!" she said. "'Nough of that!" She tried to pull it away, but I wouldn't let it go. Then I felt her cool cheek against mine. She smelled faintly of cinnamon. I saw the side of a brown breast between buttons on her blouse. I didn't care.

"Boy, y'burnin' up! Y'get back into bed!"

"Gotta—" I mumbled. She pushed me by the shoulders. I fell back against my pillow. The room moved around and around. I gagged and tried to vomit. But couldn't. I had nothing to throw up. I felt her fingers pressing around my neck. It hurt.

"Mizzus Hickok!" she called. "Y'better come! Jim's ailing!"

Beside Hannah, Mother appeared wiping her hands on a towel. She touched my forehead. Her fingers were dry like paper. She frowned. "Your throat hurt?" I nodded. She looked at Hannah. "You stay with him. I'll get Horace to ride into town for the doctor." She handed the towel to Hannah and left.

Hannah sat down on the edge of my bed. She used the towel to wipe the sweat from my face. "Y'just lay there now and everything will be all right."

"I'm dying," I mumbled miserably.

"No, Ah don' think so," she said. But I knew she was worried. She always got that syrupy sound to her words when she was worried.

I closed my eyes and saw black shadows dancing between dead trees.

I felt another hand on my forehead. I opened my eyes and stared into Doc Simpson's eyes. I saw a huge wart beside his nose. Two black hairs grew out of it. He smelled like medicine. Like hoarhound drops and castor oil. Peppermint. All mixed together.

"Scarlet fever," he said. He craned his head around to talk over his shoulder. "There's a lot of that going around now. There isn't much we can do for it. Just have to let it run its course. Keep him covered and make him drink lots of water with a little peppermint and carbonized petroleum jelly in it."

He rose and looked down at me. He shook his head and sighed. "We lost the Adams baby over at Homer to it just yesterday."

Mother made that *tch-tch* sound with her tongue. "So sad. Harriet and Harvey must be taking it badly. I'll send a pie over."

"No other way to take it," Doc Simpson said. He sighed again. "Just wish I knew what all we could do for it." He patted me on the head. It hurt. "You take it easy, James."

He left with Mother. Hannah came over and looked down at me. "Scarlet fever. Keep y'warm and y'burning up and all. Humph! Keep y'cool to brings yer temp-er-achur down, that what needed! A touch of belladonna and some calomel and aconite, I think. Mix it with a little bacon rind. That what y'need." She bent and kissed my forehead and gently patted my cheek. "Y'jus' lay there an' leave ev'r'thing to me."

She left and I looked out the window. Cold sunlight. In the books no one died when the sun was shining. But I knew that wasn't right. You could die just the same if the sun was shining or not. I closed my eyes and imagined my friends at my funeral. Yellow candles on the altar. My coffin. And Hannah singing.

> *"Amazin' grace! How sweet the sound*
> *That saved a wretch like me!"*

Pretty and sad. I shivered. I wanted to cry, but I didn't want anyone to come in and see me crying. I liked that song, though. The words were pretty and sad. And that made me cry. The pretty and sad words.

"Here." I opened my eyes. Hannah stood beside my bed. "Sit up." She put her arm under my shoulders and lifted. I sat up and leaned my head against her soft breast. It felt better than my pillow and I wished she would lie down with me and let me lay my head there and sleep there. I tried to tell her that, but she laughed and said, "Y'too young for that. Here. Take this." She shoved a spoon in my mouth. It tasted terrible.

"Yuck," I said. I tried to spit, but my mouth was too dry.

"Drink this, now," she said. She put a cup to my lips and I drank, tasting beef broth. It felt warm and good as it slid down my throat. She put the cup on the floor and leaned me over. She tugged at my nightshirt. "Let me get this off y'all."

"I'll be naked!" I croaked. I wrapped my arms around myself to keep her from pulling it off. She laughed.

"Y'all ain't got nothing Ah ain't seen before," she scolded. "But we gots to rub this lotion on y'rashes and get a clean nightshirt on. This one's done soaked wet."

And I let her pull it off me. I shivered as she spread lotion over my back and under my arms and across my neck. She pushed me back on the bed and spread lotion over my chest and stomach. I felt myself moving when she spread the lotion in my groin.

"Y'all ain't that sick y'can do that!" she said. She laughed again. Deep. Like a man would laugh.

"Hannah," I said, embarrassed.

"Don't worry," she whispered. "Ah won't tell. Now, sit up again so's we can get this clean nightshirt on y'all."

It felt cool and clean on me, and when she left I closed my eyes and thought about my friends at school doing their sums and stuff and wished I was there instead of laying in my bed. The light was soft in the window. But it was nice. And then the darkness came again upon me in long, rolling waves. I heard the mumble of people's voices riding on the waves. I saw a small boat sailing toward me, rocking over the waves. Two people were in it. One was a woman with curling coppery-red hair and sparkling green eyes. The other was a short man with a great hooked nose. His eyes burned. They scared me.

> *"Sing, little sparrow, let me hear*
> *Your song now for all the year"*

I opened my eyes. The curtains had been drawn back and gold sunlight poured in upon the puncheon floor. Hannah sat in a spindly-backed rocker. She stared out the window, singing. I felt cool. I smelled lavender and lemon verbena, and the sheets beneath me were fresh.

"Hannah," I said. My voice sounded normal. She turned her head and smiled. She rose and came to me, laying her hand across my forehead. It felt warm.

"Well, y'feelin' better," she said.

"I'm thirsty," I said.

"Uh-huh. Ah just bet y'are." She walked to the window and took a glass off the sill. She came back and helped me up. She held the glass to my lips. I drank thirstily. I lay back down. I felt hungry. I told her so. She beamed at me.

"That's good. Ah'll get y'some soup." She turned to go and I stopped her.

"Hannah." She looked back at me over my shoulder. "I love you."

She smiled. "Ah knows y'do, young Jim. Ah knows y'do."

CHAPTER 10

A GREAT fire, banked high and flickering, rose and fell on the wall. The smell of fresh bread was heavy in the room, and beneath it I could smell the cinnamon of fresh apple pie. Father sat in the slat-backed rocker in front of the fire. He looked thin and pale, his beard a gray shadow over his gaunt cheeks. He held his Bible in his hands. His fingers looked pale and translucent and I imagined I could see the bones under them as he slowly turned the pages, reading passages at random. Mother moved quietly in the kitchen. My sisters played with rag dolls on the braided rug in front of the fire. I sat on the deacon's bench with Lorenzo, listening to Father read in a reedy voice.

" 'For rebellion is as the sin of witchcraft, and stubbornness is as iniquity and idolatry—' " He paused and stared into the flames. His eyes looked vacant for a moment; then he seemed to bring memory back as he looked over at Lorenzo and me. He tried to smile, but the smile looked terrible. The slack flesh of his jaws hung down. "That doesn't mean that you owe blind obedience to another, boys." He was upset by what Reverend Cowley had preached at Christmas services, a stern warning to those rumored to be helping slaves escape from their legal masters.

"The law," he had intoned, his eyes burning righteously out at his congregation, "is the law. If one transgresses against it, then one is defying authority. That cannot be. Man must have order in his life or he is nothing more than an animal, lurking around in the dark woods! God warns us to be obedient or we shall suffer the lion out of the forest and the wolf of the evenings and a leopard will come among us and tear us to pieces, because man's transgressions are many and his backslidings have grown to abominations. Destruction upon destruction will come down upon us and the whole land will become spoiled. The trumpets of the Armageddon will sound and the light of heaven will no longer shine upon the plains. The Lord says that the land shall become desolate and every city will be forsaken!"

Father shook his head. "No, boys, Reverend Cowley was wrong. When something is wrong, you must not blindly follow it. You must remember what is right and believe in yourself. Can you do anything less than Jesus?"

I glanced at Lorenzo and frowned. He caught my look and shook his head slightly as if to warn me not to question Father at the moment. I didn't need his warning. Father had been slipping in and out of the present for the past couple of weeks. A lump came into my throat. I hated to see his mind wandering around in dark places where none of us could go. I wished Oliver was there to help us, but he had left home and gone to California along with others, looking for gold. Horace and Lorenzo had taken over the running of the farm, doing the chores, while I spent my time in the woods and fields, hunting meat for our table. Horace resented this but had to acknowledge that I was the better shot and since powder and ball was expensive, it was sound practice to leave that to me.

I had traded squirrel and raccoon skins from animals I had caught with a couple of double-springed No. 4 English Rattraps for an old flintlock pistol three years before and discovered that I could hit about anything I aimed at. From that it was a practical step to Father's rifle and shotgun. I began wandering the hills, hunting squirrels, rabbits, and prairie chickens and, at least once every two weeks, a deer that I hung in the smokehouse behind the barn. Mother and Father were not pleased—Father most of all, as he wanted me to study for the law, and Mother because she wanted me to be a preacher—but we needed meat for the table. I learned what I could from *The Trapper's Guide* and *The Life of Kit Carson*, reading at night in my attic room after the others had gone to bed. I traded the furs and Father's rifle at the Green Mountain House for a better one and a cap-and-ball revolving pistol and practiced as much as I could.

"You must remember that, boys," Father said, and I brought myself back to the present, listening to him as he warned us about the evils of slavery. His eyes looked fever-bright in the firelight. "Do not sacrifice your beliefs because another tells you that the law forbids you to have them. Man makes laws, but God gave you good sense to figure out if the law is just or not."

Then his eyes glazed again and he frowned, groping for the thought he knew he had. I let my mind wander again as he bent his head and began to awkwardly rifle the pages of his Bible, searching for a passage to help him remember. The winter had been harsh and wolves had moved in from the hills and deep woods. Nahum had lost a milch cow and a new calf to them and other farmers had complained about losing stock as well.

"William, William. We need your boy James," Nahum said after church while we huddled in the cold on the wagon, waiting for Father to climb in and drive us back home. Nahum glanced up at me. He sighed, his breath coming out in a frosty cloud. He clapped his gloved hands together. "I'm sorry, William, but your boy is the best shooter in these parts and these wolves have gotten out of hand. Mrs. Wilson lost five of her best layers just last night."

"James has school, Nahum," Father said mildly.

"William, William," he said, shaking his head. "I wouldn't ask, but we"—he paused to indicate a small group of silent, somber-faced men dressed in black who had gathered around them—"we can't afford to lose any more stock. Times are hard, William. Sometimes, we just have to do things we don't want to."

"No," Father said. "I won't compromise James's schooling. Once you leave school, Nahum, it's twice as hard going back to it."

I knew what he was talking about. He had lectured all of us many times on the need for us to take responsibility for our own actions. But, he had emphasized, we also had to remember that some things took a great amount of self-discipline and the moment we relaxed that discipline, we would find it twice as hard getting back into the swing of things.

"The devil just watches for such moments, boys," he'd said. "Then he pounces upon you. The minute you relax your discipline, you'll find it almost impossible to get your nose back on the grindstone. That's why we have so many ne'er-do-wells along the road today. They never got the gumption back to make something of themselves after they slipped away from self-discipline." Father had been reading Mr. Emerson's essays with great relish.

Nahum eyed him steadily for a moment, then shook his head. "William, I don't know any other way of putting it. There isn't one of us here who wouldn't do it if we could. But the pure fact is that we can't. We have to stay back and protect what we have. But we can't keep an eye on everything all the time. We need James. We *need* him, William. He can carry the fight to the wolves, track them, get rid of them while we guard our stock. Can't you see that that is the only possible solution? Can *you* afford to lose any stock, William?"

A low grumble came from the others around Father. He turned his head and studied the others; then his shoulders slumped. "All right," he said. "I'll give James a week." He raised his head and fixed me with his piercing blue-gray eyes. "But *only* a week, understand?" He was speaking to the others, but I knew that he meant me.

I nodded. "Yes, Father. I'll do it for a week. Then I'll go

back to school." I looked down at Nahum. "I'll start tomorrow, sir. But today is Christmas. I'm spending that with my family."

Relief spread over Nahum's face. He nodded vigorously. "Yes, that will be all right. Certainly, James, we don't want to take you from your family. By all means."

Father climbed into the wagon and looked down, studying the men. "All well and good, gentlemen. But there are costs to this, as well." A cautionary look came into the eyes of all. "There's powder and shot to be considered. And James should be rewarded for his time."

"There's the bounty," Nahum began, but Father cut him off.

"That's to be understood, Nahum," he said sternly, and all there knew that there would be no arguing with Father on this matter. "But his powder and shot are operating expenses you can't expect James or his family to bear."

"William, William. You will benefit just as much as the rest of us," Nahum said, frowning.

"Yes, that's true," Father said. He gathered the reins. "But I have no intention of bearing all the expense. We shall split it among all of us. *All* of us," he added, staring hard at Beaufoy, who was known for his stinginess. Beaufoy looked away, then back at Father, and finally nodded.

"I'll pay the first foray," George McLaughlin said, stepping forward. He looked up at me. "You swing by the farm tomorrow, James. I'll give you a horn and some shot to get you started."

My heart leaped as I glanced over his head to where Sarah and Josephine sat, waiting in the wagon. Sarah looked away from me, her cheeks reddening, but Josephine smiled and a devilish look came into her eyes. "Thank you, sir," I said, looking back to him. He nodded.

"That's good of you, George," Father said. He glanced at

the others. "I think that's the way to do it. When James needs more powder and shot, he'll go to the next one on the list. In alphabetical order. That's only fair, I think."

The others nodded grudgingly, but Beaufoy spoke up, saying, "Is that *after* McLaughlin?"

A look of quiet disgust came over Father's face. He lifted his chin. "No, we'll start with the beginning of the alphabet, I think. You'll be after Adams, Beaufoy."

"That don't seem right," Beaufoy complained. "I mean, Nashe should rightfully come after McLaughlin. Seems to me, anyway."

"You objecting to the terms, Beaufoy?" Nahum asked dangerously.

Beaufoy took a quick look around at the grim faces of his neighbors and sensed them pulling away from him. He shook his head. "No, no. That ain't what I'm saying. It's just that—no, nothing. All right." He looked up at me and said sourly, "You come by my place next, Jim." But I could see the angry glare in his eyes and made a mental note to watch myself when I went around to his farm. I didn't know what it was, but I sensed something not right with him.

"Yes, sir," I said.

Father nodded curtly, flicked the reins over the backs of our horses, and pulled away from church, heading home. A strange exhilaration swept through me as I contemplated the brief vacation I would have away from school. It was a boy's dream! Freedom to wander through the woods and fields, hunting. Father glanced at me and shook his head slightly. Immediately I wiped the smile off my face, but he had seen my pleasure at being given permission to be truant from school.

"Priorities, James," he said softly. "Always remember your priorities. All other things are momentary and temporal. Joy is fleeting. It comes to us only in brief spurts." He coughed, a hard, wracking cough that wrenched his back into a crooked question mark. "And then," he managed in a strangled voice, "you are left with reality. With life." A bitter smile flashed across his lips and then disappeared. But in that smile I read the future. And it was black and grim.

CHAPTER 11

A GREAT fire, banked high and red, flamed in the fireplace, but dinner was not yet on the table. Mother bustled around in the kitchen with Hannah, both stepping nimbly over and around my sisters, who played at helping them prepare Christmas dinner. The cooking smells wafted into the room where we sat before the fire, I on a small stool beside the hearth while Oliver and Horace and Lorenzo lounged around on the floor. Father sat in his slat-backed rocker, his feet resting on the toasted boss.

"You will be careful tomorrow, James," Father said suddenly, sternly, startling me. I looked over at him and nodded.

"Yes, Father," I said. "I'll be careful."

He cleared his throat, started to speak, then sighed and shook his head. "I don't know what to tell you, James, other than to be very careful. Wolves aren't like other animals. They're like people. Crafty, and you don't know what they will do until they do it. But if you always expect the worst, then you'll be ready for anything that happens." He grinned wryly. "Not a very good endorsement for man, though, is it? Still, one has to wonder what man has become over the years, and I suppose this is as good a time of the year to do it as any other. I don't see much where man has really progressed. There is a lot of hatred out there, boys. A lot of hatred. You'll have to work with it the best that you can."

"Mizzus Hickok sent me in with some hot cider for y'gentlemens," Hannah said, coming into the room with a tray filled with cups of steaming cider. She passed among us, bending forward to let us select our own. She smiled at me and I smelled baking upon her. My head swam suddenly and I stammered out a "thank you" as I lifted a cup from the tray, cradling it in my hands that suddenly felt big and awkward.

"Thank you, Hannah," Father said. He sipped and nodded appreciatively. "This is very good. Just the right touch of cinnamon and clove."

"Little brown sugar does it good, too, Ah think," Hannah said. She nodded at us. "Dinner'll be ready in a few more minutes. Soon's we get the fixin's ready."

She left and Father leaned back in his rocker, resting his cup upon the arm of the chair. "I think that was a propitious delivery, boys," he said. "This is not the time of year to be talking about the frailties of man. James, would you hand down my Bible for me? I think it is time that we remember what this time of year is about."

I rose and took his Bible from its resting place on the mantel and handed it to him. He took another swallow of the cider and placed the cup on the small table at his elbow. He took his glasses from the table and slipped them on, placing the wire hooks carefully over his ears. Then, he slowly, lovingly, opened the Bible and began to read.

" 'There was in the days of Herod, the king of Judaea, a certain priest named Zacharias . . .' " and I let my mind slip away from his words, sipping my cider as I thought of the morrow and where I would start my hunt—at the McLaughlin pasture where wolves had brought down a mother that had tried to defend her newborn calf.

Then Mother came in with Hannah, both bearing the

Christmas dinner, and I watched as Father rose painfully
from his chair and crossed to his place at the head of the
table. We all crowded around at our usual spots with Hannah
sitting on my left. She had a small puff of powder clinging
to her dress just above her breast. She caught me looking
and smiled at me and my stomach gave a kind of lurch as it
did when I swung out from a hanging rope over a deep hole
in Tomahawk Creek just as I let go.

"Now," Father said, and I took Hannah's hand in mine
and Lydia's small hand in the other as we formed our circle
around the evening table. Father cleared his throat and
closed his eyes, raising his face to the ceiling. I knew he was
looking beyond the ceiling to the heavens and imagining
God on his throne. I knew it, but I pushed the thought aside
for the moment, concentrating on the plump turkey, trussed
and skewered, its skin a basted golden-brown. I had collected that turkey within an hour of taking my stand in the
woods above the tiny salt lick above Tomahawk Creek
where I had prudently scattered a couple of handfuls of corn
every day for a month.

"Bless us, O Lord, and these thy gifts which through thy
bounty we are about to receive through Christ our Lord.
God grant us peace; God grant us wisdom; God grant us
patience that we might do thy work as we walk through thy
world. Give us the strength to avenge the persecuted and—"

Why did Mr. Beaufoy refer to his tallywhacker as a turkey?

"—lead us not into temptation. Amen."

We all "amened" after him and pulled out our chairs, sitting. For a few minutes we busied ourselves, passing our
plates up to Father, who carefully carved the turkey, filling
them with whatever was in front of us as we passed them
back down to their temporary owners. Then we ate, being
careful to chew our food and not gulp it lest we draw a stern

rebuke from Mother about the healthful need to chew each bite twenty times before swallowing.

Once, Lorenzo asked if that included water and was given the chore of washing and drying everything on the dining table to familiarize him with the peculiar attributes of water and why his question was a sarcastic rejoinder and not a serious one despite his protests after the penance was pronounced.

"Father?" Lorenzo said. Father looked up, fastidiously wiping his mouth on a napkin. "Do you think I could go along with James? I mean, he might need someone to watch his back in case another devil of a turkey creeps up on him." He smirked at me. I shook my head.

"A tree'll do that job just as good as you, I reckon," I answered. Lorenzo laughed.

"Well, James, I don't know. Seems to me I remember—"

"I would think you all would do better if you focused on what this day is all about," Father said quietly, but with enough authority in his voice that we knew better than to push the issue. Whenever Father didn't get enough time to complete his Bible thought for the day, he would stubbornly hold it in his mind until he had exorcised it, even if it took the daylight hours to finish it.

"William," Mother said politely. "It's Christmas. I think the boys are all old enough to know the day without being reminded of it."

"It's only one day out of the year, Polly," Father said patiently. "And I don't think it hurts them one bit to recall purpose over pleasure. The Lord is patient, my dear, but patience is not endless."

We glanced at one another, trying to recall the reason for Father's words. Horace shook his head slightly and I sighed and glanced at Hannah out of the corners of my eyes. She caught my look and smiled again. I felt my face grow warm and took a large bite of sweet potatoes. Too large. I started coughing and grabbed my water glass to wash the bite down.

"Moderation, James!" Father snapped. "How many times have we told you—"

"Sorry, Father," I managed between coughs. "Wrong pipe. That's all."

"The wrong pipe comes from the lack of attention. I hope that you pay closer attention tomorrow when you are alone out there."

Lorenzo cleared his throat. "Uh, Father, about that—"

"I think James will be able to handle the problem quite well on his own," Father said quietly. "Besides, I'm not about to lose two sons to this adventure. You have school, Lorenzo."

"Not for two more days!" Lorenzo objected.

"And that time can best be put to studying after you finish your chores," Father said firmly. "That is enough about all of this. Now, who can tell me the parable about the Prodigal Son? Horace?"

CHAPTER 12

THE DAY came up cold and gray, with swollen clouds hanging low over the grove. The dampness of the day clung to me as I moved into the trees, following the frozen path of the wolves. Behind me, the crows cawed urgently as they came back to the feast of a doe they'd pulled down after I had frightened them away with my approach. I noticed that a fresh track had been added to the old ones. One wolf had come back for a couple of feedings. I moved cautiously through the trees, making my way slowly through the brush to minimize the scratching of branches against my canvas trousers and coat. I held my Hall-North percussion rifle at port with a gloved hand while my right hand I kept naked against the time when I might need it urgently.

Halfway through the grove, a prickling sensation began on the back of my neck. I eased across a clearing and placed my back against a tree, carefully searching the underbrush for the reason for my unease. I frowned, listening to the deep silence. *Deep silence! Where were the squirrels? The jays? Sparrows?*

I stared all around the shadowy order of the clearing, moving my thoughts in time with my eyes. For a brief moment I felt panic as a shadow moved; then I relaxed as it came stationary again and I could see it was only a small bush. Fat flakes of snow began to fall, but I remained where I was, shifting my weight slightly, working my toes beneath their two layers of socks in my boots, willing the cold outside my body.

And then I smelled the wolf, a musty, deep smell that seemed to gather at the back of my throat. I swallowed and tasted the smell and knew he was close and that he was watching me, waiting, waiting—

I straightened and dropped my arm holding the rifle, half-turning to the clearing to make it look like I didn't know he was there. Still he didn't show himself. My hand moved along the barrel of my rifle. It was icy cold. A strange melancholy settled over me as if I was half-awakened from a dream and didn't know the passing of time. I shivered. Then, somehow, I knew he was coming. I took a deep, quick breath and turned, bringing the rifle up to my shoulder as I did so. The wolf was halfway across the clearing when I came around. He growled low in his throat at my sudden move and tried to turn, but the force of his rush was against him. I brought the bead of my rifle down upon his chest. He half-turned, giving me his shoulder, and I squeezed the trigger.

I didn't hear the sound of the shot behind the rush of blood pounding in my head, but I felt the thump of the rifle as it recoiled against my shoulder. The ball took the wolf in the shoulder, knocking him over. He yelped and his paws scrambled in the snow, trying to push him erect. His head twisted and he snapped at his shoulder where the bullet had taken him. Then his eyes glazed and he stretched out slowly, his paws digging at the snow in the last panic of life. I took a deep breath and leaned back against the tree. My head felt suddenly clear and I became aware of the fine outlines of the trees, the twigs on the undergrowth, the dead leaves that had yet to fall from their twigs.

I waited until his legs stretched out stiff, then slowly approached and nudged him with the toe of my boot. Suddenly I remembered that my rifle was empty and I hastened back to the tree and placed my back to it as I reloaded the Hall-North. I had to try twice to place the percussion cap on the nipple, but at last I finished. Again I approached the wolf and nudged him. A wave of disappointment came over me along with deep regret and, strangely, a small sense of exhilaration. I took a deep breath, smelling the harsh bite of the wolf's blood. I dragged the carcass of the wolf close to the tree. I leaned my rifle against the tree, close to hand, then took out my skinning knife and squatted over the wolf.

Heavy snow had begun to fall before I was finished, and I could feel the cold working its fingers deep under my coat. My toes were numb and my hands mottled blue. I rolled up the wolf's coat and scrubbed my hands as clean as I could with the snow, then took a pair of gloves from the deep pockets of my coat and pulled them on. I rose, stamping my feet until they began to tingle, then gathered the wolf's coat and my rifle and began to make my way back home. The woods had become dark and deep as I emerged from their depths and forced my way through the gathering drifts across the home pasture. By the time I stumbled into our front yard, I could barely see the outline of our house through the blowing snow.

I stepped up onto the porch and dropped the wolf pelt onto an old hide-bottomed chair, then tried to open the door, but my hands wouldn't turn the knob. I knocked on the door with the butt of my rifle. The cold had found me beneath my coat by now. I felt chilled to the bone. I knocked again, swinging the rifle butt hard against the door. Suddenly it opened and heat rushed out, nearly staggering me. Hannah stared at me as if Harpe's ghost had suddenly appeared in front of her.

"Why, James!" she exclaimed. "What in the world?" She stepped forward, taking my rifle from me. "Y'look frozen half to death! Y'get in heah! Come on now!"

I stumbled and nearly fell over the threshold. My feet felt like two lumps of ice. I took a deep breath and winced as hot air rushed into my lungs.

"Where . . . Where's Mother? The others?" I managed. I tried to unbutton my coat, but my fingers couldn't feel the buttons and I couldn't push them through the buttonholes of my coat. Hannah pushed my hands away and quickly unbuttoned my coat, hanging it on a hook beside the door. She pushed me toward the fireplace. I stumbled over the rug and would have fallen had she not grabbed me by my arm and held me up.

"Y'daddy took a turn to the wuss shortly after y'left for the woods," she said. Her finely arched eyebrows pinched together in a frown. "Y'brother Horace was goin' to ride foah the doctor, but y'mama thought it better if they jus' hitched up the team and took y'daddy into town. Save time that way. She right, of course; by the time Horace rode in and back agin, why, they-all would have been in town an hour at least. Ah don' know what to tell yuh. But Ah don' think they'll be back tonight." She glanced out the window where the thick flakes had turned to hard snow rattling against the panes. The wind began to moan around the eaves. "Ah think they'll stay over at the Green Mountain House. If not there, then somewhere in Homer."

My teeth began to chatter.

"An' heah y'is freezin' in them wet clothes! Tch. Tch." She clucked her tongue in disapproval. "Y'get out'n those wet clothes right now while I gets y'a blanket to wrap in!" She bustled into Mother and Father's room and came back with a bolster while I was still trying to work the buttons on my shirt.

"Heah," she said impatiently, brushing my hands away. She ignored my protests and within seconds had my butternut shirt unbuttoned and was pulling it off my shoulders. She wrapped the blanket around me. "Now, y'slip outta them pants. Whilst Ah gets y'a hot drink! Men!" she snorted derogatorily as she headed with my wet shirt to the kitchen. "Not one-a them's got the sense the good Lord give a jack-rabbit!"

I slipped out of my pants and wrapped the blanket around me and pushed a small stool in front of the hearth and dropped thankfully on it. Slowly, I began to thaw, but the wind whistling around the eaves made me huddle deeper into the blanket. Hannah appeared with a cup of hot tea. She shoved it into my hands, commanding me to drink. I sipped, tasting peppermint and honey. I drank deeper.

"Good. That's good," she said with satisfaction. "Warm yer insides up and y'won't catch pee-no-mea." She disappeared back in the kitchen and reappeared with a small jar of Balm of Gilead ointment. She opened the jar and the odor of wintergreen spread in the room. "Open that blanket so's Ah kin rub this on y'chest an' back," she ordered.

"It's cold," I complained, teeth chattering.

"James Butler Hickok, y'do as Ah say!" she commanded sternly. Her black eyes held that no-nonsense look.

Automatically I opened the blanket. Her fingers swiped a generous amount of the ointment on her fingertips and rubbed it on my shoulders and back, moving in small circles as she worked cold knots out of my muscles. Her hands slipped over my shoulders and down onto my chest, rubbing. Slowly, my muscles began to relax as the warmth from the ointment and the fire worked their magic. My eyelids began to droop.

"There!" she exclaimed with satisfaction. She stepped away from me. "Now y'get y'self inta bed. Go on now, y'hear?"

Obediently I rose and stumbled toward the stairs. I nearly fell and again she caught me. "Now y'stop this nonsense, y'hear, James? Y'gets y'self up to bed!"

"Yes, ma'am," I said sleepily. I didn't remember ever feeling that tired. I forced my feet up the stairs and fell onto my bed. Dimly I was aware of Hannah covering me with blankets. Then I slept.

CHAPTER 13

GRAY DAYLIGHT shone through the muslin curtains Mother had hung over the small attic window when I awoke. Wind still moaned around the eaves and the rafters creaked and popped overhead. I took a deep breath, smelling the faint odor of wintergreen and balsam from the ointment that Hannah had rubbed on my chest. I sighed and stretched beneath the blankets piled on top of me, squirreling deeper into the warm nest I had made while I slept. I felt drowsy and content.

The stairs creaked and I turned my head to watch Hannah peek over the top. She saw me awake and smiled, coming the rest of the way up. She came across and put her hand on my forehead, feeling for a fever. She nodded, satisfied.

"How y'feel this mornin'?" she asked.

"Fine," I said. "Is it still snowing?"

She nodded. "Yes, and it don' look like it gonna let up for another day. Maybe two."

"I wonder how Father is," I said, frowning.

She hesitated, then shook her head slowly. "Ah don' know, but—" She shrugged. "It only a mattah of time, James. But Ah think y'know that, don' yuh?"

I sighed, feeling a lump beginning to form in my throat. "Yes, I know it. It's just that not knowing is worse than knowing."

She nodded. "Ah knows. But we kin only wait. Nothin' more kin be done. 'Cept take care of what's heah. Now, if'n y'feel up to it, the cow needs to be milked and fed and other chores needin' to be done. Ah kin gather the eggs—"

"No," I said, interrupting her. "There's only need for one of us to go outside. That should be me. Some hay'll need to be pitched down and I reckon I'd better muck out a couple of stalls."

"Y'dress warmly, heah?" she said.

"The work'll keep me warm," I said. Without thinking, I threw back the covers and sat up before I realized I was naked. Hannah took a step backward, then turned her face away. Her face grew darker. I blushed and grabbed my blankets, covering myself. "Sorry, Hannah," I said.

She made a shoo-shoo gesture with her hands and turned back to the stairs. "Ain't seen nothing Ah ain't seen befoah," she said. "Ah'll get y'breakfast ready while y'dress."

Hannah had eggs and bacon on a plate waiting for me by

the time I got dressed and made my way down from the attic. I was ravenous and wolfed everything down, wiping the last of the egg yolk and grease from my plate with a piece of fresh-baked bread. Hannah nodded approvingly as I pushed back from the table, well sated.

"Y'did a fair amount of damage to that," she said, clearing my plate from in front of me.

"It was great, Hannah. Thank you," I said. I glanced out the window and sighed reluctantly. "Well, that cow isn't going to get milked or the stalls cleaned with me sitting here."

I rose and crossed to where my coat hung on a peg beside the door. I shrugged into it, buttoning it tightly against my chin. I wrapped a scarf around my face and pulled the flaps of my hat down over my ears. I pulled a pair of leather gloves out of the pocket of my coat and opened the door, gasping as the wind struck me hard. I stepped outside and quickly shut the door behind me. I could barely see the barn through the swirling snow. I lowered my head and forced my way through the deep drifts.

I reached the barn and had to kick snow away before I could open the door. I hurried inside and pulled the door behind me. The barn was cold and dim, but I could see Jenny, our cow, waiting in her stall. She heard me and lowed, telling me she wanted to be milked. I glanced at the other stalls and saw that Horace or Lorenzo had already mucked them out and spread clean hay. I silently thanked my brother as I took a stool and pail and made my way to Jenny's stall.

"There now, old girl," I said soothingly as I slid into the stall beside her. "I'll bet you're glad to see me."

She lowed again and I laughed and sat beside her and began pulling on her teats. The milk came in a long, hissing rush and I leaned my forehead against Jenny's warm flank as I settled into milking motion. When I finished, I threw some hay for her, shoveled out the manure from her stall, and gave her a small bait of corn in celebration.

"There, old girl," I said, patting her rump. "I'll see you around supper time, all right?"

She grunted and lowered her head, methodically working her cud. I laughed again and picked up the bucket of milk and walked to the door. I braced myself and swung the door open just enough for me to slip out. Again the wind seemed to take my breath away. I shut the door hurriedly behind me and pushed my way again through the drifts back to the house. I went around to the kitchen door and opened the door, stepping inside, pulling the door shut hard behind me to make it latch.

"Oh!" Hannah exclaimed, and squirmed in the zinc bathtub she had pulled over to the fire, trying to cover herself with a washcloth.

I stood, staring openmouthed at her full breasts, her heavy thighs tapering into well-muscled calves.

"I-I-I'm sorry," I stammered. I gestured with the milk pail. Milk slopped over onto the floor. "I finished milking," I said lamely.

"An' y'were goin' to clean the stalls, too," Hannah said, huddling down in the bathtub. It did little good, though. I could still see the tops of her naked breasts and knew the rest of her was naked, too.

"Horace or Lorenzo already did that," I said. I tried to look away, but her gleaming nakedness drew my eyes back to her like nails to a magnet. My temples began to pound.

"James!" she said.

"Sorry. Sorry," I mumbled. I forced myself to turn around. I became aware of the milk pail in my hand and automatically turned again to place it on the counter.

Hannah had just stepped from the tub. She exclaimed and hurriedly tried to wrap a towel around her. In her frustration, the towel kept slipping away. Before I knew it, I was next to her. She stopped, staring at me her eyes big and luminous. Gently I took the towel from her and wrapped it around her. She smelled like cinnamon. My cold fingers touched the skin of her shoulder. She shivered. I bent and kissed her. For a moment she stood stock-still, shocked. Then she tentatively kissed me back. I kissed her again.

And again.

The towel dropped.

She stood naked in front of me, her eyes downcast.

A tiny pulse beat rapidly in her throat.

I touched it gently.

CHAPTER 14

I OPENED my eyes to moonlight streaming in through my window. I rose and walked naked across the wooden floor and pushed the muslin curtains aside. A full moon stood high in the sky. Behind it I could see the cold glitter of stars. The storm had passed. I sighed and stretched in the cold of my room, then hurried back to my bed. Hannah raised herself up on one elbow as I slid in beside her. Her naked breasts pressed against my chest. I caught my breath and I took her in my arms and kissed her. I slid my hands over her back and felt welts.

"What happened?" I asked.

She leaned back away from me, then sat up and turned away. The blankets fell away from her shoulders to gather in folds around her hips. I saw the criss-crossed marks on her back and touched them gently.

"What happened?" I asked again.

"That what a blacksnake do when a woman sasses her

master," Hannah said harshly. "Ah was took down to the barn with all the other niggers standing around and the master had another nigger lay it on me. Then he salted me."

"Salted?" I asked.

She sighed. "They's rub salt over my back. After they's done wi' whippin'."

She looked over her shoulder at me. I sat up and wrapped my arms around her and kissed the welts on her back. My hands cupped her breasts. She moaned.

"I'm sorry, Hannah," I said hoarsely.

She shook her head. "It take two to do this, James." She rolled over on top of me and pulled the blankets up over us. She looked down into my eyes. "But Ah don' think there'll be much of this later."

"No," I answered regretfully. A great sadness filled me. "No, I don't expect there will be."

Two days later, I awoke, trying to figure out what had awakened me. The night seemed still, dark. I glanced at the silver moonlight coming through the window. I listened hard. Then I heard excited cackling. I threw back the covers and leaped from bed.

"What—" Hannah said groggily, raising herself.

"Something's in the henhouse!" I exclaimed, pulling on my pants. I stamped into my boots and hurried down the stairs. I paused to shrug into my coat, then grabbed Father's shotgun from the corner of the kitchen and stepped outside.

I paused to let my eyes adjust to the dark. Whatever it was, the hens were in a right ruckus. I stepped down off the steps and hurried as fast as I could through the drifts toward the house. I could smell the hot, sickly, rich smell of live chickens on the cold air. Halfway there, I saw a shadow dart from the edge of the house and run lightly over the snow. I recognized the brush and raised Father's shotgun, sighting carefully, swinging the barrel slightly. I squeezed the trigger and felt the shotgun kick against my shoulder. A gray cloud rose from the barrel. I took a step to the side, my finger automatically sliding to the second trigger. Then I saw the fox lying on the snow, his legs kicking weakly in his last tremors.

I pushed my way through the snow, keeping the barrel of the shotgun up. His blood was black on the snow in the moonlight, his coat red rust. The chicken lay a short distance away. I sighed, lowering the barrel of the shotgun. The moon cast an eerie white light upon the snow, making it almost like daylight. I felt a strange sense of regret as I bent and picked up the fox. His head rolled back and his tongue lolled out the side of his sharp teeth, dripping blood.

I turned and trudged back to the house, being careful to hold the fox away from me so the blood wouldn't spatter against my pants or coat. Hannah, wrapped in a quilt, was waiting at the door when I came back to the house. Moonlight played off her coffee-colored skin. She seemed one with the night and I paused, staring admiringly at her. She glanced from the fox in my hand to my face, and I read the admiration in her eyes. She smiled softly, sadly, then turned and went back to the steps, climbing slowly to my bedroom. I heard the rustle of the blankets and the creak of the rawhide webbing as she settled back into my bed. I looked down at the fox. I sighed and took a piece of old rawhide lacing hanging from a hook on the back porch. I made a quick loop and hung the fox from the hook by his front paws.

I turned and looked to the east; the sun had yet to throw false morning into the sky. I took a deep breath and let it out slowly, watching the mist rise up in the cold. I glanced again at the fox. A glaze had settled over his bright black eyes. Yet they seemed to be looking into me, and for a brief moment I imagined him saying, *You have killed me, but the brief life I lived, wild and free, is a life to be remembered.*

I shivered and went into the kitchen. I stood Father's shot-gun back in the corner and went up the stairs. I climbed into bed and Hannah turned to me. Tears glinted in her eyes. She rested her head upon my chest and I felt the warmth of her tears slide onto my chest.

And I held her close.

CHAPTER 15

I WAS in the barn, finishing the milking of Jenny, when I heard the wagon slow and Lorenzo's voice call out in the clear, cold air. I rose, taking the bucket of milk with me, and walked outside the barn, squinting my eyes against the hard glare of the sun off the snow. I waved and came down to the front of the house. Lorenzo looked tired, with purple half moons under his eyes. Mother looked as if she had been pulled through a thicket by her curls. Father was pale and hollow-eyed.

"James," Lorenzo said, nodding. I placed the milk pail on the ground and took the reins as he handed them to me. "Did you get any wolves?"

"One," I admitted. "And a fox that got into the henhouse one night." Mother looked up quickly at that, concern show-ing in her face.

"How many did we lose?" she asked.

"One," I said. "But I got it back. Hannah fixed it the next night for supper," I added casually, nodding as Hannah came out the door.

Mother nodded and sighed. "One. Well, long's it didn't go to waste. I guess we should be thankful that more weren't lost."

"Yes'm," Hannah said. She nodded shyly at me. "James took care of that right away. Next morning, he repaired the coop so no more foxes could get in."

Mother frowned, glancing between the two of us. Hannah's face turned a shade darker. I glanced up at Father, pretending not to notice how Mother's lips compressed into a hard, straight line.

"Father, how are you?"

He looked at me, puzzlement showing in his eyes. He looked at Mother. "Polly? Where are we?"

"We're home, William," Mother said, sighing. "Home." She glanced back at Hannah, frowning.

Hannah pretended not to notice and bent, picking up the pail of milk. "Ah'll just bet y'all could do with a bite to eat. Ah'll go an' take care of that."

She nodded pleasantly and left. I reached up to help Father down from the wagon. He gave me a quick look of fear and clutched Lorenzo's arm. Lorenzo looked down at me and shook his head.

"He's been like that ever since we took him in," Lorenzo said. He stepped down and reached up, helping Father as he stepped clumsily out of the wagon box and stumbled over the wheel to the ground.

"What happened?" I asked, standing back so Mother could take his other arm.

"Well, we don't know," Mother said. "That day when you went out hunting he got to watching the weather, and when it started to snow he got to fidgeting and worrying about where you were. When the snow began to gather and you still weren't home, he started pacing back and forth in front of the door and window, fussing about how you might be lying out there, hurt, in the woods someplace. Horace tried to tell him that you were all right. So did Lorenzo." I glanced at him; he nodded. "But he just wouldn't believe them. Then he started to get himself ready to go out and find you and bring you home. We tried to stop him, and then he just sort of, well"—she shrugged—"collapsed. There isn't anything else to say about it. Horace was going to ride in after the doctor, but I figured it would be faster if we just took your dad in to him."

"That's what Hannah told me," I said.

"Uh-huh," Mother grunted as they helped Father over the threshold into the living room. He stood still as she began to take off his hat and coat. "Speaking of which"—she eyed me sternly—"you two were alone out here together. Everything okay?"

"Sure," I said, feeling my ears grow hot.

Her lips grew harder. "You sure, Son?"

"What couldn't be right?" I asked.

She studied me for a long moment, then sighed and slowly nodded. "All right. I guess I'm just jumping at shadows. The past few days have been hard, being in town with your father and not knowing how you were."

"Where are the girls?"

"We left them off at the McLaughlins' on the way past," Mother said. She shook her head. "They're too young for this sort of thing. They don't understand what is wrong with your father."

"I'm not certain I understand, either," I said.

Mother sighed. "Well, we can only place our trust in the Lord and hope that he will guide us and make all things right."

I didn't answer. I was beginning to have a pretty dim opinion of the Lord lately. Father had lived his entire life trying to help others and now the good Lord was making him go through life like a child. I remembered Mr. Deasy reading to us about how man went through seven ages—

"It would behoove you all to listen a bit instead of carrying on like a bunch of hooligans and harlots!" he said, fixing the class with a stern look over the tops of his steel

reading spectacles. "And if you don't, I'll make certain that your parents find out about your behavior in school!"

We settled instantly. Most of our parents needed little excuse to whale a bit of learning into us with razor strops or broomsticks. Or silence. I didn't mind the occasional whippings so much as I did the silence that came for days when I did something that brought Mother or Father's disapproval. Botje started to sass Mr. Deasy back, but Lorenzo nudged him and gave him a warning look and Botje dropped his chin into the palms of his hands and propped his elbows on the plain plank that was his desk.

"That's better," Mr. Deasy said. "Now, class, pay attention. This comes from Shakespeare's As You Like It—"

"Short and sweet is how I like it, but I don't think we're gonna get it," muttered Botje.

"What's that?" Mr. Deasy said, raising his voice sharply.

"Nothin'," Botje said sullenly.

"Very well." Mr. Deasy cleared his throat, then began:

> " 'All the world's a stage,
> And all the men and women merely players:
> They have their exits and their entrances;
> And one man in his time plays many parts,
> His acts being seven ages. At first the infant,
> Mewling and puling in the nurse's arms.
> And then the whining schoolboy, with his
>   satchel,
> And shining morning face, creeping like snail
> Unwillingly to school. And then the lover,
> Sighing like furnace, with a woeful ballad
> Made to his mistress' eyebrow. Then a soldier,
> Full of strange oaths, and bearded like the pard,
> Jealous in honour, sudden and quick in
>   quarrel,
> Seeking the bubble reputation

Even in the cannon's mouth. And then the
  justice,
In fair round belly with good capon lined,
With eyes severe, and beard of formal cut,
Full of wise saws and modern instances;
And so he plays his part. The sixth age shifts
Into the lean and slippered pantaloon,
With spectacles on nose and pouch on side,
His youthful hose well saved, a world too wide
For his shrunk shank; and his big manly voice,
Turning again toward childish treble, pipes
And whistles in his sound. Last scene of all,
That ends this strange eventful history,
Is second childishness, and mere oblivion,
Sans teeth, sans eyes, sans taste, sans
  everything.' "

But Father, as near as I could figure it, had been cheated of a few of those ages. So much for God.

He had not made this life sweeter than that of a painted pomp. And I, I determined, seeing Father shuffle on his forgotten feet into the house, would not find myself a player in that show.

I turned and looked across the fields a blinding white from sun glancing off the unspoiled snow. *No,* I determined, *I will not end like this, shuffling through life and not knowing it.*

CHAPTER 16

THE WIND moaned around the eaves and I could hear the dry rustle of the autumn leaves shuffling off from where they had fallen and rustling in the trees where they stubbornly clung to the branches. I shivered although I was warm from my place beside the fire. I looked at the hot coals and watched, fascinated at the motion of the heat swirling slowly, forming images that appeared in strange succession among the glowing embers.

"Jim?"

I blinked and turned to Father, sitting in his rocker near the corner of the fireplace. My cheeks felt warm from the heat pouring from the fireplace. He bent forward and I felt his hand cool against my cheeks.

"Are you all right?"

"Yes, sir," I said. I glanced back at the fire. "It's just that—"

I stopped and stared in fascination as a ghostly figure formed itself, writhing, hollow-eyed, and mouth-gaped.

"Yes?" Father prompted. I shivered again and turned away, searching for and finding his eyes bright with concern. I took a deep breath and shook my head.

"Nothing, Father. Sometimes I get these strange feelings. I can't explain them, but they make me uneasy."

He pursed his lips, contemplating me searchingly. Then he sighed and ruffled my hair and leaned back in his chair. He locked his thumbs under his jaw and stared, brooding, into the fire. His thin face was drawn and white, and firelight flickered on the deep hollows of his cheeks. He remained silent for a long period. Time passed and still he stared silently into the fire, his eyes distant and seemingly focused upon nothing.

I sighed and turned away at Mother's voice gently reminding me that it was time for bed. Lorenzo complained and she stared at him with her unblinking hawk's eye. He rose and moved quietly toward our room. I pushed myself to my feet to follow him, but Father spoke out, stopping me.

"Jim, wait a moment. I wish to speak with you."

"It's his bedtime," Mother murmured.

Father smiled at her. "I know, Polly. But I wish to speak with him for a minute or two. We won't be long."

Mother shook her head at the suggestion that Father wanted to speak alone with me. She sighed and put away her knitting in the small carpetbag in which she stored her yarn and sewing supplies at the side of her chair.

"Don't keep him too late," she said to Father. "Tomorrow is a busy day. Boys grow while they're sleeping."

"They are all busy," Father said quietly.

Her lips tightened as she studied him; then she shook her head and took herself silently away.

I stood, waiting while Father studied me carefully. Then he gripped the arms of his rocker and said, "Jim, you must always fight against those dreams you have."

I shuffled my feet nervously. I knew he was concerned about me. But I didn't think my occasional reveries were much more than the mystical wanderings of a boy's mind filled with visions of adventures he had read about and wanted badly to experience.

"It's nothing, Father," I said. "I'll make sure it doesn't happen again."

Father stared searchingly into my eyes. Slowly he shook his head and said, "No, James, I don't want you to stop reading and thinking about what you are reading. But I think it is time that you realized a few things that dreams can only suggest.

"There will come a time when you will have to make a choice about what to do. Sometimes a man has to forget himself to help others who cannot help themselves. There are times when the law is not enough. Remember the story I told you about Samson?" He waited until I told him that I did; then he continued. "Some men are wily enough to escape justice. Others are strong enough to avoid the law's reach or powerful enough that the law cannot touch them. These men cannot be reasoned with and . . ."

He paused again, frowning as he gathered his thoughts.

"You must remember that good men are often blind to what they *know* they should do but are reluctant to believe. Jacob had to have his thigh broken by an angel. Paul had to be knocked off his camel and struck blind on the road to Damascus and suffer that blindness until he saw with his inner eye the truth he was meant to see. Even Jesus had to resort to violence a time or two when reason failed— remember when he lashed the moneylenders out of the Temple?"

A strong gust rattled the windows in their frames. Father glanced toward them. "This will blow a good storm down from the north—if I don't miss my guess."

He fell into a silent reverie for a long moment. His eye appeared to be studying something in the distance. I sighed. Father had slipped again into the other world. I rose and started toward my room. My hand was upon the doorknob when his voice stopped me.

"Jim."

I turned. "Yes, sir?"

"You're a good boy, Jim. Read Mark thirteen before you go to bed."

I sighed. Father was getting more and more insistent upon assigning reading passages from the Bible to one of us who happened to catch his eye. Tonight, it appeared, was to be my turn. "Yes, Father," I said, resigned.

He nodded. "Good night, James," he said, and rose.

"Night, Father," I answered.

He pressed his palm to the small of his back, stretching, then shuffled to his bedroom. He closed the door quietly. I sighed and walked to his chair and took his Bible from the small walnut table next to his rocker.

I opened it to Mark 13 and settled down in front of the fire to read it. Twice. But still I didn't understand it. I read the chapters before and after but could not understand why Father was so insistent that I read that particular chapter. I knew the words and the warnings Jesus gave his disciples, but I couldn't connect those words with Father's words.

I closed the Bible irritably and sat, staring into the fire, trying to comprehend why Father wanted me to read Mark 13. I brooded upon the reading and tried to work it out carefully in my mind Still the reason eluded me.

Sighing, I opened the Bible again and turned to the story of Samson—always one of my favorites, enjoying the strength of Samson, his dedication to his people, Delilah (I had a few secret dreams about that woman!), and his betrayal and his nobility in the midst of that betrayal and his death.

"What is it you do not understand?"

The voice startled me. I sat up and looked around. A long-haired man—blond hair—sat in Father's rocker. He was clean-shaven and wore a white robe. He was barefoot and I wondered how he could stand going unshod in that weather.

"I do not feel the cold as you do," he said.

"Oh," I said, then leaped to my feet, heart thudding frantically in my chest. "How did—"

"I hear your thoughts," he said easily.

"Who are you? What are you doing here?" I asked, working hard at controlling the sudden surge of fear in my belly.

He smiled. "You know who I am. You have read enough about me."

I shook my head, puzzled. A look of boredom flitted over his face.

"Tch. Tch. I thought you were wiser beyond your years. But apparently I was mistaken."

"I think," I said slowly, edging toward Father's gun, "that you'd better explain yourself, sir."

A twinkle came into his frost blue eyes. He leaned back in Father's rocker and studied me with a bemused expression.

"Or you will do what?" His eyes flickered to Father's gun and back. "Use that? Well, go ahead; take it."

I took a long step and reached for the gun, but when my fingers closed upon it I found I could not lift it. I strained, but it seemed as if the wood of the stock had taken root or merged with the very wood of the house itself.

I whirled and threw myself at him. His eyebrows rose in surprise and he raised his hand to stop me. A smile played teasingly around his lips.

"Are you wanting to wrestle?" he asked mockingly. "I wrestled a couple of times before with man."

I stepped back and frowned at him. What was this nonsense? "If you aren't a man, then who are you?"

He nudged the Bible on the floor with his toe. "Genesis thirty-two," he said.

I ignored his gesture. "When Jacob wrestled with an angel? It's one of Father's favorites. We all know it well." I looked at him closely, ready to give him the lie back in his throat. "Now you want me to believe you are Jacob? Try harder."

He smiled gently. "Not Jacob. The other one."

I felt my jaw drop as the meaning of his words seeped into my tired mind. I shook my head in disbelief, but even while I was denying him, the stray moments began to slide neatly into place. Yet I didn't *want* to believe him, because that would give meaning to all I had been prepared to deny.

"Yes," he said to my silence. "My name is Gabriel."

Without thinking I said, "You're an angel."

"Thank you," he said, smiling.

"I mean—" I stopped, flushing with embarrassment. I didn't know what I meant.

"I know," he said. I started at his words. He shook his head. "Don't think anything about the impossibility of things, James."

"What do you want?" I blurted, then bit my lip, as the tone of my voice was sharper than I intended.

He laughed, though, and I breathed a deep sigh of relief, for I remembered the story told how Zacharias had doubted Gabriel's word and been struck dumb for his trouble. A brief vision of what it might be like walking through the rest of my days struck mute flashed across my mind. I cleared my throat, uncomfortable with the thought.

"Why do you suppose your father asked you to read Mark thirteen?" Gabriel asked.

I sighed and shook my head. "I don't know," I confessed. "Sometimes he does things like that to me or Horace or Lorenzo and we don't know why."

"Then why do you do it?" he asked.

"Because he's my father and asked me to read it."

"*Asked* you?" he said gently.

I nodded. "Oh, I know he tells us to read it, but he wouldn't say anything if we didn't. It's one of those things that"—I paused—"you just do," I finished lamely.

"Yes, I know. You've said that before. But *why*?"

"Because he's my father," I said again. I shook my head. "That's enough for me."

"Because your father asked you to," he said, smiling. "That's all you need to know, isn't it?" I nodded and a satisfied expression came over his face. "That's all our Father asks," he said. "That you do what he asks."

"Yeah," I grunted. "I picked that up. But there's something there that I really don't understand as well. I don't pretend to know everything about why I'm told to do this or do that. It's enough that I'm told and do what I'm told."

"Yes," he said. "But you would like to know, wouldn't you?"

I shrugged. "Yes, of course."

"Your father was about your age when he was told to read Mark thirteen," he said conversationally.

For a moment I didn't comprehend what he was saying; then understanding came to me. "You mean, *you* told him?" He smiled gently. "Why?"

"Because we wanted him to know that there are times when men like that are needed. The world needs the peace-makers, but it also needs the warriors who will let the peace-makers work. Sometimes a strong hand or fist is needed to make people see reason." He shrugged. "And in some instances, the left hand of God must go to work."

"The left hand of God?" I shook my head, puzzled. "I don't understand."

He shook his head. "That's the dark side, the terrible vengeance that rises from the anger of God. There are some who must do that work, too. Sometimes a rare man comes along who must walk in that darkness and do the Lord's work among the violent. David was one of those. Sometimes the darkness swallows those men up and they become that which they once fought. Saul, Absalom, others." He shook his head, his lips pressed grimly together. "It isn't a place for some, either. Your father was one of those."

"You mean—" I shook my head. "No, not Father. He's a kind man—"

"Now," Gabriel said gently. "But for a time he was one of the left hands of God. But it takes an unusually strong man to do that work. One who is not afraid of walking through the darkness. That's why I suggested that your father have you read that passage."

"*You* suggested?"

He nodded. "Oh yes. We are seldom far away from your father these days. This is the time when he needs us the most."

"What time is that?" I asked, but he shook his head.

"It is not given to man to know the comings and goings of time yet to be spent," he said. "But this I will tell you: There is a need for you. There will be times when you will have to stand alone against great odds. There will be times when you will have to walk alone in darkness and live among those who have fallen away from God's grace. Remember always that where good lives, evil is a neighbor. But never forget that you are human, James. That is the most important."

"I won't," I said softly.

He nodded and then disappeared. I blinked and looked around, but I was alone.

And then I awoke, stiff with cold. The fire was long gone out. I shook my head; dreaming again. I had better get to bed before Mother came out and found me still up. I looked down at the Bible lying open in my lap: Mark 13.

I had been reading the story of Samson.

A chill went through me that had nothing to do with the cold.

CHAPTER 17

ABOUT TWO weeks later, Mother acted queer. I recognized the mood early when I came into the kitchen for breakfast. She glanced at me, surly, her thin mouth pulled tightly down at the corners, her blue-gray eyes stony. I sighed and took my place at the table, sitting straight, my hands in my lap, holding myself as quiet as a shadow and hoping to get through breakfast before her tongue scraped the flesh off my bones.

She cleared her throat and I sighed inwardly, mentally flashing over yesterday, searching for anything I might have done that could result in a coring.

"You were late coming home last night, James," she said, and my heart sank at the brittle tone in her voice.

"Yes, ma'am," I said carefully. I glanced at the door, willing the others to come in. Sometimes Mother eased off a bit when all of us were in the room together. That didn't mean that we were automatically exempt from one of her forays; it was just that there might be such a clamor that she would temporarily forget her intentions as she tried to keep up with all the goings-on around her. Time was our friend, for Mother kept herself so busy that something would happen to distract her and occasionally one of us could escape her intentions.

"You know when you're supposed to be in," she said. It wasn't a question, but I answered it anyway. Silence wasn't golden when Mother was in one of her moods. She took such a tactic as a weakness, and her tongue would get wagging harder than ever as she lathered herself up and took to waxing eloquent.

"Yes, ma'am," I said, and braced myself for the battering.

"Why?"

For a moment I was dumbfounded as I stared open-mouthed at her. She glanced over her shoulder. Not a muscle twitched.

"Why?" she repeated.

"I—I was helping Old Man Josiah load his wagon with apples," I said. Her eyes narrowed and I rushed on. "His man went into town Saturday and didn't come back on Sunday. Josiah needed to get the apples before they began to turn. He asked if I would help."

She cast a quick reproving look at me. "*Mr.* Barnes, James," she said quietly.

I shivered and stammered defensively, "He told me to call him Josiah."

"He was just being polite. You should never take advantage of a man's politeness, James. You respect your elders. Your turn will come. There's no need to hurry it along."

"Yes, ma'am," I said. I knew better than to press my argument when those deep lines drew down at the corners of her mouth.

"Did you get the apples loaded?"

"Yes, ma'am. We finished late by lantern light. J—Mr. Barnes said he would drive them over to Troy today."

"He pay you?"

I hesitated and she turned from her place by the stove to stare at me, waiting for my answer. I wasn't quite certain how to answer her. But I knew it wasn't the time for one of my stories. This was the time for truth.

"No, ma'am," I said.

She nodded. "He offer?"

"Yes, ma'am. But he's had a run of bad luck lately and I figured he needed it more than we did."

A small tic pulled her lips into a grimace, and she pushed her shoulders back, rolling her head slightly to help remove a crick in her neck. For a moment I thought that I was going to be given another tongue-lashing; then the tic spread into a quiet smile.

"You're a good boy, Jim," she said quietly. My cheeks began to burn and I looked back at the doorway, hoping Lorenzo would come in. "Good boy" usually followed an admonition to always walk in the footsteps of the Lord, to mind the Ten Commandments, to—

"Jim, there comes a time when you're going to have to make a choice," she said. I perked up. This was a new one I hadn't heard before. "There are going to always be a lot of Mr. Barneses around who can't do for themselves. They're good people, but they just can't help themselves when others come against them. I have a hunch that's what the good Lord put you here on this earth for—to be helping others."

I flushed deeply and looked down at the table. I didn't want to say what needed to be said at this point, but I couldn't let her go on about my becoming a missionary or a preacher. I knew that Father had hopes that one of us would go in that direction, but I sure didn't have any inclination for filling that dream. I had read Cooper's *Leatherstocking Tales* through half a dozen times and Carson and Boone and, well, just about everything I could get my hands on that told the doings in the Far West. The West was yanking hard on me each day and I knew that someday I would have to go there. Some nights I even had dreams about adventures there—me and Carson, usually—but a couple of times nightmares pulled me up out of sleep and I awoke drenched in sweat, my heart pounding like I'd sprinted a mile or two, but I couldn't manage to recall what had frightened me so, even though I would lie awake there until false dawn came and the sky was painted with pink streaks.

"Mother," I said carefully, "I don't think I'm cut out to be a preacher."

She nodded solemnly and said, "Nor do I, Jim. You got too much devil in you for that. But I think you're strong enough to turn that devilment into good. You just have to remember purpose. But be careful, Jim. Be careful. The devil is a sly one. He's a trickster that hides in the shadow of good. A slick one. That's why I said you have to remember purpose and look for what his suggestions might bring upon you and others. It isn't going to be easy going for you and I think a lot of the time you're going to have to be unhappy, but don't let your sadness take you down the wrong path. Don't go looking for the easy road. If the Lord wanted life to be easy, we'd still be in the Garden of Eden. But we aren't. It isn't Matthew, Mark, Luke, or Peter that you have to read, Jim. Look at Revelation. It's there you'll find your purpose in life. John's your man. Follow what he says. And remember that there are some among us who aren't meant to turn the other cheek but to help those that do. There's always going to be someone who will pop them on that cheek no matter how many times they turn it, and they get tired of hitting them, why, they'll more than likely take a knife or gun to them."

She paused, looking away from me off into the distance. "Your father was like that once, James. And he still is—to a degree. But sometimes when his mind strays he forgets purpose. That doesn't mean he's a weak man, though. I've seen strength in him when others walked away. But there's a lot of goodness in him, Jim. Now I know he likes to read to you and tell you some things. What was that book he was reading to you and Lorenzo the other day out under the sycamores?"

"Blake, Mother. He was talking about Milton? You know, *Paradise Lost*?"

"Oh yes," she said, and this time a broad smile lifted the light into her face and her eyes softened. "Oh my, yes. I remember him going on about that. He doesn't care much for Blake, does he?"

"No, ma'am," I said. "Leastways, not that I can see. He was going on about how Blake was wrong and Satan wasn't the strongest character in *Paradise Lost*."

"Uh-huh. Well, do you know why Milton has that fellow seem more interesting than others?" I shook my head. "It's just what I've been talking about. Satan likes to hide behind a screen of good. Sin is always far more beautiful than good, Jim. Always. That's why it gets folks to go to the left rather than the right. Milton was a smart one, Jim. He weaves a sense of goodness around you, then socks you *wham!*" She brought her hand down hard upon the table, making me jump in surprise. "Just when you least expect it. But you read on and you discover just how hard the devil can be and how the goodness just overcomes him all the time. But it takes a special person to resist him all the time."

I cleared my throat when she paused to reflect some, and said, "Yeah, I know, but Reverend—"

"I know what he says," she said, breaking in impatiently. "But he's wrong. Oh, there's strength in his words and they're good words, but he's wrong about always turning that cheek. Remember what I told you. There's always someone going to pop you when you do it if you're fool enough to keep turning. Even Christ resorted to violence on occasion, and there hasn't been a better man walking this good earth. Remember when he whipped those money changers out of the Lord's Temple? He wasn't too gentle that time. And remember when Satan came to him and tried to tease him into walking in the devil's footsteps instead of the Lord's? Why, he wasn't too gentle then, either.

"No, Jim, history is full of men who walked in the Lord's footsteps and carried a big stick or sword or club." Her eyes became distant and a soft smile came across her face, making the hard planes disappear, and for a moment I saw the young girl who had drawn Father's eye and made him camp on her doorstep until she said yes. I think that was the closest I ever felt to Mother, for I sensed a soft goodness to her and a certain girlish giddiness that made her seem . . . vulnerable, I guess. I don't know how to explain it any other way.

"There's going to be a time, Jim, when you will have to be the left hand of the Lord." A sadness came into her eyes and, for a moment, I thought I saw the glimmer of tears gathering, but she turned away and busied herself at the counter, cracking eggs and whipping batter in a heavy mixing bowl. "I know you're young for this talk, Jim, but I've seen how you stand up to those that try to take advantage of the others. That Botje boy, for example. He's a bully, a no-account that isn't ever going to amount to anything. But he'll make life miserable for any he senses to be weak. I know you've had a few spats with him and you'll have more. But always watch your back. People like him won't come straight on to you when they discover they can't beat you. They're sneaky and not worth the spit to drown a grasshopper. He isn't ever going to change; you only have to look at his father to know that—and his mother," she added as an afterthought. "The fruit doesn't fall far from the tree and that fruit was spoiled at birth—carried that rottenness right from the core into the fresh ripening. I know what the Good Book says about goodness in everyone and always looking for the good and having patience—I guess I know Job as well as any—but, Jim, that doesn't mean that the Lord doesn't have his folks on this earth as well as the devil does. The Lord put Samson down here to help his people and Joshua to help his. David was a great warrior as well as a great king. Alas, Absalom! Absalom! I see no reason why you think you have to be a preacher to do the Lord's work, Jim. There's a wildness in you, but that wildness can do his work as well." She shook her head. "I wish it could be otherwise, but there you have it. Your father should have been the one to give you this talk and maybe he will yet. But what you did for Mr. Barnes you're going to have to do for others as well. There are those who just won't listen to reason, and those are the ones you're going to have to put reason to. Someone has to do it. No reason why that someone isn't you. Remember that the Lord didn't spend his time in the Temple but went down in the city where the sinners were. He knew that those who were good didn't need his help as much as the sinners—although there's a lot of whited sepulchers among those who pretend to good—and that's probably where you're going to have to go as well, where you'll find the sinners. But watch your back," she said again warningly. "I have a bad feeling about that. A premonition, I think, and I hope to God I'm wrong. Now how do you want your eggs this morning? And how many?"

I reckoned about a half-dozen and she could whip them all up together, if she wanted. She smiled and pulled fresh bread out of the warming oven and put it on the table with a saucer of fresh-churned butter, heavy yellow with rich cream. I pulled the pitcher of buttermilk to me and filled the heavy glass by my plate and drank thirstily. I buttered a few thick slices of bread while Mother readied my eggs. She slid them off on the plate, and by the time she added a few slices of hickory-smoked bacon I already had half of them settling comfortably in my stomach. She reached across and ruffled my hair and I nearly choked on a mouthful of bread at the suddenness of her gesture. Mother just wasn't free with hugs and kisses among us menfolks, although there was a tenderness there that ran deep. She laughed delightedly at the startled look on my face, and for a brief moment I felt close to her and smiled at her girlishness as she relaxed the stern role she had to hold against those times when Pa's weakness came over him. I knew then that she had had to grow older before she should have and take a hard line in life where she should have been able to laugh and dance and enjoy spring instead of always walking in the fall. But because she had to shoulder the burden of Job I knew that she had given me words I needed to ponder on and think carefully about before I became another Kit Carson or Andy Burnett or "Broken Hand" Tom Fitzpatrick or Jedediah Smith, that quiet, Bible-toting mountain man whose sobriety had made him as much a legend as had his adventures.

CHAPTER 18

SPRING CAME quickly that year, the ice breaking from Vermillion Creek and Tomahawk Creek in late March, and a sudden warming spell displaced April showers. Mr. Deasy celebrated spring the way he always celebrated spring, taking his classes through his Chaucer, pronouncing with relish the opening lines, slowly, with great pomp,

> " 'Whan that Aprill with his shoures soote
> The droghte of March hath perced to the roote,' "

while staring with dreamy eyes around the room and out the windows to where the sun shone brightly upon the new grass.

By the end of April when the showers had still not come to lift the sun's heat, we discovered as we had each spring the joys of truancy and swimming in Tomahawk Creek. Oliver had left for California to find his fortune (and we hoped ours) and I had taken his place, working on Dan Carr's farm near our own while Lorenzo and Horace managed our place. We needed the money, what with Father spending more and more time staring vacantly into the fire and holding his Bible in his hands but seldom reading from it. He had his good days when he would do small chores around the house, but we always had to check Jenny if he had been milking, as he sometimes would not finish the job. We couldn't afford to let Jenny get milk fever.

On May Day a heavy rain fell, and the next day a bunch of us went swimming down at Tomahawk Creek. Botje's cousin, John Betts, was visiting from Peru. He was bigger than most of the other boys and took great pleasure in swimming underwater and pulling the younger boys down, dunking them. I took an immediate dislike to him. Wylie McKenzie had come with us to the creek. Although he couldn't swim, Wylie liked to paddle in the shallows, looking for freshwater clams.

I was lying on the thick grass of the bank, letting the sun dry me, when suddenly Wylie screamed. I sat up and saw Wylie in deep water, flailing his arms wildly as he went under. I glanced over and saw Betts dressing quickly.

"Help!" Wylie bawled.

I leaped up and ran to the edge of the creek. I cleared the shallows with a low dive and swam to Wylie. I grabbed him, tucking his chin under my arm, and pulled him to shore. He lay, crying and puking, on the shore.

"Good work, James," Lorenzo said quietly. He nodded to where Betts was tying his shoes. "He threw him into the deep pool after Wylie told him he couldn't swim."

"He—hurt me," Wylie sobbed.

"Little punk," Botje sneered. "You wanted to come along and play with the big boys. It's your own fault."

"Leave him alone," I said quietly.

Botje glanced at me; then his cousin came up to stand by his shoulder, placing his hands on his hips, smirking. Botje laughed. "And what you gonna do about it, Hickok?" he challenged.

I lashed out, popping him on the nose. Blood spattered against his face like a ripe tomato. His cousin stared open-mouthed; then I grabbed the collar of his shirt, spun him around, and reached between his legs, grabbing.

He howled with pain and tried to push my hand away, but I jerked, bringing him up on his tiptoes, and crow-hopped him down to the edge of the bank. His shrieks went up the scale until he sounded like a young girl screaming at a ghost. I took a deep breath, then lifted and threw him forward. He flew over the water, his hands going immediately to cup his groin. Then he landed with a flat *splat!* in the water.

"Pa'll get you for this, Hickok!" Botje bawled, holding a dirty handkerchief against his nose.

I moved toward him, but he turned and ran away into the woods. I turned to watch as his cousin dragged himself like a drowning rat from the creek and lay, crying, on the bank, holding himself tenderly. I brushed the water from my arms and legs. I glanced at Lorenzo as I dressed. A wide grin split his face.

"Well?" I challenged. "You got something to say?"

He spread his hands, shaking his head. "No, no. Not me. I expect his old man"—he nodded toward Botje's cousin—"will, though. And you know Botje's dad will."

"Let them," I said, finishing dressing. I walked over to Wiley. "Come on," I said gently. "I'll take you home."

"Thanks, Jim," he said, eyes shining. He snuffled and wiped his nose with his hand. "When I get big, I hope I'm just like you."

"When you get big"—I smiled—"you might be better than me." I glanced at Lorenzo.

He nodded toward the woods where Botje had disappeared. "Better watch your back. He won't come at you to your face, but I don't doubt he'll get a bunch of guys together and come after you."

I laughed and punched him gently on the arm. "I've got you to do that," I said.

"I won't always be around, Jim," he said seriously. "I'll do what I can while I'm alive, but I won't always be with you. Best you remember that."

"I'll remember," I said. I turned to Wiley. "Come on; let's get you home."

Word spread quickly about what I had done. The next day at school, Mr. Deasy handed back the spelling test he had given us. I sighed as I saw all the corrections marked on my paper. I could read the words and understand them, I could speak them, but I never could spell them. It was the damnedest thing, I thought wryly.

"Good job," he whispered, bending close to my ear. I smelled the peppermint on his breath and the faint hint of tobacco beneath. We all knew he smoked, but we kept it quiet for fear our parents would fire him for his "weakness."

I frowned at the paper. "But I failed."

"I wasn't talking about the test," he said. He smiled. "*Arma virumque cano*. Spelling is something that you can correct with time, Mr. Hickok. Courage and care are not."

I glanced over to where Sarah McLaughlin sat. Her face was shining as she smiled at me. I ducked my head, feeling my cheeks beginning to burn.

When I got home that evening, Mother met me at the door. She gave me a slight smile and said, "We had a caller today."

"Oh?" I said casually. I shifted my books from one hand to the other.

"Yes," she continued. "It seems Mr. Botje came by to complain about you."

"Sorry, Mother," I said.

She shook her head. "Don't be, James. Lorenzo told me everything. You did what was right. Although," she added, "I don't think you should have hit that boy in the nose. I understand that it's broken and they had to take him into Homer to get the doctor to look at it."

"Well"—I looked away from her— "I guess I didn't think."

She folded her arms and studied me for a long moment. "No, James, you didn't think. You just acted. But there are times when action is better than procrastinating. I think this was one of those times. A person can't help being what they are." She paused, then nodded toward the bedroom. "Your father wants to see you."

"Father?" I said, surprised. She nodded.

"Yes. He's aware of things. For the moment."

I heard a click in her throat and saw tears spring to her eyes before she could turn away. I glanced over her shoulder into the kitchen and saw Hannah looking at us. She nodded and smiled. I walked into the bedroom, pausing just inside the door. Father lay on the bed, gaunt, his beard showing a salt-and-pepper stubble against his hollowed cheeks. But his eyes looked clear. He gestured and I walked over to the bed and sat on the edge. I could smell the sour sickness on him. He reached for my hand. I let him take it. He smiled and a lump came into my throat.

"Well, James, I hear you have been at it again."

"Yes, sir. I guess I have."

He squeezed my hand gently. "I heard what your mother said. You mustn't ever think that we are disappointed in what you do." He sighed and took several short, shallow breaths. "James, I know I haven't had much to do with you lately—"

"It's all right, Father. I understand," I said quickly.

"—but I want you to know that there are a few people in this world who are put here to do what you did the other day." He smiled. "Christ tells us to turn the other cheek, but God doesn't mean for us to be alone and defenseless, either. He puts people here to help those who cannot help themselves. There comes a time when evil must be faced by someone who is not meant to turn that cheek. Those are special people, James. Special people. They don't come along except once in a rare while. For all of his greatness, Charlemagne only had twelve of them for his entire world. I think that God means for you to be one of those men, James. You will not have many friends. You will be alone much of the time. But I think God put you here for doing what you did the other day."

"Yes, sir," I said.

He coughed, a long, wracking cough that shook the bed. "Be careful, James. Be very careful. You have a special gift and there will be many temptations to misuse that gift. Be certain that you use it only for right. And be careful. Don't unleash the fury upon anyone unless it is the only resort left. Remember this, James!" He squeezed my hand fiercely.

"Yes, sir. I'll remember."

"Good. Good," he said. A great weariness seemed to come upon him. "I think I'll sleep for a bit, now, James."

"All right, Father," I said.

I rose and left his bedroom. Mother looked at me, but I shook my head and took my rifle and went outside. I went across the pasture to the trees and made my way to a small glade in the middle where a tiny spring bubbled past a salt lick. I settled back, out of sight in the bushes where I had sat so many mornings and evenings, waiting for a deer to come. I waited there now, not for a deer so we would have venison, but because it was something to do. Waiting in the stand gave purpose to thought. But I didn't know what to think about Father's words. His dying was in the way of quiet contemplation. *There will be time later,* I told myself. *There will be time.*

I settled in to wait.

I saw a flash of brown and gently brought my rifle up, waiting. A doe stepped out into the small clearing, head up, nostrils working as she tested the breeze. But I knew she couldn't smell me, as the breeze was into my face and she had come from the west, where my scent wouldn't carry to her. She crossed to the small stream and bent her head, drinking daintily. I waited, knowing that a buck would follow her in a few moments. That was the way nature worked; the male waited, watching for danger.

I heard him before I saw him. A slight scraping of twigs brushing against his side. A soft hoof fall. Somewhere a squirrel scolded. A jay chattered. Then he was there, almost by magic, head up, eyes watching. Six points on his rack. He moved forward gingerly, almost regally. I waited until he was beside the doe and she stepped back from the stream. When his head started down, I eased the hammer back, muffling the sound with my hand. Still a tiny *click!* sounded, almost inaudible. His head came up swiftly, twisting as he glanced from side to side. I centered the sights just behind his right shoulder and gently squeezed the trigger as he took a step back away from the spring.

The bullet took him high above the shoulder. He staggered, then turned, leaping away, the doe running in front of him. I reloaded, then came out of the thicket and crossed to where he had disappeared from the clearing. A bright splash of blood lay on the dead leaves. I glanced up at the green leaves and saw a few bright drops of blood. I nodded and moved forward, trailing him cautiously.

I tracked him for an hour through the woods before finding him lying upon the ground where he had finally dropped. A small pool of blood lay near his shoulder. I approached cautiously and nudged him with my foot. He didn't move. I looked around but couldn't see the doe. I sighed and squatted on my heels, studying him. A whitetail buck. Big. It was a long ways back to the house, and I wasn't certain if I could drag him that far through the thick woods. But the McLaughlin place was just past the line of woods. In fact, I could just see the outline of the split-rail fence that marked the edge of their west field. Perhaps I would be able to borrow a horse from him to take the buck home.

Meanwhile, I field-dressed the buck, then took a small rope and hoisted the buck well into a tree and high enough off the ground to keep the varmints away from him. The carrion birds I couldn't do anything about, but the offal I left should keep them occupied until I could return with a horse.

I hurried through the woods and climbed over the fence on McLaughlin's pasture. I called out as I neared the barn, then went inside, in case Mr. McLaughlin was there. But the barn was empty. I stood my rifle against a stall and went back to the tack room, thinking he might be in there, repairing harness, but it, too, was empty. I had shut the door behind me when a husky voice spoke from the front of the barn.

"Good morning, Jim."

I glanced around and saw Josephine standing in the doorway, one hand on her hip, the other braced against the door. Wisps of crisp dark hair blew gently around her face; her eyes were big and wide and dark, sardonic. Her lips were full like strawberries. Sunlight shone from behind her, outlining her curves. She glanced down at my hands, then exclaimed. "You're hurt!"

She rushed forward before I could explain, taking my hands and looking closely at me. I smelled rosewater on her. Her brunette hair fell softly around her face and over her shoulders in natural waves. She had a tiny mole on one cheek—a beauty mark, some called it. Her green eyes rose to mine as I said, "No, I just shot a deer and need to borrow a horse to get it home."

"Pa's not here," she said, but she didn't drop my hands as she stared intently into my eyes. I began to feel uncomfortable, awkward. I was conscious of her breasts pushing hard against her dress. The tip of her tongue appeared redly between her full lips. Then she stood on tiptoe, throwing her arms around me, kissing me hard.

"Jim—" she panted.

"Josephine, I don't think—" I stammered, but then she

kissed me again and pushed me back to a stall where we fell onto a mound of soft hay. I slipped my hands around to push her away and froze as they cupped her breasts and she moaned. She rose to her knees, her long white hands going behind her back, releasing the buttons to her dress. She shrugged her shoulders and her dress fell in folds around her waist. She stood and pushed the dress down over her generous hips. She kicked her dress from her and slid her undergarments away, standing naked before me.

"Josephine," I said hoarsely.

She smiled and stretched languidly, her large breasts moving slowly. Then she lowered her white hands and slid them down over her hips. My eyes were drawn hypnotically to the thick curly black triangle between her legs. She spread her legs and I swallowed heavily and reached for her.

The gloaming had begun by the time I emerged from the trees, leading the horse I had borrowed from the McLaughlin place. The buck lay over the back of the horse. Lights were on in practically all the windows, and several buggies and wagons were in the yard. I frowned and led the horse around to the back porch. I tied it to a post and entered through the kitchen. Hannah was making coffee. She looked up, relief spreading over her face.

"Where y'been?" she asked. "Horace and Lorenzo both went out looking for y'and come back hours ago empty-handed."

"Hunting," I said. I gestured toward the door. "I got a buck on a horse out there. I had to go to the McLaughlin place to borrow a horse to bring it back. What's wrong?"

"Y'daddy," she said. "He died about two this afternoon. He was calling for y' all morning up to the time he went." She came over to take the rifle from me. She took a deep breath; then a hard look came over her face and I saw hurt in her eyes. "I reckon it was deer y'was huntin' all right. I can smell it all over yuh. Roses?"

I ignored her and started for the living room.

"Y'better wash some of that smell off yuh," she said sharply. "There's enough smell of death in this house today. We don' need no moah."

I turned toward the pump and splashed water over my hands, scrubbing the blood from them with a bar of gray soap. I splashed water on my face, dried with a towel Hannah silently handed me, then went into the living room.

The low murmur of voices stopped when I entered as heads swiveled to meet me. They stared curiously. I saw at a glance that George McLaughlin was there, standing by the door, a cup of coffee in his hand. Nahum Gould, Abner Westgate, the Wixons, and others stood in tiny groups in the room.

Mother sat in her rocker before the fire. Lorenzo and Horace stood at her shoulder. She looked up; quiet fell over the room. I saw the relief leap into her eyes. "James," she said. "We were afraid something had happened to you."

"No, I'm all right," I said. My ears started to burn. I crossed to her and bent to kiss her cheek. She smiled wanly and patted my cheek. Her nose twitched, and I knew she smelled Josephine on me. I rose and turned toward the room.

"I'm sorry to have caused you all to worry. I shot a buck but had to track him down." I glanced at George McLaughlin. "He made it all the way through the woods to your north line. I had to borrow a horse from your place, Mr. McLaughlin, to bring him back. He's tied up out there."

"We'll take care of him, James," Abner Westgate said, putting his cup on a small table. He looked at Beaufoy. "Come on. Least we can do is hang the deer for him in the smokehouse."

Beaufoy looked unhappy at the prospect of work, but he obediently placed his cup on the sideboard and followed Westgate from the room. I glanced at Mr. McLaughlin. He nodded.

"That's all right, James. You're welcome to the loan. No harm done."

My cheeks felt hot, but I held his eyes as I thanked him. I turned back to Mother. "I'm sorry I wasn't here, Mother."

"Well, who knew he would go this quickly?"

Tears threatened to spill from her eyes. We had been prepared for a long time for Father's passing, but no matter how long you've had to prepare for it, death is always a surprise. I guess it's because we really hope in our hearts that it won't come even though common sense tells us it's going to happen. We still hope for miracles, regardless of how old we are, because we still have lingering doubts about the promised land our preachers insist is going to be ours when we die. I remember once I asked Father that if everything was going to be so good for us once we died, why didn't we hurry up and get it over with so we could enjoy the better place? Father looked at me, his brow furrowed in thought, and said, "You know, James, I've thought about that a lot. I guess it's because this is supposed to be sort of a training ground for us so we can prove to God how worthy we are."

I let it go after that. Whenever Father got into his teacher's voice I knew it would be a long time before he got out of it, and the sun was shining that day and the shad flies were out along the creek and the bass were jumping. There were more things for a boy that day than dry, dusty words. But I sensed a hesitance to him, almost as if he was telling me more what he wanted to believe than what he believed.

CHAPTER 19

I PAUSED, leaning on my shovel, wiping perspiration from my forehead. I glanced up at the hot sun. Noon. Or close enough to it, I thought, and took a deep breath, arching my shoulders back to relieve the tightness in my muscles. I glanced at the others near me, working on the Illinois and Michigan Canal. I shook my head ruefully. It was a long way from the quiet woods where I once wandered with a rifle, hunting. But work was where one found it these days. I frowned and glanced down the long shovel line to where the straw boss, Charlie Hudson, stood in the shade of an elm tree. He wouldn't move from there in this July heat except to bully one of the smaller men on a whim when he thought the man wasn't working as fast as he should.

I shrugged and turned, staring down the long line of the canal laid true by a surveyor's plumb. A lot had happened since Father's death. We had been forced to move back to Homer, where Lorenzo and Horace put their money together and bought a small house for us. I had planned on following Oliver out west, but Lorenzo had taken me aside one day and quietly laid out our finances. The family couldn't afford to have me move. Father's sickness and funeral and all had been costly to the family and we needed every hand working to bring in money.

Work was scarce around Homer, so I went up to Utica and found work as a driver on the canal—except for those times when everyone had to lend a hand to dredge the bottom after rains filled the canal with silt. Then we all had to dig a section free.

I shook my head and sighed, turning back to the side of the canal. I started to work my way back into the rhythm, bend, lift, scoop, throw. It was easy work once one caught onto the rhythm, and I let my mind stray back to the weekend when Lorenzo had shown us a clipping from a Kansas newspaper about an argument between the Kansas "Free Staters" and the Missouri "Border Ruffians" who were squabbling over the land claims in the Kansas Territory.

"I think we should give some thought to this," Lorenzo had said quietly.

"What?" I asked. I leaned back against the porch railing, shading my eyes against the sun to look at him. He sat in Father's old rocker, studying the newspaper. He turned it so I could read the headline. I shrugged. "We have enough fights right here with the whites and the blacks. What do we want to go to Kansas for and mess in that trouble?"

"I don't care about that," Lorenzo said. "But there is land available there for the taking."

Interest struck me and I turned back to look at him. I nodded. "Go on."

"According to everything I've read, Kansas land is deep and rich. Good land for farming," he said. "Level and not rocky. In most places," he added. "And it's cheap land, right now. Prices are bound to go up once the place gets settled. I think maybe we should take a little trip over there and check it out. If the price is right, we might consider moving the family over there." He glanced at the village and shook his head. "There sure ain't much here for the Hickoks anymore. I think it's gonna get worse, too. Stock and grain prices are starting to fall a bit."

"Well," I sighed, "I sure could use a break from that canal. When do you think of going?"

"I don't know," he answered, snapping the paper in his hands. "Soon, though. The longer we wait, the more prices are going to change."

The shovel struck a stone, jarring me clear back to my shoulders. I stepped back and worked the blade under it and stepped hard on the lug, levering upward. Slowly the stone rolled up from the ground and over, rolling down the bank to land with a splash in the water. The noise caused the others to look up from the work questioningly.

"You there!"

I turned and looked back toward the elm where Hudson lolled. He was looking in my direction. I waited.

"We're taking things outta the water, not throwing 'em in!" he said harshly.

"An accident," I said quietly.

He cupped his hand around his ear and leaned forward from the waist. "Eh? What's that, Hickok?"

I drew a deep breath, feeling resentment creep in. "An accident," I said louder. "A rock rolled into the water."

"Well, get it out, you damn fool! Don't just stand there lickering around on your shovel. You ain't gettin' a dollar a day to lollygag at water lilies! Put some back into it!"

I turned back and started shoveling. Anger worked in me, destroying the rhythm, and I found myself beginning to pant in the heat as sweat trickled down from my brow, stinging my eyes. The blade struck another rock, turning the shovel in my hands. I tried to work the blade under it, but the rock was too big. I sighed and began digging around it, exposing it. The rock was too big to lever out. I jammed the shovel into the freshly turned earth and turned, starting back to where we had a team hitched to a drag bar.

"Now where the hell do you think you're going?" Hudson demanded as I walked past him.

"I need the team to pull a rock," I said without pausing.

I stepped down to the team and ran my hands along the back of the wheel horse. "Good boy," I said softly, stepping behind him and picking up the reins. I clucked softly, pulling gently on the reins, turning the team toward the canal path. I flicked the reins lightly across their backs. "Let's go, boys," I said.

Obediently they stepped off, moving slowly down the path, the links on the traces jingling musically. I walked behind them, taking care that they didn't get too close to the edge.

"Jesus Christ!" Hudson exploded as I started to pass him. "You gonna take all day? Get those horses moving!" He stepped forward and grabbed the reins from my hands. He gathered the slack and started whipping the leather across their backs. "Hey! Haw! Haw! Goddamnit! Move, you bastards!"

He lashed out again at the horses. Startled, the horses lunged forward. The drag bar whipped forward, smacking Hudson's ankle. He howled with pain.

"You sumbitches!" He sawed the reins back, pulling viciously on the bits, stopping the horses. They stood trembling, confused as he kept the reins tight and started to whip the horses with the long leather straps trailing behind in the dust. They grunted from pain.

I stepped forward and yanked the reins from his hands, easing the tension. "Shh. Easy, boys," I said soothingly. The horses shuffled nervously, then relaxed. I felt a blow on my shoulder and stumbled. I dropped the reins and turned to face Hudson.

He was red-faced with fury, and tiny bubbles of spittle gathered in the corners of his mouth. "What do you think you doing, boy!" he shouted. "Who the hell do you think you are?"

He jabbed a stiff forefinger in my chest. I stepped back, stumbling over the drag bar. I caught myself and stood, staring hard at him.

"Keep your hands to yourself," I said warningly.

He laughed and stepped forward, jabbing me again with his hard forefinger. "Goddamnit, boy! You telling me what to do?"

I took another step backward to gain my balance. He mis-

understood the step and contempt spread in his eyes. He
stepped forward again and started to jab me in the chest. I
slapped his hand away and used both hands to push him
away from me. He stumbled backward, lost his balance, and
fell, landing square in a pile of fresh horse apples. Laughter rolled up and down the bank of the canal as he pushed
himself up.

"Sumbitch!" he shouted, and swung a fist at me.

I slapped his hand away and stepped in close, swinging
a short hard right to his jaw, knocking him backward into
the horse apples again. Laughter rose from the men gathering around us. He lay stunned on the ground, gathering his
wits.

"Serves him right," someone said.

"Get him, Hickok," another said.

"He's had it coming for a long time."

Hudson pushed himself up, shaking his head to clear it.
He glared at me, then lifted his shoulders and settled his
feet. His fists came up.

"All right," he said. "You want a piece of me? You got it!"

He feinted and I turned to catch the blow on my arm, but
he pulled the punch back and hooked low for my belly. I
tensed my muscles just as the blow landed, but he was a
large man and the air *whuffed!* from my lungs. I saw his
knee coming up for my face but couldn't turn away as he
caught me on the nose. Something snapped and I felt blood
on my face.

"Shit," someone said. I heard it dimly through the roaring in my ears. I took a step to the side as Hudson tried to
slam a fist into my ear. I felt the wind as it passed my cheek.

I caught his arm with my hand and jerked him forward.
He staggered and tried to butt me with his forehead, but I
ducked under him and shifted my grip to his shirt, bunching it in my hand. With my other hand I grabbed him between the legs, squeezing. He yelped with pain. I took a

deep breath and hunched my shoulders, lifting. He squealed like a pig. I felt his hands trying to push my arm away. I bent slightly at the knees, then shoved him toward the sky.

"Gawd!" I heard someone breathe. "That's gotta hurt!"

I turned toward the canal and took a short run to get momentum, then threw Hudson into the water. His arms and legs whirled for a moment; then his hands went automatically between his legs. He belly flopped into the water and went under. Immediately he came back up, splashing his arms around him.

"Help! Help!" he roared. He went under again and came back up, strangling from a mouthful of water. "Help! . . . Can't swim—" He went under again.

"Let him drown," someone said.

"Hell," another said, and sat down, pulling off his shoes. He took a deep breath and jumped into the water as Hudson went down again. He came up splashing his hands weakly as the other man grabbed him by the hair and started pulling him to the bank. His face went under and he started strangling. The other man grabbed a tree root hanging out from the side of the bank and pulled Hudson to it, keeping his face out of the water. Reluctantly others reached down to pull the straw boss up onto the bank. He sprawled on the canal path. His stomach worked and water vomited out of his mouth as the other man pulled himself out of the water with the aid of the root.

"You'd better get away from here, Hickok," someone said. I turned and recognized Adams, a small man who had been the butt of Hudson's viciousness a few days back. He gestured toward Hudson lying in a pool of his own vomit, panting for breath. "He'll press charges against you. Bet your life on that!"

"It was self-defense," I said quietly. I looked at the others around me. They looked away, embarrassed. "You all saw that."

But no one would meet my eyes except Adams, who took my arm and led me away from the small group. He paused beneath the elm tree, his lips pressed tightly together. His eyes were hard and angry, but I could read the resolution in them.

"Yes, it was self-defense," he said lowly, so I had to bend forward to hear the words falling softly from his lips. "But these men need their jobs. They have families to feed. If Hudson presses charges, they won't jeopardize their jobs."

I recognized the finality to his words and shook my head ruefully. "I don't know what you all expected me to do," I said.

"About what you did," Adams said. "None of us would have, but that's because we can't afford to, much as we'd like to. You're young; you can find work elsewhere. There ain't nothing keeping you here. Go, now! Before he has a chance to get the law down on you."

I took a deep breath, looking back at the knot of men standing around Hudson. No one bent to help him, but neither did they look in my direction. I nodded slowly and turned without another word and headed down the canal path, away from the group.

PART TWO

Kansas

Regions of sorrow . . .

CHAPTER 20

I SHRUGGED my back around to ease the strain where it had settled in the hollow of my shoulder. My feet felt puffy, and I was a bit worn from the long hike in the sun. Lorenzo and I had been on the road for a spell, making our way to St. Louis. It seemed the logical thing to do, as work was getting scarce to find around home.

Lorenzo wasn't as itchy as I was to leave home, but the prospect of the good land fairly cheap in Kansas was appealing. We needed to do *something*, as Father's death had left us in poor straits. So that June Lorenzo and I set off on foot to make our way over to Kansas and file for a homestead. We hoarded our money carefully along the way, laying up off the road at night to keep from being robbed while we slept. But I hadn't expected St. Louis to be as big as this.

We walked down into town, trying to stay out of everyone's way as we made our way through the streets. Hunters and trappers made their way along the street while the townsfolk held to the wooden sidewalks. Lorenzo gawked at the sight of a couple of simpering ladies who batted their eyelids coyly from beneath the parasols they twirled in invitation.

"Look out!" someone shouted.

I turned and saw a wagon bearing down on Lorenzo and pulled him out of the way just as the driver sawed on the lead horses, swearing a blue streak at us as he careened down the street in front of us. Lorenzo turned to look at me, shaking his head.

"This ain't for us, Jimbo," he said.

"No, Billy Barnes, it *is* for us," I said, trying to joke him with his nickname. But he just shook his head and turned back to the street, hugging the side as close as he could get.

We made our way without further incident down to the post office to see if we had any news from home and were surprised to find a letter waiting us.

"This ain't good," Lorenzo said worriedly. We found a bench against a storefront and sat down to read it.

Dear Brothers,

Mother isnt well and took her bed when you two left after 3 days. We dont no wat to tell you more the doctor said he aint certain wat ails her. But you no Mother she dont want you to worry and says that you aint to come home but to go on about your buzness and try and find a good and decent christian place where we can make a new home.

Luv, yr sister
Lydia

Lorenzo looked up, his eyes narrowed in concern. "What you think we ought to do, Jim?"

I pointed at the letter. "Well, we don't know what's wrong with her and we have her words that we should be setting out to find a new place for the family. I think we should go on and do just that."

Lorenzo rubbed his hand along his jaw. "I don't know," he said doubtfully. He fingered the letter and opened it and read it again. "Anything could be happening to her."

"Yes, that's right," I said impatiently. "She could even have a bellyache or just a bit of that womanly thing that took her to bed once in a while. In the meantime, I say let's get on with our business."

I rose and picked up my pack, looking down at him.

"Let's go on down to the riverfront and see if we can find a way upriver that isn't going to break us."

Lorenzo shook his head but folded the letter carefully and stuck it in his pocket. He rose and picked up his pack and gave a deep sigh. I grinned at him.

"You look like the portent of doom, Billy Barnes," I joked.

"I can't help worrying about Mother," he said somberly. "She's alone now that Father's gone."

"She's not alone," I objected. "She has Lydia and—"

"And?" Lorenzo paused in the street, raising his eyebrows. "And what about you or me, or Oliver could come back from California or—"

"You want to go back?" I asked quietly.

He turned away from me, his face a study in pain, gnawing on his long lower lip. "It's just that I've gotta hunch that one of us should stay back there to keep an eye on things." He faced me. "Times are changing fast, Jim. Too fast, I'm thinking. There should be a man at home."

I stared at him silently for a long time, then squared my shoulders. "All right then. One of us goes back and the other goes on. That way we got both ends covered." I dug into my pocket and pulled out a coin. "Should we flip for it?"

He shook his head. "No. I know you don't want to go back. It wouldn't be long until you found some other reason to move away. You got a restless spirit, Jim. I'll go back and take care of things at home until you find something."

Slowly I put the coin back in my pocket. "You sure about this?" I asked.

He nodded. "Yep. Just as sure as I am it's gonna be a hot one the rest of the day." He made an exaggerated sweep of his brow and pretended to shake sweat off the palm of his hand. I laughed and clapped him on the shoulder.

"All right then! Let's head on down and see if we can find me a way to get to Kansas. We'll take our leave down there."

Together we marched down to the river. I knew that Lorenzo felt bad about leaving me alone in that strange town, but rather than feeling dejected, I felt my blood sing with relief at the prospect of adventure that lay before me.

CHAPTER 21

T HE WHISTLE blew long and hard and I clambered eagerly over a pile of cotton bales to stare at the dock where the *River Queen* was putting in. Finding a ride up-river hadn't been as easy as I thought. Most boats were too expensive and fare would have put a big dent in what little money I had. Lorenzo had given me most of what we had brought with us so I could prove up on a claim somewhere, and I was reluctant to place a large chunk of that on floating wood. The pilot, however, took a good look at me and said I could ride as far as Leavenworth as long as I was willing to help load cargo. That seemed like a fair exchange to me and I took him up on that.

"Well, Bill," a voice said as a rough hand clapped me on the shoulder. "It looks like this is gonna be the end of the line for you."

I turned to grin at Jim Voorhees, the cargo master. He was about as round as he was tall, but there wasn't much fat on that frame. For some strange reason, though, he had taken to calling me "Bill" and the rest of the crew followed right along regardless of how many times I corrected them. I guess he had heard me calling Lorenzo "Billy Barnes" and somehow thought I was Lorenzo since we looked alike although we were a few years apart.

"I guess so," I replied. I looked back at the crowd gathering at the dock. "It looks like we've got a greeting party. Is that usual?"

Voorhees frowned as he studied the growing crowd. He shook his head. "Well, we always draw some—all boats do—but this boodle don't look quite chirky." He glanced up at the wheelhouse. "I think I'd better see what the cap'n wants to do about this."

"What's the matter?" I asked. But he was gone before I got an answer.

I turned back to watch the crowd draw nearer as the steamboat edged closer. They milled around, staring at us as we approached, their faces sullen. Some shook their fists. And then I heard them shouting, demanding that we pass by. I frowned, wondering what resentment they could possibly have against a steamboat docking. Then I saw that the people in front held those in back away with cudgels. I stepped back in the shadows under the second deck and lounged against the wall, watching.

As the captain carefully placed the steamboat against the dock and the loading planks were let down, a heavily mustached man came aboard, blocking others from leaving.

"Say, what is this?" a salesman asked irritably. "What do you think you're doing?"

The man shook his head. "Sorry, sir. But the folks here have decided that no passengers are going to disembark here. We already got enough trouble hereabouts with Abolitionists and proslavery folks tearing at each other's throats that we don't need no more adding more fuel to the fire." He lifted his head to look at the other passengers waiting to leave and said, "I'd appreciate it if you folks would just go on back to your cabins now. You all are gonna have to go on to the next stop. Leavenworth ain't for you."

Angry murmurs rose from the passengers. A few of the

crowd shook raised fists at the men on the steamboat. I turned to a well-dressed man leaning casually against the cabin wall, smoking a cigar.

"Excuse me, sir," I said politely, and waited while he turned his head and looked carefully at me before nodding.

"What is it, boy?"

"I don't understand why those folks don't want to let us off the boat. It seems to me that if we paid our fare to get here, why, then we should be allowed to leave if we want."

He nodded, a small grin working its way around his cigar. "Yes, it does seem that should be the way of things, doesn't it? But"—he pointed his cigar at the dock—"those folks are a bit more interested in their wants than others' rights. There's gonna be a few elections around here soon and a lot of people are trying to make Kansas go proslavery. They figure by eliminating the competition they have a better chance at getting that to happen."

I frowned. "Doesn't seem right to me. A person should be able to make up his own mind about what he wants."

The man gave me a quick look up and down, then shrugged. "Doesn't matter, though, does it? It doesn't look as if you are getting off the boat anyway." He flipped his cigar over the side of the boat and, turning, thrust his hands into his pockets and strolled toward the back of the boat away from the sunlight.

I glanced around, then noticed that a team of roustabouts had elbowed their way aboard and were beginning to carry cargo ashore. The people stepped aside, ignoring the roustabouts as they came ashore, shouldering their burdens. I nodded and made my way down to the cargo. A large white man with a stump of a cigar clenched tightly between his teeth stood directing the men, glancing occasionally at a clump of papers he held tightly in his sweaty fists. He scowled at me as I came up to him.

"What you want?" he asked.

"To go ashore," I said bluntly.

"Yeah," he grunted. "And souls in hell want ice water. Don't look like you're gonna get your chance, though, does it?"

"There are ways," I said, shrugging. "What needs to be taken ashore?"

He glanced at my bag, then raised his eyebrows. "Boy, you're just asking for trouble."

"No, sir," I said. "Just a box to carry ashore."

He placed his hands on his hips and considered me, his eyes beginning to crinkle at the corners as the thought pleased him. "I sorta like your style. A bit wild, but that'll carry you a ways, I'm thinking. What's your name?"

"That's Bill Hickok," one of the rousties said as he huffed his way past, carrying a load awkwardly over his shoulder. "He's a good lad."

"Jim," I corrected automatically. "I'm Jim."

The foreman shook his head. "Bill suits you. Well, Wild Bill, let's see if we can get you ashore." He glanced around. A man was struggling with a wooden crate just too big for him to get his arms around it. "Soakey!" The man turned his head. "Let this fellow give you a hand."

Soakey gave me a quick look, then ducked his head with thanks. "It ain't heavy, but I just can't get a grip on it."

"That's all right," I said. I tossed the sack containing my belongings on top of the box and took the back end. Soakey turned around, knelt, and lifted the edge of the box against his own back.

"Let's do 'er," he said, and together we made our way out of the hold and up to the gangplank.

"Just a minute," the foreman said. He pulled a rangy man over and whispered into his ear. The man grinned, glanced at us, then nodded. He grabbed a light box and scurried ahead of us.

I watched as he made his way onto the gangplank, then

pretended to lose control of the crate and bump hard into the center of the group of citizenry stubbornly holding tightly to the center of the wharf. They stumbled, a few arms windmilling, hands clutched and grabbed at one another; then a small knot tumbled off the edge of the pier into the water.

Shouts of laughter and curses rang up through the air. A couple of men took issue with the man who had lost his balance and started to swing their fists at him, but he ducked, lowered his head, and swept forward like an angry billy goat, piling another bunch of onlookers into the water.

In the confusion, Soakey and I made our way ashore and into the warehouse. I helped him stack the crate on top of a pile, then reclaimed my sack of belongings.

"Thanks," I said, shaking his hand.

He grinned and wiped the perspiration from his forehead with a red bandanna. "Good luck to you," he said. He pinched his nose between thumb and forefinger, snarkled, and blew a clump of snot on the weathered boards of the warehouse floor. "We gotta put up with that crap all the time. Does a man good to see some of those do-gooders get a bath and it not even being Saturday."

I laughed, waved, and cautiously made my way out of the warehouse, shouldering my war bag as I went.

Outside I saw an old man, wild-eyed, wringing his hands and flinging them wide. "Oh, by God," he cried. "I forgot him. I forgot little Paul Williams! I left him out there for the Injuns to scalp, and him only seven years old! Another apple of God's eye gone to wild! Gone!" He lowered his arm and pointed at me, his eyes boring madly into mine. "Right is needed upon the plains! Right and God's good strong hand! Needed! Before any morality and religion can come upon that sand of Gomorrah!"

"I wouldn't mind him much, if'n I were you," came a voice from my shoulder. I turned to look at a man dressed in homespun, his pants held up by canvas gallowses. He heaved a sack of flour into a buckboard and paused, eyeing me carefully.

"If'n I don't miss my guess, you're not far from the plow," he said. He grinned to take any sting from his words. "I'm Bill Williams. I gotta small place just west of here." He glanced at the madman dancing now in the streets to the music of his own madness. "And I ain't seen an Injun out there for most on six years or so. The cavalry keeps them pushed farther back in the hills so's they don't come down onto the flats much a-tall."

"Jim Hickok," I said, returning his smile. "And you'd be right about the plow. 'Cept that was mainly my brothers, although I took a turn or two when time was needed, and harvesting everyone was needed. Rest of the time"—I shrugged modestly—"I got the meat for the table."

"Good shot, are you?" he asked, eyeing me shrewdly.

"Yes, sir," I said. "Just seems to come natural-like to me."

"Ah-huh," he said skeptically, placing his hands on his hips and turning his head so he could stare at me. He was a full head shorter than I and much thinner, more rawbone and rawhide than muscle. But I could see the deep yellow calluses upon his hands and knew that he didn't farm sitting in the kitchen and sipping coffee. "Well," he said dryly, "I reckon you have come to the right place for that natural ability. But if you're looking for work, I'm falling behind upon my plowing, thanks to these rains." He shook his head. "A farmer can't do without rain and can't do with too much." He laughed. "And right now, we're in between. If you can handle a double-blade and don't mind early and late hours, I can use you. Give you room and board and five dollars a week. It's only temporary, mind!" he cautioned, holding up a dirt-begrimed finger. "Only till the plowing and planting's done. Wish I could keep you on full-time, but"—he shook his head—"these aren't the times for making that sort of commitment. But it'll give you the time to look around and see where you are and what you want to be doin'."

I was grateful for his offer and took him up on it at once. I threw my war bag into the back of his buckboard and followed him into the store to help him load the rest of his purchases. The inside of the store was dim, and it took a moment for my eyes to clear. I saw where Williams's purchases had been bagged off to the side with old flour sacks and gunnysacks. Mr. Lewis, who owned the store, was busily working his account books, pretending to ignore the other customer who stood leaning against a post, working something from between his teeth with a dirty thumbnail. His hair hung long and greasy to his shoulders, and scabs showed above his dirty cheeks and beard where lice had been working freely. He had big wrists and hands that hadn't been washed in a month of Sundays. He wore Bulchers, the left one flapping free of its sole, Kentucky jeans, and a linsey shirt that had started out blue-striped but now appeared muddy. He had a big knife stuck in his belt and snickered when his eyes fell upon me.

"Well, whatta we got here? You just get off the boat, boy?" His voice was harsh and grated upon the senses like a plow blade rubbing across a granite stone.

Williams threw him a look as he shouldered another bag. "He's working for me, Casey, so leave him alone."

"Don't look like he'd be much trouble," Casey said. He tapped a dirty fingernail against the handle of the big knife. "Tell me, boy, you pro or against?"

"I don't want any trouble in here," Mr. Lewis said worriedly. "You two just take your differences out into the street to settle them."

"We ain't got no differences. Yet," Casey said lazily.

"And we won't have," I said, taking up two of the sacks and following Williams out the door.

Williams stepped into the back of the buckboard and packed his sack tightly against the boards. He leaned in close to take the ones I carried and said in a low voice, "That man's trouble when he's been drinking and I ain't never seen the time when he wasn't. You stay out here while I get the rest. There ain't much more."

He climbed out of the buckboard and went into the store while I stood on the boardwalk, waiting awkwardly for him. At last I reentered the store and found Williams, both arms loaded with sacks, being confronted by Casey. Mr. Lewis was nowhere to be seen.

"You hired a boy and you don't know where he stands, Williams? Seems a bit careless to me. Especially the way folks are feeling around here," he said.

"Kansas has always been a free state, Casey," Williams said evenly. "It don't take no piece of paper in Washington to change that. Besides, I mind my business and I expect others to mind theirs."

"Well now, I don't know about that. Senator Atchison says—"

"Makes no difference what Senator Atchison says," Williams interrupted. "He's in Missouri and this is Kansas."

I knew what the argument was about. Or what it *should* have been about, except Casey was obviously spoiling for a fight with anyone he could taunt into meeting him. Senator David Atchison was the leader of the proslavery forces in Missouri and had been speech making up and down the rivers claiming that it could be a disaster to have a free state as Missouri's western neighbor. I had read one of Atchison's *Platte Argus* editorials on the boat coming up the river in which he'd said: "Stake out your claims and woe be to the Abolitionists who shall intrude upon it or come within range of your long rifles or within point-blank shot of your revolvers."

"Damn me if I don't think you are one of them no-acccount Free Staters yourself, Williams," he said.

"You know what I am, Casey, and I know what you are. Now get out of my way."

"Anything I can do to help, Mr. Williams?" I said.

Casey turned slowly, grinning, to face me. "Well now," he said, leaning forward, and I could smell the Old Monongahela on his breath and knew that he wouldn't be listening to reason, filled up with Dutch courage the way he was and all. I also figured there was no reason to stand there listening to him talk himself up into courage, so I simply reached forward and plucked the big knife out of his belt. His mouth dropped open. "Hey!" he began, but I didn't let him finish. I flipped the knife over so I gripped it by the blade and smacked him with the heavy handle right between the eyes. He stood for a moment, his eyes crossing to see where the hurt came from; then he crashed forward, falling face-first onto the board planks of the store. I reached down and grabbed the filthy collar of his shirt and lifted him. A bright red splotch showed on the floor where he had broken his nose in the fall. I dragged him out of the store and around the corner to the alley, his heels bumping down the steps. I left him there with the knife buried in the dirt beside him. Then I thought better of it and stepped on the knife from the side, snapping the blade from the hilt.

I went back to where Williams had finished loading the buckboard and was already on the seat, holding the reins between his fingers. When he saw me, he slid over to make room. I climbed up beside him and he clicked his tongue against his teeth and pulled the off rein, turning the team in the middle of the street. He clicked his tongue against his teeth again and the team broke obediently into a trot, their harness jangling musically with their movement.

He glanced at me. "What'd you do with him?"

I shrugged. "Just pulled him into the alley in the shade

where he won't get sunstroke. He'll have a sore head when he wakes up. I broke his knife, though. Accident."

"Ah-huh," Williams said. He spit over the side of the wagon. "Surely must've had a hard head."

"I reckon," I said.

CHAPTER 22

LEAVENWORTH WASN'T much more than a spit on the map about that time, and I felt little inclination of staying within its boundaries of muddy streets and warped boardwalks. It was a forbidden country where human passions were venerated to excess and restraint pushed to the limits. Most of those who lived in Leavenworth were of one hard slant or the other: either for slavery or against it. Either way, one was certain to come to blows at one time sooner or later if he stayed in the town. I couldn't see much future in that, so Williams's offer was a good one for me.

He had a nice little farm just southwest of the town where a creek bent in a wide oxbow as it meandered its way down toward the Missouri River. Primroses and elderberry and plums stood along its banks. I could see why he had chosen it for his homestead. It was just below a good stand of walnut and just up from some hickory and oak. Willows dangled leafy tendrils over the creek amid some buttonwood, and his house had been built beneath a huge cottonwood to give it shade during the hot summer days. I knew there was game there, for we had chased up prairie chickens and I had heard wild turkeys gobbling back along the creek. The road we followed took us over unbroken prairie, and I couldn't keep my eyes off the western reaches, where I saw blue lupine and wild strawberry.

"Yes," he said, and I glanced at him and realized he had been reading my mind.

"It's beautiful," I said.

He smiled sadly and shook his head. "For now it is, but there will be enough coming like me who will plow all that under. Can't stop progress, and I suppose there's good about that, too. A man digs down into that black earth and sees how it's been veined with water for hundreds of years and he feels a certain sacredness about him. But by then it's too late."

I nodded as the wagon rumbled over a wooden bridge. I took a deep breath, smelling the water flowing under the bridge, a perfect distillate made of spartina and the albumen of eggs. A stream of mallards coasted in with the current, and a bass jumped beneath an overhanging willow where dragonflies hovered. Spotted butterflies fluttered around the bank along with bluebottles. Near the reeds growing next to the bridge I could see the warm, thick slobber of frog spawn growing like clotted water and heard the croaking of bullfrogs sounding their maleness arrogantly to one another, calling for their mates. I could understand why Williams farmed here; he had found his paradise, and I felt a tug at my spirit at the possibility of emulating him. Yet even then I felt the fantasy of the moment as a bright porcelain of my soul. I ached for the serenity of the life Williams had, but the moment was a strange, wandering wisp of desire, for I could not see myself hunched over the plow or my children and their children rolling around my heels on the puncheon floor of my house, a copy of the home that I had just left.

I felt, instead, the need of the land and the people in it and knew that I would not be able to live a life of any normalcy for long despite my desire. I heard, in the middle of all that Eden, the distant echo of my father's voice and looked to the horizon, expecting to see a knight on horse making his way over the plain. But then I saw only blue sky and endless prairie filled with patches of walnut, hickory, oak, elm, willow, some buttonwood, and mostly cottonwood around the creeks and tanks. The water here had cut through a limestone hill, giving a slight tang to the taste, and the flowers across the prairie were brilliant, with blue lupine, primroses, wild strawberry, elderberry, and plum blossoms and chokecherries along the creek banks.

I heard the call of a quail, the challenging tom-tomming of a prairie chicken, the nervous gobble of a wild turkey. A strange peace fell over me and I found myself wanting to throw myself down on the long-stem bluegrass and inhale the virgin beauty of the prairie, to smell the acrid dark soil. I felt not as if I had come home but that I had at last found home. It didn't take much for me to see myself living my life fully and quietly and contentedly on the wide steppes of the Kansas prairie for the rest of my life.

CHAPTER 23

A S YOU plant the harvest row, you implicate the mellowed silence in hopes that the crop will not be diseased, the wheat will not rust, the corn will be knee-high by June, and the north will not send down drifts of snow until the crops are brought in after the first frost. The sun seems to brighten as you build each row, straight as an arrow behind two bow-necked Percherons, your hand callused from gripping the oak handles of the plow, guiding it carefully through the rich black earth that rolls up with a musty smell of the ages that have passed through time and time again.

I paused in the noonday heat of the field to drink cold water from the oaken bucket Williams's boy brought out to me. Perspiration dripped freely from me and my muscles felt loose and relaxed, although there was a steady ache across my shoulders that I knew would go away in time after the first rows were readied. I looked across the neatly turned furrows to where blue smoke rose lazily from Williams's chimney and past him to where Richard Budd's fields butted against Williams's fields and where the smoke rose from Budd's chimney straight up in the windless air.

For a brief moment I felt lonely and ached for my home and Mother's cooking, Hannah—but then I sighed and turned away, my hands again gripping the plow handles. I clicked my tongue against my teeth and slapped the reins gently across the Percherons' backs. Peace replaced the loneliness in my breast as the plodding hooves of the great beasts moved rhythmically across the land.

I guided the plow, turning at the end when we came to a split-rail fence and retracing my way over and over again. There was a certain music in the monotony and I listened to it, feeling it within me. And then it was over before I knew it and the sun seemed to drop below the horizon with a soft *whoosh!* I pulled the Percherons to a halt and eased the harness over their shoulders, walking them back across the black furrows to the house. Already I imagined I smelled the dew, but it would be hours before the moon would come up, at first red, then softening to white as it traveled over the prairies, and then the dew would begin rising from the warm earth. I sighed, contented with my lot, already regretting that my work here was only temporary, as it would be over at Budd's place. And then—

I shrugged with the unconcern of youth. Something would offer itself; something always offered itself to the youth. Uncertainty belonged with the aged. I was foolish enough to believe that and yet wise enough to know the frailty of the moment.

Memory is the country of the usable past when one is aware of mistranslations, mistakes, the inevitability of misinterpretation of experiences, leaving man in his age with an imperfect view of his life and the momentary importance of his actions. And his regrets for those actions. And then he realizes the strength of those battalions filled with malignant subterranean demons of dreams and then the black indwelling spirits come to him and he realizes the forlornness of his past as he plays out the hallucinatory placement of our days.

CHAPTER 24

RELUCTANTLY I rode back to Leavenworth with a farmer going in for supplies. After Williams had no more work for me, I moved over to Budd's place and finished plowing his fields for him, planting, repairing fences. I split enough firewood to carry him through the winter, and then he ran out of things for me to do. I debated about making my way farther west, but something made me realize the futility of that. The planting season was almost over and little would remain for a farmer except to quietly tend his crops and take care of the odd jobs around his farm that are little more than routine. Reason told me that I would quickly find myself out of work with increasing rapidity as the summer moved toward its rendezvous with fall. I thought about trying to file on a hundred and sixty acres of land that had easy rolling hills to it with a heavily timbered creek running a loop halfway around it. Kansas took you prisoner and never considered amnesty or an early parole. There was a quiet sense of insinuation to the land that once you stepped onto it you belonged to it forever.

Leavenworth had become a town filled with sullen individuals who stared suspiciously at one another, trying to decide who was pro- or antislavery. I thanked the farmer and stepped down from the wagon, easily shouldering my bag as I pondered my next move. I turned to make my way toward the land office. A man stumbled out of a bar and nearly knocked me into the street. I grabbed a post for balance as he bounced off me, missed his step off the boardwalk, and sprawled into the street. He lay still for a moment, then pushed himself up, cursing, and turned to face me.

"Watch where you're going, bud!" he exclaimed, slapping dust from his shirt and pants.

I stared at him coolly. "You're the one who ran into me," I said quietly.

His eyes narrowed. "I don't take no sass from someone still wet from his mother's milk!"

I placed my bundle carefully against the wall of the store behind me as he made his way back up onto the boardwalk. He came close to me, his face inches away, and I realized he was not as drunk as I had first supposed.

"The question is," he said, "what I should do with you."

"Walk away," I suggested. "If you're wise."

Laughter went up from a small group of laggards and layabouts who had gathered with hopes of seeing a fight. I glanced around quickly, noticing where they were, and took a half step to my left to keep my back free. That half step caught my opponent unaware, and his fist slashed through the space where I had been, throwing him off-balance. I quickly set myself and struck him hard on his kidneys, straightening him.

He grunted and swung around, trying to backhand me, but

I had been through this with my brothers and many school-yard scraps. I leaned back away from him, then stepped in close, hunching my shoulders, swinging quick, short blows into his midsection. His breath *whooshed* from him and he bowed forward. I took a step back and laced him with a hard uppercut I brought from my hip. He straightened, his eyes glazed, and for a moment he appeared balanced; then he fell backward, senseless, into the street, his arms outflung as if he'd been crucified.

"Break it up, boys," a voice said behind me.

I turned quickly, taking a step back and to the side in case a blow followed the words. But the speaker stood quietly, staring at the others. He wore the uniform of a colonel and the others sneered at him and a couple spit at his feet, but they were moving away when they did and he ignored them. He turned to me, eyeing me speculatively.

"You have a good set of shoulders on you, lad," he said. "I'm Colonel Harvey." He nodded at the man still lying senseless in the dirt of the street. "And obviously you can handle yourself quite well."

"Jim Hickok. I wanted nothing to do with that," I said quickly, thinking that he might consider me the instigator of the fracas. But he smiled at my words.

"I know," he said. "I could see it coming when he"—he nodded at the man in the street—"collided with you. It was quite deliberate, you know."

"Deliberate?" I frowned, shaking my head.

"Oh yes," he said, folding his arms over his chest. He tapped his left shoulder with his gauntleted fingers. "Quite deliberate."

"But why?"

He shrugged. "They wanted to see what side you were on."

"Side?"

"Pro- or antislavery," he said. He glanced around Leavenworth. "That issue has been brewing in the town for quite some days now." He laughed dryly. "I'm afraid that the whole town—if not the country—is going to erupt over this slavery issue. And other things," he added as an afterthought. "The slave issue is just the spark for the powder keg. But things are going to get worse since that John Brown episode. Where do you stand, by the way?"

His question nearly caught me off-guard, but I had been watching the others as well, the woodsman in me attuned to the temper of those around me, feeling the tension like a tautly strung fiddle bow.

"My father used to be a part of the Railway," I said quietly. "Until he died. I do not believe anyone has the right to own another. John Brown?"

He nodded at my words. "A self-styled minister. Has his own idea about religion, though. Very Old Testament. You didn't hear about the Jeremy Ridge Massacre?"

I shook my head, frowning. "I didn't know the Indians were up."

He laughed shortly. "They aren't. That was Brown and three of his sons. After a little altercation between the anti- and proslavery forces here in Leavenworth, Brown took his sons to Jeremy Ridge and brutally hanged and burned three proslavery men he caught there. According to what I heard, he preached a long sermon while they were burning on their ropes, saying he was sending them to the fires of hell with a head start on burning. That's why I'm here: to catch Brown. If I can."

He sighed and clapped his hands together. "But it turns out that both the Free Staters and proslavery folks don't like the military stepping in. You'd almost think it was a private feud and no outsiders are allowed by mutual agreement. Yet we are about the only law that is here now."

"What about the marshal?"

He shook his head. "He varies from day to day, depending upon his strength and the amount of backing he gets from whichever side he favors. Law!" He nearly spit the word. "This is a huge joke. The law is whoever is in charge."

"Isn't that the normal way of things?" I asked.

His eyebrows rose. "A bit of education as well as a strong back, I see. Well, the governor, Wilson Shannon, resigned and Daniel Woodson, the territorial secretary and staunch proslavery supporter, took his place. He promptly proclaimed the territory to be in open rebellion and had Dave Atchison bring in his so-called Grand Army of Missourians to help him keep the peace."

Atchison, a florid, sociable huge man who was inordinately fond of horses, hunting, and fishing, accompanied his pleasures with frequent nips from a bottle of whiskey he kept near him at all times. He liked to brag that he was born in Frogtown, Kentucky, where he was the "biggest frog in the puddle."

I nodded at this. "I've heard about him. They say he won't listen to any reason or argument that doesn't support his own feelings."

"He's an extremist. In all things," the colonel added. "At any rate, he got into a battle with Brown, and while he fought with Brown and his people Jim Lane took an army of Free Staters to Lecompton. It looked like a war was going to get started, but Colonel St. George Crooke stopped it with troops from here.

"That kept an uneasy peace alive until the new governor, John Geary, could arrive. He promptly dismantled the militia and forced Atchison out of Kansas."

"And how do you figure into this?"

Colonel Harvey gave me another appraising look. "I command a small force of Free Staters. We could use a scout."

For a moment I didn't understand his meaning; then I

shook my head. "I don't have a horse or a gun or anything. And what makes you think that I would make a good scout?"

A wintry smile touched his lips. "I can tell," he said quietly. He glanced down again and I felt a momentary embarrassment at the poorness of my person reflected by my homespun shirt, worn pants, and laced boots. "You may dress like a farmer and you may have worked as a farmer, but you are no farmer." His eyes touched mine. "It's in the eyes," he said.

I nodded sagely, although at that moment I didn't understand what he meant. Much later, after Ellsworth, I knew that he had seen the hunter in me and that was enough for him. What else I needed to know I could learn later, for there are some things that come only with experience. But for that experience to take there needed to be a foundation, and although I was young, I had that foundation from my roamings through the woods, learning the various songs and calls of the birds and how to read the silence that falls at man's approach, knowing the body of the woods, the lobe and larynx of bushes that are as familiar as my own palm, the sound of quail and grouse taking flight and tail feathers drumming poetry into the slipstream of the wild geese. I knew the golden days of the woods when leaves turned varnished yellow and rattled fall's music to those who paused to listen to it.

And so I became a scout, and a man who lived on Crooked Creek gave me a horse and rifle and revolver because he was too stumped up with arthritis to take his place with Harvey but still felt the need to make an obligation for his beliefs. I scouted for Harvey and narrowly missed being captured by the federal troops at Hickory Point when Harvey sent me to Lecompton for supplies.

After that Harvey disbanded his Free Staters and I became a pilgrim for a while and wandered from town to town with my fiddle and a dog that picked up with me on the road

to Mill Creek. I played for my supper at many dances and
the dog—I named him Fritz for no particular reason—
would yawn with boredom until I played "Buffalo Gals," at
which point he would rise on his haunches, lift his head to
the ceiling, and yowl the chorus along with me:

> *"Buffalo gals, won't you come out tonight,"*

much to the amusement of the merrymakers with me.

It was at Mill Creek that I met up with John Owen, who
gave me a pallet in his cabin after a dance, and it was at his
place that I improved myself with a pistol, a heavy Dragoon
revolver, using oyster cans for targets. Owen had married a
Shawnee woman, Patinuxa, a descendant of Logan, chief of
the Mingo who turned against the settlers after the Yellow
Creek Massacre in 1774 when most of his family was wiped
out. They had one child, Mary Jane, but fever took Patinuxa
and Owen never quite got over losing his wife so young.

Together Owen and I made our way around the countryside, squandering our days at church socials and town gath-
erings where I fiddled and he plucked at his banjo, feeling
the wildness of dark juices working to keep us from sainthood as blushing young women flirted with us beneath the
stern and watchful eyes of their mothers safely behind tables laden with cakes and pies and decorated with wild
cherry blossoms and prairie flowers in bacchanal glory.

Kansas, however, was an unstable place as arguments became bitter between those wanting Kansas to be a free
state and those wanting it to be a slave state. The slightest
mention of politics in a saloon—and sooner or later talk always comes around to politics where men bend an elbow—
would draw a fiery rebuttal from someone and a fight would
commence with friends and neighbors joining in on one side
or the other.

The strange thing was that I had lived long enough by this

time to see the thinking on each side. The South needed the slaves for economic prosperity—the slaves had become such an ingrained part of that society and culture, both founded on agriculture that needed cheap labor to prosper. The North believed firmly in Jefferson's words that all men were created equal. The hot-blooded Abolitionists, however, were trying to ram their one-sided opinion down everyone's throats—not a good way to try to win an argument. Still, I always remembered Hannah and the look and feel of her back heavily scarred where a blacksnake had been used to try to teach her docile acceptance of her betters. But it was hard, very hard, especially when I saw what people like the self-appointed "reverend" John Brown did to those who disagreed with their position.

Despite the newspaper columns that lauded him as the greatest Abolitionist hero of his time, Brown was a vicious fanatic—preaching against slavery and insisting on rigid adherence to the Old Testament—and it was, in my opinion, due to him that Kansas soon became known as "Bleeding Kansas." It was his sons, however, that started the whole affair. Five of his twenty sons came to Kansas and staked out claims south of Lawrence and set up Brown's Station to suit their purposes. When a group of bushwhackers came across from Missouri and harassed them, one of them sent word back east to their father and "Goodman" John Brown hastened west with a wagon loaded down with rifles and sabers.

By the time Brown got there, the "Wakarusa War" was in full swing, with the Missouri boys raiding in Kansas one night, the Kansas boys raiding in Missouri the next. All given, no one really knew who was one up on the other. Goodman John immediately formed a group of men he called the Pottawatomie Rifles, named after a creek that ran through his boys' properties south of town where proslavery riders raided free-state settlers.

Now I don't rightly know what happened next, but I have a hunch the lid blew off the simmering pot when an assassin wounded the Douglas County sheriff, a staunch proslavery fellow. Goodman John led his rifles to Lawrence to help protect the town from a proslavery group—renegades, bushwhackers, many of whom later rode with Quantrill and Bloody Bill Anderson—that threatened to come across the river from Missouri to retaliate. It wasn't long after that Senator Charles Sumner from Massachusetts delivered his speech "The Crime Against Kansas" and was savagely beaten with a cane by Preston Smith Brooks, a member of the House of Representatives.

Sumner's beating settled things in Brown's mind, and through some twisted reasoning Brown led his sons down to Pottawatomie Creek to regulate matters. They slaughtered five men there, hacking them to pieces with their sabers, in the name of freedom for the slaves. From there, Brown started out on his holy war against Missouri and all who opposed his views.

I disagreed with Brown's tactics—Lord, but anyone with common sense would have disagreed with him—but I always remembered Hannah and that formed a restlessness in my spirit and when Owen and I heard about Jim Lane putting together a tatterdemalion free-state army near Highland to fight against those ruffians coming across from Missouri, more of a peacekeeping force, really, we decided to join him.

CHAPTER 25

WE HEARD the crackle of gunfire, steady though sporadic, as we came into town. Owen frowned and glanced over at me.

"Sounds like a spat going on," he said.

"I don't think so," I said. "It sounds too steady for that. Let's take a look."

We followed the sound down an alley to a stable. Behind the stable, a shooting contest was in process. We dismounted and stood on the outskirts of the crowd, watching. A short, squat man stood, arms folded, watching critically as the men took turns firing at targets set up fifty yards and staggered from them. Each time one of them missed, he shook his head and spit a long stream of tobacco juice. The ground was soaked brown in front of him. Impulsively I walked up to him. His gray eyes flickered toward me, then back at the contest. I could see he was not very impressed.

"Your boys don't seem to be doing very well," I said.

One of his eyebrows jacked itself high and he turned, glowering, toward me. He spit, narrowly missing the toe of my boot. "Well, young'un," he said. "You think you can do better, there's your chance."

I shook my head, grinning. "Sorry. I didn't mean to upset you. It's just that they look like they could use a lot of practice."

"Uh-huh," he said, his jaws working furiously on the plug of tobacco that bulged his left cheek. "Well, son, out here, you be critical about a man's shooting, you better be willing to show your own. And," he added, reaching inside his pocket, "to make it interesting, what say thirty dollars says you can't beat the best of 'em?"

"Take it," Owen said from my elbow. I turned and looked down at him. He nodded. "I'll cover it."

I took a deep breath, feeling my blood sing with the challenge. I nodded and slipped the Dragoon from my belt. The man grunted and stepped forward waving his arms.

"Cease fire!" he barked. The men paused, dropping their weapons down by their sides, turning to look curiously at him. "Men, we have a young'un here who doesn't think you are any great shakes when it comes to marksmanship."

Eyes swiveled angrily toward me. I felt myself go red under their stares but met their gazes calmly.

"Well, Colonel Lane, let's see what he can do with that hog leg he's holding!" a voice yelled from the crowd.

"Colonel Lane? Jim Lane?" I said. The man turned to me, nodding. "Well, it's you we came to find," I said, feeling my embarrassment grow.

"Well, you found me," he said. He glanced at Owen standing behind me. A tiny smile tugged at the corners of his lips. "But we still have a little matter to settle before we engage in amenities, I think. Now," Lane said, turning back to the men. "Where's Fitzpatrick?"

"Here, Colonel," a voice answered, and a tall, thin man with black hair stepped from the crowd of men. He wore a pair of pistols belted high around his waist, butts forward. His trousers had been stuffed into the tops of his high boots. He wore a linen shirt with a patchwork vest over it. A high-crowned hat, dented in the middle, had been pulled low over his eyes. He glanced at me and smiled faintly.

"Well, Fitzpatrick, what do you say? You want to take this young'un on?"

Fitzpatrick studied me for a moment, then shrugged. "Makes no difference to me," he said. "Whatever you want."

"All right," Lane said. He folded his arms and nodded toward Fitzpatrick. "Let's see what you can do."

Three men grabbed fresh targets and ran downrange to set them up.

I stepped forward and held out my hand. "I'm James Hickok," I said.

He took my hand briefly. His hand felt soft in mine and I knew instinctively that he was no farmer. "Fitzpatrick," he said. "Most folks just call me 'Fitz.'" He looked me up and down. "This could be costly. You got the money?"

Annoyance swept over me and I grinned at him. "I reckon I can afford a dime or two." I nodded downrange. "You want to go first?"

He turned and drew his pistols quickly. I noticed that he didn't cross his arms across his chest to grip his pistols but drew them with a flickering twist of his wrist. When his right hand came level, he fired, then alternated left and right until he had ten shots off. He lowered his pistols and nodded and a man ran down to check his target. I glanced down at his pistols.

"Navy Colts," I said admiringly.

He nodded, looking automatically at the Dragoon in my hand. "That's pretty heavy for infighting. You might think about going to a lighter caliber."

I flushed and raised the Dragoon, conscious of its weight but holding it as negligently as I could. "I can handle one of these."

"Didn't say that," he said. "Just said that sometimes a smaller caliber and lighter gun is better." He held one of his pistols up. "The charge don't mean nothing if you can't hit what you're aiming at. And if you can, then a Navy works just fine. And it's lighter. You can get at it quicker."

"Seven out of ten in the eye!" the man called from downrange.

"Not bad," I said.

Fitzpatrick nodded. "Could've been better, I suppose." He

looked again at the Dragoon. "You got an extra cylinder for that? Or we going to wait while you reload?"

"I have an extra," I mumbled, stepping past him. I raised the Dragoon, firing rapidly. Then I slipped the lever and palmed the cylinder out, replacing it with another I took from my pocket. I snapped it tight and raised the pistol, firing rapidly four times as I brought it level. I lowered the pistol, feeling the sting of the back charge in my hand as the man raced down.

"Not bad, I'm thinking," Fitzpatrick murmured from beside me.

The man turned slowly, shaking his head. "Ten outta ten!" he called.

I heard a rumble of disbelief from the crowd behind me. Fitzpatrick smiled down at me. "Think you can do it again?" he asked.

"Why not?" I said, emboldened by what I had just accomplished. "Should we stretch the distance some?"

His eyebrow twitched, but he nodded, and two men raced off to move the targets back. We walked back to a small table that had been laid with powder and ball, and reloaded our pistols.

"How's your arm holding out?" Fitzpatrick said conversationally.

"All right," I said.

"Uh-huh," he said, rocking the hammers to test the action. "But I'm betting that you feel the weight if you fire long, right?"

I didn't comment, suddenly aware of the weight of the pistol. Then I realized the subtlety of his remarks, calculated to turn my mind from shooting to the discomfort the Dragoon caused. I shifted the weight of the pistol to my left hand and clenched and unclenched my right to work the tension from my arm. Together we walked back to the firing line. The men slipped to the side after placing the fresh targets. Fitzpatrick nodded.

"No reason we both can't shoot," he said. "Unless you think you might be bothered by my noise."

"Nope," I answered. I raised my pistol and began firing.

Fitzpatrick followed my lead, but I noticed he took more time to aim this time than before. We stepped back after setting our shots and a man ran down, counting first Fitzpatrick's target and announcing that he had nine out of ten in the bull. A satisfied roar rose, congratulating him. Then the man turned and looked at my target. The uproar died as he slowly backed from the target and looked back at us.

"Ten out of ten again," he said disbelievingly.

The crowd fell silent. Fitzpatrick shook his head. "Well, I'd say that you've beaten me and beaten me square, by God!" He grinned and offered his hand.

"Shoot again!" someone yelled, but Fitzpatrick again shook his head.

"Nope," he said. "There's no sense wasting powder. This 'Wild Bill' has beaten me and done it properly. None here's gonna object to that, far as I'm concerned." He turned to Lane, who stayed at the side, impassively watching us. "Colonel, you could do worse than signing this one up."

"Both of us," Owen said. He came forward, clapping me on the shoulder. He looked at Lane. "And I'd say you owe us thirty dollars for that. Give it to Jim here."

"Good going, Wild Bill!" someone shouted. I flushed at the nickname given to someone good with pistols.

The crowd clapped and someone gave a wild shout and a hat went sailing up in the air. I felt myself blushing and looked over at Lane. He came forward and handed thirty dollars to me.

"I think you're right, Fitzpatrick," he said. He looked at Owen and nodded. "There's a place for both you and Bill here. How old are you, son?" he said, turning toward me.

"Nineteen," I stammered. Suddenly I felt as awkward as a schoolboy in his presence and glanced down at the toe of my boot. "And I'd sure as certain like to be with you and your boys!"

"Then you shall be," he said, shaking my hand. "You're the best shot in three hundred."

And on that we were enlisted in his Frontier Guard, as he liked to call them. I sort of attached myself to him as his bodyguard along with Owen and we traveled around the countryside together, with Lane stumping for election to the U.S. Senate part of the time and the rest of the time patrolling the border. Once in Grasshopper Falls when Lane was delivering a particularly fire-breathing speech denouncing the so-called Border Ruffians as the spawn of Beelzebub, I noticed a dirty man with a beard start to slip his pistol from his holster. I stepped forward with the Dragoon in my hand and stared at him for a long moment before he replaced his pistol and slunk away. Lane never noticed, caught up as he was in his oratory.

Not long after this, a territorial grand jury, made up solely of proslavery folks, indicted some of the folks in Lawrence, citing them for treason along with a bunch of other crimes so vaguely stated as to be ridiculous. They sent a U.S. marshal along with a posse of Missourians to arrest them. But after the marshal served the warrants and told the posse to go home, they went on a rampage instead, tearing Lawrence apart, setting fire to the buildings, looting the stores, and shooting at anything that moved. Whiskey flowed like a river among them.

We heard about what was happening in Lawrence and headed that way as soon as we could get horsed. So did Goodman John Brown along with his sons and a few others who believed along with him that slavery was an abomination against God. But we were too late. The Missourians had slipped back over the border after drinking

Lawrence dry and pretty near leveling the town. Brown took it all personally and declared "those barbarians have to be shown that we, too, have rights." He ordered his men to horse and they took off for Pottawatomie Creek, where they dragged five men from their beds and hacked them to death with swords already bloodied from the time before. They washed their swords free of blood in the creek and I guess it ran red. After that, people began to refer to our place as "Bleeding Kansas." But Lane's army had nothing to do with that. Brown went his own way; we went ours. I think Brown was really more interested in spilling blood to show the South that they couldn't be riding across the border and messing around with Kansas politics. He was more of an "eye for an eye" man instead of "turning the cheek" and forgiving.

We found out that many of those who had come across into Kansas joined up or were from Atchison's Grand Army of Missouri—not much of an army, really. More a group of men who had decided the unsettled times were ready-made for their unsettled ways—a bunch of hell-raisers out to have a little fun. I don't think they were much better than Brown and his boys. But then again, we weren't, either, I reckon now with a bit of hindsight—the calf wouldn't get out of the barn if the door had been shut properly in the first place, Father always said, and thinking about it now doesn't shut it then. But we didn't think then. We reacted just like Brown, although, I think, with a bit more civility.

Lane's men finally met up with Atchison's Grand Army of Missouri on Bull Creek, fifteen miles north of Osawatomie. But before we could engage in anything other than a few minor skirmishes on the flanks, Colonel Philip St. George Crooke came up with a squad of troops from Fort Leavenworth and demanded that we all disband and go home. None of us wanted to take on those troopers, who were better armed than we were and had the look of seasoned veterans about them, so we slunk away with our tails between our legs, much to the name- and catcalling of the troopers. But Lane allowed that there was a time when discretion was called for and that there wasn't any reason to be ashamed. There would be plenty of other chances, he said, for us firebrands to earn our spurs.

And he was right. I soon learned that the Third Commandment could be suspended on occasion. The border broke out in a series of barn burnings, lynchings, and killings from ambush. A rightly named guerrilla war that Brown and others like him took to with relish. We had our moments, too, but I could see that things weren't going to amount to much after a few months and soon Owen and I found ourselves back in Monticello, Kansas, where Owen became a supervisor and I the town constable, thanks to a commission issued by James Denver, who was acting as the territorial governor.

I also filed a claim on a hundred and sixty acres, and between being a constable and working my claim I felt subsumed by function. But I still had time for Owen's daughter, Mary.

Ah, Mary! When I first saw her, I felt as if a mule had kicked me in the stomach and Hannah's memory slipped into the background. I remember standing face-to-face with Mary in the moonlight and watching the pale light shimmering silvery off the prairie grasses rolling gently in the night breeze like dark waves. We put our arms around each other and the future seemed spread out before us in a familiar intensity. My hands curved as if seeking the handles of a plow and I smelled the rich Kansas earth and imagined the crops that could be planted and raised from it.

CHAPTER 26

S HE LAUGHED and I was aware of being involved in her laughter and being a part of it. Her teeth were accidental stars in the night and I felt my breath slip from me in short gasps, inhaled automatically in momentary recovery. I lost myself in the dark cavern of her throat where her heart beat, pulsing in the night like a gentle ripple in a backwater stream.

I dreamed the dreams of a farmer with Mary lying beside me in the pale moonlight, watching the annealed stars and low-hooked moon. Her lips trembled beneath mine and her bronzed skin seemed to glow from an inner fever and together we made plans to wed. I built a cabin on my claim, taking great pains to make it as comfortable as possible. I bought a milch cow and put up hay, planning to serve one year as constable before settling down with Mary. I wrote to Mother and told her about Mary and that, I imagine, was the beginning of hard times between Mother and me. She dispatched Lorenzo to talk me out of marrying beneath her station.

The last fingers of leaves clutched and sank into the wet bank of the creek while the wind blew lightly, rattling the dried limbs of the trees like old bones. An uneasiness seemed to stalk the land in the cruelest month and I lay in bed, mixing memory and desire, half-asleep, half-dreaming. Mary was visiting her folks and broken images slipped through the dimness and I saw again the disapproving face of Mother, thin-lipped, hollow-cheeked, wearing a mobcap and widow's weeds and looking like the dried husk of a

spinster. Broken images slipped across the land of my
dreams where the eyes of Jesus saw nothing.

I heard footsteps shuffling, a cold wind suddenly wafting under my door, an exclamation and sudden hush.

I awoke, momentarily confused, then rose and crossed
silently to my window and peered out. Torchlight ran red on
sweaty faces grim with determination. I recognized some
of them—proslavery men whose hatred steamed in the
night. I thought I smelled the whiskey on their breath that
gave them the courage to come to my cabin like rats creeping through back alleys. The first torch flew toward the roof
of my cabin and I turned, grabbing as many possessions as
I could, crossing the cabin to the back, where I dived through
a window and rolled like a log into the darkness. I cocked
the Dragoon and fired at a dim shadow. It staggered, then
howled like a gut-shot dog.

"Jesus! He's out!"

I fired again, deliberately holding low as two rushed in
to help the first. A leg snapped backward as the heavy ball
struck it and the figure tumbled onto the ground. I worked
my way backward, down to the creek, and slipped over the
bank and through the shadows away from the cabin while
curses and screams of pain dented the night.

Morning dawned, gray in the early light with a milky fog
rising from the creek bed. I came cautiously out of the
buffalo-berry bushes where I had hidden in the night. I carried the heavy Dragoon pistol loosely in my hand, ready
for whoever was foolish enough to show himself. I paused
before the smoking ashes of what had been my cabin, listening to the birds sing themselves awake, and knew that I
was alone.

A few charred timbers still stood, but even the stone fireplace had cracked from the heat of the fire and fallen in on

itself. A self-pitying lump came into my throat, but I swallowed it away and stared at the remains of my cabin while cold anger seeped through me, settling like ice in the pit of my stomach, forcing emotions away. I wanted the anger now, *needed* the anger now, to justify the burning of my cabin as a personal attack upon myself and not upon my beliefs. To believe otherwise was to admit being naïve, and I was vain enough to want to believe I was important enough for others to want to destroy. But I was deceiving myself by making myself a martyr to the cause of antislavery. I felt noble, enriched, bitter, working myself into a justification for the morality of my intentions. I fully intended to find the men responsible for burning my cabin. But deep down I knew such intentions were futile, for the men I wanted would have witnesses that they were nowhere near my cabin when misfortune struck.

"Jim?"

I dropped to the ground, spinning around, cursing at my carelessness at not hearing him approach. I rocked the hammer back, automatically aiming at the figure in the mist. He threw up his hands, backing hastily away.

"It's me, Jim!"

I took a deep breath and let it out slowly. I gently lowered the hammer and pushed myself up from the ground. "Hello, Lorenzo. Bad timing to come up on me that way."

Lorenzo dropped his hands and moved in to me. "Damn it, Jim! You took seven years off the backside of my life!"

"Lucky I didn't take *that*," I said defensively. "What are you doing creeping up like that without announcing yourself?"

"Why the hell are you so touchy?" he retorted.

I gestured at my cabin. "That's why. Some boys came around last night and burned me out. Almost got me as well."

"Yours?" I nodded. "Looks like it was a pretty one. I

knew you had registered a claim, but I didn't know you had built already."

"Yeah, well, I had a reason," I said, sighing. "Now I reckon I'm just going to have to start again."

"Uh-huh," he grunted. He glanced at me sideways. "The Indian girl?" he asked deliberately offhandedly.

I bristled at the tone of his voice, recognizing the distaste under his question. I turned toward him. "What do you mean?" I asked quietly.

"You know what I mean," he said defensively. "Mother almost had a stroke when she read your last letter, thinking that you were contemplating marrying her."

"I am," I answered.

"Jim," he said solemnly. "She's an Indian."

A wave of anger washed over me. I had been fighting against this prejudice for almost six months—nearly being killed a couple of times—and now I was hearing the same words from my brother that I had been hearing from the pukes and crackers I had been chasing into Missouri. I felt the heat of my anger flood up into my cheeks, and the copper taste at the back of my throat told me I was close to losing control. Somewhere a jay called, raucous and loud. A squirrel answered angrily. I took a deep breath and turned back to face my brother, willing the anger away.

"I never thought I would hear that from you, Lorenzo," I said, shaking my head. "After all we did with Father, running the Negroes back and forth to get them away from their owners. Why, we even took in Hannah, if you remember." I felt a twinge of memory at the mention of her name and looked away. Lorenzo caught it.

"I remember," he said, giving me a hard look. "And don't think I don't know about the two of you. I never said nothing, but you can bet I wanted to ream your butt. What would Mother had said if she'd a-had a baby? Would've destroyed her. She wouldn't have been able to lift her head up at all in town or church, what with people snickering whenever she passed."

I flushed. "You don't know what you're talking about," I mumbled. But I knew he could tell I was lying. Unless I was spinning a story, I never could tell an out-and-out lie. I always flushed redder than a first-kissed schoolgirl at a church social.

"Yeah, you keep saying that. All licorice and horehound drops."

"Does Mother know?"

He shrugged. "I don't know. I *think* so. But with Mother you can't rightly tell everything. Sometimes she gets that prim twist to her mouth and you know she's holding her tongue although the words wanna burst outta her." He held his hand up warningly as I felt my eyes grow hard and harsh words leaped to my lips. "Now, Jim, remember that she's a bit old-fashioned. She's willing to help folks, but she don't think chickens should mate with eagles—the chickens cannot fly that high and might get hurt. Some people are like eagles; they are made to fly high. Others are made to be part of the earth. Your little Indian girl belongs there, Jim. You belong up among the eagles."

"Very literary, Brother. But what makes me so that I should fly among the eagles? Because I'm white?"

He hesitated and, I have to give him credit for doing so, blushed. But his lips were tight with resolution as he met my eyes. "Yes, that's part of it. Being white, you come from a different world than she does. You don't fit in her world and she doesn't fit in yours."

"What are you talking about?" I exploded, waving my arms around at my burnt cabin. "I built this for us. I planned on farming this land. If this wasn't becoming a part of the earth, I don't know what the hell it was! I thought I was far enough from the border to keep those Missourian ruffians away." Suddenly I felt as if the air had been punched out of me. I waved my hands awkwardly, limply. "Hell, they spent most of their time raiding the river bottoms east of here. There's a Blue Lodge not far from here and those damn Masons always raid to the southeast. But I reckon that's no insurance that they would continue to do that."

"It isn't a matter of what you *want* to do but what you're *meant* to do, Jim," he said. A hint of sadness seemed to touch his eyes for a moment, and in that moment it was like looking into a mirror and I saw myself in the unhappiness behind his solemnity and behind that solemnity I felt the distance that I was going to have to ride and the loneliness with that distance.

I turned away and stared at the charred timbers of my cabin. A half wall still hung blackly together with the stark frame of a window balanced precariously on top of it. I looked through that frame and a low fog seemed to rise from the creek. In the fog I saw the shadows of aging soldiers in an ancient war, and a great sorrow descended upon me and I knew that sorrow would be with me constantly and I would know joy only briefly. The changing seasons would bring little relief, and the little happiness I would feel would be taken away quickly by bitter time. Faintly I heard Lorenzo clear his throat, and I took a deep breath, facing him once again.

"Did you recognize any of them?"

"Thought I did," I answered slowly. "I winged a couple, maybe hurt 'em a little more seriously, but there's gonna be my mark on more than one who came here."

"Word has it that you've joined the Free-State Militia— the Redlegs. If there's any truth to that, you've got reason enough to have some of those boys coming to your house for a bit of Hickok barbecue." Lorenzo frowned. "Those boys are nothing but trouble, from what I've heard. I hope you haven't thrown your lot in with them."

I shook my head emphatically. "I rode with Jim Lane for

a while *before* he formed the Redlegs, but I didn't like him. Couldn't trust him. I found out later that when he first came to Kansas he boasted he'd just as soon buy a nigger as a mule. But he changed his tune when he took a hard look at the Free Staters. No, I won't join a man who can't make up his mind or changes it when the wind blows differently. Man's got to be constant. I left him months ago."

Lorenzo watched me hard for a few moments before relaxing and saying, "All right. Let's leave it at that. I heard from a letter you wrote to Mother that there was a section with about a hundred of acres on it you thought we should go after."

"There was," I said. I took a deep breath, trying to push the anger down inside of me. "But right now I want to rethink that."

He frowned. "But—"

I shook my head. "I mean it. You can file on it if you want—I'll show you where it is—but what Mother said needs some thinking over."

"You have to remember what Mother is like," he said.

"I do remember and that's the trouble," I said. "I remember how many nights you and me rode with Father to pick up some Negroes and take them on to the next stop. She never said anything against that. So why now is she all of a sudden set against Mary Jane? No," I continued when he started to argue with me, "no, don't say anything right now. I'm angry." I gestured toward the smoking ruins of my cabin. "I don't think I want to build another cabin right now. There's just too much hatred going on. Both at home and here."

Lorenzo said he could wait a bit while I thought it over. He took a job working for a farmer north of Monticello. I found a job driving freight between Independence and Santa Fe.

Still a restlessness within my spirit dug away at me like

spurs in the flanks of a restless gelding. The prairie hills rolled away from the wagons slowly, like brown waves upon an endless sea, lulling me into a certain lassitude that drugged my mind sometimes, making me feel like I was a sailor lost upon the Sea of Galilee. A couple of times I almost fell off my horse as I guided the wagons from one town to another.

One day I rode out a ways ahead of the freight train, checking the coulees and gullies for renegades who had been preying upon the wagons near Leavenworth. I rode over a small hill and saw a young man struggling against a couple of bearded buffalo hunters. His horse stood ground-reined a few yards away. As I watched, one of the hunters dug a fist into the youth's stomach. He leaned over, gagging, as the two of them bore him facedown upon the ground. One of them sat on his head as the other pulled his pants down, skinning them off as smoothly as a skinner's knife cutting through a buffalo hide.

I shook my head and nudged my horse with my heels, riding down to them. They were so intent upon their purpose that they never heard my horse's hooves moving through the long bluestem grass. The youth kept struggling gamely, but it was a losing battle against those men who were intent upon having their sport with him.

"Ain't nothin' like a fresh one, eh, Luke?" the one standing between the boy's legs said. He hooked dirty thumbs into his belt and pushed his pants down around his ankles. His legs gleamed like dirty ivory in the noonday sun. "Hold 'im now. I'll return the favor."

"Ain't fair, Ned," the other complained, trying to grab the boy's hands. "You allus seem to get the fresh'ns while I come in second."

Ned grinned. "This here one looks fresh enough that it won't matter none."

"There's that," Luke snickered obscenely.

I slid the Dragoon from its holster hanging from the pommel of my saddle and rocked the hammer back. The hunters froze, then turned slowly, craning their necks up and squinting against the sun to where I sat on my horse.

"What you want?" Ned demanded, hawking and spitting. His teeth gleamed dirty yellow in his bearded face. I could smell the buffalo stink on both of them—like meat left too long in the sun. The day seemed to narrow down to a small world that held only the four of us.

"Anything I hate is a buffalo man taking advantage of a boy," I said, feeling the anger burning through me like hot oil. "Let him up."

"Now," Ned whined.

"Your choice," I said. "Let him up or I'll knock you off him. I'll put a bullet through you big enough to let a jackrabbit find daylight."

"Better do it, Luke," Ned said.

Suddenly the two of them moved left and right, their hands scrabbling for their weapons. As Ned came up with a long skinning knife in his hand the Dragoon roared, knocking him back onto the ground. He screamed and his hands gripped the hole in his belly as he curved into a fetal position against the pain soaring through him. Luke turned white and started to run, but he forgot his pants gathered around his ankles and sprawled on his belly across a scrub prickly pear cactus. He yelped and rolled away, then dived for his rifle lying where he had carelessly dropped it in the grass. I waited until he tried to bring it up, then shot him in the forehead. His head jerked backward, the top of his skull fragmenting.

I glanced over at Ned, who convulsed once, his legs twisting in agony; then he lay still. I sighed and lowered the hammer on the Dragoon and looked at the boy still stretched on the ground.

"You can get up now," I said. "They won't be bothering you anymore."

He rose and kept his back to me as he picked up his pants and stepped into them. He tucked his shirttail in, keeping his face down and away from me. His hair was long and yellow-white and fell forward in twin curtains that covered the sides of his face. I could see the red on the back of his neck. I sighed and stepped down from my horse, taking a water bag with me.

"Well," I said, walking up to him. "I'm James Hickok." I pulled the wooden stopper from the canvas bag and took a long drink, then reached around and handed it to the boy.

"Go ahead," I said. "Have a drink."

Wordlessly he took the bag and tilted it up. He had fine features and was older than I first thought but still looked about ten years younger than me. His eyes, I noticed, were blue-gray. He poured a little water into his hand and splashed it across his face, then handed the bag back to me.

"Thanks," he mumbled. His cheeks were still pink beneath a soft furze that was the beginning of a future beard. I could see the embarrassment taking a hard hold upon him.

I took the water bag from him and walked back to my horse, draping it over the saddle horn. "You know," I said conversationally, "there are some things a person just can't help. There comes a time when you do everything you can and if the numbers are against you, you're still going to come up short."

I stepped into the stirrups and swung up onto my horse. "You did everything you could," I said gently. "There's nothing to be ashamed of."

He turned and lifted his head, his eyes shining. "Thanks," he said gruffly. "I appreciate what you done."

I shook my head. "You'd do the same if things were the other way around. And they could have been that way." I

looked at the boy's horse still standing patiently to the side.
I didn't see any weapons. "Especially if I wouldn't have had
a gun, either." I pointed down at the bodies. "But now you
do. Get what you want from them. They aren't going to be
needing anything, keeping the devil company the way they
are now."

I turned the horse as he called out.

"I'm Bill. Bill Cody!" he shouted.

I looked over my shoulder and smiled at him. "Pleased
to meet you, Bill Cody," I said. "Maybe we'll meet again."
I touched the brim of my hat and lifted the horse into a trot
away from them.

"I'll remember this!" he shouted, and I waved again.

I was certain that he would remember it, but I didn't think
that I would see him again despite my words. The land was
big and empty, with nothing but miles and miles between
homesteads and towns, and the chances of coming upon a
person twice in a lifetime seemed as remote then as those
of reaching the full harvest moon.

I soon pushed the matter from my mind as I turned my
thoughts back to Mary Jane. Like I told Lorenzo, I needed
time to think about what had happened, and that was a
mistake on my part. Maybe I was trying to follow Mother's
way or maybe I was trying to make up for her about not
being there the day Father died while I was spending that
time with Josephine, tumbling around the barn on spread
hay—I don't know. Either way, it was a mistake to stay gone
so long away from Mary Jane. I had made up my mind to
settle down again on the acres I had claimed despite
Mother's concern and take Mary Jane for my wife. Mother
could sort the problem out herself. But when I came back
from my first trip, Mary Jane had already decided for me:
she had married a doctor named Harris. At first, I tried to
bury my disappointment in a bottle of Old Hickory, but

that didn't last long. Her image soon disappeared from my memory until I could only remember her name and a faint outline of her form. When I could no longer remember what she looked like, I took a job on a stage line.

CHAPTER 27

I CAME to like the work along the Old Santa Fe Trail that wound up into the hills of the upper reaches of the Arkansas River before turning along the River of Lost Souls and climbing into the Raton Mountains in New Mexico. That became a little hairy, working the stage along those steep gorges and ravines, but smelling the jack pine and spruce in the early mornings and when it rained made it all worthwhile. I had never seen such hardness in a land before, but there was something intoxicating about it that pulled me right into its bosom and made me love it.

Somehow, my name got lost along the way and everyone took to calling me "Bill." I don't really remember when it became permanent, but I guess it was when I took to raising the teams I was driving into a gallop when we came to the outskirts of Santa Fe in order to shake the kinks out of the passengers' spines after they had been sitting for so long.

One day, we came rolling into Santa Fe in a cloud of dust, a lady in the coach screaming that we were going to be killed at that speed. I nearly ran over a little sandy-haired man dressed in buckskins who had been crossing the street, but he skipped nimbly out of the way as I pulled the team to a stop in front of the station.

"Oh, God!" the woman inside said loudly. "Oh, God! We made it! We made it! Praise be the Lord!"

"Yes, ma'am," I said, stepping down and opening the door for the passengers. "But he didn't have his hands on the reins. I did."

She gave me a murderous look, indignantly slapped my hand aside, and descended to the ground. She nearly stumbled when her knees buckled, but the small man leaped over and steadied her by the elbow. She jerked her arm away with a decisive and dismissive, "Men!" and, throwing her chin out in front of her like a logger's elbow, stormed on down the street toward the hotel.

"You really should be ashamed of yourself!" a drummer in a dusty bowler squeaked as he stumbled out of the coach.

"Oh, shut up," said a burly man dressed like a banker, with a heavy gold chain across his vest, pushing himself out of the coach. "It relieved the boredom." He stepped down and brushed the dust from him, nodding at me. "You sure woke us up, son. Good job."

"Thank you, sir," I said. He reached into his vest pocket, removed a dollar, and handed it to me before crossing the plaza toward the bank. I watched him as he moved away, then felt a gentle tap on my shoulder. I turned around and found the small man facing me. His eyes met mine steadily.

"That was quite a trick," he said softly, musically. "But you damn near rode me down."

I glanced at the dollar in my hand and stuffed it into my pocket. I grinned at him. "Well, you managed to get out of the way, didn't you?"

"I did," he said. "But there are some who might not have been able to. You need to start thinking about them instead of the fun you're having at the time."

I started to retort hotly, but he had a bearing about him made me draw the words back, considering, before I threw them out to the air. I think it was in the eyes; yes, it was in the eyes. No fear or apprehension showed, which was unusual, as he was fully a head shorter than I and looked to be about as big around as my thigh. If not for the buckskins and his square shoulders, I would not have given him a second glance. But his eyes—that is where the character lies, where the truth lies, and although I didn't know this at the time, I sensed it and had learned enough in my short time on the plains by then to pay heed to my senses.

"You're probably right," I said tactfully—words cost little but can gain you much, I thought—"but after a time on the trail, it seems just natural to want to let the horses out. They know they're near the end, too, and look forward to getting the harness off. But I apologize."

He stood silent for a long moment, studying me to see if I was being sarcastic or my words were sincere. Then he relaxed and a faint smile touched his lips beneath his sandy mustache. "You know," he said, "few people would offer an apology to someone out here even if they were wrong and knew it. It signals to most that they are weak—they think—and so they stubbornly maintain they are right."

I grinned at him. "So I shouldn't apologize?"

"No"—he shook his head—"that's not what I'm saying. A man needs to be honest to himself at all times. He should be honest to others as well, but most of all he has to be honest to himself and willing to admit when he's made a mistake. I'm just giving you a bit of advice, that's all. Not," he hastened to add, "that I'm free with it, normally, but I've got a hunch that you haven't been out west long. Most people see apologies as a weakness. You may have to fight someone sometime when they try to take advantage of you for apologizing."

I shrugged. "No sense worrying about it. When it comes, it comes."

"Uh-huh," he said, his eyes studying mine carefully.

Suddenly he held out his hand. "I accept. I'm Christopher Carson. Most people call me Kit."

I could feel my mouth dropping open as I took his hand. "*The* Kit Carson? I've read about you so much I think I could recite your life backward. Why, when I was a boy"—I felt the silliness of my words as I spoke them and the red burning my cheeks, but I couldn't stop myself from gushing—"I tried to imitate you in the woods back home. I read your autobiography until the pages wore out."

"Yes, well, uh, thanks," he stammered softly. He looked around quickly as if searching for a way to escape. He pulled gently on my hand and I suddenly realized that I was gripping it as if I intended on owning it forever. Sheepishly I released it and rubbed the back of my neck and wiped my hand down the leg of my trousers, not really knowing what to do with it but feeling like I never wanted to wash it again and feeling stupid for feeling that way. I never had many heroes in my time, but here was one standing in front of me as plain as day, although he was smaller than I thought he would be and looked like he could drown in a cup of water.

"Sorry," I said. "There I go again: apologizing. It's just that I never thought—well, hope I didn't make you mad."

"No, no, you didn't. It's just a bit much, you know, when people treat you like you're something special when you ain't."

"But, Mr. Carson—"

"Kit," he reminded me gently. "Kit. Please."

"All right. Oh." I shook my head. "Sorry. I'm James Hickok."

He cocked his head, squinting quizzically at me. "Any relation to a Bill Hickok I'm beginning to hear about?"

"Oh, some people call me that," I said, feeling my cheeks redden again. "Look, can I buy you a drink—or a cup of coffee—as a way of apologizing? Maybe we could start over?"

He glanced up at the sun, pressed his lips together thoughtfully, then nodded. "A cup of coffee would be nice. I don't drink much. I kind of like knowing what I'm doing and saying. Drink can grab a man by the throat and make him a fool, and I don't seem to have much trouble doing that by myself without the help of drink. But come on, I know a small place where we won't be bothered, and tonight I'll show you the Santa Fe that appeals to your age."

He led me to a small restaurant run by a Mexican just off the plaza. The coffee was strong but seasoned with cinnamon and rich cream. I finally relaxed in his presence, and slowly he began to share his adventures with me—or, at least, what seemed like adventures to me but were regarded by him as just everyday occurrences in his life as a mountain man. I began to ache for a share in his nostalgia, but I knew those days were gone and there was no way I could bring them back by trying to live in the past. Dreams, I know, are fine, but they are only dreams to be enjoyed and not the mystic revelations of a possible life.

That night, he was as good as his word—he always was—and we began our night sojourn around Santa Fe with a stop in the bar of the United States Hotel. When we pushed our way into that smoke-filled room, I saw immediately that it had become the meeting place for the mountain men. Most in that room were more Kit's age than my own, and I knew that he had made this the first stop to show me the life that had been and the stubborn men who refused to acknowledge the passing of time.

Hunters and trappers, wearing old smoke-cured and fringed buckskins, crowded the bar, drinking and bickering among themselves about the relative merits of various traps. Hawkin rifles were held carelessly or stood in corners and leaned against the bar within easy reach of callused hands. Bowie knives bristled at their belts along with small hatchets. Beneath the smoke I could smell old grease and a faint hint of pine needles. A few hailed Kit and motioned for him to join them, but he shook his head, politely declining their offer of drink, and nodded in my direction to show that he had already committed himself to my company.

On second glance, I had to amend my first opinion, recognizing merchants from Santa Fe, traders, freighters and teamsters, and Mexican entrepreneurs arguing softly in the corners away from the mountain men. The room was loud with noise as people bargained and quarreled, some singing raucous and sentimental songs. The noise began to infiltrate my senses and slowly I became aware that English wasn't the only language being spoken in the room. I heard French and Spanish and against a door leading to a back room stood four or five red-faced men arguing in German. I realized that this was the cosmopolitan center of Santa Fe, a refuge for lonely men, some of whom had made their way from the trail and mountains, all seeking a brief respite from their loneliness in the river of whiskey and warm beer that they poured liberally down parched throats.

Here Kit had a short drink—indeed, I don't think he would have been allowed out of the room had he not had one—and then we proceeded to an L-shaped flat-roofed adobe house down in the Mexican quarter. It was much darker down here and we walked in the center of the street as a precaution against suddenly being accosted from the shadows of the alleys. The room was filled with poker tables and a roulette wheel and high-banked dicing tables. Monte seemed to be the favorite game, for four of the tables had been designated for that play. The banks there were stacked with Spanish doubloons and Mexican gold and silver along with paper script.

A man threw up his hands and stepped away from one of the tables. On an impulse, I took his place. Kit gave me a questioning look but stood near my elbow as I placed some money on the worn green felt covered with the faded painted face of a snarling tiger in front of me. I lost the first round, then the second, as the bored-looking dealer slapped the shoe in front of him, slipping the losing and the winning cards from its lip. I decided to try once more when a woman came up and dropped a hand on the dealer's shoulder, leaning down to speak lowly in his ear. Her voice carried to me, but she spoke in Spanish. Kit nudged me and I bent toward him, listening as he said, "That's Señora Dona Gertrudis Barcelo. She's in charge of the monte play here." I glanced over at the woman smoking a small cigarillo. She wore a black satin dress, her shoulders bare, hair piled in curious curls held in place with a ruby-crested band. A black velvet band was around her waist and neck. Her black eyes danced toward us and caught and held mine boldly. I nodded politely toward her. A tiny smile moved her full and painted lips, bringing dimples into each cheek.

"Be careful there," Kit murmured from beside me.

"Why do you say that?" I asked quietly.

"She just told the dealer to let the handsome young American win," he said quietly.

"Then we should play a little more, don't you think? I would hate to disappoint her," I said as a recklessness came over me. I reached over and coppered my bet. I glanced at her and saw her fingers tighten on the dealer's shoulder. She gave me a tiny nod as the dealer slapped the shoe and slipped the cards out smoothly. I won and placed another bet on the king of spades, letting my winnings and original bet ride. Again the dealer slapped the shoe and swiftly drew two cards, the first the loser and the second the winner. Again I won.

"You'd better stop while you're ahead, Bill," Kit said softly. "I wouldn't take advantage of her. She's letting you win now, but you go much further, you're going to have to oblige her."

"Would it be all that bad?" I asked.

He nudged me gently with his elbow. I followed his gaze toward the side of the room where a young man in a suit sat on a chair placed on a small platform high above the crowd. He held a Greener, the twin muzzles pointed in my general direction. He glared at me, the muscles working in the corners of his jaw.

"Who is he?" I asked.

"Her current lover," he said. "Funny thing about her lovers: They don't last long. She's sort of like a black widow. Of course, it depends upon how good they are, I expect. Both in bed and out. That one's got a shotgun, though. Man would have to be quick and good to beat that. Besides," he said dryly, turning to me, "cards are the devil's prayer book. Haven't you heard that before from a parson somewhere?"

I laughed, feeling the recklessness moving up from my belly to my shoulders, that feeling a man gets when he figures he can whip his weight in wildcats. The room became suddenly bright and clear and I smiled across the room at the young man on the chair. I raised a finger to my hat and saluted him mockingly.

"Don't be a fool!" Kit said sternly. "You won't win down here. Maybe uptown, but not down here. Look around you."

Obediently I looked around. At first I noticed nothing; then suddenly I became aware that with the exception of a couple of mountain men and a muleskinner, Kit and I were the lone white men in the room. A few had become aware of the young man's interest and were staring, openly hostile, at me. I glanced across at Señora Barcelo. She smiled faintly back and I could read the invitation in her eyes. But then I noticed the fine, hard lines at the corners of her eyes, the rough skin scarred by smallpox beneath the rice powder she had used liberally on her face and shoulders. I imagined what she would be like beneath me in bed—*if you get that far without being cut in two by the Greener,* I thought. I tried to tell myself that he would not be stupid enough to use it in a crowd this size, since a shotgun doesn't recognize a particular person but treats all the same, impersonally and deadly. Then again, infatuation makes a person do dumb things. *Just like you were about to do.*

"You know," I said to Kit, "I think you have a very valid point there." I scooped my winnings up from the table and weighed them carefully in my hand, then placed my winnings in my pocket. "Man really shouldn't tempt fate when he's already had a look at the other man's cards." But I stepped back reluctantly from the table, feeling the pull of the cards and aching to buck the tiger again.

"Glad you see it that way," Kit said. "You can always come back later, you know. I wouldn't—but then, I'm older than you and been that way before."

"What way's that?"

"Letting your pecker do your thinking for you," he said dryly. Then he raised his voice so all at the table could hear. "Come on. There's a couple of other places I want to show you."

I nodded politely at Señora Barcelo. She raised her left eyebrow, and her full lips curved as she gave a tiny sigh. I smiled and followed Kit to the door. But I made a mental note of the narrow adobe-lined streets we had taken to get to the casino. I knew I would be back; discretion may be needed, but opportunity will always come to the patient man. And I knew that Señora Barcelo and I were not finished. Yet.

Kit and I took a small, dark alley smelling of acrid piss and rotting garbage to move over one street. I noticed we turned in the same direction and admired Kit's cautiousness. If we were being followed, they would follow the other street in one direction or another, not thinking that two *gringos* would take a narrow and dark alley in Mexican town.

"Where we going?" I asked.

Kit laughed. "Well, I figure if you're getting an itch, I

should take you to a place where you might be able to scratch it without gettin' yourself cut into with a scattergun." He nodded in the direction we were walking. "Not far down there is a *cantina*—a dance hall, really—and although you gotta be a little careful about which *señorita* you move with, you might get away with it."

"They don't have scatterguns there, I suppose?" I said.

He shook his head. "No, but they do have knives. And most know how to use them. That happens, don't be a hero. Just draw your pistol and point it at them. There may be a hothead or two down there, but usually that cools them off."

"Sounds like you have a lot of experience in this," I said.

"I have a lot of experience *living* here," he said. "That's all. Remember that you are dealing with humans, with people, and not with patterns. You can never predict with a certainty what others are going to do. It's best that you remember that, Bill. It will do you good later. You may *think* you know someone, but it's always best to be cautious and think that you ain't got the slightest idea what the other fellow is going to do. That way, you won't be surprised when you're wrong—and I have a hunch that you're going to be wrong-thinking more ways than one. Best not to be wrong-actioned, too."

I walked quietly beside Kit, thinking over what he had just told me. There was a lot of philosophy in that, enough to hold a man a lifetime if he paid attention to it. I figured coming from Kit Carson, it was something to do, and made a mental note to remember everything that he said and apply it to whatever it was that I was doing.

We arrived at what appeared to be an adobe house. Kit didn't knock, however, but threw the door open and strolled in. Music poured out, striking me in the face with the intensity of its scales. I took a step inside, nearly stomping on Kit's heels. The room was smoky and heavy with perfume and sour sweat. Over in the far corner, a couple of men

plucked guitars and another sawed on a fiddle while a fourth
squeezed a concertina enthusiastically. Kit said something
and I bent down closer to his lips. Heels thudded hard
against the pegged wood floor as young men and women
danced the fandango, their feet going a mile a minute while
they stared hard into their partners' eyes, their faces set in
a disdainful manner. The women swirled their skirts back
and forth with a practiced hand, exposing a flash of a crimson or bright yellow petticoat and slender calves. A few
bolder ones brought the skirt up a little higher to tease their
partners with a flash of dusky thigh. One, I noticed, had a
red ribbon tied around her thigh and her breasts bobbled like
scoops of brown sugar dropped into boiling water.

"You'll have to be a bit careful here!" Kit said, nudging
my side with his elbow.

"I thought this was different than the place we just left!"
I protested.

"It is. Except tonight there's gonna be a bit of trouble!"
He nodded over to our right. I turned and noticed a young
señorita waving a fan ineffectually in front of her. She wore
a bright red dress with a white off-shoulder blouse that
plunged nearly below her brown breasts bulging over the
top. She had a red comb seated high in her glossy black hair
gathered on top of her head to leave her slender neck exposed. Men clustered around her like dogs who'd cornered
a bitch in heat. She laughed, enjoying their antics as they
pressed against one another, each trying to force the other
out of the tight circle. A lull came in the music and two
rushed away toward a table where a huge punch bowl stood
to get her a drink.

"Yep," Kit said, shaking his head. "It was a mistake coming here. There's gonna be trouble there."

"How do you know?"

"I know her," he replied. "That's Lupe Garcia. She'll play
those boys till one of 'em gets hurt. Then she'll go sparkin'

with the winner." He spit as if a foul bug had suddenly darted into his mouth. He nearly struck the foot of a man who turned angrily toward us, his face set in righteous indignation. But the expression hastily left his face when he recognized Kit, and he turned away from us, forcing a path through the pressing crowd. "That's her usual game. I've seen it happen too many times, but"—he sighed heavily—"there's nothing to be done about it."

As Kit spoke, a flurry of excitement broke out between two hotheaded men dressed alike in short, highly embroidered jackets and tight pants that flared at the ankle. Their black hair, slicked back straight off their high foreheads, gleamed in the yellow light from liberal applications of macassar oil. They were quickly separated, but their black eyes flashed deadly signals and challenges at each other.

"That didn't seem to take long," I answered.

"I don't know," Kit said doubtfully from beside me. "I got a funny feeling that this ain't over yet."

He proved prophetic. One of the youths said something and the other laughed and taunted him. I don't know what he said, but I could recognize scorn and ridicule in his tone. The other youth flushed and, turning, strode furiously out, to the amusement of others clustered around the woman. A few minutes later, the youth reappeared, his face set in marble lines, cold fury seeping from his black eyes. He called across the dance floor. The other youth looked up, then said something to the young one standing next to him. He hitched his pants higher and swaggered out the door, slipping a hand behind his back. He staggered back in almost immediately, his hands pressed against his chest. He tried to call out for help, but the words were lost in bubbles of blood bursting from his lips. He dropped to his knees, then slowly fell forward onto his face and lay still.

The music stopped and everyone pushed forward around the young man to see what had happened. But there were

too many of them and interest quickly lagged. The fiddle
player began a bouncy tune and the dancing began again.
A couple of men picked up the body and carried it outside and returned so quickly that I knew they had dumped
the body in an alley to get it out of the way until they felt like
dealing with it later.

Kit sighed again. "This was a mistake. Come on; let's get
out of here before the usual riot begins. This is no place for
a white man. I don't relish a knife in my ribs. Especially if
I can avoid it by simply leaving." He looked up at me and
smiled at my frown. "You've spent too much time reading
those damned dime novels. Don't believe a word of them.
If I had killed as many men as they claimed I have, why,
we'd be standing here talking alone."

"But you did kill some," I said quickly.

He threw his head back and stared up at me, frowning.

"I didn't mean that the way it sounded," I added.

"Yes," he said slowly, "I've killed some. But there ain't a
night go by when I wish I hadn't. At least," he corrected
himself, "some of them. A few needed killing. There was
no way to reason with them. Best to have gotten them out
of the way when I did."

We left the dance hall. I heard rats scurrying and squeak-
ing and fighting over something in the alley, but I didn't look
to see what it was. I had a feeling I knew and think Kit
knew, too, for he turned up another street. I followed hard
on his heels, our feet kicking puffs of dirt high so flecks
shone briefly like quartz flakes in the light pouring out of
windows.

"I don't mean to say that I served up myself as judge and
jury and executioner, but sometimes a man has to do just
that." He glanced up at me and nodded as if to confirm his
thoughts. "You stick around here long enough and you'll
know what I mean by that. There's some people who just
won't live and let others alone. Those are the ones that you

are going to have to take care of so other folks have a chance to make a life." He shook his head. "It ain't right, but sometimes you just have to weigh the balance of one wrong against the other and decide which one will do the least amount of harm."

I turned his words over and over in my mind, committing them to memory as we made our way through the warm and humid Santa Fe night. We worked our way back uptown to where the money flowed easier and the liquor was better. The women were prettier in these places—for the moment— but in some I could already see the hardness of their lives setting in behind their eyes. A few had already attained a slate-hard blankness that gave the lie to their curved lips and flashing teeth when they smiled automatically at the men around them. I noticed it was the drunkest men who went with them into back rooms and up the stairs. To this day I can remember that, my first walk on the wild side of life— glasses clinking, sometimes bursting; out-of-tune pianos spranging tinnily; chips rattling along with dice; and a pretty, hennaed-haired woman singing in a whiskey-husked alto. She wore a black dress with a yellow crinoline under it that whisked around her thin calves as she strutted back and forth across the stage. Marabou feathers curled from a ferronniere around her high forehead and barley-sugar curls to drape across one cheek. I saw a fiddle and bow lying on top of the piano and walked over and picked them up. The piano player, a colored man with red garters pulled up on the sleeves of his crisply starched white shirt, never missed a beat as he grinned up at me and asked if I could play. I plucked the strings, testing the notes, then nodded, waited to hear the melody line in his song, then slipped rapidly into it with him, sawing softly in the background before taking the lead. The woman glanced in surprise at me. I winked back at her and a brightness came into her eyes as she hip-swung her way over to me and leaned down from the small stage. I glanced down her bottle green bodice at the creamy tops of her round breasts and felt my face grow hot and nearly bumbled a measure but caught myself and grinned up at her.

She winked and hip-swung her way saucily back across the stage, her blond curls bouncing in time with her bubbling breasts, drawing cheers from those men paying attention. But her eyes kept flickering back to mine.

"I think you made your conquest tonight," Kit said from beside me. "And it's a lot safer."

I glanced down at him and laughed, feeling delight make my cheeks burn rosy, and I nodded. He clapped me on the shoulder.

"I'm leaving you for now. No, no, stay here," he said as I went to lay the fiddle aside and go with him. "I need some sleep. I'm taking a pack train up to Taos tomorrow. If you're up that way, stop by. Everyone knows where I live."

"I'll do that," I said. I smiled down at him. "And thanks for what you've done. I appreciate it."

"Don't think on it," he said. He clapped me on the shoulder again, then turned and slipped easily through the crowd. Few noticed him leaving, most seeing him and ignoring him as they would their shadows on the ground on a hot summer day.

I turned back to my playing. Someone placed a drink near my shoulder and I nodded my thanks. The colored piano player glanced longingly at it.

"Help yourself," I said.

Surprise washed over his face, and he maintained the rhythm in the bass while he took the glass and sipped a large mouthful of the whiskey. He replaced the glass and swished the whiskey around in his mouth, swallowing it in stages. He smacked his lips.

"I'm thanking you," he said. His voice sounded musical, a soft drawl on his words. I grinned at him again.

"Why, think nothing of it," I said. "How about 'Louisiana Gals' next?"

Effortlessly he slipped into it. The woman onstage gave us a startled look but slipped into the song, sashaying around as if someone had oiled her hips. The room was becoming decidedly warmer.

"That's Rose," the piano player said. "An' I'm Ned."

"Hickok," I answered. "Jim Hickok." Then for some reason—I'm still not sure why—I added, "But folks call me 'Bill.'"

He gave me a quick look, then nodded. "Bill it is, then." He lifted his head and called out, "Rose! This here's Bill."

She winked at me. "And a wild one he is, I'm betting."

I winked back and knew the night was mine.

CHAPTER 28

SNOW WAS beginning to fall, thick flakes floating lazily down, but it hadn't begun to gather yet, and I knew that over Raton Pass and down in the valley the snow hadn't begun to fall. It would—that I knew—but it always came first high up. I shivered and tried to burrow deeper into my coat. My gloved hands held the reins tightly as my legs gripped the gelding's ribs. I had gotten the first wagon over the pass and down onto the flats, but there were seven more to guide up and over. I had found work with the freight company of Russell, Majors & Waddell as a wagon master after tiring of driving the stage. At first, I had nearly

refused their offer when they told me I had to take a pledge
not to drink or quarrel or fight with another employee and
be honest—did they want a saint or a wagon master?—but
then I figured it was only sound business and an old-timer
with the company laughed and said that as long as anything
I did didn't come to their attention or cause them any
trouble, they would pretend I was living up to the letter of
the pledge. I signed on and was sent first to Platte Crossing up on the Nebraska flats near Fort Kearney. There I met
Jack Slade and knew that the old-timer was right: As long as
the work was done the way they wanted it, they would turn a
blind eye toward the deed.

Slade was a short, slim man with long black hair and a
certain madness lurking deep in his black eyes. He always
wore a black shadbelly coat and low-heeled Wellingtons. I
felt his eyes upon me as I swung down from my horse near
the watering trough. I dusted my shirt and pants, easing the
pistol in its sheath at my waist with my elbow. I took a tin
cup from the pump at one end of the trough and drew water.
I drank deeply, tasting the cold, sweet water, poured another cup, and drank it. The day was hot—the sun nearly
boiling my brains out through my ears—and I had ridden a
long and hard trail up from Julesburg.

I lowered the cup and placed it back on the bent wire hook
wrapped around the mouth of the pump. I took a bandanna
from my neck, washed it out in the trough, and used it to
wipe my face and neck. I tied it back around my neck and
moved up toward the station.

Slade stepped out the door. "Welcome to Horseshoe Station. May I help you?" he said courteously. At first I thought
he was just a polite, neatly dressed worker, the type one normally doesn't see at a station on a wagon route. It was then
that I noticed his eyes.

"Hello," I said, trying hard to look as if I wanted to be

friends. "I'm Hickok. The company sent me up from Santa Fe to learn the route." I turned, looking around the station at the prairie. "Nice place."

"It is that," he said quietly, gently. "I am Slade. Joseph Slade. Most people call me 'Jack.'"

I felt a tingle run through me when he said his name, although I had known in advance that I was going to report to him. I suppose I had been apprehensive the long way up the road from Santa Fe, knowing that I was going to work briefly under one of the most deadly killers in the West. I glanced down at his vest and his watch chain. I had heard—as who hadn't?—how Jules Reni, the founder of Julesburg at the California Crossing on the South Platte, once had stolen some horses from the company. Slade went to get them back and Jules shot him with a double-barreled shotgun and emptied six shots into him with his pistol, leaving him for dead. Jules should have made certain that Slade was dead before he left, but I suppose he had been confident that Slade would not survive his wounds. Most men wouldn't have, but Slade had recovered and found Jules at Pacific Springs, where he brought him down by placing a deliberate ball in his thigh. Then Slade tied Jules up at a fence post and demonstrated his marksmanship with his pistol, breaking his knees and elbows with pistol balls, pausing to reload deliberately, then resuming his target practice, taking care not to kill him. At last, when Jules was barely conscious and coherent, Slade walked up to him, drew his knife, and slowly cut off his ears while Jules screamed and whimpered. Then Slade cut his throat. He wore Jules's ears as a watch fob.

I glanced up at him. A faint smile crossed his face. I sensed that he knew what I was looking for when my eyes dropped involuntarily to his vest. I felt my face grow warm.

"Well, come on in," he said softly, stepping back and motioning toward the station.

"Thanks," I managed through the wary thickness in my throat. He fell in beside me as I walked toward the door. I noticed the sign over the door, the letters burnt black with a hot iron: VIRGINIA DALE. I paused, looking at him.

"Virginia Dale?" I asked, puzzled. "I thought this was Horseshoe Station."

"It is," he explained. "But the house is Virginia Dale. My wife," he added. "The company owns the station, but I own the house." He nodded at the corral and barn fifty yards away. "That's actually the station over there. You can use it to stay in, if you wish. We don't use the rooms set aside for a manager. Instead, we had this built for ourselves."

I stepped in through the door and paused, my eyes taking in the clean white walls, the framed pictures hanging on them, the comfortable chairs—Belter furniture, I guessed, noticing the carved rosewood—and a circular sofa in the center of the room not that far from a stone fireplace. Deep carpets covered the puncheon floor that had been stained and waxed until it glowed like soft golden butter around the edges of the carpets. Crystal glasses had been arranged neatly around a crystal decanter filled with amber liquid— whiskey or brandy, I thought—on a small table beside one of the chairs. A bookcase filled with books stood against one wall. Starched lace curtains had been pulled back to let in sunlight from the large window looking out onto the wagon yard.

"Nice," I managed, dumbfounded at the unexpected luxury. A smile broke from his thin lips.

"Yes," he said. "Virginia and I are quite fond of our comfort." He raised his voice, calling her.

A handsome woman, voluptuous, pigeon-breasted, with wide, generous hips, came out of the back room. She wiped her hands on a dish towel she was carrying, eyeing me speculatively. I felt the force of her presence deep in my stomach and wondered just how long I was going to have to stay.

I swallowed. "Pleased to meet you, ma'am," I said. I waited for her to stretch out her hand and breathed a silent sigh of relief when she didn't.

"And what do you want here?" she asked suspiciously.

I was taken aback by her directness and looked down at Slade for help. He smiled.

"Now, Virginia, he will be our guest for a couple of days while he learns the route," he said. "I told you about his coming a week ago. Remember?"

"Are you here to replace Jack?" she asked brusquely, her eyes narrowing, making her look as if she'd bitten into a sour lemon. "If so, why, you can just climb back on your horse and get out of here. I'll give you a head start before—"

"Virginia," Slade said again. His voice stayed unchanged, but there was something about the way he uttered the word that caused her to draw up and take a half step back away from us. "Mr. Hickok is here to learn the route. That is all. Now, would you be kind enough to fix a little lunch for us? It is nearly noon and I believe Mr. Hickok might like a little repast after his long ride."

She nodded and, turning, walked away from us. I watched her buttocks swing and knew there was no corset or bustle under that dress. Not, I remember thinking, that she would need one. For a moment I had a crazy picture of the thin Slade locked between her meaty thighs; then I drove the picture from my mind.

"You must forgive Virginia," he said softly, crossing to the decanter. "She is very protective and suspicious of company men who are sent here. Not," he added, pouring two glasses full with the liquid, "that we have all that many visitors other than a few overnighters on their way across the trail. We are left pretty much alone out here. That's one of the reasons we prefer to live like this. Drink?"

He held out one glass, waiting as I crossed to take it. It was a bit early in the day, but I figured I had never needed one before to calm the nervous flutter in my stomach. I sipped cautiously. Brandy. And expensive. I took a large swallow as Slade watched approvingly.

"I expected whiskey," I said, lowering the glass.

He laughed, delighted. "I appreciate your candor, sir," he said. He motioned toward a chair. I glanced down at the spurs on my boots. "Oh, don't worry," he said. "It is a risk one takes when one tries for comfort out here."

I sat down gingerly and, placing my glass on the small table covered with a neat pile of magazines at my elbow, took my spurs off and tucked them beside the leg of the chair out of the way.

"Now then," Slade said, making himself comfortable in the other chair opposite. He sipped from his glass. "Tell me the news in Denver."

And so began a nervous week with Slade. But by the end of the time, I had become friends with him and his wife had come to accept me, even graciously offering to do laundry for me before I left. Slade may have been a hard man when he was drunk, but he maintained a rigid control over his drinking while I was a guest with him. I later discovered that he went on sporadic drunks and when he did he was totally unpredictable, as dangerous as a blind rattlesnake in a tight room.

One night, a horse whinnied, awakening me. I caught up a pistol and slid to the door of the barn and peered out. Indians had let down the bars to the corral and were quietly moving the horses and mules out. I brought up my pistol and aimed at the Indian nearest the corral. I squeezed the trigger. He yelped and threw up his arms, crumbling to the dirt.

At once wild cries filled the night and the horses bunched, then wildly galloped through the opening in the corral. I fired again and missed, then took a step away from the doorway, trying to see through the dust billowing up from the hooves of the animals. Shots slammed into the wood where

I had been standing and I dived flat behind a water trough. I peered cautiously up over the edge and saw the Indians galloping away, leaning low over their horses' necks. I snapped a shot at one but missed.

Then they were gone.

I heard someone running and dropped to a knee, bringing the pistol up.

"Hold it!" Slade said, skidding to a stop. He waited until I lowered the pistol, then came up to me.

His eyes glittered like black diamonds in the moonlight. He held a shotgun in his hands, but I could see his pistol belted around his waist. I smelled brandy on his breath as he took a quick look around. His eyebrows went up as he frowned.

"Indians?" he asked.

I nodded. "I got one," I said, gesturing at the corral.

Slade grunted and hurried forward. I followed him, stepping to the side warily to keep the Indian in sight. I had heard stories about how they suddenly seemed to come to life, and I didn't want to find a knife in my stomach. I didn't have to worry. My bullet had caught him between the shoulders.

Slade rolled him over, kneeling to study the figure carefully. He nodded and rose.

"Kiowa," he said. "A long way away from their land. But who knows where their land is anymore?"

"How can you tell?" I asked.

He pointed at the scalp and the moccasins. "They club their hair like that when they're on a raid," he said. "See how the leather is stitched with one layer overlying the other? Only the Kiowa sew like that. It's something you pick up after a while," he said as he caught my frown. "Just be patient." He clapped me gently on the shoulder. "You did pretty good, catching one like that in the dark with a pistol." He glanced down at the Dragoon in my hand. "Especially a heavy load like that."

"Should we saddle up and go after them?" I asked.

He shook his head. "No. Indians usually leave a couple back to catch white men foolish enough to go galloping after them at night. We'll wait until morning and pick up a couple of men from the Pony Express station and anyone else we can find. It'll be safer that way. We'll be able to move faster than they will. Those horses will be pretty spooked and it'll take all they have to keep them from scattering over the land."

The next morning, though, we were in the saddle before light and at the Pony Express station, where we found three others. I was surprised to see Cody.

"Howdy." He grinned, coming up, his hand outstretched.

I was surprised at him. He had grown quite a bit and his shoulders were heavier with muscle. He was clean-shaven, with tired rings around his eyes.

"Well, I'll be damned!" I said, shaking his hand. "How've you been?"

The guarded look slipped from his eyes and I knew then that he was worried I would let slip how we had met, but that was in the past and, as far as I was concerned, over. I never have thought that we built up debts in the world. There just is too much of the world to worry about who was one up on the other.

"Fair to middlin'," he said. He jerked a thumb over his shoulder. "I've been riding for the Pony lately."

"It's good you boys know each other," Slade said. He nodded at the others who came out of the station. "Indians drove our stock off last night and we could use a bit of help getting them back."

"What's it pay?" a burly one growled.

Slade's eyes narrowed. "My gratitude," he said softly.

The man shook his head. "That and a dollar would buy a shot of whiskey," he said.

A dull red began to move up Slade's neck, but he held his tongue and shrugged and turned to the rest of us.

"Well, whoever's going with Bill"—he nodded at me—"and myself, saddle up. We have to get on the trail or they'll get too far ahead of us."

The burly one shook his head and turned back to the station. "You all go on without me, you want," he said. "But ain't no way I'm putting my scalp lock out for a reddie to grab without something coming back in my poke for it."

Slade's eyes narrowed as he watched the burly one disappear into the station; then he sensed my stare and turned. A cold chill washed over me and I went to my horse, covering my discomfort by fumbling at my cinch. The blackness of hell laced with leaping fires had just opened up before me.

"Mount up," Slade said softly, and we all swung into our saddles and followed him as we cantered out of the yard.

We crossed the trail five miles out. A blind man couldn't have missed it or failed to follow it. Slade sent me ahead to scout to keep the party from running into an ambush, but the Indians were more intent on putting distance between the stage station and them and pushed ahead hard. We were smaller and could move faster.

The trail led straight to Powder River and up to Crazy Woman's Fort and to Clear Creek. I found their camp by midafternoon and rode back to wait about five miles from them for Slade and the others to come up to us.

"Well?" Slade demanded as he reined in his lathered horse beside mine. Dust caked his face, and his eyes burned from the mask into mine. I remembered what I had glimpsed hours before and suppressed a shudder.

"They're camped about five, maybe six miles east of here," I said. "It's a dry camp and will be hard to come up on them. But we can if we wait until dark, I think. There's

a shallow vale that comes down to them from the north.
That'll keep us from being highlighted if we're careful."

He nodded with satisfaction. "Good job, Bill," he said.
"You've done well." He turned to the others. "We'll wait
here until dark. Sit and loosen your girths and let your horses
breathe. We'll have a bit of hard riding tonight."

Cody looked around, frowning. "Mr. Slade?"

Slade turned to him, sitting back in his saddle, an eyebrow raised.

"Uh, aren't we a bit exposed out here?" Cody asked. "I
mean, sir, that maybe one of the Indians will send someone
out to check their back trail?"

Slade glanced at me.

I shook my head. "No, I don't think so," I said. "They've
been pushing fairly hard and there isn't that many of them.
They'll keep their guards close to the horses to keep them
from straying. We should be all right."

Cody nodded, but his face still clouded with misgivings.
He swung down and loosened the cinch on his horse, then
sat on the ground, looping his reins around one wrist to
wait.

"You're learning," Slade murmured to me. "How'd you
know that?"

I shrugged. "Common sense," I said. "It's what I'd do. I
can't figure an Indian would do more than that."

"Maybe," he said. "But always remember that you need
to also think what the Indian *shouldn't* do as well. Just
when you think you've got them figured out, they'll do the
opposite. Common sense doesn't mean a damn thing to an
Indian. That's a mark of a civilized man. I think you're
right, though. What do you have up there? About six?"

"Five," I said. "And one looks hurt. I might have winged
one last night. I figure that he'll stay back, and one to care
for him, while the other three split a guard among them.
They've been pushing hard and they'll be tired as well. Even

Indians have to sleep sometime." I shrugged. "I don't know. I could be all wrong. But it just *feels* right to me."

"And that's what you need to go by," he said. "Go by your feelings."

We waited until the moon began to rise; then we tightened our cinches and the others fell in behind me as I rode in a wide detour to bring them down from the north upon the Indian encampment.

I was right; there was only one guard, and he rode slowly around the horses to keep them from straying too far. I didn't see Slade slide from his horse, but suddenly the Indian jerked upright and slipped from his horse. I hurried forward in time to see Slade rise from the ground, a long-bladed knife gleaming wet-black in the moonlight. He smiled.

"One," he said softly.

He slipped the knife into its scabbard and circled his hand over his head. We mounted and rode forward. When we were within fifty yards of the camp, Slade suddenly slapped his heels hard against the sides of his horse. It squealed in pain as Slade's rowels drove into its sides, and leaped forward.

Then we all were galloping hard behind Slade, riding down upon the camp. The Indians leaped to their feet, but a barrage of gunfire seemed to slam them back onto the ground. As quickly as it began, it was over. I became aware I was holding my pistol in my hand, but I hadn't fired it. I slipped it into its holster and turned away from the others beginning to dismount.

"Cody," Slade said, "you go with Bill and see if you can gather those horses. I'll want to move out as soon as we can. There's no telling how close we might be to other Kiowa. No sense in taking any chances."

It took Cody and me most of the night to gather the horses and mules. A couple of the others came out to help us, and by gray light we had all our horses and mules and the Indian horses as well in a tight herd. Slade grinned and waved to us, and we began to drive them back to the station.

We arrived near sundown, weary and worn, and Cody and I put the animals into the corral. They bunched up at the water trough. Cody looked over at Slade as the station manager rode up to the house and dismounted.

"I don't think I'd want to cross that man," he said thoughtfully.

"You'd be wise not to," I said. "He's killed quite a few who have tried to run his trail. And he isn't fussy how he does it, either."

Cody's eyes settled on mine. I shook my head. "Let's put up our horses and get cleaned up. I'm hungry."

Obediently he followed me into the barn.

I have to give Slade credit for taking care of those who had helped him. By the time Cody and I had cleaned up and put in our appearances up at the house, Virginia and the cook had readied a supper for us and Slade had set out bottles of whiskey. By the time the dark had gathered, we were all pretty mellow and Cody was nodding sleepily in his chair. We heard a horse coming and I stepped out into the shadows under the porch to wait for the rider to show himself.

It was the burly man who had refused to go with us. He reined in and sat on his horse, staring at me.

"Cody here?" he asked.

"He's here," I answered.

"You tell that little bastard to get his ass back to the Pony station. He's supposed to be riding the next shift due in a couple of hours."

I shook my head. "You'll have to get someone else to ride it," I said. "He's been in the saddle all day helping us bring the stock back."

"I don't give a shit what he's been doing," the man said. "It's what he's going to do that interests me."

I felt someone beside me and turned to find Slade staring out at the man. His eyes were flat and cold and I could smell bay rum on him.

"I think Mr. Hickok has told you what needs to be done," he said softly. "Now I'd be obliged if you'd ride on back and see to it. That Cody boy has been wearing himself out in the saddle and needs to get caught up on his sleep. Boys grow while sleeping, you know. But you're a full-grown man and surely know that."

The man shook his head and spit a black stream of tobacco juice on the steps leading up to the porch. "I just said my words," he said stubbornly. "You get that kid back there or he can find hisself another job come morning."

Slade stepped down off the porch and to the side. "And you, sir," he said harshly, "can climb down off that horse and scrub your spittle from my step."

"Be damned if I will!" the man said.

I don't know if he moved toward his pistol or not, but Slade's appeared as if by magic in his hand and I saw the flare from the barrel and heard the *splat!* as the bullet struck the other man in the chest. He hunched forward, then fell backward as his horse reared in fright. Slade slipped forward and seized the bridle, speaking soothingly to quiet the nervous mount.

I sighed and craned my head, looking at the leaden sky and trying to gauge the daylight left. It would be close to dark before we finished, I reflected sourly, and that would be pushing the mules up and over the pass and hoping a lead one didn't become stubborn and stop. They did that on occasion and wouldn't take another step until they were damn good and ready, never minding the whip you laid across their backs. Fact was, you'd be better coaxing them like you would a woman.

I smiled as I thought of Rose waiting for me back in Santa Fe. I had no illusions; I knew there were others in her bed when I was on the trail—she had too large an appetite for waiting faithfulness—but when I returned, there was no one. Although, I reflected as the gelding picked his way over the rocks, some of the men didn't understand or *want* to understand why she dropped everything when I came back and spent her time with me instead of spreading her favors around.

I shivered from the cold and hunched deeper into my coat. I slipped into a remembrance of the last time I had seen Rose.

She had long, thin white hands with long nails, cool against my skin. Like ivory, only soft. Below I could hear the out-of-tune piano jangling merrily and the susurring murmur of voices, indistinct but there. Her golden hair lay long down her naked back and I lifted it away to walk my fingers over the bumps in her spine. She moaned, and her heavy breasts moved back and forth across my chest. Across the room I could see the old drawing of an old bearded man in priestly robes, holding a cross high from whose center a red heart appeared, lights radiating from its center, and and she moaned and her mouth came hard upon mine feeling fire flaming through it into mine setting a blaze going going and I thought about the day when I had to leave for St. Louis to bring the other freight train back and I thought about the road and how it curved gently across the prairie as golden as her hair waving like golden waves in the golden light when the sun was near dawn and streaks of red came like carmine blush across the blue blue sky and and and

The gelding shied and drew me from my daydream. I dropped my hand down along his neck, patting it gently, soothing him, instantly alert. "Easy, boy," I whispered. "What is it?"

And then I smelled it: rank, musky, thick in the throat. I looked around for the source, my eyes probing the darkness between the deep green of the jack pines. Then I heard a low growl and took my hand away from the gelding's neck, feeling for the pistol at my belt. Two cubs scampered back into the shadows, and at the same moment an old sow grizzly bear lumbered out of the deep pines, gathering speed as she came toward us.

The gelding screamed with fright and reared suddenly. Caught unaware, I tumbled backward off him, landing hard on the ground, my head striking a stone. Stunned, I heard the gelding's hooves hammering the trail back down the way we had climbed.

I rolled over and saw the bear still coming, faster. I clawed my pistol from my belt and, rising to my knees, fired as rapidly as I could. I saw the bullets strike, her flesh flinch, but she only groaned and never slackened her pace. The hammer of my pistol clicked on a spent cap. I dropped it and rose to my feet, backing away from her as I drew the bowie knife. Then, she was on me. I felt her hot breath, fetid from rotten meat; her tiny eyes rolled wickedly. I threw up an arm and felt her long claws rake through my coat and down my arm. I felt the scream bubbling up in my throat as another paw crashed down on top of my head, clawing my scalp away. I fell and tried to roll away. Her claws ripped through my pants and legs. Black smoke drifted across my vision. I swung wildly with the knife and felt the jar as the blade bit deep into her, striking bone. My hair hung down over my eyes, and I stabbed blindly, felt the blade sink in, and twisted my wrist, ripping up. She roared with pain and picked me up, wrapping her thick arms around me, claws digging into my back. Her mouth gaped wide and came down around my head. I felt her teeth grating on my skull and stabbed again and again, ripping the blade up as fast and hard and deep as I could drive it, ripping, ripping—

And suddenly she went slack. I felt her guts roll hotly out of her belly onto my legs and boots; then we fell, she pinning me beneath her. The air exploded from my body and the black smoke came again, but this time, it stayed—

CHAPTER 29

I SAT in the sun's rays, feeling the warmth seep in and relax my muscles, listening to Sarah Shull's husky voice singing the old ballad. She couldn't have carried a tune in an oaken bucket, but there was a sensuality to her voice that hammered away at a man's innards. A dove called mournfully from down at the creek. Lazily I opened my eyes and rolled my head against the rough logs of Sarah Shull's cabin across from the Rock Creek Station, searching for the dove in the sun-dappled cottonwood trees towering over the little creek. I heard the music of water running over rocks and a couple of logs that had been placed to make a small dam for swimming and fishing just above the deep ruts scored in the earth by iron-cased wagon wheels making their way over the Oregon Trail.

I had the smell of the earth in my nostrils, warm and dank. I heard Fritz lapping water from an old bucket near me and reached down automatically to scratch his ears. I smiled as he walked slowly away so that I was scratching close by his tail. Fritz was a mongrel who had discovered the Muddles' bitch about three miles away. I figured it must have been his first encounter, for he seemed to be in an extremely agitated state the past four days. I glanced down at him. He turned brown eyes up at me.

"You old phony," I said affectionately. He grunted with pleasure, then moved down the cabin wall and plopped down in the shade, one ear falling over an eye. I watched his brown and white body pant in the heat, then slow as he dozed. A bee bumbled its way around us for a moment, then streaked off to the side of the cabin where Sarah Shull had planted hollyhocks. I shifted position and grimaced as scar tissue tried to stretch. I sat up and gently massaged my left arm to ease the ache. I glanced across the creek to where the Rock Creek Station stood. Jane Holmes—I called her Mrs. Wellman, as she was the common-law wife of Horace Wellman—was out hanging up laundry on cords stretched between two wooden Ts tamped into the earth about fifty feet from each other.

I frowned, remembering how the company had sent me to Kansas City for a doctor to take care of me and then moved me to the station, where I could work as a hostler while I healed. I was weak then, terribly weak, and could barely shuffle around the yard, let alone pitch hay. But Doc Brink, a sometime hired hand, was always willing to help out, laughing and joking good-naturedly to help me forget the pain. He rode occasionally for the Pony Express, which also shared the station with the Central Overland California and Pike's Peak Express Company owned by Russell, Majors & Waddell. Dave McCanles, who had built the station before selling it to the company and moving to a new ranch along the Little Blue River, had been swaggering arrogantly around the station lately, demanding that Horace Wellman, the new superintendent for the company, pay him the rest of the money the company owed him for the station. Unfortunately, the company was teetering on bankruptcy and there was nothing that Horace could do.

I knew what McCanles was capable of. He was a bully of the first sort and had taken to grabbing me and throwing me to the ground whenever he came upon me, then standing, laughing, over me as I tried to struggle with one arm to my feet. There wasn't much I could do, though, except try to stay out of his way. I was barely strong enough to use a hay rake, let alone my pistols that I kept in a satchel beneath my bunk in a small room at the back of the large barn where the horses were stabled during foul weather. Wellman kept a fringe-topped surrey there, too, for the Sunday outings whenever they could get away—which was practically never.

I sighed and cautiously stretched. No, nothing good was going to come of McCanles and his nearly daily visit to the station these days. It didn't help that McCanles favored the South while I had foolishly made my feelings regarding slavery known in a lax moment with a bottle of whiskey and a few hardcases I had mistakenly earmarked for friendship down at the juncture where Rock Creek flowed into the Little Blue River, where catfish and bass lived lazily in back pools, ready to snap at a grub or manure bug impaled upon a hook. Foolish! Foolish! McCanles knew my place in the gathering of sides within a day or two of ill-fated afternoon fishing.

McCanles had a number of "wannabes" hanging around him at the time, playing to his pompous preening and posing. The number varied, as many became disgusted with his bullying and left the euphoric inner sanctum where he admitted those who placated his favor. He was a burly man, strong as an ox, with curling black locks that he painstakingly combed over his collar. Unfortunately, although he was usually closely shaved, he had a disdainful appreciation of soap and water, and when he stood upwind and close to me I nearly gagged from the sour stench reeking from his clothes.

He had been a sheriff of Watauga County in North
Carolina—or so he claimed; I have my doubts—and came
to Rock Creek with Sarah, his lover, after his wife discovered that their marriage did not reside in the Garden of
Eden but rather on the slopes of Mount Purgatory. Perhaps
I should say he "fled" North Carolina, for had he stayed, the
courts would have stripped him naked of his mercenary
belongings and awarded everything to his legal wife and
children. North Carolina took a dim view of philandering—
when the event was brought to the law's attention. I think it
was the narrow view of the Baptist convention that had a
throttlehold upon the political machine of the state. The
Baptist crowd finds sin in everything except the making of
jelly—provided that is not done upon the Sabbath.

When McCanles came to Rock Creek, he established a
station on one side of the waters and on the other a ranch
where he placed Sarah and against whose log cabin I lazed
away the day while I mused wonderingly on what prompted
him to send for his wife and children after he had settled in.
If a man was looking to live in a hornet's nest, that was one
way to do it.

Jane looked across the creek, noticed me lounging about,
and waved. I waved back, admiring her beauty and natural
figure that needed no corset to set an hourglass figure upon
her womanly frame. She was far better-looking than Sarah
Shull, but Jane was dedicated to her husband and such dedication put a damper upon other men's thoughts. *Or would
have,* I thought suddenly, *if that man wasn't Dave McCanles.
Could that be the reason for his hard-nosed attitude toward Horace?*

I frowned, musing at a couple of dragonflies darting
around each other a few feet from the hollyhocks. When
Russell, Majors & Waddell organized their Pony Express,
they had thought to lease the Rock Creek Station, but Mc-

Canles had convinced them that they would be better off buying it from him at one-third down and the rest in three-month payments.

I suppose that was a good arrangement, but setting up a new enterprise on a shoestring budget doesn't allow much leeway for unseen expenses, and Russell, Majors & Waddell had been plagued by several—Indian raids upon outlying stations, the sudden disappearance of stock, exorbitant expense accounts turned in by station managers for supplies, equipment, wages: The list went on and on, and before long, the firm found black ink becoming a scarce item in their ledger books.

McCanles let the first month's payment ride, but when the second month rolled around he began to get ugly, hovering over Horace, who was half his size, his apelike arms threatening to encompass the smaller man in a death hug, sausagelike fingers jabbing his point home in Horace's skinny chest as the Roman legionnaire's hammer had driven forth the herctical nails into the sacred hands and feet, demanding payment. But Horace could do nothing and finally agreed to accompany McCanles to Brownsville to ask Benjamin Ficklin, the line superintendent, to make good the account.

That had been three weeks ago and the party had yet to return. That didn't bode well, although there were numerous possible explanations for their tardiness. Unfortunately, I could think of only one, since I had not been paid myself during the same period that McCanles had been waiting for his money.

Soft arms crept around my neck, startling me. I smelled her sweet breath as she breathed gently upon my ear.

"Jim, you've been sitting here for hours now. Can't you think of something better to do with your time?"

I turned my head to Sarah and found her rosebud lips a

scant inch away. I kissed her and felt the giggle rise up from her breast, shaking her. I leaned back, staring sternly at her.

"Woman, is this such a laughing matter to you?"

"No," Sarah said, freeing one hand to brush a stray tendril of honey blond hair off her fine forehead. Her cornflower blue eyes stared merrily into mine. "But you forget that Jane can see what you are doing."

"What *we* are doing," I corrected, slipping my hand over her generous haunch. Her eyes turned smoky gray, and her nostrils widened as she breathed deeply, her large breasts moving against my arm. "You forget," I added slyly, "that it takes two to play this tune."

"Ah, Bill," she said.

"Jim," I corrected, but she ignored me and turned, plopping herself onto my lap. She squirmed slowly and I felt myself responding to the movement of her buttocks. She looked half-lidded at me. A trickle of perspiration ran down from her temples along the line of her jaw, down her thin neck, past the quickening pulse-beat in her throat, to disappear under the collar of her calico dress.

"Whatever," she sighed indifferently.

I smelled fresh-baked bread on her and a hint of Pears Soap from the bath she had taken earlier and the earthy smell of her want. I grinned at her and pressed my hand harder against her hip. I could almost feel her blood humming through her veins as she slumped against me.

"Let's go inside," she whispered hoarsely. Her teeth bit my earlobe none too gently and the wild recklessness exploded within me.

"Now why would we do that on such a sunshiny day?" I asked, teasing.

She began breathing heavily, swearing gently. Her arm slipped from around my neck and I felt her groping, trying to push her fingers behind my belt. I laughed and her eyes widened.

"Dammit, it's not funny!" she said furiously.

"Of course it is," I said, and rose. She slid off my lap, catching herself unsteadily upon her feet. I wrapped an arm around her waist and led her into the cabin.

CHAPTER 30

I WAS at the station with Mrs. Wellman when McCanles rode up with three others, demanding that we vacate the premises immediately. Mrs. Wellman stepped out of the cabin to try to talk with him, but McCanles refused to listen to her.

"You send your man out," he said. "I want to settle with your husband. One way or the other." He laughed, rolling his big shoulders, confident that he would win whatever battle Wellman tried to put up to keep control of the station.

"He won't come out," Mrs. Wellman said, a bit embarrassed.

I glanced over at her husband, crawling under a bed at the far end of the cabin, and felt a surge of disgust go through me at a man hiding behind a woman's apron strings, but I knew that he was no match for McCanles any more than I was in my weakened condition. I sighed and stepped into the doorway. McCanles saw me and his eyes narrowed.

"Well, well," he said. "Hickok. I got a bone to pick with you, too, Dutch Bill."

"James," I said softly. "My name's James."

"I don't rightly care one way or the other what your name is," he said boldly. "You want to take a hand in this, come on out and we'll settle it like men."

I shook my head. "You just go on about your business,

McCanles," I said. "You're not wanted around here. In fact, you're trespassing."

"Trespassing!" His eyes bulged with fury. "Why, you, you—I own this place until I'm paid in full. And that's been a damn long time coming! Now I want all of you to get off this here property right now!"

"Nope," I said softly. I touched the handle of my pistol at my belt. McCanles caught my gesture and settled back in his saddle, eyeing me narrowly.

"Very well. Then send Wellman out or I'll come in after him," he said. He touched a long blacksnake draped over his saddle horn and I knew full well what he had planned for Wellman.

I shrugged and stepped back inside, but I drew my pistol and held it ready at my side. McCanles kneed his horse around to the front door of the station, where he had a clear view of the inside of the station except for a calico curtain that partitioned the front room into two bedrooms. I stepped up against the edge of the curtain so I could keep him in sight. McCanles saw me and yelled, "Come on out and fight fair!"

"What kind of fair fight you planning on, McCanles?" I said loudly. "A cripple and an old man. That the type of odds you favor?"

"You sumbitch," McCanles said, and swung down from his horse. He pulled his pistol from his holster as he stepped inside the cabin. He saw me and grinned, raising his pistol to take aim. I knew in that instant that he had not come for Wellman or to take possession of the station. That was his excuse. He had come for me. I could see it in the excitement in his eyes and then I felt my pistol leap in my hand. Gray smoke separated us for an instant, but I heard the heavy, meaty *thuwunk!* and knew my bullet had struck him in the chest. I stepped around the side of the curtain and saw Mc-Canles sprawl across the threshold.

At the same instant, the three with him leaped from their horses and ran toward the house. One of them, Jim Woods, I later discovered, started in through the kitchen door with pistol drawn. I fired twice, wounding him. He reeled away as Jim Gordon, McCanles's foreman, tried to come in the front door. I winged him with a quick shot from the hip. He staggered out the door.

"Let's get out of here!" Woods hollered, and he and Gordon ran for the trees along Rock Creek. That yell must have spiked Wellman's blood with a dose of bravery, for he climbed from beneath the bed by now and ran outside, snatching a grubbing hoe from where it leaned against the side of the house. Doc Brink, who had been working in the barn at the time, appeared with a scattergun.

"Come on! Let's get 'em!" Wellman yelled, and took off after them, whooping like an Indian on the scalping trail.

The third man wasn't a man, I noticed. It was McCanles's son, twelve years old, who gathered his father in his arms, tears spreading down his cheeks.

"Kill him! Kill him!" Mrs. Wellman screamed hysterically. She pointed a trembling finger at the boy, but I shook my head and slipped my pistol into its holster.

"There's been enough of that around here," I said quietly.

I meant the death of McCanles, but seconds later I heard the boom of Brink's shotgun. I ran toward the creek and saw where Brink had killed Gordon with a double blast, the pellets ripping a huge hole in his back.

I heard screams rising from a patch of weeds to the side of the house and raced there just in time to see Wellman finish chopping the life out of Woods with the grubbing hoe. He turned to look at me, the craziness showing in the whites around his eyes, his clothes and face spattered with blood.

I sighed heavily, knowing no good would come of this, and made my way back to the station.

I was right: The courts found all of us innocent, especially after a couple of people swore they had heard McCanles planning to whip Wellman to teach him not to welsh on a deal. But what came out of this was a story that came to be known as "The Massacre at Rock Creek Station" and I found myself the sole hero of that fight, thanks to people like George Ward Nichols, who wrote a highly warped account of the fight in *Harper's New Monthly Magazine* that came out after the war.

But it was the war that drew me next. What war doesn't do that to the young and foolish who have been named after kings and raised on the nobility of man in diversity?

CHAPTER 31

THE HEARING was held in Beatrice before T. M. Coulter, Gage County justice of the peace, but despite the charges brought against me by the McCanles faction, I was found not guilty.

Immediately afterward, I left Rock Creek and was nearly to Fort Leavenworth, where I hoped to pick up work on a wagon train heading west, when a rider came galloping past in a cloud of dust, wild-eyed and bushy-tailed, yelling at the top of his voice that we were at war. I pulled the brown mare I was riding to the shade of a cottonwood and dismounted to sort through some options. I loosened the mare's girth and leaned back against the scabrous bark in the sultry heat and watched the mare as she nuzzled a swath of brown grass with halfhearted interest. But I sensed that I had to get involved in the war; there was something more than an adventure waiting in front of me; it seemed as if I was coming toward a reckoning. The idea of being a soldier didn't appeal to me, and my still-weakened condition would have kept me from enlisting anyway. But I could be a scout or a wagon master. I sighed and scrunched down against the side of the tree, tilting my broad-brimmed hat over my eyes. Within moments, I was asleep.

I awoke with a start, feeling a certain tension in the air. A small runnel of perspiration trickled slowly down my back. Tiny hairs prickled along my arms like I was in an electric storm. I took a long, slow breath. A sour smell seemed to wash over me, and I knew I wasn't alone. Then I heard a small sound like leather scraping softly over small pebbles and rolled quickly to my right, palming my pistol as I came up on my knees.

Two men, filthy and bearded, gaped at me. Their clothes looked caked with old dirt and grease and smoke from a thousand fires. One held a long-bladed dagger. I dropped the barrel on him, rocking the hammer back on my Navy Colt. I swept my second pistol from my belt and leveled it at the other as he tried to bring his Sharps rifle around.

"Hold it, boys," I said, although each was at least twenty years my senior. They froze and I used the moment to look around; my mare's bridle was tied to an old, spavined mule standing with drooping head in the sun. The mare shuffled her feet nervously. I couldn't blame her; the mule looked as tattertatted as the men.

"You know," I said conversationally, "there isn't a court in the land wouldn't hang you in a minute for what you boys are trying to do."

"A-huh," the one with the rifle grunted. He spit a long stream of tobacco juice at a rock, missed. "Wal, ther's many slip twixt here and there. An' yuh ain't out of heah yet." His rheumy eyes shrewdly considered me. He glanced at the one with the knife. "Ah don' think you can make both of us."

"Like you said," I answered, "there's many a slip between fact and expectation."

His rheumy eyes shrewdly gauged me, trying to decide if I was the trouble I was promising. He glanced over at his partner and shook his head. "Yuh could be good enough to put the move on both of us, but Ah don' think so," he said slowly.

"Like you said," I answered, "there's a lot of slip between doing and expectation. I guess it amounts to one thing: Do you feel lucky?" I waved both pistols. "It seems to me I have enough for both of you."

Broken yellow teeth peeked from his tobacco-stained lips. He nodded. "As Ah 'spected, boy. Yuh ain't got enough salt on yuh or yuh wouldn't be puttin' that much faith into luck."

I smiled faintly and rose to my feet, taking a step backward and to the side, narrowing the gap between them. "Oh, I wasn't counting on luck," I said. "I thought *you* were."

"Boy, yuh sure have sand. Ah'll give you that," he said. "Wal, guess we'd better know yer name so's we know what name to bury yuh under."

"Hickok," I said. "James Butler Hickok."

I watched as the dagger man's eyes widened. "Lem," he said urgently. "That's the one who did for those folks up at Rock Creek Station. Yuh 'member that drummer telling us 'bout it over that jug last week?" His eyes flicked back to mine. "Yuh that one, boy?" I nodded. Slowly he replaced the dagger into the top of his calf-high boot. Twine had been wrapped around the arch to hold the boot together.

"They say he kilt six there faster'n a man could blink," he said. He held dirty palms up. The lines were ridged with caked dirt. "Ah don' want no hand in a game like that."

Lem gave me a hard look. His eyes traced me slowly, noting the pallor in my color, the hollowed cheeks, and he shook his head.

"Yuh talkin' hell on wheels, Seth," he said. "Yuh take a look at this feller? Harsh wind blow him clear to Alabama."

Seth shook his head and turned away, deliberately leaving me his back as he walked to the mule. "Yuh 'cide for y'self, Lem. Me, Ah don' cotton to no hastened grave. This heah world's harsh 'nough for gettin' by. But Ah ain't in no hurry to step inta the other on a chance it'd be better. Leastways Ah know what to 'spect heah."

He reached the mule and deliberately untied the mare and dropped the reins upon the ground. The mare took a couple of skittish steps away from the mule and stood, ears pricked, watching nervously. Seth pulled himself upon the mule's back and drummed his heels against the mule's ribs, gigging him forward. The mule took a couple of steps, then stopped, dropped a loose pile on the dust, and moved forward reluctantly.

"Seth!" Lem yelled. "Gawd dum yuh! That's my mule!"

"Then cum with him," Seth said without looking back.

"Seth!"

But this time Seth ignored him, kicking the mule as hard as he could, but the mule ignored him and continued his steady plodding down the road. Lem sighed and shook his head in despair and looked again at me. I thought for a moment I saw resignation in his eyes, but then his features hardened.

"Yuh see how 'tis," he said, but I heard no regret in his voice. A lone dove called, and down by the creek a jay answered.

"It'll be a mistake," I said warningly. "You can just walk away from it all. You'll have to leave that Sharps behind, though."

He glanced down at the rifle in his hands and slowly shook his head. "No, reckon Ah couldn't do that." He raised his eyes and I could see the uncertainty gnawing at him and knew then he was going to try to swing the barrel of that Sharps. Even as I spoke I could see the decision take hold and squeezed the Navy's trigger.

The ball took him square in the chest, punching him back into the sunlight. He gasped twice and lay still. I took a long deep breath and let it out slowly.

"Wasn't much of a choice," I said. I picked up the rifle and checked it. The rifle was far cleaner than him. I was surprised. A man normally keeps his weapons as he keeps himself. I heard a wagon coming and dropped the Sharps on top of him before walking out and gathering the mare. I stepped in the stirrup and swung up, settling in the saddle as a farm wagon hoved into view, a gaunt and bearded fellow in clean overalls sitting in the spring seat. He reined in his team and stared from me to the dead man on the ground. I nodded at him.

"That man's name is Lem," I said. "That's all I know. He tried to steal my horse."

"Don't look like he made it," the man drawled.

I pointed at the Sharps. "That rifle's got the cost of a burial in it."

"Then why don't you take it?" the man said in a reedy voice. "He sure ain't gonna know the difference."

"I don't need a rifle," I said. I touched mine in its scabbard beneath my leg. "I have one."

"Saw that," he said. "That's why I figure it's as you say. Even if it wasn't"—he shrugged—"don't matter none to me. But what's to keep me from just taking the rifle and leaving him?"

"Depends on you," I said, and nudged the mare with my heels. "Reckon nothing would stop you as long as you don't mind listening to yourself each day."

I lifted the mare into a canter and rode after Seth. I caught up to him in a few miles. He glanced up at me, alarm in his face. I paused long enough to tell him about Lem and the farmer, then rode away toward Fort Leavenworth.

CHAPTER 32

A T FIRST I joined Lorenzo, who was working as a wagon master, but I soon took on a job as a special policeman under Lieutenant N. A. Burns, who was the provost marshal at Springfield. That didn't last long, either, however, as I quit when they shorted me pay and, not long after, Brigadier General John B. Sanborn hired me as a scout. That was, in a way, the beginning of the legend of Wild Bill—although the McCanles incident at Rock Creek was beginning to make the rounds as well—and I spent most of the war either scouting for the Union or else behind enemy lines, trying to find out Confederate plans.

A pearl gray mist sifted over the trees and road down through Arkansas as I rode a mule above the road through the tree line, looking in vain for the Confederate soldiers that were supposedly in the area. I knew I was close to Pea Ridge, but in the mist I found the road appearing and disappearing and then it was gone for good and I was lost. Not a very good position to find oneself in when he doesn't know where the enemy might be.

"All right now, y'all just rein in that mule and sit tight."

The voice startled me, coming from the mist as it did. I reached automatically for my pistols, but a shot *popped!*

by my ear and I froze. "Raise 'em," the voice said again, patient and amused.

Slowly I raised my hands. A couple of gray-clad men suddenly appeared beside my stirrups. One of them, the speaker, moved a wad of tobacco around in his cheek and spit on the ground, staring up at me, bemused at my appearance. I wore heavy boots, canvas pants, a butternut shirt—not embroidered; I didn't want to be shot as a bushwhacker by one of my own—and a slouch hat with a broken brim. I carried a pair of Dragoon pistols, .44 caliber, so heavy that they would have pulled my britches down if I hadn't helped my belt along with a pair of leather suspenders.

"Take his pistols, Jed," the man said. He laughed as he watched the Dragoons be taken from my belt. "Son, y'all should put wheels on them things and pull 'em around as cannons. Now, who are yuh and whar you headed?"

"Butler," I managed around the sudden dryness in my mouth. "Jim Butler. I'm just headin' away from those folks behind me. Bunch of fellows in blue coats. They burnt Daddy's cabin and shot his pigs and—"

He held up his hand, near choking on his plug from laughter. "Son," he gulped and spit. "Now Ah ain't no such fool as y'all seem to think. Nor is Jed there. There ain't a damn pig around here for fifty mile or we'da found 'em instead of livin' on coon and possum and drinkin' acorn coffee like we been for the past couple of weeks. Hell, boy, get y'all's story down 'fore y'all spit it out at a man and try to make 'im y'all's fool. All right. Ah reckon Ah know what y'all is." He nodded at Jed. "Take 'im back to camp and give 'im to the captain. Mayhap the boy'll come to his senses and tell the truth when he's standing 'fore a firin' squad for being a spy."

"Spy?" I shook my head and spoke as anxiously as I could manage. "Mister, I don't know what you're talking about. I'm just what I told you and I know there ain't no pig around behind me. I'm from Missouri and this here's Arkansas, near as I can figure. I'm looking to join up."

He shook his head, beaming merrily at me. "Boy, y'all just ain't got quit in your words, do yuh? Well, take him back to camp and let the officers sort 'im out. Mayhap he's tellin' the truth; mayhap he's lyin'. One means he could be good for us, and t'other, well, hell, a bullet will take care of that."

Silently the other man nudged me with his rifle. I climbed down off the mule and waited while he tied my hands behind my back; then I stumbled through the mist in the direction he pointed. He followed, leading my mule behind him.

We must have walked a mile or two; then suddenly the mist lifted from a hollow and I saw what I had been looking for camped down around a tiny brook under a bunch of trees. I don't know how many there were, but I could see groups of men huddled around tiny fires all down through the hollow and around a bend of the creek.

We made our way down the slope and were stopped by a young lieutenant and a couple of whiskered soldiers who lacked the humor of the one we'd left behind. The lieutenant eyed me carefully, then looked at the soldier behind me.

"Well, Allen, where did you find this one?"

Jed spit and jerked his head back the way we had come. "Back there," he said quietly. "Me and Ben found 'im riding this here mule above the road. Looked kinda suspicious and all, what with the road being just a hill away and all. Mean, why would he be ridin' there instead of in comfort on the road if he weren't looking for us?"

"Because I didn't know the damn road was there," I said. "Hell, I been trying to stay out of Yankee hands for the past two weeks. Why would I want to take a chance on a road anyway, not knowing friend from foe in this damn fog?"

"Uh-huh," the lieutenant said. His eyes looked unfriendly and I knew at once he didn't believe me. "Well, we'll just take him on up to the captain and let him decide."

But he couldn't decide, either, and I was led right up the ranks until I was before General Sterling Price. I reckoned I was in deep water that was getting hotter and hotter as we went deeper and deeper into that camp. Every time we passed a campfire the men would rise and step forward to study me carefully. I kept getting more and more edgy as we went along, fearing that sooner or later someone was bound to recognize me. The Union wasn't the only one with scouts out; the Rebels had them out, too, and whether they knew it or not, I knew that the Union army wasn't that far behind me. I hadn't been on the trail more than a day. The Union and the Rebels were closer than anyone thought.

"General?"

Price turned around, staring at me. His uniform was neat and clean. He wore a beard that looked like it was trimmed daily.

"The guards found this man wandering around out along the line. Thought he might be a spy."

Price pursed his lips, studying me. His black eyes remained expressionless. I knew instinctively that bluster wouldn't win him over, so I stared back at him, waiting, somehow feeling that silence was my best defense at the moment. At last he nodded and said, "Well? What were you doing out there?"

"Looking for you," I said. It was the truth and I felt he would hear that in my voice and maybe, just maybe, I could fool him after with a lie.

He smiled faintly. "And how did you know I was in the area?"

I shook my head. "Not *you* precisely. I don't know you from Adam. I was looking for a camp of any Southern soldiers."

"Why?"

So I spun my story again, watching him watch me, listening to my words. I forced myself to remain calm and tried to speak over the fluttering in my stomach and hoped that my bladder, threatening to burst at the time, would not betray me.

When I finished, he nodded and said, "Well, I know that there are Union soldiers around here somewhere. There has to be. Where I don't know." He nodded again at me. "You've had some education; I can see that. But you're young. . . ." He paused, furrowing his brow. "All right. I'll give you the benefit of the doubt." He nodded at the captain behind me. "Untie him and swear him in. We can't give you a uniform, because we have none to spare. You stay here with me as a runner, though. We'll put you to use there."

I didn't have any reservations about that. I knew why he was keeping me close at hand. He did mean to give me the benefit of the doubt—Price had a good reputation for being fair that he had earned while serving in the Missouri General Assembly and even in Congress. He had even been Missouri's governor for a term or two. But I didn't have any illusions; I knew he would have me shot in a minute if he thought I was a spy—I couldn't be anything more, as I wasn't in uniform.

And so I went to work for Price, watching, learning, memorizing, waiting for my chance to get away. Two weeks passed and I knew that I had to be making a move soon or else I would be listed as a deserter—if I wasn't listed so already.

Then one day Price told me to take a message to Archibald S. Dobbin north of Pea Ridge. I borrowed a chestnut—a fine mare with a white blaze down her face—that I knew had bottom and rode to find Dobbin. I wasn't exactly sure where Dobbin and his men were, but I did have a rough idea of Pea Ridge. I found them about a hundred yards from the river and delivered my message that he was to engage the Union army under Curtis only if they came across the river. He laughed and said he had no intention of trying to cross the river with the Union boys dug in the way they were but to wait a bit and he'd write a note for me to take back to Price.

I rode down toward the river where a group of men were sitting around a fire, having a cup of coffee—not the acorn mash Price's men were drinking, either, but real coffee, which set my mouth to watering. One of the men looked up and saw me sitting on the chestnut and asked if I would like to join them.

"Hell," a sergeant said. "Y'all gonna give coffee to every young'un wet behind the ears that comes this way won't be none left a-tall for the men."

I stared at him for a second while the man who had spoken to me stood uncertainly half between the sergeant and me. I stayed on the chestnut and laughed at the sergeant. I nudged the horse forward and took the cup of coffee from the man. The tin cup burned my fingers, but I took a swallow and sighed as it burned its way down, then sighed again as I felt its magic work through my stomach.

The sergeant was annoyed at the man for letting me have the coffee and started to complain when I spoke up.

"Hey," I said softly. He looked up at me, his brown eyes challenging me brazenly. "I'll bet you a dollar I can ride closer to the river than you."

His eyes widened at that. The man who gave me the coffee turned away, hiding his grin behind a cough.

"Well? What's it going to be?" I continued. "You been sitting there flapping your lip about being so damn brave and all, how about it? You game for a buck?"

He looked uncertainly from me to the river about a mile distant. He rubbed the palm of his hand over his lip, staring at the Union line on the other side, trying to gauge just how close he could get to the river without being shot.

"Hell," I said, tossing the empty cup to him. He fumbled before catching it and swore when the dregs splattered his tunic. The others laughed. "Tell you what I'll do. I'll give you a mark and you see if you got the nerve to follow."

I reached down and pulled their guidon from the ground where it was stuck.

"Hey!" he said, raising a hand to snatch it back, but I kneed the chestnut away from him. I laughed, feeling a certain craziness swing giddily through me.

"You want it, come and get it!" I shouted, and kicked my heels against the sides of the chestnut.

She leaped forward, reaching full gallop quickly, her hooves kicking large gouts of the wet earth behind her. I heard the sergeant swear and call for his horse, and bent low over the chestnut's neck, urging her on.

A shot snapped by us from the Union lines and I stuck her reins between my teeth and whipped my hat off and waved it back and forth. Another shot came and I swore and waved the hat harder, then leaned over the chestnut as we neared the river. I dropped the guidon as the chestnut didn't pause but leaped into the river and began swimming for the other side. I slipped out of the saddle, placing her between myself and the Confederate shore. Bullets from behind us began to kick up the water as it dawned on the Rebels that they had been played for fools and a barrage from the Union side answered them. I glanced back over the top of the chestnut and watched as the sergeant and a small party turned their horses to gallop back from the river. Then the sergeant threw up his hands and tumbled from his horse. The others lay low over the backs of their horses and put the spurs to their sides, galloping away.

The chestnut climbed the bank, dragging me with her, as a squad of soldiers hurried over, their rifles covering me cautiously. I shook the water from my hair and grinned at them.

"Thanks for the help, boys," I said. "My name's Hickok. Who's in charge here?"

That was what happened, although by the time Nichols got done with the story I had raced the sergeant to the river, then leaped over it, turning in midair and firing with my pistols, killing half a dozen or so Rebs before my horse's hooves touched the ground on the other side. I think Nichols had me killing that sergeant, too, but I didn't. Fact is, I barely got away with my life and my grinning at the end was more relief than anything—relief that I wasn't shot by either the Confederate or Union soldiers.

There were other adventures as well, including one where Quantrill damned near killed me and another one where I almost killed Bloody Bill, but somehow the truth of those got lost in the stories and the stories got lost in the truth and over the past years all that got mixed up with whiskey and rye and each other, and I doubt if I can even remember everything about what happened during the war. I do remember one time, though, because I still can't explain it and never did tell anyone else about it for fear they would think I was a fool and a liar. I don't mind the latter, but the former is valuable only insofar as everyone knows you've been joking around with them at the end. Somehow, though, what happened in those Arkansas woods never seemed like a joke to me.

The day came slowly in a gray swirling mist settling in for a long stay over Wilson's Creek. Those weeks earlier, I had signed on as civilian scout with the Union army at Fort Leavenworth and was taken by General Niles Becker, a vain and arrogant man with well-oiled black hair swept back from a fine high forehead. But he was a bit too cautious and reluctant to move forward until the entire terrain was well scouted. Yet he put limits on the distance for the scouts, preferring to keep them close at hand in case the troops had to suddenly move elsewhere. It seemed like he wanted to know but yet he didn't want to know—which left his scouts scratching their heads more than once, trying to figure out what to do next.

Report after report came back negative from scouting trips over Missouri's rough terrain, and I began to get a strange feeling that something wasn't right. I knew that Rebels were around because I never found a single head of livestock in all the forays I made through those hills. Yet I found no one, even though I worked myself deeper and deeper into the hills and woods.

"You boys stay close," General Becker said when I requested permission to make a deep scout into southern Missouri. "If we get orders to move out, I don't want to have to send someone looking for you."

"But, General," I said, feeling frustration building up inside. "General, I'll always be able to catch up. You can't move that fast that I won't be able to find you. An army this size leaves a mighty big trail."

"Sir," he said, suppressing his irritation. "We are training for rapid deployment."

And I knew by the note of finality in his voice that the subject was closed. I could have suggested that I might find the golden goose or Boru's Harp by going over the next ridge and gotten nowhere.

"Besides," he said disdainfully, "we have over five thousand soldiers here. If a Rebel force large enough to launch an attack against us was anywhere near, we would have known about it by now."

"Nice to be certain," I muttered, and left.

The woods seemed still, dark, and deep under the low gray falling slowly over Wilson's Creek. A damp cloying smell like swamp gas and mold seemed to wrap around us. I couldn't shake the feeling that everything was all wrong as I squatted on my heels over a cup of coffee, huddling as close around the small scouts' fire as I could to keep the swarms of mosquitoes away. Voices became soft murmurs and all of us threw uneasy looks out at the gray bank rolling in toward us.

At last I tossed the dregs of my cup on the fire and made my way to the picket line to get my horse. Perhaps I would feel better if I rode around the ridgeline and made certain that we really were alone. The quiet pressed down upon us and I heard the edgy but quiet arguments of the men who felt it, too, as I rode through the camp.

Then I was among the wet trees, slowly making my way across the creek and into the trees. I heard a *clunk!* and instantly thought of a rifle barrel accidentally striking against a cannon. A muttered curse followed. I reined in and froze, trying to find the direction of the noise, straining to hear. My mare's head suddenly jerked up and her ears pricked and twitched. I nudged her and she moved forward. A swirling mist coiled slowly around us like a Hydra's breath. Suddenly a little breeze swept a hole in the cloud and I saw a small battery of cannon being pulled into position by Rebel soldiers. At the same time, a lieutenant in a plumed hat turned and saw me and froze in astonishment, his jaw dropping down to his gray tunic.

I whirled the mare around and clapped my heels hard against her ribs. She grunted in surprise but sprang forward, her tiny hooves flashing as she flew back toward our camp. I heard the lieutenant's warning shout. Then the roar of the cannon and whistle of shot as it rose out of the trees. The ground trembled when the shells landed ahead of me, and then the screaming began. Tiny pops sounded, then the buzz of angry bees as balls zipped past my head from the wild firing of our troops shooting madly into their own fear.

"Goddamnit! I'm coming in!" I bawled, and bent forward over the mare's neck as we splashed into and across the creek. I reined in in front of Becker's tent and slid quickly out of the saddle. I burst into the tent and encountered Becker pulling on his boots, eyes wild.

"What's going on?" he demanded, rising and stamping his feet to settle them in his boots.

"You're under attack, you damn fool!" I snapped. "A force of ghosts suddenly materialized along with phantom cannon"—another shell burst nearby, followed by the screams of injured men—"and is blowing the hell out of your troops who don't know they aren't supposed to be hurt!"

"That's enough, Mr. Hickok!" he said. "When one can keep his head—"

Another explosion came, nearer than the last, drowning out his words. Suddenly it dawned on me that the Rebels probably had placed spotters in the trees around the camp days before to mark out targets.

"Damn!" I said. The commanding general's tent would have been one of the first marked. I turned and ran out of the tent.

"Mr. Hickok! Come back! I haven't finished—"

A loud *whoosh!* came overhead and I dived headfirst behind a fallen tree as Becker's tent disappeared under a direct hit, cutting off his indignant yell. My ears filled with the roar of exploding shells, and shrapnel rattled through the trees above me. Leaves and sticks and bark rained upon me, followed by a cloud of black dirt and dust.

"General Becker! General Becker!" screamed a captain. "What'll we do? What'll we do?" I sat up and spit dirt from my mouth and wiggled my little fingers in my ears in a vain attempt to clear the ringing. The captain saw me and ran toward me.

"Where's the general?" he cried.

"Dead, I think," I said, and pointed at the hole where his tent once stood.

The captain turned and looked, stunned, at the hole. "But," he stammered, "where's the general?"

"In heaven or hell, and right now I don't care which!" I shouted. Then I heard that wild ululating Rebel yell and swore. We were being attacked in force by Confederate cavalry. It was too late to form a line or redoubt or whatever plans Lyon had drawn up in the past weeks to cover what he calls "contingencies."

"Tell the men to fall back away from the creek!" I shouted. "If we can get some distance between us, we can make a stand. Maybe," I added.

But we couldn't. The men were already running with wild abandon through the woods. Some of the other scouts found me, and together we fought our way clear, slicing our way through the Rebel cavalry toward the east, hoping to beat a flanking movement. We didn't bother with trying to rally our soldiers; that would have been a mark of vanity to expect that we could. I had no doubts that this day would be a momentous day for the Confederate forces. My first experience in war had ended in complete disaster.

CHAPTER 33

ISRAEL PUTNAM and I rode across the bridge spanning Wilson's Creek and immediately turned south into the shadowed woods of bare trees reaching black arms toward the leaden sky. Spring was late in coming, and although it was April, it was colder than a witch's behind. I huddled inside my deep-pocketed canvas coat, shivering as we made our way cautiously through the damp trees and

bushes. Silence covered us like a thick blanket. No squirrels chattered angrily at jays coming too close to their nests,
no birds sang warnings to others, as we plodded along a
bare deer trail that wove its way around trees, down to the
bank of the river, and back into the middle of the woods.
Israel rode in front of me, the back of his beefy neck wrin-
kling as he swung his gaze from left to right and back again,
his gloved right hand resting lightly on his pommel near a
holstered Dragoon Colt revolver. Automatically I touched
my own Colt .44 caliber Dragoons hanging on either side
of my saddle horn, loosening them in their holsters.

We rode down a hill and into the boundary of a valley,
damp fog wrapping itself around us as we descended. I
ached with weariness and I was cold, my nose red and snot
dripping into my mustache, freezing almost immediately,
and I felt uneasy, that feeling I always got when I knew
someone was watching us and I couldn't see him. I cast back
to the night before when Tan Jenkins, shot to holes, rode in
on a lathered horse and reported a guerrilla force moving
south to link up with Confederate forces near Pea Ridge.
After the Becker debacle, General Nat Lyon had lost no time
in ordering Israel and me to saddle up and go find them.
Lyon was a fire dragon for certain, constantly looking for a
war even if he lost a third of his men or so. He had his eye
on politics after the war and knew a good war record would
bring in lots of votes from the zealous New Englanders who
eagerly read his daily reports back to the home newspapers
with the eagerness of a sinner looking for a Messiah to follow. I didn't much care for Lyon, although I had to admire
the results of his recklessness.

"Boys," he said once as we were having a cup of coffee
before heading into our blankets for the night, "victory
comes only to those who don't flinch away from gunfire."
He had pointed into the darkness. "Back east there's a young

man called Custer who said he always rode to the sound of
the guns, and he's right. You don't win battles sitting around
campfires, telling everyone how good you are while running
a cleaning rod through the bore of an unfired rifle. You have
to get up and take the fight to the enemy to keep him off-
balance. Like a fighter." He rose to his feet and danced a
bit on the balls of his booted feet, throwing lefts into the
darkness, hooking with his right. "Don't let him get set and
choose the ground upon which to fight you."

A loud *awk!* brought me from my dreaming, my hand
half-drawing one of the Colts from its holster while I looked
around quickly for the source of the noise.

"Crows," Israel said sourly, pointing upward.

I glanced at the gray sky showing through the nude black
limbs. A flock of crows circled in slow, lazy gyres, climbing and dropping down nearly to the highest branches of the
trees before swinging back up, ever in a circle.

"They see something," I said softly.

"Ay-uh," Israel grunted. He reined in his horse and stood
in his stirrups, trying to see ahead on the deer trail. "I don't
like this, Bill. The back of my neck's just a-crawling. I got
a hunch we're being injuned."

A gray shadow moved at the edge of my vision. I slipped
one of the heavy Colts from its holster, cocking it as I turned
toward the movement. A she-wolf, bags heavy with milk for
her pups, melted like twilight into the darkness of the brush.
My skin prickled. I took a deep breath, smelling the damp
and mold from the moss in the scaborous bark of the trees.
She turned to look back at me just before she disappeared,
her yellow eyes gleaming at me like the devil's lanterns.

"Don't think nothing's worse than a she-wolf with pups,"
Israel said softly. I glanced at him, his jaw bunching as he
worked a wad of tobacco he'd stuffed into his cheek. His
brown eyes looked nervous, darting around the woods. "And
something's got her up and moving to draw it away from

her litter. Otherwise, she'd a-held tight to her pups, waiting us out as we rode past."

"You ever get tired of being right?" I asked anxiously. My pulse seemed to shudder as blood pounded in my temples.

"She's crossed our path," he said solemnly, his head turning to his left.

I leaned away in my saddle to look around him and heard the snap of a rifle ball passing where my head had been only a moment before. Then guns roared from the bushes and half a dozen balls slammed into Israel, blowing him backward off his saddle. His horse screamed, reared, and galloped away. I dropped the knotted reins over the neck of my horse and drew the second Dragoon from its holster and blazed away at the bushes. My horse gave one leap, then grunted and hunched down and seemed to draw in upon herself. I kicked free from the stirrups and dived out of the saddle as she crumbled to the earth. I landed hard in a pile of dead leaves next to Israel. His eyes looked wildly at me, his mouth open and gasping for air. I glanced down at his chest and saw the blood bubbling out.

Lung-shot, I thought automatically. I snapped a couple of shots at a quivering bush and heard a yell of pain. The firing eased for a second and I stuffed one of the pistols under my belt and rose, seizing Israel by the collar and dragging him around behind the thick bole of an oak. Bark flew off the side of the tree, stinging my cheek.

"Bill!" Israel gasped, clutching at my coat, pulling me down. The tree shivered as bullets pounded into its trunk. "I'm finished. End it and get away."

I ignored him and leaned around the tree and fired at a figure that broke from the brush, running toward us. The heavy ball took him in the belly, doubling him over and knocking him off his feet. He yelled, his hands flying up in the air, a pair of pistols slipping from them as he rolled on the ground, clutching the big hole in his belly, trying to push away the pain. He screamed and screamed again; then a bullet came out of the brush and blew the top of his head away, silencing him.

"Tan was right," I said. "Guerrillas are here. They're the only ones who kill their wounded rather than leave them behind. No soldier would do that."

"Joe Shelby, I reckon," he gasped, his face white beneath his scraggly beard. "Get the hell out of here, Bill!"

"I ever tell you my name's James?" I said. I slipped the cylinder out of a Dragoon and dropped it into my pocket, taking a loaded one out of the other pocket and snapping it into place. I laid it on the ground and placed a fresh cylinder into the other Army, then checked the Navies in their holsters at my waist. Both seemed all right and I replaced them, slipping a thong over the hammers to secure them. I cocked the two heavy Dragoon Colts and peeked cautiously around the trunk. White smoke seemed to hover beneath the layer of fog above us, slipping slowly over the deer trail, disappearing into the bushes. I yawned, trying to clear the ringing in my ears.

"You think I give a rat's ass about that now?" he gasped. His head jerked back from a sudden stab of pain, banging into the ground. "Ah, Jesus!" He pulled his hands away from his chest and looked at them, bright red. "Lung-shot."

It wasn't a question, but I treated it as one. "Yep," I said. "Reckon so."

"That finishes it," he said. He wiped his hand on his pants, then hawked and spit into his hand and stared at the bright red-spotted spittle. "Ay-uh. Well, I'm between shit and sweat." He moved, rolling over, gasping with pain at the movement. His hands clawed his pistols from his belt. "I reckon you'd better get back to Lyon and tell Old Dragon Breath that we found his Rebels for him."

"Israel," I began, but he cut me off.

"Git," he said firmly. He looked at me, his eyes clear from pain for a moment, but I knew he hadn't long. It was that look of calm resignation one gets just before death washes over him. "I can hold them for a few minutes." He lifted his pistols, wincing from the effort. "Barely feel any pain now at all. That's pretty bad. Well, I got twelve shots and I'll get at least one of them with it. Promise you that. Now clear out of here. I'll cover while I can."

I reached out and squeezed his arm. "You want me to tell anyone?"

He shook his head. "Nope. Don't have no one 'cept a brother back in Springfield. He's a shopkeeper back there. Don't put up much with guns and such. Flour and sugar man. A made Quaker, I think. You might tell him if you get back there."

"I'll tell him," I promised.

He jerked and fired and I heard someone scream. "Well," he said with satisfaction. "I got the one I promised you. Now you don't haul ass, you ain't gonna be tellin' no one nothing."

"Been good knowing you, Israel," I said. I rose to my knees and blasted away at the bushes, then leaped to my feet and sprinted away from the oak, trying to keep between it and the bushes.

"Get going, Wild Bill!" he yelled. "Come on, you butternut-shirted sonsabitches!"

I glanced back and saw him firing away at the bushes, then slipped behind a close stand of hickories and lost him. I jammed one Colt into my belt and used my free hand to push branches out of my way, keeping the other Dragoon up and cocked, ready for anyone who tried to stop me.

Then the firing stopped behind me, and I knew Israel was finished and the guerrillas would be along behind me soon, if not now.

I suddenly found myself beside the river and paused,

looking for a hiding place. Behind me, the guerrillas came closer, moving cautiously now, as they sensed that I had been cornered. I saw a dead log washed up from the last spring flood and made my way to it, reckoning that it would give me a little cover and if I could hold them off until dark, I might have a chance of slipping away through the brush.

Little hope, I thought sourly as I settled behind the log, facing back the way I had come. It wouldn't take a Grant to figure out that I could be flanked by someone willing to get a bit wet.

A bit wet.

I crawled to the edge of the bank and looked up and downriver. I saw what I was searching for about a hundred yards downstream where the river cut back into the bank, then swung away in a tight oxbow, looping around almost upon itself before turning and heading south again. A natural overhang stood at the top of the river's curve, with a tangle of willow roots and swamp grass forming a kind of curtain over whatever lay behind. It wasn't much, but if it was deep enough—I glanced over the bank to where a young alder had washed, bobbing gently in the undulating waves that came from the current.

I rolled over and looked quickly back over the dead log. No one had yet to break out of the tree line, but that didn't mean they weren't in there watching and waiting for me to make the first move.

I chewed the end of my mustache thoughtfully. It was risky, but options weren't presenting themselves at the moment. I sighed and rolled back to the edge of the bank and slipped off into the water, trying desperately to hold my pistols in one hand above the water to keep the powder dry. Whatever was in my coat pockets was immediately soaked and useless. If I was cornered, I had twelve shots and then my heels if I was lucky. But I knew the chances of outrunning a guerrilla were slim and none. Those folks in their embroidered butternut shirts were far more used to these woods than I was. I had to try to think my way out.

The air exploded in a gasp as the cold water seeped through my clothes. My legs went numb almost immediately and I gritted my teeth tightly to keep from crying out. Gently I edged the alder free from its mud anchor so the water wouldn't muddy itself. Then a good tracker would know instantly what had happened. I took a deep breath and worked the tree out into deeper water, into the current, and let myself sink down to my neck behind the trunk of the tree, trying to hide the hand holding the pistols in its branches.

The tree swung gently in the current, floating tantalizingly slowly downriver. I resisted trying to speed it up, knowing that everything had to look as natural as an apple hanging on the tree. Then I saw a small group of figures edge out of the shadows and make their way cautiously toward the dead log. Had I not been watching for them, I would have thought them to be the very shadows themselves forming a thicket of the imagination, the way the guerrillas blended with the trees and bushes at the edge of the woods. Their leader straightened and cast a quick look around. He pointed toward the alder tree and the others turned, bringing their rifles up. I gave up on keeping my powder dry, jammed my pistols back behind my belt, touched the Navies to ensure they were secure in their holsters, and took a deep breath and went under the water as a fusillade struck the trunk of the tree and the water on the other side.

I felt the tree press against me as the current turned it slightly to make the bend. I took a chance and slipped up to grab a quick lungful of air. The cutback was just in front. I ducked under the water again and opened my eyes, peering through the silt. My lungs burned as I tried to work my way through the web of roots, hoping that there was a little space behind where I'd be screened from the river and the other side of the bank. Finally, I had to force my way up or drown.

I found myself against the wall of the bank, the grass overhang nearly touching the water. In front of me were roots and root tendrils forming a thick screen. I edged the heels of my boots against the bank to form a small grip and dug my fingers deep into the clay to hold myself still and keep ripples from working out of the cut into the open water. By now I couldn't feel much of anything and fought to keep myself from shivering, gritting my teeth tightly to keep them from chattering.

The thump of horses' hooves came through the small cut from overhead. I breathed shallowly, hoping that they hadn't noticed how the river had taken a large dig out of the bank before looping its way around the oxbow. Voices murmured, but I couldn't make out the words. Then the horses began moving away, but I remained where I was, as someone might have been trailing behind to catch the odd fellow trying to double back on a trail. It was a favorite trick of the Southern boys to leave a couple riding drag. A lot of good men went under because of that trick.

I waited for an hour or so more and had started to work my way out through the veil of willow roots when a king-fisher swooped toward the bank, then turned abruptly and darted away. I sank back to where I had been and gritted my teeth against the cold that seemed to seep into my very bones. Even my teeth ached from the chill when twilight began to fall. When I could no longer see through the veil, I decided to take my chances and cautiously crawled and pawed my way through. I swam downstream and around the bend to where a small cove tucked back up among the trees. I made my way into the cove, then hauled myself, dripping wet, out of the river. I touched my pistols automatically. The Navies were still in their holsters, but I had lost the Dragoons somewhere during my time in the water. I was so cold that I hadn't even felt them slip from my belt.

A cold breeze slipped down from the north, and despite my attempts to keep my teeth from chattering, my body seemed to be consumed by Saint Vitus' dance. I stood on the bank and swung my arms and tried to run in place to warm myself, but my feet thudded upon the ground like blocks of ice. Dizziness washed over me, followed by waves of cold and hot. I gave up and started to make my way around the cove, hoping that I was upstream from the bridge.

I traveled for hours; then night fell without warning, and I knew that I was hopelessly lost in the dark woods. I stumbled and fell over twisted roots that seemed to throw themselves up in my path. Brambles clawed at my clothes and ripped into the flesh of my hands when I tried to push them away. A strange savageness came out of the darkness, wrapping itself in thickly muscled arms around me. Bitter death seemed to breathe upon my collar.

Somehow I blundered off the one true path that seemed to be looping its way through those woods. I felt warm, then hot, then cold, then hot again, and a cold perspiration began to bead and flow down my face, chest, and back. I panted from the exertion of my efforts. I knew I was going downhill only because one foot always planted itself lower and lower. Then I saw a light in the trees and made my way toward it, hoping that luck was still with me.

I found a small tavern in a clearing back from a small trail. A weathered sign swung, creaking on an ancient hook. I could just make out ARIAL'S KEEP. Strange name for these parts, I thought, and cautiously worked my way around to the front, coming in from the south out of the way of the north breeze. I wanted to be downwind of any horses that might be hitched out front.

I peeked around the corner of the tavern. No horses. Cautiously I approached the door and gingerly leaned my ear against it, trying to hear inside. Silence. I pulled a pistol from its holster—whoever was inside wouldn't know the powder was wet and useless and, I hoped, wouldn't be bold enough to challenge a man already holding a pistol—took a deep breath, and cracked open the door. I peeked inside but saw no one. A fire blazed cheerfully in the cobblestoned fireplace. A pot of stew bubbled merrily, its rich odor floating out upon a slight draft through the open door, making my mouth water. My eyes blurred. I rubbed them with the heel of my hand. The door jerked open and I staggered inside. I tried to turn, but my balance was gone and I sprawled on the floor, my pistol skittering away into a corner of the room.

I heard the door slam shut and tried to rise, but my arms were weaker than my resolution and I thumped back to the floor again, staring up at the log trusses of the ceiling as they swam around as if a swing in a breeze. I heard a rustle like lone bat wings on a hot summer night—but it wasn't summer, I told myself, barely spring. Remember that: barely spring.

A pair of bare feet beside me. I noticed the thickly ridged yellow-casted toenails and caught a glimpse of the heavy yellow pads of callus under the balls of the feet. The ankles were trim and went up into sturdy calves, but the rest of her legs flitted in and out of the darkness folded under her green and white calico dress—green and white? I frowned, trying to remember if there were such colors in calico. The dress swam and disappeared and I realized what I had thought to be green and white was soft gray, a plain gray dress, clean and hard-ironed, that spread around generous breasts, tucked in at a narrow waist, and ambled down over ample hips. The dress rustled and her face swam down to me, lantern-jawed, with luminous black eyes and premature silver hair. Her face was smooth and deeply tanned, so one might take her for an Indian except for the golden sheen of her flesh that could have only been given her by the sun. Her heavy breasts pushed against her dress as she leaned over

me like a forest mother, her generous eyebrows furrowed
in concern.

Lightning flickered through the windows, flashing across
her face like a burning brand. Thunder boomed hard on its
heels—*boooooo-arrrrr-maaacccchhhhhaaaaa-aaa-aaa-
aaa*—and the fire flickered and ducked and danced in answer. Tallow candles dimmed—had I seen them before? I
no longer knew as memory began to shatter and separate
into tiny pictures: Israel jerked and fell from his horse; tiny
spurts of red fire like animal eyes flickered from the bushes;
Father stepped from the grave with the grave still clinging
gravely to him, flesh hanging in gray strips, hair in gray tangled knots, eyes hollow and accusing, a strange, earthy
smell wafting from his decaying flesh to me. . . .

"Y'burning up, mister," she said, her voice soft and musical, rolling over me like warm water. Her hand pressed
against my forehead, wiping away the cold sweat. "Y'all
been out there long? Must've been," she said, answering her
own question. "This heah's Ah-real's Keep. Y'all welcome
heah. Don't matter at all to me what y'are. Not many find
their way heah through those dark woods."

"Water," I croaked.

She nodded, then rose. I closed my eyes, trying to still
the red-crazy images darting and dashing around in my
mind. A dipper of cold water pressed against my lips. I
drank thirstily, but somewhere between my fevered gulps I
drifted away into darkness and

*a fiery wheel came spinning out of the darkness pulled
by rearing black horses with flying manes and fierce eyes
blazing leaping over flaming ditches gullets where every
flame strives against another flaring blue then a yellow-
red hurtful to the eyes and the flames reached over hungrily trying to seize me as I stepped into the chariot and
met a man with long flowing black locks and burning eyes
and shoulders bursting his tunic and I knew this was the*

one who wrestled with the gods and angels and he said I was among the captives by the Chebar River when a whirlwind came out of the north bringing with it a great cloud and a fire that folded and unfolded upon itself and within that fire I saw four men with four faces and four wings and they glowed like burnished brass as bright as burning coals and a spirit entered me and I felt words pressing against my brain saying Son of man I send thee to the children of Israel to a rebellious nation that hath rebelled against me and sinned against me like impudent children and I have chosen you to go among them as a watchman and say unto the wicked that they will die and his blood will I require at thine hand and then Father came toward me dripping the grave around him and said I was another Jacob who deceived his father's trust by wearing goat sleeves so he would be as hairy as Esau and I protested but knew of my betrayal of his death and his life with Josephine as he lay dying and suddenly I saw Hannah staring at me with accusing eyes and then she moved away from me falling rapidly away as if someone was pulling her backward into darkness and

I awoke in a strange room, my throat raw and my mouth dry. I seemed to be floating, light-headed, around the timber-walled room. I smelled lavender and tried to lick my lips from feeling like parchment. My tongue felt bristles and I rubbed my hand over my chin, expecting to feel my chin smooth, and felt, instead, a nascent beard. Wonderingly, I tried to remember when last I had shaved, and could not. "Yesterday?" I said the word aloud.

"Longer, I'd say."

The soft voice twanged at my memory. I rolled my head and saw the forest maiden sitting in a straight-backed wooden rocker, watching me carefully.

"Y'all been heah a long time."

I remembered suddenly Israel and our assignment. "Gotta get back," I murmured. The words made my throat hurt. My gun belt hung on the bedpost next to my pillow. She caught my glance and nodded.

"They're loaded. Ah thought you'd want that," she said.

I nodded and tried to sit up, but I was too weak and fell back against the bed.

"Gotta . . . gotta . . ."

"Uh-huh. Thought you'd think that way, too," she said. The chair creaked as she stood. "But a man's gotta find such things out for himself. Won't do no good at all trying to tell him."

She walked to the bed and rested her hand on my forehead. I felt the thick callus on the palm but the gentleness, too, and it felt cool and good lying there. She frowned for a moment, then nodded, and her eyes smiled down at me.

"Y'all still got a bit of the fever, but it's passing by right good now, Ah'd say." She pursed her lips *like twin rosebuds* and her thoughts seemed to nudge into mine.

Won't do no good at all to be gettin' up and goin' now y'all safe here and won't take long at all for y'all to fall sick out in the wet woods and then the bushwhackers will find y'all for certain and it'll be all up with y'all then swinging from a white oak tree and your body burning—

I shook my head weakly. "Where am I?"

"Y'all know that," she said calmly. "Think back."

Memory came flooding back in a mad cycle of shadows. I saw myself riding behind Israel, saw the winking flash of red gunfire, the bright spurt of blood from Israel where the bullets struck him, heard the *ka-rrracck!* of the bullets passing, the sound of Israel's last stand, felt the thorns as I crept through the bushes, the cold river, the sound of bullets ricocheting off the water, the deep dark woods, rain—I shivered—and the sign, but I couldn't read it in the misty darkness

ARIAL'S KEEP

whispers whispering

I said the words aloud: "Arial's Keep."

She smiled and nodded and patted my shoulder gently. "Ah'll get y'some broth," she said.

"I need to go—"

She spoke without turning. "Y'all goin' to go through that again? Being foolish just like a man."

"No. Sorry. You're right," I stammered. "Wait." She paused and glanced over my shoulder. "How did you know I wanted my pistols?"

She shook her head, smiling with irony. "Why else would y'carry them like that? A man'd be a foolish one indeed if'n he went walking around these woods heah with unloaded pistols."

"But the powder—"

"Common sense. Y'all were soakin' when y'came in heah. Stands to reason the powder would be damp."

"Of course," I murmured, feeling foolish for the asking.

"Yes," she said.

"What is your name? Sorry." I blushed. "I'm forgetting my manners—I should have asked that before."

"Helen Caroline Ernst," she said. "And I'm not married." She smiled faintly as I blinked in surprise.

"Then, Arial?"

"It's always been named that."

"How long?"

"Always," she repeated, and nodded at me and went outside.

I sighed deeply, trying to focus my thoughts, but they seemed to dart and slide around like swallows on the wing, here, there, everywhere, slipping easily away when I tried to grasp them. Then I frowned, remembering words that had not been spoken. Where had they come from?

The door opened and she came back in, carrying a bowl of broth with a horn spoon lying out upon the lip. Steam rose

from the bowl. She heeled the door shut behind her and
came to my bed, sitting on the side next to me. A tiny smile
flickered at her lips as she spooned the broth from the bowl,
blew gently upon it, then carried it to my mouth. I opened
my mouth automatically and felt the hot beefy broth slide
over my tongue and down my throat. I coughed, a hard,
racking cough, and felt something break loose in my chest
and flood up into my mouth. She held out her hand.

"Spit," she commanded.

I hesitated for a moment, then meekly complied. She
wiped her hand upon the apron she had tied around her gray
dress, then took another spoonful of the broth. Like a baby
bird I opened my mouth, this time tasting a bit of honey. I
frowned.

"What's the matter?" she asked.

"I—" But I couldn't answer. How could I explain the differences in taste to her without sounding ungrateful? *Best,*
I thought, *to keep silent about what you don't know and
what might hurt her.*

"Wise idea," she said, and held another spoonful to my
mouth. I swallowed obediently before registering that she
had spoken to my thoughts and not my words.

"How did you know? What I was thinking, I mean?"

"Some things a man is not given to know," she said
calmly. "Heah." She placed another spoonful next to my
lips. I swallowed, tasting something strong, like horsemint
with something behind it—tag alder bark? I didn't know,
but I knew there was meadow cabbage in it, maybe some
lobelia—Indian turnip?

"Yes," she said.

I started to speak, but a warm drowsiness came over me.
Drugged—I fought against the approaching twilight, then
felt her cool palm again upon my forehead.

"Y'all still feverish a bit," she said softly. "But sleep now.

When y'awake—*everything will be all right and y'all will be able to walk some, but y'all will still be weak, but sleep now, sleep*

a strange humming came to me, softly at first, then building into a lullaby, and I clung to the melody, feeling it work its magical way into my senses, numbing them gently, gently taking them into slumber—

the sedge had withered from the lake and no birds sang in the warm still of the air then she came my forest maiden walking across the meadowland to me and knelt by my side and her gray dress slipped from her shoulders and gathered softly in folds at her waist before sliding down her shapely thighs and she stood naked before me gloriously naked her breasts falling gently to the side large nipples like ripe plums and the soft fold of her stomach folding gently into the tangled weave between her legs and she knelt beside me and slid into my arms and her lips fastened gently to mine for a moment for a moment only and then pale kings and princes drifted slowly by smiling sadly but knowingly at me and I felt myself a prisoner but a willing prisoner and—

I awoke rapidly, the dream remaining with me for a moment before slipping away into the tattered darkness momentarily in my mind. I looked around the room; I was alone, my clothes washed and neatly ironed, hanging over the straight-backed rocker close beside my bed. My Navies still hung in their holsters beside the bedpost, but the thong had been slipped away from their hammers. I lifted one from the holster, feeling the familiar curve of the butt settle handsomely into my palm. I slipped the cylinder from the pistol and checked it: fully loaded, the caps seated firmly upon the nipples. I replaced the cylinder and slid the pistol back into its holster.

I rose, steadying myself by gripping the bedpost until the soft blackness disappeared from my eyes. I crossed to the chair and began to dress, smelling something faintly like clover wafting from my clothes. I took a deep breath and tried to lift my gun belt from the bedpost, but although I had checked one of the revolvers only moments before, I now found the weight too much for me and was forced to leave them hanging from the bedpost. I frowned, moving my fingers, trying to work the stiffness from them, feeling supple energy flowing into them. I tried to lift the pistols again, but this time they seemed to be nailed to the bedpost. I couldn't lift them a quarter inch.

I gave up and walked to the window and looked out; pandemonium reigned among the birds, suggesting great events to take place. The day seemed different, almost as if the light had shifted and a shadow had swept over the trees and left something behind it, a darkening, a chill. Then I saw her moving through the line of the woods, grubbing among the dead leaves, among the wood scruf, looking for something that would give moment to time, meaning to a meaningless remembrance, looking for reality under the camouflage of the accidental.

I tried to open the window to call to her, but I couldn't budge it and the effort made me weary. I crossed back to the bed and sat, then fell back onto the pillow, telling myself that I would only rest another minute.

I awoke on a bare hillside above a small lake from which the sedge had withered. Coming toward me was a young woman with a garland of flowers in her hair. She bent and kissed me and a lily appeared on her brow and a decided dreadfulness entered me. Her foot was light as she approached, her eyes wild, and when she fell in my arms I heard a sweet moan rise from her lips. Quick pictures of pale kings and princes swept in front of my eyes. I closed them and gathered her into my arms. Her filmy gown fluttered over us like an opaque cloud, and when the cloud lifted she was gone and I stood clad in strange armor not far from a saddled gray horse grazing.

"Orlando!"

I turned, feeling the heaviness of my armor upon me. I opened my mouth to ask who was Orlando, but instead strange words came forth, strange but familiar: "Yes, milord?"

A man dressed in mail sat upon his horse, a magnificent black stallion. A golden circlet crowned his head.

Charlemagne.

The name whispered out of the shadows to me. It felt familiar and *I knew him*!

"You will be the rear guard as we make our way through the pass at Roncesvalles. Select your men." He smiled at me and a warm feeling swept over me. "I don't think you will need many. There has been no trace of the Saracens since we left Pamplona."

A man all in black rode up beside him. His face looked like a somber cloud had rested upon it until it melted permanently into the flesh.

"Ganelon," I said with distaste. My hand dropped down to my pistol and found the hilt of a great sword. My fingers closed comfortably, familiarly, around it. My other hand found an odd horn at my waist.

He smiled faintly at me; his black eyes, the type that some women called sad, stared savagely, glittering, at me. His hand went to his own sword strapped on his saddle.

Charlemagne nudged his horse between us, his eyes flashing angrily.

"Hold, you war hounds!" he snapped, annoyed at the animosity between us.

Ganelon's lips lifted in a snide smile. "Again you are lucky, Orlando," he said contemptuously.

My blood raced hotly through me. I stepped around the king's horse. I slipped my sword from its sheath and slapped Ganelon smartly upon his thigh.

"Come down with your blade, Ganelon!" I challenged. "Come down to your death! 'Tis been well earned."

"Enough!" Charlemagne roared. "Put up your sword, Orlando!" I hesitated and glanced up at him. His black eyes were flat and hard. "It's not a request, Orlando! It is my command!"

I stepped back, unwillingly sliding my sword into its sheath.

"What is it, Ganelon?" Charlemagne demanded, his eyes holding me in place.

"The army is ready to march, my liege," he said, his voice undergoing a fawning change that brought a hot flush to my cheeks.

"Very well," Charlemagne said. "Return to them. I shall be along shortly." Ganelon tapped his breast in an almost insolent salute and rode away. Charlemagne glanced over his shoulder at him, then back to me.

"You must learn to control your anger, Orlando," he said harshly.

"He is a traitor! I know this, my king!" I replied hotly.

"And how do you know this? No," he said, holding up his hand as I made to answer. "No, I do not want to know this now. But when we return to our home, you will prepare and present your charge formally as should be done. I cannot have such malevolence between my paladins. There must be peace and harmony between them or else they will lose the strength that makes them worthy of helping those who are oppressed." His lips pressed into a hard line beneath his beard; then his eyes softened.

"You are my favorite, Orlando. You are destined for greatness. Men will sing about your bravery and deeds long after we are all dust. Ganelon will be forgotten. But for now"—a hard edge came into his voice—"I have a need for all my paladins. *All* of them," he repeated slowly for emphasis. "Am I understood?"

I bowed my head. "Yes, my king."

"Then choose your men. We leave immediately after."

He wheeled the mighty black and rode away toward the waiting army.

I sighed and walked to my horse. He raised his head at my approach and nickered in greeting. I patted his neck affectionately. "Well, my friend," I said softly, "I think that no good will come of this. But we have to make do. We have to make do."

A dread seeped uneasily into my veins as I mounted and rode toward the waiting men to make my choices, feeling hollow and cold inside.

I made my decision and stood aside while Charlemagne rode past at the head of his army in the company with Ganelon as his companion. Several Saracen heads topped the lances of the army as it passed.

I sighed and turned, studying the small troop that I had chosen to remain behind with me. We had driven the Saracens away, but they had also been weaker than they should have been, and I thought that they had been bringing Charlemagne's forces ever southward over the mountains and to the sea. Yet Ganelon assured the king that nothing was amiss, everything was proceeding according to plan. I didn't trust him.

A shadow seemed to fall over me as the last of Charlemagne's army passed, leaving me alone with my small force of men.

"Well," Oliver said from beside me. "What now?"

I shrugged. "Obey the king's wishes. That worthless King Marsilius is supposed to meet us at the pass of Roncesvalles to pay tribute to Charlemagne. We are to collect it and bring it with us."

Oliver made a face and stared around at the rugged country. "A good place for an ambush, you ask me, though no one ever does, so I do not know why I waste words and breath."

"Because you like to hear yourself talk," Eggihard said teasingly. "You would rather sit on the silks and satins of the king's court than upon an honest man's leather. Right, Anselm?"

Anselm grinned. "True enough in Oliver's case. He was always one for the ladies."

"Stuff that nonsense," Oliver said gruffly.

"Enough," I said, laughing. "We may have need of Oliver's gift of gab before we are home. Meanwhile, we have need of his eyes." I stood in my stirrups and noted a large cloud of dust to the southwest. I pointed to it. "And here comes Marsilius with his tribute for Charlemagne's coffers, or I miss my guess."

Anselm frowned as he studied the approaching cloud.

"Perhaps it isn't my place to say, Orlando, but that seems to be a lot of dust for someone bringing tribute. 'Tis an army's dust, I'm thinking."

"Uh-huh," Oliver said, suddenly sober. He set his spurs to his horse and rode away. "I'll check it!" he called back over his shoulder.

"Eager, isn't he?" Eggihard said. He grinned. "I happen to know that a fine barrel of wine will have been delivered by the time we get back." He put a finger alongside his nose conspiratorily. "As seneschal, I distribute the wine—"

"Something's wrong!" Anselm interjected.

We turned as one, watching Oliver gallop back faster than the canter he would have assumed if all had been right. He reined in beside us in a cloud of dust. I suddenly became aware of the barren landscape, the harsh rocks rolling up against the hills.

"Well? What news?" I asked.

"It's as you suspected," he reported grimly. "That bastard Ganelon—"

"Well?"

"I wish this was yesterday. Then we would have the full

army here. Marsilius is coming! Oh yes, he is coming! But bearing arms as his tribute, and the whole world is with him!"

The others gathered around me. "Better blow your horn to warn Charlemagne," Anselm suggested.

"Let's wait a moment," I said.

The others exchanged glances as Archbishop Turpin rode up.

"What's wrong?" he asked.

"Betrayal of the highest order," Anselm said. "Marsilius, being the good king that he is, has decided to give cold steel in lieu of the promised gold for his tribute."

"You had better warn Charlemagne," Turpin said to me.

"That's what we have been telling him, but he wants to wait!" Anselm said in exasperation.

I ignored them and galloped to the top of the Roncesvalles Pass. I reined in and studied carefully the sea of men marching toward the pass. Death's wings fluttered past me and I felt the old restlessness returning. I looked down in the valley to where the trail through the pass began.

"You miserable little valley!" I murmured. "The blood shed here today will be your shame forever."

I turned and rode furiously back to my little group. I nodded at Oliver. "You were right, my friend. Marsilius the traitor is coming."

"Then hadn't you better signal for Charlemagne to rejoin us?" Anselm asked nervously.

I shook my head. "And fall into the trap? No. Only as a last resort."

"I don't think it gets any more final than this," Oliver muttered, drawing his sword.

"Even if I did sound the horn," I said, "I do not think Charlemagne would return in time." I turned, studying the rocky terrain around us, and nodded.

"If we had to meet them, this is a better place than most.

Marsilius will have to come up to us, and only a part of his men at a time."

"The sea only throws one wave at a time against the land, but eventually it works its way," Eggihard said. "Even granite cliffs give way to it."

"But for a while, the cliffs are triumphant," I cried. "Where is it written that man will escape death?"

"I just wanted to put it off a little longer," Anselm said, drawing his sword. He settled his helmet firmly on his head. "If that be the way of it, though, then let's get on with it!" His teeth flashed whitely in an eager grin.

I drew Durindana, the sword that had been Hector's at Troy, and roared, "Away to the Saracens!"

As we rode down upon them, I prayed that the Virgin Mary would take pity upon my men. As we neared the front line, I looked back at my comrades and said, "All for himself and Saint Michael for us all! We are all perfect knights!"

"Perfect fools maybe!" Oliver said, but a grin spread his lips and his eyes shone with the promise of battle before him.

And then we fell upon the Saracens, and such was the deceptiveness of our charge that great confusion reigned. We took advantage of them, slicing through their ranks like the Lord's flail. The air filled quickly with dust and the cloying odor of blood. A large din rose from the floor of the pass of Roncesvalles until I thought the whole world would know what was happening. Men and horses screamed their death song; others cursed. Heads flew from shoulders to be trampled under the feet of heavy chargers.

But there were too many, and one by one the paladins fell from Saracen blade and spear. My blood trickled from a hundred wounds. Then I saw Oliver standing alone in the midst of fallen warriors. His face was a mask of blood flowing from his terrible wounds. I cut my way through the Saracens separating us. Oliver heard me but could not see me through a veil of thick blood over his face. He struck hard, but I blocked the blow with Durindana, the only blade that could have withstood such a blow without shattering.

"What, Cousin? Do you fight for the Saracens now?" I asked.

Oliver laughed and wearily lowered his blade. "I beg your pardon, but I can see nothing. The curtain of death has drawn close around me."

"'Tis only blood," I objected.

"Aye, mine," he said. "I die. Some traitor has dealt me a death blow in the back."

"I shall take you someplace safe," I said, bringing his horse to him. He mounted and sat determinedly.

"No," he said. "Lead my horse into the thick of them so I may avenge my own death."

I led him through the heart of the Saracens, our swords hewing a street out of flesh. By the time we reached the other side, blood poured from another fifty wounds hacked upon me.

"Rest here," I panted, helping Oliver from his horse. "I will ride to the hill and sound my horn. It is time to let Charlemagne know what has happened to his rear guard."

Oliver laughed painfully. "*Now* you decide to toot that damn thing. But when you return here, you will find only the grave man."

He sat down with his back against a rock, drew two last deep breaths, raised his sword, then died, frozen in defiance.

I sighed and rode to the top of the hill and raised the great horn to my lips. Twice I blew it, the second time louder than the first, blood bursting from my lungs. I blew the horn again, the dark gray mist creeping ever closer toward me as my blood flowed freely from my wounds. The horn burst and blood poured from my mouth and nose—

The door flew open and armored soldiers rushed in followed by Agravaine, who swaggered, sneering, toward me. I heard a sharp, indignant gasp and a naked body rose from me, clasping a coverlet to her breasts. Her golden hair lay tousled on her bare shoulders and her sea green eyes flashed angrily.

"How dare you enter my chambers in this manner?" she demanded.

"To arrest traitors, my queen," Agravaine said mockingly. "On the king's orders."

She slumped forward, the coverlet nearly slipping from her hands.

"Lancelot," she whispered.

I pushed her back and rose, naked, from the bed. Agravaine laughed.

"Well, Lancelot," he said. "And how fares it tonight? I see your sword is at ready use!"

A great loathing surged through me. "You go too far, Agravaine," I said.

He drew his sword and touched me lightly upon the left nipple, pressing the skin to near breaking.

"I go too far? And what about you, Lancelot?" A mad grin stretched across his face. "This will bring the king's favor to me instead of you, Lancelot. You and"—he looked deliberately at—

Guinevere.

Again the whisper of a name flitted across my mind, lifting images of our love—naked bodies in the flickering firelight, clutching each other furiously as we pressed closer, trying to merge our flesh and souls into one—from the depths. How long? I couldn't remember. It didn't matter. She was the world to me. But Arthur—

"—and your trollop burn at the stake for treason!" he finished with a satisfied licking of his lips.

Blood pounded through my veins. My muscles swelled, and I slapped his sword away with my left hand. I stepped forward, grasping his shoulder and pulling him to me. His breath, reeking of onions, exploded in my face. I spun him around, grasping his sword arm by the wrist with my right, twisting it behind him. I levered it up hard between his shoulder blades, hearing and feeling the tendons snap in his shoulder just before he screamed in pain.

We stood for a moment in grotesque meeting, shaking hands—dear long-lost brother, kinsman, lord, thane—then I took the sword from his hand and slipped my arm around his neck, bringing his head sharply into my shoulder. I heaved upward and felt his neck crack and dropped his suddenly lifeless body to the floor.

"Look out!" someone—Gareth, I thought dimly—cried out just before I swung the sword, beheading him. His headless body stood stock-still for a moment; then the nerves in its legs jerked spasmodically, making two backward steps, the fountaining blood spattering those behind, briefly blinding them.

The blade danced in a blur of its own devising as I stepped forward among them, felling them as a scythe would stalks of wheat.

I watched coldly, dispassionately, as they fell away from me, feeling the invincible, familiar power surging through me. My strength grew, seeming to sap theirs from them. Panic came upon them, and they fled screaming toward the fireplace at the far end of the room, pushing and shoving, each trying to get behind the other. A mad laugh leaped from my throat and I felt my lips spreading in a smile I saw reflected in the terror in their eyes. I started forward, the blade singing in my hands as all do when I heft them—

"Lancelot! Save yourself!"

I turned toward her. She pointed toward the door, the coverlet slipping away from a white cone-shaped breast whose ruby tip I had kissed—was it only minutes before?

"Go!"

"My lady," I began.

"It is my order!" she shouted. Her eyes widened fearfully. "Look out!"

Without thinking, I swung the blade over my head, blocking a sword stroke from Garse, who tried to take advantage of my brief unguarded moment. I spun, sliding the blade down his blade, then reversed the stroke and ripped sideways, gutting him.

He screamed and fell to his knees as he tried to press the thick, bloody worms back into his bowels. I spun away from him on the balls of my feet, swinging the sword in a tight arc. I severed one man's arm at the shoulder. He spun away from me, the stump spurting blood around the room, upon others who stepped back reflexively from him.

I took the moment to dash from the room. I glanced down the hall. Armed men came up the stairs toward me. I turned and ran down the hall into the chapel, slamming the door tightly behind me. I drove the blade deep into the wood beneath the door lever, jamming it. Then I ran to the stained-glass window. A candle flickered bravely in a red glass chimney on the altar. I paused and looked up at the crucified figure on the cross above the altar.

"Keep her safe until I can return for her," I begged.

I seized a candelabra from the altar and raced to the window, shattering the glass and breaking it free from its frame with three blows. I dropped the candelabra to the floor and stepped gingerly out onto the stone sill.

A great banging came from the iron-strapped door behind me. I glanced down at the waves of the moat lapping softly in the pale moonlight far below me.

A hundred feet? I pushed the thought away and, taking a deep breath, leaped up and away into the dark, praying—*"Guinevere, Guinevere, Guinevere"*—softly as I fell into the inky blackness of the waters. . . .

Guinevere . . .

. . . standing tied to the stake, wood piled around her, the flames beginning to leap toward her as I charged through the gate into the courtyard, my sword slashing and hewing a path open to her. Her lips formed my name and I heard the din of battle behind me as those knights still loyal to the two of us protected my back. I rode up behind her, my horse dancing, wild-eyed, squealing in terror from the flickering fire. I swung the blade down, severing the ropes binding Guinevere to the stake. I seized her arm and pulled her up behind me, then let my charger race away from the fire. Men fled from his hooves, but still he trampled some.

"Away! Away! The queen is safe!" I cried. Obediently the others fought their way back to the gate, then turned and galloped after us, away from Camelot—

> A gentle knight was pricking on the plaine,
> Ycladd in mightie armes and silver shielde,
> Wherein old dints of deepe woundes did
>   remaine,
> The cruell markes of many' a bloody fielde;
> Yet armes till that time did he never wield.
> His angry steede did chide his foaming bitt,
> As much disdayning to the curbe to yield:
> Full-jolly knight he seemd, and fare did sitt,
> As one for knightly giusts and fierce encounters
>   fitt.

I awoke bathed in sweat and glanced around the room. I was alone. I sighed and closed my eyes again

and then a mythic ancestor came out of the forest old and bent with grief his hand trembling upon a cane that he leaned on to shuffle forward hesitantly one step at a time his shaggy head covered with wild white hair shaking from side to side as if he could see into the depths of the woods

around with his ash gray eyes in the dark hollow sockets of
his head and he said do you hear the pain carried on the
wind it is the cry of wasted lives and he laughed when I did
not answer and asked if I dared to drain the world of its
light and smiled and beckoned to me to join him among the
trees but I was afraid and remained frozen where I was and
he called to me on the wind saying come journey with me
through the centuries and learn to walk decades with your
steps I took a willing step

Her hand gripped my shoulder, shaking me awake. She
smiled down at me.

"Y'all been sleeping for a long time," she said. "I see that
y'got up and did a little moving around. That's good. Y'all
need to get your strength back, and that ain't gonna happen
lyin' around in a bed for me to wait on yuh."

"Thank you," I said. "If you will just give me a hand—"

I tried to sit up, but she pushed me back against the pillow. "Ain't no reason to be pushin' it, though. It takes more'n
a day to get over the hackin' and coughin' y'all been doin'
since I tucked y'into that bed."

"I'm grateful," I said, trying to push against her hand. I
felt a fine sheen of perspiration begin to form from my efforts. "But I have to get back across the river."

"Uh-huh," she said, and laughed. "Y'all may have to get
back across the river, but it'll take y' a while. There's many
a bushwacker between here and there. I'd wait awhile. Another day or two won't make any matter."

"You don't understand—" I began, but her eyes began to
glow and I found myself drawn into their depths

Better than you think. But you still ain't going anywhere
until you're ready. Won't make another bit of difference at
all despite what you think. The pattern's been cut and the
fabric sewn and there ain't a way that you can change that.
Not a way. 'Sides, you ain't got a horse

"I need one," I mumbled. "I can buy one—"

Not here you can't. But good things come to him who waits. And you need to wait.

Look.

"Gotta get back—"

and she slipped her hand behind her back and her dress fell again from her and naked she climbed in beside me naked and her lips caught hold of mine and I felt my soul lift up from inside me and go winging away into the dark and I begged for it again and felt her lips again hotly upon mine and her legs wrapping themselves lithely around me and I tasted hell or heaven in her lips and then I heard her laugh and felt—was it scorn not love—

Again I awoke and found myself naked and wary. Then memory came back to me and I threw the covers back from me. Wonderingly I gazed down at my naked self and frowned to find my clothes neatly gathered upon the rocker. Had I dreamed everything? No, I decided, I could not have dreamed it. Not all. Not everything.

The door opened and she came in again, smiling at me. Embarrassed, I fought to bring the covers quickly over me, much to her amusement.

"Do y'remember?" she asked. I gave her a startled look and this time she laughed, the notes of her laughter tinkling like silver bells. "Don't tell y'all have forgotten!"

I shook my head, managing a weak smile. "No, I haven't forgotten. I'm not certain that I will forget anything."

She laughed again, amused at my youthful gallantry. "Perhaps not," she said graciously. "I hope not. Y'll have to remember everything at all times if y'all are going to succeed."

"Succeed?" I frowned. "At what?"

"At what y'all have been chosen for," she answered calmly.

I shook my head. All this was becoming too obscure for me to grasp. A sound came as if a painter was falling down his ladder *rumpababababababagalharaghtakammminar-ronkonnbrontonnertoohoohordenenthurnu!* and I jerked upward, turning quickly toward the window, one of my pistols slipping into my hand before I thought of it as if by magic. I glanced down at it, then at her.

"Yes," she said in reply to my unspoken anxious expectancy. "There is a bit of magic to it. There is always magic."

"Magic." I felt a laugh bubbling up inside me but fought to keep it away.

A wry smile twisted her lips, her eyes hooded, and she shook her head slightly, recognizing my disbelief in the single word. "Y'all don't know the wind, but it is there when y'least expect it. There's no reason to think other things cannot exist as well in a like manner, is there?"

"I suppose not," I said. "But what magic would you be talking about?"

"Y'all'll know before you leave," she said cryptically. I tried to ask her more questions, but she held up her hand, staying my tongue. "Enough for now. Y'all be ready to leave in two days. *In two days,*" she emphasized when I started to object. I sighed and looked down at the pistol.

"No, y'all can't do that," she said, intercepting my thought a moment before it came to me.

I looked wonderingly at her, thinking the thought at the time: *I could force you*—and knowing instinctively that I couldn't. I let my hand with the pistol drop to my side and then and only then realized again that I was naked and felt the burn of embarrassment flush over me. She placed her hands on her hips and laughed merrily at my discomfort as I tried to cover myself with my hands.

"All right," she said, bemused. "Come on down when y'are ready. But leave your pistols behind. Except that one," she said roguishly, glancing at my hands. "Y'all won't be needing the Colts tonight. As to the other, well, we'll see."

She turned and left the room, closing the door gently

behind her. I crossed to my clothes, pausing to slip the Colt back into its holster, and again dressed. It seemed as if only minutes before I had stepped into my clothes and felt them softly warm me against the chill of the room. I tried to lift the gun belt again from the bedpost, but it seemed again as if it had been nailed in place. I could take the pistols from their holsters, but when I tried to turn with them toward the door they seemed to weigh my arms down, impossibly heavy, and I replaced them in their holsters.

I crossed to the door and gently lifted the latch. The door swung smoothly open, revealing the hallway leading to the flight of stairs downward. Firelight danced its shadows on the timbers of the wall opposite the banistered railing across from me. The wood looked hand-rubbed with molten candle wax, shining dully, richly, in the dim light. I walked cautiously to the stairs and looked down. The planked table had been richly set with a white linen cloth. The dishes glittered silvery and candles burned steadily in tall silver candlesticks in the center of the table. I noticed that four places had been laid for dinner and frowned, wondering who the other two would be, then catching my thoughts warily before they could escape into the magic—if there *was* such a thing—and betray me. Candles flickered in the wooden sconces pegged into the wall, casting a dancing light over the room.

"Come on down," she called.

I looked quickly for her, and for a moment I wondered if the words had been spoken or if they had been thoughts slipped into my mind. Then I saw her beside a spinning wheel, wearing a white dress with a low neckline and what looked like green ivy embroidered around the neck and hem. The sleeves were long and wide and edged in ivy, too. Her feet were bare and her silver hair glinted in the light as if it had been freshly washed and brush-dried. It fell softly over her shoulders. A wreath of tiny red rosebuds had been woven and circled her forehead. Her black eyes danced merrily, tiny lights like shooting stars coming toward me. She gestured, and I obeyed, walking slowly down the stairs.

I glanced at the spindle on her wheel and frowned, trying to put a name to the color she was spinning, but it seemed to change color as I watched, shining, then darkening, then exploding into a series of ripe colors—blue, green, yellow, orange—before fading softly to shades becoming darker and darker until a single black thread was drawn. I blinked and the spool seemed to leap up shimmering in sunlight and then disappeared.

"What—"

"Does it matter?" she said. She frowned, tilting her head to the side.

"I remember your spinning."

She shook her head. "But it isn't wise to tell man everything." She smiled to take the sting from her words. "Y'all been born for violence, James. But y'all are needed." She shrugged. "Ah 'spect y'all know that, though. Or have an inkling. There's good and bad in all people and all people taste the side of each a time or two. But Ah have a feeling y'all going to eat more from the right side of the platter. At least, that's why you were woven."

I shook my head, frowning, and started to speak to ask her to explain her strange words, but then I felt a cold breeze caress my neck.

I turned quickly. Two men stood behind me. My hands instinctively went to my waist, clawing for pistol butts that were not there. I swallowed and backed warily away from them until I bumped into the table. They watched me soberly, without speaking. She came forward and put her hand on my arm.

"Don't be frightened," she said lowly. "They are not here to harm you."

I looked at them carefully and saw that they were weaponless—or at least, I could see no weapons on them.

Each was dressed in a Prince Albert coat with checkered trousers, a red sash around his waist. They wore white ruffled shirts with a white scarf tied around their throats. Their boots were highly polished and reflected the light of the room back into it. Their long blond hair had been carefully combed and fell to their shoulders. For a moment I thought I was staring into a coming reflection of myself, but they moved into the room and the thought slipped away from me on swallow's wings. Each took a seat at the table and waited as she pulled me to a place at the foot of the table, then seated herself at the head.

She smiled down at me. "Drink your wine," she said gently. Automatically I lifted the wine to my lips and tasted it. Like honey. And I drank deeply before I knew I was drinking it. I placed it back on the table and looked from one man to the other, trying to understand the unearthly aura that exuded from them, a negative radiance like dark light.

"There is a need for you," the one on my right said gently. "A great need. Now and in the future."

"By whom?" I asked. My tongue felt thick and I looked suspiciously at my wineglass. It was full again, but by whose hand I did not know.

"You will know," the other said. He turned to the first speaker. "Like Achilles?"

It was a question before I knew it was a question and the other shook his head, saying something, but I was not listening to his voice

a short life and not always a happy life and you will be alone until the end but you will never know family for a man like you there is no family and the happiness of children is a myth for others who will envy you and hate you and you shall know both by their envy and hatred and although there will be some who will become close to you do not expect to find your salvation in them for that will be only through your deeds and your responsibilities

I heard a noise at the door. She raised her eyebrows, looking at me, and nodded slightly. I rose and crossed over the tightly pegged floorboards and opened the door. A marvelous black stallion stood there, saddled. He was alone. I walked out, speaking softly to him.

"Whoa, boy. Where's your master? Easy now," I crooned as I placed my hand gently upon his neck. He turned his head toward me and I saw that he was blind in one eye, a film covering it like a sheet. I glanced at the saddle and started, noticing the saddle was mine and the Army pistols in holsters on either side of the pommel were mine as well.

"What?—"

I turned toward the tavern—

And saw nothing. A twilight gloaming was coming over the woods and I heard the cawing of crows in the distance. My hands went to my waist and I felt the familiar weight of my pistols, snugged in their holsters. I glanced down at the heavy canvas coat over which they had been buckled. My pants were fresh and clean and warm against my legs. I moved my toes inside my boots and felt the heavy woolen socks in which they had been encased.

The horse snorted behind me, and I turned, suddenly aware that I held the reins in my hand. I looked at him wonderingly.

Black.

Where did that word come from? I said it aloud and the horse nodded his head.

"Black. Your name is Black," I said automatically.

He grumbled deep within his chest and twisted his head from side to side, hearing or seeing something; I couldn't be certain.

"What is it, boy?" I asked.

I glanced around at the woods; we were alone all right. As alone as anyone could get in a late spring woods.

Where is Arial's Keep? And where is the woman? Where is Helen Caroline Ernst? Where is—

A jay chattered angrily near us. I glanced around, half-fearfully, expecting—anything. I drew one of the Navy Colts from my waist and cocked the hammer, trying to penetrate the gloom beginning to deepen around me like a pearl mist.

you are disappointing me James you men are all tragedians looking for the romance of atonement but you won't find it here and you won't find it in the war although that is where the story of Bill will begin to find its ending now go to your beginning for you know what is expected what is needed of you

Swiftly a picture flashed upon my memory and I held it tightly for one crystal clear moment. Helen coming toward me in a filmy gown, her beauty radiating through the garment, nearly blinding me. There was a terrifying earnestness in her face and I knew that I had become her lover and she my guardian, a figure more deeply felt than motherhood. Then everything seemed to confront me at once: Father's death, Josephine, Mary, another Mary, a couple of women whose names I no longer knew if I ever did, Kansas, and, briefly, a glimpse of the last call of fate in a blurred image of dead branches, twisted, bone white, stripped of bark, nude, and then the picture was gone and I stood alone in the clearing, clean and alone, my pistols freshly armed, a black horse moving restlessly beside me.

I turned and mounted. I pulled on the reins, trying to turn him to the left, but he shook his head. *Annoyed.* I loosened the reins, dropping my hand to the pommel, comfortingly near the Army pistols. Black turned to the right and moved confidently off through the woods, his hooves finding a trail where none existed. I crouched low over his neck, watching the growing dark in the bushes half-fearfully, but Black gave no evidence of others being in the woods with us as he made his way through them as sure-footed as if he was on a graded highway.

For an hour or better we rode like this, and then we emerged into the twilight of a turned field and I smelled the earth, musty and dank beneath his hooves as he picked his way across the furrows to the road. He paused, flicking his mane, then turned decidedly toward what I took to be the west, although there were no stars to guide me, only a crescent-shaped moon beginning to appear, a milk white outline at first, slowly deepening into yellow, then bloodred.

I heard the hollow *clud-clud-clud-clud* of his hooves as we crossed a wooden bridge. A burned-out schoolhouse loomed on our left; then a small graveyard appeared on our right, the white-pine planks used as tombstones stretching up from the black ground like bones. We passed under a leafless gnarled oak tree and then I saw the flickering of campfires on a broad hillside and wondered if I was seeing Union or Confederate fires, but it didn't seem to matter at the moment, for I felt as if I was riding through a vision— not a dream, for a dream lacks sustenance and I could smell and hear and feel the night around us and the bunching and releasing of the black's muscles as he lifted into an easy, ground-gaining lope toward the fires.

I didn't touch my pistols but left the path to the horse, trusting in him to find the way for me.

An hour later, we were among the tents of a Union regiment and the men were shouting and calling me by name as they rushed toward us:

"Wild Bill. Wild Bill. Wild Bill—"

CHAPTER 34

THE SUN came up as red as Sally's bloomers: a fiery red that seemed to rise and expand until the red covered the whole of the horizon. It began to bleed over the rest of the sky, and with it came the breath of brimstone, harsh and biting upon the nostrils. A sulfuric yellow haze began to roil by the treetops.

"Damn," Peter Pelican breathed silently from beside me.

I rolled to my side and looked at the youth. He was looking with awe at the sky, shaking his head. "What's the matter?" I asked.

He jerked his head, indicating the sun. "Pa was a preacher," he began. "He see a sky like that, we'd be hearing the words of Revelation being shouted at us from the time he first saw it. That's the sign of the apocalypse, Jim. Sure as I'm sitting here, that's what the world's gonna look like when the four horsemen come ridin' out of it."

"You believe that?" I asked.

He shrugged. "Reckon it don't mean a thing if'n I believe it or not. Can't stop the sun from rising; can't stop the horsemen from ridin'. Might as well make the best of it we can."

I nodded and rolled back over, peering cautiously over the bluff down into the Rebel camp. I put a glass to my eye and sorted out the colors flying near General Ben McCulloch's tent. I remembered the words I had had with Curtis, who had insisted that we try to pick McCulloch off with some of his staff after I came back with a report of the camp. I didn't think that Curtis would have gone for this, but he had and here I was, again behind the lines with young Pelican, who was the best shot in camp with a rifle. I looked down at the Springfields on the ground beside us. Both had been fitted with telescopes as long as the barrels, and the bullets had been carefully loaded by Pelican. I looked back at the camp and saw the general's striker go into his tent.

"Get ready," I said, and picked up my rifle, settling myself comfortably. Out of the corner of my eye I watched Pelican carefully wipe the barrel of his Springfield and squirm into position.

"You get the first shot," I said. "Make it a good one." I recalled my words with Curtis as I began to breathe deeply, slowly.

That isn't the way I fight, Curtis.

War is war, Hickok. People die in war. It doesn't make a difference if it's in battle or not. You know that. You've done it before.

Doesn't mean I have to like it. When it comes my turn, I sure as hell hope I see the man who does it. I want it to be a man with sand, not someone with a good eye.

"Here he comes," Pelican breathed.

I looked through the scope and watched as McCulloch came out, holding a cup of coffee. He slapped his chest with the other hand and took a long, slow breath, reveling in the morning. He was as predictable as running water. We had been watching him for four days and his routine never varied. Now he would take a long sip from his coffee.

"Take him," I said softly.

Pelican grunted. I heard his breath slip slowly from his lips and then a loud *crack!* as he squeezed off the shot. I watched and saw the tent flap jerk beside McCulloch.

"Damn!" he said.

Without thinking, I held a half foot above McCulloch's head and squeezed the trigger. The rifle lurched back hard against my shoulder, the telescope jamming me under the eye. For a moment I was blinded; then I heard Pelican's gleeful shout, "You got 'im, Jim! You got 'im!"

I blinked the fog out of my eye and looked through the glass to where McCulloch lay motionless on the ground, soldiers swarming around him.

"Take as many as you can," I said, and slid a cartridge into the Springfield.

Pelican's rifle sounded. A major threw up his arms and slumped to the ground. I fired randomly and watched as somehow I managed to hit another soldier. The shot hadn't been well aimed, but somehow I had managed to hit another. Pelican began to shoot deliberately and every shot seemed to strike home. I fired another couple of shots, then noticed a mounted patrol sweep out of the camp to our right.

"Time to go," I said, and squirmed back from the edge of the ridge. I ran low to where Black stood, trembling anxiously from the gunfire. I mounted and watched as Pelican swung up on his mule.

Together we turned and rode hard, heading back toward our lines. The day had been good for the Union, but it still left a bad taste in my mouth. There wasn't anything honorable in doing what we had done. Perhaps we had shortened the war by a few days; perhaps not. But man was meant to live and die honorably. McCulloch had just died.

I turned in my report and gave Pelican credit for the kill. But Pelican was a product of his daddy's preaching and lying just wasn't in him. He had already told the others around the camp how he had missed and I had shot McCulloch.

Curtis, however, believed me and not the rumor running like wildfire through the camp. He granted my request to be transferred to Captain John Kelso's command as a scout. I didn't care much for Kelso—he was wild and careless with his men but extremely lucky, and I had learned by now that luck was better to have than all the careful planners who wouldn't make a move unless they had a dozen confirmed scouting reports.

CHAPTER 35

SOMEONE KEPT kicking the sole of my boot. I opened an eye and saw John McKoan grinning in the gray light of morn. I sighed and rolled away, wrapping myself deeper into my blankets.

"G'way," I mumbled. "I was up all night."

"I know," McKoan said. He squatted and placed a cup of coffee near my head. "But Kelso has an idea that we can make a raid down through Elkhorn Tavern and Van Buren."

"What?" I sat up, kicking my blankets away. I sat up and reached for the cup of coffee, swearing as I burnt my fingers. "But that's—that's—"

"Yeah, we told 'im," McKoan said. "But he thinks a small group can do a bit of damage and take the Rebs' attention away from the front. Sort of a"—he motioned with his hand as if sliding butter across a table—"detraction action."

I stared at him in disbelief. "Detraction action? What the hell?"

He laughed and turned his head, spitting a long stream of tobacco juice that narrowly missed my blankets. "Wal, that's what he calls it. Don't know what he's thinking, but it's enough for him to get antsy, and you know what he's like when he gets that way."

I sighed and stood up, sipping cautiously on the coffee. "Yeah, I know," I said disgustedly. "Well, if this don't make the cat piss milk!"

But Kelso had made up his mind and there was no changing it. We rode out of camp that night, which made me even more nervous, since we didn't know where our patrols were and at night all uniforms and men look alike. The Kelso luck held, though, and we crossed the river and into the trees and made a mad race down through Rolla and Springfield and back across Wilson's Creek to Elkhorn Tavern.

We came down hard on a couple of camps, surprising the sentries and riding through, shooting wantonly into the tents and sleeping forms around the fires. We didn't wait to see the damage that we did but continued on our wide detour, riding recklessly and with wild abandon deeper into the Confederate territory. I thought about the Fatal Sister and wondered if we would pass Arial's Keep, but we didn't and I'm not certain what I would have done if we had. But then I wasn't certain anymore if that had indeed happened. But I didn't have time to dwell upon such thoughts, as Kelso kept us moving at a lathered pace throughout the night.

We pulled up for the night in a hickory grove and kept a sharp watch, but no Confederate patrols came near us. That night we rode on toward Elkhorn Tavern, and that is where we ran across a small Rebel patrol accompanying a couple of young women in a carriage toward General Buford Hacker's camp. I pulled up in a thicket and watched as they went by and frowned as I saw the two women sitting primly in a carriage with riders flanking them on either side.

I waited until they disappeared around a bend in the road, then nudged Black with my heels and rode down a ravine to where Kelso and the others waited. He was on his feet by the time I drew Black in. McKoan and John Allen and Zeke Stone rose, Stone groaning and complaining about his lumbago but still moving as spryly as a man half his age.

"Yes, Mr. Hickok?" Kelso said. "You have found something, I take it."

His eyes gleamed with a fanaticism that made them burn with green fire. He rubbed his gauntleted hands together anxiously.

"Don't know," I said, taking a canteen of water from McKoan and drinking thirstily. I lowered the canteen. My teeth ached from the cold water, but I still felt a sheen of perspiration on my face and scrubbed my hands over the stubble on my chin. I felt dirty and hated that more than anything.

"Well?" Kelso said impatiently.

"A small patrol went by escorting two young women in a carriage," I said.

"Whores for the camp," Zeke said with satisfaction.

"No," I said, shaking my head. "I don't think that's right. They seemed to be under guard. Riders flanked them. I don't know." I took my hat off and wiped my head, scrubbing my hands through my hair. "It just didn't 'feel' right, you know, Captain?"

Kelso pursed his lips and stared thoughtfully back at me. Allen shook his head. "Don't mean a damn thing," he said. "For all we know, Zeke could be right. Be the first time, I know, but he's gotta be right oncet."

"That's what I call confidence," McKoan said, spitting.

"What do you say, Mr. Hickok?" Kelso asked, his eyes burning into mine. I felt the heat of his desire and knew he was willing to go after them.

I took a deep breath and shook my head. "Well, it just didn't look right to me. I think those ladies were prisoners." I shrugged. "And hell, if I'm wrong, we can't be any worse off than we are now, can we?"

Zeke laughed and said, "Damn if you ain't right, Bill. Ain't one of us coming out of this alive, so might as well be shot for a fish as a carp."

"Now what the hell does that mean?" Allen demanded. "Hell, you don't make no sense at all. Captain, that ain't—"

Kelso shook his head. "Doesn't matter. I know what he was trying to say." A reckless grin plastered across his face. "Mount up, men!"

"Oh shit," Allen sighed, and went to his horse, a mean bay that tried to take a chunk out of his leg each time he stepped into the stirrup. He kicked it automatically and the horse screamed in fury. "Well, dammit, if we're gonna get killed, let's get on with it!"

Kelso clapped his hands with satisfaction and leaped onto his sorrel and motioned for me to ride ahead. I led them down the ravine. Black moved anxiously under me, sensing the battle coming, heading toward the patrol. I took a hard hand on the reins. He threw his head angrily, mouthing the bit as if he could chew through the metal. His neck arched; his mane flew back and forth as he snorted in disgust.

I led the patrol through the woods and across a pasture on a wide detour, guessing where the road would loop back again, keeping a creek on my left as I rode. We came out of the trees just as the patrol came into view. The lieutenant in the lead pulled up, startled at our sudden appearance. I dropped the loop of the reins on Black's neck and slammed my heels hard against his sides. Black squealed with fury and leaped forward. I lifted the Army Colts from their holsters and thumbed back the hammers as I rode down upon the lieutenant. He opened his mouth to yell, but I snapped a shot off that struck him in the chest, somersaulting him backward off his horse. Then I rode into the patrol, gripping Black's sides hard with my legs as he drove into the side of a horse, his yellow teeth snapping, tearing a chunk out of the horse's neck. I shot his rider, then shot another and turned in the saddle to snap a shot at a third as Black wheeled and charged the trail rider. I raised my pistol, then saw shock cross his face and a bright scarlet flash explode from his chest. He fell from his saddle and his horse turned and galloped away. I pulled Black up and turned, raising my pistols, but it was over; all were dead.

I looked back down at Kelso and the others, staring openmouthed at me. Zeke grinned and waved his long rifle.

"Well, you didn't git 'em all, Wild Bill!" he chortled.

"Damnedest thing I ever saw," Kelso said as Black cantered back to him. "And folks call me crazy."

I reined in and looked down at the ladies. One of them, blond-haired with flashing blue eyes, laughed, her full lips spreading generously over her face, lifting into dimples in her cheeks.

"Yes, I'd say you are one wild man," she said.

"We thought you might be in difficulty, ma'am," Kelso said, gallantly tipping his hat at her.

"And we were," she laughed. "Mary Ladd and I have been accused of spying for the Union." She shrugged. "But now it seems that our accusers aren't around anymore. I'm Susannah Moore." She smiled archly at me. "And I'm eternally grateful, sir, for your gallantry."

I grinned down at her as Zeke spit disgustedly. "Hell," he grunted, "you'd think Wild Bill was winning the war all by hisself!"

PART THREE

Paladin

He snatched the lightning shaft from heaven

CHAPTER 36

PERHAPS WHAT began it all ends it all. I don't know—that is one of the mysteries I haven't been able to solve and know, now, that I never will. I know the mystery—the cruelty within people that cannot be excised with a burning brand despite all the assurances of our priests and preachers—

The war ended and for a while I cast around like others who had fought in it, trying to decide what to do next. For a while I hauled freight, working as a teamster for McFadden & Co., but I quickly became bored with the slow-moving wagons rolling over the brown plains. I hunted a bit and thought fleetingly about going up into the mountains and becoming a mountain man, but I knew that was only a maudlin dream held over from the youth that I no longer was. I went home to visit Mother, but I had been gone too long to belong there anymore and I soon made my way to Springfield, looking halfheartedly for a job but not knowing what it was I wanted to do. Springfield wasn't much to shine a lantern at, but it was the largest excuse for one in that part of the state. An uneasy pall seemed to hang over the town even on the sunniest days as former Rebels and Yankees moved nervously through the streets together. Most, however, seemed to be looking for the same elusive moment to present itself and tuck them beneath a blanket of success. But moments like that have to be made to happen, and few showed any inclination to become that involved in the day.

I was infected, too. A restlessness had seemed to enter my soul and I soon found myself irritated and angry at others who meant to do me no wrong but still somehow managed to easily offend me all the same.

I began to gamble recklessly and for a while Lady Luck smiled favorably upon me as coins and chips seemed to flow steadily over green felt and scarred pine tabletops toward me. But I took little satisfaction in my growing finances, boredom quickly following upon the heels of the brief exhilaration of winning.

I met Dave Tutt at one of the tables in one of the saloons and took an instant dislike to the man. It's strange how sometimes a man can meet another and find the hackles rising upon his neck. But that was the way with Tutt. I knew he had been a Rebel and probably a bushwhacker—he had that look about him: arrogant, lip-curling, and a chip on his shoulder large enough to be a loblolly pine. But the real reason we rubbed each other raw was Susannah Moore.

Susannah—long blond hair, breasts that moved beneath her dress when she walked despite all she tried to do to hold them still, and, in the dark, soft white skin that seemed to glow beneath my hand. Any male who stood around her breathed deeply and I knew what they were smelling, for I smelled it as much as they—the salt of the woman who wants a man. Susannah wasn't particular about any man, although when she stayed with one she was true to him until she left and then she never went back. That was her own strange code of honor. In her mind, I suppose, it kept her from seeing herself as "loose" or a "soiled dove" or an "adultress," which were the terms most often flung the way of women like her.

Susannah was none of those; she was just a woman who met men on their own terms and hers. Nothing more.

But Tutt, well, Tutt was different. He had a cruel streak in him that others sensed whenever he was near and stepped wide of him—all of which fed his arrogance and made him strut more, the cock of the boardwalk in Springfield.

I wouldn't play cards with him, because he was a poor gambler—he always lost, and when he lost he drank, and when he drank he became ugly and unreasonable and as certain as the rising of the sun that he was immortal. Father would have called it the bravery of Achilles, which wasn't bravery so much as it was an arrogant assurance of his own moment in time.

Tutt had come upon the game in The Lyon House and tried to sit in, but as I had started the game, I refused to let him play. He turned red with rage; then his face went strangely white and he smiled and picked up my watch, saying, "I reckon you owe me this much from the last time we played."

I laid my cards on the table and looked up at him. "I've never played with you, Tutt," I said quietly. "And I never will."

"You think you're too good for me, don't you?" he challenged, a wild recklessness coming into his eyes.

"No," I said carefully. "I *know* I'm too good for you."

The room became silent as all eyes turned toward us. Tutt hesitated, an uncertainty flashing momentarily in his eyes; then he, too, felt the eyes of the room and knew he had gone too far to simply replace my watch and walk from the room.

He forced a laugh and dropped the watch in his shirt pocket, then said, "You can have it back when you bring my money to me. I'll be in the square tomorrow at noon." And he walked from the room.

I excused myself from the table and rose and left quickly to reclaim my watch, but by the time I made it to the doorway he had gone. I knew, however, that he would be in the town square in the morning with my watch: He had already said that, and if he did not show up at the appointed time he would be laughed out of Springfield, and a man like Tutt can take no laughter directed his way.

The next day at noon, I was waiting in the square when I saw him take my watch from his pocket, pretend to consult it, then step out into the sunlight, holding the watch in his left hand.

"That's enough, Tutt," I called warningly. "You've taken this too far."

"Too late for that!" he said. "Come and get it."

I started across the square and he pulled his pistol from its holster and let it dangle at his side. I placed my hands on the butts of my Navy Colts and continued across the square until only ten feet separated us. His eyes glittered black hate at me from beneath the brim of his hat. He laughed again, but it was a nervous laugh, and then he was caught up in the moment.

"You know I don't give a damn about this watch," he said softly.

"I know," I answered. "But it's her choice to make. Not yours. Not mine."

"With you gone, there won't be much of a choice left!" he said. Something moved in his eyes, and I knew he was finished talking. I twisted my wrists, flipping the pistols from their holsters. I fired as I leveled it, and saw the bullet strike him in the middle of his belly, knocking him down. His pistol flew from his hand. I stepped forward and took my watch out of his hand.

"You were a stupid man, Tutt," I said softly. "Is anything worth the dark?"

His eyes looked frightened for a moment; then the tendons of his neck stretched hard as he tried to jerk himself away from approaching death. He moaned and I knew it would have been a scream had not his throat contracted suddenly, shutting off all sound, shutting off life. A glaze came over his features, and his muscles relaxed into the dirt.

I sighed and turned back to the crowd, holding the watch in one hand, one of the Navy Colts in the other. I saw metal flash and said sharply, "I hope there's not another stupid person here. It was a fair fight."

My friends Jim and Art appeared then, each holding a shotgun. The hostility of the crowd immediately vanished and they turned away, dispersing. A couple came forward to carry Tutt to the undertaker's house and I walked toward the nearest saloon to wash the brassy taste out of my mouth.

I was arrested shortly after the Greene County coroner returned his report and had a bench warrant issued for me for killing Tutt. But two days later the charge was reduced to manslaughter, and some friends put up a two-thousand-dollar bond to bail me out of jail. Captain R. B. Owen then pulled a few strings and talked John S. Phelps, one of the leading attorneys of the time, into taking my case. Phelps made short work of the charges against me, rounding up witnesses who swore Tutt had fired first—that didn't take long, as almost the entire town had witnessed the battle—and I was acquitted.

I thought that was the last of that affair, but I couldn't have been more mistaken. The local newspaper, the *Missouri Weekly Patriot,* tried to scrape my hide away with a series of articles, lashing not only me but the jury as well within the sanctified safety of its editorial columns. But I refused to rise up against the writer, recognizing instinctively that I wouldn't win in a war of words and knowing full well that nothing would be gained by hauling him out into the street and thumping him. But I didn't know how such a controversy appealed to others. People always want to know the dirt upon a fellow even if he's cast as a hero. Fact is, I think if a fellow is a hero to some, there's others who don't rest until they've dug something up to tarnish his reputation. Most men aren't happy unless they can make others more miserable than themselves. Then they're happy. I suppose, however, that it was the idea of finding a hero in peacetime to take the place of those lost with the end of the war that brought Colonel George Ward Nichols to Springfield in search of me.

I was playing cards in Springfield with a couple of friends when Clark came into the saloon, saying, "Jim, there's a Colonel Nichols asking for you over at the hotel." He grinned. "Says he wants to talk to the great hero Wild Bill Hickok."

I swore softly as the others around the table grinned at me.

"Hero, eh, boys?" Wallace said, chuckling. "Maybe we ought to just give up while we can on this here game and give him our money."

"I'll get it anyway," I said, spreading my cards out. "Three queens."

Wallace laughed and tossed his cards in. "Thought you were bluffing, Bill," he said congenially.

"I didn't," Art said. "Figured you for the queens, Bill, and knew you didn't have the fourth 'cause I buried it in the deadwood. Three kings." He laid them gently in front of him, smiling gleefully. I shook my head in irony as the others broke into laughter.

"So what do you want to do about the colonel, Bill?"

I nibbled on the edge of my lip as I thought for a second. "He really a colonel?" I asked.

Clark shrugged. "Claims he is. Fact is, ask him once and you'll understand how he won the war single-handedly, thanks to his genius. But I guess all those writers are that way."

"I beg your pardon," Bob White said stiffly, leaning back in his chair. Bob had been a correspondent for some eastern paper during the war and took slurs upon his former occupation as a personal insult. "That is a gross generalization made by a fool."

"No offense," Clark said easily. "Present company excepted."

"Yes, I imagine," Bob said. He looked owlishly at me. "Well, why not have a bit of fun with him? Let's give him a hero."

"I don't know," I started doubtfully.

"Oh, come on!" Art said gaily. "Don't be such a stuffed shirt."

The others grinned at me. I threw up my hands, surrendering. "All right. Let's see what we can come up with."

Eagerly they tossed their cards aside. Bob brought glasses and a bottle of Monongahela from the bar. We all took a glass. I leaned back resignedly as the others put their elbows on the table and began to talk animatedly, arguing gleefully as they built a proper hero's life for Wild Bill Hickok.

Colonel Nichols looked eagerly around the lobby as he tripped down the stairs of his hotel. He spied me sitting on a medallion-back sofa next to a Hepplewhite chair near the corner. He made a beeline toward me, his eyes shifting nervously around the room, sizing up the "color" for the article I suspected he had already written and was looking for a few details to plug in and give it the ring of reality. A grin tugged at my lips. Everyone in the lobby was from the poker game and dressed in the dime novel's idea of what a westerner should wear, after an hour spent in Martin's Mercantile choosing their costumes. Even Bob had dressed up in a pin-striped collarless shirt with a huge yellow bandanna spread over it. He wore a broad-brimmed hat with a crown tall enough to hide a pony keg of beer in it and sheepskin chaps with an old revolver tucked awkwardly in his belt. I hoped it wasn't loaded or he'd probably shoot his nuts off pulling it out, as the blamed fool had cocked it before jamming it under his belt.

Deke wore a fire-engine red shirt and blue bandanna under a rawhide vest, a wad of tobacco bulging one cheek like a foraging chipmunk.

The others sprawled in rainbow colors around the room, affecting the bored look of fresh-washed cowboys the fourth day off the trail.

"Mr. Hickok?" Colonel Nichols said, halting in front of me.

I rose and stretched out my hand. "Call me James," I said.

"You are 'Wild Bill' Hickok?" he said anxiously.

I thought I heard a giggle and looked toward Bob. I could tell from his bright eyes he was having a hard time holding his laughter in. I glared at him. He made a strangled noise and looked away.

"I don't really care for that," I said uncomfortably. "That's just something the folks hung on me."

No mistake about it; Bob stuck his knuckles in his mouth, trying to stifle the giggles.

"Wild Bill," Nichols breathed with relish, pumping my hand like he was trying to draw water. "You don't know how long I've been looking to meet with you! Ever since I heard about the McCanles massacre—"

"Yeah, well, you know," I said, uncomfortable with his beaming presence and his reference to the fight at Rock Creek Station that I had been trying to put in history ever since the courts had found me not guilty of murder.

He beamed. Positively beamed. I felt myself growing red with embarrassment. "I'm Colonel Nichols," he said, drawing out his title so I had a half hunch it was self-awarded. Fakes make a ceremony out of what they pretend to be while those who have brought themselves up by their bootstraps don't feel the need to lay their rank out on the table in front of anyone. But for the next quarter hour he oiled my ears with his gab and stories about the glory he'd earned, looping his way up and around just about every major battle I'd ever heard about—except the Trojan War; somehow he missed that one—and, as near as I could tell, the North owed him a debt of gratitude for having saved it from a terrible fate at Gettysburg.

Toward the tail end of his tale, I gave Bob a dirty look and tapped the handle of one of the Colts holstered, butts forward, at my waist. Bob laughed and looked deliberately away, pretending he hadn't noticed me. I sighed and turned my attention back to the colonel, who hadn't noticed my attention lapse, just as he wound up his lecturing.

"But enough about me," he said modestly, his lips spreading in another smile that would have blinded an Indian a mile away with its brightness. "Tell me about yourself, Wild Bill."

He leaned back in his chair, looking with high expectations at me. I nodded, staring back at him for a minute, until a tiny frown began to appear between his brows and his eyes began flickering nervously away from mine.

"Something wrong?" he asked uneasily.

I shook my head and leaned forward conspiratorially. He leaned back away from me for a second, but I motioned for him to lean forward. He hesitated, then slowly bent forward, his eyebrows jerking up and down in question.

"I don't know," I said, frowning and nodding toward Bob. "But that fellow over there looks just like a face on a wanted poster I've seen hanging around the sheriff's office. No, don't look!" I said sharply as he started to turn automatically in the direction of my nod. "You might give us away."

"Us?" He swallowed and his eyes started their wild dance again. "Why. Yes. Yes. Of course."

I nodded and gave him a grim look. "And if I don't miss my guess, he's got his gang with him, too."

Nichols's face became grim, but a welcome joy seemed to creep into his eyes. His tongue crept out and wet his lips nervously. "Ah, gang?"

I pursed my lips and shook my head. "Some of the most bloodthirsty rascals who ever came down the wood," I said. "Robbed a bank over in White River and killed eighteen people before riding out. Then they rode back in for pure orneriness and killed another six or seven before they rode away. Three of the dead were women."

"Women?" he replied with relish, and I could read the headlines of his stories gleaming in his eyes. A fine sheen of perspiration appeared on his forehead.

"Yes," I said, lowering my voice. "One a grandmother."

"Grandmother," he repeated. His cheeks began to look a little flushed with anxiousness. Again he licked his lips. "Ah, maybe we should get some help."

"No time for that," I said. I took an old Manhattan from beneath my coat and pressed it into Nichols's hands. He looked like he might faint from glee in his chair.

Bob caught the motion and gave a thumbs-up to the others. "Look out, boys!" he roared. "It's Wild Bill Hickok!"

He drew the pistol, accidentally nudging the trigger as it came out of his pants. Most of us had loaded our guns with blanks before starting off with the joke, but Bob had put a full load in the revolver and a streak of flame shot out a foot long from the barrel, setting his trousers on fire. He yelped and dropped the pistol and began slapping at his groin with his palms to put out the fire. The others stared open-mouthed at his wild dance, forgetting their roles.

I swore and leaped to my feet, drawing my pistols as I came out of the chair. "You boys have been terrorizing folks long enough! Now you've got"—*aw, hell*, I thought, and swallowed gamely—"Wild Bill to deal with!"

I almost threw up as I said those lines and decided the hell with the rest of the speech the boys had written. I started shooting, and the others snapped out of their trance, drew their pistols, and began firing back. Out of the corner of my eye, I saw Nichols dive out of his chair and fall flat on the floor behind me. I emptied one pistol as Nichols rose to a crouch and stretched his pistol over the arm of the sofa, shooting with grim satisfaction in Bob's general direction. The fire crept up Bob's pants, and he howled and slapped wildly at his groin. The others began grabbing their bellies and falling to the floor, dying dramatically, caught up in their finest hour. All of them discreetly spilled flat bottles of snake oil mixed with chicken blood we had gotten from the butcher on their shirts, then stuffed the bottles back under their shirts and sprawled grotesquely on the wood floor.

All save Bob, that is, who jerked spasmodically out the door, britches flaring, and jumped into the horse trough. A small cloud of steam rose up. His shoulders slumped in relief for a second; then he climbed out of the trough, water streaming from his clothes, and limped painfully, spraddle-legged, down the alley.

A white fog filled the lobby. I peered through the smoke and nodded satisfactorily. "Well, Colonel, reckon we got them all." I stumbled for a second, trying to remember the name Bob had given himself, then gave up and invented one. "Short-armed Bob's heading for Hades even now as we speak!"

Nichols rose from behind the arm of a heavy chair, waving his pistol. He saw the "dead" bodies and his face broke into a wide smile and he dusted off his suit.

"We did?" he said, then added, "Well, by God, so we did!"

He handed the pistol to me and started toward the "bodies," but I caught his arm. He gave me a puzzled look.

"What?"

"One of them might be playing possum," I said solemnly.

"What?" he asked, looking blankly at me.

"One of them might be waiting for us," I said loudly. "Faking, you know?" I roared. I knew what the problem was—their ears were ringing from the pistol shots made louder in the room than they would have been out in the open.

Art finally heard me and jumped up, leveling his pistol at us. Nichols roared angrily as I pulled a double-barreled shotgun, sawed off six inches in front of the chambers, from beneath my coat, rocked back the hammers, and tripped the triggers. It sounded like a cannon in that narrow lobby. The recoil damn near knocked me back on my ass, but I caught the back of Nichols's chair and managed to remain upright. Clark threw himself backward as Nichols charged toward him, windmilling his arms furiously. His foot stepped on one of the pistols and rolled out from under him.

"Ark!" Nichols yelled, stumbling, trying to catch his balance. He failed and fell forward, his head smacking into the walnut leg of a table. His eyes rolled up in their sockets. He tried gamely to rise but fell, unconscious, to the floor.

"I'll be damned!" I said.

Art opened an eye and, not seeing Nichols standing beside me, rose cautiously. "What's wrong?"

"I think he knocked what little brains he had out," I said, kneeling beside Nichols. I pressed my fingers against the side of his throat and felt his pulse beating. "No, the hero of the War Between the States is still alive."

"You sure?" Art asked, coming forward. He squatted, looking at the bump rising like a mountain on Nichols's forehead.

"I think I know a dead man from a living one," I said dryly. "Help me get him into the chair."

Art helped me raise Nichols and sit him upright in the chair. Deke, sensing something was wrong, rolled his head around. He saw the two of us standing beside the chair. "What're you doing?" he asked.

"He knocked himself out," Art said disgustedly.

"What?" Deke climbed up, giving us a disbelieving look. He nudged the others with the toe of his boot.

"I didn't stammer," Art said sourly. "Shit. It all went beautifully."

"What? What?" Jim asked, rising. "That damn cannon's got my ears ringing like a blacksmith's anvil," he said reproachfully, glaring at me.

"It was your idea," I said, lifting the shotgun and looking at it disapprovingly. "If I had shot loaded in this, I would have wiped out half the town with its spread. Here." I tossed it to him. He wasn't expecting it and it struck him on the forehead. His eyes crossed; he wavered for a second, then collapsed to the floor unconscious.

Art threw his hands up in the air disgustedly. Then he noticed Bob was gone. "Where's Bob?" he asked.

I explained quickly. He shook his head. "Damn, this thing's turned to horse poop real fast."

"Shit," Deke said automatically.

"That's what I said," Art said.

"You said 'poop.' There's a difference," Deke said defensively.

Nichols moaned in his chair, moving his head slightly back and forth on the tatted throw over the back of the chair.

"He's coming around," I said.

Without thinking, Art whipped out his pistol and whacked Nichols on the head. Nichols slumped deeper into his chair, a second lump already forming on his forehead.

"Now why did you do that?" I asked, feeling frustration climbing up through me like a raccoon scaling a tree.

"He would've seen us," Art said.

I shook my head. "You boys grab Jim and get him out of here."

"What are you going to tell him?" Art said.

"I'll think of something. Maybe I'll tell him he got creased."

Art motioned at his forehead. "That don't look like no bullet to me."

"Maybe he won't know the difference," I said.

"If he really was—is—was a colonel, he will," Deke said mournfully.

"Bullets can do the damnedest things, though," Art said philosophically. "Come on, Deke. Let's get Jim and go find Bob."

"You might try the widow's place," I called as they hoisted the unconscious Jim between them and made their way awkwardly out the door.

The hotel clerk came forward, holding a couple of glasses and a bottle of whiskey. He shook his head as he handed them to me. "Pour a little of this in him," he said.

"Let's get him up to his room first," I said.

The clerk helped me raise the colonel to my shoulder, then followed me with the whiskey and glasses as I carried Nichols up the stairs. We laid him on top of his bed after removing his coat and tie. I unfastened his celluloid collar as the clerk wet a towel in the hand basin, wrung it out, and brought it to me.

"All right," I said. "I'll take it from here."

He left as I folded the towel and placed it over Nichols's forehead. I sighed, poured myself a drink, and pulled a chair up next to the bed and sat, waiting for him to awaken.

The next day, I put a shaken but swaggering Nichols on the noon train heading east. His head was swathed in bandages, giving him a piratical look. He pumped my hand enthusiastically and promised he would, by God!, write the truth about Wild Bill Hickok. He climbed aboard and waved his broad-brimmed hat with a grandiose gesture as the train pulled out from the station.

I thought that was the last I would hear about Colonel Nichols, but six months later Bob came into The Lyon House holding a copy of *Harper's* in the air.

"Here it is, gentlemen!" he crowed. "The true story, part one, of Wild Bill Hickok!"

"You sorry-assed son of a bitch," I said accusingly. "And after all I've done for you."

He ignored me as the others clamored for him to read it aloud. He cleared his throat, made certain that a glass of whiskey stood at his elbow to lubricate his speaking facilities, and began.

WILD BILL

Several months after the ending of the Civil War, I visited the city of Springfield in Southwest Missouri. Springfield is not a burgh of extensive dimensions, yet it is one reason why it was the *point d'apari* as well as the base of operations for all military movements during the war.

On a warm summer day, I sat watching from the shadow of a broad awning the coming and going of the strange, half-civilized people who, from all the country round, make this a place for barter and trade. Men and women dressed in queer costumes; men with coats and trowsers made of skin, but so thickly covered with dirt and grease as to have defied the identity of the animal when walking in the flesh. Others wore homespun gear, which oftentimes appeared to have seen lengthy service. Many of those people were mounted on horseback or muleback, while others urged forward the unwilling cattle attached to creaking, heavily laden wagons, their drivers snapping their long whips with a report like that of a pistol-shot.

In front of the shops that lined both sides of the main business street, and about the public square, were groups of men lolling against posts, lying upon the wooden sidewalks, or sitting in chairs. These men were temporary or permanent denizens of the city, and were lazily occupied in doing nothing. The most marked characteristic of the inhabitants seemed to be an indisposition to move, and their highest ambition to let their hair and beards grow.

Here and there upon the street the appearance of the army blue betokened the presence of a returned Union soldier, and the jaunty, confident air with which they carried themselves was all the more striking in its contrast with the indolence which appeared to belong to the place. The only indication of action was the inevitable revolver which every body, excepting, perhaps, the women, wore about their persons. When people moved in this lazy city they did so slowly and without method. No one seemed in haste. A huge hog wallowed in luxurious ease in a nice bed of mud on the other side of the way, giving vent to gentle grunts of satisfaction. On the platform at my feet lay a large wolf-dog literally asleep with one eye open. He, too, seemed contented to let the world wag idly on.

The loose, lazy spirit of the occasion finally took possession of me, and I sat and gazed and smoked, and it is possible that I might have fallen into a Rip Van Winkle sleep to have been aroused ten years hence by the cry, "Passengers for the flying machine to New York, all aboard!" when I and the drowsing city were roused into life by the clatter and crash of the hoofs of a horse which dashed furiously across the square and down the street. The rider sat perfectly erect, yet following with a grace of motion seen only in the horsemen of the plains, the rise and fall of the galloping steed. There was only a moment to observe this, for they halted suddenly, while the rider springing to the ground approached the party which the noise had gathered near me.

"This yere is Wild Bill, Colonel," said Captain Honesty, an army officer addressing me. He continued:

"How are yere Bill? This yere is Colonel N——, who wants ter know yer."

Let me at once describe the personal appearance of the famous Scout of the Plains, William Hickok, called "Wild Bill," who now advanced toward me, fixing his clear gray eyes on mine in a quick, interrogative way, as if to take "my measure."

The result seemed favorable, for he held forth a small muscular hand in a frank, open manner. As I looked at him I thought his the handsomest *physique* I had ever seen. In its exquisite manly proportions it recalled the antique. It was a figure Ward would delight to model as a companion to his "Indian."

Bill stood six feet and an inch in his bright yellow moccasins. A deer-skin shirt or frock, it might be called, hung jauntily over his shoulders and revealed a chest whose breadth and depth were remarkable. These lungs had had growth in some twenty years of the free air of the Rocky Mountains. His small, round waist was girthed by a belt which held two of Colt's Navy revolvers. His legs sloped gradually from the compact thigh to the feet, which were small and turned inward as he walked. There was a singular grace and dignity of carriage about that figure which would have called your attention meet it where you would. The head which crowned it was now covered by a large sombrero, underneath which there shone out a quiet manly face; so gentle is its expression as he greets you as utterly to belie the history of its owner; yet it is not a face to be trifled with. The lips thin and sensitive, the jaw not too square, the cheek bones slightly prominent, a mass of fine dark hair falls below the neck to the shoulders. The eyes, now that you are in friendly intercourse, are as gentle as a woman's. In truth, the woman nature seems prominent throughout, and you would not believe that you were looking into eyes that have pointed the way to death to hundreds of men. Yes, Wild Bill with his own hands has killed hundreds of men. Of that I have not a doubt. "He shoots to kill," as they say on the border.

In vain did I examine the scout's face for some evidence of murderous propensity. It was a gentle face, and singular only in the sharp angle of the eye, and without any physiognomical reason for the opinion, I have thought his wonderful accuracy of aim was indicated by this peculiarity. He told me, however, to use his own words:

"I allers shot well; but I come ter be perfect in the mountains by shootin at a dime for a mark, at best of half a dollar a shot. And then until the war I never drank liquor nor smoked," he continued, with a melancholy expression; "war is demoralizing it is." Captain Honesty was right. I was very curious to see "Wild Bill, the Scout," who, a few days before my arrival in Springfield, in a duel at noonday in the public square, at fifty paces, had sent one of Colt's pistol-balls through the heart of a returned Confederate soldier.

Whenever I had met an officer or soldier who had served in the Southwest I heard of Wild Bill and his exploits, until these stories became so frequent and of such an extraordinary character as quite to outstrip personal knowledge of adventure by camp and field; and the hero of these strange tales took shape in my mind as did Jack the Giant Killer or Sinbad the Sailor in childhood's days. As then, I now had the most implicit faith in the existence of the individual; but how one man could accomplish such prodigies of strength and feats of daring was a continued wonder.

In order to give the reader a clearer understanding of the condition of this neighborhood, which could have permitted the duel mentioned above, and whose history will be given hereafter in detail, I will describe the situation at the time of which I am writing, which was late in the summer of 1865, premising that this section of country would not to-day be selected as a model example of modern civilization.

At that time peace and comparative quiet had succeeded the perils and tumult of war in all the more southern States. The people of Georgia and the Carolinas were glad to

enforce order in their midst; and it would have been safe
for a Union officer to have ridden unattended through the
land.

In Southwest Missouri there were old scores to be settled
up. During the three days occupied by General Smith—
who commanded the Department and was on a tour of
inspection—in crossing the country between Rolla and
Springfield, a distance of one hundred and twenty miles,
five men were killed or wounded on the public road. Two
were murdered a short distance from Rolla—by whom we
could not ascertain. Another was instantly killed and two
were wounded at a meeting of a band of "Regulators," who
were in the service of the State, but were paid by the United
States Government. It should be said here that their method
of "regulation" was slightly informal, their war-cry was, "A
swift bullet and a short rope for returned rebels!"

I was informed by General Smith that during the six
months preceding not less than four thousand returned
Confederates had been summarily disposed of by shooting
or hanging. This statement seems incredible; but there is
the record, and I have no doubt of its truth. History shows
few parallels to this relentless destruction of human life in
time of peace. It can be explained only upon the ground
that before the war, this region was inhabited by lawless
people. In the outset of the rebellion the merest suspicion of
loyalty to the Union cost the patriot his life; and thus large
numbers fled the land, giving up home and every material
interest. As soon as the Federal armies occupied the
country these refugees returned. Once securely fixed in
their old homes they resolved that their former persecutors
should not live in their midst. Revenge for the past and
security for the future knotted many a nerve and sped
many a deadly bullet.

Wild Bill did not belong to the Regulators. Indeed, he
was one of the law and order party. He said:

"When the war closed I buried the hatchet, and I won't fight now unless I'm put upon."

Bill was born of Northern parents in the State of Illinois. He ran away from home when a boy, and wandered out upon the plains and into the mountains. For fifteen years he lived with the trappers, hunting and fishing. When the war broke out he returned to the States and entered the Union service. No man probably was ever better fitted for scouting than he. Joined to his tremendous strength he was an unequalled horseman; he was a perfect marksman; he had a keen sight, and a constitution which had no limit of endurance. He was cool to audacity, brave to rashness, always possessed of himself under the most critical circumstances; and above all, was such a master in the knowledge of woodcraft that it might have been termed a science with him—a knowledge which, with the soldier, is priceless beyond description. Some of Bill's adventures during the war will be related hereafter.

The main feature of the story of the duel was told me by Captain Honesty, who was unprejudiced, if it is possible to find an unbiased mind in a town of three thousand people after a fight has taken place. I will give the story in his words:

"They say Bill's wild. Now he isn't any sich thing. I've known him going on ter ten year, and he's as civil a disposed person as you'll find hereabouts. But he won't be put upon.

"I'll tell yer how it happened. But come inter the office; thar's a good many round hy'ar as sides with Tutt—the man that's shot. But I tell yer 'twas a fair fight. Take some whisky? No! Well, I will, if yer'l excuse me.

"You see," continued the Captain, setting the empty glass on the table in an emphatic way, "Bill was up in his room a-playing seven-up, or four-hand, or some of them pesky games. Bill refused ter play with Tutt, who was a professional gambler. Yer see, Bill was a scout on our side durin the war, and Tutt was a reb scout. Bill had killed Dave Tutt's mate, and, atween one thing and other, there war an onusual hard feelin atwixt 'em.

"Ever sin (*sic*) Dave come back he had tried to pick a row with Bill; so Bill wouldn't play cards with him any more. But Dave stood over the man who was gambling with Bill and lent the feller money. Bill won bout two hundred dollars, which made Tutt spiteful mad. Bime-by he says to Bill:

"'Bill, you've got plenty of money—pay me that forty dollars yer owe me in that horse trade.'

"And Bill paid him. Then he said:

"'Yer owe me thirty-five dollars more; yer lost it playing with me t'other night.'

"Dave's style was right provoking; but Bill answered him perfectly gentlemanly: 'I think yer wrong, Dave. It's only twenty-five dollars. I have a memorandum of it in my pocket down stairs. Ef it's thirty-five dollars I'll give it yer.'

"Now Bill's watch was lying on the table. Dave took up the watch, put it in his pocket, and said: 'I'll keep this yere watch till yer pay me that thirty-five dollars.'

"This made Bill shooting mad; fur, don't yer see, Colonel, it was a-doubting his honor like, so he got up and looked Dave in the eyes, and said to him: 'I don't want ter make a row in this house. It's a decent house, and I don't want ter injure the keeper. You'd better put that watch back on the table.'

"But Dave grinned at Bill mighty ugly, and walked off with the watch, and kept it several days. All this time Dave's friends were spurring Bill on ter fight; there was no end ter the talk. They blackguarded him in an underhand sort of way, and tried ter get up a scrimmage, and then they thought they could lay him out. Yer see Bill has enemies all about. He's settled the accounts of a heap of men who lived

round here. This is about the only place in Missouri whar a
reb can come back and live, and ter tell yer the truth,
Colonel—" and the Captain, with an involuntary movement,
hitched up his revolver-belt, as he said, with expressive
significance, "they don't stay long round here!

"Well, as I was saying, these rebs don't like ter see a man
walking round town who they knew in the reb army as one
of their men who they now know was on our side, all the
time he was sending us information, sometimes from Pap
Price's own headquarters. But they couldn't provoke Bill
inter a row, for he's afeared of hissel when he gits *awful*
mad; and he allers left these shootin irons in his room when
he went out. One day these cusses drew their pistols on him
and dared him to fight and they told him that Tutt was
a-goin ter pack that watch across the squar (*sic*) next day ast
noon.

"I heard of this, for every body was talking about it on
the street, and so I went after Bill and found him in his
room cleaning and greasing and loading his revolvers.

" 'Now, Bill,' says I, 'you're goin to get inter a fight.'

" 'Don't you bother yerself, Captain,' says he. 'It's not the
first time I have been in a fight; and these d——d hounds
have put on me long enough. You don't want me ter give up
my honor, do yer?'

" 'No, Bill,' says I, 'yer must keep yer honor.'

"Next day, about noon, Bill went down on the squar. He
had said that Dave Tutt shouldn't pack that watch across
the squar unless dead men could walk.

"When Bill got onter the squar he found a crowd stanin
in the corner of the street by which he entered the squar,
which is from the south, yer know. In this crowd he saw a
lot of Tutt's friends; some were cousins of his'n, just back
from the reb army; and they jeered him, and boasted that
Dave was a-goin to pack that watch across the squar as he
promised.

"Then Bill saw Tutt standing near the court-house, which yer remember is on the west side, so that the crowd war behind Bill.

"Just then Tutt, who war alone, started from the court-house and walked out onto the squar, and Bill moved away from the crowd toward the west side of the squar. Bout fifteen paces brought them opposite to each other and about fifty yards apart. Tutt then showed his pistol. Bill had kept a sharp eye on him, and before Tutt could pint it Bill had hi'sn out.

"At that moment you could have heard a pin drop in that squar. Both Tutt and Bill fired, but one discharge follwed the other so quick that's hard to say which went off first. Tutt was a famous shot, but he missed this time; the ball from his pistol went over Bill's head. The instant Bill fired, without waitin ter see ef he had hit Tutt, he wheeled on his heels and pointed his pistol at Tutt's friends, who had already drawn their weapons. " 'Arent' yer satisfied, gentlemen?' cried Bill, as cool as an alligator. 'Put up your shootin-irons or there'll be more dead men here.' And they put 'em up and said it war a fair fight.

"What became of Tutt?" I asked of the Captain, who had stopped at this point of his story and was very deliberately engaged in refilling his empty glass.

"Oh! Dave? He was as plucky a feller as ever drew trigger; but Lord bless yer! It was no use. Bill never shoots twice at the same man, and his ball went through Dave's heart. He stood stock-still for a second or two, then raised his arm as if to fire again, then he swayed a little, staggered three or four steps, and then fell dead.

"Bill and his friends wanted ter have the thing done regular, so we went up ter the justice, and Bill delivered him self up. A jury was drawn; Bill was tried and cleared the next day. It was proved that it was a case of self-defense. Don't yer see, Colonel?"

I answered that I was afraid that I did not see that point very clearly.

"Well, well!" he replied, with an air of compassion, "you haven't drunk any whisky, that's what's the matter with yer." And then, putting his hand on my shoulder with a half-mysterious half-conscious look in his face, he muttered, in a whisper: *"The fact is, thar was an undercurrent of a woman in that fight!"*

The story of the duel was yet fresh from the lips of the Captain when its hero appeared in the manner already described. After a few moments' conversation Bill excused himself, saying:

"I am going out on the prarer a piece to see the sick wife of my mate. I should be glad to meet yer at the hotel this afternoon, Kernel."

"I will go there to meet you," I replied.

"Good-day, gentlemen," said the scout as he saluted the party; and mounting the black horse, who had been standing quiet, unhitched, he waved his hand over the animal's head. Responsive to the signal, she shot forward as the arrow leaves the bow, and they both disappeared up the road in a cloud of dust.

"That man is the most remarkable character I have met in four years' active service," said a lieutenant of cavalry, as the party resumed their seats. "He and his mate—the man who scouted with him—attempted the most daring feat that I ever heard of."

As there appeared to be no business on hand at the moment the party urged the lieutenant to tell the story.

"I can't tell the thing as it was," said the young officer. "It was beyond description. One could only hold their breath and feel. It happened when our regiment was attached to Curtis's command, in the expedition down into Arkansas. One day we were in the advance, and began to feel the enemy, who appeared in greater strength than at any time before. We were all rather uneasy, for there were rumors that Kirby Smith had come up from Texas with all his force; and as we were only a strong reconnoitring party a fight just then might have been bad for us. We made a big noise with a light battery and stretched our cavalry out in the open and opposite to the rebel cavalry, who were drawn up in line of battle on the slope of the prairie about a thousand yards away. There we sat for half an hour, now and then banging at each, but both parties keeping pretty well their line of battle. They waited for us to pitch in. We were waiting until more of our infantry should come.

"It was getting to be stupid work, however, and we were all hoping something would turn up, when we noticed two men ride out from the centre of their line and move towards us. At the first instant we paid little heed to them, supposing it some act of rebel bravado, when we saw quite a commotion all along the enemy's front, and then they commenced firing at the two riders, and then their line was all enveloped with smoke, out of which horsemen dashed in pursuit. The two riders kept well together, coming straight for us. Then we knew they were trying to escape, and the Colonel deployed our company as skirmishers to assist them. There wasn't time to do much, although, as I watched the pursued and their pursuers and found the two men had halted at what I could now see was a deep wide ditch, the moments seemed to be hours; and when they turned I thought they were going to give themselves up. But no; in the face of that awful fire they deliberately turned back to get space for a good run at the ditch. This gave time for two of their pursuers to get within a few yards of them, when they stopped, evidently in doubt as to the meaning of this retrograde movement. But they did not remain long in doubt, for the two men turned again, and, with a shout, rushed for the ditch, and then we were near enough to see that they were Wild Bill and his mate. Bill's companion never reached the ditch. He and his horse must have been shot at the same time, for they went down together and did not rise again.

"Bill did not get a scratch. He spoke to Black Nell, the mare you saw just now, who knew as well as her master that there was life and death in that twenty feet of ditch, and that she must jump it; and at it she went with a big rush. I never saw a more magnificent sight. Bill gave the mare her head, and turning in his saddle fired twice, killing both of his pursuers, who were within a few lengths of him. They were out of their saddles like stones, just as Black Nell flew into the air and landed safely on our side of the ditch. In a moment both the daring scout and the brave mare were in our midst, while our men cheered and yelled like mad.

"We asked Bill why he ran such a risk, when he could have stolen into our lines during the night?

"'Oh,' said he, 'mate and I wanted to show them cussed rebs what a Union soldier could do. We've been with them now for more than a month, and heard nothing but brag. We thought we'd take it out of them. But'—and Bill looked across the greensward to where his companion still lay motionless—'if they have killed my mate they shall pay a big price for it.'

"Bill must have brought valuable information," continued the lieutenant, "for he was at once sent to the General, and in an hour we had changed position, and foiled a flank movement of the rebels."

I went to the hotel during the afternoon to keep the scout's appointment. The large room of the hotel in Springfield is perhaps the central point of attraction in the city. It fronted on the street, and served in several capacities. It was a sort of exchange for those who had nothing better to do than to go there. It was reception-room, parlor, and office; but its distinguished and most fascinating

characteristic was the bar, which occupied one entire end of
the apartment. Technically, the "bar" is the counter upon
which the polite official places his viands. Practically, the
bar is represented in the long rows of bottles, and cut-glass
decanters, and the glasses and goblets of all shapes and
sizes suited to the various liquors to be imbibed. What a
charming and artistic display it was of elongated transpar-
ent vessels containing every known drinking fluid, from
native Bourbon to imported Lacryma Christi!

The room, in its way, was a temple of art. All sorts of
pictures budded and blossomed and blushed from the walls.
Six penny portraits of the Presidents encoffined in pine-
wood frames; Mazeppa appeared in the four phases of his
celebrated one-horse act; while a lithograph of "Mary Ann"
smiled and simpered in spite of the stains of tobacco-juice
which had been unsparingly bestowed upon her originally
encarmined countenance. But the hanging committee of
this undersigned academy seemed to have been preju-
diced—as all hanging committees of good taste might well
be—in favor of *Harper's Weekly;* for the walls of the room
were covered with wood-cuts cut from that journal.
Portraits of noted generals and statesmen, knaves and
politicians, with bounteous illustrations of battles and
skirmishes, from Bull Run number one to Dinwiddie Court
House. And the simple-hearted comers and goers of
Springfield looked upon, wondered, and admired these
pictorial descriptions fully as much as if they had been the
masterpieces of a Yvon or Vernet.

A billiard-table, old and out of use, where caroms
seemed to have been made quite as often with lead as ivory
balls, stood in the centre of the room. A dozen chairs, filled
up the complement of the furniture. The appearance of the
party of men assembled there who sat with their slovenly
shod feet dangling over the arms of the chairs or hung
about the porch outside, was in perfect harmony with the

time and place. All of them religiously obeyed the two
before-mentioned characteristics of the people of the
city—their hair was long and tangled, and each man
fulfilled the most exalted requirement of laziness.

I was talking a mental inventory of all this when a cry
and murmur drew my attention to the outside of the house,
when I saw Wild Bill riding up the street at a swift gallop.
Arrived opposite the hotel, he swung his right arm around
with a circular motion. Black Nell instantly stopped and
dropped to the ground as if a cannon-ball had knocked life
out of her. Bill left her there stretched upon the ground, and
joined the group of observers on the porch.

"Black Nell hasn't forgot her old tricks," said one of
them.

"No," answered the scout. "God bless her! She is wiser
and truer than most men I know on. That mare will do any
thing for me. Won't you, Nelly?"

The mare winked affirmatively the only eye we could
see.

"Wise!" continued her master; "why, she knows more
than a judge. I'll bet the drinks for the party that she'll
walk up these steps and into the room and climb upon the
billiard-table and lie down."

The bet was taken at once, not because any one doubted the
capabilities of the mare, but there was excitement in the
thing without exercise.

Bill whistled a low tone. Nell instantly scrambled to her
feet, walked toward him, put her nose affectionately under
his arm, followed him into the room, and to my extreme
wonderment climbed upon the billiard-table to the extreme
astonishment of the table no doubt, for it groaned under
the weight of the four legged animal and several of those
who were simply bifurcated, and whom Nell permitted to sit
upon her. When she got down from the table, which was as
graceful a performance as might be expected under the

circumstances, Bill sprang upon her back, dashed through the high wide doorway, and at a single bound cleared the flight of steps and landed in the middle of the street. The scout then dismounted, snapped his riding-whip, and the noble beast bounded off down the street, rearing and plunging to her own intense satisfaction. A kindly-disposed individual who must have been a stranger, supposing the mare was running away, tried to catch her, when she stopped, and as if she resented his impertinence, let fly her heels at him and then quietly trotted to her stable.

"Black Nell has carried me along through many a tight place," said the scout, as we walked towards my quarters. "She trains easier than any animal I ever saw. That trick of dropping quick which you saw has saved my life time and again. When I have been out scouting on the prarer or in the woods I have come across parties of rebels, and have dropped out of sight in the tall grass before they saw us. One day a gang of rebs who had been hunting for me and thought they had my track, halted for half an hour within fifty yards of us. Nell laid as closc as a rabbit, and didn't even whisk her tail to keep the flies off, until the rebs moved off, supposing they were on the wrong scent. The mare will come at my whistle and foller me about just like a dog. She won't mind any one else, nor allow them to mount her, and will kick a harness and wagon all ter pieces if you try to hitch her in one. And she's right, Kernel," added Bill, with the enthusiasm of a true lover of horse sparkling in his eyes. "A hoss is too noble a beast to be degraded by such toggery. Harness mules and oxen, but give a hoss a chance ter run."

I had a curiosity, which was not an idle one, to hear what this man had to say about his duel with Tutt, and I asked him:

"Do you not regret killing Tutt? You surely do not like to kill men?"

"As ter killing men," he replied, "I never thought much about it. The most of the men I have killed it was one or t'other of us, and at sich times you don't stop to think; and what's the use after it's all over? As for Tutt, I had rather not have killed him, for I want ter settle down quiet here now. But thar's been hard feeling between us a long while. I wanted ter keep out of that fight; but he tried to degrade me, and I couldn't stand that, you know, for I am a fighting man, you know."

A cloud passed over the speaker's face for a moment as he continued: "And there was a cause of quarrel between us which people round here don't know about. One of us had to die; and the secret died with him."

"Why did you not wait to see if your ball had hit him? Why did you turn round so quickly?"

The scout fixed his gray eyes on mine, striking his leg with his riding-whip as he answered,

"I *knew* he was a dead man. I never miss a shot. I turned on the crowd because I was sure they would shoot me if they saw him fall."

"The people about here tell me you are a quiet, civil man. How is it you get into these fights?"

"D——d if I can tell," he replied with a puzzled look which at once gave place to a proud, defiant expression as he continued—"but you know a man must defend his honor."

"Yes," I admitted, with some hesitation, remembering that I was not in Boston but on the border, and that the code of honor and mode of redress differ slightly in the one place from those of the other.

One of the reasons for my desire to make the acquaintance of Wild Bill was to obtain from his own lips a true account of some of the adventures related to him. It was not an easy matter. It was hard to overcome the reticence which makes men who have lived the wild mountain life, and

which was one of his valuable qualifications as a scout.
Finally he said:

"I hardly know where to begin. Pretty near all these
stories are true. I was at it all the war. That affair of my
swimming the river took place on that long scout of mine
when I was with the rebels five months, when I was sent by
General Curtis to Price's army. Things had come pretty
close at that time, and it wasn't safe to go straight inter their
lines—"

I had heard enough and let my thoughts drift back over
the stories that Nichols had embellished so much in his article—I could hardly recognize them—but he had caught a
hint of the story for the duel between Dave Tutt and myself.
It wasn't so much the watch as it was Susannah Moore,
whom Tutt had been trying to talk into bed ever since I had
known him. As to killing his "mate," I had no idea where
that came from and I was certain that if Tutt was still alive,
he would have wondered what mate Nichols was talking
about as well.

As to the war—well, there were moments, and then there
were moments, but nothing like the stories Nichols claimed
he had heard. Yes, there had been nearly four weeks when
I was lost in the woods and sick after Israel's death, but that
was a private matter that I kept to myself. I had made the
long shot on a Confederate colonel that everyone said was
impossible and there was as much luck in that shot as skill
as I had held high over his head and hoped the bullet
would loop itself down at the right moment and it did. I
remembered the battle of Wilson's Creek, running supply
wagons from Rolla to Springfield with Lorenzo, fighting
at Pea Ridge in Arkansas with Curtis—where I had made
a lucky shot at a Confederate officer, knocking him into a
ditch, but it was not General Ben McCulloch, as everyone

claimed—among several other places. But there is a long
way between truth and the storyteller and—

I became aware of the silence in the saloon and glanced
around. The others were looking expectantly at me, grins
wide on their faces. I wondered what all Bob had read to
them, then knew I had to say something.

"If I ever talked like that, my father would have given me
a tongue-lashing that would peel paint off a fence," I said.

The others collapsed in peals of laughter, whooping and
hollering at my statement. I felt a dull red mounting to my
cheeks and shook my head. "And damn the man who can't
tell a stallion from a mare. Black's blind in one eye and she's
a he and—"

All of which made them laugh even harder. I gave up in
disgust and left, my ears burning from the lies of Nichols
and promising myself that I wouldn't go through another
episode with another writer as long as I lived. But once a
person has such a story written about him, he is no longer
the private person he wants to be; he has become a public
person, and the public does not care for the truth. The lies
are much more interesting to them and that article became
the springboard for hundreds of others until I couldn't recognize any resemblance to me at all.

In time, I became lost in that identity, the Scout of the
Plains, the killer of Indians and badmen. Charlemagne
would have been proud to have me as one of his paladins,
and in some of the stories I thought I recognized a vague
resemblance to those stories Father used to read to us on
cold wintry nights with the wind whistling outside and the
fire roaring up the chimney and sending warmth back into
the room. But any further chance at those days was gone
forever after Nichols's story came out. The rest of my life
was spent being the legend, not the man. But I had had
plenty of warning about that.

CHAPTER 37

F ORT RILEY stood upon the Kansas plain like a large keltoid scar while the land rolled gently in end-less brown waves away from it from horizon to horizon, no beginning, no ending, just countless miles in any direction one looked.

Black's hooves kicked up a fine sifting of dust as he moved down the road toward the fort. Although it had been a long ride from the Ozark hills, he still moved effort-lessly through the heavy heat that brought crinkly heat waves rising in the distance against the low hills. A thin trickle of sweat ran down my spine and my mouth felt like a wad of cotton had been stuffed in it. My eyes stung and my skin prickled beneath my blue shirt and the inside of my thighs felt chafed from rubbing so long against the saddle leather.

There had been no rush to leave Springfield, yet I felt the time had come after I lost the election for marshal. Strangely, I didn't seem to care as much as those who had supported me. They took it hard and threw dark looks at the gleeful celebrants the night the results were announced. A restless-ness had come over me in the past few weeks along with a certain infamy that hung over me as I moved along the Springfield streets after Nichols's article became familiar to the people. Boys dogged my footsteps, wooden pistols tucked into waistbands in emulation of me, adopting my walk as their own. Women tilted their heads and coquett-ishly batted eyes at me. I picked up many scented handker-chiefs dropped "accidentally" in front of me as their owners sashayed past me, balancing parasols over their shoulders. Men either sneered in derison or teased me relentlessly in saloons and cafés. Yet there were some who cast withering glances at me and spit when they spoke my name.

A normal life was no longer an option for me. At least, not in Springfield. And the easy money flung recklessly over the gambling halls by ex-soldiers frantically searching for a taste of the excitement they had known in the war began to dry up. When an offer came for me to return to working for the government, I seized it and left for Fort Riley, taking a roundabout way to pay a strained visit to Mother. But I didn't stay as long as I had planned. Resentment still ran high within each of us despite the four long years that had passed while I was in the war. Although Mary was a distant memory—I could scarce recall her name—Mother's meddling still rankled me, while she considered my anger unwarranted and became angry herself, a defense she had used all her life, even when she knew she was in the wrong. I left with a sour taste in my mouth and my guts churning, riding Black in the general direction of Fort Riley as I thought about the wire that had found me while I was working my way through the mellow stage of a bottle of Old Hickory.

The field officers at Fort Riley were going ragged trying to bring order to the post from the chaos that had engulfed it after the end of the war. When Captain R. B. Owen was appointed the assistant quartermaster at Fort Riley, he sent a wire to me in Springfield asking me if I would come and help out as a deputy U.S. marshal. The teamsters and soldiers were often at odds with each other, and fights were frequent and often deadly. The army had fallen into a deplorable state after the war, with several recruits enlisting for the sole purpose of being sent west, where they promptly deserted after stealing horses and mules from the army stables and corrals. The scouts did not help matters, either, by siding with the teamsters against the bullying of the soldiers.

I rode into the fort and noticed a teamster and soldier rolling in the dust behind the stables, cursing and striking wildly at each other. I paused for a moment, then shook my head and rode on until I found Owen's office. Wearily I dismounted and tied Black to a post, made a halfhearted effort to dust myself, then climbed the steps and entered the office, ducking my head as I crossed under the short doorway. I paused for a second to allow my eyes to adjust to the cool dim light inside, then found my hand being seized and heartily shaken by Owen.

"Bill! Damn, but if you aren't a sight for sore eyes!" he exclaimed, beaming at me.

I returned his grip and nodded. "Got your wire in Springfield and it just seemed like too good a chance to pass up," I declared. "You say you have a problem here?"

His face fell and he released my hand and moved behind his desk to his chair, motioning me to another across the desk from him. "Yes, a severe problem," he said. He gestured toward the window. "We are in danger of losing control of the fort unless something can be done quickly. We are losing horses and mules almost every day as someone deserts and takes them with him and I don't have enough troops to mount a regular provost marshal patrol. In fact," he added gloomily, "I don't know which soldiers are honest enough to put on such a patrol even if I had enough to go around."

"Uh-huh," I said, stretching until the kinks popped out of my back. "And you want me to do what, exactly?"

Owen made a face. "A bit of everything, I'm afraid. I've secured an appointment for you as a deputy U.S. marshal, but you will not report to Tom Osborne, the United States marshal for Kansas. For all practical purposes, you will report to me or the commander. Marshal Osborne is a bit upset about this, but"—he shrugged—"he hasn't been able to help us, either, being tied up with the rest of the state and all. No, we need someone for ourselves. We can also use your expertise as a scout." He grimaced. "Ours are a bit less than competent and I'm not certain if I would trust them to find water in a horse trough. Fact is, I planned on making you the chief of scouts. You will have total authority to do your job."

He slid the badge and my appointment across the table to me.

"We'll put you up in officers' quarters. That way, you'll have a bit of privacy and I think that will send a message to the others that change is coming. It might make your job a bit easier. But," he said, waggling a finger at me, "don't think that this is going to be a cakewalk. You are going to have one hard time bringing order here."

I yawned and slipped the badge and paper into my pocket. "Well, if it's all right with you, I'd like to get a bath and cleaned up a bit and Black taken care of before I start. I'd also like a meal. How about tomorrow?"

Owen shrugged and leaned back in his chair. "One more day won't make any difference. Fact is, I thought about sending you out after a couple of deserters who left sometime last night. They took nine good Arkansas mules with them as well."

"All right," I said, yawning again. My eyes felt sandy and at the moment all I really wanted was a bath and bed. "I'll get after them first thing in the morning. Black could use a rest, though. Okay if I take another mount?"

"Take what you want," he said magnanimously. "I'll have a pack ready for you by sunup."

"Sounds good," I said, standing. I shook his hand. "I'll help myself to a mount once I see your stock."

I left and winced as the hot sun blinded me for a moment. Black grunted disconsolately and I grinned at him and stepped down, untying him. "You old phony," I said, rubbing him between the eyes. "You'd grumble if you were the only stud in a field of mares and had a bait of oats at your beck and call."

Black shoved me with his nose. I laughed again and took his reins and walked him across the parade ground to the remount stables. A burly man wearing a dirty pair of faded red longhandles worked an anvil on a blacksmith's bench. Heat from the forge rolled out in an acrid wave. A sorrel stood hip-shot next to him, head drooping in the heat as it waited patiently to be shod. He glanced up at me, then at Black, and shook his head. He spit a long stream of tobacco juice and shifted his cud past rubbery lips to the other cheek.

"That there ain't no army horse," he proclaimed.

"Nope," I said. "He's mine." I started to lead him into the stables beyond, but the smithy dropped his hammer and stepped in front of me, placing a soot-blackened hand against my chest to stop me.

"You ain't listening. Ain't no horse but army horses coming in here," he said. Sweat stood out in huge drops upon his face and I could smell the sour odor he hadn't washed off in at least a week. "I gotta 'nough to do with these damn sojers bringing in their nags what with having to deal with another's. Take him on down to Junction City and stable him there."

"I'm working here," I said quietly.

His eyes ran rudely up and down; then he laughed and shook his head. "Don't look like it to me. What you workin' at?"

"Deputy U.S. marshal," I said quietly.

"Uh-huh," he said, and shook his head. "But that ain't makin' cotton with me. You think you bringing that nag in here, you're barking at a knot, sure as a skunk smells."

"Couldn't smell any worse than you," I said impatiently. "Now step aside—"

I could see the punch coming in his eyes before he had

time to draw back his fist. I twisted at the hips and threw a fist deep into his gut just above his belt buckle. He sucked in a gulp of air and the cud slipped down his gullet. His face turned a shade green as he sank to his knees and spewed a bile green and yellow mess onto the hard-packed dirt in front of the forge.

"Sorry," I said, "but I'm just too damn tired to waltz around with you." I fished the badge out of my pocket and held it down in front of his watering eyes. "Now you paste an eyeball on this and take real good care of Black here. Nobody else is to ride him, and if they want to know why, you tell them Marshal Hickok has said no. Understand?"

He nodded, and strangled noises came from his throat. He gagged again and turned his head. The cud of tobacco plopped in the middle of the mess in front of him. "Ain't Wild Bill?" he gasped.

I sighed. "There's some who call me that. Good as name as any, I suppose."

I led Black down to a stall at the end of the stable and unsaddled him. I found a brush and worked him down as he contented himself with a small bait of oats. When I left the stable an hour later, I saw word of my arrival had spread. Soldiers watched curiously as I made my way back across the parade ground to the officers' bathhouse.

An orderly silently took my saddlebags and bedroll and said he would take them down to my quarters. I had the third room. He had drawn a bath for me, but he was afraid the water had cooled some. I told him that was all right and he left, grateful that I hadn't made him heat up more.

I stripped and eased myself into the tub and relaxed as much as I could. But at twenty-eight I was at nearly six-three and around a hundred eighty pounds, and tubs on army posts weren't made that size. Still, I was grateful and slowly soaked away the knots of travel.

CHAPTER 38

I LEFT the post at false light, riding the sorrel the smithy had been shoeing and tugging a high-stepping mule behind me with a camp pack tied tightly with a diamond hitch. The smithy was all apologies for his conduct the day before and quick to make amends, his eyes straying constantly to the twin Colts at my waist. I read his concern and tried to make him feel at ease but knew my reputation made him wonder if I was sincere.

I swung a wide loop around the post until I found the trail of the two deserters and the nine mules. I smiled to myself at their confidence, as they had made no attempt to hide it, electing instead to ride steadily toward the southwest. I sighed and settled back in the saddle and pointed the sorrel down the trail after them. I let the horse make his own track. I had a suspicion that the deserters would change mounts quite a few times among the mules, electing to ride steadily for a day or more before making camp, wishing to put as many miles between them and the fort as possible. I had only the sorrel and, in a pinch, the mule and was outhorsed. But there's a funny thing about a man who thinks he's in the clear: He gets lazy, and I was counting on that happening, if not at the end of this day surely by the next or the one after that. The trick was not to wear my mounts out too early in case the deserters caught sight of me and made a run for it.

It took two days, and in the evening of the second I caught the flicker of a campfire tucked up in a stand of cottonwood trees on the banks of the Little Arkansas River. I reined in and tied the sorrel to a tree and settled down to wait for an hour or two.

When the half moon climbed up by the Dipper, I rose and made my way downstream. One of the mules caught my approach and snorted and I froze, my heart leaping; then I heard the twin snores coming from the blanket-wrapped forms curled around the embers of their fire. I shook my head; they were lucky a roving band of Indians hadn't come upon them. It was a misconception of most white men that Indians didn't fight at night. Something about their souls losing their way to the happy hunting grounds if they were killed in the dark. But that wasn't true; the happy hunting grounds didn't exist and most Indians had nothing against the cover of darkness.

I simply walked into the camp and dropped a couple of branches on the fire and waited until it flared up. Then I took a glowing branch and held it against the foot of one of the deserters. He yelped and came clawing up out of his blankets, grabbing his foot and howling as he rolled around on the ground.

The other sat up quickly, fumbling for his pistol, then froze as I stuck the barrel of one of the Navies between his eyes and rocked back the hammer.

"Uh-uh," I said quietly. "You don't want to do that."

"I don't want to do that," he parroted, his eyes crossed and staring hard down the shiny barrel.

I reached and took his pistol from him and stepped back. "Keep your hands in plain sight," I cautioned.

The other man was trying to blow on the bottom of his foot to cool it as he hopped down to the river. He fell on the clay bank and jabbed both feet in, puddling the burnt foot in the shallows to cool it. He sighed and looked back at me.

"What's the big idea?" he demanded, then saw the pistol in my hand, and his eyes widened. He raised his hands up to his shoulders. "Look, we ain't got much, mister, but you're welcome to it. Just leave us one mule, will you? It ain't civilized to leave a white man without a ride in hostile country."

"It's stupid for a white man to camp by a fire in hostile country, too," I said. "You should have had your dinner, then moved camp a few miles away. You're lucky to have your throat in one piece."

His hand automatically cupped his throat. "Who are you?"

"I'm Deputy U.S. Marshal James Butler Hickok and you two are under arrest for desertion and stealing army property," I said.

"Aw, shit," the other man said. "I told you we should've hid that trail. But no, you hadda ride on down. 'No one'll come after us,' you said. And now look at the mess we're in." He looked up at me. "Say, you wouldn't consider—"

"Nope," I said. "I wouldn't. Now let's just get ourselves ready to return to the fort, shall we?"

"It's the middle of the night!" the man with the burnt foot said.

"It is that," I answered. "And I want to put a little distance between us and this place just in case there's a hunting party of Indians out and about."

"I'll get my boots," he said, standing and wincing.

"Nope," I answered. "We'll just leave the two of you bootless. Be a lot easier on me if you have to think about it before you decide to take off."

"This—this—ain't no white man treat another like this!" he sputtered.

"Yes, they would. Especially in this situation. Now unhobble those mules and get up on one. Don't use a saddle. I want you riding bareback."

They looked at those mules with their sharp-ridged backs, and their shoulders slumped in dismay.

"Have a heart," the first man begged. "We go two miles

rubbing up and down on those spines and we'll have sores to gall a grizzly."

"And no thoughts of running, either," I answered. I motioned with the pistol. "Let's get moving. Now."

CHAPTER 39

WE TOOK four days to get back to Fort Riley. One day we had to lay up in a little wash while we waited on a Kiowa hunting party to work its way by us—not that there was much to hunt, but the Kiowa were a long way from their hunting grounds and probably figured they'd better keep an eye open for the Comanches, who took a dim view of trespassers in general and thought the whole world was their walking ground. I couldn't blame them; from what I had seen, the white man wasn't far behind in making his claim, either.

When we finally rode in through Fort Riley's gates, Captain Owen grinned from ear to ear as he ordered the two weary troopers to be taken to the guardhouse. He glanced up at me and said, "You look like you could use a wash and a rub from the inside out."

I scrubbed my hand over my chin, grimacing at the rasp of bristles, and said, "Well, I allow as to how you're probably right, but I think I'd just as soon have a bath and shave and sleep for a day or two."

Captain Owen shook his head. "Not that I'm begrudging you that, but we have General Sherman here, since you've been gone. He's putting together an expedition up north and needs someone to guide him. Someone who knows that country," he added.

I swore and sagged in the saddle, feeling the weight of the miles like a steel anvil upon my shoulders. I shook my head. "When?"

"You have about six hours, I'd suspect," Captain Owen said. "Of course, who knows with that Blood and Thunder? He gets a burr under his saddle, he'll be wanting to go."

"Uh-huh," I grunted, and turned my horse away, heading toward the stables. "Well, you tell him that if he wants me to scout for him, to head due north if he wants to leave before I'm ready. I'll pick him up. He won't get into any trouble in that short distance."

"Tell Sherman?" Captain Owen asked incredulously. "Might as well tell the wind to stop blowing. You'd better be ready when he's ready. He waits on no one."

"Then you'd better get Cody to scout," I called over my shoulder.

"Cody's not here, dammit!" he said, raising his voice. "And I wouldn't want to be the one to tell the general anything he might not want to hear! Men have been ruined for less than that!"

And so, six hours later, I found myself on Black's back, gritty-eyed but washed, and heading north up toward the Rock Creek country I had left so long ago, as we made our way up to Fort McPherson with a detachment, including Dr. William Finlaw and his family. Dr. Finlaw was scheduled to be the new post surgeon, and Sherman decided that rather than send a separate troop to accompany him to the fort, we'd just make a little detour and drop Dr. Finlaw and his family off at McPherson on the way. This was typical of Sherman, though; impetuous and impatient at all times, he somehow managed to temper that with a bit of common sense at the crucial moments that kept him mortal and human.

The third night out, I was sitting with Dick Curtis, another scout, by our campfire when a small girl appeared hesitantly at the edge of the fire.

"Hello," Curtis said. "What's your name?"

I looked up and noticed the little girl staring solemnly at me. I smiled at her and went on with cleaning my Navy Colt, figuring that she was just wandering around before bedtime like most kids do when they're bored but don't want to go to bed.

"Sally," she said timidly.

"That's a pretty name," Curtis said. "Your mommy and daddy know where you are?"

She didn't answer and I looked up to catch her nodding, still staring at me. Then I realized it was my hair, which had grown long and now hung over my shoulders. I smiled again at her and suddenly remembered that I had a stick of peppermint candy in one of my saddlebags.

"You like peppermint?" I asked.

Her eyes lit up and she nodded. I smiled and slipped the cylinder back onto its axle and snapped the barrel in place. I laid the revolver aside and wiped my hands on a bit of rag before pulling my saddlebags to me. I rummaged around for a bit, then found the sack and pulled it out. I was wrong; there were two sticks of peppermint left.

"You been holding out on me, Bill!" Curtis said accusingly. I grinned at him and held the candy out to the girl. Most of the dime dreadfuls made a big deal about the drinking habits of the scouts and westerners, but few ever said that most of those who lived on the plains and in the mountains had a sweet tooth and often had a piece of hard rock candy whenever they sat down with a glass of whiskey. I was no different. There were times when rolling around a piece of candy in the cheek made one feel better after a long hard day on the trail when one really didn't dare drink.

"Well, to tell you the truth, Dick, I totally forgot I had it, what with the hurrying up and everything before we left the post," I said. The little girl fastened her eyes upon the bag but hesitated until I shook it at her. "Go on—take it," I said. "Better you should have it than this old man and me."

Timidly she came forward and took the candy from my hand, then surprised me by reaching out to touch my hair.

"It's like silk," she said solemnly. "Like Momma's. Why do you wear it like that? My daddy doesn't."

Curtis started chuckling and reached over to pour himself another cup of coffee from the pot we had placed next to the fire's coals to keep warm. "Now let's hear you with that one, Wild Bill," he said.

She glanced over at Curtis. "Why does he call you Wild Bill?" she asked me.

I shrugged. "It's just a name someone stuck on me. My name's really Jim."

"My daddy told me about you," she said, turning to look at me with wide cornflower blue eyes. "Did you really kill all those men?"

Curtis coughed, but I refused to rise to his snorting and chuckling. I shook my head. "Well, I don't know about all because I don't know what your daddy told you," I said. "And it really isn't important. I just do the job that I'm supposed to do."

"But you have killed some bad people," she persisted.

"Yes, I have shot some bad people," I said. "To keep them from hurting others."

"I guess that's all right," she answered, then turned to look back into the dusk as her mother called her name.

"I think I'd better go now," she said. "Momma gets worried if I don't come when she calls."

I rose and dusted off the seat of my trousers and held out my hand, bowing courteously. "Well, Mistress Sally, would you like me to walk you back to your wagon?"

She giggled. "You're silly," she said, but she placed her hand in mine and together we crossed the camp to the ambulance where Dr. Finlaw and his family had made their beds. A twinge of regret came over me as I felt her tiny hand in mine and I had a strange premonition that I would never have any children or know the warmth of a family of my own. By the time we arrived at the Finlaws' cook fire, a lonely melancholy had settled over me.

"Hello, Mr. Hickok," Dr. Finlaw said when he saw the two of us. He glanced at Sally, still clinging to my hand and sucking on one of the peppermint sticks. "What have you got there, Sally?"

"Wild Bill gave it to me," she said. She looked up at me. "Isn't that right?"

"Yes," I said, "but you could do me a big favor by calling me Jim."

"I like Bill better," she said.

"And Mr. Hickok would be even better," her mother said, coming up to gather her. She nodded politely at me. "I hope Sally didn't bother you, Mr. Hickok."

I shook my head. I sensed her concern behind her politeness and knew she worried as any mother would if she found her child in the presence of a man who had blood on his hands.

"I enjoyed her company," I said politely. "I don't get a chance to talk with children much. It's a relief."

She quirked an eyebrow at that, then said, "Tell Mr. Hickok good night, Sally. It's bedtime."

"Good night, Mr. Hickok," she said dutifully.

"Good night, Sally," I said.

"Will you stay here with us?"

I raised my eyebrows at that and glanced at her father. He smiled faintly and gave a tiny nod.

"Sally has nightmares when we're out here like this," he said. "She's afraid the Indians will sneak her away." He made a gesture. "It's all those stories she's heard."

"I wouldn't be afraid if Mr. Hickok was here," she said.

"No Indian would want to come around someone named Wild Bill."

I smiled and went back to the fire I'd been sharing with Curtis and gathered my belongings and carried them back to the ambulance and spread out my bedroll under the wagon. I slept under that wagon for the rest of the trip, enjoying the time in the evening and early morning when Sally would stay close to me.

When we hit the Blue River, I took her bullfrogging in the sloughs and slipped and fell with a loud *ker-splash!* in the water when my foot rolled over a dead branch submerged in the shallows as I was reaching for a particularly large bullfrog. She laughed and laughed when I struggled up, a water lily hanging over my shoulder but still holding the squirming frog in one hand. I glared at him and said, "Well, you're one for the roasting pan!"

That set her off laughing until she had to hold her sides and sit on the bank. We caught a mess of bullfrogs and took them back to camp, where her mother rolled their legs in flour and fried them up for a fine supper.

All too soon, however, the trip came to an end and Sherman's expedition made its way up to Fort Kearney, where I scouted for some short patrols while Sherman debated about mounting a large expedition up into the Dakotas to chase the Sioux. I hoped the weather would start to change and hold him in the fort until spring. I knew what it was like being out on the prairie in winter and didn't relish trying to scout through drifts and spending my nights curled in blankets as close to a fire as possible, hoping my toes wouldn't be frozen by morning.

Common sense held Sherman out of the Dakotas, however, and he returned to Fort Riley. There I met Henry M. Stanley, who had come west as the correspondent of the *New York Herald*. We met in a saloon and I could tell right away that he was looking for stories and on impulse I spun him a few yarns, watching his eyes widen as he scribbled with a short pencil on a handful of papers he always carried in the pocket of his coat. Later I would remember that short pencil must have shortened his memory some, too, for when I read some of the dispatches he sent back to his paper I could scarce recognize the stories I had told him in the whoppers that emerged from those yellow pages. A careful check of records would have shown Stanley that I couldn't have been in two places at once, but those writers like Stanley are too impatient for that. They just want to see the story in print and find their pockets a little heavier with the jingle the stories bring.

While the army decided to settle in and began to winterize itself, I took advantage of the fall weather to make my way over to Kansas City for a last fling before the snow came. Market Square turned out to be quite a haven for others who were having their last fling as well. Buffalo hunters lounged around along with a lot of professional gamblers and some scouts like me. Wyatt Earp was there along with Luke Short, who liked to sit with me in the cool evenings, sharing a bottle or two while we discussed Shakespeare. I remember Short had a likening for *Henry V*, while I thought *Hamlet* was a better play. I was grateful that Dad had insisted we study Shakespeare and for the schooling I had, as, frankly, I took a better shine to Short than I did to some of the others who preferred to wrap their hands around bottles of whiskey and talk about what they'd left behind out west.

I also took to a new game I'd heard about but never seen—baseball. Kansas City had a team they called the Antelopes that played against other town teams on a field they'd made ready at Fourteenth and Oak streets. There was a great rivalry between the Antelopes and the Atchison Pomeroys, and when the Pomeroys came to town for a game a riot had evolved when the Pomeroys drove the umpire from the field, halting the game before either side had won. They decided to play the game again the next Saturday and this time find an umpire that couldn't be driven from the field.

I was sitting in Jake Fourcade's room at Fourth and Main, having a quiet game with Short, arguing about *Richard III,* when one of the city fathers came up and cleared his throat. I looked up and politely pushed my chair back from the table to hear what he had to say.

"Uh, Mr. Hickok, a couple of us have taken note that you've been coming to the Antelopes' games and . . ." He hesitated, swallowing nervously.

"Yes?" I said. "I hope that's all right. I'm kind of getting to like that game. Never saw it before."

"Yes, well, no," he stammered. "I mean, no, there's nothing wrong with that; it's just that— Look here, would you be willing to umpire a rematch with the Pomeroys next Saturday?" He fidgeted and sweat began to bead upon his forehead. "What I mean is, well, those rascals drove our umpire away just as we got up a couple of runs. We want someone that they won't drive away and will last until the game's over. It's a matter of pride," he said. "I mean honor."

"Well, Bill," Short laughed. "What would Richard do in a time like this?"

"I don't know," I said, "but I sure know Henry wouldn't run away."

He laughed again and pushed his chair back, tossing his cards into the middle of the table. He rose from the chair—he was short in more than just his name—and, placing his hand over his heart, gesturing like Booth with the other, declaimed:

> *"He which hath no stomach to this fight,*
> *Let him depart; his passport shall be made,*
> *And crowns for convoy put into his purse:*

We would not die in that man's company
That fears his fellowship to die with us.
This day is called the feast of Crispian:
He that outlives this day and comes safe home,
Will stand a tip-toe when this day is named.
And rouse him at the name of Crispian.
He that shall live this day, and see old age,
Will yearly on the vigil feast his neighbours,
And say, 'Tomorrow is Saint Crispian':
Then will he strip his sleeve and show his scars,
And say, 'These wounds I had on Crispian's day.'
Old men forget: yet all shall be forgot,
But he'll remember with advantages
What feats he did that day. Then shall our
*   names,*
Familiar in his mouth as household words,
Harry the King, Bedford and Exeter,
Warwick and Talbot, Salisbury and Gloucester,
Be in their flowing cups freshly remembered.
This story shall the good man teach his son;
And Crispin Crispian shall ne'er go by,
From this day to the ending of the world,
But we in it shall be remembered;
We few, we happy few, we band of brothers;
For he to-day that sheds his blood with me
Shall be my brother; be he ne'er so vile
This day shall gentle his condition:

"And gentlemen in England, now a-bed
Shall think themselves accursed they were not
*   here,*
And hold their manhoods cheap whiles any
*   speaks*
That fought with us upon Saint Crispian's day."

"Damn," someone muttered, "but that Short has a way with the words."

Short grinned and cocked an expectant eye at me. I rose and gave a mock bow, sweeping my hat off, and, holding it over my breast, said:

> "There's the respect
> That makes calamity of so long life;
> For who would bear the whips and scorns of
>   time,
> The oppressor's wrong, the proud man's
>   contumely,
> The pangs of deprized—"

"'Disprized,'" Short interrupted. "For Christ's sake, quote accurately."

"Shut up," I muttered, and continued:

> "The insolence of office, and the spurns
> That patient merit of the unworthy takes,
> When he himself might his quietus make
> With a bare bodkin? who would fardels bear,
> To grunt and sweat under a weary life,
> But that the dread of something after death,
> The undiscovered country from whose bourn
> No traveller returns, puzzles the will,
> And makes us rather bear those ills we have,
> Than fly to others that we know not of?
> Thus conscience doth make cowards of us all;
> And thus the native hue of resolution
> Is sicklied o'er with the pale cast of thought,
> And enterprises of great pith and moment
> With this regard their currents turn awry,
> And lose the name of action."

"Shit, Hickok ain't no slouch at those words, either," the same man said loudly as a smattering of applause followed the end of my speech.

"Not bad," Short said grudgingly. "I always wondered: What are 'fardels'?"

I started to give him the definition Father had drummed into us, but the man beside me cleared his throat. I looked down at him.

"Excuse me," he said. "That was well done and all, but, er, what, that is, will you umpire the game?"

"Yes," Short said, drawing himself up as much as he could—his head came bare to my shoulder and damn if he didn't remind me then of a cocky rooster. "That's just what Wild Bill's been saying."

"Jim," I muttered, but to no effect. "Dammit—"

"A man is nothing but his name," Short said. "And Jim does not fit well with your demeanor. Rather a Bill—nay, a Wild Bill art thou!"

"Oh hell," I said. "Yes, I'll umpire your game."

The man beamed and shook my hand enthusiastically, pumping my arm as if trying to draw water from a reluctant well.

And so it came that I found myself behind the home plate that Saturday, umpiring a game I knew little about. Not knowing what an umpire should wear, I had decked myself out in a silk hat, brocaded vest, calfskin boots, a velvet-collared frock coat, and a fine shirt with starched ruffle. I wore a red sash around my waist and placed in it a pair of ivory-handled Colt Navies that had been given to me by Senator Henry Wilson after I had guided his party on a short trip into the plains. I have to admit that I certainly made the best-looking umpire the Antelopes ever hired— Short's words, not mine.

The game started and soon it was apparent that the Antelopes were the better team, and they jumped out to a big 15–0 lead. That was when the Pomeroys decided to try me a bit. A big, broad-shouldered man with hands like a blacksmith's came up to bat. Shorty Anderson was pitching for the Antelopes and whizzed one by the plate.

"Strike!" I called.

The batter stepped back away from the plate and glared at me. "That was nowhere near the base!" he snapped.

Shorty noticed the batter's attention was on me and took the opportunity to whip another ball across the plate.

"Strike two!" I called.

"What the hell?" the batter yelled. "Goddammit, I wasn't ready!"

"That's your problem, not mine!" I said. Out of the corner of my eye, I saw Shorty winding up to heave another ball across the plate. "But if I were you, I'd keep my eye on that pitcher."

"You sonofabitch! We're being homered!" he yelled at his teammates. He waved one huge fist under my nose.

I didn't wait; I hauled off and punched him on the buzzer, knocking him backward. He staggered, trying to keep his feet, but one foot rolled over a bat and he sat down abruptly on the ground as Shorty pitched another ball over the plate.

"Strike three! You're out!" I called.

The Pomeroys started out onto the field, but I stepped in front of the plate and hooked my hands around my pistols and stared at them.

"Something wrong with the call?" I asked innocently.

A couple started forward but were jerked back by their teammates. I glanced at the batter as he struggled to his feet, blood streaming down his nose.

"No, no," he mumbled. "Guess I should've been paying attention to the game."

He went back to his teammates as the Antelopes jogged

in to take their place batting. The game proceeded without a hitch to the end, and the Antelopes won, 48–28, and Short appeared with a carriage to give me a ride back to Market Square. People cheered as we rode slowly down the streets. It was one of my finest moments.

CHAPTER 40

A LL THINGS come to an end, however, and I had to make my way back to Fort Riley. I found the fort a changed place in the month I'd been gone. A new regiment of cavalry was being formed—the Seventh—with a new commander: Lieutenant Colonel George Armstrong Custer, who persisted in wearing the brevet rank of general he'd been given during the war. He was a colorful sort who appealed to me, wearing his blond hair nearly as long as I did (although I could tell his was thinning faster than mine on top), and had a liking for fringed buckskin coats with his general's stars sewn on the shoulders and a flashy red silk scarf around his neck.

But it was his wife, Elizabeth, that drew my attention more. Her eyes seemed to follow me around the room whenever I was in it, making me feel a bit hot and uncomfortable from the frank intensity of her stare. I hoped Custer wouldn't notice it, and as far as I know, he never did. But whenever his attention drifted, I found her standing close to me so that a feather would barely have been able to fit between us. She wore a cinnamon scent that seemed to roll up from her shoulders and high breasts, and there were times when I'd leave their home and make my way to the saloon to drink away the stirrings that she rose in me.

I spent most of my time, however, down in the Solomon River valley, which was a favorite hangout for the riffraff that were trying to strip the fort of its horses. Cody came to join me at the fort, and together we made a big dent in the thieves that had taken to settling in shanties and soddies in that valley.

But Cody couldn't be with me all the time and there came a time—December 22 in '67, I remember—when I found myself at a crossroads saloon somewhere in Jefferson County up in Nebraska. I had been following the trail of some horse thieves and the night came down cold with a hint of snow to it, so I decided to wait out the night in the saloon rather than get caught in a snowstorm along the trail.

It was a sad, evilly run place with barrels and stoned planks serving as a bar. Whiskey was drawn from a keg, the bartender ignoring the few dusty bottles that stood on a short plank table behind the bar. The walls were earth bricks and the chairs were old wooden boxes that were gathered around a potbellied stove at the back of the room.

Heads turned to look at me when I walked through the door. The hackles rose on the back of my neck as I recognized the unfriendliness of the herders who had made their way, like me, to the saloon to wait out the storm. For a moment I thought I didn't know anyone in that place and almost turned and left, but then I thought, *The hell with it.* The room was warm and I could keep my back against a wall. Then I saw Seth Beeber, Jack Slater, Frank Dowder, and Jack Harkness—four cusses who were friends of a couple of men I had taken to Fort Riley for stealing horses.

"Well, well," Beeber said when I stepped up to the bar, elbowing my way to the end to put the wall at my back. "Would you all look who came in?"

"Hickok," Slater answered. His ferret eyes stared unblinking at me. "Thought I heard you'd lost your fine hair down at Sandy Creek."

"You heard wrong," I said. I motioned to the bartender, who drew a glass of whiskey and placed it silently in front of me. I tasted it and my throat tried to close against the trickle going down. I frowned and said to the bartender, "What'd you do? Throw in a couple plugs of tobacco and some rattlesnake heads?" I pushed the glass away from me and pointed to the dusty bottles on the table. "Let's try one of those—unless it came from the same barrel."

"Cost is two bits more," he said. His teeth were blackened stumps in his mouth.

"And a clean glass," I said, noticing the rim of dirt around the one I'd just sipped from.

"What's the matter, Hickok?" Dowder sneered. "You don't want to drink with us?"

"No," I said frankly. "I'm particular about who I drink with."

I took the drink the bartender poured from one of the bottles and had started to raise it to my lips when Harkness suddenly reached out and gave me a shove. The whiskey splattered into my face. I dropped the glass and backhanded him across the face, splitting his lip, knocking him back and away from me.

"Better stop this before it gets serious," I said.

"Bastard!" Harkness yelped, and tugged at his gun. The other three went for their pistols at the same time. I flipped one of the Navies out and shot Harkness in the jaw. Beeber's bullet struck me in the right shoulder, staggering me. Two other bullets fanned the air where I'd been. I slipped the second pistol out with my left hand and fired rapidly. My first shot took Beeber in the head, snapping his head back. My second ripped a hole in Slater's throat. Dowder fired hurriedly and missed and I took the moment to put my bullet in the middle of his face. I glanced down at Harkness, but the fight had left him, as he gurgled and bawled, holding his shattered jaw in both hands.

I felt blood dripping down my shoulder and looked at the room, suddenly aware that I was vulnerable. A man rose from one of the tables and came over to me. I looked at him carefully and he pulled back his coattails to show he was unarmed.

"I helped doctors during the war," he said. "You want, I'll see to your shoulder." I followed him to a back room where he stripped the shirt back from my shoulder. The bullet had gone clean through and he clucked to himself as he took a clean towel and poured a generous dollop of whiskey on it.

"Lucky," he said. "I thought I might have to dig it out, and I ain't got no probe to be carving down in your shoulder with. It might have been messy."

He clapped that towel on my shoulder and I let out a yelp as the raw whiskey burnt into my shoulder, and wondered how much luckier I could have been. But he was a good man and I was lucky to find one in that place at that time.

But I've always been lucky in that respect. Whenever I've needed someone, I've had someone around to give me a hand. Lady Luck, however, is a fickle lady, and sometimes one can press her too much. But I was young and foolish then, and life seemed to be better when I pushed my luck. And I took great satisfaction when Lady Luck stayed with me through one narrow scrape after another and men would wag their heads in admiration and swear up and down that I had the luck of the angels riding with me and cast jealous glances in my direction. I didn't realize at the time that I was building a reputation that would make too many men jealous and wanting the same reputation for themselves and figure that going through me would be a shortcut to the reputation that they wanted. When I was older, I tried to explain that to a writing fellow once, but he wouldn't do the story I wanted because it didn't have the color that he thought people wanted to read. The truth never does and truth is an unwelcome bedfellow for the young.

I think the best example of Lady Luck probably came the time that Jack Harvey and I were making our way back to Fort Hays after we'd been sent out on a scout by Custer. About thirty miles west of Hays, we found a man who had stumbled across a band of Indians and had been cut and gashed and scalped. He was almost done with this life and looking into the darkness waiting for him, but he told us that he and five others had been attacked by a party of Indians numbering roughly fifteen. The men had split up, hoping to draw the Indians away from one another and hoping that the Indians would chase one or two for their sport and game, but the Indians came after him, then went after the others. He remembered hearing their screams; then he took one last deep breath and let it out in a wheezy gasp and died.

"Reckon it'd be best if we didn't stick around and bury him, Bill," Harvey said. I glanced up, irritated a bit, knowing that Harvey had a dim regard for life in general, but I saw that he was staring back along the trail that we had just left. I rose and looked over his shoulder at a dusty cloud rising and swore.

"I think I know what that is," Harvey said pointlessly. "And I don't really feel like tying into numbers that would raise a cloud like that."

"I agree," I said, and caught Black up by the reins, mounting. Harvey threw a leg over the buckskin he was riding and we made our way down to a small gully cutting south of where we had found the man. We reined up and crept up to peek over the rim of the gully to see what the Indians decided to do. I noticed that fresh scalps hung from the manes of their horses and figured they remembered that they had left that man alive and had come back for some more fun. Then one big fellow noticed our shod tracks leading away from the man's body, and he yelped something at the others and pointed in our general direction.

"Shit," Harvey muttered, and scuttled back away from the lip of the gully and leaped on his buckskin. He didn't wait to see if I was following him—truth be told, I wouldn't have waited for Harvey, either; common sense dictated the other would be following—but galloped away, bending low over his horse's back as the Indians came along the lip of the gully, trying to get close enough to shoot down upon us.

"At the next bend, turn around and shoot!" I hollered at Harvey as Black came up behind him.

"Fuck that!" Harvey shouted, bending lower.

"We need to stop them a bit somehow if we're to get out of this!" I yelled.

Harvey swore again, then whipped up his rifle as we thundered around the bend in the gully. I pulled my pistols from my belt and clamped Black's reins in my teeth. The Indians came recklessly around the bend after us and we opened fire, dropping two of them. I don't know who hit them and don't care. It was enough that two fell, as the Indians turned away and ran back to regroup and rethink their possibilities.

Harvey and I decided to leave them to their thinking and turned and galloped back on down that gully and Lady Luck was with us, as it widened out into a sandy bed of a dry river. We left the gully and took a wide detour around a stand of willows, heading toward Fort Hays. About that time, however, I reckon that big Indian managed to convince the others that only two horses had made the tracks they were chasing and here they came, yipping and yelping along our trail, hell-bent on having a bit more fun with a couple of white men.

"You got any more ideas, now would sure be a good time to use one!" Harvey yelled.

I glanced over my shoulder; the Indians were gaining on us and I could feel Black beginning to labor between my legs. I glanced at Harvey's buckskin and saw the foam-flecked sides and knew he wasn't going to be good for much longer. Then I remembered something I'd read during the war when Custer had said he always rode to the sound of the guns and that the best defense was an offense. When in doubt, charge.

"All right!" I shouted. Harvey gave me a quizzical look. "When I say, 'Now!' wheel that horse around and we'll charge them!"

Harvey's look turned to skepticism, then certainty that I was mad. "What? Are you out of your goddamned mind? We're a bit outnumbered here!"

"And our horses aren't going to last to the post at this pace!" I said. A reckless grin pulled at my lips. "So what have we got to lose?"

He shook his head and swore a long and blue streak, but his right hand plucked a Colt Army from its holster over his pommel.

"Let's do it, then, before common sense takes over!"

"Now!" I shouted, and wheeled Black hard to the left. The buckskin grunted and followed, and I let out a large yell and clamped my heels to Black's sides.

He gave a loud snort, his head came up, and I felt him reach down inside himself for that extra bit as we charged directly back at the Indians. I slipped the reins between my teeth and pulled my Colts and began shooting as rapidly as I could thumb the hammers. Beside me, Harvey's big Army boomed continuously.

A big hole appeared in the chest of the big Indian leading the others and his face took on a surprised look as he tumbled backward off his pony. The other Indians slowed, staring at us in wild surprise; then as one they wheeled their ponies and beat a hasty retreat. Another one threw up his arms and fell off his pony, bounced twice, then lay still, but no one turned to pick him up.

I pulled Black in and sat, breathing deeply, as Harvey came up beside me, gasping. His buckskin hung his head, sides heaving. Harvey glanced over at me.

"You are one lucky sumbitch," he said. He slammed the Army back into its scabbard. "But you're madder than a bee-stung wolf! Sometimes I think you gotta foot in heaven and hell and friends in both places!"

We made it back to Fort Hays without any problem.

CHAPTER 41

THE 1867 winter closed tightly over the prairies, and General Hancock, who'd been sent out to bring the Indian "troubles" to a close, was called back east to take up duties more suitable for his stodgy mind, and this time the army sent Major General Phil Sheridan out to take charge of the campaign against the "savages." But the army never gave Sheridan additional troops. He was still outnumbered roughly six-to-one. But Sheridan realized that he needed to compensate for his inferiority in numbers by setting up an intelligence system, and for that he relied upon his scouts.

When July came, the Indians broke out of their territory, the Cheyennes slipping away from their reservation near Fort Dodge and immediately cutting a large swath, murdering the settlers around the Council Grove area. Large bands of Comanche and Kiowa heard about their sudden success and slipped away to join them. Soon the valleys of the Saline, the Solomon, and the Republican had a gray haze from burning homesteads hanging over them.

Sheridan sent columns out in pursuit, but the Indians managed to give them a slip. The days slipped into weeks and the weeks into autumn, and only then did the attacks upon the settlers and ambushes upon patrols began to slacken. Sheridan then decided upon a winter campaign. Although the scouts tried to tell him that a winter campaign was a big mistake, Sheridan was adamant, as he was certain the soldier was better equipped than an Indian. He sent one column under Custer to strike at the Cheyenne villages along the Washita while another under Colonel A. W. Evans would come up from Fort Bascom. General Eugene Carr would lead a third column out from Fort Lyon in eastern Colorado. The plan was to push the Indians into a center somewhere and crush them, somewhere around the headwaters of the Red River. I was sent to the Fifth Cavalry at Fort Lyon and spent late autumn riding dispatch back and forth from Carr to Sheridan at Fort Hays.

Not long after I arrived at Fort Lyon, Carr sent me out on a lone scout to the north to see if rumors about Cheyenne raiding parties were true. I came across a burnt wagon on the grassy bank of Kiowa Creek with dead bodies lying naked and mutilated in splashes of blood. I could tell from the tracks that a large band of Indians had come through and that the tracks were fresh. Figuring that the Indians might be flush from their victory and a bit careless, I rode to Gomerville, fifty miles southeast of Denver, to get some volunteers to help me track down the band.

Gomerville was a small town that sprang up around a sawmill that had been built along a creek. Most of the men there knew someone or a family that had been killed by the recent marauding Indians, so I had little trouble in getting volunteers to ride with me. With thirty-four men, I rode rapidly to the area between Kiowa Creek and the Republican River, but the Indians seemed to have vanished into thin air.

For eight days we scouted that territory; then on the ninth we rode to a high table mesa near Sand Creek to use as a vantage point. That was a big mistake. The plain below us was covered with Cheyenne and no sooner did we appear on the top of the mesa than we were spotted.

"Jesus Christ!" Bob Anderson breathed as he saw all the Indians below us. There must have been nearly a thousand. "I think we're a bit outnumbered, Bill!"

"Jim," I said automatically. "Yessir, I'd say that we were. In fact, I think it would be best all around if we left just as quickly—"

"Bill!"

I craned my head and looked over at Johnny O'Dell, a young rancher. He was staring back at the trail we'd used to come up onto the mesa.

"I don't think you're gonna like this! I sure as hell don't!"

I nudged Black and rode back and looked down: A war party had come around the mesa and cut off our retreat. I shook my head. "Well, boys, I'd say we'd best get to work. All of you get something to dig with and start making a big hollow all around here. It's sandy enough that we should be able to get a good barricade up fast."

"I don't know," O'Dell said doubtfully. He squinted up at the sky. "There's a good two, three hours of daylight left. That's enough time for those reddies to make a couple of charges."

"Get to digging!" I snapped. I wheeled around. "Tom Riley, Bill Garrison, you two unlimber your rifles and keep those Indians down as much as possible. Remember that they have to come up the hill, so you have to lower your sights a bit. Aim for the horses. That'll slow them down some."

No sooner were the words out of my mouth than a small band of young warriors charged up the side of the mesa toward us. I slipped a Henry out of my saddle and stepped down from Black. Fred Gomer took the reins and led Black to the rear as I knelt behind a sandstone and began firing. I dropped two Indians from their horses before Riley and Garrison joined me. The next volley killed three more, and the others turned abruptly and rode back down to join their elders, sitting on horses and watching the rashness of youth.

The next three hours seemed to crawl by as the three of us moved from one side of the mesa to the other, shooting down to keep the Indians away while the others dug furiously to shelter the horses and men. At last, the sun began to slide down the horizon and I pulled the others together for a quick meeting.

"We have to face facts," I said. "We can't hold out here indefinitely. Someone's going to have to ride for help."

Garrison shook his head and looked down at the milling Indians. "I'd say anyone who tries that is bent for certain upon suicide. He might get through, but there's a better chance up here than down there. Who knows? They might get tired and go off and leave us. I've heard about that happening."

"True," I said, "but that happened where the defenders had food and plenty of water. We've got some food that we can ration out, but all the water is what we brought up here with us in our canteens. And I don't know if we have enough ammunition to hold out for any length of time." I pointed down at the Indians. "And don't think those Indians haven't got an idea what they're up against. They have a pretty good idea about our problem just as we do."

"So," Riley said, "who's going to go?"

They glanced around at each other, refusing to make eye contact. I gave a deep sigh. "Well then, I'll go. Black's had a bit of rest and he should be able to show those Indian ponies his heels."

"Ain't gonna say I wish you weren't going, Bill," Garrison said, shaking his head, "but I'm grateful that you're willing to give it a shot. I don't think much of your chances, though."

"Well," I said, straightening. "If I don't make it, one of you will have to try next. And another after him."

I walked over to Black and took my canteen from my saddle. I filled my hat full and let him drink, then smoothed the blanket under the saddle and tightened the cinch. Black's ears perked and I knew he knew that something grand was going to happen. He grumbled happily, deep in his throat.

"All right, old boy," I whispered, patting his neck and running my hand down his nose. "You're gonna have to fly like the wind. I hope you're ready."

He tossed his head and mouthed the bit as I climbed into the saddle. The sun had dropped full below the horizon and blue twilight was coming like a dark blanket over the land as I eased off the top of the mesa and began to walk Black down the steep side. Keeping a Navy in one hand, I let him pick his own way. I hoped we'd get down to the flats before being spotted. That'd give us a little more edge than coming at a gallop down the side of the mesa onto the flatland.

And Lady Luck was with us. We managed to get a couple hundred yards across the flats before an Indian spotted us. He gave a loud cry, and I put a bullet in his chest as I kicked Black hard in the ribs. Black screamed and charged forward. I heard an arrow sing past my ear and saw flashes of gunfire in the darkness. An Indian appeared in front of us, but Black hit him with his shoulder, spinning him away. Another tried to run his pony into us, but the pony was no match for Black. I fired at the gun flashes near us and ignored those that winked a short distance away. Suddenly I sensed we were beyond them. I held the reins in my teeth as I replaced the cylinder on the Navy with a fresh one and holstered it. Then I bent low over Black's neck and urged him on.

We had about fifty miles to go and I don't remember ever

watching the moon skate so slowly over the night sky. But then we were in Gomerville and I was yelling for relief riders. About twenty-five saddled up, but when I tried to exchange Black for another horse, none were to be had. I patted his neck and gave him a hard look in his one good eye.

"You'll have to do it, boy," I said. "I don't like doing this, but we have no choice!" Black tossed his head again and nickered.

I mounted and led the men back toward the mesa. We rode hard, as I wanted to get back while night still hung over us so the Indians wouldn't see how small a party we were. It was a hard ride, even harder going back than coming, but it was still dark when we charged down upon the Indians, hollering for all we were worth, shooting everywhere. The Indians didn't bother making a stand but rode away from the valley as fast as they could go.

When we rode up to the top of the mesa, a quick glance told me no one had been killed. I swung down from Black as Garrison grabbed my hand and pumped it.

"Goddamn, Bill! I didn't think you could make it!"

I glanced at Black, legs trembling from the strain of the past hours, head hanging low. I could hear him gasping for air and loosened the saddle to give him all the slack he needed. But I knew that ride would have been too much for any horse, even Black. I shook my head and patted him along the neck, feeling tears spring to my eyes. Garrison moved up beside me and ran his hand down Black's back.

"I'm sorry as hell about your horse, Bill," he said. "Windbroke, ain't he?"

I nodded, unable to speak.

"Well," Garrison said, "he's got a place in my home pasture and barn for as long as he lives. I promise you that. It's the least we could do."

So, thirty-four men were saved, but I lost Black, the best

horse I've ever owned. I rode back there a few years later
and Black was still alive, his muzzle gray now, but he recognized me and came up and nuzzled me and it was all I
could do then to keep from crying like a baby.

Not long after that, I made my last ride for the army. I didn't
know it at the time, of course, but it all happened when Cody
and I found a bull train loaded with Mexican beer winding
its way along an old trail. Cody and I watched that train for
a couple of hours, then decided that it would be better if we
took that train to the boys who most needed it: Carr and his
troops, camped south along Turkey Creek from Fort Evans.

It didn't take much, just a bunch of hollering and shooting over their heads, to convince those Mexicans that they
were set upon by bandits and raiders. They turned and ran
back south, heading for the Rio Grande, leaving Cody and
myself in command of the beer train.

We took that beer back to Carr's command and, well, we
made a little profit selling it in pint cups to those boys. Of
course, it didn't take long before tempers started flaring here
and there, and Cody and myself weren't helping matters
along any, having sampled the beer along the way back to
make certain it didn't "turn" on us.

Carr decided that Cody and I were a bad influence and
set us to riding dispatch again. I was sent to Fort Wallace
and made the whole trip without a hitch. I was returning to
Fort Lyon when I saw a buffalo grazing near Sand Creek.
Feeling a bit peckish, I dropped him and carved out a steak
to broil over a driftwood fire on a gravel bar in the creek bed.
I had just finished when suddenly seven Cheyenne warriors
appeared on the bank above the stream and charged down
toward me, shout and yelling as if the devil were at their
hindmost.

I had no time to make it to cover but drew my revolvers

and managed to drop four of them before one of the three remaining managed to get close enough to throw his lance into my right hip. I put a bullet in his head as I fell to the ground, spoiling the aim of the other two braves, who overshot me. As they wheeled their horses, I took advantage of the stationary targets and dropped them with a ball each.

I was sorely hurt, though. I tied up the wound as best I could, then started to ride back toward Fort Lyon. Every step that horse took jolted me so that I swore a thousand bees were taking a bite out of the raw edges of that wound. I'm not certain what happened finally, but I managed to come upon a small band of woodcutters not far from the fort but fell out of the saddle before they could help me.

I woke up in the fort's hospital with Cody sitting on a rough-hewn stool beside me. He grinned and held out a bottle of whiskey when he saw I was awake.

"Well, Bill, for a moment there, we all thought you were cashing in," he said. I took a small sip of whiskey and started hacking and coughing as it burnt its way down my throat. I gestured toward a cup of water and Cody held it while I drank thirstily.

"Tell you the truth," I said after opening my throat up with water, "I was certain about that, too."

Cody's eyes traveled to the lance I'd brought back with me. "Looks like a Dog Soldier's lance," he said. "How many were there?"

"Seven."

"And how many did you account for?"

"Seven."

He shook his head. "You're a regular hell on wheels, aren't you?" He took another drink from the bottle and smacked his lips. His pale blue eyes were as shiny as new-minted dollars. "What you going to do with that lance?"

"You want it?" I asked, reaching for the bottle of whiskey. I took a cautious sip and held my breath as it slid down my throat.

His eyes lit up. "You mean it?"

"It's yours. Just make certain that I have enough whiskey to get through this."

"It's a deal," he promised.

And he was as good as his word. But my hip refused to respond to treatment and became infected despite everything the army surgeon tried. At last, I decided I'd go home to recuperate and that spring found myself back in Troy Grove, where my sisters and mother spoiled me with cookies and pie and cake. But the wound became even more infected, and finally we had to call in the doctor from town to open the wound up again and scrape the bone.

After that, I healed rapidly and soon the old familiar restlessness came upon me again. When fall came, I bade everyone good-bye and made my way back to Fort Hays, thinking I'd pick up scouting again. But when I arrived, I found Hays City had grown into a bunch of saloons and dance halls with gaudily dressed women cavorting around in paint and ribbons among the board shanties and tents and false-fronted buildings. Hays set right on the old Santa Fe Trail, and long trains of canvas-topped freight wagons made their way up that trail from New Mexico on a regular basis, carrying trade goods, and Fort Hays had grown to include nearly two thousand soldiers, including the Seventh Cavalry.

Brawls were daily and numerous, and with the east–west railroad coming through, the town was booming and law was an afterthought. The day belonged to those who could take it.

CHAPTER 42

THE DOG days of August. And the day had been no exception to the rule—hot and muggy—sweat running in streams off a person who was hoping for night when surely it would be cooler but it wasn't and the dust hung like a brown curtain in the air that turned to muddy runnels when someone walked through the droplets that seemed to be hanging in the air and gathering granules like iron filings to a magnet and music bounced like leaden notes around the darkness off wooden storefronts and posts and windowpanes until it all seemed to merge into a jackannery of noise—

"Bill!"

I sighed and tossed my cards into the deadwood on the table. I took my hat off, pulled a handkerchief from an inside pocket of my coat, and mopped the perspiration from my forehead. I looked disgustedly at the brown tinge left on my handkerchief, folded it, and replaced it in my pocket.

"What is it?" I asked.

Jess Bowden stood just inside the doorway, gasping for air, pointing frantically behind him. "Mulvey and some of his cronies got John Lee treed."

I shook my head tiredly, then rose from the table and made my way out of the saloon. I stood for a moment, letting my eyes adjust to the brightness while the sun beat down hard on me, setting my temples to pounding like a blacksmith's hammer on an anvil. The sun took the drench right out of a man and I felt the whiskey I had drunk while playing cards begin to churn in my stomach. I glanced down the street to where Bill Mulvey and some cowboys down on their luck had hoisted John Lee up in the air with a rope around his chest. They had thrown the other end over a rafter beam and tied it to a hitching post. They passed a bottle back and forth. One would take a drink, then step forward and slam a fist against John Lee.

I drew a deep slow breath, checked the ivory-handled .36 caliber Colt Navy pistols in their holsters, and started down toward them, my boot heels echoing hollowly on the board-walk.

Mulvey saw me coming and stepped aside, lips peeling back from blackened teeth. He slipped a pistol from his holster and held it low by his side. "Well, well. Hickok. Wondered when you'd get down here."

I nodded at John Lee. "Cut him down, Mulvey."

His eyes narrowed. He took a long, deliberate drink from the bottle and tossed it to one of the others. He wiped his hand on his dirty shirt. "Uh-uh. Don't think so." His eyes went flat. "All we wanted was a bit of credit so we could get some supplies."

"That's why people have jobs," I said. "A man's reputation gets him credit. You can't expect something to be given to a nobody who can't even hold a job swamping out a saloon's spittoons."

I watched his eyes grow wide; then the dull liver red flush came suddenly into his face.

"Damn you—" he said thickly, and I flipped the pistols out of their holsters and fired. The bullets struck him in the belly. The pistol flew from his hand as he fell backward to the ground. For a brief moment he looked stunned; then the pain hit him and he screamed and clutched his belly and tried to press the pain away.

I looked at the others staring openmouthed at my pistols. "Well?" I asked softly.

The one holding the whiskey bottle swallowed with difficulty. "We was only funnin'," he said.

"Cut him down," I said. "I don't want to tell you again."

He nodded and pulled a knife from his pocket.

"Doctor! Help!" gasped Mulvey. "Christ! The pain! Ahh!"

The cowboy stepped over Mulvey and, hand shaking, cut the rope holding John Lee from where it was anchored to the hitching post. John Lee fell in a heap on the boardwalk.

The cowboy looked uncertainly at me, wet his lips, and glanced at Mulvey. His face turned dirty white under the grime and tan.

"Now what?" he asked.

"How fast can you run?" I asked.

"What?"

"I said"—thumbing the hammer back—"how fast can you run?"

You never saw the like of it in all your born days. The bottle fell from his hand, and before it hit the ground the cowboy and his friends were high-stepping it down the street, legging it for all they were worth toward the Hays City limits as if the hounds from hell were chomping on their heels, saliva dripping bloodily from their great jaws, sweat sluicing off their bodies and running in rivulets to muddy the street, horse apples flying behind the heels of their booted feet.

"Damn you, Hickok! You've . . . killed me!" Mulvey said from between teeth gritted against the pain.

I looked down at him as he gave a last terrified scream, eyes bulging in terror as they looked down the long, dark path into the abyss.

And I heard the running feet of the righteous coming down the street toward us.

"Migawd!" someone said in an awed voice.

I slipped the Colts back into their holsters. I pointed at Mulvey and ordered he be taken to Halloran's Funeral Parlor and John Lee to Doc Adams's office. I started to walk toward the jail and the crowd parted like the sea spreading before Moses.

"God, ain't he the cold one?" someone muttered.

But I ignored them all, forcing myself to walk nonchalantly to the jail. I opened the door and stepped in, shutting the door firmly behind me. Then I ran down the corridor to the back door letting out to the alley and barely made it before my gorge rose mightily and I vomited the leavings of my lunch and the whiskey I had drunk into the silted dust of the alley where none but a battered one-eyed cat could see the loss of dignity and the clay feet of the knight-errant that reminded him constantly that he was, after all, only a man.

For a while I thought that killing Mulvey would be the last of it, that word would spread and others would avoid me. Word spread, all right, but it had the opposite effect; it brought others to me, trying to be the one that took down Wild Bill Hickok. Always, though, I ruefully remembered the woods and Israel and Helen Caroline Ernst's words or the words that came from the vision she had woven magically around me and knew instinctively even while I hoped otherwise, that those who came to me were being brought to me for killing, as a sacrifice, if you will, to the god who would allow others to live on land fought for by others like those I would kill who did not want to give up what they had earned—not even for civilization, for it was a rebellion against civilization that had sent them out to the West in the first place. And now they were being told that they were no longer wanted: Move farther west, mister gunmanpathfinderhuntermountainmanadventurer, for the frontier is a frontier only briefly, a mere grain upon the sandy beach of time, and there is no longer any room for you here.

But I knew that it was for those who came after that I had been sent for and it was for them that I would fight even though my fighting would eventually mark even me as one who had to be banished in order for civilization to continue to grow. That is the make of humanity; it uses the people it needs for the moment, then discards them upon the refuse pile of time.

There wasn't much to Hays City, Kansas, although the city was growing rapidly. Buffalo hunters, skinners, hide pullers—all those connected with buffalo hunting used it as a place to sell the hides they had taken from butchered bison. Gamblers, pimps, and prostitutes began to flock to Hays City as well as did the soldiers who were stationed a mile away at Fort Hays. I read in the paper once where I told a reporter that "there was no Sunday west of Junction City, no law west of Hays City, and no God west of Carson City." But I don't remember ever saying anything like that and I didn't know the reporter from Adam.

Hays City was filled with mule whackers and stores filled with everything that would appeal to a man's pocketbook on payday. There was the huge Othero and Sellars warehouse that employed only Mexicans in its freighting business. North and South Main streets flanked the railroad track from Chestnut to about one-half of a block west of Fort Street. North Main held the Capless and Ryan Outfitting Store, Leavenworth Restaurant, Hound Saloon & Faro House, Hound Kelly's Saloon, the justice of the peace's office, M. E. Joyce, Tommy Drum's Saloon, Kate Coffee's Saloon, Mose Water's Saloon, R. W. Evans's Grocery Store and Post Office, Cohen's Clothing, the Perry Hotel, M. J. R. Treat's Candy and Peanut Stand, Cy Godard's Saloon & Dance Hall, and on the far corner "Nigger" White's barbershop. There were several places where the soiled doves roosted and stood on balconies, displaying their charms in their scanties, calling boldly down to riders.

Not long after I killed Mulvey, I was having a game in Tommy Drum's place when Jim Curry, an Irish locomotive engineer, saw me sitting with my back against the wall and stormed up to the table, waving a pistol, claiming he was going to shoot me. For a moment I thought I was going to have to draw on him, but Tommy Drum started dancing around us, jabbering about how this wasn't right and for Jim to put up his gun and that he'd buy champagne all around. I swear he looked just like an excited rooster prancing in a hen yard, and I burst out laughing. Jim goggled at my laughter, then glanced at Drum and started laughing as well and put up his gun, mumbling something about how Ida May wasn't worth it.

I knew then that Ida hadn't been the clean catch I had thought she was when I took her to my bed, and resolved then and there that I would be a bit more careful with another's charms in the future. I also knew grimly that I had better be in constant practice, for there would be some like Jim Curry who wouldn't want to kill me for the sake of a spurned love; there would be some who would be looking for the reputation that came with killing someone who had already killed another.

In September, Samuel Strawhun came to town, spoiling for trouble. I sighed when I saw him ride into town, knowing that we would be locking horns before long. I had known him in Ellsworth, where I had been living with Indian Annie. The sheriff, E. W. Kingsbury, had needed a bit of help one day when Strawhun and his cronies got drunk and tried to tree the town. We took their guns away and, since there were more than the jail could hold, tied them to a stock corral until they sobered up. The trouble was that some sobered up faster than others, but we didn't dare let one loose until all were sober enough to be let loose, for fear that the one untied would find a way to free the others who would still be drunk enough to want to finish the job they had set their minds to doing.

I was standing next to John Bittles when Strawhun rode into town. I heard John sigh and turned to look at him.

He shook his head and spit into the dust of the street. "Sam Strawhun. I knew things were too good to last."

"You know him?" I asked, surprised at his statement.

"Yeah," he said disgustedly. "I know him. Everyone in

Hays knows him. He tried to take on A. B. Webster at the post office when A.B. told him that the vigilance committee had his name on the short list. He and a Weiss fellow went into the post office and banged around A.B. and then tried to kill him. But old A.B. isn't to be reckoned that way, you know. He managed to get to his pistol and put a pellet in Weiss's belly down low where it could do the most damage. Strawhun ran away and left Weiss on the floor. He's no damn good and as yellow as the day is long. Watch your back, Bill," John said warningly. "He won't come at you head-on unless he has a couple of boys with him. But he will lay for you."

"I'll remember that," I promised, and walked on down the street to where Strawhun had ridden in front of Odenfeld's Saloon on Fort Street. Strawhun had just swung down from his saddle and was tying his horse to the post in front of the saloon.

"Strawhun," I called.

He ducked under his horse's neck and peeped over the saddle at my approach. His brown eyes blinked nervously, shifting back and forth like a cornered lizard. He stepped out and around his horse, keeping his hands well away from his pistol.

"Hickok," he said. "I wondered where you had run to."

"Run? Why, you two-bit snake rustler, who ever had to run from you? Run?" I shook my head and planted my feet. He suddenly looked unhappy, shifting back and forth in his boots, badly scuffed and run-down at the heels. One pocket of his shirt, which had obviously been a stranger to the washboard since he bought it or stole it from a clothesline, had been partly ripped off. His pants bagged at the knees. "You've got iron. Settle your problem now."

His glance darted around at the curious on the boardwalk, a cowboy sitting on his pony in the street, warily watching the two of us. Strawhun tried to laugh, but it came out shrill, like a schoolgirl goosed by the class bully.

"Sure. Right. And which of these good folks would come to help you?" he sneered.

I stepped toward him. He backed away so rapidly that he ran into his horse. Startled, the horse lashed out with its left hoof, catching Strawhun in the buttocks, lifting him in the air, and throwing him forward. He landed *whumpp!* on his belly, his face slapping forward into a fresh pile of horse apples. He rolled over, gasping for air. I stepped forward and slipped his pistol from its holster.

"I'll leave this with the bartender in Odenfeld's, you sorry-assed cat—" I held my tongue, for I sensed ladies around, but Strawhun caught my drift. I could see it in his eyes, glittering mad, but he lacked the sand to do anything about the madness within him. "You can stay two days. One to wash the trail dust off, if you ever do"—I backed a step away from the stench lifting off him—"and another day to get yourself supplied. But then you got three options: hit the trail, take the train east or west, or go north." I nodded in the general direction of the cemetery. "That's it, Strawhun. Two days. No more."

I left him in the street dust and walked into Odenfeld's and handed his pistol—a Beals .36 caliber Remington that had seen much better days; its hammer looked like it had opened more than one can of beans—to Jackson, the bartender, with instructions to return it unloaded to Strawhun once he was certain that he was leaving town.

I should have been a bit more cautious, but I was too mad for horse sense, as Father used to claim I lacked. He was right; I have found Father to have grown wiser over the past twenty-some years. In fact, he seems to grow wiser each day—

Two days later, Strawhun and a couple of men he had

befriended—hide hunters down on their luck—tried to clean out Odenfeld's Saloon. I suppose they meant to rob it as well, but Jackson sent the swamper out the back door to get me when he saw which way the stick was floating.

Glasses were flying out of the saloon as Rattlesnake Pete Lanihan, my deputy, and I came close to the saloon. I stopped and picked up a couple and handed them to Pete. "Watch yourself," I said softly, then stepped into the saloon about 1:00 p.m. and found one of the hide hunters standing in the middle of the floor, his face flushed with drink, weaving back and forth, his pistol swinging recklessly in his hand. Strawhun leaned against the bar, watching hungrily, his eyes glittering. I glanced around quickly, noticing the rest of the bar huddled behind the stove at my left, poised, ready to duck left or right if the hide hunter started shooting.

"Drop the pistol," I said loudly. He swung toward me, epithets falling foully from his lips. "Drop the pistol. Now."

He squinted, trying to make out who had the nerve to say anything to him. I stepped forward as he hesitated, caught his pistol by the barrel, and twisted it in his hand. His finger caught in the trigger guard and popped like a dry stick in winter. He screamed and staggered away, clutching his hand, the broken finger pointing crazily away at a right angle.

I nodded at Pete, who stepped to the bar with the glasses in his hand and placed them on top of the bar. I laughed and said, "Boys, you shouldn't treat a poor old man this way. Glasses are expensive."

"I'll throw them out again, if I want," Strawhun said.

I watched him out of the corner of my eye as I studied the other hide hunter. "Then they'll carry you out of here, Strawhun. I told you to leave in two days. Your time's up. Walk out, climb on your horse, and leave."

The other hide hunter raised his hands belt level, pulling his dirty coat aside to show me he hadn't a handgun. But I noticed his Sharps rifle leaning behind him against the bar. I heard a noise and I glanced over at Strawhun. He had stepped away from the bar, starting to draw his pistol, but froze in an awkward pose, his prominent Adam's apple swallowing with difficulty.

"Well," I said softly. I smiled at him and saw him cringe inwardly. A wild glee rose in me, then an icy calm. "You're halfway there, boy. You want to travel the rest of the way north?"

He wanted to give it a try—everyone in the saloon could see how hard he wanted to try—but he was about a quart low on nerve.

"Pull it or back off," I said. "I've got more to do than stand here jawing with a pig-sucking scum like you."

He shook his head and wet his lips nervously. "I don't go against a stacked deck." He glanced over his shoulder at Jackson, who raised his hands and moved down the bar, away from the action.

"Don't take no account of me," he said. "You're on your own."

I stood, silently waiting for Strawhun. I watched as he began to tremble.

"Who else is going to back you, Hickok?" he whined, trying for bravery, but everyone saw his fear. Someone chuckled and Strawhun's face turned dull red beneath the dirt and scraggly beard covering his weak chin. "Say something, damn you!"

I remained quiet, letting the silence build up between us. The room stayed quiet except for that one snicker. A light drift of cigar smoke wisped between us and the room began to narrow down to one thin shaft of light as I focused on his face. For an instant I smelled the sour odor of his fear; then his hand started moving. I flipped my right Colt Navy out of its holster, firing as it came level. The .36 caliber bullet struck him in the forehead. His head snapped back, suddenly becoming too heavy for his scrawny neck. He fell backward, dead.

"No!" Pete shouted. I turned to see the other hide hunter starting to lift his rifle, but he had forgotten Pete, who stepped forward and laid his pistol alongside the hide hunter's head. His eyes rolled for a minute; then he crumbled into the sawdust on the floor, out cold. I took a deep breath, smelling the acrid smoke left from my shot. *Brimstone, an old friend*—

"Good work," I said to Pete. I pointed at the hide hunter, who cradled his hand, whimpering from the pain of his broken finger. "You. Come here." For a moment he looked as if he was going to refuse; then he stumbled forward. I took a knife from his belt and pointed at his partner. "Drag him down to the jail."

"My hand—" he began, but I cut him off.

"That isn't a request," I said, tossing his pistol to Pete. He caught it deftly and held it down by his side, thumb ready on the hammer.

"Yes, sir," the hide hunter mumbled, and bent, grabbing his partner's leg with his uninjured hand, tucking it under his armpit. He leaned away from the weight, dragging the hide hunter toward the door.

I glanced over at the crowd. "Would a couple of you gentlemen mind dragging that man down to the undertaker's?"

Four men stepped forward and quietly bent to lift Strawhun from the floor. Outside, I heard the hide hunter's head *thunk-thunk* down the two steps to the street. Silence deepened; then Jackson stepped to the middle of the bar and announced the saloon was buying the next round. Slowly the others crossed to the bar, giving me a wide berth. I sighed and walked to the door, knowing that two killings in two months was going to draw criticism from some and hoping that the vigilance committee would back me against the angry voices that would soon be raised.

I stepped into the middle of the street and looked up at the stars. Suddenly I thought of Nichols's story and realized the grim fascination that as funny as we had taken it at the time, it was my death warrant. There would be others beside Strawhun who would be coming to town to make trouble, hoping to become famous through a shortcut.

I turned and walked heavily toward the jail, feeling a black depression begin to drop over me like a shroud.

I didn't have long to wait. The next night, a shot buzzed past my ear like an angry hornet as I made my rounds. I crouched, my pistols suddenly in my hand, as I faced the alley. I heard heavy footsteps pounding the dust. I straightened slowly, realizing what had happened. I looked down at the pistols in my hand, remembering the strange encounter I had during the war, the warning of the strange visitors. I sighed and carefully placed my Colt Navy pistols away.

I took to avoiding strong lights and dark alleys. I made my rounds down the center of the street. When I had to enter a saloon, I pushed the doors hard against the wall to make certain no one waited to catch me unaware. I always stepped in to the right or left, varying it at whim so no one could predict my movements upon entering, sliding along the wall so no one could get to my back. People noticed the change in my behavior, but there was a certain respect in their glances my way.

The good reverend tried to raise enough holy disgust at the two killings, but A. B. Webster and the others on the committee refused to listen to him. At one time, A.B. told the reverend—*Ticklor? Yes, Ticklor*—to mind his own flock and let the townsfolk herd their own sheep. Wolves were more common there than in the reverend's square building at the end of town.

But my time, I realized, was limited, as more and more

problems came my way from Fort Hays. I had taken a warrant to the commander at the time, Colonel George Gibson, to take Bob Conners, who had murdered a drover near Pond City and was arrested by Deputy U.S. Marshal Jack Bridges and deposited in the stockade, to Topeka for trial. But Gibson refused to release Conners to me, claiming that I wasn't duly appointed by the governor.

The real reason, however, was that I had posted the town off-limits to the soldiers until Gibson decided to run a bit of discipline on the troopers, who had a history of raging through the town on payday. Finally tired of warning the soldiers to behave themselves, I tossed a couple of them in jail and held them over for trial. Gibson tried to take them out under his authority as commander of the fort. But I declined to release them to him, and when his adjutant tried to push his way into the jail I calmly told him that he could join them if he wished.

This made Gibson angry, and cooperation between the fort and the town fathers became lost in the shuffle. Grudgingly, however, Gibson issued orders to his men that they would serve time in the post guardhouse if they caused any trouble in town. This stopped the partying troopers in their tracks for a while, but it was an uneasy solution to the problem and I was very unpopular with the soldiers for quite a while.

My unpopularity didn't lift when General George Custer came to the post as commander, although George and I got along better than one would expect. George was intent upon making a name for himself with the papers back east and had no intention of letting the soldiers mar his reputation with a bit of drunken behavior.

It was his wife, Elizabeth, however, who intrigued me more, and that brought on more trouble from George's brother, Tom, who fawned over Elizabeth—Tom and George called her "Libby," but I always referred to her as Mrs.

Custer when we were in company and later as Elizabeth whenever she came to town to shop, accompanying her whenever she took a ride out in the prairie.

I remember the day I met her at Fort Hays, riding my sorrel to the post after I figured the Custers had settled in to introduce myself, although George and I had known each other for years. I had worked briefly with George as a scout in '67. I didn't think George would remember me, but he did. That was one thing about George: He was quick about remembering people, because he never knew when they might be able to push his legend along a bit a ways down the line.

The day was bright and sunny and my sorrel had been groomed until his hide shone like polished leather. He was well fit from a good diet of oats and trim as I rode him out to Big Creek every day to practice with my pistols. Fort Hays had been at the mouth of North Fork of Big Creek where Smoky Hill Trail crossed the stream, but when the railroad came in the fort was moved fourteen miles up Big Creek. I no longer wore my buckskins, having traded them in for a Prince Albert coat and checkered pants, and had discarded my holsters—save for when I rode out on the prairie and was going to be gone for a while—for a red sash, as I could feel the pistols always that way and they came more readily to hand when I had to draw them than they did from the deep holsters. I always wore a broad-brimmed hat to keep the sun from my eyes.

This day, however, I planned on riding on out in the prairie to visit some homesteaders after my call at the post. I wore top boots, riding breeches, and a dark blue flannel shirt with a scarlet set in front to match the scarlet neckerchief that trailed down the side of my neck and chest. The sorrel was feeling his oats and pranced in a huff when I rode him to the Custers' home and dismounted.

Tom Custer opened the door when I knocked on it. His

eyes widened slightly, then narrowed when I introduced myself again to him. Although George (his wife and friends called him Autie, but I could never for the life of me figure that one out) was always polite and never drank a drop of liquor, Tom was quite a randabout who got drunk quite frequently—a dangerous time, because there wasn't an ounce of fear in Tom and a man like that who got drunk could be a handful for anyone. I didn't know it, but a streak of cruelty ran in him, too, for a few weeks later I arrested him when he got drunk and rode his horse into a saloon in emulation of me in that damn Nichols's story and tried to make the horse climb up on the pool table. When the horse wouldn't, Tom pulled his pistol out and shot it, saying, "That'll teach the dumb son of a bitch!"

"It's the lawman from Hays: Hickok," he said over his shoulder.

A murmur came from within and he stepped grudgingly aside and motioned for me to enter. I removed my hat and stepped over the threshold and came face-to-face with a beautiful woman, realizing almost too late that it was George's wife. She had glossy auburn hair, gray eyes, and a waist I could easily span with two hands. Her eyes widened and a faint scent of lilacs came from her. I found later she wore lilac scent in the company of her husband, jasmine at other times—

"My sister-in-law; Mrs. Custer," Tom said sourly from my shoulder.

"Ma'am," I said, and made a small bow. She presented her hand and her eyes widened in surprise when I gently kissed it.

"My, a gentleman here, of all places!" she exclaimed, a lovely rosy flush touching her high cheekbones.

"I think he's here to see Autie," Tom said quietly.

"Of course," Elizabeth said, but her eyes held mine boldly, commanding. "Whatever would he be doing here otherwise?" I caught a glimpse of mischief in her smile at me; then what I came to call her political mask dropped over her face.

"Marshal Hickok?" a voice called from the other room.

I nodded at Elizabeth and stepped cautiously around her, conscious suddenly of her breasts pushing against her bodice. "Excuse me, ma'am," I said politely.

As I walked in his office George rose, extending his hand to me. I took it, remarking silently to myself on the strength of his grip. A self-assured mantle seemed draped over his shoulders and I recalled the stories I had heard about the boy general during the war who had fearlessly thrown his men into battle against the Confederates but also about his uncanny sense of attack that had him emerge victorious at every encounter.

"James, isn't it?" he said, catching me off-guard for a moment. I had been called "Bill" so long that my given name seemed foreign to my ears. Then I nodded and smiled back at him, feeling myself leaning toward the bright aura that seemed to be sparking from him. His golden hair lay as long as mine across his shoulders. He wore a bright red scarf at his throat and his uniform was freshly pressed. I had heard stories that he bathed every day, as I did—a fact that had started a new enterprise in Hays, as others had taken to following my example.

"General," I said, noting that he accepted the title as if he had been permanently posted in that rank and did not carry it as a brevet only—an honor that he clung to from the war even though he was technically only a lieutenant colonel commanding the Seventh Cavalry.

The room was a monument to his successes, souvenirs of battle hanging on the wall: a tattered Rebel guidon, Indian pipes, hatchets, a quilled breast guard, bows and arrows in deerskin quivers, photos of himself—he was a bit vain in that regard—and rifles. His dogs raised their heads at my entrance, eyeing me questioningly. One thumped its tail a few times on the floor and the others took this as a sign of good intent and went back to sleep in front of the small fire burning cheerfully in the fireplace.

"What can I do for you? Is this a formal visit?" he asked, motioning me to a chair. He offered a cigar, which I refused, and I noticed that he closed the humidor firmly before Tom's hand could reach into it.

"No, informal," I said easily, holding my hat in my hand. "I'd like your assurance that we won't have any repeat misbehavior of soldiers in Hays." His eyes narrowed and I hastened to add, "We've had a few unfortunate problems in the past with troopers getting drunk on payday and trying to force their, ah, attentions on some of the wives and daughters. Your predecessor gave us a bit of trouble with this, and I'm trying to stop any trouble before it gets a chance to start."

"You've got to expect some blowing off of steam," Tom said, butting into our conversation. I caught a hint of anger in his voice and turned to meet his stare.

"I'm not saying that they can't come into town," I began, but he interrupted.

"Yes, I'm certain of that. Hays makes quite a haul from the army payroll, doesn't it?"

I felt my shoulders stiffen with a sudden awareness of the animal anger beginning to seep from him. A challenge seemed to flicker from his eyes to mine and I nodded slowly.

"Very well," I said softly. "Have it your way." I stood, still looking at Tom but feeling George's annoyance behind me. "But anyone who causes trouble in Hays will visit my jail. Anyone," I repeated for emphasis. "Officer, enlisted man, hired help—I don't care. *And* they'll face charges in town, not here."

"You have no authority," Tom started, but this time I interrupted.

"I'm wearing my authority," I said.

His eyes dropped to my chest, but I was not wearing a badge. A puzzled look started to form in his eyes and I tapped the ivory handles of my Colts, drawing his attention to them. His face tightened with anger.

"That's enough, Captain," George said from behind me. The formality of his tone brought Tom to stiff attention. His eyes stared off into the distance, anger still sparking from them, but the rigorous discipline of the soldier held him in check.

"Marshal," George said authoritatively, and I turned to face him. "I thank you for your concern, and rest assured that punishment will be double that which you mete out in town for any who behave dishonorably. I will see to that personally," he added, staring hard at Tom. He was displeased with his brother's behavior, but he was a fellow officer *and* his brother and I knew that there would be exceptions made.

I made my thanks and took my leave. Outside, I found Elizabeth dressed in riding clothes, wearing a campaign hat over her auburn curls, a feminine copy of her husband's coat tailored to emphasize her breasts. She was mounted on a pretty sorrel mare.

"Marshal," she said warmly as I emerged from Custer's quarters. "Would you mind accompanying me on my morning ride?"

"I'll get my horse," Tom said brusquely from behind me. Her eyes flashed at him and then her husband's voice called for him from inside. He stared furiously at me for a long moment, then reentered the quarters, closing the door behind him.

"Be happy to," I said, untying the sorrel. I swung easily into the saddle and stared down at her. A flush began to climb the white column of her throat. She laughed throatily, and together we rode through the gate onto the prairie, following the creek south away from the fort.

A week later, the Seventh Cavalry took to the field and Elizabeth came to town, finding me in my office where I was filling out overdue paperwork. I looked up as she entered, wearing a pearl gray satin dress, her hair gathered at the back and falling in careful curls to her shoulders. She wore a tiny gray hat with a black band perched on her head. Her eyes were wide, and tiny lights glimmered from them.

I rose and said, "May I help you, Mrs. Custer?"

"Mrs. Custer?" She laughed. "Why don't you call me Libby? Everyone does."

"Then," I said gallantly, "I shall call you Elizabeth. I don't wish to be everyone."

An eyebrow arched as she studied me carefully. "Very gallant," she murmured. She pronounced it *"ga-lant"* and I felt a smile forming.

"Easy when I'm in the presence of a charming *woman,*" I said. For a moment I almost said "lady" but changed my mind, emphasizing the latter.

"I have heard about you, Wild Bill," she said. I winced and she smiled a bit wickedly. "Yes, I heard my husband call you James. But Elizabeth deserves her Wild Bill." She took a deep breath as she spoke, and I motioned to a chair.

"Would you like to sit, Elizabeth?" I asked.

"No," she answered. "I think I would like to go for a drive. Would you mind accompanying me?"

"What about your brother-in-law?" I asked pointedly. "I understand he is your usual escort."

"My brother-in-law is a bit too enamored of me," she said matter-of-factly. "And he is out in the field with my husband. I'm alone."

Her eyes met mine with a studied frankness and I felt her magnetism deep inside me. I stepped around the desk and started to take my hat, but she came past me, shutting the door firmly. Then she turned and moved close to me, her arms slipping around my neck, pulling me down and kissing me firmly, pointedly.

I caught my breath and stood awkwardly, frozen by the suddenness of her action. She leaned back away from me and said breathlessly, "But there will be no complications, Wild Bill. None, do you understand? I will not leave Autie and we will be *very* discreet. There will be no scandal. Autie will be president someday and I will not permit anything to keep that from happening."

"But—" I started.

She laughed softly. "I know about his . . . liaisons," she said. "The weeks that he's been away—what soldier's wife doesn't expect that? He writes every day, but I can tell when he's been unfaithful. His letters have a certain regret about them, the words feel a bit ashamed when I read them, and I know."

"And that makes a difference?" I asked.

She shrugged and I felt her breasts move against my chest. "Of course it does," she said. "A woman is no different from a man." Her eyes darkened and I read the anger in their depths. "I am a woman, not an icon, despite what everyone tries to make of me. You know that. I can tell, so don't deny it. A woman has the same needs as a man. And I have no intention of—" But I bent and kissed her, shutting away further words that I did not want to know. Confession may be good for the soul, but not for embarking lovers. There must remain a mystery. And there remained a mystery between Elizabeth and myself, although given her wild abandon in bed, I wondered at Custer's willingness to chance losing her for the sake of a momentary fling. But Custer's arrogance would not let him think for a moment that he wasn't always in full command of every situation surrounding him. That would eventually be his downfall.

Tom, however, quickly sensed something was happening

between Elizabeth and myself. I caught his glare whenever he rode into town or business took me to the fort. A couple of times, he pressed deliberately close to me, a challenge that most men would not ignore. But I kept away from him as much as possible. His attention to Elizabeth, however, forced us to be only that much more discreet in our affair and to take extra pains to keep it so secret that George and everyone else had not the slightest hint of Elizabeth's infidelities.

"Bill?" Elizabeth Custer asked. I turned, looking at her.

"Yes?"

She smiled at me, her generous lips curving up into twin dimples. Her eyes danced mischievously. "You look good today," she began. I looked automatically into the mirror she had hanging beside the door where Custer could check himself before stepping out into the fort where his admiring public waited. I did look good, I thought, studying my reflection: long blond hair brushed carefully, just touching my shoulders, a small-fringed buckskin jacket over a bright blue shirt that matched my blue-gray eyes, sash with my old army belt buckled over it and twin holsters that I wore when I went out scouting hanging on each side, the Navy Colts butt forward. A bowie knife nestled behind the left holster. I glanced on down at the leather trousers and Wellington boots I had brushed before coming to meet Custer at his quarters.

"You're another Narcissus," she said accusingly.

I flushed, recognizing how she had set me up by appealing to my vanity. And I was vain then. I knew it and wasn't bothered by it until someone brought it to my attention. Like Elizabeth. Or Bill Cody, who had been teasing me since I'd met him when he was a boy riding for the Pony Express. That had been a long time ago and many bottles of whiskey.

"The other day you called me 'Orpheus' when I was sawing away at my fiddle at the Officers' Dance," I said, smiling over at her.

"Ball." She grinned. "It was the Officers' Ball. You never did get that right, did you?"

"A dance is a dance, whatever you want to call it," I said, shrugging. I looked in the mirror again. Maybe I was a touch narcissistic, but what the hell? I looked damn good. Not as good as I looked in my marshaling outfit: cutaway coat, flowered vest, ruffled white shirt, salt-and-pepper trousers, string tie, high-heeled boots, and a broad-brimmed hat to keep the midnight sun out of my eyes. I wore the same outfit when I went to New York to meet Cody at the Brevoort Hotel. The damn cabdriver tried to charge me five dollars for a two-dollar fare and threatened to take three dollars out of my hide when I wouldn't pay the extortion. I left him on his back in the gutter.

"I guess it is at that," she laughed. She glanced around to see if her husband could see us, then stepped close, pressed her perky breasts against me, and gave me such a deep kiss that I thought I was going to pass out for lack of air.

I came up swimmingly just as Custer entered the room. Fortunately, Elizabeth had pulled away and was reknotting my red scarf around my neck. He grinned and crossed, kissing her on the back of her neck.

"Just can't resist mothering everyone, can you?" he said.

She smiled and gave him a quick kiss that wives long married give their husbands to bid them good-bye. "You men always need someone to look after you," she said. She pulled his shirt collar out from under his jacket. "I never saw a man who could take care of himself. You all need a woman around."

She glanced at me and gave me a wicked grin. "Right, Bill?"

I felt my face growing hot, remembering the last time

we'd been together while her husband was out on patrol with
Buffalo Chips White as his scout instead of me. Custer was
a lucky man; Elizabeth was quite gifted in bed.

Elizabeth Custer answered when I knocked on the door to
Custer's quarters. I took a step backward, unmanned to a
degree by the force of her presence. Her round breasts
pushed against the dress she had chosen that resembled an
officer's uniform on top but then swept down into the generous curve of her hips before falling to the floor.

"Yes?" she asked. "What is it, Bill?"

I pulled my hat from my head and said, "I was told to
report to General Custer as soon as I arrived," I said.

A faint smile touched her lips. "Well, he isn't here. He
rode out this morning with Buffalo Chips. I understand he's
going to be gone for a couple of weeks on patrol with White
and Tom."

She meant Custer's brother Tom, who had been a pain in
my side ever since coming to Fort Hays. There was something between the two of us that just rubbed each of us raw.
I nodded and said, "Well, ma'am, if you'd be so kind, just
tell him that I stopped by as he asked."

"Excuse me, Mr. Hickok, but I'm forgetting my manners.
Won't you come in?" She stepped back into the house,
swinging the door wide before I could refuse. I glanced
around; nobody seemed to be paying us any particular attention, so I took a deep breath and stepped inside. She shut
the door behind me and came around in front, taking my
hat and hanging it on the hat rack.

"It's almost dinnertime and I'm dining alone," she said.
"Won't you join me?"

"Well, Elizabeth, I'm afraid I haven't had a chance to
bathe yet—"

"Nonsense, Bill, you are quite all right. But if it's a quick wash that you want"—she gestured toward the back—"you'll find a washroom at the rear."

"Thank you, ma'am," I said. I was splashing water on my face before I realized that she had taken control of the entire situation, assuming that refusal was not an option that I had. I grinned sourly at my reflection in the mirror. Why was it that women always try to take control? The hell with it. I slipped out the back and hotfooted it over to the post barber and bribed the boy to heat up some water for a quick bath.

I couldn't have been gone more than twenty minutes, but in that time the table had been set, the meal placed, candles lit, and the servants dismissed for the night. She waited primly on a Hepplewhite chair made from mahogany with a satinwood veneer. Her black satiny dress fell off her shoulders and tucked neatly up under her breasts to bring them bubbling over the top like ivory balls. The sleeves gigot sheers. I took a deep breath and smelled the light scent of roses.

"Well, Bill," she said lightly. "You seem to have been a while."

"Yes, ma'am," I said, standing awkwardly in front of her. "That I have." I tore my stare from her breasts and studied the various trophies Custer had hung on his walls. One wall was filled with horns: antelope, deer, a pair of elk, with framed photographs sprinkled between them.

"Autie likes his trophies," she said dryly.

Something in her voice drew my attention back to her. Her eyes looked brittle, unamused, for a moment; then laughter rolled back into them. "My husband is a hunter, Bill. Of any game."

"Yes, ma'am, I know that," I said. I glanced back at the trophies gathered on the wall. A buffalo head had been mounted close to the ceiling and threatened to dominate the room. I pointed at it. "I was with him when he collected that one."

She rose and came over to stand close to me. This close, her scent bewildered my senses.

"Yes, I know. In fact"—she waved a hand at all of them—"I know about them all. Even the one he gathered down on the Washita. But you weren't there then, were you, Bill?"

"Call me James," I said. "That's my name."

She shook her head. "No, but I will call you Bill. James suggests far more intimacy than I intend."

I stepped back and stared down at her. "Ma'am? I'm sorry, but I'm not much good at these parlor games."

Her laughter rang through the room. Then she placed her hands deliberately behind her. I heard buttons slipping through their holes in the fabric of her dress; then the gown gathered in a soft black cloud at her feet. My eyebrows nearly pushed themselves off my forehead. She stood naked except for a pair of black net stockings held on her alabaster thighs by white garters with tiny red rosebuds upon them.

I gulped and glanced at the door. She laughed deeply. "It's locked, Bill. Don't worry. We won't be interrupted."

"We won't?" I asked stupidly. I couldn't take my eyes off of Custer's luck. I had never seen anyone so closely resembling pictures of old Grecian sculptures of Aphrodite before. She could have modeled for any of them with her high breasts, rounded to perfection, with large nipples pointing toward me. Her waist tucked in, her belly flowing smoothly down to her thighs and her heavy red-gold triangle between her legs.

She crossed to me and stood close, her breasts rubbing gently over my stomach. "We have all night, Bill. *All night,*" she emphasized. Then she placed her arms around my neck and kissed me deeply and I forgot about everything except wondering where the damn bed was.

I awakened in the early morning, sated, Elizabeth's head tucked in the hollow of my shoulder, her leg thrown across my belly. I kissed her gently and she opened her eyes to smile at me. "Are you hungry yet?" she asked.

"Not for food," I said, nuzzling her cheek.

She slapped my arm playfully. "You're insatiable. I like that." Then she drew away from me and sat up, back on her heels, looking down at me. Her eyes went serious. "I like this, Bill, but this is all it will ever be."

"I know. We've had this conversation before."

She touched my lips with her forefinger and ran the nail down my neck and chest to my groin. I shivered She smiled. "Bear with me. I want to emphasize our relationship. I won't leave Custer," she said. "I *can't* leave Custer. Oh, I know he's cheated on me—especially with that Cheyenne girl that he brought back from the Washita River when he destroyed Black Kettle's village. They had a son, I believe. I don't know. I was back in Michigan visiting family during that time." Her lips hardened. "Do you know a woman can always tell when her man has slept with another woman?" I shook my head. "It's true. We can always tell. It was in his hesitance toward me. And then there was the quiet talking whenever I came around. Eventually a couple of friends discovered what had happened and told me. At first I was hurt, then thought I would leave him. But"—she shook her head—"I couldn't. I have become a part of the Custer legend, you see. Just as much as if I rode with him constantly. And there's a good chance that he'll be president someday. George Benton, the New York publisher, is already laying the groundwork for Autie. I can't jeopardize that. You understand?"

"You mean you haven't jeopardized it with this?" I gestured at the bed. She laughed merrily.

"No, I haven't. Who would believe you? And besides," she purred, settling down upon my chest, "I don't think you are looking for any long involvements, either. Or am I mistaken?"

"You minx," I said, laughing in spite of myself. "You planned this all along!"

"Yes, I did," she said.

"And Custer had not sent word for me to meet him as soon as I arrived from scouting?"

She shook her head, her tresses trailing over my bare chest. "No. Are you mad?"

"I should be."

"But you're not."

"No. No, I'm not."

And I pulled her close, devouring her anxious lips, feeling her hands move hotly over my body, her legs wrapping around my waist—

Almost as good as Agnes Lake Thatcher, whom I met later—

But trouble wasn't far down the line, and trouble always seems to put an end to everything pleasant with me. I lost the election to my own deputy, Rattlesnake Pete, although I was really ready to leave Hays anyway. The town and the county were slow in paying me, forcing me to send a demanding letter to them:

ELLIS COUNTY

To J. B. Hickok Dr.

To services as policeman 1 month and 19 days at $75.00 per month $122.50. I certify that the above account is correct and remains due and unpaid.

                                             J. B. Hickok

But my salary was short in coming, and following my defeat at the polls I took a brief vacation in Topeka before returning to Hays to try to collect what I was owed.

Dust. I remember the dust of the day. Hot. Sweaty. July 17, 1870. I was frustrated at not receiving my money and went into Paddy Walsh's saloon to have a drink that evening. The air hung like a fur coat over everyone, stifling. Five or six soldiers sat in a corner nursing their beer. I ignored them and walked to the bar. Paddy met me, smiling a welcome.

"Bill," he said pleasingly. "Damn, but you're a sight for sore eyes."

"Paddy. How about joining me in a drink?"

He grinned. "Now isn't that a fine thing to be saying to an Irishman? And what fool would be ignoring an invitation like that?" He reached beneath the bar and pulled out a dark bottle, winking at me as he did. "And we'll just start with a nip from the private stock."

I laughed and took the glass he offered, sipping. "How have you been, Paddy?" I asked.

He drank and sighed, nodding slightly toward the soldiers in the corner. "There's been the ups and the downs. Oh, I'm saying nothing against Pete, you understand, but there's a bit of a problem between himself and the soldiers. Right now, he's out of town after the person who cut out a couple of Jake Mason's cattle and we've had a wee bit of trouble—"

"Here now, is that a bottle of whiskey from the good land?" a rough voice said at my shoulder.

I glanced over, recognizing Jerry Lonigan and John Kelly, both in uniform, the sleeves of Kelly's blouse showing where sergeant's stripes had recently been taken. He grinned at me, his red face bloated with drink. I sighed inwardly and casually moved a half step to my left, putting distance between the three of us. I had had trouble in the past from both of them and knew they were baiting me, trying to draw me into trouble.

"It is that," Paddy said quietly.

"Well then, let's be having a glass," Kelly said.

"'Tis a sharing I do only with my friends," Paddy said. He nodded toward the other soldiers in the corner. "Be a good lad and go back to your suds with your mates."

Lonigan placed both hands on the bar, leaning over it to glare at Paddy. "So you'll be having a drink with the little miss here and ignore the men? Now what would that be making you?"

"The owner of the bar who's telling you to take your business elsewhere," Paddy said, his voice tight with warming. One hand dropped down beneath the level of the bar and I knew if it came up there would be a wooden bung stopper—he called it a shillelagh—that had ended more than one would-be brawl in his saloon when he crowned the fighters with it.

Kelly looked over at me, his eyes moving slowly over my hair. "Y'right, Jerry, me friend. 'Tis a fine set of curls on that head. Now, d'yuh suppose he would be willing to treat us?"

I recognized the insult in his words. "Keep a civil tongue in your head, Kelly," I said.

He beamed and turned toward me, his hand reaching out to push me in my chest. He froze as I brought a pistol up, cocked and pointing at his bulbous nose that glowed like a red bull's-eye lantern. "All right, you bog jumper," I said softly. "You want trouble? You've got it."

His eyes narrowed as he looked down the barrel of my pistol. "'Tis not a gunman I am and you're no man if you won't be meetin' another with something 'sides iron."

"That's no problem," I said. "Put your pistol on the bar. You, too, Lanigan, then go back to your friends."

The two unbuckled their belts and laid them on the bar.

Lanigan walked back to the table with the others and stood beside it, watching. I smiled at Kelly.

"Back off, Kelly. Five steps backward."

Grudgingly he moved. I slipped the other pistol from my sash and laid it on the bar, holding the other steady on him as I slipped the Prince Albert from my shoulders. I handed it across to Paddy along with my other pistol and stepped toward Kelly.

"Now you satisfied?"

"Lad, you just made the biggest mistake of your wee life," he said, and swung a meaty fist at my jaw.

I swayed back and away, then stepped forward, hooking him low in his big belly with my left, and when he bent forward raked the heel of my palm up and over his chin, splitting his lips wide, shoving him away from me. He staggered backward and I stepped forward, hitting him again in the belly and this time hooking sharply with my right to his jaw, holding my elbows close in at my sides. His head snapped backward, his eyes crossed. He swung another clumsy right at me, but I slipped under it and hit him twice in the belly and snapped my head up, catching him on the point of his jaw. His teeth came together with an audible *click!* and he fell backward like a cut tree, crashing into a table, upturning it.

"Well," I said, turning toward Paddy. "That's that."

He started to smile; then his eyes closed warningly. I started to turn, ducking at the same time. A beer mug caught me a glancing blow on my temple, dazing me. I caught myself against the bar.

"Here now! Fair play!" Paddy shouted.

But the soldiers ignored him, swarming over me. A fist caught me on the jaw, stunning me. Another struck me in the belly, but I had tensed myself as I fell back against the bar and little damage happened. Then another glass smashed against my forehead, and I felt a cut open above my eyebrow.

I levered myself up with my elbows on the bar and kicked out blindly with both feet. I connected with someone, heard him yell, and for a second I had breathing room. I slipped down the bar, striking out instinctively as someone came in from my right side. With satisfaction I felt bone give way, followed by a yelp of pain; then I caught a glimpse of metal.

"Bill!"

I half-turned and caught my pistols as Paddy flipped them to me.

"Look out!" someone shouted.

I fired at the flash of metal and heard someone scream from pain. A shot snapped past my ear. I fired at the flash in the gray smoke that began to fill the space between me and the soldiers. I fired again and heard the wet *smack!* as my bullet hit someone, where I couldn't tell. Dimly I saw Kelly rise from the floor and grab at his pistol on the bar. I snapped a shot at him and saw the bullet take him in the belly. He staggered, screamed, and fell to the floor, his head going forward as he grabbed the pain.

And then, quiet.

I stared at the two soldiers still standing. I motioned at them angrily, indicating the wounded on the floor. "Pick up your people and get out of here," I said furiously. "You wanted to buy into this, now you pay the piper. Get back to the fort where you belong."

"And you'll not be coming in this place again!" Paddy said emphatically. I glanced over my shoulder and saw him shouldering a shotgun, the barrel cut down to eighteen inches or less, at the soldiers. One blast from that would take out everybody in the room, and the soldiers knew that. Silently they helped the others to their feet; then two of them hoisted Kelly between them and they left.

Paddy sighed and lowered the shotgun. He glanced at me. "You'll need a bit of patching, Bill," he said. He poured another glass and slid it over to me. "But if I were you, I wouldn't be wasting much time on my aches and pains in Hays. Soon as Tom Custer hears about this, he'll be in after you, and there's nothing you can do about that with Pete out on the trail. The army's the law when the law's gone."

"I know," I said quietly. I downed the drink, shuddered against its bite, and took my coat, shrugging into it. I slid the Colts back into the sash and took a towel from him, pressing it against my forehead to stop the bleeding. I glanced at the repeater clock on the wall, noting the time.

"Be seeing you," I said, and stepped outside. I walked down to the station and caught the 9:05 train heading toward Topeka. I didn't draw a clean breath until the train pulled away from the station, ten minutes late as usual.

I never saw Elizabeth again. Nor George or Tom Custer, for that matter, although I heard about them several times. I still remember her, though, the soft nights, her wild abandon, and her fanatical devotion to Custer. A strange combination never resolved.

CHAPTER 43

ABILENE—"CITY of the PLAIN"—was a typical town, running from the east to the west. Texas Street ran next to the railroad while Cedar Street truckled south from the railroad about five blocks from Mud Creek. But it was A Street that was most important, for this was where Joe McCoy built his Drover's Cottage, three stories with a hundred rooms for the cattlemen bringing herds up from Texas and the buyers waiting to bid hotly for the mossyhorns those Texas randies pulled out of the brush.

The Alamo was the best saloon, but there were plenty of

others ready to splash tanglefoot out into shot glasses for the cowboys after they'd had long overdue baths and dipped their tallywhackers in willing cyprians down in the Devil's Addition where they held their red-light practice. The Alamo had three sets of double-glass doors that folded back, and large paintings of nude women with "more bounce to the ounce" hung on the walls. Yet there were other saloons suited more to the wild man's fancy, such as the Bull's Head, the Applejack, the Old Fruit, the Elkhorn, the Pearl, the Lone Star, and the Longhorn. I don't think there was a cattle town in Kansas that didn't have a Longhorn Saloon.

The "proper folk" of Abilene tried to maintain law and order in their town by hiring Tom Smith to be marshal. Smith, however, didn't believe in using firearms, preferring to pound a sense of right and wrong into those who'd strayed with his huge fists. But fists don't match up well with guns, and Smith was soon killed while trying to arrest a ne'er-do-well.

About that same time, McCoy was elected mayor and sent Charlie Gross to find me at Fort Harker, where I was playing poker and running a losing streak. I was offered the job of marshal of Abilene at $150 a month and 25 percent of all fines collected in court. I took office on April 15, 1871.

I do not believe there are angels hovering protectively over us, but there well could be apostates walking in our shadows. They wait to take advantage of our mistakes—and we all make them.

I have.

Neither love nor prayer can bring Mike back since I put him by mistake in the earth.

That was indeed a grave night.

I remember everything about it from the taste of the peppermint candy I had eaten to calm my stomach after a supper of steak—I seem to taste the cloying flavor even now—to the tiny shadows dancing at the edge of my vision.

Somewhere, someone was banging out "Buffalo Gals" on a piano badly out of tune and the boys were whooping it up in the thick of the night. A haze of dust hung in the gloaming, creating halos around the lighted windows.

A few of the stalwart stodgers were down in the church trying to drown out "Buffalo Gals" with "Rock of Ages," singing in ancient, reedy voices, but even if it had been Sunday there weren't enough Christian voices to drown out the songs of pleasure. A few black-garbed women had earlier marched down the street followed by old Mose Harper diligently pounding a bass drum so loudly that he drowned out the sheaves they were trying to bring in, much to the amusement of a few liquored-up cowboys who stood on the corner smoking hand-rolleds while catching their second wind to have another go at chasing the elephant.

Beside me, Joe, the fire dog that had adopted me, sat on his brown-spotted haunches and occasionally moaned a long, sad refrain to the music—much to the annoyance of the Ladies Brigade led by the mayor's wife, Ida.

She had a nose like a blue heron and a chin like a pelican followed by a goiter that turned liver red and flounced back and forth like a turkey's wattles when she got angry, which was most of the time—which was why the mayor spent as much time as he could sneak in at Mexican Lupe's small house down by the cattle pens. He figured he was safe enough down there because Ida was certain that all Mexicans were in league with the devil, and would rather be caught outside without her bustle than be within a hundred yards of Lupe's place.

Ida was always accompanied by the Widow Johnson—I swear, it seems like every town I've been in has a Widow Johnson in it and every one of them is scrawny-necked, pigeon-breasted, and has a face that looks like it's been savaged with an ice pick. The widow and Ida were quite a pair, each gifted with a tongue that could lash varnish off a mahogany bar. And given to using it with a frequency that challenged the rising of the moon.

I remember once when the Widow Johnson got to haranguing a pair of cowboys fresh from Texas without the trail dust washed off them yet and the back of their throats parched dry as the desert wind from New Mexico chasing tumbleweeds over the Chisholm Trail. They took it for a while—like most Texas cowboys, they had a healthy respect for women—but when she raised a question about their mothers (one *never* questions a Texan's mother whether one knew her or not) one of them draped a noose around her middle and pulled her squawking like an upended chicken into a water trough. When that failed to cool her ardor, they tired quickly of their game and raised her up over the Bull's Head saloon sign. One of them used his bowie knife to quickly divest her of dress, bustle, and, well, everything and left her dangling there, red-faced with embarrassment, turning this way and that, trying to hide her nakedness and not knowing which part, north or south, to cover first. The children got a quick education in the female anatomy—although since she had ventured on her own down toward the cattle pens, there weren't many children who lived there who hadn't had an eyeful of a naked woman more than once.

When I finally arrived there to cut her down, tears were flowing through the caked dust on her face, but I swear there was a new light in her eyes, hidden behind her fronted indignation—excitement, if I'm any judge (and I am)—and I reckon I was right on that, because this Widow Johnson left town on the next stage. I found her six months later in Wichita in one of the upstairs rooms of The Oriental, rouged and happy in her rebirth.

But Ida worried at my days and nights like a dog at a fresh butcher's bone, caterwauling about the degradation *proper women* (I know what that implies but hanged if I can *un-*

derstand the difference) had to undergo in that lawless and godless community. She enlisted the aid of just about every churchgoing woman in town, berating me for not doing my duty by shutting down the dens of iniquity flourishing in town. Finally, I tired of listening to her and her friends and did just what she and the others asked—much to the consternation of their husbands, who finally put their collective foot down and forbade their wives from dabbling in politics when the husbands discovered taxes would have to go up 3,000 percent to make up the differences in the budget normally covered by the "weekly fines" once levied upon the cyprian practitioners. In no uncertain terms, the ladies were told to concentrate on other godly activities, setting women's suffrage back a decade or so.

But all that happened long before I killed Mike by accident.

Sometimes I wonder if there is a God and if Father wasn't just whistling a hopeful tune in the dark with all his quiet lessons by the flickering firelight at night before the hearth after the supper dishes had been cleared and all of us had gathered to listen to him read from the Bible.

Funny that I should remember them now—why?—

I think it all began—I *know* it all began; what do I think I'm doing by pretending ignorance?—when the governor didn't act quickly enough to provide law for Hays City to satisfy the citizens who elected me to be the marshal or sheriff. I never was quite certain which office I legally held, but it was enough at the time to satisfy the citizens of Hays City, who really were interested in only two things in a sheriff: his reputation for handling pistols and his reputation as a man killer.

I had both. And it didn't take long for me to have to prove it. Once a person has a reputation for that type of work, someone is always trying to take it away from him. I have *never* understood why anyone would deliberately go out of his way to want such a reputation, but there are always those madmen who equate strength and power with murder.

The warm night spread over us like a soft blanket. I relaxed at the table in the back, my chair resting against the wall, watching the room contentedly, enjoying the night for what it was and trying to forget what it would become in a couple of days when the trail herds began pouring up in beefy waves like a sick cantankerous sea over the Chisholm Trail from Texas. Abilene waited impatiently, anxiously, for their arrival. The dry goods stores had filled their stock with the latest hats and shirts and pants and broadcloth coats, the women's shops had their hat stock with delicate feathers and veils and stylish sunbonnets refilled, with Chicago, Boston, and New York labels sewn in them by seamstresses in Cleveland to double their prices, the general stores had laid in supplies of preserved foods—namely, peaches, to satisfy the sweet tooth of some cowboys—and cases upon cases of liquor and countless barrels of beer had been stored in the back rooms of the saloons.

Unfortunately, the riffraff also arrived early, gamblers in velvet-collared pearl gray coats over brocade vests. Two gamblers sat a couple of tables away from me even now, practicing their deals. I watched as one tried to deal a hand of "seconds" around the edge of the table, and sighed, knowing he would be one I would have to deal with sooner or later if he tried that trick on a sharp-eyed Texas cowboy who knew his game—and practically all of them did. I hoped it wouldn't end in a burial, but, I shrugged philosophically, that was a risk one took when one played with such foolishness.

The door pushed open and "Pie" Downstreet, the "printer's devil" we called him, although he was the editor of the local paper, staggered in, eyes peering redly through the dim light left by the burning peg lamps on the walls. His long coat hung loosely on his narrow shoulders hunched like a vulture's wings. His white shirt was ink-stained, but his string tie had been carefully knotted at his throat. He needed a shave, but he wore his derby cocked at a dignified slant over his forehead. Tufts of graying blond hair stuck out from under the brim. He weaved for a moment in the doorway, then made his way to the mahogany bar, freshly waxed and gleaming wetly. He tapped with a finger on the bar and Muggins, the barkeep, looked up from his place at the end where he had been polishing glasses with a dirty towel to remove water spots.

"What can I do for you, Pie?" he asked solicitously.

"A little whiskey if you will, my good man," Pie said, forming the words carefully. "This is a sad day for all." He squinted through the gloom and shook his head. "And there's not a man jack of you knows why."

One of the gamblers looked up, showing mild interest. "Someone die?"

Pie nodded and slowly picked up the glass poured him by Muggins. He turned it slowly, admiring the way the light refracted off the whiskey's amber surface. "Yes. A lot of people." His eyes looked into the distance for a moment; then he said solemnly, "Here's to the death of the sovereign state of Georgia."

"Aw, hell," the gambler said, disappointed. "Another damn Southerner."

I sighed again and picked up my glass, draining it. I rose, settling my coat over my shoulders and loosening my pistols in the red sash around my waist. Pie was normally an easy-goer, but when he had "drink taken"—as he put it—a craziness would come over him at times and he became sullen and morose and belligerent, taking offense easily.

He drained the glass quickly and set it precisely in the

middle of the bar. Muggins took one look at Pie's face and reached under the bar for the sawed-off billiard cue he kept there.

"Pie," he said warningly. "Let's not do anything we'll be sorry for. I'll give you a final tot on the house and you make it a night. What do you say?"

Pie gave him a long dignified look, then drew himself up and straightened the settle of his coat over his shoulders. "I thank you for your hospitality, Mr. Muggins, and the libation offer, but there's a little matter of an insult to settle."

He started to turn from the bar. Muggins began to raise his stick, but I shook my head warningly and stepped up beside Pie, laying my hand on his shoulder, pressing him back against the bar, keeping him from turning.

"Now, Pie, I don't want trouble tonight. I'll have enough of that in a few days. So let's have a quiet drink and then I'll walk you home. After," I said, turning pointedly toward the outspoken gambler, "this gentleman conveys his apology."

The gambler frowned and leaned back in his chair, his hands slipping under the edge of the table. "I don't apologize to drunks. Especially Southern trash," he said.

Beside me, Pie took a deep breath, air whistling through his teeth. He tried to turn again, but by now I had the collar of his coat in a firm grasp.

"Mister," I said softly, "that wasn't an option. You made a mistake. Own up to it. And"—I glanced at the edge of the table to where his hands had disappeared—"don't be foolish enough to compound it. Bring your hands up slowly." I rested the palm of my right hand lightly on the pistol nestling butt forward, my wrist curved slightly for a twist-draw if needed.

Indecision flickered in his eyes and briefly I felt a cold chill run through me. Then Muggins spoke up from behind my left shoulder.

"You want I should throw them out, Marshal Hickok?"

The gambler's face turned pasty white. He swallowed with difficulty and carefully raised his trembling hands above the edge of the table and rested them on the green felt surface. They twitched as if he had palsy.

"Hickok. Sorry. I didn't know."

I shook my head. "Shouldn't have mattered," I said. "Now it does. You've got three choices: Take the first train east or the first train west. Miss either one and you go north next."

"North?" A puzzled look came over his face. His partner coughed. The first gambler looked questioningly at him.

"He means Boot Hill," the second said apologetically.

The first gambler's head swiveled back to me. "You throwing me out of town? Last I heard, this was a free country. Lincoln made it that way when he freed all the niggers and we beat the hell out of those Southern bastards who didn't believe he could do that."

"The country is," I said gently. "But this town isn't. Here I make the rules who stays and who moves on. You've got the mark of trouble about you, and that I don't need. Now or later. So I'm just taking care of that now." I looked at the clock on the far wall. "I think you've got about an hour to get your things together. The nine-oh-five is due through then." I waited for a moment, but he continued to stare at me. I released Pie's collar and took a step away from him. I shifted my balance to the balls of my feet, feeling the cold chill race through me again, prickling my skin.

"It's not much of a choice, but it's the only smart one to make," I said softly.

His partner cleared his throat noisily and I divided my attention between the two of them.

"I heard about what you did at Rock Creek Station," he said. I waited, remaining silent, watching. It was his game now. I was just one of the players. He waited for me to answer, and when I didn't he rubbed his nose with the heel of his hand. "I heard about that shot you made at Hawkin's Ridge in the war. How far was it? Some say a mile, but that seems a bit far to me. Probably an exaggeration, I'm thinking. Right?"

"Damn fool," Pie muttered from beside me. The gambler's eyes crossed to him, growing ugly. "You're talking yourself into being brave and right into your grave."

Then, just as suddenly, it was over. The gambler threw up his hands. "Not me," he said quickly. "I was just making small talk. You know?" he added, looking my way.

I nodded. "Yes. I know. It's dangerous talk, though. You go along with your friend now, and don't come back to Abilene again. Understand?" Indecision flickered in their eyes. "We don't know your names, so there's no shame to follow you. But again, there'll be only 'Anonymous' on your headboard if you push this. Nobody will know what happened here unless you tell them."

Silently they rose and quietly left the saloon. I waited for a minute in case one of them suddenly found his nerve up again, then relaxed and turned back to the bar.

Wordlessly Muggins slid a tumbler of whiskey in front of me and one in front of Pie. He poured a third glass for himself.

"Well, I'm glad that came to nothing," he said. He raised his glass to ours, and we drank to our good fortune.

"No loss with those two," he said, lowering his glass. "I marked them for trouble when they first came in. They were too smug, you know? As if they already had the game they were planning on playing won." He closed one eye and leaned his elbow on the bar. "You handled that real well, Marshal. And I thank you."

"My job," I said, finishing my drink.

He shook his head and made a motion with the whiskey bottle, but I placed my hand over my glass.

"No, sir," he said. "You could have killed them and no one would have faulted you for that. You'd have been doing your job that way, too." He nodded, pressing his lips together. "And most would have—'cept for Tom Smith, I reckon. He would have just used those big fists upon them." He shook his head. "Glad to see it end the way it did."

"A killing doesn't solve anything," I said. A faint picture of Father appeared at the edge of my thoughts. A bitter smile crossed my lips.

Remember, James, he who lives by the sword dies by the sword. But sometimes there are those who are destined to that life. There was a time when even God needed the warrior Michael and Charlemagne his paladins. Sometimes, a certain man is needed, but that doesn't mean he gets a free ride out of it. A killing is always a killing whether it is needed or not. And few escape a return stroke once they swing their sword.

"You all right?" Pie said curiously from beside me.

I blinked my way back to the present. I frowned, shaking my head. This drifting was happening more and more lately. A dangerous time for someone marked by others. I glanced into the mirror behind the bar and for a brief moment felt a shock run through me at the recognition of the lined face staring back from what looked like a soft halo. My eyes had been bothering me lately, aching. When had those creases started to appear? I couldn't remember although I stared into the shaving mirror every day.

"Come on," I said roughly to Pie. "I'd better walk you home before you take it in your head to lick half of Abilene."

He finished his drink and handed the glass to Muggins. "Ah, that's kind of you, Marshal, but the night still has heels on it and hasn't started yet to tiptoe into dawn. And I, for one, am thinking a trip to Mrs. Mack's fine house would be a fine way of settling the hours into a calming state." He produced a battered pewter flask and handed it to Muggins. "Fill it up, sir, to give us the strength for our journey to the fine manse where the good widow still directs others into how to lock their shins around a man's worthy middle."

Muggins raised his eyebrow at this but took the flask, stoppered it with a small funnel, and filled it with the good whiskey he kept beneath the bar, Tennessee samplings left behind by traveling salesmen trying to increase their territory.

I shook my head. "I think not, Pie. But I'll walk you to Mrs. Mack's if that's where you want to go."

He blinked watering eyes at me and took his flask from Muggins, carefully restoring it to the inside pocket from whence it came.

"A gentleman indeed!" Pie exclaimed. He turned, sliding one hand under my elbow, gesturing eloquently like a Cicero with the other. *"Vidi aquam egredientem de templo a latere dextro. Alleluia!"*

Muggins leaned forward, beckoned, and whispered across the bar. "Do you understand him when he gets into that?"

"Yes," I replied. "It's loneliness. And fear."

"Fear?" He frowned. "Of what?"

I shook my head. "I don't know. It's general among all men. For some, it's growing old." I couldn't help glancing again at my reflection in the mirror. Muggins caught my look and nodded.

"I understand," he said. "Especially when you're alone, right?"

I smiled, following Pie's gentle pulling on my arm. "Yes. Especially when you're alone."

"Salvi facti i sunt. Ad deam qui laetificat juventuteng meam," he slurred.

"Damned if I know what you're saying. I take it you were an altar boy," I said. I stumbled a bit, trying to match my step to his shambling stride. He laughed at what he thought to be my clumsiness.

"Come, Marshal, let us make our way to Mrs. Mack's mantrap," he said.

I glanced back at Muggins, who shook his head and made his way from around the edge of the bar. "I think I'll just close up," he said resignedly.

"It's a bit early for a saloon to be closing, isn't it?" I asked.

"Yeah," he grunted. "But tonight's a bit empty." He glanced around. "Besides, there's nothing more lonely than being alone in an empty saloon at night. I think I might just call it an evening and get some rest while I can."

Pie and I made our way down the boardwalk. When we passed the Bull's Head tavern, a voice came from the shadows, caressing us with false interest. "Hello, boys. You interested in searching out maidenheads?"

Pie paused, weaving slightly as he tried to peer into the shadows. "That you, Cissy?" he asked.

"Go to hell, Pie," the voice said. "I'da known it was you, I woulda kept my mouth shut."

"La belle dame sans merci," Pie said, placing his hand over his heart. He doffed his derby in her direction.

"Don't be doffing that come-to-bed hat of yours to *me*!" she said sharply. Then a note of new interest came into her voice. "But who's that with you, Pie? What long drink of water is that beside you?"

She came swaying out of the shadows into the pale moonlight. Her crimson dress shone wetly like dark blood. Her net stockings looked like spiderwebs wrapped around her thin legs. She eyed me boldly, but for all her pretending, I knew she recognized me. She bent forward, pretending to study me, allowing her bodice to drape open and her buddies to move tantalizingly like old ivory cones in the moonlight.

"Ah now, Cissy, you know full well this man," Pie said. He wagged an admonishing finger at her. "You're being a bit frivol', aren't you? Looking for a bit of a roll with the good marshal here? A nip and tuck? A quickie in the alley?"

She ignored him, her black eyes boldly eyeing me. "My goodness! So it *is* the marshal. My, my, my." She straightened, arching her shoulders back, posing provocatively. "I hope I didn't say anything wrong." She slipped her pulpy tongue between her lips as if pretending to offer me a kiss, but I knew the fakery in her gesture for the reality she meant.

"No," I said, my lips spreading into a grin. "You've said nothing wrong. But I'm not interested. Sorry."

She pouted and threw her head back, making her hair flounce at the back of her neck. Then she laughed throatily.

"So," she said. "You're after helping this old rousty down to the red house, eh? Down to old Mrs. Mack's? Well." She cocked her head to the side, eyeing me saucily. "You might go that far and fare the worse for your walking."

"Not tonight, fair Cissy," Pie said hastily.

"And why not tonight?" she snapped back, annoyed. "Do you think you hold the hours in your hand to dole out when you want like pennies to a beggar?" She thumped herself between her breasts with her thumb. "I can walk where I want without begging your permission, you old pirate! I haven't forgotten how you left me in the morning hours without so much as a kiss for my time!" She looked at me, pointing an accusing finger at Pie, now rocking back on his heels to put as much distance as he could between him and her fury. "I demand you arrest this man, Marshal!"

"Oh?" I struggled to hold myself serious. "And what charges should I bring against him?"

"He stole . . . He stole . . ." She paused, shaking her head. "First, he took advantage of my 'charms,'" she said delicately, "when I was in a soft moment. Then, he left me without so much as a thank-you and . . . he stole my garter.

Black with tiny red rosebuds upon it! But"—her eyes grew steely—"he raised dangerous feelings I didn't know I had!"

I looked at Pie, who was squirming in embarrassment. "Did you do that, Pie?"

"Ah now, that was a goodly time ago and I can't remember everything that's happened since the end of the war—"

"Ah," she said disgustedly, making a gesture as if brushing him from the night. "You're like all the rest of them who fought, always blaming the war for something you don't want to have anything to do with! When are you going to forget the war and get on with your life? Besides," she continued, "you are a liar!" She stepped boldly up to him, backing him to a porch post. "You are a lying whoreson—"

"'Tis the pot calling the kettle black!" he said. He swung around behind the post, placing it protectively between them. "Keep her away from me, Marshal! Before I lose my temper! A woman with an adder's tongue has a bite to her as well! She speaks poniards, and every word stabs: If her breath were as terrible as her terminations, there were no living near her; she infects to the North Star!"

She spun on her heels and stared up angrily at me. "Well?" she demanded. "Are you going to arrest this romper or not?"

I shook my head. "Not," I said.

She stared at me in disbelief, then threw up her hands, spitting the word, "Men!" as if it was a curse that had been placed upon the whole earth. Then, turning, she stomped back into the shadows.

"Whew!" Pie said. He pulled a dirty handkerchief from the sleeve of his coat and wiped his face. "That harridan will be the death of me yet!"

"Maybe you should just give back her garter," I suggested. "And perhaps a little something to soothe her ruffled feathers?"

"There's wisdom in the simile," he said solemnly. "But

for all of that, she's a whore. Still . . ." His voice trailed off musingly as he looked in the dark where she had disappeared. He pulled the flask almost absentmindedly from his pocket and took a drink. He offered it to me, but I shook my head and he returned it to his pocket. "Still," he repeated, "in a way so are we all."

Then he brightened and, holding his hat to his head, craned his head upward, studying the heavens. "'Tis nearing the very witching time of night when the churchyards yawn and graves gape wide and hell breathes out a contagion to the world!" He grabbed my arm, pulling me urgently down the street. "And it's best the time for all who would run the wild-goose chase to take themselves well away to the hellsgate and Queen Mack."

"Yes," I said. "I think that would be most prudent—to get you off the street."

"I sense a mockery in your words, Marshal, but no matter. Time marches on and opportunity with it. We must hasten to catch it!"

I sensed a strange urgency to his words and remained silent, following him as we hurried down the street to Mrs. Mack's house. The whorehouse sat on the edge of the town on a little rise above the streams that trickled from the cattle pens draining into the creek. Stones had been haphazardly placed to guide the unwary foot over the soggy ground. A rich smell rose from the streams and grounds, raw and nearly overpowering, but Mrs. Mack had directed the planting of rosebushes and lilac bushes, jack-in-the-pulpits, lilies of the valley, rose of Sharons, mimosa, all scented flowers that bloomed continuously until the first killing frost, masking the cattle smell effectively, creating a tasteful garden in the middle of swamp and squalor.

"Ah, the abode of Circe!" Pie said as we approached.

The three-story house gleamed whitely like a marble tomb, although lights shone cheerfully from many windows and a strange cascade of notes fell from inside in a series of five. I couldn't recognize the song, but the line was simple enough that I wished for my fiddle, wanting to join the anonymous player in a tune or two.

We stumbled up onto the porch and Pie hammered on the freshly enameled red door. It opened quickly and Mrs. Mack stood in front of us, dressed in a blue silk gown that did much to hide her age. She held a drink in one hand and stared affectionately at Pie.

"Well," she said, the word rasping in her throat. "I was wondering if you were going to make it tonight." She glanced at me and her smile tightened perceptively as she recognized me. "Are you helping him, too, Marshal?"

My eyebrows rose in puzzlement. She nodded and her smile slipped to sadness. "You don't know. I see. Well, come on in, you wastrel boys!" She stood back, throwing the door open wide. I caught a glimpse of an emaciated black man sitting at the piano, improvising, the sleeves of his red pin-striped shirt held tightly to his thin biceps with red garters. A young cowboy, his hair still gleaming from his recent bath, sprawled on a lion-footed couch with a fleshy blond whore on one arm and a sober-faced Indian, long glossy hair as shiny as a raven's wing falling to her waist, on the other. Both were half-naked.

Pie stepped through the doorway, lifting his hat from his head, piously intoning, *"Introibo ad altare Dei."* He stopped in the center of the room, blessing the four cardinal directions and, by default, all in the room.

The blonde beside the cowboy gave a squeal upon hearing him and leaped away from the side of the cowboy, hopping across the red and gray Oriental rug to throw her arms around Pie's neck, hugging him tightly.

"Pie!" she said happily.

"Ah, Zoë," he said, patting her rump affectionately.

The cowboy looked annoyed and started to gather his legs

to rise. I stepped through the door still held open by Mrs. Mack. The cowboy glanced at me, then paused and looked again. I saw within him the same hellfires that burned within me. But I did not see a shadow of goodness that could cool those raging fires and turn the man-host away from his trespasses.

"I know you?" he asked, a touch of insolence to his voice.

"You don't know how long I've been waiting for you!" Zoë exclaimed.

"Ah, yes. 'Tis nice to be missed," Pie said.

"Perhaps," I answered easily. "Where you from, cowboy?"

He stiffened, his face closing tightly with anger. I couldn't blame him; it wasn't a question that one asked another in the West until they had ridden together for a month or two—and perhaps even not then. I knew a couple of old-timers high on the divide who didn't know each other's given name, yet they had been together in that cabin for the better part of twenty years. But it was a question a marshal had to ask—or *better* ask—from time to time simply to be prudent. There was no reason not to answer the question when an officer of the law asked it—unless there was a cloud along a person's back trail or, more often I had found, he wanted to create the *illusion* of a cloud to impress someone, usually a young woman. But the women in Mrs. Mack's had known those men who did not need to impress anyone, and looked upon such youthful posing as pure posturing.

"Getting a bit personal, aren't you?" he asked.

"Goes with the job, kid. Take it easy," I said.

He flushed. "I ain't a kid and you can stuff easy up your butt!" he said hotly, his face red like spoiled liver with anger.

Pie cocked a red-flashed eye over Zoë's bare shoulder. "Now there stands a man whose empty words threaten to loose a hurricane!"

The cowboy flushed fiery red, going all hot around the eyes as anger flexed through him. "Shut up, you old fool! I don't need no lip from you, either!"

"Oh?" Pie asked, raising his eyebrows innocently. "And what do you need from me?"

The cowboy started forward, his fists clenched tightly at his sides.

"And you don't need nothing here, either!" Mrs. Mack said, stepping forward, blocking him. "Get your hat, cowboy, and hit the trail!"

He swayed for a moment, his lips curling into a sneer. "You're throwing me out of a whorehouse? Nobody throws me out of a whorehouse! Especially an old whore like you!"

"Get out," Mrs. Mack snapped. "You can just go on down to Buck's Livery. He's got a nanny goat out back. Either that or go back to pulling your tallywhacker on the trail, 'cause it ain't gonna get pulled in here!"

"That's it!" I said. I grabbed him by the shoulder and spun him toward the door. He turned back, swinging wildly. I shifted my weight, dropped my left, and when his eyes followed it automatically threw an overhand right hard against his jaw. He dropped like a sledgehammered steer. I grabbed his feet and pulled him out of the room. His head bounced like a nursery ball down the three steps from Mrs. Mack's porch. I dragged him over to the corner of the yard and left him under the lilac bushes planted there and went back inside.

"Well played, thou just and faithful servant!" Pie cried, peeling Zoë from around his neck and applauding.

A cuckoo clock on the wall began crying: *Cuckoo! Cuckoo! Cuckoo!*—

I glanced at it: eleven.

Mrs. Mack stepped forward, her fingers touching me lightly on my cheeks. Rice powder seemed ingrained in every pore of her face. She had blended kohl half moons under her eyes and deeply rouged her lips and cheeks scarlet. Her hennaed hair had a fresh look and the scent she wore had an expensive musk to it.

I could tell she was old by the tired lines she had artfully hidden and the world-weary knowledge that she kept half-hidden behind green eyes. Yet she carried a sensuality with her like the mantle of Aphrodite discreetly draped over her shoulders.

She smiled gently, and I knew she had seen interest quicken in my eyes, but she shook her head.

"Thank you again, Marshal. A woman—even an old whore—likes to be reminded she is still wanted. But tonight belongs to Pie."

Zoë immediately stepped back, looking chagrined. "I'm sorry, Pie. I didn't know what day it was."

I frowned, looking at the old editor and the tears gathering in his eyes and sprinkling his cheeks like diamonds. He nodded, patting her gently on the shoulder.

"June seventeenth," he said kindly. "I don't expect you to remember, my dear. It's enough that I do." He looked at Mrs. Mack and corrected himself. "*We* do."

"Yes," Mrs. Mack said softly, placing her hand gently on his arm. Zoë took his hat from him and stepped back respectfully, courteously waiting.

"Thank you, Zoë," Pie said. He smiled at Mrs. Mack.

"Ned," she said. The piano player looked over his shoulder. His eyes were puffy and yellow, and I knew if I stood next to him I would smell the sick-sweet scent of opium.

"Yas 'um?" he mumbled.

"Play 'The Drover's Waltz,' " she said.

A look of mild surprise came into his eyes. "It that time o'year, 'gin?" he mumbled. Then, his fingers stretched and flexed and the groups of five rolled sweetly into the waltz. Pie held his arms out and Mrs. Mack gathered the hem of her gown in one hand and stepped into them. They swayed

together for a second, picking up the rhythm, then slipped
gracefully into the dance.

Dimly I was aware of time shifting, Pie wearing a frock
coat with watered-silk facings, a starched shirt with mother-
of-pearl studs, long trousers ironed tightly, with his feet
encased in highly polished Congress boots; she in a moon-
lit blue gown with matching shoes, dance card held around
one wrist by a gold ribbon, her gloved fingers resting lightly
on Pie's gloved palm. The years fell away, and I heard the
strings of an orchestra, the low murmur of polite talk, yet
Pie and Mrs. Mack were oblivious to it all, lost in the world
of their own making. I sensed coaches waiting, carefully
groomed horses restlessly shuffling hooves on cobblestones,
uniformed men cordoning off a crowd of the curious pressing close to catch with eager eyes a glimpse of the world
they could never have. Then others danced by—one who
could only be a mayor or governor or senator or perhaps all
three, with a plump, partridge-pouting-breasted dowager in
black in his arms.

And then they were gone.

As were Pie and Mrs. Mack.

I blinked, then felt a small hand in my own, leading me
to the spangled couch. Zoë smiled gently up at me as we
sat together. Her hand slipped over my thigh as she leaned
into me, twisting her shoulders so my hand seemed to naturally cup her breast and her nipple pressed urgently against
my palm. Her breath had a faint hint of garlic to it, not un-
pleasant. Her forehead was smooth alabaster, her nose aq-
uiline, hooked slightly at the end above bow-shaped lips. A
tiny mole stood at the corner of one eye, both eyes the color
of deep-blue mountain lakes.

"What is so special about the day?" I asked.

She sighed and tiny tears squeezed out of those deep-blue
eyes. She snuggled closer to me and her hand slipped between my thighs.

"It's the night when Pie's wife died trying to give birth," she said lowly. "Both of them. The baby, too, I mean. At midnight."

"And what does that have to do with Mrs. Mack?"

"She was, is, his wife's sister."

"Sister?"

"Happened fifteen years or so ago this very night," she said. "Ever since, they have spent the night together."

"Fifteen years? How would you know all that? You're not that old."

She smiled sadly. "There's not a whore anywhere doesn't know that story. It happened in Atlanta during the war. It's sort of like real love, you see?"

"No," I said. "I don't see that. I just see two tired old folks trying to remember better times."

"Maybe," she said. She lay quietly against me, fondling me absentmindedly, her thoughts elsewhere.

Ned shifted his song again into the handful of five notes he had been noodling with earlier. I wished again for my fiddle. Then a song began to emerge from the abstract chords and runs. I closed my eyes, concentrating, trying to remember.

James.

The word whispered softly from the air. I opened my eyes, seeking the speaker.

James.

A command then. The voice familiar. Then, suddenly, Father stood before me, black burial suit moldering, his face leper gray, blue-circled hollow eyes staring mesmerizingly into mine.

James. Repent. Now. Leave this den of iniquity.

"I cannot," I said.

"Pardon?" Zoë said.

You fornicated while I lay dying.

"Accident," I muttered. "Who can tell the comings and goings of man?"

"Are you all right, Marshal?"

You learned your lessons well. But you were the death of me.

"No."

"Shall I get you a drink?"

Yes. With your disobedience. Now I say to you: Leave this whoresden and return to your mother.

I shook my head. "Too late for that."

"For a drink?"

Too late? It is never too late to repent. Lift up your eyes unto the Lord. Knock upon the door and it shall be opened unto you.

"And the wicked if I leave? Will they inherit the earth? No, Father, it is too late to repent, too late to begin again."

"Oh, Marshal. What is it?"

And his face seemed to soften under its gray shade and then I felt the ache of his love come across the room between us on his ashen breath. He began to slowly weave back and forth like the shadows of dappled leaves in a sunlit slow breeze.

James. James. James.

"I'm Bill now, Father. James is no more."

No more.

"Remember? Once upon a time a knight—"

Not long now, James.

My mouth felt dry. "Father?"

Slowly the specter faded, leaving behind only the hint of a whispered, *Not long.* I started, leaping to my feet. Zoë fell away, clutching the arm of the couch to keep from tumbling to the floor.

"What—" she began, confused.

I looked across the room into the mirror bracketed with

deer antlers. My features looked drawn and gray and old. Cuckolded by fate. An antique smell of mold and dank earth permeated the room. I recognized the smell: like old battlefields filled with rotting bodies and covered with heavy, cold fog.

I walked shakily to the window and looked out. Zoë came with me and anxiously pressed against me. My face felt damp from perspiration. I looked out into the darkness, glancing toward the lilac bushes where I had unceremoniously dumped the young cowboy. The ground was vacant beneath the bushes. I nodded toward them.

"Did that cowboy give his name?"

"Calls himself John Wesley Hardin," she said. I glanced down at her. She frowned, concerned. "Why? Do you know him?"

I shook my head. "Never heard of him."

She looked relieved. "He said his boss sent him ahead of the herd to look things over. I think he was lining up buyers."

I nodded. The name of a minister, but there was hell in that boy, and a coldness in the pit of my stomach told me I would be seeing him again, soon.

Cuckoo. Cuckoo. Cuckoo—

"Bill?"

I looked down at her face, blurred around the edges now in the half shadows by the window. She looked soft and vulnerable, needing.

"It's after midnight. Do you want to go to bed?"

I glanced at the stairway, then overhead. I felt the need, too.

"Yes," I said softly. "Yes. I think I would like that."

She sighed and snuggled her head against my chest. I placed my arm around her, holding tightly to her youth as we climbed the stairs to her room beneath the eaves.

CHAPTER 44

THE HOUSE seemed empty when I came down two hours later from Zoë's room. I felt strangely nervous, on edge, although there was no reason for me to feel that way. The whiskey had worn off, and although I was tired, everything appeared bright and lucid. The piano player was gone; the whores were gone. I breathed deeply through my nose, smelling the cheap perfume, whiskey, other strange scents that were not strange in that house. I glanced into the mirror between the antlered hat rack on the wall beside the door to check my dress. A tired old man looked back, and briefly, for a scant moment that burned itself into my mind, I saw the face of my father in mine.

"Cuckolded by fate, aren't we, Father?" I murmured. Then the image changed and I saw myself with fine lines criss-crossing my forehead like a scout's rudely drawn map. Suddenly I felt old, as old as the hills, and the weight of time burying itself upon my shoulders like the stone of Sisyphus. And, like Sisyphus, I felt as if all I was trying to do kept rolling back down on top of me, burying me. Briefly I saw hills studded with dark pines, a gulch with a small stream running like a snake through it, tents and quick buildings tossed up to serve the citizens slogging through muddy streets, and dimly I heard strained-string twanging of banjos playing "Buffalo Gals" and an out-of-tune piano or two rattling out jangling noise that only the player could appreciate.

"Buffalo gals, won't you come out tonight . . ."

merged with

"Once in the dear, dead days beyond recall
When on the world the mists began to fall."

I crossed to the window and looked out again at the lilac bushes, half-expecting to see the cowboy I had lain there still there, although I knew he had been long gone. A strange premonition came over me. I felt empty, brooding, as if something vital had been taken from me.

I sensed someone beside me and looked down at the Indian woman I had seen earlier on the couch with Zoë and the cowboy. She looked tired, with bruised half moons under her eyes. A tiny red mark appeared on the side of her neck. I glanced around the room, but we were alone.

"You don't remember me, do you?" she asked, her full lips smiling slightly, ironically.

I studied her carefully—her skin shone like burnished copper, her breasts full, aureoles large and nearly purple, legs short and muscular but finely shaped. There *was* something familiar about her. But what? Slowly I shook my head.

"I'm sorry," I said regretfully. "Should I?"

"Annie was my sister," she said softly, her lips curling back from white teeth.

Indian Annie. Annie Liffey.

Ellsworth, 1867. Smoky fall had draped itself upon us and I breathed deeply as I rode on Black into Ellsworth, a quarter of an antelope tied behind my saddle. I rose early that morning and saddled Black, riding out mainly to clean the sour saloon taste from my mouth and the cigar smoke fog from my lungs. I breathed deeply of the cold air on the prairie and lifted the reins. Black needed no further urging and broke into a ground-gaining lope that he could carry all day if necessary. I sensed the joy in the one-eyed horse as he shook his head, his long mane flashing in the gray light as he sensed the open space in front of us.

I let him run for a long while, until his skin was shiny with sweat, but his breathing was still deep and easy. I turned him away from the road. He plunged with joy into the deep buffalo grass and grama grass that swept in undulating waves in front of us. We moved up and down the hills. I let him pick his own way. Finally, he came to Fossil Creek and dropped down into a trot until he came to the edge of the water. Then he snorted and bent his head, drinking the cold, clear water. I sensed movement at the edge of my vision and turned to see a small herd of antelope coming down a ridgeline a short distance away.

On an impulse, I slipped from the saddle, sliding my Henry out of its scabbard. Black froze as the reins hit the water in front of him, standing rigid as a statue. I faded away from his side into a stand of willow beside a thick bunch of bluestem grass. I settled into the grass and quietly levered a round into the Henry's chamber. I waited patiently as the antelope continued down the ridge, moving toward the stream. Then the leader saw Black and stopped, his head coming up swiftly. His tail raised warningly like a rabbit's scut. The others behind him scattered left and right. I drew a bead on his chest, held high, and squeezed the trigger. The bullet took him in the white blaze of his chest. He took a wild leap left, ran a few paces, then dropped, sliding on the thick grass.

I rose and watched the other antelope race away. Black snorted and tossed his head, turning to stare from his good eye, trying to see what had happened. I crossed and slid the Henry back into its scabbard and patted Black on his shoulder.

"Meat, boy," I said, and mounted, riding him over to the dead antelope.

And now I came in the back way to Ellsworth, making my way to a small shack at the back of the Grand Central Hotel. A cold wind started skating down from the north across the treeless prairie. I reined in beside the shack and sat for a moment, wondering why I still stayed in Ellsworth after losing the election for sheriff. I had carried the town— perhaps that was why I still stayed—but the rest of the county had decided E. W. Kingsbury would be the better man. I knew the good captain—an honorary self-appointment, I suspected—and I suppose for the county he was. Cattle rustling had risen along with horse theft, and I had a hunch it wouldn't be long before the entire country broke wide open.

I sighed and stepped down from Black and untied the antelope quarter and carried it inside. Annie turned from the table where she had been making bread, her forearms white with flour, a smudge alongside one high cheekbone. I paused, staring fondly at her. Her lips spread in a smile. Her eyes dropped down to the antelope quarter. She nodded approvingly.

"Fresh meat. We'll have stew or steaks tonight?"

I laughed delightedly at the way she made a statement a question. "Steak," I said.

She nodded. "Stew tomorrow." She came forward to take the quarter from me, pausing to kiss me quickly.

I grabbed her and kissed her deeply until I could feel the passion move up inside her. Then I released her and stepped back and away from her. Her eyes glinted blackly at me, her nose widening as if gathering scent on a breeze. Then she lunged forward, catching me unaware. Her momentum drove me backward until the backs of my knees caught the edge of the bed. I fell backward and she tumbled onto me.

"You don't get away that easily," she muttered darkly.

"Didn't think I would." I grinned.

"Damn you," she breathed. . . .

"Sophie?" I said.

She nodded. "You do remember. Just needed a little nudging?"

A wave of nostalgia washed over me as I recognized the habit of her sister ingrained in her, the making of a statement into a question. Images flitted across my memory, then fluttered away on bat's wings.

"Yes," I said. "I remember you. But not like this."

She shook her head. "Times are hard. Especially for half breeds. That damn Custer and his men. You know?"

I nodded. I knew. Everyone knew about the Washita and how the Seventh Cavalry had massacred the Cheyenne and some odd hangers-on despite their peaceful lodging under the American flag that Black Kettle flew religiously outside his tepee under the mistaken guise that it offered protection from xenophobic Americans. The newspapers had made it out to be a major victory for Custer, thanks to his pet reporters he took with him on all his campaigns. He had learned early the advantage of publicity.

"Not everyone's a Custer," I said. "There are quite a few good men around."

She gave me a strange look. "Yes. I didn't mean to hurt you. What was between you and Annie was between you and Annie. Besides"—her lips split in a rueful smile—"who am I to point a finger and shout about whoresons?"

I shrugged. "Who is anyone?" I cupped my hand under her chin and lifted it and kissed her gently on the lips. Her eyes shone up at me and then a tear ran slowly over her high cheekbones and down her golden skin.

We didn't become lovers that night but soon after. Zoë was a bit miffed for a while, but Judd Harkin started paying her a moon-eyed attention, riding in from his ranch two or three times a week, and her attentions turned elsewhere.

Sometimes, though, when the pale moonlight slanted in just right through Sophie's window and caught her face in a certain light I would see Mary's face and then a great sadness would well over me again at what I had lost and the

world would seem a sadder place for me and I had a hint of
what Pie was going through each June.

Once I tried to talk to him about this, but he cut me short,
saying with a twisted grin, "All the world's a stage and we're
all playing various roles upon it. Didn't you know that,
Bill?"

CHAPTER 45

I WAS walking past the stage when a woman stepped in
front of me. I touched the brim of my hat automatically
and made to step around her, but she stepped back in front
of me. I frowned and took a half step back, studying her
carefully; then a smile broke over her generous lips.

"James Butler Hickok, you mean to say that you don't recognize me? And after all we were to each other once?" she
said, pouting. She arched her shoulders back, bringing her
breasts up brazenly, and I smiled.

"Hello, Susannah Moore," I said. "It's been a long time
since Springfield."

"Six years," she said, her voice low and husky as I remembered it. My stomach felt weak and I grinned.

"Six long years," I said musingly. Lights glittered in her
eyes and her pink tongue flickered out like an adder and
damn if those six years didn't seem to melt away. She and I
had set up housekeeping in a small cottage south of the
tracks, but I could tell that there wasn't anything to us other
than a healthy desire for each other's bodies. When we
weren't making love, we fought like cats and dogs, and then
she took to taunting me about Dave Tutt, and, well, I had
put her on the next train going west, figuring she would find

herself another "house" somewhere down the line. When that train finally rolled out of sight, I had breathed a long sigh of relief.

I strolled on down to the Alamo Saloon and went in to have a drink to celebrate my good fortune. Mayor Joe Mc-Coy was having a midafternoon toddy and offered to buy a round for the two of us, saying he had a little thing he wanted to discuss with me.

"By the way, Jim," the mayor said, "we will have a circus in town next week."

"A circus?" I shook my head. "You're asking for trouble, Joe. A circus always brings shills and crooked games with it."

"There will be a lot of spending, too, though," McCoy said.

I stared into his eyes and knew that any further argument was useless. The mayor and other businessmen had already imagined the money they would deposit in the bank during the week that the circus was in town. For that they would put up with minor nuisances, which would really be my problem anyway. Yet I had to voice my opposition, if only to be on the record if something drastic went wrong.

"I'm going to be pretty shorthanded next week," I said. "I have to send some prisoners over to Abilene with a couple of deputies. All of us will be pulling double duty as it is without the problem of the circus being in town. This is a bad time for it to be here."

McCoy frowned at me. "Would there ever be a good time for you, Mr. Hickok?"

"Frankly, no," I said, honest to a fault. "Circus people cause more trouble than they're worth."

"People need an outlet for amusement, Mr. Hickok," Ted Henry said. I turned my attention to him. "The normal mundane passing of life must have a few thrills to it."

I laughed. "I thought we had that when the trail herds

came through. Wasn't that enough excitement for everyone?"

McCoy sighed and stared at me. "What do you have against a circus?" he asked.

"I have nothing against the circus coming to town," I said patiently. "I just want to wait until my deputies are all ready. We're shorthanded enough since I had to send a deputy down to Wichita and bring back Tom Jackson for stealing that homesteader's horse, and my other out trying to track down that cowboy who put the knife to the parson's hand when he tried to hit him."

"The parson going to be all right?"

"Yes," I said, shaking my head. "But he thinks that little cut on his hand has marked him like the wounds of Christ. He's going to be big trouble unless someone has a talk with him."

"By 'someone' I suppose you mean me."

"Who better?"

He shook his head. "I hate talking to Parson Jonas more than I did taking a dose of salts as a kid. Well—"

The sun was beginning to slip over the horizon as I decided it was time to make my way to the circus tent pitched outside of town. I really didn't want to go, but my deputies were busy checking the saloons and whorehouses down by the cattle pens, so the lot fell to me. I promised that I would make a quick appearance to remind people that the law was still around despite roustabouts who seemed to carry a carefree, romantic reckless abandon for rules and regulations. When I was a child, I had loved the carnivals and circuses when they came to the county, but I knew as an adult, as an officer of the law, that petty thievery often accompanied the circus on its rounds, with pickpockets and pitchmen often teaming together to relieve a person of his hard-earned wages. An appearance was needed to cast a bit of doubt into their minds. Yet I did not delude myself; my appearance

would not keep absolute order. I would have to deal with
several complaints before the circus left town.

I stepped inside the tent, pausing to let my eyes adjust to
the flickering light coming from torches strategically placed
around the periphery of the tent. Someone in the crowd
spied me and called out.

"Bill!"

"Wild Bill!"

"It's Wild Bill!"

I nodded at the calls, for the banter that greeted me was
nothing new. I glanced around at the crowd seated beneath
the tent, flattered at their recognition, yet a strange premonition seemed to lodge within me. Something timeless upon
the gray warm air within the circus tent, fluid and personal.
The dim noise of the crowd rolled over me like waves and I
looked up at the roof of the tent and saw a man in tights flying through the air from one trapeze bar to be caught by the
hands of another and thrown back to the bar he had just left.

For some inexplicable reason, my heart trembled and I
felt my breath come faster as a wild spirit seemed to pass
over my limbs. I felt as if I, too, was soaring upward and
outward, rising to meet the sun beyond the canvas limit of
the tent. I felt . . . purified? Yes, purified and radiant, and
my soul seemed to rise from the lethargy of my dull spirit
that had lodged within me for days, weeks, and months.

"Ladies and gentlemen! Mrs. Agnes Lake Thatcher!"

My eyes flicked back to the center ring and a dizziness
swept over me as I saw a woman standing beside a horse.
She wore a pair of crimson tights that failed to hide her
sweeping muscular thighs, her hips, the smoothness of her
belly and rise of her breasts. She wore her auburn hair up
on top of her head. One arm stretched toward the applauding crowd. Then she leaped gracefully upon the back of
the horse and urged it into a lope around the center ring.
She seemed magically changed from the human to a part

of the horse. Her long, muscular legs gripping the sides of
the horse moved rhythmically with the horse, her hips riding gently with the rise and fall of the horse. A small
black-fringed skirt around her hips seemed like the feath-
ering of soft down as it fluttered. Her breasts moved tantalizingly beneath her thighs. Her face became flushed and
her lips parted with excitement as she rose to her feet on
her horse's back, her feet confidently gripping the horse's
hips. A strand of hair slipped free and curled over her
forehead. She brushed it away irritably.

Then she leaped up in the air and flipped her feet gracefully over her head, landing gently upon the back of the
loping horse, her arms spread for balance. And then she was
in constant movement, like quicksilver, flowing over the
horse's back from one side to the other. The crowd ap-
plauded wildly and I felt my heart hammering in my chest.
I touched the pistols at my waist, calming myself with their
familiarity.

And then her eyes met mine accidentally in quiet suffer-
ance of my stare. She withdrew her eyes, then suddenly
looked back, her eyes widening, holding mine, and I felt a
force pass between us as if she had allowed my image to
pass into her soul. She curled herself around on the back of
the horse, gracefully crossing one leg over the other as she
brought the horse to a stop in the center of the ring. Her heel
nudged the side of the horse and I saw her rich, full lips part
as she murmured and the horse bowed to the crowd.

And then she was gone, riding across the ring away from
me, waving at the crowd. She disappeared through an opening in the tent across the ground from me. I took a deep
breath and, turning, went back outside. I paused in the cool-
ness of the evening and glanced back into the flickering
torchlight inside the tent. A couple of painted clowns in
baggy clothes had moved into the center ring, arguing with
each other.

I turned and walked away from the tent, heading back to town. A rim of the new moon rose into the black waste of the sky, throwing silver light upon the road leading into town. I walked along the edge to keep the dust off the shine of my boots. A new, wild life seemed to be singing in my veins.

I made my way behind the big tent to where a small caravan had arranged its wagons in a tight circle to form a miniature hamlet. I paused uncertainly, then caught a passing clown and asked where I might find the Thatcher wagon. He gave me a narrow look, glanced at the marshal's badge on my vest, then pointed wordlessly at a large wagon near the center of the hamlet. I could feel his hostility seeping from him in waves but couldn't blame him. I was certain that they had been rousted several times by other marshals during the past few years. But then I couldn't blame the marshals, either; I understood their reluctance to put up with circus folks. There had been too many cases of riotous behavior in some towns that had allowed the circuses to pitch tents on the outskirts. Usually it began in saloons when some of the roustabouts decided to "let down their hair" after a performance—usually the last one after they had packed and were getting ready to pull out. Sometimes they had left wreckage in their wake, disappearing in the night when the law tried to find them. A couple of times, banks had been robbed. Or saloon owners. Or both. I had no intention of letting any of that happen in Abilene. I figured the best way was to let the circus owners know to head off trouble before it got a chance to start. Besides, I couldn't get the picture of Mrs. Thatcher out of my head.

I shook my head as I approached the wagon. *Quit this nonsense. You're only asking for trouble. Rule one: Never fool around with a married woman. Leave that for Cody and the others.*

I knocked politely on the door and heard a voice call out to come in. I opened the door and stepped inside. She was alone in the wagon, costumes and the careless litter of a single person scattered throughout the living space. The crimson tights had been tossed on a small bed attached to one side of the wagon. She sat at the long end in front of a mirror and tiny table littered with makeup, powder, brushes, and rouge pots. She leaned forward, looking in the mirror as she wiped the stage makeup from her face. The robe she wore gaped wide and I had a quick look at her generous breasts before she looked up at me, gasped, and leaned back away from the mirror, her hands quickly pulling the robe closed around her neck.

"Yes? What is it?" she asked anxiously.

"I'm Marshal Hickok, ma'am," I said politely, removing my broad-brimmed hat. I brushed my hand quickly over my hair, smoothing it. I straightened my shoulders, and my head bumped against the ceiling. I felt cramped in the narrow space. "Mind if we have a little talk?"

Her eyes narrowed, the flesh drawing tight across her high cheekbones. "And if I did?"

"Well," I said quietly, "I reckon we'd have it anyway. Is your husband about somewhere?"

She sighed and stood up. I was surprised at how short she was. She had looked taller in the ring. She had a lot of spring in her legs, I thought, looking down automatically. Her bare feet were highly arched, her ankles well formed.

"Sorry, my husband died a few years ago. I own the show now. Marshal?"

I glanced up, feeling my ears begin to burn, realizing that she had caught my stare and read my thoughts. "Sorry, ma'am," I said. "But I thought I would have a bit of a talk with you and make certain that nothing goes wrong during your stay in Abilene."

"I see," she said. Her eyes shone brightly at me. I could feel the anger behind them. "So you are warning us to stay out of your town?"

"No, ma'am," I said, shaking my head. "But I don't want your people going up above the Deadline."

"Deadline?" she asked, puzzled.

I nodded. "This is a drovers' town, ma'am. A lot of cattle herds come up to be shipped back east. We've got a section of town reserved for them. I reckon it'll do for you folks as well."

"And if we need supplies?"

"There's a couple of general stores there that outfit the cowboys and outfits that come in. Some saloons as well and"—I flushed—"more than a few houses for the men if," my face burned, "they, well, you know," I finished lamely.

A tiny smile curved her generous lips. "You mean whorehouses, Marshal."

"Yes, ma'am, I reckon that's what I mean," I said, suddenly irritated by her boldness.

"And if we decide we want to go up into the other part of town where the 'respectable' folk live? What then?" Her voice dripped with contempt.

"I'll arrest them," I said quietly. "This isn't an option I'm offering, ma'am. It's a telling. Don't go above the Deadline. You have no reason to go up there. And," I added deliberately, "that doesn't mean you get a free rein below the Deadline, either. The same rules apply to you folks as to the cowboys when they come up from Texas. No guns. No fighting. I'm not saying you can't have fun, but don't let it get out of hand."

She eyed me narrowly for a long moment, then said, "How many deputies do you have, Marshal?"

"Three," I said. "But don't let it come down to that, ma'am. You'll lose."

"I think we have you outnumbered," she said.

I sighed and replaced my hat. Her eyes widened slightly at my deliberate movement. I touched the ivory handles of the Navy Colts in my sash, drawing her eyes to them. "The choice is yours, ma'am. And your people. I'm giving you fair warning. Don't go above the Deadline."

"Have you spoken to the mayor about this?" she asked challengingly.

"I don't need to, ma'am," I said.

"It seems to me that you might be overstepping your bounds, Marshal," she said. "You aren't—"

"But I am, ma'am," I said, interrupting her. I met her hard stare. "Don't go above the Deadline."

"Good day, Marshal," she said firmly.

I nodded. "Good day, ma'am. Enjoy your stay in Abilene."

I opened the door and stepped outside, closing it gently but firmly behind me. I stood for a moment in the afternoon sun, thinking regretfully about the need to be the law and how my life wasn't mine own to live as I wished. I looked thoughtfully at the closed door, then walked away from the temporary hamlet. I had a hunch that I hadn't seen the last of Mrs. Thatcher. There was a lot of strength in that woman. She didn't like limitations being put upon her. I had made a mistake asking for her husband. That was carelessness upon my part. A couple of questions put to circus folks would have told me everything I needed to know. But what is done cannot be undone.

I was right, though. The next day I came across Mrs. Thatcher coming out of a dress shop above the Deadline. She threw her head back, green eyes looking at me challengingly. "Good morning, Marshal," she said.

"Good morning, Mrs. Thatcher," I answered. "I think you have strayed a bit."

"Have I?"

"Yes, ma'am." I pointed down the street to where a sign stood in the middle, dividing the town in half. The Deadline. "That's where the line ends. Where the sign is."

"I can read, Marshal," she said.

"Then you know that you are above the Deadline."

"Yes." She gave me a defiant look. "It isn't fair, Marshal. We have the same rights as everybody."

"That's true, ma'am," I answered. "But your rights end at the Deadline. It's not that I have anything personal against you, ma'am, but if I allow you to come across the Deadline, that sends a signal to your people that it's all right for them to come across as well. And that could mean trouble later. I don't intend on having trouble later. Preventive medicine is always better than the sickness."

She flushed and bit her full lower lip. "Are you saying that we're a sickness upon the fair people of Abilene?"

"No, ma'am. But you could be. I'm just quarantining you, that's all. Just like a doctor would the measles, cholera, or typhoid."

She swung her hand to slap me, but I was too quick. I caught her wrist and held it tightly as she tried to pull back away from me.

"And you're under arrest, ma'am, for violating the Deadline and for attempting to assault an officer of the law," I said, turning and pulling her toward the jail.

"Oh! You . . . you . . . brute!"

"Yes, ma'am," I said. I lengthened my stride deliberately to keep her off-balance, stumbling after me. People turned to stare at us as we passed, but I hurried along, ignoring their questioning looks.

I opened the door to the jail and pushed her inside. She recovered her balance like a cat and, turning, lashed out again at me. This time, however, I failed to catch her wrist and her hand struck me stingingly across the face. Without thinking, I slapped her back, staggering her. I reached out, grabbed her shoulder, pulled her reticule from her, tossed it on my desk, and propelled her toward the cells. We were alone, the night drunks having been cleared out and taken to court for fining earlier by one of my deputies before he went off-duty from the graveyard hours. I scooped the keys off the top of the desk and pushed her into the first cell, locking the door firmly behind her. She spun and threw her weight against the bars.

"This—this is intolerable!" she said angrily. Her eyes were bright with frustrated tears.

"No, ma'am," I said. "This is what happens when you don't follow the instructions of the law. I won't have anarchy in my town. Even from a beautiful lady."

The last caught her up for a moment; then she remembered herself and said, "I demand to see the mayor!"

"After you see the judge, ma'am," I said.

"Very well. Let me see the judge then."

"As soon as you cool off, ma'am," I said. I turned and walked behind my desk, seating myself. I opened the drawer, removed the ledger in which we kept our arrest reports, and dropped the keys into the drawer before shutting it. I opened the ledger, took up a pen, dipped it, and began to fill out the report.

"Your full name, ma'am?" I asked.

"You know my name!"

I sighed and leaned back in my chair. "Ma'am, I know your name, but this is a formality. I don't mean any offense, although," I added, "you certainly have given me enough cause not to treat you like a lady."

A hot retort leaped to her lips, but she pressed them tightly together, staring at me. I waited. At last, she said, "Mrs. Agnes Lake Thatcher. Widow."

"Thank you, ma'am," I said, leaning forward, writing. "Age?"

"That, sir, is an impertinence!"

"Shall we say twenty-five?"

That caught her up short. I knew she was older than that; I could see it behind those green eyes that stared hypnotically into mine. Her features softened and she turned away, crossing to the narrow cot. She sat gingerly on the edge.

"Whatever you say, Marshal," she said wearily.

I started to fill out the report, then stopped and drew a line through her name. I closed the ledger and stared thoughtfully at her. Her eyes met mine; then a wry smile came across her lips.

"I'm sorry, Marshal. I was wrong."

I nodded, waiting.

"I should have stayed below the Deadline," she said. "But a person gets tired of always being regarded as a second-class citizen. I guess I was warned by one sheriff or marshal too many. But you could at least have given us the benefit of the doubt until we did something to give you reason for warning us like you did."

"That's the point, ma'am," I said. "I didn't want it to come to this. I didn't want any unpleasantness like this. Below the Deadline's not all that bad."

"But it isn't right—"

"Yes, ma'am, it is right. Folk have a right to live the way they want. You chose your life just like these folks chose theirs. I wouldn't put up with anyone going down across the Deadline to cause trouble down there any more than I would having folks from below the Deadline come up and cause trouble up here. The fathers of this town have decided how they want to live and I enforce what they have made law. Doesn't matter if I agree with it or not. That's not my job. I was hired to enforce the law, not to stand judgment against it. That's what I do. That's all I do," I said deliberately.

She nodded slowly. "I said I was sorry, Marshal. Very well. I'll stay below the Deadline and I'll keep the circus people down there. Does your law have compassion for someone who apologizes?"

"Yes, ma'am," I said. "I can give you another chance to stay below the Deadline."

She glanced at the jail door when I didn't move toward

it. A tiny frown marred the space between her eyebrows. "Well then?"

"There's still the charge of attempting to assault an officer of the law," I said. "That's a more serious matter."

Her shoulders slumped. "All right. Let's go see the judge and get it over with."

"I can fine you, ma'am, if you wish to plead guilty. We won't need to go before the judge unless you wish."

"Yes, yes," she said, waving her hand. "I plead guilty. How much is the fine?"

"Dinner tonight with me at the Drover's House," I said.

Her head jerked up and she stared through the cell bars at me, her green eyes boring into mine.

"Dinner," I repeated. "Nothing more. Just dinner."

She studied me carefully, then nodded, a slight smile softening her features more. "You are an enigma, Marshal. That means—"

"I know what it means, ma'am," I said, rising and taking the keys from the drawer and crossing to her cell. "I can read."

Her smile widened, bringing a strange, ethereal beauty to her features, taking the hardness from behind her eyes. "My words come back to haunt me," she said musingly. "Very well, Marshal. Dinner. After the last show?"

"Yes, ma'am," I said opening the door to let her out. "And it's James, please."

"I think I prefer Bill," she said, stepping out of the cell. She stood close to me for a moment. I could smell the cologne she had used and a hint of Pears Soap behind it. Tiny wrinkles slipped out of the corners of her eyes and her forehead had a fine trace of wrinkles across it. A tiny softness appeared below her chin. I was conscious of the swell of her breast and how tiny her waist was—I felt as if I could span it with my two hands, although I knew I couldn't—and a womanly swell to her hips.

"May I have my reticule, Bill?" she asked softly.

"Yes, ma'am," I said, stepping away from her and taking it from my desk. I handed it to her. Our fingers touched and she held the touch a second longer than necessary to keep it from being an accident.

"Agnes, please," she said. "Call me Agnes. I'm old enough for that." She walked to the door, then looked back over her shoulder. "And it's been a while since I've seen twenty-five."

I shook my head slightly. "Not for me it hasn't."

She laughed, deeply, richly. "You are a strange one, Bill."

And that began our affair. Not that night, though. But the next night she came to my room, and when she slipped out of her clothes my breath caught achingly in my chest as she stood naked in front of me, her full breasts dropping a little to one side after being freed from their restraint, her belly smoothed, curving down into the dimple of her navel, then a slight swell down to where tiny lights from the lamp in the room glinted off the red-gold triangle between her legs, heavy, muscular thighs swelling, then dropping down to well-formed calves, and then she stepped forward, pressing herself against me, and I thought back to the first night with Josephine and Hannah and now it felt like the first night again and a shyness came over me, startling me with its urgency, and I remembered all the other women briefly, their faces and bodies flitting like shadows across my memory like Annie's and her features appeared before me and then faded blurred by the thoughtlessness of time and slowly other images appeared slipping in and out of memory and then it was autumn and Lorenzo coming to see me to tell me not to marry Mary and oh God I thought I was going to burst when Josephine and I tumbled upon the bed of leaves beside Tomahawk Creek for the first time and I thought then that I didn't love her and that it probably wasn't fair that I would do that with her and know I wasn't going to marry her but then I thought as well as her as another and I knew then that I wasn't the first in that well-plowed field and I knew that it was all right because she was enjoying herself as much as I and teaching me a lot more than I had ever known even after watching the cows and pigs and horses and I felt a stallion myself as we slipped naked and sweaty beneath the dappled leaf shadows and again in the gentle running waters of Tomahawk Creek and again and again until I felt knowing and experienced and everything became easier and the firelight flickering over Hannah's dusky body turning it almost golden and and I felt the deep urgency of Agnes and knew it to be far more than the urgencies I had felt before with the others and I felt her mouth against mine and her tongue pressing gently against my lips and then I tasted a bit of the cinnamon and hint of apple on her tongue from the pie she had had for dessert and Hannah's deep kiss that almost drove me out of my mind with desire and then I felt Agnes's hands unknotting the sash from around my waist and then unfastening my belt and my salt-and-pepper trousers fell to the floor and she was sliding my coat off my shoulders and suddenly we were naked on the bed and a fire seemed to be licking across my flesh and . . .

CHAPTER 46

P IE AND I were strolling by the stream behind Mrs.
    Mack's place, enjoying an after-supper cigar, when her scream rent the night, tearing the moon to tatters. Even over the lowing of the cattle upstream I could hear the shouts and felt the terror racing through the dark. Then out of the dark stumbled Ned, Mrs. Mack's piano player, holding a

matted cloth dripping red—black in the moonlight—tightly against his cheek.

"It Mrs. Mack's, Marshal," he said as loudly as he could. He winced but gritted his teeth and continued. "I tried to stop him, but he git me with a skinnin' knife! He got Zoë upstairs in onna dem rooms doin' turble things to her!"

I swore and threw my cigar away, racing for Mrs. Mack's. I heard Pie lumbering along at my boot heels, wheezing as he ran as fast as he could. My boots thundered across the porch boards and I threw open the door. Sophie saw me and nodded solemnly, pointing toward the stairwell.

"Third door from the left on the second floor," she said as I pushed my way through the crowd hovering like carrion eaters at the foot of the steps. I shoved the mayor away. He cursed as he stumbled and sat down abruptly. I ignored him and took the stairs two at a time.

I pulled a pistol from my sash, simultaneously slamming my foot against the lock, breaking the door out of the frame. Zoë lay curled into a fetal ball on the floor. Over her stood a hulking buffalo hunter, fresh from a bath, but the stink still clung to him like rancid suet. He held a braided rawhide quirt in one hand, a knife in the other, the quirt singing as he smacked into her flesh. Blood spurted from the bruised flesh and she screamed again.

"Hold it!" I yelled. He looked up, wild-eyed, then back down at Zoë. His arm slashed her again. "Goddamnit, I said stop!" I roared.

He paused for a moment, staring at me, then kicked her once with his round-toed boots. She moaned and tried to roll away from him. He lashed her twice with the quirt.

I swore and stepped forward, swinging the barrel of my revolver hard against his nose. He yelped and stumbled backward. The backs of his knees hit the bed. His arms windmilled as he tried to keep his balance, but I had followed him and struck him again on his nose. He fell backward, the knife flying into a corner. He raised both hands to his nose, holding it.

"Guddam yuh, yu bwoke muh nood," he muttered. Blood ran between his palms, dripping onto his shirt.

"Next time, stop when a lawman tells you," I said.

"Whyg? Sheg onlyg a whoge," he said.

A wave of anger came over me as I listened to him claim his rights for having bought her services for the night. I had heard this before when buffalo hunters bragged how they had bought an Indian squaw for some of the meat from buffalo they had slaughtered, then left her without her nose in the middle of the prairie. This wasn't the first time I had had to come into a whorehouse, either, to set things right with a customer who thought his two dollars entitled him to a slave for the night.

I glanced down at Zoë. She stared up at me, both eyes nearly swollen shut. Her nose bent off to the left and there were cigar burns over her arms and shoulders. She cupped one hand close to her naked breasts, but I could see that at least two of the fingers in the hand had been broken. Her back and stomach had bloody welts from the quirt and there was one long cut down a thigh that had to have come from the knife in the corner.

I felt the muscles in my jaws work as I turned back to the buffalo hunter. "You are one sorry son of a bitch," I said softly. "Get up. You're under arrest."

He stared dumbfounded at me, not believing what he was hearing. "I'm arrested for the likes of her?" He jabbed a thick forefinger at Zoë on the floor. "Since when's it against the law to take what's coming to you?"

"What's coming to you?"

"I bought her! She owes me!"

"I didn't want to do it, Bill," Zoë sobbed. "He wanted me

to whip him, but I couldn't do it. I offered to give him his money back, but he wouldn't take it! Said a deal struck was it and if I wouldn't do him, then he'd do me." She sobbed.

"Get up," I said.

A sullen look came into his eye. "You wouldn't be so much without your pretty pistols, would you?" he said contemptuously.

"Now you've really done it," Pie said from the doorway. "You sorry bastard, you're gonna get what's coming to you now."

I stepped forward and jammed my pistol hard in the hollow of the buffalo hunter's throat. He gagged, then froze as I cocked the Navy. "Get up. Real slow, but get up."

He rose, the quirt dangling from his wrist.

"Take that off and toss it on the bed."

He slipped it off his wrist and dropped it on the bed.

"Turn around."

He frowned but did what I told him. I jammed the pistol barrel against the back of his neck to let him know it was still there. Then I reached down and gathered the quirt and nudged him toward the doorway. The crowd gathered stepped back hurriedly as we came slowly out of the room.

He reached the head of the stairs and I placed my foot on his butt and pushed. He stumbled forward, then rolled head over heels down the stairs. I was right behind him, and when he pushed himself up, shaking his head, I jerked him onto his feet and whipped the barrel of my pistol back and forth across his face, letting the pistol sight rake across his flesh, tearing it. He yelled and stumbled backward, his hands trying to block and catch my hands.

"You asshole!" he screamed.

He turned and ran for the door, jerked it open, and stepped outside. I followed him, and when he had taken a few steps I put a bullet in the ground next to him.

"The next one's in your back!" I shouted.

He froze, then slowly turned as I stepped down, coming toward him. A cold recklessness came over me as contempt for him welled up from deep inside of me, burning like a paschal fire. I jammed my pistol back into my sash and walked slowly up to him, rolling my shoulders, loosening them. He frowned when he saw the pistol put away.

"All right, you wanted it," I said.

His eyes narrowed suspiciously; then a leer came over his ripped lips. "You ain't gonna get away now, Marshal. This is my game!"

He threw a lumbering right hook. I leaned back away from it, then stepped left and away from the left he tried to sneak behind the hook. He grunted as his fist caught nothing but air, swishing around to his right and throwing him a bit off-balance. I swayed forward, digging my right hand into his short ribs, feeling them give way. He gasped and reeled, then tried to back-heel me. I stepped away from his foot and kicked him hard up between the legs. He screamed and fell to his knees, hunching forward, head slamming hard into the sloppy ground. His shoulders heaved as he tried to draw a breath past the pain in his groin. I reached down and raised him up by his collar, and when he stood half-erect I looped a left under his cheek, straightening him. A quick left-right-left combination drove him backward. He fell down again. This time I put my boots to him, kicking him again and again as he tried to roll away from me.

"'Nough!" he gasped.

"I'll bet that's what Zoë said, too, didn't she?" I said.

I let him climb to his feet, then stepped in and beat him again, dodging as he tried to swing two heavy fists at me. He came up against a corral, and I wedged him there, settling into a rhythm as I hit him with short, hard blows, keeping him from falling, drawing back just enough to punish him without putting him out.

Suddenly he bawled loudly like a bull calf just castrated

and rushed forward. I stepped away, balancing myself on my toes, expecting him to turn, but he ran instead for the stream. I drew my pistol and, taking careful aim, shot him in the ass. He screamed and fell forward into the stream.

The crowd rushed forward, but he never showed again. Later, when I tried to track him in the daylight, I found where he had come out of the stream near a stand of willows, but I lost him when he went across the cattle trail. It didn't matter. By then, the anger had left me and all I wanted was a prisoner to take before the judge.

But when I turned back toward Mrs. Mack, the crowd watched silently as I made my way through them to the whorehouse. They remained silent while I passed, but I could feel the uneasiness spreading through them as they wondered what had been unleashed in their town. Yes, I wanted to tell them, it was below the Deadline, but it was still Abilene and if it happened down there, couldn't it happen up where the respectable folks lived?

I kept silent, letting them puzzle it out on their own. I went up the stairs to where Zoë now lay on the bed, the other whores gathered around. Sophie was carefully washing away the blood with a clean towel when I entered.

"I saw what you did," Mrs. Mack said, stepping forward. She nodded at the other girls. "Most here did. Thank you, Marshal. It's been a long time since someone stood up for us."

I shrugged. "There's no difference between you and others, Mrs. Mack. You chose your profession and it's an honorable one as far as I'm concerned. You have the same rights as others."

I walked toward the bed, but she placed her hand on mine, stopping me.

"Anything you want anytime, Marshal, you come here and we'll get it for you," she said emphatically. "And you can leave your wallet at home, if you know what I mean."

A murmur of assent rose from the other girls. I nodded and turned my attention back to Zoë as Pie came through the door. He took one look at Zoë and shook his head.

"Ah, yes," he said. He swayed a bit from all the drink he had taken. "It's a sad affair of which we speak. But weep no more, my dear, for he has walked through the watery floor of the river, baptizing himself by walking through the waves. One can forgive him his Bluebeard tendencies as he tried to mount his way to the heights of Olympus, there to encounter his own furry Aphrodite. He did not, my dear Zoë, mean to harm you. He sought, instead, penance from your hands. You should have been quicker in giving it to him, but his Greek ways would not allow him to accept that which he asked."

"Oh, shut up, Pie; you're not making any sense," I said. "You want to do something useful, quit your nattering like an old washerwoman and go fetch the doctor."

Pie drew himself upright, gripping the lapel of his long coat in his right hand as if he intended on delivering an oration. His eyes blinked lazily, owlishly, but bright lights sparkled in their depths.

"I don't want to hear it, Pie," I said quietly. "Not now. Nor does Zoë."

He frowned, then glanced again at Zoë's battered features and nodded. He hurried away. I turned my attention back to Zoë.

"She going to be all right?" I asked Sophie.

Sophie turned her dark eyes upon me. I nearly fell into their depths, but she nodded and went back to cleaning Zoë's wounds.

"She will need to have a doctor's care for a while," Sophie said. She touched Zoë's thigh. Zoë moaned in pain. "That will have to be looked after. Stitches, I'm afraid. But there is more that you cannot see. He used that whip inside her, too."

A quick gasp came behind me. I glanced at the women standing around the bed, their hands pressed against their mouths, their eyes as they stared at the battered figure on the bed.

"Don't you worry, honey," Mrs. Mack said, patting Zoë's hand. "We'll take care of you."

"She can't hear you," Sophie said.

"Well, we will!" Mrs. Mack said as if Sophie had been doubting her word.

I sighed and pushed my hat to the back of my head. I glanced around the room and saw the man's saddlebags lying in the corner of the room. I crossed to them and opened them. They were filled with money. I stood and carried it back to the bed.

"It looks like he came straight here after selling his hides," I said. I opened the bags so Mrs. Mack could see. Her left eyebrow twitched and she nodded.

"Well, it all goes to Zoë," she said stoutly. "She deserves it after all this."

"Yes, she does," I said. I closed the saddlebags and draped them over my shoulder. "Tomorrow I'll put it in the bank in her name. Meanwhile, after the doctor has seen her, we'll move her up to the Drover's House, where she can rest."

"That's over the Deadline," Mrs. Mack said, eyeing me narrowly.

"Yes," I said, turning toward the door. "It is. I'll have a room made ready for her and send a buggy down to bring her up. Better yet, tell the doctor I said for him to take her up there himself."

I walked out of the room and down the stairs, heading for the Drover's House. The mayor caught up with me halfway there.

"I heard what you were intending on doing," he said, breathing heavily from his run. "I don't think that's such a great idea."

I stopped and stared at him. He walked on two more paces before he realized I wasn't beside him. He stopped and turned back, a puzzled look on his face.

"You make one exception, you're opening the door," he said. "The law's the law and—"

"There'll be about ten more trail herds coming through here in the next month," I said. "You want my badge now? Because it won't make any difference one way or the other. She's going up to the Drover's whether it's a good idea or not. The question is, do you want me as the law or just another citizen taking her up there. Your choice."

He stared at me, then drew a deep breath. "You're a hard man, Hickok."

"That I am, Mayor," I said, walking around him. "That I am."

The Drover's didn't want to rent a room for Zoë until I leaned over the counter and stared hard at the clerk for a moment, letting the quiet do my talking for me. Finally, he flushed and mumbled how he was probably going to be fired for it but pushed the register across to me. I nodded and wrote "Zoë Butler" in the register.

"That her real name?" he asked, reading upside down.

I stared at him again. He turned nervously to the keys and took down No. 8. "It's at the end of the hallway upstairs," he said. "It'll be quiet there."

"And pretty much away from the rest of the guests, that it?" I asked, taking the key from his fingers.

"You can't go pushing people around like this, Marshal," he protested, his nerves finally easing off.

"Yes, I can," I said quietly. "I don't like to do it, but I can only take so much hypocrisy in one town and Abilene's just used up its quota. Anyone says anything, you refer them to me. Otherwise, just leave her alone. The doctor will be giving her some prescriptions and directions of things to do. She needs anything, I expect you'll do her running for her.

Right?" He hesitated. I drew a deep breath and tapped the key against the handle of one of my pistols. "Do you want to compound the mistakes made this evening?"

"Yes, sir," he said glumly, "I'll take care of her."

"That's good," I said softly. "And if you run into any trouble or someone tries to trouble her, I want you to get me immediately. Night or day. Doesn't matter. That woman's been through more than any woman should have to. *Any* woman," I said slowly, emphatically. "And keep those damned sky pilots away from her. They want to save her soul, tell them I said to get down on their knees in their own church and do the praying there."

"Yes, sir," he repeated. "I'll do what you say."

"I know you will, Harvey," I said kindly. "You're too smart to do otherwise. When do you go off?"

He glanced at the repeater hanging on the wall. "Midnight. In two hours."

"Swing on down to Muggins's place," I said. "I'll buy you a drink."

His eyes brightened and he looked much happier as I stepped out of the Drover's and made my way back toward Mrs. Mack's place, pausing at the livery stable to tell Stumpy Waters to hitch up the doctor's horse and buggy and bring them down to Mrs. Mack's.

Zoë healed slowly, and I made certain that it was a peaceful healing. I let her friends come up from below the Deadline, and when the Ladies Brigade tried to object I told them they would be better off in the church asking God to forgive them for their hypocrisy for trying to keep sinners away from his divine judgment. For the next few weeks every time I encountered one of them on the street, she turned her head, pretending not to see me from under her parasol.

Then came the time when Doc Blake came to me and told

me there was nothing else he could do for her, but that she needed the help of some specialists back in Chicago.

"Sorry, Bill," he said, rubbing his hands across his tired face. "But there's only so much I can do here. Gunshot wounds, sewing up a few knife cuts, delivering a baby now and then, listening to the reverend's wife complain about her womanly problems, that I can handle. But whatever that buffalo hunter did to her up inside's going to have to be fixed by someone who knows his way around in there better than I do. This is going to take a specialist. Now there are a couple I know about back in Chicago, but . . . well"—he scrubbed the knuckles of his hand furiously across his scalp—"how's she going to get there? It's going to be expensive, too. We're not talking about anything simple here."

"Don't worry about it," I said. "I'll take care of it."

"You?"

I nodded at the skepticism in his voice. He started to say something else, then shrugged and left, making his way across the street to the Drover's House. I sighed and rose, settling my pistols in my sash. I took my hat off its peg by the door, flicked some dust off its brim, and left for Mrs. Mack's place. I had an idea but wasn't certain if I could swing it. I knew, however, that Mrs. Mack hadn't always been in the business, not until it became the only option left to her. I swung by the newspaper office to catch Pie up on the problems. He promised to put a plea in the paper but warned me that probably not much would come from it.

"These people have their own standards," he explained, wiping ink off the tips of his fingers with a rag soaked in kerosene. "And their standards don't dip low enough to include whores. Sorry, but that's the way it is. I got a couple hundred I can let her have. That's the best I can do."

"It's a start," I said, and left, continuing on my way to Mrs. Mack's.

I shouldn't have worried. All that woman needed was a

cause to get her lickerish up and moving. By the end of the week, she had deposited about seven thousand dollars in Zoë's account and her girls were looking hollow-eyed and sore from helping in their own way. Pie was right; the good folks of Abilene hadn't raised even a thousand toward helping Zoë. But with what had been in the buffalo hunter's saddlebags, Zoë was well off.

When I put her on the train heading east she began crying and clung to me, pleading with me to go with her. But I didn't. I watched as the train chugged out of sight, taking her away from Abilene. Inside I felt a small loneliness in the hollow of my stomach, the type one feels when a good friend moves away. We hadn't been friends, but Zoë had come to mean something to me. I hadn't figured out just what yet, but I knew there was something special that had just left my life, and a sadness came over my spirits.

CHAPTER 47

FIREFLIES DOTTED the streets at the corners as we made our way through the deserted streets. Faint piano notes tinkled in the night so faintly that they seemed imaginary. The whole town seemed to breathe shallowly, like a giant beast awaiting its prey that it knew would be coming—wolves at a water hole, waiting for the sick to make their way to it.

From beneath the boardwalk in front of the Bull's Head, Dooley the Dwarf, his hair like twists of dry straw, crawled. His mad eyes flickered left and right, anxiously seeking the children, the bane of his existence. A scabbed weal over one eye told of their cruelty. His eyes caught us and he winced, crawling backward in puffs of dust until he was half-again into his den. Then he paused, raising his head, sniffing the air questioningly.

"Grrahut?" he said, hawking and spitting phlegm in the dust before him.

"One must always honor the idiots," Pie said. "They are today's jesters who formerly advised kings with their merriment."

"Grabst. Kthogue arat lacht mucht grimbacuch gluch clach bucht—"

"Yes, yes," Pie said, nodding seriously as Dooley spoke urgently, his hands twisting and jerking passionately with his speech. Pie reached into a pocket, removed a small coin, and handed it to Dooley. The idiot took it, his eyes slanting this way and that slyly. He bit the coin experimentally, nodded, and it quickly disappeared among his rags. He looked questioningly at me.

"Grubh vohim?" he said.

I reached into my vest pocket, removed a dollar, and handed it to him. He snatched it eagerly and slipped it somewhere upon his person. Then he lay his fingers aside his nose conspiratorially and said, "Ban, ban, Ca-Caliban."

"You've made an invaluable friend with your generosity," Pie said. "Most noble of you."

Dooley nodded vigorously and scuttled backward, disappearing under the boardwalk.

Pie nodded, patting my shoulder, knighting me as a comrade in adventure. "I'm proud of you, Bill."

"He's an idiot." I shrugged.

Pie gave me a look of disappointment. "'Tis better to be lowly born, and range with humble lives in content, than to be picked up in a glistening grief and wear a golden sorrow."

I shook my head. "All right, Pie. You've lost me."

Pie looked at me solemnly. "I wonder at times whether men really trust themselves with men. All too often, men satisfy themselves with the foppery of the world that makes them react like fools when they are sick in fortune." He gestured toward the boardwalk where Dooley had disappeared. "One must never challenge the fates, Marshal. A man's good fortune at times comes at his heels. Mad people often have great wit and others look away from them, for they do not understand their thoughts, and because they do not understand, they fear them and drive them away if they can. If not, they ignore them and pretend that they are not there. They become shadows, and as shadows they are privy to the secrets of others. One must never take the station of others for granted lest one become the fool and the fool the sane."

"If you say so," I said solicitously. I wanted no argument with a drunken man. One never wins. And an *intelligent* drunken man always emerges victorious. When Bacchus touches a man on his shoulders, he imparts as well a semblance of truth.

CHAPTER 48

I HEARD a noise and, turning, spied Dooley stumbling down the street, toting a grimy flour sack of rags, bones, and old pieces of metal that clinked and clanked with his step. He stopped before me and grinned, his teeth blackened stumps in his mouth. An overwhelming stench seeped from his open mouth. I averted my face, nodding at him, and tried to step around him, but he stepped in front of me, shaking his head.

"Gach! Gach!" he said urgently, his eyebrows waggling seriously. I remembered Pie's words and inwardly sighed. I smiled pleasantly at Dooley and took another dollar from my vest pocket. I tried to hand it to him, but he shook his head violently.

"Gach! Gach!" he said emphatically. He pointed toward the Bull's Head and then pantomined shooting me. I slowly nodded.

"Yes, I know there are people there who would like to kill me. But I am ready for them," I said slowly, patting the revolvers at my waist.

He shook his head, muttering quickly some unintelligible noise, then glanced around covertly and scuttled sideways around me like a broken-legged crab. He jabbed me hard in the back with his forefinger, simulating gunfire. Then he came around in front of me again, bowing and nodding grimly, pointing again at the saloon.

I frowned. "Someone is planning to murder me? Shoot me in the back?" For a second I felt ridiculous, talking to an idiot as if he were an equal. But he nodded and I knew then that madness is only a matter of perspective.

"Would you happen to know who?"

He nodded vigorously and pretended to deal cards, then pulled an imaginary pistol from a shoulder holster. He rolled his shoulders, threw his chin toward the sky, and swaggered around in a circle, smoothing his cravat, had he worn one.

"Phil Coe?"

He stopped and nodded solemnly at me. I patted his shoulder gratefully, conscious that it was the same gesture I used on Joe, my dog, who sat panting patiently at my heels. Dooley grinned and twisted his shoulders pleasantly.

"All right. Thank you, Dooley," I said. I again offered him the dollar, but a hurt look came into his eyes and he turned away from me. For a moment I was puzzled; then I had a rare insight: Dooley didn't want my money; he wanted my friendship.

"Dooley." He glanced over his shoulder at me. "Would

you like to have dinner with me tonight?" A sudden light of hopefulness shone in his eyes. He nodded. "Very well," I said. "Meet me at the Chinaman's at six this evening. All right?"

He grinned and nodded and turned to go.

"Dooley."

He glanced back.

"It would be nice if you would bathe first. Here." I again stretched the dollar out to him. His eyes narrowed. "No, no," I said. I pointed across the street to the barbershop. "I want you to get a shave and a haircut and a bath. I'll stop by and have Mr. Goldman bring you some new clothes. All right?"

He frowned for a moment, sticking his tongue into his cheek, thinking.

"It would be a favor to me," I said.

His lips split into a grin, and he nodded, clapping his hands with excitement. He took the dollar, touched his forehead with a dirty finger, and scurried across the street toward the barbershop. I walked down the street to Goldman's Store.

The bell jangled as I walked inside. Goldman looked up from the ledger where he had been entering figures. He nodded, carefully marked his place with a pencil, and closed the ledger. He rose, pulling his sleeve guards off as he came toward me.

"Yes, Marshal? How may I help you?"

"Hello, Samuel," I said. I glanced over at the counter where he had neatly folded pants and shirts. "I need some new clothes. But they're not for me." He nodded, hands folded patiently in front of him, waiting for me to explain. "They're for Dooley." His eyebrows rose. "I'm taking him for dinner tonight. Would you be so kind as to take him an outfit? He's over at the barbershop getting cleaned up."

"You surprise me, Marshal," he said.

I raised a quizzical eyebrow. "Why's that?"

"I didn't expect to find compassion in you, given your reputation," he said bluntly. "There's not many would do anything for the unfortunate among us despite their . . . 'Christian' pretenses." He spread his hands. "Of course I'll follow your wishes, Marshal."

"And bill me," I said.

"At half-price," he said. He smiled faintly at my surprise. "If you are willing to help Mr. Dooley, then who am I to take advantage of your generosity? We have a story about that among my people."

"The Good Samaritan?" I asked.

He shook his head. "I see you are familiar with more than I thought. No, but it will do as a simile." I turned to go, but he stopped me, saying, "Do you know where Abilene takes its name?"

"Luke three one?" I said.

He smiled faintly. "That I would not know. But it is a region west of Damascus where one finds the tomb of Nebytlabil—the tomb of Abel, slain by Cain. The first murder, Marshal."

"Yes," I said. "Too bad it wasn't the last. But men are more prone to follow bad examples than good. That's why there's a need for people like me."

"Yes, perhaps. But I still think it would be best for all concerned if there were no more guns at all—even yours, Marshal."

A heavy weight seemed to descend upon my shoulders and I felt the years press heavily upon me like the weight of the stars upon the shoulders of Atlas. I nodded respectfully and left, pausing outside to let my eyes adjust to the harsh sunlight.

A group of cowboys galloped recklessly by, raising a cloud of dust, weaving around two women and a child crossing the street. One woman screamed, throwing her hands fearfully in front of her. The second hunched protectively over the child.

The cowboys reined in in front of the Bull's Head. Laughing and calling coarsely to each other, they flipped the reins of their horses over the hitching rail in front of the saloon and swaggered in, clapping each other on the shoulder as if they had just pulled a successful prank.

I sighed and crossed the street toward the Bull's Head, pausing to check at the barbershop and tell Clem that Samuel Goldman would be bringing clothes around for Dooley.

"Goldman?" Clem asked, moving carefully around a patron's lathered chin with his razor. "The Jew?"

"Yes, the Jew," I said calmly.

"I hope he doesn't want a bath," Clem complained. "He'll leave a line of grease around the tub! Damn Jew!"

"Leaving it dirtier than those buffalo hunters coming in?" I asked, irked by his prejudice. He winked at me, supposing he had found a like believer.

"Far as I can tell, one and the same. Grease is grease and it takes a heap of scrubbing to get something like that clean," he said, nodding his head like a weather vane in rhythm to his own words.

"You might try climbing into it yourself now and then, Clem," I said. He glanced suspiciously at me. "You can't keep getting by with the lavender bottle."

He started to reply, but a gunshot cut off his words. I turned and stepped cautiously from the barbershop, my hands hovering around my pistol butts. Across the street, a small crowd of cowboys had gathered outside the Bull's Head. In front of them stood Phil Coe, Ben Thompson, and the young man I had rousted out of Mrs. Mack's place. I couldn't see any pistols out, but that meant nothing in the Devil's Addition, where gamblers and cowboys had pretty much a free hand—as long as they didn't terrorize the citizens by galloping through town on their way to the saloons and bawdy houses.

I sighed and strolled across, noting my deputy, Mike Williams, shadowing me from the boardwalk opposite. Mike was a good man who usually stayed in the jail, but we had emptied the jail that morning, taking the drunks and cowboys to court. Now he watched my back as I strolled up to the small crowd of men. Ben Thompson gave me a cool grin, but Coe's eyes burned with a maniacal hatred. I understood where that hatred came from: A young lady, Susannah Moore, had left him and moved in with me when I left the Drover's Cottage for a small two-story house at the south end of town. But we had argued constantly, as she was in the market for a husband and I wasn't looking for a wife—it wouldn't have been fair, given how tenuous marshaling was—and she soon moved out for another gambler who had a small house in the Devil's Addition.

Damned, though, if the red-haired lady who was living with Coe at the time didn't show up on my doorstep a couple of days after Susannah left—*what was her name? Beth? No, Bessie, I think. It could have been Emma Williams, but I think she was more in Hays or Ellsworth*—and that pretty much was the last nail in the coffin for Phil Coe. I had taken to watching my step carefully around him.

Now Thompson was another sort. I had hauled his faro table out of the back room a week before when I found out they were using a San Francisco shoe in the game—a slap on top released a spring that allowed the dealer to slip out the second card or third card, if he wished, leaving the winner on top a loser if the bets were in favor of one way or the other. Things didn't improve, either, when I had the Bull's Head sign altered somewhat to make it more appeasing to the gentle sensibilities by painting out the genitalia. Coe was little more than an obnoxious drunk, but obnoxious drunks are dangerous when they get a load on and sense their own invulnerability. I had more respect for Thompson, who had shown how deadly he could be with his pistols.

"Hello, Ben," I said, coming up to them. I stopped about eight feet short of the crowd, far enough that I could keep all hands in view. I recognized the young cowboy from Mrs. Mack's. He wore a brace of pistols in brazen view against the posted policy. Thompson nodded at me.

"What's going on, Ben?" I asked, keeping my voice light but firm.

"Damn dog," Thompson said, smiling widely. He pointed across the street. I knew without turning he was pointing at Joe, my dog. "Thought I'd get rid of it." He shrugged and nodded at the young cowboy. "I pointed him out to Wes here, but he missed."

"Lucky," I said, eyeing him steadily. "That happens to be my dog, Ben. And you know it. What are you up for?"

The young cowboy stirred and strutted forward. "All this over a goddamned dog?" He laughed. "Why, back home in Texas we'd shoot anything that wasn't where it was supposed to be. Dogs or niggers. Makes no difference. Come to think of it, Mesicans come under that, too."

He eyed me boldly, challengingly. I smiled at him. "I think you'd be better advised leaving your guns somewhere they won't get you in trouble. This bunch could cause you a bit of a problem."

"I can take care of myself," he boasted, standing as tall as he could. His eyes shone like agates. "Course, you want, you could take them. If you think you're man enough."

"Foolish talk," I said. "I'm not impressed, and if you get killed trying it, these folks aren't going to be impressed, either."

"I don't plan on being the one dying," he said. He hunched his shoulders dangerously. "I don't know what you plan."

"On living," I said.

"Kill him," someone said—I thought I recognized Coe's

voice—and the young cowboy started to draw, but by that time I had flipped the Navies out of my sash and had one cocked and leveled at the center of his face. The other I kept pointed between Thompson and Coe.

"Bad mistake," I said.

"You think you can get all of us?" he blustered.

"I don't have to," I replied, feeling a trickle of sweat drop down my spine. "All I have to do is kill you and these other two. The others won't want a piece of that. And if they do"—I shrugged—"you won't know about it. That worth dying for?"

He half-pulled his pistols and I rocked the hammer back on the Navy with my thumb. "Another inch," I said softly. "Another inch and you're dead. Make no mistake about it. Anyone shoot me or not, you're dead. Just as certain as the sun. You want that?"

He shook his head and let his pistols drop into their holsters, slipping the thong over the hammers to secure them. I nodded but kept the pistol leveled at his face.

"What's your name?"

"John Wesley Hardin," he said sullenly. "Some folks call me Little Arkansas."

"I got paper on someone that fits your description," I said. "I'd think it a wise choice if you'd climb into your leather and head out of town."

"Now?"

"Better now than never, don't you think?" I asked.

His face flushed. "This is the second time—"

"And there won't be a third," I said, fixing him coldly with my eyes. I lowered my voice so only the two of us could hear. "The next time, I'll kill you. Make no mistake about it. This isn't a game for me despite what you think. You can say whatever you want to whomever you want once you're out of Abilene. Doesn't make any matter to me."

He turned silently and walked to his horse tied to the

hitching rail in front of the Bull's Head, mounted, and rode out of town. I had a strange premonition that I would be hearing about him again before long, but at the moment I was more concerned with Thompson and Coe. I lowered the hammer on the Navy and turned to face them, keeping my pistols in my hands.

"You are one sorry son of a bitch, Thompson," I said, looking down on the pudgy gambler. "You and that pretty boy partner of yours—"

"Who the hell you calling a 'pretty boy'?" demanded Coe, taking a half step forward. I brought the pistol up slightly and he stopped, glaring at me.

"I'll pluck that beard of yours hair by hair, you don't shut up right now," I warned. I looked back at Thompson. "Next time, try and do your own dirty work instead of getting a half-cocked kid to walk your talk," I said.

"Maybe I will," he said, his face flushed beet red.

"Uh-huh. And pigs will fly," I said.

I was pushing and I knew it, but things had come to a head enough that it was time to make an example of someone and I couldn't think of anyone who might make a better example than the two in front of me at the moment. But I knew, even as I spoke I knew, that neither one of them would make a move toward his pistols and their standing among the Texas boys had just gone down a peg or two. That was enough for now.

I slipped the pistols back into my sash and backed away a couple of steps, then turned and made my way down the middle of the street. I heard muttering behind me but couldn't make out the words and knew that I had nothing to worry about. Only after the muttering stopped. But it didn't and I walked confidently down the street away from them.

CHAPTER 49

I T DIDN'T take long, however, before things came to a head, and quickly. Thompson left town to meet his wife and children in Kansas City. The town council told me to shut down the Bull's Head but decided to leave it open after Coe sold out to Tom Sheran. But Coe didn't leave town. He hung around the fringes, gambling a little here and there. Once, when he was roaring drunk, he announced to the world that he was going to kill me before frost, and I had no illusions that it was only drunk talk. Coe would do that, but not where anyone could see him.

The city council had dismissed all of my deputies save Mike Williams, who had taken to walking the rounds with me at night until the hours settled a bit. I was grateful for his company, as it gave me another pair of eyes when I walked down through the Devil's Addition.

I remember the night.

October 5.

Mike and I had stopped for a nightcap at the bar in the Novelty Theater when I heard a gunshot come from the Alamo on Cedar Street. I knew there was bad trouble, as the Alamo catered to a different clientele than the other saloons. The Alamo had three sets of double-glass doors that were folded back on hot nights. Several paintings of voluptuous nudes lolling on velvet settees hung around the walls. The bar was one of the longest in town, with a gleaming mahogany top fitted with brass. It was a place where the stockmen played, not penny-ante gamblers.

"Stay here," I said to Mike as I moved away from the bar.

"You need someone at your back," he protested, starting forward. I stopped him.

"No, not tonight," I said "I'd just as soon you stay out of the way."

I hurried across the street, slipping into the back door of the Alamo and pushing my way out through the front. I saw a mob of Texans, mostly drunk, weaving in the street around Phil Coe, who stood in the middle of the street, waving a pistol. I took a deep breath and stepped down to face him.

"You fire that shot, Coe?" I asked.

"Damn dogs around here," he said, grinning broadly. "I almost got him, too."

"What dog?" I asked coldly, feeling the hatred welling from the crowd like a flood wave. "Where?"

"Well, hell, he got away," Coe said. "But what the hell? A dog is only a dog. Right?"

"All right," I said quietly. "Drop your gun on the ground. All of you drop your guns," I repeated, raising my voice. "Drop your guns and leave town. And you don't come back, Coe. I've had enough of you."

"*Damn you!*" he exploded, and started to raise his pistol.

I flipped the pistols out of my sash and fired as they came level. The bullets took Coe in the abdomen. He dropped the pistols and sank forward, his hands pressing against the sudden pain that stabbed hard deep inside him.

"The rest of you—"

A shadow flitted at the corner of my eye. I saw light glinting from a pistol barrel and whirled and fired. Mike grunted as the bullets hit him in the chest. He fell dead to the ground.

"My God," someone said in the sudden hush. "He's kilt them both. An' one a friend."

Rage rushed through me as I saw Mike stretched lifeless on the ground. I turned slowly to the crowd, rocking the hammers back on both pistols, a hot recklessness driving rational thought from me.

"You all have just thirty seconds to get out of town," I

said. "Then I'm going to kill every man jack of you. This town is closed to your type. Now, you coon-swyving sons-a-bitches, play your hands!"

They scattered like pasteboards in a whirlwind, leaping upon horses and galloping out of town. Within minutes, I was alone in the street with the dead Mike Williams and the dying Coe. "You . . . killed . . . me . . ." Coe gasped.

"I reckon so," I said. A bartender peeked out of the Alamo. "Go get the preacher. Get the doctor, too, if you want. It won't make a damn bit of difference. But before you do, close and lock your doors. This town is shut down."

And with that, I roared through the town, shutting down all the saloons and gambling houses. Even Mrs. Mack's place locked its doors. Within an hour, I walked the silent streets. Coe had been taken to his cottage near the school-house in the southwest part of town. He was a while dying, but I couldn't feel any remorse for him. I had Mike placed in a coffin and sent home to his wife and family in Kansas City.

Two months later, I resigned, knowing full well that I no longer had the heart for the job. Whenever I went to arrest someone, I sensed Mike coming to help me out of the shadows. A couple of times, I narrowly escaped injury when the shadows coming from the corner of my vision turned out to be friends of the man I was arresting. I knew I no longer had the heart for the job. But the days of the cattle drive were pretty much over anyway by this time. I left Abilene and went to visit Colorado Charley Utter for Christmas. I loved the mountains during Christmas—the snow-capped peaks, the sharp, crisp smell with a hint of pine. I think it was the nostalgia of Christmas as well that held me as it always did, for I could never pass a Christmas without remembering the ones I had had as a boy back in Homer. Charley opened his house to me. And then shortly after that I went to Springfield, where Cody found me.

CHAPTER 50

"**B**ILL," CODY said, coming into my dressing room at Niblo's Gardens New York, I think it was. Cody had found me in Springfield, where I was broke and trying to make a living gambling, which is hard when you're broke and gambling has been declared illegal by the Springfield blue bloods. He had sidled up to me at the bar and told me he was putting together a Combination, acting out stories of the Wild West.

That threw me for a minute and I looked at him closely and asked, "The Wild West?" Cody always seemed to speak in capital letters. "What do you mean, the 'Wild West'?"

But he waved away my question impatiently and went on about how a fellow named Ned Buntline had put together this show and it was tailor-made for people like us and we would make more money than we could burn in a lifetime of autumns if we went on with it. My options were kind of thin at the moment, so, with some misgivings, I said yes.

I should have realized what the East was like when a cabbie took me from the train station to the hotel where Cody was staying and tried to charge me double. When I refused, the cabbie tried to pound it out of my hide and I left him unconscious in the gutter. Cody had bailed me out of that one, so I thought I would give the show a try.

I glanced in the mirror at him, standing behind me. He closed the door gently behind him and I sighed, knowing what was coming. Last night had been a disaster. I had a mental blackout and couldn't remember my lines. Ned Buntline had been furious, but Texas Jack Ohumurado had thought it funny and regaled the patrons in the many saloons we had passed through in New York City after the show with accounts of my ad-libbing.

"Bill," Cody said in a stage whisper. "I don't like it. I think there're Injuns around. I gotta funny feeling on the back of my neck."

The spotlight hit me in my eyes. I saw twin halos spinning in front of me like comets. "You want to take that damn light out of my eyes?" I asked, shading them with my hand and looking up at the operator managing the light from the balcony.

Cody looked baffled for a moment. The actors playing Indians froze in tableau around the stake to which they'd tied Molly—what the hell was her last name?—artfully enough so her breasts were all but hanging free, and I had to admit that they were good-looking breasts, as I'd seen them on the times when she managed to slip away from her husband and make it to my room, which was every time when we didn't have an afternoon performance.

"What say, Bill?" Cody said, stalling for time.

"I said to take that damn light out of my eyes," I said irritably.

"Why, Bill, 'tisn't a light but the sun," he said. I recognized Kate's line, but damn if I could remember what I was supposed to say next.

"Well, it sure ain't the moon," I said, trying hard to remember the foolish line Buntline had written. I still couldn't. Something like, "Well, I reckon we ought to scout around and see if we can find those rascals." But the line just wouldn't come. My eyes were beginning to ache from the harsh light shining into them. The audience tittered, recognizing that I was lost in the wilderness of bantering words.

"Well, my neck's just a-itching," Cody said, coming back to the script.

"Hell," I muttered, "maybe you should wash it now and then."

The audience roared with laughter. Texas Jack nearly doubled over, his voice keening with his giggling behind us. Molly hooted from the stake. Even the Indian actors were trying not to break into hooraws, desperately holding on to their stage stoicism. Buntline's eyes glittered with anger when I glanced at him. But I stood nearly a foot taller than him and had once upended him in a rain barrel when he got a little cocky like the bantam he was.

Cody, however, was another story and he wasn't laughing as he stared somberly into the mirror at me. I could smell the whiskey he had drunk "to clear his pipes" as he readied himself for the matinee.

"I know," I said. "But that damn light shining in my eyes just drove the words out of my head. Besides, they're just crap anyway. You and I know that isn't what happened. Hell, you never killed Yellow Knife anyway in a duel. You shot him with your Sharps from a hundred yards away."

"That doesn't show very well on the stage," Cody said. He lifted his hand automatically, smoothing his goatee, running his thumb along his mustache on his upper lip. His eyes were red-lined from the night's drinking and foolish with the blue smudges he insisted on putting around them and the heavy rice powder he had dusted his face with to cut down the glare from the stage lights. He looked like an old whore. I told him so.

"Now, you see, Bill, that's just what I mean!" he said, annoyed. Cody was a good man, but he just never seemed to come down off the stage at that time. He even held his character when he called it a season and went back to North Platte to his Scout's Ranch. He was always Buffalo Bill Cody and whatever the hell he had decided to be the next season: Indian Fighter, Man-Hunter, Chief Scout of the Plains—whatever.

"You've got to learn what people want and give it to them. Their heroes have to be larger than ordinary men

and that's what we are supposed to be out there." He flung
his buckskin arm dramatically toward the stage behind the
door and slid one booted foot forward. I glanced at the
thigh-high boots he ordered specially made for him from
Fort Worth. Texas Jack always swung by to pick up his
leather order when he came north to join Bill in Kansas
City, where they met each year to put the show together.

"You've got to give people what they want," he said.

I remembered when I thought that was what I was doing
when I was marshaling. That was before the fracas in
Abilene when I killed Mike accidentally. Those were good
times, if a bit stressful, always watching my back, automatically reading the shadows when I made my rounds late at
night through the streets, waiting for cowboys to make up
their minds when I braced them for stepping over the bounds
I allowed as to whether they were going to turn their pistols in or use them, Phil Coe—

"Bill," Cody said impatiently. "Bill, are you listening to
me?"

I shook my head and glanced up at him in the mirror, then
back at myself, seeing the tired lines drawing my face tight,
my hairline beginning to track up on my forehead, remembering when I tried to open *The Great Buffalo Chase at
Niagara Falls* and going bust—a thousand dollars in the
hole—getting drunk as a skunk when my creditors fore-
closed on the show and letting a cinnamon bear we had
brought along as an exhibit out of his cage to roam the
streets, laughing insanely as people ran screaming from him
as he ambled through the streets, pausing to gobble down a
bunch of sausage an Italian had on a pushcart. The Italian
tried to shoo the bear away, but the bear, who had been
around humans since a motherless cub when Red Feather
had found him and raised him—I never figured out why he
did that; I would have given odds that he, being an Indian
and all, would have killed the cub and used his fur for

something—but the bear grabbed the Italian and licked him affectionately, positive that he had found a friend in that friendless city where people had been poking him through the cage bars with pointed sticks when one of us wasn't watching. A bunch of bystanders managed to free them, and the bear, sorrowful at losing a friend, ambled down the alleys, scavenging garbage bins for food. I remembered the look on the three policemen's faces when I told them to put up their pistols when they drew them to shoot the bear and hoping that they would do it and not make me live up to my reputation by using the pistols beneath my hands and the bear going *Umph! Umph!* behind me as he grunted his way through some spoiled meat outside Delmonico's. The judge took a dim view of my actions although the bear was safe by that time in a cage at the zoo.

That did it for me until Cody found me, broke in Springfield and no way to make a stake at the tables after a bunch of rich wives with nothing else to do pushed through a reform policy that outlawed gambling. Cody found me lounging around Market Square, looking for something to do. I damn near didn't recognize him in a long fur-trimmed coat that he'd had copied after a picture of some lord or baron in a magazine, a brocaded vest with a gold watch chain spread across his belly. The links on that chain were heavy enough to pull a ferry across the Mississippi River.

"Bill," he said, leaning an elbow comfortably on the bar, a tumbler full of whiskey close at hand. "Bill, I'd like to have you come back to New York with me. Buntline's putting together a play he's calling *Scouts of the Prairie*. There'll be me, him, Texas Jack, and Colorado Charley in it. You'll make up the fifth. We'll have a gay time of it all."

"Have it," I grunted, draining my glass of whiskey. "I've had it with show business. I lost my shirt on that Wild West show I tried to take back east."

He shook his head, glancing sideways at his profile in the

mirror behind the bar. "Hell, Bill, there'll be no risk to you. You'll draw a salary of a hundred a week to start. More later, I expect, after it becomes a hit."

A hit. Well, I never could say that Cody didn't have confidence. He never did think that he'd come out on the short end of a rope in anything he did. I guess that's why he managed to live grandly even when he had no money. He managed to convince everyone around him that there was gold in buffalo chips.

I started to say no, but then I remembered I was thirty-six and didn't want to spend any more time scouting for the army and tired of bending a pistol barrel over some cowboy's hard head. So here I was, giving out such lines as, "The Indians are upon us!" and "Fear not, fair maid! By heavens, you are safe at last with Wild Bill, who is ever ready to risk his life and die, if need be, in defense of weak and defenseless womanhood," which caused a bit of snickering and such from drinkers at whatever bar I wandered through.

"Goddamnit, Bill!" Cody said, exasperated.

"Yeah, I hear you," I said. "Hell, everyone in the theater hears you."

"Well?"

"Well what?" I asked.

He rolled his eyes and stuck a fist on his hip, glaring at me in the mirror. "What are you going to do? Buntline's having a litter of kittens over your actions last night. And that ain't—isn't the first time. You're getting worse as we go along instead of better. You're losing it."

"Well, whatever 'it' is that I'm supposed to be losing I don't know. But this 'play' "—I made my voice heavy with sarcasm—"is nothing more than a pile of manure. Why don't you give the people the truth?"

"I just told you—"

"I heard you. But they seemed to enjoy themselves last night. They laughed," I said defensively.

"This isn't supposed to be a comedy," he said patiently. "People know the West isn't funny. It's serious. People die out there. Horribly. Indian attacks—"

"Save it," I sighed. "I know what goes on out there as well as you do. It's not all killing Indians and outlaws. Hell, I play my fiddle about as much as I shoot my pistols. Say, you remember that dance we threw together at that church social—where was it? Wichita?—when you disappeared with the good reverend's wife and those kids found you a humping away down by the river like two jackrabbits and she yelled that you trapped her? That reverend sure was mad as hell at you! I think if he'd had a pistol he would have blown a hole clean through you."

"I remember you laying a pistol alongside his head to stop him from slapping his wife around—damn it, Bill! This is serious!" he said. But I could tell that his heart wasn't behind his words. For all of his pretending and posturing, Cody was a plainsman and damn good at it when he didn't have an audience around demanding that he be Buffalo Bill and not Cody. "Buntline is threatening to take us to court!"

I studied him for a moment, until he flushed and looked away, his hand straying once again to stroke his goatee, thumb his mustache. "And what," I asked softly, "is Buntline going to take us to court on? Being too stupid to learn lines? Why did he hire us anyway?"

"You know why he hired us," Cody mumbled, looking away. "You got any whiskey in here?"

"You've already loosened your pipes enough," I said dryly.

He ignored me and went to a small table by a chair in the room where I had left a whiskey bottle and tumbler. He poured a tumbler full, sipped it. His eyes raised in surprise.

"Tennessee sipping whiskey? Since when have you drunk anything other than Monongahela?" He took another appreciative drink.

"Since a few people like my performances," I said, motioning to the tiny bar in the corner where my costumes hung behind a dressing screen.

He crossed over and drew the curtain, his eyebrows rising nearly to his failing hairline. "Glory be to Bob!" he breathed. Cases upon cases of whiskey had been stacked back there. He opened one idly, almost reverently. Then he turned and pointed an accusing finger at me.

"All this gold and you weren't going to share with your old pard?" he said, the words rolling in proper declamation from his lips. "After all we've been through together?"

I shook my head. "We weren't really pards, Cody. You went your own way most of the time, leaving me to mine. Help yourself. I can't drink it all."

He took two bottles from the case and stuck one in a pocket on each side of the long fringed buckskin coat that hung nearly to his knees. He cleared his throat and drained the glass, placing it back on the small stand.

He shook his head. "Try, will you, Bill? Buntline takes himself seriously, and that's a dangerous man."

"Any man is dangerous who takes foolishness seriously," I said. I held up my hands as his lips pressed together angrily. "I'll try. I promise. I'll try."

He nodded and crossed to the door, pausing to say, "I know you will, Bill. I know this isn't exactly your campfire, either, but there's a lot of money here if we play our cards right. A lot of *easy* money. Easier than we ever made in all our lives."

"My father used to say that easy money usually had the devil behind the door, spending it," I murmured.

He stared soberly at my eyes in the mirror, then nodded

slowly. "Your father was undoubtedly a wise man. But money spends the same no matter where it comes from. It ain't, doesn't, got a conscience. See you onstage."

He closed the door behind him as I continued eyeing the reflection of a young middle-aged man growing rapidly older before his time. I noticed the soft blurring around the edges of the figure in the mirror and wondered idly if it was a problem with the refraction of the mirror or if it was an ominous sign of the time coming when I would slip into the other world behind the mirror.

That night, while Buntline was declaiming about "dirty redskins" and how we (the white men) had to get rid of the varmints if we wanted to civilize the West, the spotlight operator made the mistake of shifting the light to shine in my face. I was ready for him this time and drew my pistol and shot the light out.

The pistol shot, coming at that particular time, when Buntline was waxing eloquent in some speech he had cribbed from Shakespeare, took him by surprise and the beans and steak he had eaten for dinner took that moment to explode from his concentration. A loud *brrraaaaakkkk* followed hard on the heels of the pistol shot like a distant echo. The audience collapsed. Even the fabled stoicism of the "Indians" broke apart onstage and Molly, tied to the stake (I never could figure out why, as she was playing an Indian woman named Dove Eyes) and supposedly filled with fear, laughed so hard that tears dug gullies through her thick pancake makeup. Cody turned his back to the audience, his heavy shoulders shaking with deep barrel laughter, while Texas Jack sank on his heels, his high-pitched giggling sounding over the guffaws onstage. Charley Utter snickered and ran offstage, holding his nose, which only made the audience laugh harder.

Buntline stormed over to me, his face livid with anger.

"You son of a bitch, that's it! I'm not putting up with another goddamn thing from you!"

I looked down at him. "I warned you about that before, you cocky little bastard."

Enraged, he drew back his fist and swung at me. I leaned back away from it and jabbed him in the nose with a quick left. His nose popped like an overripened tomato and blood spattered his beaded buckskins. He staggered backward, lost his balance, and fell solidly on his butt. A stunned look spread over his face; then he scrambled to his feet and ran at me, fists flailing wildly.

I stepped in and dug a right into his belly. That did it for his insides. He bent double, gasping for air while air ripped out through his butt.

Brrrrrrraaaaaaaaaaaaaaccccccccchhhhh! Pft! Pft!

That was pretty much the end of the play that night, as the stage manager wisely dropped the curtain over the whole fiasco, symbolically dropping it over my stage career as well. I didn't wait for Buntline to fire me or file charges on me. I left the stage, grabbed the few possessions I had in my dressing room, and headed back to my hotel room.

I checked out, leaving the room charges in Buntline's name, and worked my way through the saloons over to the train station. In the last one, an Englishman came up and touched my long hair wonderingly, saying, "I say, are you an Indian or a white man?"

Which affront I was drunk enough not to take. I knocked him flat, announcing to an openmouthed crowd, "That's what I am."

I walked across the street and took a train to Topeka, breathing a deep sigh of relief only when the train thundered across the trestle over the Ohio River, feeling the tightness of the past months seep from my shoulders, my very bones. The two bottles of whiskey I had drained by then helped, too. I didn't come away from that trip with much of any-

thing except blue-tinged glasses I had to wear after a foot-
light exploded near me when all the scouts were supposedly
snuggled around a campfire on the plains, listening to me
tell a story.

CHAPTER 51

F OR A while I moved around the place and finally got
word from Cody and Colorado Charley that they were
planning on doing a bit of hunting and if I could meet them
in Cheyenne—

The message came at the right time. I needed to get away
from Kansas, where I was getting tired of trying to cool off
the hotheaded youngsters looking for a fast way to get a reputation, without killing them. I usually managed to get
close enough to bang them on the head with one of my
pistols—which was a good thing for me, as my eyes had gotten to the point where I wasn't sure anymore who was
friend and who I should shoot if they yelled my name from
more than twenty-five feet away.

So there I was stepping down from the train in Cheyenne,
wearing my dark glasses to keep the sun from burning my
eyes, squinting, trying to find the damn Republican Hotel,
where I was to meet Colorado Charley. I finally found the
damn thing, checked in, and made my way back downstairs.
I was heading for the bar when I heard a gasp and then,
"James? Is that you?"

I turned and peered through the permanent gloom and
saw a shapely figure hurrying toward me. I could tell by the
skirts that it had to be a woman—I thought I knew the voice,
but time places a trick on a man's memory in more ways

than one—but I didn't know her until she was standing in front of me.

"Agnes?" I said hesitantly.

She laughed and I watched the color come up into her cheeks. Her eyes sparkled and she put out a hand to touch my arm. "I thought that was you—"

I was glad to see her, and all ideas of exploring the bar pushed themselves right out of my head. We went over to a corner and sat, I taking the edge, where I could keep as much of the room in focus as I could. We talked for hours, then went to eat, and then I escorted her to the house where she was staying with her friend Minnie Moyer.

"Why don't we get married?" she asked suddenly. A mischievous smile curved into dimples.

I was a bit taken aback at this and hemmed and hawed, trying to find a way of stepping back from the proposal in a gentlemanly way, but suddenly I remembered everything that had come up since Abilene—my fling in show business, gambling, drinking—and I wondered why I should not have what other men my age had.

"I don't know," I said, giving her a chance to back away. But she didn't. She stepped in close and I smelled the lilac of her perfume and I remembered the fine time we had had in Abilene and the letters that she wrote to me at least once every two months and everything I had for myself after all those years in the West and suddenly nothing seemed as important as marrying her and nothing seemed to make more sense than marrying her, and I figured, *Hell, that's two out of three or four, and what better odds could a person ask for?* Better than hunting for a third or fourth queen on a new deal from a fresh deck, and it had been a long time since I had seen a fresh deck.

"All right," I said.

A stunned look came over her face; then she squealed with joy and leaped into my arms and the next day, March

5, 1876, Agnes and I were married by Reverend Warren in S. L. Moyer's home, and after spending the night in the Republican Hotel Agnes and I headed for Cincinnati for our honeymoon and where I thought, briefly thought, I suppose in the passion of the moment, that I would be able to hang up my guns.

I didn't find out until much later that Agnes had known I was going to be in Cheyenne because she ran into Cody, who had been drinking all day and told her in a rash moment that he was meeting me in Cheyenne to go hunting. Agnes beat him to Cheyenne on her own hunting party and bagged her own game. She was hesitant to tell me, but when a couple shares a wedding bed there comes a time eventually when one has to rest, and that means talk. At first she was afraid I would be angry, but after I thought it over for a second I realized that I was pretty fortunate to have someone like Agnes go to all that trouble for a broken-down gunfighter.

"Bill," she said after a little over a week in Cincinnati, "I heard about an eye doctor in town who has had pretty good luck treating folks with eye problems. Why don't you go to see what he has to say?"

I pushed the newspaper away from my face and stared across the room at her. She sat in front of the window in a soft halo that outlined her. I didn't say anything while I thought over what she had said. I really didn't want to go to the doctor—I suppose I already knew what he was going to tell me: that I should have been a bit more careful with consorting with cyprian devotees—but I really couldn't think of a good excuse to give Agnes without hurting her feelings. And that I wasn't going to do.

So Agnes made an appointment for me, and the next day but two I found my way to a Dr. Roderick Thorpe's office, where he examined me and then said, "Mr. Hickok, I'm afraid I have bad news for you."

"Uh-huh," I grunted, reaching for my hat. "I reckon I have a good idea what it is you're going to say."

He caught my hand for a moment and quickly released it when I turned to stare at him. He was close enough that I could see how unhappy he was about having to give me the news and how nervous he was by the perspiration popping out on his forehead.

"I am sorry, Mr. Hickok, but you have what is called glaucoma. You probably got it from your mother or father and they from theirs. We don't know much about it; I can give you some drops against the pain, but"—he shrugged his shoulders—"there really isn't anything we can do about it. Usually we find this in older people, but that doesn't mean that it can't occur in young men, either."

"I understand," I said, turning away from him.

"I would like you to see another man, however," he said, following me to the door. He shoved a piece of paper in my hand. "A doctor in Kansas City on the Missouri side—Dr. Joshua Thorne—who might have a different opinion and who might have a remedy or can offer you some more advice. I am sorry, sir."

"It isn't your fault," I said, and gave him a smile.

The smile disappeared, however, when I stepped down into the cold wind whistling through the Cincinnati streets. I had no illusion at all about what the good doctor was trying to tell me gently: I was going blind and I didn't have that much time until I would be completely blind. I think I knew I was heading that way when I was in Hays City and noticed how some people had gentle halos around them like angels and perhaps I should have mentioned that before, but at the time and in that place it would have been deadly to let it get out that Wild Bill Hickok had eye problems. I would have been dead in a week.

"Well, of course we must go to Kansas City," Agnes said

when I told her what Dr. Thorpe had said. "We'll leave on the train the first thing in the morning."

I reached out and pulled her to me and kissed her as gently as I could. I felt the slight tremble of surprise on her lips and I think she knew even then what I was going to say. But I said it anyway, telling her that I wanted to go to Kansas City alone and then go back to Cheyenne and from there up into Deadwood, where the latest gold strike had been discovered. I worked hard at convincing her to let me go alone, telling her that I had better see if I could find some quick money up there against the time when I would be blind and unable to find any work. Finally she agreed to my suggestion when I told her I would only be gone six months at the most.

The next day she saw me off on the train to Chicago, where I would change over for one to Kansas City. She cried when we left and held close to me and finally walked away, her shoulders shaking. For a moment I was tempted to go after her and tell her that I had changed my mind, but I didn't. I already knew no jobs waited for me in Cincinnati regardless of whether I had healthy eyes or not. And I already knew—even before the train chugged out of the station—that I couldn't let myself be a burden to her. I loved her too much for that.

PART FOUR

Legend

All ashes to the taste

THE TRAIN pulled into the station in Chicago. I stepped down stiffly and sighed, looking around. I had a long wait until the next train left for Kansas City and wondered what I would do to kill the time. There were always bars, but I felt a certain reluctance about going into a bar. I half-smiled at the strange change in me that seemed to have come since my marriage to Agnes, but there it was. I knew that I would eventually be back in the bars and back to playing poker, but in the meantime, I didn't want to have anything to do with the strange company of men that I knew I would find there.

I walked out of the train station into the cold, gray weather, shivering slightly when the cold struck me. I turned and walked briskly down the street, intending on stretching my legs for a couple of hours, and thought I might as well see what sights I could.

I had just turned up Michigan Avenue when I heard a woman's voice behind me.

"James? That you?"

I glanced over my shoulder at a well-dressed woman standing in a doorway, a package under her arm. I took my hat off my head and gave a half bow. "Yes, ma'am. It is. But it's a long time since anyone called me by that name except my mother and brothers."

She laughed, the sound tinkling like silver bells. "You don't remember me, do you?"

I frowned, stepping closer so that I could bring her more

in focus through the blue-tinted glasses I was wearing after Dr. Thorpe recommended that I wear those until after I had seen Dr. Thorne.

Vanity.

I shook my head.

"I'm Zoë."

For a moment I was confused; then I remembered the battered woman I had put on the train in Abilene so many years before. *How many? How many?*

"I'll be damned," I said. I started to hold out my hand, muttering the pleasantries one makes in such situations, but she stepped close and stood on tiptoes to kiss my cheek.

"It's been a long time, James," she said.

I felt a moment's confusion, then realized that she had never before called me James. Always Bill. Always. I smiled at her. "Yes, it has."

She cocked her head on the side like a towhee and regarded me for a second before saying, "I heard about your little escapades in the theater."

I laughed. "Well," I said ruefully, "there's some that just weren't made for traipsing the boards. That's what they call it, acting, I mean."

"I know," she said. I realized the changes in her, the sophistication that came only after long study. I was impressed.

"So what have you been doing with yourself?" I asked in the sudden awkwardness that fell between us.

"Not much," she said, smoothing her dress in front of her with that automatic gesture she had used so many times when she wore nothing but a wrapper and stockings held up with red ribbons. A pang of memory came flashing back to me, but I pushed it away. "I invested a bit of money with a 'friend,'" she finished.

I nodded. "Good for you. You're doing well then?"

"Oh yes. Nothing to want." But her eyes said something different. I pretended not to notice.

"Married?"

"No, you?"

I nodded and watched her face tighten for a minute; then she laughed. "Well, would you think it bad if a woman like me would invite you for dinner?"

I shook my head. "I would be honored to have dinner with a woman like you, Zoë."

A wetness sparkled in her eyes for a second; then she laughed and stepped next to me, tucking her hand beneath my arm. "Then come on. We'll find a cab and go home. It's the maid's day off, but I can—"

"Why don't we eat at a restaurant? No sense you going to any trouble," I said.

She cocked her head at me like a towhee again. "You afraid to be alone with me, James?"

You little minx. "No," I said. "All right. If that's what you want."

"I owe you that, James," she breathed quietly. A dark shadow slipped down over her eyes and between us.

"You don't owe me anything, Zoë," I said. "Let's not think about that, all right?"

"All right," she answered, her eyes sparkling again. "Let's enjoy ourselves."

I laughed and we walked to the corner, where we found a cab, and took it to her house. I sat in the kitchen enjoying a glass of whiskey with her while she cooked. Then she opened a bottle of wine and we ate—

We were sitting on the couch when she turned to me and said, "Why did you marry, James?"

I was nodding sleepily from the meal and wine and felt a moment's confusion. Then I realized what she was asking.

"Because . . . I fell in love," I finished lamely. But she had caught the hesitation in my voice and smiled sadly.

"That's not it, is it?" she asked.

I shook my head.

She regarded me silently for a second, then said,

> *"Can I be less desirable than she?*
> *Less interesting? Less beautiful? Can mortals*
> *Compare with goddesses in grace and form?"*

"No," I replied. "When my Agnes walks, she treads upon the ground. But I was not meant to belong in the East; I do not belong here; I belong where I am needed."

Angry lights glinted in her eyes. "Have you looked at yourself lately?" she demanded. "You are nearly blind and whiskey-bloated. You are right; you are not Odysseus. You look more like Falstaff, staggering around, proclaiming your honor. But"—her gaze softened but not the intensity of her words—"you are no longer the young man who tamed Hays City and Abilene and scouted for Custer. You have earned your rest." She fell on her knees in front of me. "The West is for young men, James. At least those who do what you do. Put away your guns."

I squinted at her, working hard to bring her into focus. The lamps in the room had a soft glow around them. Her golden hair shone softly around her like a halo. I shook my head regretfully. She sighed and rose, walking to the window.

"Is it because of me?" she asked lowly. "Because of what I once was?"

I glanced involuntarily at the nude painting of her hanging on the wall and remembered the photograph she had had made of her naked and given to me after I had shot the man who had beaten her while she was at Mrs. Mack's house.

"No, that has nothing to do with it," I said.

She turned from the window and pressed her hands together tightly in the folds of her dress. She gave me a crooked smile, but it had no happiness in it.

"They say once a man has tasted the forbidden fruit it no longer holds a fascination for him."

"And some men like a fine whiskey that's been well aged in oaken barrels."

She stared at me for a long time, her hair, newly cut in the day's fashion, seemed to glow around her again, and I sighed and pressed the pads of my fingers against my eyes, rubbing softly at the ache, softly rubbing the pain away from the muscles of my face.

"James," she began, but I interrupted her.

"I no longer know the boy who was James," I said softly.

"You told me once—"

"James is dead, Zoë. Can't you see that? Only Bill is left." I shook my head. "When a wolf gets too old for the pack, he must leave or be killed. I don't have that luxury."

"You have become your own legend," she said slowly.

I nodded. "Whatever Bill is. Wherever I go, I'll always be Wild Bill."

"I think that's what you want," she said, an angry note creeping into her voice. "You *want* to be the legend. All your life you have been building the legend. Well, now you have it!

"How does it feel to be Wild Bill?"

I shook my head and felt the years pressing hard upon me. My knees ached, and whenever the weather changed I felt the pain throughout my body, the old wounds reminding me constantly that they were there. My hands—I glanced down at them, spreading my fingers, studying the large knuckles, the slight involuntary trembling, critically—had lately been giving me trouble in the mornings. Sometimes they were so stiff that I could barely buckle my belt. I rolled a poker chip back and forth over my knuckles to keep them from becoming stiff during the day. Even my feet were prone to swelling during the night, so much so that I could no longer order boots from Fort Worth—the last the boot-maker had made so many years ago belonged to a younger man, to James, not me.

"It's what James wanted," I said. "Bill wants to be James."

She came back to the couch and sank down beside me. I lifted my arm and placed it around her, pulling her close. This close, I could see the tears welling in her eyes.

"Funny, isn't it?" I said. "A boy wants to be a man, but the man wants to be the boy."

"It wouldn't make any difference if you could reverse the sands of time," she said. "You would always be what people want, what people need you to be. What I needed you to be back in Abilene." She sighed. "I'm sorry for being un-grateful. If you hadn't helped me then, I wouldn't be here now."

"I don't know about that," I said. I touched the tip of her nose and used my thumb to wipe away the tears. "I have a hunch you would have been here now anyway. You weren't made to be a happy whore, Zoë."

"I wish it could be Zoë Hickok," she said mournfully. "But that wouldn't do, would it?"

I grinned and shook my head. "Some writer would get to investigating and find out about Abilene. Here you are in-vited to the theater and into the proper houses. You're much better off being Zoë Butler than Mrs. Hickok. But," I added as her full lips drew down into a pout, "you could be Mrs. Butler." She frowned, uncomprehending. I smiled and gen-tly touched the softness under her chin. "My full name is James Butler Hickok."

A new dawning crept into her eyes. She wrapped her arms around my neck and kissed me gently upon my lips. I rose, picking her up in my arms, and carried her into her bedroom, pausing just before the threshold. Her opulent curves pressed against my chest. I felt the trembling of her heart, and the answering beat of my heart begin to thud faster in my chest. On her mantel, the clock struck gently the witching hour of the night.

"It's the best I can offer," I said, hesitating.

"It's enough," she said. Her lips brushed my neck just above the collar. "But just tell me you love me. You don't have to mean it. Just once is all I ask. That's enough."

"Zoë, I love you," I said, and for that moment, I did. I carried her over the threshold as a new bride and gently laid her on her bed behind the lacy bed curtains. I bent and kissed her, long and deep, as tenderly as I could. The quickening of her breath ruffled the hairs of my mustache.

"Yes," she said breathlessly. "Yes, James, I will be your bride. Yes, you will always have Mrs. Butler to come back for. Yes, I will. Yes."

Later I rose in the dark of her bedroom, slipping from beneath the quilted comforter and walking naked as Adam before the serpent's teasing across the floor to the window. I parted the curtains cautiously. Snow fell, big flakes tapping gently upon the windowpanes. Spring snow. A bad time, but the time had come for me to set out upon my journey westward. I looked back at Zoë sleeping peacefully from our newly wedded lovemaking, curled into a warm ball beneath the comforter. I studied her face and her hair and wondered what she had been like in her youth, in the first bloom of her girlish beauty. A strange but friendly pity entered me, and I felt tears forming in my eyes and I touched them wonderingly, trying to remember when last I had shed a tear. I looked to where our clothes lay in a marriage mix upon the floor. A petticoat string lay across the floor from beneath the ball of my checkered trousers. I couldn't remember any tears before this and thought that this must be love and perhaps I had not lied when I had told her I loved her—as much as James could have loved her, perhaps, before he became Wild Bill, who only had left the moment to pass boldly into the dark of the other world, which was better for him than to fade and wither dismally with age.

I became aware of the air of the room chilling my shoulders and pulled the curtains tightly closed to shut out the night and crossed through the room's dark, quietly feeling my way back to bed with my knobby toes.

Yes, I thought, slipping under the comforter and stretching out beside her. It was time to begin my journey to the West. But not tonight. Nor tomorrow. Nor, perhaps, the next day. No, not the next day. Before then. Otherwise I would stay and age dismally until I became a dried pod, but in that time I would forget the joy of being James one last time and Bill would destroy what was between us at this moment, this *final* moment, when James had come back into the world but even now was already beginning to slip away into the dark as Bill thought of his westward journey.

I turned in to her, kissing her eyes until their lids butterflied beneath my lips, wanting her at that moment desperately to help push away the final dark for one brief moment until James entered it forever.

She smiled up at me sleepily, her bare arms rising to caress my shoulders. "James—"

CHAPTER 53

D EADWOOD.
No light, rather darkness visible.

A gray day spreads over the gulch as I saunter down the muddy road. Frost was on the surface of the water barrel when I rolled out from under Colorado Charley Utter's wagon and washed my face and shaved. I dressed and then nudged the pile of blankets heaped over Charley. Soft snoring ceased. His head poked cautiously out and dark eyes blinked heavily at me.

"What the hell you doing up in the middle of the night?" he demanded, yawning.

"Day's half spent and you're still lolling around like a whore after an all-night party. And you call yourself a mountain man," I scoffed. I nudged him again with my toe. "Come on," I said. "Let's go down to the Chinaman's and get a hot bath. My bones are creaking and need a bit of lubricating."

He yawned again and motioned vaguely at the wagon box overhead. "There's a bottle in the back left. Under the tarp. Lubricate and be happy." He started to pull the blankets back over him, but I bent and yanked them off. He yelped.

"Goddamnit, Bill! It's the middle of the foggin' night!" he complained, shivering in the cold morning air.

"It's late," I said sternly. "If you're going to go tomcattin' all night long, you can damn well get up and earn the day."

He sighed and grabbed a blanket to wrap around him as he rolled out from under the wagon. He stood, swearing softly as he worked the night out of his muscles. His legs were a mass of scars from the unwelcome attention of a bear and at least two arrowheads and a rifle ball that he still carried somewhere. He limped in a tiny circle, then went to the barrel and panned water. He splashed it vigorously on his face and chest, then toweled dry. He picked up his razor and stared at it for a moment before shaking his head.

"All right, we'll go to the Chinaman's," he said. "I can't face a cold shave today." He yawned and stretched again, looking around our campsite on the creek above the town. "There's something about the day that ain't right, Bill."

"What do you mean?" I asked, feeling the bristles rise on the back of my neck. I shivered suddenly and looked around the camp. Thirty feet away, most everything was a blur, and I stared hard, trying to focus upon the brush.

"I dunno," he said, shaking his head. "But something feels bad about the day." He glanced at me. "Stop squinting. It's a feeling, that's all. Like the day was made for something that's yet to happen and something that you won't like."

I nodded, taking him seriously. A man who had lived life like Charley seemed to develop a sixth sense that warned him about things that were about to happen. That's why men like Charley had managed to keep their hair as long as they had despite the years they spent in the high mountain country and around Indian camps and mining towns. It came from being away from man for long periods at a time. I had had it once when I was scouting for the army and in the war, but I had spent so much time since then in towns that it had slipped away from me. Or maybe I was just too damn tired anymore to pay attention to it. I felt like I was a hundred years old lately, my hands stiff in early morning, aches where I had never had aches before, and times were at night when I would sometimes wish wistfully for a bed and mattress instead of the cold ground under my blankets.

I shivered. "Well, you get any more specifics, you let me know," I said. "Get dressed now. Let's go to the Chinaman's. I need a long hot soak."

He turned away, grumbling to himself about how damn men were inconsiderate of another who had spent a long day's night familiarizing himself with the layout. I laughed as he stood on a camp stool and reached over the tailgate of the wagon and pulled a bottle of Old Hermitage out from under a tarp. He pulled the cork, took two long swallows, then replaced the cork and tossed the bottle to me. I damn near missed it, fumbling with it before wrapping both hands around it.

"Getting old, Bill. Time was you could have caught that

with one hand without looking," Charley said, stepping gingerly down from the stool. He squatted and retrieved his clothes from where he had neatly folded them under the wagon.

"You're no spring chicken yourself," I said. I took a long drink from the bottle. "I've never seen anyone gimp around as much as you in the morning, complaining about this and that. You'd think the world had been made for you and the rest of us are just trespassing."

"Uh-huh," Charley said, pulling his leather britches on and slipping the fringed shirt over his head. "Well, we have to look at things from a practical side. I've known you what? Ten years? At least all of that. And you been burning that candle from both ends. I think your wick has finally found the flame in the middle. Look at you: damn near blind— don't worry; I won't let anyone know; my mother raised no stupid children 'cept my brother—and you're still playing Wild Bill. Why don't you cut your damn hair, put away your pistols, and enjoy what time you have left?"

I laughed and turned away, heading up the gulch toward the town where "Chinese Bob" had build a bathhouse next to the creek. I could hear Charley muttering to himself as he struggled to catch up. I passed him the bottle as he came close. He took another drink and shuddered. "I could use a steak," he said.

"We'll go get something after the bath," I said firmly. "You're beginning to ripen a bit yourself."

"Uh-huh," he said. He sniffed at his armpits and frowned. "You may be right about that."

I smiled and kept silent. Charley was one of the most fastidious men I had ever seen. Next to myself, of course. I never had liked being dirty—a strange dislike for one who lived on the frontier, where bathhouses were few and far between. But I had taken more cold baths and washes in streams and creeks than I could ever remember in a month of Sundays even if I was inclined to put my mind to it, which I wasn't.

We steamed a long time in the Chinaman's house, feeling the whiskey work its way out of our pores. After a half hour, both of us felt a bit more human and we made our way down to Alice's Restaurant, where we ate steak and potatoes and drank a pot of coffee. Charley decided he was going upriver to Lead and check on some property up there—he had this idea about making a fancy house for those miners who wanted something other than a tumble and poke with overworked girls in Deadwood—and I decided to go on down to McNutt's place and see if I couldn't scare up a game.

A dog yelps in an alley next to me and my hand reaches reflexively for one of the ivory-handled Colt Navies in a sash around my waist. The alley is just a blur in the gray light, and I tense for a moment, ready to draw, then relax and chuckle silently to myself. "You're jumping at moonbeams," I say.

I continue on down the street to Saloon No. 10 and enter. The saloon is a bit crowded for this early in the day, but not as bad as it had been the night before. Red, the bartender, notices me and waves me over, placing a glass of whiskey and an egg in front of me.

"On the house, Bill," he says.

I nod. Red has taken to me since I drove a brace of drunken miners and a wolfer out who had decided to take issue with his speed of service a week back. Fact is, I had to be careful, since he refused to take my money and wanted to keep my glass full all the time. I thank him and crack the egg and drop it into the glass. I drink it in one pull, replace the glass, but before I can put my hand over it, Red fills it again from the private bottle he keeps under the bar.

"Thanks, Red," I say.

He brushes away my words with a quick wave of his hand.

"My pleasure, Mr. Hickok," he says. A miner calls for another round from down the bar. Red shakes his head and turns away from me. "The game's still going," he says over his shoulder, and nods toward the back of the room.

I turn and see Captain Frank Massey, a Missouri River pilot, still at the poker table from the night before along with Charlie Rich and Carl Mann, one of the owners of No. 10. I wasn't surprised; that game had been going on steadily for about a week now, with one or the other of us slipping away for a day or so but always returning. I walk back to the table.

"Well, look who just rolled in," Massey says, winking at the others. "You going to give us a chance to win back our money?"

I laugh. I had been a big winner the night before and there had been general grousing about me leaving the game with half the money from the table. A squint-eyed man with a broken nose who called himself Jack McCall had been busted flat and had pushed himself away from the table as I stood to leave.

"Well, you left me empty," he said sourly.

I handed him a dollar. "I never leave a man busted. At least get yourself something to eat."

He glared at me. "I don't need your handout," he said, a dull flush coming under the black beard stubble. He jammed his hands into his pockets, but his eyes fixed on the coin in my hand. I laughed and reached out and tucked it into his pocket.

"Man's got to eat," I said. "I'll be damned if I let a man go away from the table without a bit of jingle in his pocket to see him through at least one day."

Anger flashed in his eyes and his shoulders had hunched as he clenched his fists inside his pockets, but he turned away, muscles in the corners of his jaws working furiously.

"I don't believe he cared much for your gesture, Bill," said Mann.

"Some people just ain't grateful," Rich answered.

I sighed and stood, stretching. Knots popped in my back and I could feel the weariness settle between my shoulder blades. "Well, doesn't matter much to me," I said. "I just know it makes me feel better."

Mann shook his head. "Some people get insulted at gestures like that, Bill," he warned. "I'd be a bit more careful if I were you."

I laughed and sauntered out, making my way down to Alice's to get a bite to eat.

Now I laugh with the others and look at Massey. "All right, I'll give you a chance," I say. "Trade places with me."

"Superstitious, are you?" Massey jokes.

"All gamblers are," I say, grinning. "But I really don't like leaving the room at my back."

Massey nudges Mann with his elbow and winks. "Well, you can't have this one. My luck's running good with this seat and I don't want to change."

I shrug and start to turn away, but Massey says, "What's the matter, Bill? You finally afraid of something?"

I turn slowly and stare at him. A silence falls over the table as the others look nervously from one to the other, wondering how I'm going to take the accusation. I pull a stool away from the table and sit, being careful that enough space is left between the edge of the table and my pistols to clear.

"All right," I say quietly. "I'll play your game. But it better be a good one."

The others heave sighs of relief and play resumes, more subdued than before, as a nervousness settles over the table that inhibits talk. The cards run against me almost immediately, probably because I'm nervous about my back naked to the room and find it difficult to pay attention to the play. Soon I've played the last of the coin in my pockets and I turn to Red and ask him to bring me fifty dollars in chips.

He waves and I turn back to the table, staring across at Massey.

"Deal," I say quietly.

"Cards running against you, Bill?" he taunts.

I nod, knowing that it takes only one hand for Lady Luck to change her fancy, usually against those who take her for granted. She's a fickle lady and not given to those who do not acknowledge her with a touch of humility.

Massey flushes, then begins to deal.

Dimly I hear a drunken harlot singing to a beggar-man whose raggedy clothes show his sunburnt ass hanging like sourdough starter from his breeches:

> *"I have met them all, Cody and Bill,*
> *And had both of them in an hour.*
> *I adore their wonderful eyes, but still*
> *I cannot grip their thighs. . . ."*

But song is a lie. I am troubled, though, for who will remember the man behind the raunchy lines in a dance hall girl's song? A man's honor is all that survives him past the grave.

Is that the sole reality of what men like and loathe? Lies instead of truth? Dishonor instead of honor?

I am an old man looking backward upon life. It's not the years; it's the mileage in a world gone into the midnight of madness—

Eight of spades

and then there was Cheyenne and Colorado Charley and together we took a wagon train along the trail to the Black Hills following up and into the Hills to a gulch stripped of wood and called Deadwood by those who were mining the gold from the sides of the gulch and a fall rain had left the main street full of mud so that the horses and stage had a hard time coming through and then Doc Holliday climbed off the stage and Jane found him Calamity Jane who wanted to be more to me than I could take and had come overland from Cheyenne with us but she wasn't much of a beauty and didn't have the manner or features or contours that a fellow might conjure up on a lonely night and savor and she wasn't tall and leggy or even shapely at all and her nose was a bit flat and a little canted off to one side as if it had gotten in the way of someone a time or two in the past and her eyes were deep-set and green with lips that were thin enough with a touch of pout to the lower but still unvoluptuous and a little jowl and high cheekbones that would have been fashionable on anyone but her and her auburn hair had full red tints to it and was seldom waved or curled and cut short to hang just below her neck and occasionally she would let it grow longer but then it would appear greasy and gray the red dull like rust and she carried no shame of her sex with her as many women did then which made her strangely in a way pretty and vivacious but her escapades shocked the Baptist righteous who allowed a person little leeway between this world and the next and she had a way of moving her head to toss her hair back and forth away from her face but the strangest thing was how she could switch from an alley cat ready to dig your eyes out with dirty claws to a Persian kitten cuddly and warm and with a gesture leave you with an insinuation of beauty and grace that would hang momentarily in the air like lavender scent and leave a man hungry for more and she knew this because she had learned enough of what she needed to make man a fool of himself by fabricating whatever charm she instinctively knew would appeal to him but it was all sport to her regardless how seriously others might take her flirtations and I didn't take them seriously enough to suit her and she became moody but always appeared at my elbow like a cat cuddling up to its master for a saucer of milk except Jane's milk was whiskey which she drank hard and fast like a man and then the words and stories would pour boastfully from her mouth and often I would leave her there spinning yarns to whoever would buy her a glass of whiskey while I made my way back down the creek to where Charley and I had set up camp

Jack of diamonds

and the next morning the two of us would go to the Chinaman's place where we'd get a bath and have a few drinks while the Chinaman fixed us steaks and eggs and then Charley would go around looking for claims to buy and up to Lead where he finally took on a house and then decided to run a pony mail service between Cheyenne and Deadwood while I limped my way around with an old billiard cue as a cane to help me with my rheumatism that had crept up on me during the overland trip halfheartedly looking for a claim and more often than not finding a card game in a saloon with some who wanted to play with Wild Bill Hickok who was tired of being Wild Bill Hickok and who had to squint to make out his cards as his eyes were going bad until everyone looked soft with a halo around them like angels except there weren't angels in that gold camp and I knew it for there weren't no angels anywhere even in Cheyenne where I had met Agnes Lake Thatcher and married her and then went with her to Cincinnati where I thought we would be happy but we weren't happy there couldn't be happy there because I knew that I no longer had a place in this world but I couldn't tell Agnes that and that I would have to go back to the West again

Ace of clubs

and when the Deadwood strike came around I told her that I would go there and make a fortune and then we could go anywhere we wanted and she pretended to believe me and that night we made love as if we invented it and the next day I was on the train for Chicago and then back to Cheyenne where I met Charley and we put together the wagon train to go to Deadwood and found Jane at John Hunton's ranch where she got drunk and ran naked through our camp and tried to climb into bed with me and then passed out and some of the girls in the train bound for Deadwood Big Dollie Dirty Emma Tit Bit Smooth Bore and Sizzling Kate all took her into their wagon and she rode the rest of the way to Deadwood with them past Jack Boman's ranch at Hat Creek where Cody met us and told us that Custer and his men had been killed at the Little Big Horn

Eight of clubs

that sobered us up as we rode the rest of the way looking for the Sioux and Crazy Horse and Gall and Sitting Bull or White Owl to come down upon us a-whooping and a-hollering and trying to kill us but we made it to Deadwood and I could tell it was the last town for me as I rode into that town that wound along the creek like a snake between the hills and saw Charlie Storms and Jim Levy prowling around and wondered how they managed to get away from not being hanged all these years and I felt Death walking in that gulch and said to Charley Charley I feel this is going to be my last camp and I won't leave it alive but Charley just laughed as the others did who heard about that and I sat down and wrote a letter out to Agnes using a stump for a desk saying Agnes Darling if such should be we never meet again while firing my last shot I will gently breathe the name of my wife—Agnes—and with wishes even for my enemies I will make the plunge and try to swim to the other shore and I walked down and posted it to her then went to Nuttall and Mann's No. 10 Saloon where Harry Sam Young shouted his cheery greeting when I came in the door and got into a poker game with Captain Frank Massey a Missouri River pilot who had to drop out and get something to eat and then a ferret-faced man calling himself Jack McCall sat down and tried to play poker but he was too aggressive and had to buy in on every pot and before long he was broke and when he left the table I handed him some money and told him that I never left a man without a meal and he gave me a hard look and looked around the table and I thought then that I had insulted him and knew that he had played in the game only so he could say that he had played in a game with Wild Bill Hickok but he took the money and left and a couple of days later I came back into the No. 10 and came over to where Carl Mann Charlie Rich and Captain Massey were playing and asked if Mann would change seats with me so I could put my back against the wall but he laughed and teased me and I decided the hell with it and took the chair that left my back to the room and played some and lost some and then asked Red to bring me fifty dollars in pocket checks until I could get money from the camp and then I saw Jack McCall come in and look around and thought for a moment that he looked like a cornered rat

Ace of spades

but then the cards came and I laughed and said that the old duffer he broke me on the last hand but this one was going to be different then McCall shouted damn you take that and

A Historical Note

Jack McCall shot James Butler "Wild Bill" Hickok in the back of the head in Saloon No. 10 on August 2, 1876. Hickok was thirty-nine years old and rapidly going blind from "ophthalmia"—a rather broad term that covers a lot of diseases, but Hickok's apparently was a type of glaucoma or granular conjunctivitis or trachoma. The general assumption by ophthalmologists consulted in regard to the descriptions of Hickok's affliction is that Hickok suffered from gonorrheal ophthalmia. McCall was subsequently brought to trial in a miners' court in Deadwood and found "not guilty" and promptly left town for Cheyenne and Laramie. There McCall took to bragging about how he had murdered Hickok with one lucky shot—out of the six rounds in his pistol, the only one that worked was the one that killed Hickok. He was promptly arrested by Deputy U.S. Marshal Balcombe and taken to Yankton in the Dakota Territory, where he was brought to trial again. This time, he was found guilty and hanged on March 1, 1877. It was the first legal hanging in the territory. Although it would appear that McCall was the victim of "double jeopardy," this was not the case, as the court in Deadwood had no legal jurisdiction and was, consequently, an illegal court. Deadwood was an "outlaw town" in that the citizens had no right to be in the territory at the time, as the Black Hills were still legally an Indian reservation and only a federal court had legal jurisdiction.

The legend that has sprung up in regards to Calamity Jane and Wild Bill Hickok is precisely that: a legend. Despite Calamity Jane's claim that she and Hickok were secretly married, much evidence exists that shows this was an invention of hers and Hickok was not associated other than as a casual acquaintance with Jane. He was married to Agnes Lake Thatcher on March 5, 1876. She had a daughter, Emma, by a previous marriage who took Hickok's name when she entered show business. No records of any children sired by James Butler Hickok have yet come to light.

R.L.E.

BOWIE

To Jesse Everhart,
who traveled the "wilds" of Wisconsin with me
—RLE

To my family for their patience
and to my friend Randy for his.
—LCL

Acknowledgment

This work owes a special debt of gratitude to our editor, Robert Gleason, who first suggested its unusual format in Chumley's in Greenwich Village while we were visiting old haunts. May your glass always be full.

"By Hercules! The man was greater than Caesar or Cromwell—well—Nay, Nearly equal to Odin or Thor. The Texans ought to build him an Altar."

—Thomas Carlyle

Mine honour is my life; both grow in one;
take honour from me, and my life is done.

—William Shakespeare,
Richard II (I.i. 182–183)

Quod non pro patria.

—Bowie motto from family coat of arms

A. J. Sowell

According to the fashion of the day, I am obligated to take pen in hand and explain why I decided to write this book. The answer is quite simple: We need heroes more than ever now and I don't believe we can spare Jim Bowie. Of course, the heroes we need now are not the heroes that the dime novels and some of those "yellow journalists" are trying to cram down everyone's throats. No sir. We don't need those robber barons and such who think that making a pile of money makes them worthy of admiration. Money is nice, I don't begrudge a person for wanting it, but there are other things more important—especially for our young people today who don't seem to have those models to measure up to like I had when I was a youngster. Of course, I'm quick to admit that most of those heroes were real people and we knew their faults as well as we knew their qualities, and in the measuring we did, the latter greatly outweighed the former.

Strange, now that I am an old man, I am more aware of the value of having heroes than I did when I was growing up. I suppose that is a license of age. Too bad that it is wasted upon the old and not lavished any more upon the young. All too often, nowadays, I see people hustling and bustling their way through life without paying the slightest bit of attention to their children. They do not tell the stories that are necessary for children to hear, they do not read to their children anymore, and because of this, we are losing a vital part of our history as well. We can't afford to do that. We can't afford to lose men like Jim Bowie.

My family knew Jim Bowie since around 1829. But that's not so unusual. I reckon every person who lived in Texas prior to his death at the Alamo in 1836 knew Jim Bowie if not personally, then by sight, since people were prone to point out Bowie as he walked along the streets. But in our case, well, our family roots, like all family roots on the frontier, are very important, and the Sowells, like the Bowies, came from Highlander stock and Highlanders have a habit of sticking together. Bowie spent many a night discussing politics and Texas with my grandfather, my father, and my uncles.

I wasn't privy to this since I wasn't born until twelve years after Bowie's death, but I sure heard the details of some of his adventures from my kin who got it straight from the quiet man's mouth. They all delighted in filling my head with those wonderful stories. And stories were very important to a young man growing up on the edge of the frontier. He needed heroes to help him decide which road he was going to take when he became a man, and manhood came early in those days out of necessity, what with Indian problems and the renegades and outlaws thick as fleas before the Rangers took to combing them out of the Thicket and Hills District. Fact is, it seems like there was more opportunity for a young one to go wrong than to remain right those days. So heroes were important. Very important.

To know a man one must know something of his roots. James Bowie was a limb of a fine family tree. His ancestors on his father's side were Scots, Highlanders. The name "Bowie" might even be from an ancient Scottish word, buieclaiomh, *which could be translated as "the big man who carries the claymore," a claymore being a huge, two-handed broadsword. Though sometimes the clans cut down the sword or put a new hilt to it, the originals had a blade as long as six feet. The sword was traditionally carried by the clan's biggest warrior and used against men in armor. If the man was big enough and the claymore strong enough, it could cut the armored man in half.*

The Bowies were Scottish nobles and on familiar grounds with heroes like William Wallace and Rob Roy. In fact, Bowie was fond of saying that his family could trace its roots back to both Rob Roy and his wife, Helen McGregor. In fact, there seems to have been a strange parallel between James Bowie and Rob Roy, but to see that, it is necessary to explain a little about Rob Roy since heroes seem to be of little interest anymore among those who have become infatuated with the antics of villains.

Rob Roy was a bit of a rogue, but there was goodness in him: depending upon which side of the Jacobite rebellion one supported and whether he was transporting your cattle to safety or simply to his own herds.

Sir Walter Scott wrote about him and the Highlanders still tell folk stories about Rob Roy McGregor Campbell. Those stories seem to be all that are left of the man and history has built him into a legend, but James Bowie's ancestor, John Bowie, knew the man, fought with him, and was, for a time, outlawed with him.

One day, John Bowie said to Rob Roy, "Rob, we'll do no good fighting the English. They don't know the old ways, nor follow the Highland code. We'll lose if we stay."

"Aye, you're right, John Bowie, but I'll do my best to rule my land," Rob Roy replied. "But you leave with the seal of your family, and I'll wager you'll keep the Highland honor alive."

Though some uncharitable souls did speak of the certain death of a dissolute rogue who had betrayed a clansman, the fact is John Bowie moved to Northern Ireland. An uncle named John Smith asked him to move to the New World, and in 1705 or '06, Bowie immigrated to Maryland.

John Bowie had a son, John Junior, who in turn had three sons. James Bowie, who was the grandfather of the subject of this book, was one. This James Bowie lived in Edgefield, South Carolina, and married a woman named

Mirabeau. Though he died young, James and his wife had five children. One of these was named Rezin Pleasants. Rezin had a twin brother named Resa. I suppose it's hard for those not raised on the frontier to realize the hardships incurred by those who have lost a father. The male children are forced to become men even faster than usual. Back-breaking, mind-dulling labor combined with sudden Indian attacks does that.

Rezin Bowie was a "man" when he joined Col. Francis Marion—the "Swamp Fox"—during the Revolutionary War. He was only fifteen at the time and seventeen when he was injured and captured by the British.

In the 1700s, Dismal Swamp covered much of South Carolina. Oh, the people were making progress in taming the land and establishing plantations, but the Cherokees often raided the towns and plantations, and the border was slow in advancing. A maternal great-uncle of mine, John Carpenter, also one of Marion's men, said that the swamps were the most dangerous spot on earth. Besides pools of mud and quicksand that could trap an unwary person, the swamps were mosquito-infested and filled with poisonous snakes, alligators, and wild boar. A man could easily get lost in those swamps and if he did, he died.

My mother's family knew both John and Rezin Bowie. In fact, he sponsored them when they enlisted with Marion. For two years, they lived in or around Dismal Swamp. They fought many battles, but the one that was Rezin's downfall was Marion's attempt to take Savannah in 1779.

The Southern colonies were less inviting to the British than the North, so the British did not concentrate efforts at capturing the South until around 1778, when they moved into Savannah and effectively conquered Georgia with its capture in December of that year.

In September 1779, Maj. Gen. Benjamin Lincoln led members of the Continental Army against the British forces.

They could not take Savannah, so Lincoln lay siege to the city, trying to starve the defenders out. But the British general, Augustin Prevost, refused to surrender, waiting for the arrival of British troops led by Lt. Col. John Maitland. Meanwhile, Marion brought his forces to link up with Lincoln's soldiers. For some reason, Lincoln did not attack the city until Maitland's arrival. Then, he planned a three-pronged attack against the city. First, he feinted at the enemy's left, then led a strong attack at the British rear, through Sailor's Gate, and at Spring Hill Redoubt.

His plans might have worked, but Sgt. Maj. James Curry of the Charleston Grenadiers deserted Lincoln's forces and took news of the plan to Prevost. The British were waiting for the attack. Marion, my uncle, and Rezin all attacked the Redoubt on October 9, 1779. The fight lasted for hours. The British laid down a hellish fire from cannon and muskets, but Marion led his men straight to the parapet and raised the flag. Two officers were instantly killed and a Sergeant Jasper tried to save the flag, but he was killed.

Maitland counterattacked and the hand-to-hand battle lasted for well over an hour. Rezin fought well for only being a boy of seventeen. He used an old saber he had rescued from a junk pile after it was broken by a musket ball during a skirmish with Tarleton's men. He reground the point and with its basket-hilt it became his favorite weapon.

At the Redoubt, Rezin killed three soldiers when suddenly he sensed someone behind him. He whirled and found an officer swinging a saber at him. He had no time to block the blow. He caught the blade with his left hand. The sword nearly severed it. He swung his short sword into the officer's belly, then dropped to his knees, tearing off a hunk of his homespun shirt and staunching the pouring blood with it.

Meanwhile, the Swamp Fox led his men back, leaving Rezin wounded at the Redoubt. He was taken to a field hospital in Savannah, where he was treated by Elve Ap-Catesby Jones, the daughter of John Jones, a recent Welsh immigrant. Elve was immediately taken with the handsome Rezin, and in 1782 they married. She was a calming influence on Rezin, soothing his fiery temper when it threatened to explode, as it frequently did during those frontier years. They had ten children: twin girls who died in infancy, Sarah, Mary, Martha, John, Rezin Junior, James, Stephen, and David, who drowned in the Mississippi when he was nineteen.

The Bowies moved from Georgia to Tennessee, then Kentucky, Missouri, and finally, in 1802, to Louisiana, where they first took up land on Bushley Bayou near Rapides. At the time, Louisiana was a Spanish possession struggling to make itself civilized. I heard many stories about how Rezin, Elve, and their children fought the renegades who tried to take advantage of them.

One adventure in particular happened when a gang of rogues tried to squat on Bowie's land. The leader, Garreoux, I think his name was, had three others with him. He was confident that he and his men could handle an old war veteran and his brood of young children, so he camped on the Bowie plantation and began logging the ash, oak, walnut, and maple, floating it downriver to New Orleans to sell.

Rezin took his son John with him when he went to speak with Garreoux, but Garreoux only laughed at him. He insulted Rezin and Rezin's temper flared. He pulled his pistols and told Garreoux and his men to get off his land. Garreoux's response was to draw his knife and throw it at Rezin. I suppose he thought he could scare Rezin away, but Rezin was far beyond scaring by then. He shot Garreoux in the chest, handed his gun to John and told him to reload while the other three rushed him. He pulled out his knife and slashed one across the chest and shot another in the leg. John had reloaded by this time and the others decided that discretion was far better than valor—especially since the old man had just put three of theirs out of commission. They took off running.

Now, the parish sheriff was no friend of Rezin's. He came out to the plantation to arrest him and took Rezin back to the town, where he put him into the wooden jail. Elve knew Rezin had fought in self-defense, so when word leaked back to her that the sheriff—Barnett, I think he was called—was a cousin or something to Garreoux, she decided this nonsense had gone far enough.

She ordered one of the Negroes to saddle three horses while she loaded four Lancaster horse pistols that fired .50 caliber balls. She took the Negro with her and rode into town, where she confronted Barnett and told him to let Rezin out of jail. When Barnett tried to laugh at her, she handed two pistols through the bars to Rezin and pointed the other two at Barnett. Now, that may not sound like much, but those .50 caliber bores look as big as cannon when you're looking down the business end. The sheriff promptly opened the door and let Rezin out.

They worked the land along the bayou for quite a few years, always trading for better land when it came up for sale. When word came back about Texas land, Rezin began to talk about moving the family there, but he died in 1819 without ever seeing it.

I'm an old man, now, and I can see how those stories might have been embellished, but somehow, that doesn't seem to be such a bad thing. Good should be stronger than Evil. I can remember Grandpa telling me the story about how the first Bowie knife was made. I could only have been about five years old at the time.

We lived in a one-room cabin, but it was snug and warm as my family took pains to show craftsmanship in all they did. The fireplace was made with cut stone all carefully placed so as to have no chinks to let smoke back into the cabin. My father and uncles were already discussing the extra rooms that would be added come spring, but right then, at night, in the dead of winter, the atmosphere beside the fire was perfect for a story of high adventure.

Grandpa spoke like a Tennessee hill man. He never did lose that even though the rest of us had developed a Texas drawl, and his voice was always slow, the words evenly spaced, so you didn't really notice the depth of his voice or the quiet authority of his words. He was an educated man who still worked with his hands, a rarity on the Texas frontier. When he told his stories, the images just jumped and danced in your head and it didn't take much in the way of a youthful imagination to draw yourself into the picture, too.

That night of the Bowie knife story, Grandpa rocked in his chair, staring at the fire, while he slowly honed a Bowie knife, eleven inches of mirror-bright steel an inch and a half wide. The rasp of steel against the Arkansas white rock matched the creak of his rocker. His voice startled me.

"You know what this is, boy?"

"A Bowie knife, sir," I answered.

"You know how it came to be called that?"

"No, sir," I said anxiously. I settled myself on the floor beside his big feet because I knew a story was forthcoming.

"I had a little shop in the Hill Country. It was pretty wild back then. A forest primeval, hills and trees—darkness caused by shadows. I dug my shop into a cave. It seemed so much more fitting to make iron into steel while tucked within the earth itself. Just as the old craftsmen did at the dawning of the world."

He handed the knife to me. I took it gingerly, turning it over in my hand, watching the tiny lights from the fire dance off its wicked edge. He pulled his pipe from his vest and took out his little buckskin pouch of Eagle Claw tobacco

*and began to patiently fill his pipe. He watched me care-
fully as I handled that knife. When he was comfortable and
his pipe drawing well, he began.*

"*I was working late in my cave-shop. It was much drier
there than outside. A big Texas storm was raging. Lightning turned the dark night into day for brief seconds and
the sound of thunder was like a mountain falling upon
you. Those kind of nights are best spent inside where you
can forget the hobgoblins, but I had work that needed finishing.*

"*I had the forge at its hottest and the cave had taken on
a warm, red glow, when a particularly loud blast of thunder startled me. A dark figure stood in the cave's mouth.*"
*Grandpa's hand closed into a huge fist and I felt the hairs
begin to prickle on the back of my neck.*

" '*Who be ye?*' *I called out. But the figure didn't answer.
Slowly, it raised its hand and removed a rain-sodden hat.
It was Jim Bowie himself, a big man, red-haired and fair
of face. His words were soft, but when someone made him
angry, thunder clapped from him.*

" '*Mr. Sowell, I need somethin from you. There is not another man I can trust. Only a man whose blood has been
replaced with steel. Only a man whose ancestors were the
armorers of William Wallace and Rob Roy himself could
do me this favor.*'

" '*What favor, Jim?*' *I asked.*

" '*I need a new knife. War's coming to Texas, and I need a
knife that will cut the heart strings of thousands of enemy
soldiers.*'

" '*Well, can you give me an idea about what you want?*'
I asked.

"*He reached beneath the serape he wore against the rain
and pulled out a knife he had whittled out of loblolly pine.
The blade was like this,*" *Grandpa said, reaching down and
taking the knife from my hand.* "*The blade longer than*

most, short for a sword, though. Single-edged, but with a weighted back so the power of a slash would be increased.

" 'I have business elsewhere and won't be back this way for a month or so. Could you have it ready by then?'

"He knew the answer before he asked, for a Highland master armsmith always did his best work for the laird who goes to war. Especially when the laird is the greatest knife fighter of the day.

"For a month, I worked steel. Some was too brittle, some became pitted. Knife after knife I threw back into the melting pot, working back, tempering it time and again. I reformed the point to make it look like an old clipper ship and sharpened a bit of the front so that it could be used for ripping. I put on a D guard and an eagle's head pommel, invoking the old Scottish symbol. It was a miniature saber, but in the hands of a man like Bowie, it was death to the enemies of Texas."

Granddad stopped and stared right at me. "Finally, on a night just like the night of the request, the proper elements formed."

He fell silent, rocking and staring into the coals of the fire, seeing the coals of his forge in his memory. I stayed quiet, letting him remember, knowing that he would tell me when he was ready.

"Maybe, it came from the fires of Hell. I don't know if Heaven or Hell was in that knife. There wasn't another like it. Steel like a mirror, bronze the color of lightning, an ebony handle bright and checkered so it wouldn't slip in the hand, with a cross guard and the pommel like a Highland eagle.

"Jim entered as I finished edging it. He took it and looked at it closely, turning it in his huge hands. I watched him anxiously because I had made a few changes from the model he had given me and I didn't know how he would take to them. Then he looked at me and said, 'It's the finest knife ever made. What do you call it?'

"'I'll call it the Bowie knife, if that'll suit ye,' I replied.

"It suited him just fine and all the other knives that came after that are still called by the same name I gave to him that night in my cave."

Today, Grandpa's words seem a bit far-fetched, but he modeled his stories after those told by Sir Walter Scott in the books he kept on a shelf above his bed. But I called for all the stories I could get on Jim Bowie and never tired of hearing Grandpa slip into his storytelling voice. When I got older and traveled away from the homeplace, I kept a sharp ear out for other stories about Jim Bowie from oldtimers sitting in bars or around potbellied stoves whittling and chewing while they remembered when. But I always remembered Grandpa's best.

And what adventures Jim Bowie had! Riding alligators in the swamps, hunting wild cattle with a knife, duels, Indian fights, lost treasure, these fabulous tales became my favorite fare. In the daytime, I reenacted those stories, becoming in my youthful imagination Jim Bowie, while my playmates became the villains that I would dispatch with swings of my whittled Bowie knife.

I needed somebody like Jim Bowie. I needed a demigod who fought because it was the right thing to do. Later, I even joined the Rangers because I felt it was something that Jim Bowie would have done, because the frontier needed men who were willing to protect those who couldn't protect themselves.

One of the stories that was a particular favorite of mine was the story of the "Grass Fight." It seems Bowie and Fannin fought an action against a vastly greater force of Mexicans. Bowie yelled out, "Keep under cover, boys, and reserve your fire. We haven't a man to spare." I have no *reason to doubt this because Uncle Andrew was there and he never tired of telling how Bowie handled the battle. But the real point that needs to be mentioned here is that what he said is still true to this day. We haven't a man to spare. Certainly not a man like Jim Bowie.*

Today, it seems to be popular to point out another's weaknesses. I don't know why that is so popular. Everybody has a weakness or two. That doesn't matter. It's what a man does with his life that matters. And that's the reason why I decided to write this book. To set the record straight about Jim Bowie.

One of the first interviews I conducted was with Black Sam, who was a slave of Bowie's sent out of the Alamo just before its fall with a letter for Sam Houston. Unknown to Black Sam, the packet he carried also had his letters of manumission setting him free. Apparently Bowie knew that he would die in the Alamo and was performing one of his wife's last requests, to set their slaves free before both died.

Black Sam was ninety-eight years old when I found him in Los Angeles, where he was living with his great-grandson and wife. His memory was sharp, for the most part, but the picture Black Sam could give us of Jim Bowie is incomplete.

Black Sam

Black Sam was one of Bowie's slaves who was sent out of the Alamo at the end with his papers of freedom and a message for Sam Houston. It was one of the last acts of Bowie, who had remembered his dead wife's last wishes to set Black Sam free. Black Sam had been with Bowie for over twenty years and had served him faithfully during all that time, even to caring for Bowie when he went through the dark depression following his wife's death.—A. J. S.

Mars Jim? Well, he buy me oncet while I was lying in a shed down by the wharf in Naw leans, him. Aint nothing for it but that, you see. I was a rascal then, me, and the white trash who owned me was gonna take me to the Breakerman after I refused to work the cotton without water. Breakerman he wrap chains around me sos I couldnt run—heavy chains them like the swamp loggers used up in the loblolly pines—and then whip me with a blacksnake that curled the hide right off my back.

Mars Jim, why, he had come down to Naw leans to find a buyer for the lumber he and him brothers—Rezin and, well, I forgets just now, but I tries to remember, me—they cut trees in the sawmill they had in the back bayous somewheres.

I dont rightly remember much about Mars Jim, now—course, that all be good forty, mebbe sixty years ago he send me out of that place with a message for his brother Rezin. Ifn I know what coming down to happen, why I stay with him. Dont know what I coulda done different from the others once them Messicanos come down upon them, but who knows? Maybe one more gun make the difference in the right place at the right time. Happen before, it did, on San Saba—you know bout the silver mine out where the Caddos they kill the Spanish soldiers and take the silver for themselves? Thought so. It pretty much part of Mars Jims legend now.

Now, that whole thing start when Mars Jim get to seeing what the Injuns bring into San Antonio to trade once a year. Silver. But it not the silver that they dig from the ground, No sir. It the silver what already been dug from the ground and melted down into tiny bars. Oh, they tries to hide it but it dont take no smart mans to see what it was before they break it up into chunks or work it up into bands and such. It come from a worked mine.

Mars Jim take his time. He talks to the old chief and makes good friends with him. Goes back with them to theys village. Hunting, he says. Takes me alongs with him. They never seen nigger before although theys heard about one that came through many years before. Supposed to be a witch. You know, one of thems who can make sick peoples well and well people sick. Aint one of them but they dont knows that so they think it good luck to have me along with thems. Dont know what I do if I have to do something with the magic, but luck comes with us and I only have to cure a boy with the bellyache—which I do with a little bicarb of soda that Mars Jim bring along to make into breads. They mighty pleased with me and Mars Jim for that. Think it sorta breaks through this wall somes have around us.

Anyways, not long after this, Mars Jim come back from hunting with the old chief and he all excited and can hardly wait to get back to San Antonio. Seems that the old chief finally shows Mars Jim where they gets the silver. Mars Jim he tell me about this as we go back to San Antonio. Seems some missionaries—Franciscans, I think he calls them—sets the Injuns to working for them. Make them dig ore outta the ground and melt it down. That not bad, cept they treat them bad like some white mans treat niggers. Like the dock-man and the Breakerman treats me, you understand. Yes?

Now, Mars Jim, he promise the old chief that he wont tell nobody nothing about the silver mine. He tell me, course, but that aint like telling someone. I his and it like talking to hisself when hc do that. Sort of having another ear. But it only another year pass and when the Injuns come back to San Antonio, they aint friendly no more. Gotta new chief, too, they does. Mean mans who Mars Jim nearly fought with oncet in the village cept the old chief tell him that aint mannerly. Dont know quite what manners have to do with Injuns, but somes aint bad just like somes whitc mans aint bad, but on the whole I rather stick with niggers like me.

Well, Mars Jim married now with the governors daugh-ter and he and the governor get to thinking that nows the time to go back to that silver mine and bring out a load of silver and make everyone richer than they already is. The governor and Mars Jim already rich, but funny thing about that is I aint never seen a white man who have enough. Al-ways wanting more. Messicans the same way. Always want-ing more than theys already has. Cant spend what they do has but that aint making no matter.

Except in Mars Jim it was different. Mars Jim didnt care as much for the money as for the getting of it. He likely give it away oncet he gots it when he gets it.

Not long after the Injuns leave San Antonio, Mars Jim has a party together and we a-heading off to the West after them, not sos to make them suspicious—though I thinks they had those suspicions anyways—also think that new chief of theirs knew Mars Jim was coming after him cause he manage to get an awful lot of Injuns together when he finally finds the place where he wants us—but that wouldnt have made Mars Jim any less determined to go. He just naturally that way. Long with us comes Jim Coryell, Dave

Buchanan, Bob Armstrong, Jesse Wallace, Matt Doyle, Tom McCaslin, Caiaphas Ham, and Mars Jims brother, Rezin.

The sun shining bright like the Lord coming down on Judgment Day. Hotter than a griddle. Sweat already soaking through my homespun shirt before the mule I was riding and me get out of the plaza. Course I back among the pack animals along, but it clear to all there that I aint just nobodys nigger to be doing whatever it is they wants. Mars Jim see to that. I his nigger and aint nothing to nobody else.

But that day sure enough be a hot one. I cussing at it long before we clear the town. Aint much of a town, either: just a few mud shacks. One look pretty near like another cept some bigger than others and fancier inside. Should of not tempted the Lord, though, with all that cussing because it weren't long before the water came down in sheets that put Noah's flood to shame. We dont dry out no more than down it come again. And again.

Finally, about two weeks out, it stop raining for good and then I wisht it was back a-pouring as much as it want.

Took us bout a month or so—leastways it seemed so to me—to get across that land. Terrible land, it was, too. Dry most of the season cept now when we thought over again that none of the gear would dry out. Plenty of oak and mesquite for good cooking and Mars Jim and the others kept the larder filled with deer and turkeys.

Reckon it must have come somewheres north of the Llano when we run into a couple of Comanches and a Messican they used to speak for them. Seems like some younguns had stolen some horses that belonged to folks back in San Antonio and wanted to return them fore folks decided to go hunting Comanches.

Mars Jim, now, well he tell them no hard feelings by folks back in San Antonio held against the Injuns for what been done. They mighty grateful for what Mars Jim tell them and after Mars Jim give them some tobaccy and powder and shot, they ride away.

Next day, though, the Messican he come riding back, wearing out his pony like the devil at his heels! Seems they run across over a hundred Injuns following after us: Tehuacanas, Wacos, Caddos. A bit of everything.

Well, Rezin—Mars Jims brother—ast him what them Injuns might want with us and he tells us they Injuns after our hair. Dont know what they want with my woolly hair, but I get this funny feeling deep down in the pit of my stomach bout what I hears. Mars Jim, though, his eyes lit up like new silver dollars and he grins and allows how things were sounding mighty intrasting. Mighty intrasting.

The Messican he tells us that Ysayune—he the chief of the Injuns what was friendly to us?—gets to thinking bout all this and he sends the Messican on to tell us to come back and he help us him. But Mars Jim he figgers it not far to the old Spanish fort built by the mens when the Franciscans mining the silver to protects them. Mars Jim says that it best if we go there cause them adobe walls can stop a lot more arrows and bullets than a bunch of willows and mesquite bushes.

But we dont get there fore we begins to lose our horses cause it too stony and rocky and theys pulling up lame. Well, the river aint got no place to defend, sos we leave the river and rides north to where theys a bunch of oak trees with a thicket on the north. A small creek runs by it and Mars Jim decides this be the place to camp.

We dont sleeps much that night. Next morning, we pack up to move when Rezin spies the Injuns coming towards us. Injuns! he hollars and we ducks into the thicket till Mars Jim can decide what to do. Over a hundret Injuns they was.

"Well, boys," Mars Jim says. "Reckon weve got our work cut out for usns."

"Looks like it, Jim," Mars Rezin says. "But fore we do, I

think wed better go and have a little talk with them. Wont do no harm and ifn we can get out of this fix without fighting, so much the better."

Well, Mars Jim allows that wouldnt be a bad idea, so Mars Rezin, he and Mars Dave goes off to talks with them. Mars Dave he speaks a little Caddo lingo and they making a bit of friends when one Waco man waves a scalp and shouts out, How-de-do! Then, well, them Injuns begins to shoot and Mars Dave he hit in the leg.

Mars Rezin picks him up and begins to run back to the thicket and them Injuns try to run Mars Rezin down. But Mars Jim he leads a bunch of the others outta the thicket and they keep the Injuns off til Mars Rezin makes it to the trees.

Then they settles down and gets to shooting like the devil, leading his apostates at us. Yessir, I there, too, loading up Mars Jims pistols fast he could shoot them and between times keeping his rifle handy, too. When they gets in close, why that to Mars Jims liking with that big knife his. That terrible to see it. Dont know what come over Mars Jim when that knife in his hand. Seems he possessed by the devil. Face gets all white and tight like he shoes pinching the corns on his feet and his eyes, mad. I sees that once in Naw leans I. House there where Mars Jim he send this woman . . . but that story dont belong here no.

Mars Tom he killed when he try to gets a good shot at an Injun and fore long, why, they aint much left of us. Most all been shot and all been shot at so many times that no one pays any attention to balls whistling by like quail singing.

The Injuns set fire to the thicket and some try to get in on us, but Mars Jim take that knife of his and kill them. Some nights, I still hears them screaming when Mars Jim fall upon them and sees that knife of his streaming blood from it.

They runs from the thicket and bout that time a chief he

tries to get the Injuns to charge back into the thicket. But Mars Jim, he shoot him dead and the Injuns pull back to think about coming into the thicket again. Ifn they only knew that most of our guns was out of bullets cause we dassnt open a powder horn to reload what with all them sparks flying around us, we be dead now.

While theys talking about they plans, Mars Jim he gets us building a fort by throwing up piles of dirt and stones wherever we cans. We works on this through the night, thinking the Injuns come upon us at first light. But, no, they aint coming. They have enough and pulls out and leave usns alone. We return to San Antonio. Mars Jim, why, he most disappointed, but he figgers maybe the next year we try again. We never do, though.

I dont talk bout things that hurt Mars Jim no. Not that man. I dont care for some of the things he do, but he save me from the Breakerman.

Pay top dollar for me then. Happen down Naw leans way. Long time ago. Long time. Old mans mind plays tricks on him do. But I be sold at auction offn Mars Beauchamps death when his daughter sell everything and move back to Franch she. I trained for house duty, not fields. Can read some, too, I. First man buys me try to put me in cotton fields, but I dont take to that and next thing I know, Im back on the block, me, and dockman he buy me and tell me tote bale that I aint no house nigger no more and I try to tells him I that not good way to spend moneys him, but he lay that blacksnake cross my shoulders and carve his initials with it in my back him.

I try; aint no way no man not try with that snake coming fast cross his shoulders him. But aint no way I can work like others time. No way. Not brought up used to work like that no me. I house nigger. Field nigger cant do no house nigger work; house nigger can do no field nigger work no ways. Happen be that dockman—Wilson he name—he get the

Breakerman who happy with the blacksnake and take his cut at me each morning sometimes noon, too. Time today it bother me and my daughter she put the linament on it but it hurt no how anyway.

I make up my mind that I run away. They catch me they hang me good, but I dont care no more.

I remember the day, now. Remember it well although it do slip in and outta my memory at times. Memory aint what it used to be. No sir. Time was I could remember most everything, then I married up with Dulcie after Mars Jim send me back home and we free and monied, then, so we move down into Naw leans and open a restrant down in Storyville. That another story—maybes I tell it and maybes I dont. But we work that fifty years fore Dulcie she die and I works it another five before my son take over after he gets the lolapoloozing out of his system.

No, I remember that day. All I gotta do is twist wrong when the rain coming and I can remember that day. Cept there no rain that day, no sir. Just hot old sun shining down like a fifty-dollar gold piece, making the sweat run right down my back and stinging where the salt rolls into the cuts made by the Breakerman's whip. I remember that sun. And I remember them mosquiteers and horseflies buzzing around the blood on my back and biting till I thought I go mad.

That when Mars Jim come down, redhaired and gray-eyed he, and the dockman he try to impress the big white man with what he can do with the blacksnake and he curl that lash along my shoulders and knock me down. The cotton bale I carry fall into the water and he start to lean into the whip across my shoulders see me. I dont pay him no mind, though. I just trying to keep the Breakerman whip off my back. But I aint no field nigger, I a house nigger, and that why I cant work as fast as others and that make the Breakerman mad and before I knows it that old blacksnake curling around my back again.

Mars Jim dont say much. Just pick up that Breakerman and toss him into the Mississippi down where the slops sloshing against the pilings. Sure funny enough to see that but it aint good for me, Im thinking, once that Breakerman get outta that water it gonna be me that pays for Mars Jim throwing him in among the slops and the others laughing at him while he hanging onto a piling and puking his breakfast up among the slops. No sir.

I gives Mars Jim a long look and he stares back. I dont do nothing but stare at him and slowly he nods and walks over to the dockman and they begins talking and I can see that Mars Jim is working mighty hard on what he saying, but the dockman he just keeps shaking his head like he got the St. Viters Dance or something, but then Mars Jim fold his arms like this and lay his head back and stare down at that dockman and the dockman, why he suddenly make up his mind and nod. He spit in his hand and shake Mars Jims hand and Mars Jim yells to the smith on the pier to knock my chains off cause aint no way his nigger gonna insult him walking down Bourbon Street with chains clanking around the cobblestones.

That was Mars Jim. He buy me from the dockman and I go with him for many years. But not always good these places we go. But I see him many times help others like he help me him. I see him happy and I see him cry from pain when his wife and babies die. I see him the day in Baratara when we go to buy niggers from Jean Lafitte. Fact is, we find out how to get to Lafitte's place when Mars Jim take me to Pierre Lafitte blacksmith shop and have the smith break the studs off my collar.

Where was I? Oh yes. We go to Barataria Island. Day cold and wet, gray like the bayou water for a hurrican come and throw it back up on the land. Stink, I tell you. Worse than the dock in Naw leans. Much worse. What make it so the gibbet where five men hanging and feeding the gulls and kites swarming around their heads, tearing strips of meat off them like they was prime beef hanging in a tree and forgotten. Bad.

Dont rightly know what one of Lafitte mans say to insult Mars Jim, but Mars Jim, why he knock him over loop-de-loop. One smack with Mars Jim fist and down goes pirate.

For a minute there I think that we gonna join the men on the gibbet, but Mars Jim step up to Lafitte cool as rainwater and say he buy all the slaves including the culls and Lafitte just narrow his eyes down over his suety cheeks and laugh. He gonna forget what Mars Jim do to—Diego, that he name? Think so—but the other pirates there they dont let him forget what Mars Jim do so they has to have an accounting. But Lafitte, he a smart man: he wont allow no accounting until he accounts paid in full which mean Mars Jim own the slaves but if he killed, why then Lafitte own them back again along with the money Mars Jim bring with him.

But Lafitte, by then he think to be fair with Mars Jim cause he know that Mars Jim might be buying more slaves if he live. But he have what he call the honor of the society to uphold.

Well, Mars Jim allow how that seem right to him, but I see that the excitement getting upon him by his eyes. He look across the sand and see this log half-buried where the big water bring it up on the fast tide. He walk down to that and get to studying it and the next thing I see, they pirates a-nailing both Mars Jim and this Diego to this log in the sand, driving them tenpenny nails deep through their pants into the log. They give a knife to each and the pirate he try to kill Mars Jim straight off, but Mars Jim too big and cut the pirate throat with one slice. Sand turn black from the blood gushing from his throat like a fountain.

We run the slaves for near two years. Mars Jim he smarter

than other runners. No swamp sale for him. No sir. He take
niggers to the mainland and then take them north and find
the sheriff at Naw leans. He turn the niggers in to the sheriff, saying he find them him along the coast. Sheriff hold
he sale and Mars Jim take half the money for his reward.
Everything all up and up on the legal.

I know the sheriff he know what Mars Jim doing. Aint
no man catch as many niggers that way alone along a coast.
Maybe once in a lifetime all. But he can tell that he better
not call Mars Jim a liar. There something about the way
Mars Jim had at looking into another mans eyes that made
a man think twice about calling him a liar even if he was a
time or two.

Oh, that dont mean he not without honor. How you think
the judges get rich in Naw leans anyways? Or the lawyers?
Aint one of them without honor. But in the trade, why every
man looks out after himself. That business. That all.

But that aint it either, Im thinking. No, sir. Not at all. Always something else about Mars Jim that make you want
to believe him even when you knows you crazy for believing him. I guess that what bring up the big fights down at
the sandbar. Yessir, that the one between him and Major
Norris Wright except that ain't what it really is. A woman
involved there, too. Seem like always in the big fights before Texas theys a woman involved. They flocks around
Mars Jim like flies on a honey pot. Why somes even send
him gifts—mostly married womens them. They the ones
that aint gotta worry about theys reputations because theys
husband gives them respecterbility.

Mars Jim send most of them back but always send along
a little something extra sos not to insult them. He say a mad
woman be the worst thing a man could have and he just
didnt have the time to try and make things smooth with a
mad womans. Besides, some of those womans come from

pretty powerful family in Naw leans at the time. Oh yes. Mighty important some. But Mars Jim, why he play soft with them.

Cept one.

Sometimes I think she the one that make Mars Jim do crazy things like running niggers from Barataria. Seem like he always trying to get more and more moneys faster and faster. I think he have in mind making a wife of that one. But she bad. I know. Man not look at her beauty, look behind it, man can see the poison there. Bad poison.

Judalon de Bornay. Remember her name, now. No way I forget her. Mars Jim kill two men for her. Notice I says for her. Not on cause of her. That woman she likes to play with men. Make all mad for her then pit them together like buck niggers in the quarter, know what I mean? Way the owners used to bring theys big buck niggers in from the fields and fight them against each other in the quarter, back where theys a courtyard or two. Fight to the death, thems. But that aint for Judalon Bourney. No sir. She gets herself in with some bad mens and beg Mars Jim to take her out of her trouble.

First time that happen she courting this fancy fencing man and he get a little fresh with her. She tell Mars Jim the fencing man try to take liberties that only a married man should take—cepting we know that aint exactly true cause womens take the same liberties when they cans—and Mars Jim he challenges the man to a duel.

That a bad one and Mars Jim kill the man back of St. Somethings place—one of them gambling places where niggers exchange owners three, four times a night, sometimes. In an old storeroom it was. They puts both of them in there without lights, the fancy fencing man with a sword and Mars Jim with this big knife—I tell you about Domi-ique You, Lafittes man in Naw leans? No? Well it seems . . . sorry. Old man rambles at times. Well, it his knife

> ## Children of James Bowie and Ursula Bowie, née María Ursula de Veramendi
>
> Maria Elve Bowie, born April 18, 1832, in Bexar
> James Veramendi Bowie, born July 18, 1833, in Monclova

Mars Jim uses. Everybody laugh at that, knife against a sword. Nobody laugh when Mars Jim walk out without a scratch upon him and the fancy fencing man laying in a pool of blood on the floor of that storeroom.

Another time, years later and Mars Jim already married to Ursula he love so much who he send away to die. But Mars Jim and me on a riverboat that time, coming down to Naw leans after clearing up a old debts owed Mars Jim and he brothers from the time they in the land business up north. This Judalon Bourney married now to somebody who no good for her. A weak man who gambled away all theys money cept Mars Jim, why he know they aint no way that game straight narrowed. Crooked as a black cat's tail. He get into the game and catch them cheating. Onc man crazy enough to challenge Mars Jim and Mars Jim drive that big knife of hisn clean through his breast bone when the gambler try to shoot him. Strike so hard you could hear the bone break when the knife hit him.

She the reason, though, that we make maybe fifteen run with gang of niggers from Barataria and Mars Jim he get rich. But last time bad time. It all my fault. I sleep and the niggers get away and the niggers they get away after Mars Jim tells me not to chain them cause we far enough inland and away from the ocean that they wont run. But when I on watch, I fall asleep and the niggers take and creep away from the fire and run back towards the coast from which we just takes them. Stupid niggers. They run right into the Kronks, them. Cannibals.

When we catch up to them wasnt nothing left. The Kronks ate good they. Nothing left cept cooked bones and splotches of fat and grease and blood on the sands. Birds bellies heavy with what Kronks dont eat.

Well, Mars Jim, he look at what Kronks do and he shake his head and turn away. "Sam," says he, "aint no good come from all this. This a warning that we have made enough trips with slaves. We find something else to make money."

That what he tells me. But I think he just plain sick, him, of what he be doing to other men. Mars Jim never treat me like a dumb nigger and he never beat me. Never. I know what men say about Mars Jim, but he aint like that. He a kind and gentle man lessen someone push him too far. Never take sass, but never look for trouble either him.

We once down in Natchez and some mans—think his name Bloody Jack—well, he insult Mars Jim and they takes out their knives and goes to cutting at each other. Mars Jim coulda killed that man, but he dont. He cut him bad in the arm and the man just stand there looking stupid-like, blood dripping down his arm. Mars Jim, though, he just put up his knife and walks away.

Shoulda killed that man, though. Bloody Jack get some dock trash together and send them after Mars Jim who riding back to Lousanna through the canebrake. They jump him and hes best friend there. Hurt him bad, but he kill all three. Bad thing, he lose his best friend who get killed in Mars Jim place.

Another time, why Mars Jim and me over Texas way. This after his wife and children killed by the fever and Mars Jim, why, he take to drinking. For a while, I think he bout to drink Texas dry, but one day the man Houston come to him and say, "Jim, you nothing but a damn drunk and I know what Im talking about for I been there, too. Now, pull

your head outta them jugs and get to work for us. I need you.
War a-coming with Mexico and we need men like you bad."

Well, Mars Jim pull his head outta the jug and he get to
work for Houston. Lotta people they dont care for Mars Jim
cause when he drinking he not the most sociable one around.
Fact being he once throw Travis into a pond when Travis
think he can insult Mars Jim and another time he dry-shave
a man with his big knife when the man think he can take
advantage of Mars Jim when Mars Jim drunk.

But Mars Jim he have a reason for acting like that and it
a reason that all men would have if they love theys wifes
like Mars Jim love his. He do anything for her. He even send
her away when the fever come to keep her safe. But he dint
pick the best place. The fever already there. She die, but she
die only after her children they die.

I guess that make Mars Jim hate himself, knowing like
he do that he responsible for his wife dying. Her death leave
a big empty hole inside him that never fill back up. Never.
Not even when Houston ask him to finish with his drinking. Reason he stop cause he honor. At the end, it his honor
as a man that finally matter. He cant let nobody see him die
like that. Not a drunk. But the hole still there. A deep dark
hole.

Elve Bowie

Elve Ap-Catesby Jones Bowie was second-generation Welsh, a frontier woman about whom not much more need be said. She knew the harsh life of a frontier farm, how to work a plantation, and how to raise a family.—A. J. S.

So. You want to know about my son, James. I haven't said much: my one comment after his death at the Alamo has been widely quoted. I have been told it appeared in many newspaper articles. Jim's death caught me off-guard when my daughter Martha told me about it, but I knew something bad was going to happen. I had had a dream about Jim the night before and he was splashed red and around him burned a golden glow like you see around fireflies. I just knew that I was seeing my boy's spirit with a hero's halo spreading around it, turning gradually red, reflecting the fury that took over him at times. In a way, I guess you could say I was prepared for Martha's words.

"I'll wager no wounds were found in his back," I said to her. I meant that, too. Jim was never one to turn his back on danger. I don't mean that he went around looking for trouble. He was always somewhat reasonable, but when people began to push him, I would see that golden glow begin to rise up around him and then, well, it was better if you just stayed out of his way.

I didn't cry when Martha told me. Much has been said about that, too. But that's the way the Welsh and Highlander-Irish are. Death is just a part of life. The only thing that matters is how you live it. And Jim lived well.

He always liked his stories, did Jim. We came from a race

of storytellers, you know, so Rezin and I always had one or two to entertain our children when it was raining outside and they got restless. The old stories are good ones and I never tired of telling them. There's a lot of wisdom in them and I'd hate to see them lost. Rezin believed that the more you knew, the better off you'd be, so he made sure that all of the children—me, too—were given the best education that was possible.

My husband was a man of vision. That's the reason our children were so well educated for the time. Every tutor that came through the country had to stop and give lessons to our future, as Rezin used to say.

It seems like Rezin was always thinking about the future and planning for it. No one who has not been there can imagine the hard physical labor that it takes to carve a plantation out of the wilderness, and fewer see the labor that goes into converting the raw produce from the plantation into saleable produce.

"Boys," Rezin would say, "the English lord would watch men work and the profit he would keep. That's why the English lost the American colonies. It will not be the cause of us losing our plantation."

He meant the boys had to know hard labor as well as civilized behavior. He made the boys work with the slaves and because of this, two things happened. First, the plantation prospered, and second, the boys grew very strong both physically and in character.

Rezin always said that the land did not belong to you until your sweat watered it. Or your blood. Our boys sweated over their land, and as any who work the land can tell you they scraped enough skin off to spill some of their blood onto that fine black land.

Much of the land we settled was covered with oak groves. The oak had to be cut down and then dragged to the pit for cutting into planks. Many of those old trees weighed a ton or more, and they had to be manhandled into a position so the horse could drag it, then moved into position over the pit.

Once they had that oak tree over the pit where they wanted it, one of the boys would climb down into that damp hole in the ground and pull down on a whipsaw. The person above would then pull the saw back up and then the boy in the bottom would pull it back down.

Up-down, up-down, while the sweat poured off them and the mites of sawdust clung to their skin and gritted into their eyes already stinging from salty sweat. It took special people to work like that. No one today is willing to do that kind of labor. Less'n they're nigras.

Jim seemed to be able to stand the pit longer than most, and one day, took to bragging about it. His father took him aside to speak to him about that. I was on the porch, shelling peas, and heard every word.

"Jim," Rezin said, "a gentleman is both born and made. It takes good blood, and you have that. But a gentleman must also learn the rules of behavior. A gentleman doesn't brag because that only gets him into trouble. If he brags, why then, he must prove himself over and over because there's always someone somewhere wanting to test him. A gentleman lets what he does stand by itself."

I think Jim was thirteen, maybe fourteen at the time, but he marked right up, saying, "Yes, Father. But when is it bragging and when is it just stating fact?"

Rezin turned away from Jim and looked out over the land. He chewed on his lower lip for a minute, composing his thoughts.

"I think, son, any time you are being asked if you can do something and you answer with the truth, then that's fact. If you are just telling people who have no need to know, then it's bragging."

Jim seemed to mull that over for a while, then he nodded

soberly and went back to work. But I could tell that those words had an effect upon him. I think he kept those words with him for the rest of his life.

Yes, Jim's father had a major influence upon Jim. For example, Rezin was always talking about machinery around the boys, telling them that was the future of the country. He said even then that if machines could cut down on work, then we wouldn't need slaves and we'd be able to turn them free to start their own lives.

Well, Rezin heard about a machine that ground the sugarcane down in half again the time it took to do it by hand. He always talked about putting together a stake and going back East to get one of those machines. He died, though, before he could realize that dream. But Jim remembered it and in 1821, his brother Rezin and Jim bought a stream-driven cane machine and installed it on Rezin's plantation. It was the first one in the state and the boys were extremely proud of their accomplishment. But they weren't any prouder than their father would have been if he had lived to see what his boys did with his words. My husband died just a little bit before.

Now, I know this isn't what you wanted to hear, but I want you to understand that Jim was not a roughneck, not the wild man that folks and those newspaper fellows and magazine writers want you to believe. No, he was a man who was trained to be a gentleman. Rezin used the heroes out of Sir Walter Scott as prime examples of how a man should behave, and Jim took the lessons to heart. He never tired of hearing about Rob Roy and Ivanhoe, or the Irish tales of the Red Branch. Cuchulainn. Others. He was a knowledgeable man who had a keen insight into others.

Now, I don't mean that Jim didn't have a wild streak in him. He did. All my boys did. They were pretty rambunctious when out in the woods. They hunted and hunted well. Our slaves never went hungry, even during the lean years when drought hit. There was always food on our tables. That wasn't an easy thing to do, either, when you figure there were always six or seven children around and at least eight slaves and Rezin and me. Seventeen or eighteen mouths, sometimes more. All the boys learned to hunt and fish almost from the time they could walk. I suppose that's when people started calling them "the wild Bowie boys." But there was a restlessness in Jim that the others didn't have.

Jim used to ride alligators, you know. Can you picture that? He used to sneak up on a sleeping gator—there must've been a million of them in the swamp back then—and jump on his back. He held the gator's mouth shut and plunged his thumbs into the gator's snakelike eyes. (You ever look into a gator's eyes? Cold as death, they are.) Well, that gator'd run into the water and toss and turn, trying to throw Jim from its back. 'Course it couldn't see and besides, even if he could, he couldn't do much about it 'cause a gator's strength ain't in opening its mouth; it's closing it. A grown gator can snap a heavy board in two with one chomp, but a young child can keep it from opening it. Just has to watch out for his tail is all.

But I suppose the most dangerous thing Jim did was to hunt wild cattle with a knife and rope. Doesn't sound like much, I know, when you look at cattle these days, but back then, well, those cattle were mean. And smart. Jim used to climb a tree along a well-worn path and wait patiently for hours until one wandered by. Then he'd drop a loop over those horns, snub the rope around the tree, then drop down and cut his throat with the knife.

When he was young, I paddled his britches, I tell you that. Nigh to wore my hand out, I did. But, at the same time, I was pretty proud of what he did. Not many men would try to get under those hooking horns to cut the animal's throat, much less boys. Still, it was a constant battle between him and me. Eventually, he won. I just got tired of whipping him for not minding what he was told. Besides, we got to liking that fresh beef now and then. Made a welcome change from our other fare.

Fishing was something else, too. While most people would go after the perch and crappie, Jim always went after the alligator gar. You know those fish? A fighter with teeth like razors. Keeps fighting even while it's dying.

I remember another story about Jim. Once, we had a bear raiding our corn patch. Now, things were a bit tight at the time and we couldn't have our food being taken from us. I don't recall where Mr. Bowie was at the time, but young Jim decided something had to be done about it. Swamp bears may not be the size of those animals I hear about in the shining mountains, but they can still kill an ox with one swipe of the paw. There ain't as much room in the swamp, neither, as in the mountains, so it's kind of hard to take a long shot at one, you understand?

Well, this big black must've thought he was on easy street, taking corn from a woman and her little ones. What he didn't eat, why he just threw down on the ground and put his scent all over it to keep any others from eating it. Let his water on it, he did.

Jim found where the bear was entering the patch and he went out and got himself a cypress knee. He then hollowed out that log just enough for the bear to get his muzzle in, then hammered in big nails cattywampus so that when the bear stuck his muzzle in to get the honey that Jim used to bait his trap he couldn't pull it back out again. I didn't think it would work, but one night there was a fearful roaring from down at the corn patch. Jim flashed that big grin of his, took a gun and walked down and shot that bear.

I still have its hide under my bed. It feels rather nice on cool mornings when I climb out to get dressed. And I always think of Jim when I do.

When Jim was young, his favorite story was one about

Mr. Bowie, his father, and me. I always told Jim I was pregnant with him, but this happened in spring of '95 and Jim didn't come along until April of '96 and I don't think he ever did arithmetic it out.

We had just moved out to a farm in Kentucky when some ne'er-do-wells came to squat. I guess they thought Mr. Bowie was too tame to shoo them off, because they were downright arrogant about what they were planning on doing which was to take our best pasture land. Well, Mr. Bowie went down to reason with them. John and David went along with him. He had decided that it was time that the boys learn how to deal with rascals. I remember I didn't want them along with him, but when Mr. Bowie set his mind on something it was near impossible to talk him out of it.

Those men were just plain stupid. Mr. Bowie was a big man. Close to six-two, he was, and broad and strong. He had a bad left hand from a saber cut during the War. That was when I captured him, you see. We used to joke about that. Savannah it was. . . . Where was I? Oh yes.

Well, Mr. Bowie gave each of the boys a pistol. David was preparing himself for sainthood and didn't want to take one, but Mr. Bowie was firm about it and each of the boys tucked one of those big horse pistols into the waistband of their trousers. Mr. Bowie took two for himself and this saber he had cut down along with the highland dirk he'd got from his father. The dirk had the family seal on the half. He used that seal to sign documents.

They rode down to the creek where the men had decided to squat. Mr. Bowie had a special leather belt that he wore around his waist. It had two loops for his pistols and a scabbard for his saber. He wore the dirk over his left buttock at the small of his back. He carried a double-barreled shotgun across his saddle as he rode.

I remember David telling me what happened when they got to the men's camp. He said it stunk to high heaven. The men had a rough lean-to built, but that was about it. They had a bunch of cowhides staked out, drying in the sun, and a pile of oak stacked and drying. It was our wood, too, that they'd hauled from where Mr. Bowie had cut and stacked it.

"What the hell do you want?" the leader said.

"I want you to explain your camp on my land," Mr. Bowie said. David said that his father's words were so soft-spoken that he had to strain to hear them. If so, that should have been the ruffians' warning. But when you get men like that who think they own the world, you can't tell them anything.

"Your land?" The leader laughed. "Why, I reckon this land belongs as to him who can take it."

Mr. Bowie shrugged then and dropped his reins across the saddle in front of him. He looked the leader calmly in the face and said, "Why, then I suppose you'd better get to taking. Or leave. Choice is yours."

Wouldn't you know they made the wrong choice? That man raised his musket, an old Brown Bess, if David remembered correctly, and pointed it at Mr. Bowie. But Mr. Bowie drummed his heels into the horse's side and it reared, startling the ruffian so much that he hurried his shot and missed. He never got another 'cause Mr. Bowie dropped that double-barreled shottie square into his face and pulled the trigger, blowing his head clean off his shoulders.

Mr. Bowie slid from his horse with a horse pistol in his hand. That .50-caliber ball nigh tore another's head off. One of the others snapped a shot at Mr. Bowie and he took a ball in the side. The boys were trying to stop their horses from rearing, but they couldn't and they were afraid to shoot for fear of hitting their father.

Mr. Bowie dropped his horse pistol and pulled two others from his belt. He fired at the man who was aiming at the boys, and knocked the musket from his hands. He didn't do that on purpose, you understand. He just missed, that's all. He dropped the pistols and drew his knife while he rushed at the fourth man trying to load his rifle. The man tried to brain him with his musket, but Mr. Bowie slipped under it and slashed him across the stomach. The man screamed and fell down, trying to hold his guts in.

At that time, David shouted a warning and Mr. Bowie turned as the man who had tried to shoot the boys rushed at him, swinging a big axe. Mr. Bowie ducked under the swing, lifted the man across his shoulders and ran him hard against a tree. He pulled that dirk out and swung it hard into the man's belly, pinning him against the tree.

Well, that was the end of that fight. Mr. Bowie loaded the bodies in the wagon and took them into town. He turned them over to the sheriff and kept the wagon and what little they had to pay himself for the trouble and for the lumber he figured they'd stolen. He came on back home, but that wasn't the end of the story.

It seems that the good people of Eliott Springs were beginning to feel themselves somewhat civilized although for the life of me, I can't understand why what with a killing a month going on somewhere in the area. Anyway, they got the sheriff to come on out to our farm and arrest Mr. Bowie. I remember when he arrived, standing there uncomfortable like, scratching his head, wondering if he was going to get out of there alive or not.

Finally, he spoke up, saying, "Mr. Bowie, there were four men killed and even though we ain't yet found out who they are, all this killing makes us look bad. Uncivilized like, you understand? Well, I sure would appreciate it if you'd come on back to my cabin and sit a spell while we try to figure out who they is. Leastways, it'd look mighty nice to the voters if they saw me bringing you in. Sort of send a message that we ain't taking their killing lightly."

Well, Mr. Bowie sort of hid this little smile he had at times when his fancy got tickled. Me, why I was hopping mad that the sheriff'd dare take in Mr. Bowie for defending himself and what was his. I lay into that sheriff something awful, but Mr. Bowie just told me to take care of the children and leave the rest to him. He got his horse and went into Eliott Springs with the sheriff.

I waited three days for Mr. Bowie to come home, then finally I yelled at Zeke, one of our Negroes, to hitch up the wagon and take me into town. It was about ten miles and the more that wagon bumped along that road, the madder I got until by the time we got to town, I was ready to shoot someone myself.

I had a couple of pistols with me when we got to the sheriff's cabin. I climbed down and looked that sheriff straight in the eye and told him that I wanted to see my husband.

"Why, of course, ma'am. Mizzus Bowie," he stammered. He opened the door and I looked in at Mr. Bowie sitting at the table.

"All right, Rezin," I said to him. "You've had your little fun. Now, it's time to come on back to the farm and get to work. You've got a family that needs you more than this sheriff needs a prisoner."

He smiled that little smile. Oh, he knew that I missed him and he knew that I meant what I had said. He winked at me and rose, saying, "Why, of course, Elve. I was wondering how long it would take you to come on in."

"Now, just a minute," the sheriff blustered, his face all red beneath this scruff of a beard he had. "This man's a prisoner. He can't go nowheres at all."

"Oh, I reckon he can," I said smoothly. "I reckon in this instance you'd be willing to make a little exception, wouldn't you?"

I pulled one of those pistols and jammed it deep into his belly. His face turned sort of pasty white—kind of like a catfish's belly—and he decided right then and there that Mr. Bowie must have acted completely in self-defense.

Mr. Bowie and I went on back home and never heard another thing about it. Ah, but Jim loved that story. Once he said to me, "Mama, we always have to do what's right, don't we? Weren't you wrong when you took Papa from the jail?"

"Maybe," I answered. "The law's right, Jim. But sometimes, people like to twist the law to suit themselves and when they do, why then you're right when you go against it. You just have to know when you're right."

"Yes," he said, his little face sober. "That's something I'll always have to remember, won't I?"

That was my son Jim.

Mrs. Bowie's story differs somewhat from the story my grandfather told, yet so many similarities exist between the two, that I am inclined to believe the story to be true.—A. J. S.

The Deposition of Rezin Pleasants Bowie, Sr., to the Opelousas Parish Court Concerning the Recapture of an Escaped Slave on the Old March Road 1812 by His Son James

Rezin Pleasants Bowie, Sr., grew up fast on the frontier. He had not reached the age of seventeen when he joined Col. Francis Marion (the Swamp Fox) to fight the British. Shortly after the war, he married and began a new life, carving a plantation out of the wilderness. But he was never satisfied with his land and continued to move west until finally settling in Opelousas Parish, Louisiana, when it was under Spanish rule. He was a tall, big-shouldered man with red hair and high principles. He died in 1819.— A. J. S.

To the Opelousas Parish Court

Sir:

Since this is a formal document for the court of this parish I will begin by introducing myself. I am Rezin Bowie, Sr., father of James Bowie. I am a freeman and legal resident of Opelousas Parish, Louisiana. My business is the sale of lumber and crops from my own plantation. My son, who was born in Logan County, Kentucky, in 1796, the year the Harpes were on such a rampage, is just fifteen, this year of 1812.

I have been asked to briefly explain Jim's character, and to relate the incident that happened to him when he was performing an errand for me. The first can be done

William Micajah "Big" Harpe, and his brother, Wiley "Little" Harpe, were the scourge of the Wilderness Trail leading from Knoxville, Tennessee, to the uncharted West. The brothers were Tories in North Carolina until after the British surrender, when they fled to Tennessee, robbing and killing westward-bound settlers. The two giant, bearded, wild-eyed men were captured time and again but always managed to escape from the flimsy frontier jails.

Five murders have been documented in which the Harpes disemboweled their victims and filled the cavities with stones, sinking them in the Barren River.

After a $300 reward was placed upon their heads, they drifted up into the Ohio River valley and eventually made their way to the infamous Cave-in-the-Rock, a natural fortress honeycombed with subterranean passages so large that the Harpes hid stolen herds of cattle and horses in them.

Finally, the Harpes were trapped by a posse in 1799 in Ohio. Wiley escaped, but a volley of shots blew Micajah from his horse. The posse fell upon Micajah with long-bladed knives, attempting to cut off his head. As they were sawing away, the mammoth killer bellowed, "You are a Goddamned rough butcher but cut on and be damned!"

Harpe's head bounced along in a saddlebag as the posse made its way back to camp. Lack of provisions, however, led them to boil his head for supper one night. The skull was nailed to an oak tree as a warning to other highwaymen. Wiley Harpe disappeared, but legend has it that one winter after 1800 he was caught by a pack of wild wolves that tore him to pieces.

easily. He has always been raised by the teachings of the Church, and what it means to be descended from nobles of the Scottish Highlands. He has had such schooling as my wife and I can give as well as what we could hire from private tutors. He speaks Spanish, Cajun French, some of the old tongue from Scotland, and, of course, American. He understands arithmetic and has read many of the Classics, and though he has not had the advantage of reading Greek or Latin, he has become acquainted with Homer and Virgil, as well as Walter Scott and the modern writers.

My son is now and will always be a gentleman. Albeit, he also understands the rough and tumble life of the frontier and the hard work involved in running a plantation.

The second question that I am to answer in this document is somewhat more difficult. I feel this questioning comes about because people have written about my sons. These writers have called them the Wild Bowie Boys, only because they do what others might want to do, but can't stomach. James has hunted gators, aye, and ridden them. He has hunted the dangerous wild cattle with only a knife and sometimes a piece of rope.

I don't hold with these risks taken by my sons, but I do understand the excitement of youth and I also know how many precautions my sons take before they do these things. Jim is a crack shot and can throw a knife like none I've ever seen. Though he's only fifteen, he's an uncommonly tall, strong man. He stands almost six feet tall and weighs about 160 pounds.

The difficulty for which he stands before this court is one that takes very little explaining, but cannot be completely verified. Jim was defending someone less fortunate than himself. What else could a gentleman do?

Jim was traveling by Old Marsh Road on business for the plantation. He chanced upon a Flatboatman who seemed lost but was traveling in the same direction as my son. This man had in his company two black slaves. A young buck of about twenty years, and a young girl of tender years, say four or maybe five. The young girl was deformed with a twisted and crippled limb. The crippled limb was much shorter than the other, making it somewhat difficult for the young girl to walk.

The Flatboatman was described as tall, thin and sinewy. He wore the uniform of his kind: a loose blue jerkin that reached to his waist, over a bright red flannel shirt, coarse brown trousers of linsey-woolsey that covered his nether regions, and on his head he wore a cap made of untanned skunk skin, with the fur side out and the red feather of the fighter proclaiming to one and all his nature. On his feet he wore moccasins of leather and he had a wide belt from which he hung, in a poorly made leather sheath, a wide-blade, sharp-pointed Spanish dagger. The blade was about eight inches long. He also had a tobacco pouch and a small pouch carrying bits and pieces, and a shot pouch and a powder horn. Behind the belt was a smooth-bore .52-caliber horse pistol of British make, following the military pattern of 1806. His final piece of equipment wrapped around his torso was a huge blacksnake whip, with a hardwood handle.

The man was in his middle years, and had obviously learned cruelty in a misspent life, for he was tingeing the air blue with his cursing of the slave. The young slave had been carrying the child, and was now tired beyond human endurance. The Flatboatman was issuing threats amidst the cursing.

The words were all of death to at least the young girl, and probably to the young slave. Jim was simply minding his own business, but the language was barely tolerable. Jim has been taught to mind his own business.

Jim could not make out much of the cause of contention, but the man said he would teach manners to the recalcitrant slave. Then he uncoiled the whip from around his torso, and straightened it with a snap of his wrist, so that it flew out behind him. His body was aimed at the young girl, not the man.

Jim told me he asked the man if that little girl wasn't a bit young to be whipped like a field slave.

The man cursed Jim and told him to mind his own business.

"Shouldn't all men be aware of right and wrong, and so be prepared to defend the right?" reasonably responded my son to the rather unreasonable man.

This haughty villain challenged Jim. He said, So you want to fight, do you? Well, the word he used isn't really worth putting into this document, but needless to say it was a word a man must not take from another man, especially such a specimen as Jim described to me.

But, because Jim had simply been attempting to catch the man's attention so as to let his temper cool, he was willing to let the insult be ignored. But, the man continued with a string of verbal abuse that insulted me, my wife, Jim's natural mother, and his other antecedents. He proclaimed that my son committed vile acts on his relatives and animals.

Jim has an easygoing nature, so he was willing to let this pass as well, again allowing for the fact that the Flatboatman was already roused and so was not really responsible for all the words he was so reprehensibly using.

But then he snapped the whip at Jim. What else could the boy do? He had taken words no gentleman should have to and he was about to see a child whipped because she had a God-given disfigurement.

When the man hit Jim with the whip, Jim caught it. While the man was strong, he was not expecting his strength to be matched by such a youngster. Jim pulled the man off of his feet.

Jim's temper finally snapped and he pulled the handle of the whip to him. "You have no call to use this whip on me" were the very words my son reported to me as he told me about this unfortunate affair.

But the man didn't see reason and tried to drag the horse pistol from under his belt. While he rolled over and searched for the pistol grip, Jim had time to rush forward.

"First you try to whip me, then you try to pistol me," he said. Surely this can be forgiven since it was a problem that could be settled no other way.

Jim hit the man's right wrist with the oak handle of the whip. Since the man could not hold the weapon with a broken wrist, he dropped it. The Flatboatman with his left hand then tried to draw his Spanish dagger.

Jim rapped the man's fur cap, knocking it off the man's head. The man tried to roll to his pistol, but the slave picked it up and he and the young child moved a bit away from the commotion.

The man, seeing that he could not use either gun or knife, decided on rough and tumble and raised himself to charge my son. Jim stood his ground. The man rushed in and Jim fetched him a blow with the fist holding the whipstock. There was a loud crack as the man's jaw broke. But the man's momentum pushed Jim back.

The pain of the broken jaw and the power of the blow made the Flatboatman lose his footing and he fell hard. Jim regained his balance and quickly reached for the

Spanish dagger at the man's side. He flipped it away so that the melee would be handled without bloodshed.

The man got up slowly. There was no give in the man, and by this time Jim could do nothing but defend himself. The man took a very proper beating, with the outcome being that Jim left the man unconscious three miles from the village on the marsh road.

He said the man was dragged to the Gallows oak bend and was laid under the Spanish moss. Jim returned home to report these things to me, bringing the slaves and the man's weapons home with him as well. I took them along with my own weapons and went back to the spot where Jim had left the man. He was gone.

My sons do not lie to me, and so I believe the story as was told to me. And as a former justice of the peace, I knew that a proper record should be made of the incident. I reported to the Sheriff and am now making this statement for the Parish records. Of course, since the man had absconded, and a slave cannot be asked to testify, very little else can be said. Except repeating what I have said throughout. My sons are gentlemen, and gentlemen don't lie, especially to their fathers.

The last item that must be brought to the attention of the court is that after reporting to the Sheriff, I learned that the Negroes were stolen. If more details of how this was discovered are necessary, I can furnish details, but the fact that the court should be made aware of is that I communicated with the legal owner. I bought the slaves from said owner, who did not want the trouble of sending a bounty hunter to retrieve his property. The deed is on record, and can be viewed by the court.

Though this is a hearsay piece of information it should also be recorded. The Flatboatman was thought to be part of a group that stole slaves and sold them to new masters, convincing the slaves that they were slowly being moved to an area that would allow the slaves a chance to board the underground railroad and flee to freedom. I cannot attest to the truth of this last statement.

Signed,

Rezin Pleasants Bowie, Sr. (RUBRIC)

Addendum to the report by Mr. Rezin Pleasants Bowie of Opelousas Parish

Jim Bowie was sent a reward by Mr. Jean Paul Devareaux of the Picard Plantation. The U.S. Government also sent a reward for the capture of an escaped slave. In addition Mr. Bowie was allowed to keep the whip, knife and pistol of the man who stole the slaves.

Rezin Pleasants Bowie, Sr. (RUBRIC)

The conspiracy Mr. Bowie mentions in his report has surfaced several times, though generally it is not a flatboatman who is guarding the slaves.

The John Murrell of whom he speaks was a man of infamy who looted and plundered the entire southern United States. He tried to begin a slave rebellion by catering to dissatisfied slaves on selected plantations across the South, but financing his planned rebellion by stealing slaves from one plantation and selling them to another up or down the Natchez Trace.

He owned several "sporting houses" in the Swamp District of New Orleans, the Pig-Gut District of Memphis, and Natchez-Under-the-Hill. Over the course of a few years, he managed to assemble an army of cutthroats and brigands such as has never been brought together by one man in the history of the West. Among his confederates numbered many notorious men such as Bloody Jack Sturdivant and others who terrorized travelers along the Trace and the Mississippi River. Some say Murrell alone murdered over a hundred men although there is no way of verifying those numbers. He died insane.—A. J. S.

Rezin Pleasants Bowie

Rezin, one of James's older brothers, was born September 8, 1793, and lived often in his baby brother's shadow. He was an astute businessman who owned plantations and different mills and twice was elected to the Louisiana State Legislature.—A. J. S.

Brother Jim was remarkable. I know you've corresponded with John—most people begin with the oldest and work their way on down—so you know that Jim was the gentlest of gentlemen and yet he seemed always to be around when someone lost his temper and pulled him into an argument. When people challenged my brother, well, there was nothing to it but to defend his honor.

That was a common enough thing in those days, so I really don't understand why so many people make a big set-to about the duels he fought and the men he killed. People take a look at a man's record and judge him by that without thinking about the times that made the man. Even Aaron Burr, Thomas Jefferson's vice president, fought a duel once or twice as did Andy Jackson and others. But you don't see anyone making much fuss about their doings. I don't know why they do about Jim's.

Well, that's not quite right. I guess I might add a bit more. You see, Jim had a natural curiosity that led him to always being near the center of these melees. But that came natural to him. We were raised as frontiersmen of sorts. We did well by the standards of the areas in which we resided, but we never became Southern aristocrats. Seems like people have a rather narrow view of the Southern man. He's either a Southern gentleman sitting on his porch between white columns and sipping sugared whiskey or else he's poor white trash. We were neither. We started poor, but we increased our wealth through our own labor, sweating and hauling logs out of swamps right beside our Nigras.

I guess you could say that put us in the unique situation of being betwixt and between. Father taught us the meaning of being a Highland laird, and this set us apart from others and caused a few stories to spring up about us that simply were not true. "The Wild Bowie Boys" were really not much different from other young men of those days. Everyone had a streak of wildness in him that had to be unleashed at times. Boys are the same now, twenty years later, except that it seems that wildness in the young ones is more directed at hurting others than simply giving leash to a restlessness of the spirit.

Personally, I prefer great literature and music. So did Jim, but his spirit was so restless that he seemed to want to experience the whole world as quickly as possible. I went hunting and fishing with him quite a bit, but I really prefer to be around people who stimulate me intellectually, so I have a tendency of staying in the background. People took to calling me "that other Bowie" and I guess I earned the name.

Jim's curiosity manifested itself in travel. He was always on the go. One moment he would be talking to a man in a shack on the Mississippi, the next he would be in a mansion eloquently discussing politics and modern machinery. He loved the wilderness, but when he returned to civilization, he would immediately seek large crowds, immersing himself in what had happened during his absence, devouring newspapers to keep himself up-to-date about what was happening in the world. He would go to low dives on the waterfront or to fancy balls. Made no difference to him and he treated people the same wherever he went.

In a way, that was his undoing, for people don't really like to be treated like other people. Everyone thinks of himself as better than someone else. I guess people need someone to look down upon to reaffirm their own place in the world. They resent it when someone reminds them of their place in humanity. Quite often, Jim's attitude would grate on people and eventually they'd toss a challenge out to him. That took some doing, for as long as his honor wasn't besmirched, why Jim would laugh and walk away from them. That, of course, often made the other man look a fool, which infuriated him even more.

I remember one time when a young Creole took umbrage at something Jim said to one of his friends. The young man really had no business listening to Jim's conversation, but, well, people are like that, too. What they dislike in others they often have in themselves. Anyway, this young Creole sent his seconds around to where Jim was staying, telling him that he demanded satisfaction. This, of course, gave Jim the choice of weapons and Jim laughed and said the weapons would be snowballs at ten paces the next time it snowed in New Orleans.

This sort of baffled those Creoles who had never seen snow and perplexed them because they couldn't understand why someone with Jim's reputation didn't leap at the opportunity to kill someone else. But Jim never saw the necessity of killing someone just to be killing someone. There always had to be a purpose for it and words, well, words that did not question his honor never hurt him.

I remember once we were almost robbed by river pirates. You never heard that? Well, one day a letter from Jim arrived at my plantation at Avoyelles. It was sort of cryptic: "Rezin, we've got a challenge. Jim."

Well, I told my slave, Jeb, to saddle my horse while I immediately packed a bedroll, took out two pistols and a knife my blacksmith had made for me with a crossguard across its handle. I took down my long Pennsylvania rifle, climbed into the saddle, and left for Jim's cabin.

The day was gray and gloomy. It had rained the night before and the red soil was slick like grease. I let my horse pick his own way while I watched the trees carefully alongside the road. We had been having a bit of trouble with highwaymen and I didn't need a surprise. I didn't know what Jim meant by a challenge, but I suspected that it had something to do with our business, which was floating logs down the river to New Orleans for sale.

When I rode into the clearing where Jim's cabin stood, I gave out a long hello. An answering call came from behind the low log cabin. I hitched my horse to a corner butt, settled my pistols in my belt, and walked around to the log pit that Jim, his slave Black Sam, and I had built to allow us to fashion planks. Jim was in the pit; Sam was up top. Even though he had sent for me and was expecting me, Jim still spent his time working. He never seemed to rest.

Jim laughed and pulled himself out of the pit in one smooth movement. An ordinary man would have had a ladder down there but Jim just jumped in and out of that six-foot pit like others get up and off a stool. He picked me up and spun me around like I was a child and told Black Sam that he could have the rest of the day off.

We went up to his cabin and had a meal of roasted boar, washing it down with a little corn liquor he had picked up from friends of his who had a still back in the swamps. Jim was about the only one I knew who was willing to go that deep into the swamps where some of those Cajuns lived. Not because he wanted or needed liquor—brother Jim was moderate in his habits and so drank only a little—but he went into the swamps to meet people, and to see the wild country. And Jim came back while other people who delved into the backcountry swamps didn't come back out. Gator meat, we called them. People who lived that deep into those swamps didn't want outsiders coming in. I don't know why; just the nature of some, I reckon. Anyway, all that rich meat and that liquor was making me sleepy. I yawned. Jim noticed and grinned.

"A bit sleepy," I confessed. "Might could use a nap, I reckon."

"Rezin," Jim said. "We've got to get my logs down to the dock at Gallows Bend. I've got a mortgage due and I can't wait any longer for a run-together."

What Jim meant by that "run-together" referred to the habit that we loggers had come to, bunching our logs into one or two massive float rafts and shepherding them downriver to keep the log pirates from stealing us blind. Normally, one or two men could easily make a float down to Gallows Bend, but to go any farther made it a bit chancy unless there were four or five in the party.

Now, I really don't know if Jim's note was that pressing or not. Sometimes, Jim just took it into his head to clean out a nest of snakes and did it. Other times, he might just walk on past the nest and leave them be as long as they left him alone. I never could understand that. Whenever I came across a nest of snakes I always cleaned it out. The same with renegades and outlaws.

"Well, of course, I'll help you," I said. "We're brothers." But I was a bit puzzled. If he had to go only as far as Gallows Bend, then he and Black Sam should have been able to easily manage the float alone. I told him that.

"Rezin," he said quietly, "there are some river pirates working near where the Atchafalaya and Red rivers converge."

"They're moving up the river," I said quietly.

Jim nodded. A tiny smile played around his lips. "You don't look so tired, now, Rezin," he teased.

"I think I just woke up," I answered.

The problem was easy to see. Jim had to ride the current, keeping the logs floating straight and not jamming. That meant that he could not watch the bank as well as for snags in the river.

"How do you want to play it?" I asked.

He leaned forward, tiny lights dancing in his eyes as he outlined his plan. Black Sam would ride the current this time while he and I paralleled him along the bank, just inside the cover of trees. The river pirates would think Black Sam was a lone nigger that they could take advantage of, and when they made their move, why Jim and I would rush from the trees and take care of them.

It was a simple plan and I didn't see anything wrong with it except that at some places, the woods were mighty thick and the float could get on downriver ahead of us. Jim laughed and allowed he had thought about that, too, and there were only one or two places where that might happen. We would beach the float when we came to those places and have Black Sam rest a spell to give Jim and me a chance to work along the banks and get ahead of him.

We set off in early light the next morning. The forest was thick and the rains had left the ground softer than usual. We followed Black Sam without too much trouble until we got to Big Bend, which wrapped around the conflux of the Atchafalaya and Red. We helped Black Sam beach the float and Jim told him to give us two hours' head start to work our way overland before he poled around the bend.

Black Sam nodded and settled himself in the shade beneath a loblolly pine. Jim grinned at me and we took off through the woods, cutting across the bend. We were about halfway there when we stumbled upon fresh tracks. Jim looked at me and leaned close, whispering, "I think they've got an ambush set up ahead."

"Now, what makes you think that?" I started to ask, but

then we heard Black Sam singing a hymn like a young boy would walking past a graveyard at night.

Jim swore. "Damn it, he sure enough has a poor sense of time."

We moved forward a bit faster than we should have, but it was a good thing that we did for we came upon the ambush just as they tried to spring it on Black Sam. A shot rang out and for a moment, I thought they had hit Sam, but he just dropped flat on the float and picked up an old musket.

I pulled down upon one man and fired at the would-be assassin, but missed. The man rose and began running, but Jim shot him before he took more than three or four steps. Five others rushed for the raft, and Jim and I pulled out our pistols and fired at them. We both chose the same target, however, so we wasted one round although, as we later discovered, both of us had hit him dead center.

Black Sam rose to his knee and steadied his aim at the other four. They turned and ran for the woods away from the shore. In their panic, they ran right towards us. The one in front carried an axe that he swung wildly as he neared us. I caught his swing with my rifle and deflected it, coming up with the stock to catch him square on the chin. He dropped as if pole-axed.

Another had an old cutlass that looked as if it had sailed on one of Jean Lafitte's ships. He was swinging it at Jim, trying to cut him in half, but Jim danced back and forth, a grin on his lips, waiting until the man overextended a swing. Jim darted in and sank his knife deep into the man's stomach, ripping up and disemboweling him.

The other had had enough of us and took off running for all he was worth, weaving in and out of the trees, heading deeper into the woods. Jim took off after him, his long legs moving smoothly like a panther. I ran after him, reloading my pistol as I went.

We hadn't gone more than a mile into the woods when

we suddenly came upon a clearing. I expected Jim to pause, but he didn't. He gave out that panther scream of his that like to near froze my blood even though I was half-expecting it. He leaped into that clearing and bounded across the clearing, catching the men as they emerged from the crude lean-to they'd erected. The first one tried to stop Jim, but he just swerved to one side and his arm flickered across the man's throat like a cat's paw, leaving a streak in its path that immediately flooded bright red.

The second one tried to raise a pistol, but Jim's huge, knotted fist struck him, knocking him flat on his back, his feet flying up higher than his head. The one we'd chased saw all this and turned to run back into the trees. I guess he didn't see me standing in the shadows, for he ran right to me and I clubbed him to the ground with my rifle.

We tied the two survivors up with strips of rawhide and took a look at their camp. They'd been making a haul, waylaying loggers and merchants traveling the river. We found a stack of hides that had been cured and stretched, a couple of bales of cotton, indigo, and a pouch full of rings and watches that belonged to those unlucky ones who had probably been thrown into a gator hole somewhere back in the swamp.

We took the men to the sheriff while Black Sam floated the logs on down to Gallows Bend. The sheriff was mighty unhappy to see us, saying, "Well, you caught them, now you can just hold them until the judge comes on around. I ain't wastin' my money feeding scum that'll soon be on the gallows tree."

Jim complained that our keeping those renegades for the two weeks it took for the judge to arrive was one of the most expensive things he had done, but the truth of the matter was that the judge gave Jim and me all but ten percent of the loot we had recovered from the renegades, that ten percent going to something he vaguely called court costs. We made enough for Jim to clear his mortgage and for me to take another arpent of land.

But the point was that had those rascals not tried to waylay Jim's raft, then Jim probably would have left them alone. Then again, maybe he wouldn't have. Jim was mighty unpredictable in those cases. One thing he did do, however, was return a watch that he found in the loot that had *W. H. Cade* engraved on the back to a young girl back in the bayou, Sibyl Cade, a beautiful, buxom girl who had most of the bachelors in the area panting at her doorstep.

Sometimes, I sit on my porch in the twilight, sipping and remembering that time we broke up the river pirates. I think now that Jim knew what had happened to Sibyl's brother and decided that those renegades had come close enough to him. Remember what I told you before: Jim had a tendency to leave people alone as long as they didn't bother him or his friends. Whether or not that was the case in this instance, I don't know. I did discover later that Jim had a clear month left before his mortgage ran due. And I know that Jim was one of those bachelors that kept coming around her cabin. I wonder what might have come of Jim had she been able to work her Cajun charm upon him.

Sybil Cade

Sybil Cade was the first woman that James Bowie loved. She gave the following when she was ninety-seven and living in a nursing home in Opelousas. She never married and had one child. She never revealed the name of the father.—A. J. S.

Jim.

Dont think a day gone by when I aint thought about him since he went down to Nawluns and fell in with that fast crowd.

And that woman.

Cant blame him for falling in love with her. She was everything Im not.

Everything.

Beautiful.

High society.

I dont even know what fork to use or how to dance them dances they dance down there.

She ruin Jim with her fancy ways. Before he go down there and fall in with that pirate Lafitte and find how much he like them fancy clothes and all, he plain folk like me. Good folk.

I meet him at a broom-jump. You know that? Minister or priest hard to find in bayou and time comes when man woman decide to marry, why something must be done. So they gets their friends and relatives together at a cabin. Lots of music and eat and drink big, and then at midnight, someone brings a broom to center of the room and hold it low about a foot off ground and the two take hands and jump over it together. That all. They married, then.

Course, some also get married again when priest or minister come around. Dont happen all that time, though. Last one through here stay one night and go away. Think he get gator bait. Not so wrong about that. One did get gator bait twenty, thirty year back.

No, aint much use for holy man in the back bayou.

Jim aint got much use for them, either. But when I meet him at broom-jump of Cousin Ellie he handsome. Head and shoulders taller than any man there. Red-gold hair and them eyes could look right through a woman and make her soft like butter.

Smell good, too. Like he rub sweet soap all over. But that man-smell there, too. Cant keep that away. Cept with Jim, why it not raw and strong like with others.

At the dance, man name Terchett try to take me out to the cypress when I tell him no. Others watch him dragging me away, but not Jim. He knock Terchett down. Bam! One smack with his big fist and Terchett stretched out like dead.

That night he kiss me down by the cypress. I remember that. Arms like iron bars, but gentle.

Gentle.

A softness in him that other men wont let a woman see.

We begin walkin out together. Down here, that mean hands-off to other men and most people on bayou know bout Jim and his temper and stay away from that side of him.

Once while we at a birthday people they talk about Jim and his gator-ridin. Most call that a lie. Jim get real quiet and go borrow old clothes and change and we go down to the water and sure enough, theys a gator floating there like a log. Jim he creep out on a branch and drop down on top of gator and grab that gator by the jaws, squeezing hard, and jam he thumbs into gator eyes. They flop and turn all over that water and other gators see this and come in, but Jim, well, he just hollar and laugh. Finally he come out, wet, like a god he look and my heart thump against my breastbone like it trying to knock a hole in it.

That night we make love like we invent it.

And Jim ask me marry with him.

We set for that spring, but then Jim he go to Nawluns with lumber he and his brothers cut to sell from they mill. I feel funny bout that. Almost like something tellin me dont let him go. Stay way. I get cold sweats at night and bad dream, always same bad dream bout a black rooster, and I know Jim aint comin back and I feel all hollow and empty inside. Cold like when sudden wind come down from the north and burn the trees.

And I know Jim aint comin back.

But I pretend everything all right before he leave. I know he stay if I ask, but they a restlessness in him and I know that a man with that need to walk it out of him and so I say nothin. A man have to have his freedom. Cant keep tied to the house and all because then he not a man no more. Spirit break and nothin left of the man. And Jim, well, he all spirit. Take that away and aint Jim no more.

So he go to Nawluns.

And meet that girl.

I see her once and she pretty. Black-haired and black-eyed. Tiny. Not like me. Delicate. But there a set to her mouth like in a person who suck lemon. And I know she a wicked lady.

Cruel.

And she no good for Jim.

But something like that a man have to see. Aint listening to no one tell him differently. So I stay quiet and watch Jim hang around her like she a bitch in heat. Maybe she be, cause she always whinin and complainin and Jim try to make things right but never can.

Jim's mama dont like her either. Say she not woman enough for Jim, but Jim dont listen to her. Finally Jim's mama tell Jim it time for the woman to leave cause she doin nothin but whinin and Jim take her and go back to Nawluns.

Next thing, he over to Campacino and Lafitte and kill two men and he . . .

Here, Sybil's daughter interrupted, objecting to our interview. Sybil became confused and could not recall what had happened later.—A. J. S.

Well, no man like Jim. No man.

John Jones Bowie

John Jones Bowie was born in 1785 in Burke County, Georgia. He was the oldest of the "wild Bowie boys" and became a prosperous businessman and plantation owner, as well as a state representative in Louisiana.—A. J. S.

Jim was a contradiction. There's no two ways about it. I suppose we all are to some extent or the other, but Jim more than most.

He was born in Logan County, Kentucky, in spring of 1796. But he spent the most important part of his childhood in Catahoula Parish between 1802 and 1809, embracing the years between six and thirteen.

He was young, proud, poor, and ambitious, without any rich family connections, or influential friends to aid him in the battle of life. After reaching the age of maturity he was a stout, rather rawboned man, of six feet height, weighed 180 pounds, and about as well made as any man I ever saw. Taken altogether, he was a manly, fine-looking person, and by many of the fair ones he was called handsome.

People I know have a tendency to be dreamers or doers. Jim was both. Whereas most people found a passion in business or politics and used the woods for their amusement, Jim made the woods his business. I suppose if he had stayed in town and worked his charm on people he could have become president. Just about everybody who met him liked him—except those who thought his easy manner marked him as an easy man. There wasn't anything easy about Jim.

We lived on the edge of the frontier, back then. My father, Rezin Pleasants Sr., moved from the land south of Ohio, I guess in either Tennessee or Kentucky, around 1800 to a place around Bushley Bayou. He got two thousand arpents of land which he cleared with his slaves. It was hard, brutal work and very dangerous with ruffians and renegades hanging around in the woods, looking to waylay someone. A lot of people don't think about that because New Orleans was pretty settled and civilized, but the country outside the city was still frontier.

At night, Father taught us to read and write not only in English but in Spanish and some French as well. We balked at this, but he held firm, telling us that we needed to know all three languages if we were to get ahead in the world. At the time, we thought he was crazy, but we knew better than to argue with Father. Of course, he was a natural teacher, too. He knew when we had had enough of book learning for a while. Then, he taught us to shoot and hunt. Everything that appeals to young boys.

Jim was better than all of us. Smarter at his books and a better woodsman, too. He picked up things fast. He listened and then he knew and he never forgot anything he knew. He was good for us, too, for we had to learn to answer fast or else baby brother would make us look like fools.

We ran into many problems where we lived, so we had to learn how to deal with trouble without relying too heavily upon the law. Part of the reason for that was because we really couldn't trust the law. But that's not unusual. We still have that trouble today. People use the law for their own means, twisting and turning it until it represents only their own interests.

But you don't want to know about this; you want to know about Jim. Well, let me tell you a story or two.

One time we were out hunting wild cattle near Bayou Teche when Jim saw a gator sleeping on the bank. Jim had been thinking about a story an old trapper had told us about

how a gator's mouth was weak opening but real strong closing and he had figured out a way to have a little fun.

"John," he whispered, "I think I could ride that old
gator."

"Quit it, Jim," I whispered back. "Ma would tan your hide
proper if she found out what you're planning."

Jim ignored me. He usually did that when he had his
mind set upon something. I never knew a person to change
his mind once it was set and right then it was set upon
riding that gator.

"Listen. I'm going to sneak up on that old gator and go
for a little ride."

Well, Rezin was with us and he laughed at Jim. "Tell me,
little brother," he said. "How you planning on getting off
that gator once you're done riding him?"

Jim frowned and scratched his head, then just shrugged.
"Well, I guess I'll just jump off and run."

As the oldest, I probably should have said something, but
I didn't. Besides, I wanted to try it myself, but it was Jim's
idea and so I thought I'd let him go first. It wouldn't have
made any difference anyhow. I would've had to fight Jim
in order to go first.

Jim crept up on that old gator sunning himself under a
moss-covered oak and jumped up on his back. He grabbed
hold of that gator's mouth with both hands and squeezed
tightly.

That old gator woke up and took off running for the
water. Now, a lot of people think that a gator is big and slow,
but it just isn't so. We yelled, and that probably scared the
gator even more. That gator hit that water with a big splash
and swam for the deep water. I could tell Jim didn't know
what to do; he hadn't figured that the gator would head for
water and there he was. Rezin and I tried to draw a bead on
the gator, but couldn't fire for fear of hitting Jim.

Jim kept cool, though. He jammed his thumbs into the gator's eyes, blinding him. The gator started twisting and turning in the water, and Jim took the opportunity to slip off his back and get away. That gator splashed around some, snapping its huge jaws, trying to find the thing that had blinded him. But Jim got away.

Well, Rezin and me, we figured that we couldn't let our baby brother have all the fun, so we took to scouting out gators for our own little ride. One day, some people spotted us riding them and word got back to Mother and we got one of the worst tongue-lashings we ever got.

I guess that's when people started calling us "the wild Bowie boys." Or it might have been the way we hunted wild cattle. That, too, was a bit of an accident, but necessary as well.

A drought had hit the South at the time and crops were pitiful. We needed meat but shot and powder was pretty expensive so Jim came up with this idea about how to get meat for the table. Actually, I think it was one of the Indians who told him, but he made out that it was his own idea.

We waited in a tree above a cowpath until one of those horned bulls came down the path. Then we dropped a loop over its horns, tied it to a tree, then tried to sneak in under the slashing horns to cut its throat. Mother undoubtedly knew what we were doing because no bullet holes were in the hides we brought home, but she didn't say anything.

One time, though, Jim tied into one that was too big, a big, mossy-horned bull well over a ton with a horn-spread of well over four feet. He yanked Jim out of his tree before Jim could get him close-snubbed. He swung those wicked horns at Jim and nearly unzipped him from belly to chin, but Jim still had his knife and whipped it across the bull's muzzle.

The bull roared in pain and rage and started raking at Jim with his horns, but Jim rolled under its belly and reached up and slit his throat. Blood gushed down, near drowning him, then the bull fell down upon him.

Jim's pride was mighty hurt by that, but we can all use that a time or two in our lives. It took Rezin and me about half an hour to get that bull's carcass off Jim. Of course, we were laughing half the time while Jim wore out the Lord's name in vain at us, but finally we managed to pull him out from under that bull.

Jim was mighty red by that time, what with the bull having bled itself dry. It was only after we tossed him into the river to get cleaned up that we found out his knife had slipped when he went across the bull's throat, gashing his hand pretty deep.

Rezin took one look at that wound of Jim's and put his mind to work. That night, he saw Father's cut-down saber and reasoned that if a sword was built like that to save a man's hand, then a hunting knife should be, too. He talked Jesse Clift, our blacksmith, into making a knife patterned after a sword for Jim out of an old file and that was how the Bowie knife came to be made. I know a lot of people have been taking credit for it, but there's no romance to the story at all. Just plain common sense.

I told you Jim was a contradiction, and I think another story is needed to illustrate what I mean.

There was a time when Jim was seventeen that Father had to go downriver to sell lumber and he left Jim in charge of his Blue Leopard puppies. They were old enough to train and Father had told Jim to start them out while he was gone.

The next day, Jim took them out, but they still had enough puppy in them to ignore his calling. He lost sight of them and stumbled over a backwoodsman's cabin while looking for them. Turns out the man, Jean Lebeau, was beating his Indian wife with a rawhide whip when Jim came upon them. Jim knocked the man down, but the squaw ran into the house and came out with a musket and pointed it at Jim, telling him to get.

Well, that man's pride was a little hurt what with Jim knocking him down in front of his wife and all. When Jim came back that way with the pups leashed, Lebeau gave him a black look, but Jim ignored him. He'd done what he thought he should and if the woman wanted to be treated that way, why, then, so be it.

That night, Lebeau crept over to our house and took one of the pups. I forgot to tell you that Lebeau was pretty well known along the bayou for his mean streak. That was why Father had refused to sell him one of the male pups when he came around offering. I think he thought that he could get Jim in trouble with Father if one of the pups turned up missing.

Anyway, Jim trailed the man back to his cabin and told him that he wanted the pup returned. About this time, Jim was a stout, rather raw-boned man nearing six feet in height and weighing upwards of 180 pounds with shoulders as well-made as any man I ever saw. His hair was light-colored, not quite red—his eyes were gray, rather deep set in his head, very keen and penetrating in his glance. His complexion was fair, and cheekbones rather high. He was handsome, as many ladies such as Sibyl Cade called him. I suppose Lebeau thought that made him not quite a man, for he laughed at Jim and cussed him out in French and Choctaw, telling Jim he was illegitimate and that all of our family was the same. Jim got redder and redder, but when Lebeau said something about Mother being poorly paid for her favors, Jim knocked him ass over teakettle.

Lebeau went to Judge Beauvier over that, claiming that Jim had stolen his dog. He swore out a warrant for assault and battery against Jim and the judge fined Jim five dollars because Jim couldn't produce the pup that Lebeau had hid.

That was a lot of money in those days and the more Jim thought about the injustice of it all, the madder he got.

Finally, he couldn't take it anymore and went back to Lebeau's cabin. He found the pup in Lebeau's smokehouse and when he tried to bring the pup home, Lebeau came out to stop him. Jim beat the hell out of the man, leaving his face looking like a rainbow, and brought the dog back home again. Then, he went to see the judge. He found him in town and confronted him. A crowd slowly gathered, listening, for everybody around there knew what had happened.

"Judge Beauvier," he said. "That dog belongs to my father. I found him in the smokehouse where Lebeau tried to hide him. I told you he had him, but you wouldn't go out to Lebeau's place to look for him. Now, I want my money back."

"Look, youngster, my ruling was final and that's that," Judge Beauvier said.

"Even though you were wrong?" Jim said.

"Who says I was wrong? You a lawyer, now? I could charge you with contempt of court and—"

"Now, wait a minute," Jim said. "You're saying that I'm wrong?"

"I'm the law around here," Beauvier blustered. "Until you study law, you have no idea as to what is wrong." He snorted and sneered at Jim. I suppose he thought that he had young Jim on the run, but he missed the golden mist that sort of rose up around Jim. And then he made a big mistake. "I could charge you with contempt of court, but because of your lack of knowledge and your tender age, I'll forgive that."

"Let me get this straight," Jim said. "You'll forgive me for demanding that you serve justice?"

"No young whippersnapper is going to stop me in the street and challenge me with some trumped-up story . . ."

He broke off as he saw the lights beginning to burn in Jim's eyes.

"You're calling me a liar after treating me like a brawler?" Jim said quietly.

That's when he remembered that Jim was a yonker and decided that the high road was the right road. He also noticed that people were gathering around them, listening to the argument. He took heart in their nearness and straightened as tall as he could—which really wasn't very tall since he still had to crane his neck in order to meet Jim's eye.

"Yes," he said. "You are on the road to becoming a bravo and a scoundrel."

With that, Jim slapped him across the face, knocking him down. The judge yelled for help, but most there had run up against the judge's court a time or two and they ignored him. Jim reached down, hauled the man to his feet, then knocked him down again. When he pulled him back up, the judge figured he had kissed enough ground and put up a hand stopping him. He handed Jim five dollars and Jim left. The crowd cheered him as Jim walked away. The judge never did anything about the way Jim had treated him. I guess he didn't want to take on the rest of the wild Bowie boys.

Jim left home somewhere around 1814 and took up a new life on Bayou Boeuf, Rapides Parish. There, he cleared a small piece of land, but his chief means of support was from sawing plank and other lumber with the common whip-saw, and boating the wood down the bayou for sale. He was like many those days: young, proud, poor, and ambitious. He didn't have any rich family connections or influential friends to aid him in making his way in life. He made his own way. He had an open and frank disposition with rather a good temper despite what others say. He always had to be aroused by some insult, and then his anger was terrible to see and frequently terminated in a tragic scene. That judge was lucky, as was Lebeau. When Jim was possessed by anger, he couldn't be reasoned with. But I never knew him to abuse a conquered enemy or impose himself upon the weak and defenseless.

He was a man of very strong social feelings and loved his friends with a deep faithfulness and hated his enemies and their friends with all the rancor of an Indian. He was social and plain with all men, fond of music, and liked a glass in the merry mood to drive dull care away. But he seldom allowed it to steal away his brains or transform him into a beast. Except once, and that was his Dark Period that we Bowies don't talk about much on account of we feel that some things should remain in the family.

Well, you asked about Jim and I guess this sort of tells you something about him. Jim never was one to tolerate injustice whether it was directed to him or others. There was just something stubborn about him that made him wade right in and stand up against what was wrong.

In the end, it was that which killed him. That, and some other things.

Edwin Forrest

Edwin Forrest was one of America's first actors to achieve international recognition. He was powerful, handsome, willful, and unschooled, his character molded in part in New Orleans during 1829, when he was thrown into a crowd that was at once gay, sophisticated, crude, and cruel. His puissant animal vigor and sonorous utterance, coupled with his vigorous style and love for characters of rugged, primitive heroism, made him quickly popular with theater audiences beginning to tire of worn melodramas and static Shakespearean presentations by untalented actors. He numbered among his friends James Bowie and became so enamored of the man that he modeled part of his persona after him, even to challenging his employer on one occasion to a duel in a darkened room, naked and armed only with knives in emulation of a duel Bowie supposedly fought against a man named Contrecourt. Bowie was amused at the younger man's hero-worship and went so far as to give Forrest a copy of his knife. Forrest used that knife whenever possible in his many stage roles, but most often in the play Matamora.

He was most famous for his interpretation of Hamlet, playing him as a strong-willed, elemental character in revolt that mirrored his own unconscious revolt against the idealized classic drama. For that, his audience forgave him for his uncontrolled, egocentric passions, his vanity, and his arrogance.—A. J. S.

Had Shakespeare known Jim Bowie—God! What an epic! A tragedy! A triumph!

I would have played him—who better?—as a Hercules, browbeaten by a tepid society unworthy of him and fearing him for knowing itself to be unworthy of him.

Yes, he was my friend. I even forgave him for a little impromptu medley that occurred between us at St. Cyr's gambling establishment when both of us were, shall we say, taken a bit with drink and momentarily infatuated with the same woman of rather tainted reputation who had gained entrance to the establishment on the arm of yet another gentleman.

Jim and I had begun our late-night carouse through Vieux Carré following one of my better Hamlets on a Tuesday night, I remember. After fortifying ourselves with a few glasses of absinthe at a small establishment near Pierre Lafitte's blacksmith shop on Bourbon Street, we began working our way through the Quarter, one establishment at a time, stopping for the rather thirsty business of progress at every, or nearly every, saloon along the way, arriving at last at St. Cyr's.

Jim was quite amiable but I, well I, flush from my triumph of seven curtain calls, still felt the fire of the stage in my veins, and stalked to the gaming tables. My muse still smiled upon me, triumph after triumph, coin after coin finding its way into my pocket. Yes, my night was rapidly becoming complete. All I needed was a gift from Aphrodite to fulfill my evening and launch me triumphant unto the new day.

Then, *she* walked in. A quadroon of especial beauty. Eyes smoky gray, skin of *café au lait*, hair black and gleaming like a raven's wing, her breasts full and copiously displayed so that when one stood next to her the hint of aureoles could be seen, tantalizing. She was Faustus's Helen and my head became light with desire. I ached for her. The very room suddenly became charged with male want. I sensed a low, barbaric growl simmering throughout the room.

"Ah!" I cried, standing erect and gesturing towards her.

"Was this the face that launched a thousand ships,
And burnt the topless towers of Ilium?"

I walked towards her, balancing carefully on the balls of my feet. I stopped, stage center, declaiming declining,

"Sweet Helen, make me immortal with a kiss."

She laughed and curtsied and gestured with her fan for me to approach. I slipped up and leaned down to kiss gently those rich, full lips. A hint of mint lingered on my lips, and I touched it with my tongue.

"Her lips suck forth my soul: see where it flies. Come,
Helen, come, give me my soul again."

I leaned forward again, but she interplaced between our lips her fan. I frowned and started to speak when a hand closed gently around my upper arm, tugging me back.

"Enough, Edwin," Jim said softly. "You are embarrassing the lady."

I looked back at him, flaring, "How dare you upstage me, upstart?"

"I apologize," he said, ignoring my outburst. He bowed to the young lady. "We have been celebrating his triumph at the St. Charles Theater."

A tiny smile spread her lips, lifting a tiny mole at the dimple of her left cheek, in a desirable manner. Her eyes looked frankly into his for a moment, then lowered demurely as he took her hand, bowing gallantly over her fingers.

"Thank you, sir, for your courtesy," she said, her voice like soft, tinkling notes from a French music box.

"James Bowie," he said.

The atmosphere suddenly seemed charged with heat between them and a pang of jealousy quickly swept into me. I stepped forward and pulled Jim back away from her.

"This is totally unforgivable," I said. "I do not need you to apologize for me."

He laughed and brushed my hand from his arm. "You're drunk, Edwin," he said. "Perhaps we had better leave."

A fury seemed to rise inside me. I slapped his face, regretting my action almost immediately, for he had done nothing for me to give him such an offense. A gasp went up around the room. I became instantly aware of the ticking of a clock somewhere, the lapse whirling of a wheel, the clink of chips. I felt the hungry eyes of the room upon me, waiting for Jim's response to this insult.

I threw my head back to stare into his eyes and felt my heart grow cold. I looked at death, a dark emptiness, watching the color change from blue to slate-gray, his lips thinning.

"You are a fool, Edwin," he said softly. "I could kill you for that."

"I'm at your service, sir," I said. My tongue felt thick in my mouth. I swallowed past the instant dryness. I knew then I was dead, but honor does strange things to a man, forcing him into extended moments of foolishness. I was young—that is my only excuse—and the lust of a young man often causes him to mistake honor for common sense.

"You may . . ." I started to say, "name your seconds," but his fist, the size of a boulder, crunched against my jaw, knocking me over a chair. Unfortunately, the blow also knocked common sense from me (or perhaps it was relief at being treated in this manner instead of a roasted Christmas goose ready for carving). I leaped to my feet and charged him, flailing my fists like a border ruffian only to be knocked back over the chair again.

Laughter ran around the room. Stung, I rose and remembered the lessons of Jem Mace, a pugilist friend who had given me a brief stint of training. I shrugged out of my jacket and raised my fists in the accepted style and advanced upon him. I caught his next blow on my forearm and lashed out at him, bloodying his nose.

"There, you rascal!" I panted. "I'm for you!"

He laughed again, stinging me into action. I leaped forward only to find my fist caught in his hand. I cried out as his other hand grabbed me in my private parts and then swung me high overhead. He threw me like a sack of meal onto a table, knocking the wind from me. I slid off onto the floor and looked wonderingly at the strange pattern in the Oriental carpet. Then, I pushed myself erect and stumbled towards him. He shook his head and gave a great sigh.

"Edwin, you are the biggest damn fool."

"Sir," I croaked, then I saw his big fist coming towards me and . . . nothing.

I awoke in my rooms with a cold cloth lying across my forehead. I ached all over and my stomach rolled from the wine and brandy I had drunk. Suddenly, a wave of nausea rolled over me. I rolled to the edge of my bed in order not to foul myself and felt a hand drag me over a basin into which I vomited.

"Thank you," I said weakly and rolled back onto my pillow. Jim's face swam into focus and shame burned through me.

"God," I moaned. "I'm sorry."

"All right," he said and rinsed the cloth and replaced it over my head. "You've made a fool of yourself. You're lucky that our seconds weren't visiting, now. None would blame me for killing you after that."

"I know," I said miserably.

"Do you?" he said sharply. "Look at me!"

The incident with William Charles Macready to which Forrest refers occurred at the Astor Place Opera House in New York in May 1849. Forrest was acting at the Broadway Theater and had nothing to do with the disgrace that occurred on the eighth, when Macready attempted to act Macbeth and was howled down by a riotous mob of Forrest adherents who had packed the playhouse. Macready's friends convinced him to try another farewell performance on the tenth, refusing Forrest's friends admission to the theater. But they could not control the streets. A great angry mob gathered and began to stone the theater, smashing all the windows and beginning to tear down the structure to get at Macready, who had insulted their hero Forrest during Forrest's London tour. The 7th Regiment was called out to escort Macready in disguise to safety. When the ruse was discovered, the mob began to fight the militia until finally the word was given to fire. Twenty-two persons were killed by the militia in the riot and thirty-six wounded before the mob dispersed, leaving in its wake a wrecked theater and a black shadow upon Forrest's reputation.—A. J. S.

I raised my head with an effort and tried to look at him, but his features swam in and out of focus. He shook me and I almost vomited again.

"You must control your temper," he said. "Any of those in the room could have and would have killed you in a minute for what you did. You are not in their caliber. They have blazed before and you have only pretended to it."

"I have my honor . . ." I began, but he interrupted me.

Forrest had built a large home on North Broad Street, Philadelphia, and it was here where he had housed his memorabilia in a wing off the house. It was subsequently destroyed in a fire and the contents lost with the exception of the famous knife given to him by Bowie which he had fortuitously placed in another room.

"You'd better learn the difference between honor and stupidity," he said sharply. "If you leave yourself open to insult by your actions, your honor has been transgressed only by yourself, not by those who insult you then. Your honor should be defended only when someone insults you of his own will, not yours."

"I'll remember," I said, closing my eyes.

And I have, although my temper has failed me several times, such as when I caught George W. Jamieson and my wife in compromising positions, or when Macready led his friends against my Macbeth in London. When that poor excuse for an actor brought his troupe to America, I returned the favor, but he would not let it lie there and, well, I regret that my friends became overzealous and many people died, but that, I insist, was not my doing. In all things, I have since defended only slights that have been cast upon my honor through no fault of my own.

Jim surprised me a few nights later by giving me his knife as a gesture of forgiveness. I was touched and filled with awe as I held that weapon in my hands. It was the one with which he had fought duels, going naked into a darkened room with another, armed only with knives, yet another duel at Galvez-town, and the Vidalia incident. I have treasured that knife and used it several times on stage when situations called for it. I have it yet, in my house in Philadelphia in my private museum.

Yes, Jim was a friend. Nay, more like an older brother to whom I owe much that I never repaid.

Henry Clay

Henry Clay met Jim Bowie in 1832. Clay regaled many of his friends with the story of that meeting, which took place in a coach somewhere in the southeastern United States. Another traveler, William McGinley, wrote an article about the occurrence that was widely published in newspapers around the country. The famous statesman and great compromiser, who died in 1852, told this story to an acquaintance of mine. Here is the way it was told to me.—A. J. S.

I was traveling on the Cumberland Road by coach. It was an uncomfortable trip due to the fact that it was unseasonably cold, wet, and blustery. The ventilation in a coach is usually not that exceptional, yet with the weather being what it was we found no cause but to shut the leather shades to keep the inclemency out of doors.

There were three men and a very pretty little lady in the coach. The man was Bill McGinley, a businessman who was of average height and build. Altogether a pleasant companion who spoke about the topics of the day with some knowledge. He spoke thoughtfully and was never angered by disagreement.

The lady was hardly more than a girl. She was quite petite, maybe just a tad under five feet tall and with a slender build. She was dressed in good clothes, though they seemed to be not quite new, colored in shades of blue which set off both her eyes and the yellow of her hair which spilled out from under her hat.

The third traveler was a huge man. More than six feet tall, it would seem, and very broad, though these things had to

be guessed at because he was wrapped up in a huge black
cloak, and he had a black slouch hat that he pulled low over
his face. Mostly he sat quietly, either dozing or listening to
our conversation, but when he made a comment, I looked
into those firm gray eyes and heard a well-mannered, well-
modulated voice, that showed Southern breeding and dignity. Those additions to the dialogue showed both deep
understanding and quick intelligence. I was very much impressed with my fellow traveler.

I was, of course, the third man.

The first leg of the journey was entertaining and even a
little enlightening. Even though the stuffy condition in the
coach made us a bit uncomfortable, the cozy companion-
ship made for a pleasant travel.

This was to change as another man joined us. The man,
dressed in buckskin pants, a homespun shirt covered by a
leather hunting jacket, and sporting a fur cap, was a raw-
boned six-footer. Tall, lank, and unwashed, he bellowed in
the close confines of the coach, "I'm half-horse, half-alligator;
the yaller flower of the forest; all brimstone but the head
and ears, and that's *aqua fortis!*"

The man was untutored and halted our conversation
since we were forced to listen to his side of the issue which
was based on his ill-perceived, nay, ill-conceived, knowledge of the world. The man had never been out of the forest, and never been in a city larger than a few hundred
people. Though this in and of itself was not a hindrance to
all backwoodsmen, this particular specimen was proud of
his lack of thought. His philosophy seemed to be, don't
think, do.

Our mysterious passenger just rolled himself tighter in his
cloak and tried to sleep. He was soon able to, as conversation in the coach dried up like a creek bed in a drought.

The man, feeling that he had won over us poor thinkers,
pulled out a pipe and began puffing. Soon the coach was as

smoky as the common room in an ale house on Saturday night.

Our little flower began to cough. "Please, Mister, the air is too thick for you to add to."

The man's face was angular and had the appearance of an axe, and his words came out like cold steel chopping at her protests. "I paid for my place, an' if I want to smoke, nobody's gonna stop me, nohow."

Then in a blur of movement, our man of mystery threw back his cloak and pulled a huge knife from behind his neck. The blade was at least a foot long and had a brass handguard and backstrap.

"Stranger, my name is James Bowie, well known in Arkansas and Louisiana; and if you don't put that pipe out the window in a quarter of a minute, I'll put this knife through your bowels, as sure as death."

The pipe went out the window, along with his tobacco. The man did not want to incur the wrath of that fine Southern gentleman, the greatest fighting man in the Southwest, the patriot Jim Bowie.

John Bowie

In the early 1800s, there were two things that really stirred a man's blood—land speculation and politics. Texas was a new land and its new government conflicted with the older government, resulting in anger, frustration, and opportunity. For a population who equated wealth with the ownership of land, Texas was a dream come true. But problems arose.

Speculators invested money and, in some cases, risked their money against questionable titles. However, the settlers were in no mood to wait for the courts to decide ownership, so they bought land through speculators. If the courts overturned titles, the speculators would return the money to their clients and then lose their investment.

The Bowies used the money raised through Jim's slave venture to invest in land. The Bowies sold much of the land to other speculators, judges, lawyers, and politicians. This made a fortune for the Bowies and resulted in several court cases that damaged Jim Bowie's reputation.

Since he was the most visible of the Bowies, and because he was known as an adventurer, he became the villain.—A. J. S.

Since the time of the first Bowie, the family has always acquired land. My grandfather, my father, and finally myself and my brothers Rezin and Jim have always believed in owning land. We began purchasing land around 1820 and will continue purchasing land as long as the price is right and we have funds.

I have never spoken about our problems. It is best to keep

these things to yourself. I know Jim always felt the same way, that's why he had so much trouble with the death of his wife, but more of that another time. Land is the question, now.

Major Norris Wright, as sheriff of Rapides Parish, Louisiana, introduced us to a certain friend of his who purported to be Bernardo Sampayreac. Señor Sampayreac offered us sixty thousand arpents of land left from a grant made to him by Governor Miro of Spanish Louisiana. Alfred and Carey Blanchard served as witness to this meeting.

In good faith, we purchased this land, though in working out the deal, we had to borrow from numerous banks, and one problem we did not think to have was that Major Wright would often do his best to block these loans.

This would infuriate James, especially because Jim had some other difficulty with Major Wright, and these led to Major Wright trying to commit murder, and then losing his own life to Jim in Natchez.

In 1828, we were vindicated by the Arkansas State Court. Jim had just gotten out of his sickbed, and decided to move to Texas and leave all the problems and notoriety of his battle with Major Wright behind him.

In Texas, he applied for one-quarter league of land on Galveston Island. This was his right as a single man and citizen of Mexico. He knew this island well when he had certain business dealings in Texas in 1819 and 1820 with Jean Lafitte. He was soon looking at the many possibilities in Texas and started planning where investments were best.

A lot of people are not aware that we Bowies were the first to bring mechanical sugar presses into Louisiana. This was only one of the advances we made, and Jim had even bigger plans for Texas.

He discussed the financial rewards the family could gain if we were to establish cotton gins and textile factories in Texas. Considering there was fine cotton being grown there and an available port for shipping, we decided that this would be a very good investment.

Add to this the huge tracts of land available cheap and Texas appeared to be the finest opportunity for Jim. This is why he went to Texas.

James Stewart

The land in question purchased from Sampayreac was first placed in John's name, then sold to James Stewart. —A. J. S.

John Bowie sold me land that they had purchased on 22 October 1828. The land title was filed in the county records of Hempstead County, town of Washington, in the State of Arkansas.

I received title in December and applied for the land at the land office in Little Rock on 12 December 1828. The land coordinates were N.E. 13, 11 S.W., 26 W. and E. one-half, S.E. 17, 11 S., 26 W. and W. one-half, N.E. 13, 11 S.W. This was entered on the register on that day.

Much of our problem came about because we had to show how Señor Sampayreac received the grant. The court tried to prove he was deceased prior to Bowie buying the land, maybe even prior to receiving the grant, or that he was a foreigner and they also tried to prove he was a fictitious person. Though how he could be both fictional and real I am still unsure.

I believe it was these conflicting testimonies that lost the case for Sam C. Roane, the state prosecutor. The testimony of John Heberard was very important to the case since he swore to the legitimacy of Sampayreac and the grant.

In 1831, through some chicanery brought about through the Attorney General of the United States William Wirt and Roane, the verdict was overturned again and the state got my land. The Bowies made good the loss, but it still irritates me that they were able to take my land from me.

The Bowies were con men, plain and simple. There were more than 126 cases that were heard in the State Courts that had to deal with the Sampayreac land grant. It is my belief that there never was a Sampayreac. The name is incredible. In all my research, I could find no such person in any Spanish documents, and the individual could not be produced for cross-examination. Any way you look at it, the entire business was simply a land swindle.

The first case was forced into court in 1827—the same year as that scandalous duel near Natchez. The fact was that 126 land claims were being held up while we tried to prove their validity. The case went before Judges Johnson and Eskridge. I asked for a continuance in order to study both evidence in the form of this Sampayreac and Spanish law. For precedence, I cited *Soulard* v. *United States* where Chief Justice Marshall ruled that attorneys for the state sometimes need extra time to prepare for cases dealing with foreign land and property laws.

The judges refused. I do not suggest that the real reason behind their refusal lay in the fact that the Bowies and their fellow speculators sold this land to every man of influence or power within the state, and that these lawyers, bankers, businessmen and judges stood to make a very large amount of money at the expense of both the State and Federal governments.

On December 19, 1827, the case was again brought to trial. Three days earlier, on the 16th, a subpoena had been issued, clearly stating the charges against the Bowies

> ## Letter from Thomas F. McKinney to Stephen F. Austin
>
> Permit me to introduce to you Mr. James Bowie, a gentleman who stands highly esteemed by his acquaintances, and merits the attention particularly of the citizens of Texas as he is disposed to become a citizen of that country, and will evidently be able to promote its general interests. I hope that you and Mr. Bowie may concur in sentiments and that you may facilitate his views.

stemming from the fact that Sampayreac was a fictitious person, or was a foreigner and then dead, that is to say, he was dead before the land grant was issued.

A deposition was allowed into evidence from a Mr. John Heberard that swayed the judges into finding for said Sampayreac for four hundred arpents of land.

We filed a bill on December 28, 1827, that alleged due to surprise and fraud the court erred in its proceedings. We even declared that the papers used to prove the Bowie case were forgeries. Personally, I think they were drawn up by that master forger Bloody Jack Sturdivant. But I could never prove my suspicions.

On February 7, 1831, the ruling was overturned and the four hundred arpents of land were returned to the State of Arkansas and the United States of America.

Criminal proceedings against Jim Bowie were never initiated. I suppose it is because people were afraid of retaliation. Personally, if someone had been willing to file a charge, I would have been happy to prosecute the rapscallion.

I spent the better part of four years working on this problem while Bowie languished in the lap of luxury, married to a Mexican governor's daughter, an heiress by all account.

Still, we won despite everything and the government received its just due.

Mary Wells

Mary Wells, sister of General Montfort Wells, Samuel Levi Wells III, and Thomas Jefferson Wells, was the victim of a rather sordid piece of gossip that Dr. Thomas Harris Maddox heard from one of his patients and took great delight in repeating upon his various visits to the taverns in and around Natchez. It was a scandalous tale that no gentleman would have dared repeat unless he thought himself invulnerable from challenge. Mary apparently was linked to Bowie following the death of her sister, Cecelia, two weeks before Cecelia was to be married to Bowie. Of course, the scandal became even more popular when people realized that the Wellses and Bowies were cousins. Major Norris Wright took a certain vicious delight in the scandal as he had been a contender for Cecelia's hand as well, only to be thrown over rather contemptuously by Cecelia when he pressed his suit.—A. J. S.

The man had absolutely no scruples at all. None. Dr. Maddox, I mean, and as for Major Wright I have only the utmost contempt.

The whole affair began when Cecelia died just two weeks before she and Jim were to be married. Jim was totally devastated by Cecelia's death.

I get ahead of myself.

Or behind.

I . . . loved Jim more than . . .

But it was Cecelia that he wanted. Then. And in that, there was a bit of scandal as well for I was the oldest and should have been the one first married. But it was frail

Cecelia that Jim chose. Oh, I did not hate him for loving Cecelia. My love was too great. I wanted only his happiness. That was all that mattered.

Cecelia died on a Thursday and we buried her on a Saturday. Jim rode down along the river, after the funeral. When he did not return to our house that night, I rode out in the early morning, searching for him. I found him down by the willows on the lower quarter of our land along the river. I went to him and comforted him in his grief. My breast ached for him and I felt his sorrow and loss as harshly as my own, and when he put his arms around me and cried, I weakened. I went all hot under his hands, soft beneath their hardness. Maybe it was because I felt what was beneath his killer's hands, maybe not. By accident we kissed.

And we made love. Not from any sense of lust, but to find ourselves and our love for Cecelia in each other. It was an affirmation, perhaps an epiphany. By making love to each other, we confirmed our loss of Cecelia.

I cannot explain it well, but it was this one time and only once that Jim and I were together as man and woman. And it was enough for both of us to realize our loss.

But we were observed at the willows by someone. I suspect Wright. Why? He was always around, like a weasel trying to sneak into the hen house. Always ingratiating or trying to ingratiate himself within our family. But we knew him for what he was, a blackguard of the worst kind. He wanted Cecelia only because my brothers held title to a piece of bottom land that he needed to provide a docking and delivery for his crops. Otherwise, he had to haul his cotton into the Cotton House and pay the poundage rate for transfer.

But my brothers had no intention of selling the land and when he became abusive, even refused him the right-of-way across their land, doubling the distance that Wright had to transport his cotton.

And then there was the matter of his association with Colonel Crain, who had no honor at all in regards to his just and due debts, electing to challenge those who had loaned him money instead of paying them.

Wright did ask me to marry him after Cecelia refused him, but I knew that the only reason he sought my hand was for the leverage that would give him with my brothers to gain a right-of-way. I guess you could say I was partly responsible for leading him to believe I was interested in him. I was not and still am not the prettiest girl in Louisiana or Texas. My jaw is square and my brothers complain that I have a rather frank way of looking into men's eyes as if I were challenging them. That's how I knew what Wright was up to, for a man like Wright would not have paid any attention to me for my looks alone.

Wright pretty much had his own choice of women—for the most part, that is, for he had a penchant for married women—because he had that mysterious dark quality about him. Saturnine, or satanic, thin-lipped with the coldest eyes I have seen except on a snake.

I remember when he asked me to marry him. We had gone out riding together along the river road leading down to the Cuny Plantation. The day was hot and humid and I had removed my corset before riding in deference to the heat. Wright could hardly keep his eyes off my breasts as we rode, and I have to admit that I did enjoy the way he looked at me.

We pulled up to rest our horses under a large, twisted oak festooned with moss. He tried to kiss me when he helped me down from my horse, but I pushed him away and laughed at him, calling him a flirt.

"Flirt?" he said. He grinned, but I could see no humor behind his smile. "Why, I believe you are the flirt, Mary."

"That, sir, is a woman's prerogative," I answered. I took

a small handkerchief from my sleeve and blotted my upper lip and brow.

"And a man's?" he asked.

"Why, to wait upon a woman's!" I exclaimed. "Surely, you are aware of that, sir!" I added teasingly.

"Mary," he said, clearing his throat. "There is something that I have been meaning to say to you. Or ask you, rather," he said disarmingly.

"Yes?"

"I have enjoyed our rides together and, well, will you marry me?"

The proposal as it came surprised me, and I treated it as a jest before refusing it. His eyes hardened for a moment, then relaxed and he forced a laugh.

"I will take it up with your brothers," he said condescendingly. "They know more of what a woman needs during these times than—"

"I do not choose to be chattel property for any man," I said, coolly interrupting him. "I am not subject to the authority of man, nor will I allow any man to have dominion over me. Certainly no man of the like of Wright. I am free to wed as I please or not to. I do not need a husband, sir, to enjoy the benefits of the marriage bed."

"Those are not the words of a lady," he said thickly, his face turning red with fury.

"No?" I asked. "And why not? They are the words a gentleman might use. And does not a gentleman have the privilege of visiting other ladies? Why should a woman not have the same privileges? I think you are placing too much emphasis upon a maidenhead and not enough emphasis upon the maiden. If a man has a choice in such matters in this world, then a woman has the same choices."

He rode away, whipping his mount in fury after my refusal. I remember seeing flecks of foam stream back from that frightened horse's mouth and I knew I had made the right choice, although I had made a powerful enemy for not only myself, but my brothers as well.

Not long after that exchange, Cecelia died and Jim and I had our brief affair. You know the rest of the story.

I've had many lovers since then, but somehow, in the dark of the night, I always see Jim's face above mine and feel his lips upon mine and his arms holding me tightly.

It hasn't been the same since.

The Vidalia Affair

*In 1827, Bowie became embroiled in a bitter feud with the
sheriff of his parish, Major Norris Wright, who shot Bowie
in the streets of Alexandria, Louisiana. The truth of what
happened there and what happened later on the Vidalia
Sandbar is a hotly argued subject. Margaret Bowie clipped
an article out of a paper that reported the event after it happened, but neglected to either date the clipping or write
down the name of the paper and author. It does, however,
seem to have been written by someone who was an eyewit-
ness to the affair or who had intimate knowledge of what
transpired.—A. J. S.*

From a Newspaper Article Clipped by Margaret Bowie

Major Norris Wright was a moderate man. Moderate in his
dimensions, moderate in his dress, and moderate in his personal code. At least, that was how he always appeared.

I heard many different stories as to where he came from,
how he gained his wealth, and even how he came to be
called Major. I do not know which was true, though I heard
some of these stories in the presence of the Major himself.

You see, in those days, I had let myself be drawn into bad
ways. I drank bad liquor and smoked bad cigars, consorted
with bad women, [Perhaps this is one reason why the article is lacking an author—Ed.] and had the worst companions. All in all, it was a bad life, though exciting at times.

As for the Major, I understand he originally came from
Baltimore in Maryland. At that time, many men from the
North who had some skill at arms came South. Even though

Miscellaneous Data

The Wells family were the oldest and richest in the area; the Cunys and the Bowies sided with them and were called "the Old Planters." Their politics were listed as Henry Clay Whigs. The Maddox party was made up of Jacksonian Democrats.

In 1823 William Fristoe, the sheriff of Rapides Parish and a friend of James Bowie, died in office. Major Wright (some say through tricky politics) was selected to serve out the term, which ended in 1826. In 1826, Wright won his reelection in a hotly contested race. Some say Sam Wells was the opposing candidate. When Wright was killed, Sam Wells became sheriff. Wells died from yellow fever in New Orleans in 1829. He was delivering prisoners.

Norris Wright came from Baltimore with Robert C. Hyson to clerk in the store of Martin and Bryant. Hyson and Wright took over the business after the death of one of its members. In 1825 the business converted into a bank and Wright became a director. This allowed him to turn down loans from the Planters.

Samuel Wells accused Crain of killing Gen. Sam Cuny in a written statement. Since Crain allegedly pulled the first pistol, Wells called it premeditated murder. The case went to the grand jury, but no trace of it or a decision rendered by the grand jury can be found, the records having disappeared.

dueling was and is frowned upon by the law, the men of the South believed in honor above all else. A man who had the appearance of a gentleman, and knew how to shoot or use a sword, could make a large amount of money.

Sheriff Major Norris Wright was attached to a conspiracy. The Murrell Conspiracy, to be exact. You see, Murrell needed people in many different positions of authority in order for his plan to work.

The plan was very complicated, and took years to establish. However, before it could be completed, it was uncovered, and broken. Murrell went to prison, and if he hasn't died is still there; hence, my desire to keep my name secret.

Wright made money through many different channels. He had interests in several taverns, inns, and gaming houses; in these his confederates received and sold stolen goods, mostly for counterfeit money, passed information (for a price) to various and sundry thieves, worked land swindles using documents forged by Bloody Jack Sturdivant, sold bills of sale for stolen livestock, including slaves, and made enough money to be placed on the board of directors at the bank in Alexandria.

He also was both an extraordinary pistol shot and a trained swordsman. When he first came south and he needed money, like his friend Judge Crain, he would simply borrow the money and not pay it back. When it came time for his benefactor to collect his due, Major Wright would challenge him to a duel and kill him. Most of this was in his past by the time he ran for sheriff, but those of us in the clan knew it.

As sheriff and bank director he was in position to pass information and stop individuals who might cause problems to Murrell's plans, the plans of the Clan of the Mystic Confederacy. One of these individuals was James Bowie.

Of course, Major Wright also enjoyed the work, because Bowie had set up opposition to Major Wright's candidacy for the position of sheriff. Wright was a lot better hater than he appeared. I suppose I should also mention that there was a woman involved, but I'll kindly keep her name to myself, it not being fit to mention in this testimony.

Anyway, the entire Bowie clan could have caused problems. All were intelligent, cool under fire and could, if pushed, have fought anyone who tried to take what was theirs, and what would be worse is they would lead a fight to help their neighbors.

The Bowies are an honorable clan. Indeed, that is probably their biggest downfall. They have always played by the dictates of honor, even in business.

James Bowie was a very quiet and unassuming gentleman, but when aroused he was hell on wheels. There are stories which I cannot reveal here about fights on the bayous, on the river, in the gambling halls—well, let us simply say that James Bowie was not a man who could be taken lightly unless you wanted to be crippled or killed.

Major Wright started his campaign by casting aspersions on Bowie's pretension to being a gentleman. He did this by having the gamblers at his dives talk about Bowie. They called him a hard-drinking, carousing womanizer. A brawler who more often than not killed his opponents.

These words, with details invented as the gossip advanced, went straight to Bowie's ears. Bowie tracked some down. It was not exactly pleasant for the man who passed these rumors if Bowie found out. Only a few died, and those are not important.

His defense all but halted the lies.

Next, Wright thought to drive the Bowies out through financial means. The Bowies were always gambling on land. These speculations required much ready cash. Norris had the cash and withheld it at the banks. He stopped them from getting loans, the result being that the Bowies lost several good options that would have established them as very wealthy men.

All the Bowies were angry, but James Bowie was quite willing to kill the Major with his bare hands.

He received his chance one day in Alexandria.

I had just spoken to Major Wright about . . . well, maybe I'll keep that to myself, but needless to say it was something not best talked about in the open.

Let me explain this better. Alex at this time was part frontier town, part city. The town square was bordered by a tavern and an inn on the north, a blacksmith and livery shop on the east, a courthouse on the south, and several small shops including a jewelry store on the west. The stable of the inn and the livery were built almost together in the shade of a small stand of oaks. Several of these massive old trees were even used as part of the corral.

It was in the shade of these trees that the Major and I met one afternoon. We were hidden from the gawkers in the square and from most of the people moving in the street. Though there were not many, because we had chosen a time, I believe it was 3:00, where the heat of the day combined with the steamy atmosphere would keep most people from witnessing our secret meeting.

I had just whispered the message when he exclaimed, "D——!"

I prepared to flee, but he halted me with a sudden motion of his hand and a hoarse whispered word, "Stay. It's that b——Bowie."

I was somewhat taken aback. Major Wright seldom showed his emotions. He was a very moderate man. Maybe cold would be a better word.

I have never seen such a fierce expression on a man. It was as if a rough chiseled stone statue had come to life. Bowie was said to be a fine-looking gentleman, but now all emotion had been driven from his countenance. His blue eyes had changed to gray and even his sandy, almost red, hair seemed to have become aflame with his anger.

"Sheriff Wright." Bowie's tone was normally quiet, he

usually spoke with authority, but never with command, if that makes sense. He said things with such confidence that you just responded the way he wanted you to, without you ever thinking about doing anything else.

"Mr. Bowie," the Major responded with his glacier-cool tone.

"I am given to understand that you have blocked our loan at the bank." He really said that. I can hear it now even though this was almost ten years ago.

"I did." Major Wright actually sneered at Bowie. I knew why, because I saw the man's hand sneaking around to his coattails. I knew the Major had a pair of pocket pistols hidden in his long-tailed coat.

"I take it the bank is adverse to making money." Bowie was striving to keep control, but he was all fire except for that voice, which belonged somewhere at the top of a cold snow-capped mountain.

"The bank deals with gentlemen, not bravos, not men who blackball their betters."

Bowie stepped forward, and that's when Wright pulled his pistol. The explosion startled both me and Bowie, who flew backwards onto the green grass. The powder blue jacket he was wearing flared up.

Bowie jerked himself to a sitting position and beat the flames out with his hands. He then rolled to his feet.

Wright was in shock. He had expected to commit murder, not be embroiled in a battle, but a battle was looming.

Bowie growled. It was like a huge wolf was suddenly let loose from a chain. Wright was scared, something I never expected to see.

The Major tried to reach for his second pistol, but Bowie was on top of him. The Major was a man of about 160 pounds, and Bowie lifted him into the air by his neck. He then hurled the Major against the oak tree.

The Major was dazed, but Bowie went right to where he lay and jerked him up as though Wright weighed nothing. Bowie held him up with one hand and slapped him. It sounded louder than the pistol shot. Then he backhanded him. Over and over, the Major was struck.

I rolled around behind Bowie and screamed for assistance. I had and have never seen a man so easily manhandled. Bowie's strength must have been enormous.

Finally the blacksmith and some of his cronies, aided by Bowie's own brothers, pulled him away. There were about ten men involved. Bowie pushed them away, scattered them several times as though these tough frontiersmen were no more than children.

Wright, in the meantime, was unable to do more than crawl. He'd tried to potshoot a deer, and got him a wild longhorn, or a gator, or a razorback, or something like all three.

I was trying to slip away before they started asking me questions that I could not, should not answer on peril of my own life and liberty, but I heard a man ask Wright what happened.

"Bowie . . . went . . . crazy." He couldn't hardly talk. The red and purple marks on his throat gave mute evidence as to why.

"Whose pistol?" someone else asked. Bowie responded.

"Look in Major Wright's coat. I believe you'll find the mate."

They did, and I left. I needed a drink, and so I went into the tavern.

Bowie and his brothers came in just as I finished answering in the negative as to what the commotion was outside. The tavern keeper had poured me a brandy, and I moved aside to let Bowie get a drink. He was again the soft-spoken gentleman.

The Maddox Party

Dr. Thomas H. Maddox
Col. Robert A. Crain
Dr. James A. Denny
Maj. Norris Wright
Alfred Blanchard
Carey Blanchard

The Wells Party

Samuel Levi Wells III
Maj. George C. McWhorter
Dr. Richard Cuny
Thomas Jefferson Wells
James Bowie
Gen. Samuel Cuny

Spectators with Dr. Maddox

Dr. Provan
Col. Barnard
Capt. John B. Nevitt
Dr. Cox
David Woods

Date

Wed. Sept. 19, 1827. Temperature at 5 A.M. 80
degrees, at 4:00 P.M. 91 degrees, dry, with a wind
from the southwest, skies clear.

Place

Adams County, Mississippi, Sheriff Henry
Tooley, Esq.

"Why'd he try to kill you, Jim?" Rezin asked.

"I don't know, Reez." Bowie took a sip of his drink.

John said, "Why'd he stop our loan? The bank lost a lot of money. That's not good banking."

"All right, I just can't stand it. I've got to know. Why aren't you dead, brother Jim?"

"The ball hit something in my pocket." He reached into his coat and removed some dingus that I was too far away to see.

"My Mason symbol. He figured I'd blackballed him from the Lodge. Look, the ball is stuck on the eye. That'll bring bad luck."

Bowie looked at the little doodad for a moment, and then said in a voice I had to strain to hear, "I just picked this up at the jeweler. I slipped it into my pocket when I saw Wright over there by the oak. Luck sure is a strange thing, isn't it, boys?"

Bowie tossed the little amulet into a spittoon. He and his brothers finished their drink and left. I dug the Masonic pin out and kept it as proof that this story that I have related to you is completely true, and I have shown this good luck charm to the editor of this paper as evidence.

The very next year James Bowie killed Norris Wright at the Vidalia Sandbar Massacre. And this year, Big Jim Bowie, the only man who ever truly frightened me, died in Texas at some place called Bexar.

I stated earlier that Murrell scared me. James Bowie scared me even more. Even in his death I hesitate to write this, and only my desire to see history set straight convinced me to sell this article.

I began to withdraw from the Clan from that moment on. I was afraid that Bowie might discover that I was at odds with him and would then attack me. Once Murrell was arrested, I escaped and began a new life. I have lived a life that a preacher would envy ever since, and the charm I mentioned has brought me good luck.

The story I have told is a true one. I swear on Jim Bowie's Masonic amulet, the one that saved him from Major Wright's bullet.

From the Letters of Mary Wells

It is hard for me to believe that I was the cause of men spilling their blood even unto death. I was quite young in 1827, little more than a girl.

Apparently, Jim and I were discovered down along the willows that one day by either Major Wright or one of his friends. At least, that is what my brothers determined, but I have a sneaky suspicion that Annette Jeanne saw us and told Dr. Thomas Harris Maddox what she had seen. I believe she thought that Dr. Maddox would pass word on to the Major since they were friends and all. Annette Jeanne was always after the Major, but he had eyes, at that time, only for me.

Montfort, my brother, became furious when word finally trickled back to us. He immediately called for a horse to be saddled and rode into town to confront Dr. Maddox. Since he cannot see very well—cataracts, you know—he took along a shotgun. When he asked Dr. Maddox for the name of the person who had perpetuated such a lie, Dr. Maddox refused to answer. That's when Montfort went back to his horse to get his shotgun. Dr. Maddox took to running down the street and Montfort shot and killed a man standing by the barber shop instead.

Naturally, Dr. Maddox had little choice but to challenge Montfort for his actions, but Montfort refused to fight him, saying that he wouldn't fight anyone on the field of honor who wasn't a gentleman. Well, this was just what Dr. Maddox and that weasel Major Wright needed. They began to spread word about town, questioning Montfort's honor. Montfort was furious, but he knew that to fight Dr. Maddox was a useless thing since he wouldn't be able to see the doctor at twenty paces.

At last, Samuel took his place even though his eyesight was only a little better. Well, Dr. Maddox accepted and their seconds began to set the details. I planned on going to the duel with them, but on the morning of the affair, Montfort locked the door to my room and ordered the servants not to let me out until after ten o'clock, well past the time for the duel.

A Note from Thomas Jefferson Wells

I have little to say about the Vidalia duel. There were animosities present. Alfred Blanchard was there.

We had been at variance for a while. Blanchard was an unsavory man. Though he made pretensions towards being a gentleman, he was simply a scavenger.

He would hang around wealthy men and find ways to get them to spend their money on him. We would always buy the dinner, the drinks. They would often loan him money, and somehow after an evening of drinking, they would have forgotten if he paid them back. I never got so drunk that I forgot who paid me back.

His brother was only slightly better.

My major problem with Alfred, though, came about from a little set-to we had at the Alexandria Mid-Summer's Eve Ball. All the plantation gentry were there and we were having a truly wonderful evening. Alfred, of course, was intoxicated. No, that's too fine a word: he was drunk. He was making a fool of himself and was so obnoxious that he was past objectionable to disgraceful.

I made some comment to this effect and a little later while I was dancing with the pretty O'Hara girl, I heard Blanchard make an obscene comment to me. As I began to turn, he shoved his fist against me. I felt this burning down my side, and then he stepped back with a small knife in his hand.

Someone screamed and Jim and Rezin looked over and saw what had happened. They grabbed Blanchard and, at first, I wondered if they were going to rip him apart, limb by limb. But they simply threw him down the stairs and out of the ballroom. Blanchard does have friends, and they quickly got him away.

Fortunately, the wound was only slight and I was back on my feet in a day or two, ready to kill him at the first chance I could get. Of course, I could have challenged him, but the situation was not quite right. I had to wait for a long time. Until September 19, 1827.

18 September 1827

I find I must write down some of my thoughts before meeting foes on the island Vidalia in the Mississippi River.

My Friend & Cousin Sam Wells will be facing Dr. Thomas Maddox in a duel of honor on the morrow. With him will be a party of men whose interests are contrary to ours. My own enemy, Col. Robert Alexander Crain—sometimes Judge Crain—will be there as well. Perhaps we shall get a chance to settle our differences as well.

Col. Crain is a rogue. My father once made the mistake of endorsing a note for Crain despite warnings from several individuals who knew about Crain's habit of borrowing money & not paying it back. When the note came due, Crain refused to pay & my father felt honor-bound to honor his signature despite Crain. Money was scarce at the time & we had to sell some slaves in order to satisfy the obligation. That made us a bit of a laughingstock among the people of Alexandria for a while until the day Crain came out to our place & I shot him in the arm. Perhaps if my aim had been better, this affair tomorrow would never have come to fruition.

Dr. John Rippey, whose nieces are married to my cousins Montfort & Samuel Wells, once rented a plantation to Crain & when he asked Crain for rent, Crain responded that he had been insulted by Dr. Rippey, challenged him to a duel, & killed him. It was, of course, murder. Crain had blazed many times while Dr. Rippey had never been hunting let alone shot a pistol.

Crain still never repaid the money although the court, in settling Dr. Rippey's estate, did force Crain to give up the plantation. He managed a huge profit, however, while the affair dragged through the courts for nearly two years.

Strangely, Crain never could understand how I could be promoted to general over him when I was only a lieutenant of horse & he a colonel, but the answer, of course, is relatively simple: no one would serve under him as a brigadier. In fact, many individuals left his regiment following his duel with Dr. Rippey.

I suppose people in other parts of the country think we are fools with our dueling. They do not understand that given the court system we have, the only recourse left open to us is on the field of honor. That is how justice is meted out.

And that is why I must go to Vidalia tomorrow. Jim Bowie will be there tomorrow. And Major Wright. I am uncertain as to what all this portends, but I am sure that the duel will not be confined to the two principals. I am sure that Crain feels the same way.

Notes Taken by Colonel Crain on the
Occasion of Serving as Second to Dr.
Thomas Maddox in an Affair of
Honor with Samuel Wells

A meeting was held between myself, Col. Robert Alexander
Crain, originally of Fauquier County, Virginia, & Major
George C. McWhorter as seconds to Dr. Maddox & Samuel
Wells. Since the challenge was made by my principal, Dr.
Maddox, the choice of weapons resided with Mr. Wells,
who selected pistols at ten paces.

We agreed upon Vidalia Island to be the site for the
affair, about seventy miles northeast of Alexandria on the
Mississippi River.

The challenger's party will consist of: Dr. Thomas
Harris Maddox, principal. Col. Robert Alexander Crain,
second. Dr. James A. Denny, surgeon. Major Norris Wright,
Alfred & Edward Carey Blanchard, John B. Nevitt, Dr.
William R. Provan, Thomas Hunt, Col. William Barnard, &
Dr. William R. Cox, witnesses. My servant, Job, will carry
the pistols.

The challenged party is General Montfort Wells, who
will be served by his brother as an accepted substitute on
account of General Wells' poor eyesight & pleurisy. His
party will consist of Samuel Levi Wells III, principal.
Major George McWhorter, second. Dr. Richard Cuny,
surgeon. Thomas Jefferson Wells, James Bowie, General
Samuel Cuny, witnesses.

The time & date set for the meeting will be September
19, 1827 at noon.

From Colonel Crain's Journal

Sept. 19, 1827

At last I will have a chance to meet those who have opposed me for so long. I have arranged for a duel between Samuel Wells & Dr. Maddox to be fought at the Vidalia Sandbar, far enough away from the supporters of the Wellses, the Bowies, & the Cunys to ensure our safety should matters come to an expected head & we have the chance to settle all our scores at once.

I do worry about Bowie, though. I have never seen anyone quite as fierce as him &, I must confess, I am a bit cautious about him. Barnard will carry a shotgun & my servant extra pistols, though, so that is some comfort.

Walter Worthington Bowie,
Family Historian

A tendency exists among readers to accept the opinion of family members. In the case of the Bowies, however, that is a dangerous thing to do. Rezin once said that neither he nor his brother ever engaged in a duel of any kind, although several accounts exist of Jim Bowie's triumphs upon the field of honor. The below account, although flawed by time, does provide a quick sketch of the affair.—A. J. S.

The "Sandbar duel," as it was called, which took place on a little island in the Mississippi River opposite Natchez, September 19, 1827, has been more written of, perhaps, than any other of James's numerous fights. The following statement of that celebrated fight is based on a letter written two days after the duel by one of the participants and an article in a Southern paper, published a short time after the occurrence.

For many years a feud existed between two parties in the Parish of Rapides, on Red River. On one side was Col. James Bowie, Gen. Montfort Wells, Samuel Wells, General Cuny, Dr. Cuny, and McWhorter. On the other side Dr. T. H. Maddox of Charles County, Maryland; Maj. Norris Wright, of Baltimore; Col. Robert A. Crain of Fauquier County, Virginia; Alfred and Edward Carey Blanchard, of Norfolk, Virginia; and Dr. Denny composed the leaders of the two parties. Their quarrels finally resulted in arrangements for the fight on the Sandbar, the principals, however, being Dr. Maddox and Samuel L. Wells, the others as witnesses, seconds, and surgeons. After two ineffectual exchanges of shots, Wells and Maddox shook hands, but

Cuny stepped forward and said to Colonel Crain, "This is a good time to settle *our* difficulty"; Bowie and Wright also drew, and the firing became general. Crain killed Cuny and shot Bowie through the hip. Bowie drew his knife and rushed upon Colonel Crain. The latter, clubbing his empty pistol, dealt such a terrific blow upon Bowie's head as to bring him to his knees and break the weapon. Before the latter could recover he was seized by Dr. Maddox, who held him down for some moments, but, collecting his strength, he hurled Maddox off just as Major Wright approached and fired at the wounded Bowie, who, steadying himself against a log, half buried in the sand, fired at Wright, the ball passing through the latter's body. Wright then drew a sword-cane, and rushing upon Bowie, exclaimed, "Damn you, you have killed me." Bowie met the attack, and, seizing his assailant, plunged his "bowie-knife" into his body, killing him instantly. At the same moment Edward Blanchard shot Bowie in the body, but had his arm shattered by a ball from Jefferson Wells.

This ended the fight, and Bowie was removed, as it was supposed, in a dying condition. Of the twelve men who took part in the affray, Wright and Cuny were killed, Bowie, Crain, and Blanchard badly wounded; the remaining seven men escaping any serious injury. Colonel Crain, himself wounded, brought water for his adversary, Colonel Bowie. The latter politely thanked him, but remarked that he did not think Crain had acted properly in firing upon him when he was exchanging shots with Maddox. In later years Bowie and Crain became reconciled, and each having great respect for the other, remained friends until death.

A.H.W. (A Hidden Witness)

The best account of the famous Vidalia Sandbar incident comes not from the participants, who bear a natural prejudice towards the opposing side, but from someone known only as "A Hidden Witness," who happened to be in the right place. From his words, it appears that this individual was afraid for his life and was not among the "gentry" of the day. I believe it was only his addiction to strong drink that drove him to finally break his silence and give the following account of that infamous day, probably long after John A. Murrell had been imprisoned.—A. J. S.

The meeting between Dr. Thomas Harris Maddox and Samuel Levi Wells III was set for high noon, September 19, 1827, at the Vidalia Sandbar, a dueling site of note. The altercation was over a shot taken at Dr. Maddox by Samuel Wells's brother General Montfort Wells after Dr. Maddox allegedly impugned the honor of General Wells's sister by either claiming she had been impregnated by James Bowie or that she had been observed in the field with a buck nigra of rather ponderous possession. Either way, it was an insult to the Wells name and General Wells felt justified in trying to draw satisfaction from a man he deemed beneath his dignity.

It was a hot and steamy day for September. Though it never truly seems to get cold in Louisiana, the sun seemed especially warm as it reflected off the dirty sand of the beach. The six men, the two principals, the two seconds, and the surgeons, Dr. Denny and Dr. Cuny, all commented upon the unseasonable heat as they readied themselves for the medley. Their voices carried to the pile of driftwood collected in a corner of a stand of willows by the spring flood where I was sleeping. At first, I did not recognize the men, but later, after observing what had happened, I discovered their identity.

Colonel Crain and George McWhorter approached each with a nigra carrying a set of dueling pistols. [Ed. Note: These were later to be identified as a matched pair made by T. Mortimer & Sons of London, England, a .36 caliber with a rain-proof pan and roller-bearing on the steelspring.—A. J. S.] Together, they supervised the loading of the pistols after which Mr. Wells made his choice.

The two men stood back-to-back, pistols held in the ready manner. The umpire asked if any wished to make an apology to avoid the duel, but each having answered in the negative, the count was given, slowly and carefully. At ten paces, the two turned and fired and each missed. The pistols were reloaded and the count given a second time and again each missed.

At this point, they declared that their honor had been satisfied and Wells invited all to share a glass of wine with him and others who were in the edge of the wood as witnesses. I recognized those as Jim Bowie, Tom Wells, and General Cuny who advanced after Wells mentioned them. Suddenly, I heard a noise behind me and turned to see Sheriff Norris Wright and seven or eight men coming out of a stand of sweet-gum on the other side. I knew Wright. Everyone knew Wright, a more crooked man in the area would not be found. Rumors had tied him and Crain to John A. Murrell's Clan of the Mystic Confederacy. I don't know if there's any truth to this or not, but I had heard many talking about this in Mother Surgick's pleasure house Under-the-Hill. With Wright were the two Blanchard brothers, Albert and Edward, and Bill Barnard who carried a double-barreled shotgun.

I scrunched down under those old oak roots and hoped that they wouldn't decide to investigate because it sure would have been hard on me if that faction knew I was there.

Well, Crain allowed as to how he wouldn't drink with Bowie or Cuny, but that didn't stop Wells from trying again. He said he would take them over to Connelly's Tavern at Natchez and buy all a drink there. That's when Crain said, "Be damned before I will drink with you and your blasted friends!"

Unfortunately, Bowie and Cuny were close enough to hear Crain's words and at that, Cuny yelled, "This is a good time to settle our own problems, Crain, here and now!"

The General tried to drag his pistol from his pocket, but the hammer caught in his coat. Crain pulled his pistol free and raised it to shoot at Cuny, but Bowie stepped in front of the General. I suppose he thought that would stop Crain, but it didn't. Crain fired anyway, shooting Bowie in the hip and knocking him down.

He threw his pistol away and tried to draw another, but Cuny had his pistol free by now and shot Crain in the arm. Crain was a cool one and game to the core, I'll give him that—wouldn't expect much else from one of Murrell's cronies—and pulled that second pistol and shot Cuny in the left breast.

Meanwhile, Bowie pulled himself upright and drew a huge knife. Lord, if my blood didn't run cold at the sight of that blade with a brass handle. Light glinted off its edge like diamonds. Bowie started to hobble over to Crain, but Crain threw his pistol in Bowie's face and turned and ran away. I don't blame him for that. I would've run away, too, if I had to look into that face dragging a leg towards me.

The pistol struck Bowie on the forehead, stunning him. He fell to his knees, shook his head for a moment, then started to get up, but Dr. Maddox jumped on his back and tried to hold him. But Bowie was a bull and threw him off.

Dr. Cuny's Reaction to Bowie's Wounds

I write this for the layman, although my medical colleagues will undoubtedly find interest as well in the person of Jim Bowie, who withstood all the wounds he received at the Vidalia Sandbar.

Mr. Bowie is a large man a few inches over six feet and weighing close to 220 pounds. He is amazingly well-knit with a hearty constitution.

During the chance encounter, Bowie was shot four times with three balls remaining in his body, two in the left hip and one in the left shoulder. He was grazed by three other balls that drew blood and sustained a large gash upon his left hand. A pistol butt raised a large swelling on his forehead and a sword had been pushed through his sternum into his breast, necessitating its removal with forceps.

I have constantly been amazed at the resiliency of the human body but never more than I was at this time by what Mr. Bowie had suffered. He was abed for several weeks after this, but never despaired, taking the time to read and make plans for when he had thoroughly recuperated to go abroad. He is a testimony to the human spirit.

At that moment, Wright pulled a pistol and fired at Bowie, knocking him down again, but he didn't kill him.

"Goddamn you, Bowie!" he yelled, and unsheathed his sword cane and ran at him. Bowie was flat on his back, dazed from Wright's bullet when Wright stood over and raised that cane like a stake in both hands and drove it into Bowie's chest. Bowie twitched and I thought for sure he was dead. Wright must have, too, 'cause he put a foot on Bowie's chest and tried to pull his cane free, but then Bowie raised his left hand and grabbed Wright by his forearm.

Wright leaped back, helping to pull Bowie up and that's when Bowie stabbed that huge knife in Wright's belly down low and used both hands, ripping it up to Wright's breastbone.

Wright screamed, then looked down at his guts spilling out onto the ground and said, "My god, the damned rascal has killed me." He fell down, his legs twitched and convulsed, and he died, blood rolling out in a huge pool and sinking into that sand.

Meanwhile, Alfred Blanchard and his brother figured Bowie would be easy pickings, standing there with that sword sticking out of him. He pulled his sword-cane and took to stabbing at Bowie, but Bowie batted his sword away and slashed Blanchard's arm to the bone. He screamed like a gut-shot horse and Carey Blanchard pulled a pistol and shot Bowie, hitting him in the hip and knocking him down again. He grabbed his brother and ran away with him towards the woods, Alfred's arm streaming blood. That was when George McWhorter winged him with a pistol, but they got away.

Well, I don't know what else happened. It was all over in minutes. I know other shots went off—I remember hearing that double-barreled shotgun—but I don't know where the pellets went or who they wounded. I do know that Bowie and his friends had the field after it was all over.

Dr. Cuny had gone to his brother, but Crain's bullet had killed the General. He worked on Bowie, staunching the flow of blood. He tried to pull that sword out of Bowie's breast with his forceps, but the sword was stuck too deep and the forceps kept slipping away. Finally, he gave up on the sword and took to operating on Bowie right there, digging out the pistol balls and plugging the holes with linen.

I think Crain must have suddenly been overcome with

shame for his treachery for he brought Bowie a drink of water, saying, "I thought you could use this."

"Thanks," Bowie said.

"This is a hell of a state of affairs," Crain answered, looking around the field.

"You shouldn't have shot me while I was mixed up with Maddox," Bowie said.

"I figured I had to stop you," Crain said. "You're the toughest son-of-a-bitch I ever saw. Good luck."

And he left.

I stayed hid until they carried Bowie to a boat, then across the river before I came out of my cover. I felt weak and my hands shook like I was coming off a five-day drunk. I can't begin to tell you how frightened I was and took off for the north along the Bloody Trace, working my way over up to the Pinch Gut District in Memphis where I figured to lay over for a while before going down to the Swamp in New Orleans. I waited until someone gave me a picayune before I told this story, but it is true, every gospel word of it.

Bowie was taken to Connelly's Tavern across the river and carried up into a corner room on the second story. There, Dr. Cuny finally managed to remove Wright's sword from Bowie's sternum after obtaining a pair of blacksmith tongs. So deeply embedded was the sword in the bone that two people had to hold Bowie steady while Dr. Cuny applied leverage to extract the sword.—A. J. S.

*I discovered a copy of the statement made by James Bowie
after the Vidalia Sandbar fight when I had a little free
time on my hands after delivering a prisoner to Natchez
for extradition purposes. It was my first time in Natchez
and while I was taking in the sights, I suddenly remembered the Vidalia Affair. I visited the newspaper offices
and while reading the lurid account of the battle, I discovered the enclosed statement, made on either December 23
or the 24th in 1827, recorded in a reporter's notebook. I
tried to verify the contents of the notebook with court records, but those records have been lost.—A. J. S.*

Gentlemen of the Jurie. [sic]

My name is James Bowie. I am a resident of Rapides
Parish, Louisiana where I have resided for almost eighteen
years since I was a child. The accounts that have been made
in regards to the recent occurrences at the Vidalia Sandbar.
Most of what has been reported have been lies, even to the
place of the battle which was at another sandbar without
name just above Natchez.

I wish to remind this jury that I am appearing of my own
free will and that this Jury has no right to be investigating

what began as an Affair of Honor. The subsequent brawl that took place is most regretable [sic] but happened outside the jurisdiction of this court.

Dr. Thomas Maddox and Samuel Levi Wells III met in an affair of honor. I, and several members of the Wells family, attended as spectators. We stationed ourselves in the woods about two hundred yards from the Field of Honor. Others are more qualified to speak to the issuance of the duel. For the record, I saw the participants after the exchange of two shots each that apparently had no effect on either man. They then approached each other in such a way as to suggest that the affair had been satisfactorily concluded. Seeing them shake hands and taking this to mean that the Affair of Honor had been settled by mutual agreement, I and my friends went forward to congratulate the gentlemen.

Major Wright and Col. Crain and the two Blanchard brothers, Alfred and Carey, also approached the party from the opposite side. As we drew close to the duelists, Col. Crain commenced firing his pistols. Several shots were fired. Each member of the Wright party carried two loaded pistols, and both Wright and Alfred Blanchard carried sword canes as well. I, Gen. Cuny, and Thomas Wells carried a pistol each. I was wounded in the first volley and struck in the forehead with a thrown pistol. Dazed, I drew my pistol after another shot downed Gen. Cuny. Col. Crain ran from the field. I fired at him, but missed as two more bullets struck me, knocking me to the ground. Major Wright took advantage of this and rushed forward, stabbing me in the breast with his sword cane. He placed his foot upon my breast and tried to pull the sword free, but the handle came off in his hand. I drew my knife and reached up, pulling him down on top of me and stabbed him in the stomach, reaching up for his heart. He said, "Damn you, Bowie! You've killed me!" then vomited blood on me and died. I pushed him off and tried to rise whereupon Alfred Blanchard attacked me with his sword cane, slashing me across the arm as I tried to defend myself. I returned the blow with my knife, cutting him deeply, severing, as I later discovered, the leaders [sic] in his arm. He fled the field.

That is what happened. I have here, a brief summation of the affair. I offer it to you now.

I do not know exactly how to use the information I received today. I find great confusion twisting and turning within me, troubling me deeply. Today, I arrived in Houston to deliver some depositions to Court and some personal messages from my father to certain members of the Texas State Congress. It was in pursuit of the latter that my steps took me to The Yellow Rose, a discreet tavern where a man might meet a woman of the night a step above the prostitutes of Front Street and the waterfront. The tavern is a large, two-story, frame building. Next door is a saddlery, a bootmaker, and a gunsmith. It is a well-run establishment with an excellent reputation, although it is not an establishment that would cater to the gentry.

I knew the man I was looking for by sight and so did not approach the long, mahogany bar dominating the far end of the room. Instead, I elected to sit at one of the small tables scattered haphazardly around the room. I had an Allen & Wheelock .44 caliber lipfire revolver belted around my waist along with a Bowie knife made by Grandfather and a Henry rifle I leaned against the wall behind my chair. The bartender held up a whiskey glass and a beer glass. I motioned towards the latter and he filled it and handed it to a young lady to bring to my table. She hesitated long enough to ascertain I wasn't interested in anything else, then discreetly returned to the bar, giving a slight shake of her head to the bartender.

The door opened and closed behind a tall, black-haired, black-eyed man with olive skin. He stood for a second, letting his eyes adjust to the cool and dark interior. He wore a fine broadcloth suit and a stiff-brimmed Stetson that he removed and smoothed his hair with the palm of his hand. A quick smile flashed over his lips as he called out a name and waved to a man I didn't know, then he moved easily across the room to the bar, stopping to visit briefly with other men along the way. I could tell he was popular with the regulars, all wearing dark suits and ties. Only one other man in the room was dressed like I in dusty clothes and scuffed boots. He, too, carried a pistol at his belt while the others, if they were armed, had them tucked beneath their coats. His eyes glittered like a lizard's as he watched the olive-skinned man cross the room. I touched my pistol uneasily, surreptitiously removing the hammer thong and easing the pistol in its holster.

"A needled beer, please, Dave," the man said. He gave the range rider a quick look, then dismissed him and leaned an elbow comfortably on the bar

"Barkeep! Since when are niggers served with white folk?" the range rider asked waspishly. His voice was loud and carried the room. Heads turned quizzically towards the bar. The olive-skinned man swiveled his head to stare at the speaker.

"My bar. I choose who drinks and who doesn't," the bartender said. He slid a glass in front of the olive-skinned man.

"You ain't drinking that here, boy," the range rider said roughly. He took a small step away from the bar and rested his hand upon his pistol.

"Mister," the bartender began, then fell silent as the range rider gave him a hard look. He moved away from the bar and began to sidle down to the far end away from the conflict.

"What's your name, nigger?" the range rider said.

"Cuny. Norris Wright Cuny," the olive-skinned man replied. He stared unflinchingly into the range rider's eyes. "And I'm not armed."

"Just like a nigger to claim that," the other said. "But I'm willing to bet you got a razor or something tucked away somewheres. I reckon that's good enough for me."

I sighed and rose, and crossed over to the pair. "Drink up and leave," I said quietly to the range rider.

His eyes fell down to my chest, saw my Ranger badge, then shook his head and turned slightly, putting his right hand and revolver out of sight.

"Don't think so," he said stoutly. His shoulder moved slightly and I drew my pistol and laid the heavy barrel across his head. He crumbled to the floor without a sound. I bent and took his pistol, a Colt M1860 .44, from his holster and tucked it through my belt. I ran my hand over his body, feeling for other weapons and finding none, straightened and motioned for the bartender.

"Better fetch the sheriff," I said. "We'll lock this boy up till he sobers then set him outside of town."

"Thanks, mister," he said, a bit shaken by the experience. "We don't have much play like that in here. That's usually down towards the docks a ways or over at Galveston. Folks around here live and let live. Especially," he added, flicking a look at the olive-skinned man watching quietly from near my elbow, "since the War, you know."

"I can imagine," I murmured. I nodded at the man and returned to my table.

"What about his pistol?" the bartender called.

I shrugged. "Tell him you don't know what happened to it."

"You gonna keep it?"

"You want him coming back here and shooting up the place when he gets out of jail?" I asked.

"No, no," the bartender said, holding up his hands. "No, you keep it. You earned it. I guess," he amended, frowning slightly. He motioned to a burly young man with a heavy, sloping forehead. "Jimmy, you take this man over to the sheriffs office and tell him to lock him up for being drunk and disorderly."

The young man bent and easily picked up the range rider, slinging him over his shoulder and carrying him from the tavern. I sighed and slipped my hat from my head and ran my fingers through my hair. I hadn't planned on getting involved in local law enforcement, but it's easier to deal with a problem before it becomes a problem than after.

"Thank you," a voice said. I turned my head and looked up at the man called Cuny. "I do believe that man might have killed me."

"Yes, I think he would have," I replied. "He was just drunk enough to be dangerous. Some men are like that. Small men, usually, who need a bit of liquoring to remember that God didn't make them giants."

"May I buy you a drink?" he asked.

I shook my head. "No, one will do me. But you may join me if you wish." He pulled out a chair and sat.

"I'm Norris Wright Cuny," he said, stretching out his hand. I took it, surprised that it was dry and strong despite his recent close call.

"I heard," I said. "I'm also struck by its strangeness."

"Pardon?" He frowned in confusion.

"That you bear the name of two mortal enemies," I said. He laughed easily and sipped his drink.

"You know, you're the first one who made that connection," he said. "Most people know about the Sandbar Incident, but few remember the names of the participants. Yes, I suppose it's strange. Even stranger when you realize that Philip Cuny was my father and Sam my uncle. But how did you know about the Sandbar participants? That was a long time ago. Fifty years or more."

"My father was a friend of Jim Bowie," I said. "Fact is, he rode a bit with Bowie when he was younger. My grandfather even claimed to have made a knife or two for Bowie, but you know old folks and their tales."

"Yes," he said, nodding in agreement. "I'm well aware of that, as you can imagine."

"Pardon my nosiness, but why would your father name you after an enemy such as Major Wright?"

He shook his head, his lips curling in amusement. "Do you know why that incident came about?"

I shook my head. "I was told it was over the honor of Mary Wells."

"That was the excuse," he said. "But the real reason was that the Cunys, the Wellses, and the Bowies were all Whigs. Major Wright and Colonel Crain's group, rabid Jacksonians all, beat them in the election. My father thought at the time that naming me after Norris Wright might settle the bad blood between the two parties. It didn't.

"I never really knew why they used Mary Wells as an excuse," he said, leaning forward over the table and clasping his hands together. "Nobody really said what it was that Maddox said about her. But Maddox had few scruples, according to what others have told me. He thought nothing of dragging reputations through the mud if it got him a point or two at the polls. Colonel Crain was almost as bad." He paused to sip his drink. "You see, Wright wanted Louisiana to grow into statehood—a plan, incidentally, of Jackson as well for that would give the U.S. a strong reason to support expansion. But Wright saw it as a way to increase his fortune. With money, he had power, the type of power that the Masons had."

"I've heard that Bowie was a Mason," I enjoined.

He nodded. "They all were. Men learned quickly that membership in the Lodge would give them the leg up they needed to personal wealth. Now, I'm not certain, but I believe that Bowie and his group managed to keep Wright if not out of the Masons at least out of the offices they needed to consolidate their hold on the power base at the time. There was also a bit of scandal going around at the time that Wright and the Maddoxes had an 'understanding' with John Murrell—you know about him, I suppose?"

I nodded. Everyone knew about John Murrell, one of the bloodiest men who roamed the Natchez Trace and almost succeeded in seizing control of Louisiana.

"I heard stories about Murrell and his Mystic Clan. They almost managed to seize control of the South."

"Yes," he said soberly. "Few people realize how close that was. And, if you remember what I just told you, Major Wright and the Maddoxes wanted Louisiana to grow. Murrell's plan was to seize control of New Orleans and, well, you can see where some people would jump to conclusions about the Maddoxes and Murrell."

"If something wasn't already there, then I can see how that rumor would be effective," I said.

He smiled faintly. "Yes. There is that. But Jim Bowie had applied for a loan through a bank controlled by Major Wright. In reality, there was no reason for the loan to have been disapproved, as Bowie and his brothers had more than enough land for security, but Bowie wanted the loan to buy more land around Rapides Parish. That would have given him control of a very large part of Louisiana. Wright knew that and turned down the loan.

"The Bowies, however, counting on getting that loan, had made sizeable commitments to purchase land. They were stretched pretty thin and had to scramble to meet their obligations. They couldn't meet them all and lost some of the land upon which they had taken options. Wright quickly snapped up those options, isolating Bowie and his people from further expansion in Louisiana."

"That makes sense," I acknowledged. "People have done stranger things in the name of politics."

He hesitated, his eyes flickering towards the door, then

back. I could tell he had more that he wanted to tell me, but I also knew better than to push him for it. People have to make their own minds up about certain things before opening up what is really on their minds. At last, he sighed and leaned back in his chair.

"I imagine you can tell that I'm . . . colored," he said, a bitter smile touching his lips. I nodded and sipped my beer, letting him sort out his words in his own time. "For a while, I was involved in the Reconstruction." He shrugged. "That's not so unusual, but it has made me a lot of enemies. I believe that man was hired by some of them to . . . get rid of me. I know this sounds very melodramatic, but I can't think of any other reason for him to be here at this precise time . . ."

"Still a bit of a coincidence, wouldn't you say?" I murmured.

He laughed. "Perhaps I am making too much of the affair. But, if you live the life of a colored man—"

"We all have our prejudices," I said, interrupting him. "That doesn't make prejudice better coming from one man's mouth or another's."

"Yes, but you see, that is part of the answer to your question as well," he said quietly.

I perked up and drained my beer. I signaled to the bartender and held up my glass. Cuny smiled and shook his head.

"I thought you said one was enough," he said.

"I think, under the circumstances, another wouldn't be out of place," I answered.

"Good. Then I'll buy." He held up two fingers and pointed to himself. He finished his drink and sighed and leaned back again in his chair.

"My grandmother on my mother's side was a slave on a neighbor's plantation," he said after our drinks had been brought to our table. "My mother lived her life as a slave even though she gave my father eight children. But," he continued, "I hold nothing against my father for all of that. He freed every one of us and made certain that each of us received an education, even though that was not popular at the time. In fact, it was very dangerous, for some of the Southern states had laws against educating Negroes, you know."

"I see," I said slowly. "At least, I think I do."

"I'm not sure that you do," he answered. "But that is where the problem began. Even though Major Wright blocked the Bowies' loan and kept them from extending their influence beyond Rapides Parish, they were still a force to contend with due to their influence in the Masons. Now, Wright also had his eye upon Mary Wells and when she rebuffed him, Maddox decided to voice it around that she was sleeping with a black man from the plantation. The Wellses had a huge colored man who fought in a few sporting contests which had become more popular than cockfights at the time." A trace of bitterness touched his voice. "That man was my second cousin, Samuel Thomas Cuny. He was very good with his fists. Too good. He killed one of Major Wright's Negroes in a fight. That cost Major Wright a lot of money. He tried to regain it in a horse race against Jim Bowie, but Bowie had a horse that couldn't be beaten. Wright lost even more.

"It was then that Maddox told his lie and two men died because of it."

"And a legend was born," I said.

"Yes," he answered. "And a legend was born."

We sat until twilight, visiting about the ways and means of the day. I returned to my room and took up my pen to make a record of the day's (and night's) occurrences before I forgot them. But as I finish these words with June bugs knocking against the lantern shade, I wonder if Cuny told me the entire truth. His relation of the events seems to be a bit skimpy for the affair at Vindalia [sic] Sandbar. Indeed,

I wonder if Maddox told the truth and not a lie. A white woman sleeping with a black man in those times would have been ruined and the black man boiled alive in a large kettle. Even the double standard of today's times that allows a white man to sleep with a black woman does not allow the same privilege for a white woman. This, I am certain, Cuny knows as he must also know that being the son of a male slaveowner is currently politically in vogue. But to be the son of a black man and white woman or even the grandson of such a union would be socially unacceptable.

I believe somewhere in the middle the truth lies. And, I think Jim Bowie, through his love of Mary Wells, made certain that the scandal died that day on Vindalia [sic] Sandbar along with Major Wright.

James Black

James Black had a life filled with adversity. He rose to prominence, then fell into virtual obscurity. He had property, but died penniless, living through the charity of the doctor who took care of him.

He was born in Hackensack, New Jersey, in 1800. In 1804, his mother died and his father remarried. In 1808, he ran away from home, was caught in Philadelphia and apprenticed out since he refused to say where he came from.

He learned to work silver, then left Philadelphia and did odd jobs and blacksmith work. He went to work for a blacksmith named Shaw in Washington, Arkansas. Shaw and his sons did actual smithing, Black fixed guns and made knives. Eventually, he became a partner in the business.

Black fell in love with the blacksmith's daughter, Anne, and relations between the partners became strained. Black tried a new business, failed, and went back to work for his father-in-law, started a new business, and eventually failed at that when he went blind.

He spent his last years living with the doctor who tried to cure his blindness. He died in 1872.

James Black charged dearly for his knives, from fifty to one hundred dollars each. Black would sell a knife only if it passed his hickory test. Black would take a new knife and whittle a seasoned piece of hickory for one hour. If at the end of the hour he could still shave the hair off his arm, the knife was sold. Otherwise, it was discarded.—A. J. S.

Dear Air. Sowell,

You have heard that I was the inventor of the Bowie knife. This is true. In December of 1830, James Bowie came into my shop in Washington, Arkansas. Mr. Bowie rode up to my shop. He was dressed as a gentleman in gray and black and rode a great black horse. I was standing at the front, getting some air, as he rode up.

"Sir," he says, "are you the cutler, Black?"

I assured him that I was, and he introduced himself as Jim Bowie of Louisiana, Arkansas, and Texas. He asked me if I would make a special knife for him.

Mr. Bowie then withdrew a huge knife from the leather sheath at his side. He said he wanted the knife polished, and an ivory silver handle. He also ordered a new sheath also silver-mounted.

"This knife saved my life and I think it needs to be set apart, somehow."

I had heard something about his big duel over Natchez way and thought that this must have been the knife used in that famous fight. I studied it, Mr. Bowie's formidable size, and his hands, since I had heard of him as a noted Bravo and knife fighter I knew what I needed to do.

He then chose another knife so as to have it handy while I fashioned the hilt and polished the blade to a mirror shine. I spent days on this work, but even as I worked I thought and planned, and created. I knew I could improve on the design.

My method of making steel was a secret that I still keep. Before I die, I plan to give that secret to my benefactors.

The work was extremely hard and time consuming, but I made a twin of the knife that Bowie carried. I also made one that was better.

The knife I made was fourteen inches in length and

the blade was wedge-shaped in cross-section thus giving it weight for slashing or chopping. It was an inch and one-half wide. I placed a brass backstrap on it for catching the blades of others, and an S-shaped brass crossguard.

The curve of the blade to the point was not symmetrical, but went to a point that was perfectly centered. The ivory hilt was fastened to the crossguard by a brass ferrule. The full tang was weighted so that it balanced for throwing. The blade would make two revolutions in thirty feet.

The knife was a thing of beauty, but in Jim Bowie's hands, it was the greatest weapon of the frontier. When Bowie arrived at my shop, I showed him the first, and he was well satisfied. I had targets available for practice behind my shop and we retired there so that he could throw his new weapon.

He flipped the blade up and threw it. It was such a beautiful motion that there seemed to be no force in it, but the blade went three inches deep into a chunk of pine I had hanging up between uprights.

"I am very satisfied," Bowie said as we walked to remove the knife from the target.

This knife, though, was only a butcher's knife, well balanced with a beautiful hilt, but it was nothing to the ebony-handled knife I showed him next, the one I described earlier in this letter.

I had made a leather sheath from bull's hide and then had the leather polished until it shone.

Bowie was stunned. He took the knife from the sheath and studied it. His eyes glowed. I pointed at the hilt.

"Look at the initials, JB, cast in the hilt. I thought you might like this one a bit better," I said.

He turned and threw the knife at a target. The knife buried half its length through the pine and I couldn't help shuddering as I thought what would have happened had that been a man.

I charged him one hundred dollars for the two knives. Bowie showed his knife to his friends and many of them came to my shop for one like his. Many others tried to make similar knives, but none could. Not even the Sheffield Company in England.

Respectively yours,
James R. Black [RUBRIC]

Governor Dan W. Jones

The Jones family cared for Black after his blindness. Black was absolutely destitute, had no way of providing a living for himself and had no family to fall back upon for his care. He kept the secret of his process to himself, fearing that if he let that out, then he would have nothing with which to bargain for his room and board. The day finally came when he decided to release his wonderful process of making metal. Arkansas governor Jones remembers that day.—A. J. S.

Dear Mr. Sowell:

Yes, I do indeed remember James Black, a smith from Washington, Arkansas, and am quite aware of the wonderful story in regards to Mr. Black having made the first Bowie knife.

About 1831, James Bowie came to Washington, Arkansas (to visit his brother John), and gave James Black, a smith, an order for a knife, furnishing a pattern, and desiring it to be made in sixty or ninety days, at the end of which time he would call for it. Black made the knife according to Bowie's pattern, but since he had never made one that suited his own taste in point of shape, he concluded this would be a good opportunity to do so. Consequently, after completing the knife ordered by Bowie, he made another; and when Bowie returned he showed both knives to him, giving him his choice at the same price. Bowie promptly selected Black's pattern.

Shortly after this, Bowie became involved in a difficulty with three desperadoes who assaulted him with knives. He killed them all with the weapon Black had made; and after this when anyone ordered a knife from Black, he ordered it made "like Bowie's"; and still later, "Make me a Bowie knife." Thus, the famous weapon acquired its name. Other men made knives in those days, but no one has ever made *the* Bowie except James Black. Its chiefest value was in its temper, for Black undoubtedly possessed the Damascus secret. It came to him mysteriously and it died with him the same way.

Time and again when I was a boy, he said to me that notwithstanding his great misfortune, God had blessed him in a rare manner by giving him such a good home, and that he would repay it all by disclosing to me his secret of tempering steel when I should arrive at maturity and be able to utilize it to my advantage.

On the first day of May, 1870, his seventieth birthday, he said to me that he was getting old and could not in the ordinary course of nature expect to live a great while longer; that I was now thirty years old with a wife and growing family, and sufficiently acquainted with affairs of the world to utilize properly the secret which he had so often promised to give me; and that, if I would get pen, ink and paper, he would communicate it to me and I could write it down.

I brought the writing material and told him I was ready. He said, "In the first place"—and then stopped suddenly and commenced rubbing his brow with the fingers of his right hand. He continued this for some minutes, and then said, "Go away and come back again in an hour."

I went out of the room, but remained where I could see him, and not for one moment did he take his fingers from his brow or change his position. At the expiration of the hour I went into the room and spoke to him. Without changing his position he said, "Go out again and come back in another hour." I went out and watched for another hour, his conduct remaining the same.

When I came in again and spoke to him at the expiration of the third hour, he burst into a flood of tears and said:

"My God, my God, it has all gone from me! All these years I have accepted the kindness of these good people in the belief that I could repay it all with this legacy, and now when I attempt to do it, I cannot. Daniel, there were ten or twelve processes through which I put the knives, but I cannot remember one of them. When I told you to get pen, ink, and paper, they were all fresh in my mind, but they are all gone now. I have put it off too long!"

For a little more than two years he lived on, but he was ever an imbecile after that.

I hope that this does help you in trying to discover a profile of James Bowie. I never met the man, but feel that I have through the story told above by Mr. Black so many times during the years that he spent with us. I regret that I cannot give you a more complete look at Mr. Bowie. Far too often we are forced to draw conclusions about a man and his character from stories that we learn from those who claim they did know him. Unfortunately, such a claim cannot be made by me.

Respectfully,
Daniel W. Jones [RUBRIC]

Noah Smithwick

Noah Smithwick left Kentucky for Texas in 1827. Over the next thirty-three years, he worked to make the state a better place. He was a blacksmith and armorer, soldier, Indian fighter, and Texas Ranger. One of the many things he did was to make a large number of Bowie knives at his forge.—A. J. S.

In answer to your question, Jack, I did make some original Bowie knives. I made them every time I set up a forge, but the way this came about was this:

I had known Jim Bowie since around 1828, not long after we first came to Texas. In 1890, I had a forge set up in San Antonio de Bexar, which most of us called Bear, at the time.

In 1830, Jim Bowie brought me a fine blade to copy. The blade was about ten inches and maybe two inches thick. It was the one he used in the famous fight on the Sandbar. He had it refitted with ivory handles and the blade highly polished. There was even a new sheath made for it that was silver-mounted.

He asked me to duplicate his knife. It was plain that he wanted a good camp knife, and this blade would have a variety of heavy uses around the camp, and of course, as a weapon it had proved itself well in Bowie's hands.

I made the knife and gave it to him. Since people knew that I had made an original Bowie knife for Jim Bowie, using his as the model, they flocked to my forge. Depending on finish, I was able to sell them for five to twenty dollars each.

I met Bowie many times before his death at the Alamo. Though I never met his wife, I heard much about her, and after her death, I saw him reduced to tears.

I have heard much, over the years, about Jim Bowie, both good and bad, but one thing I will say is that Jim Bowie was a faithful friend. Whatever faults Jim Bowie had, abandoning a friend was not one of them.

A story made its rounds in San Antonio that Bowie got into a fight. A friend of his watched the whole thing. When the fight was over, Bowie asked his friend why he didn't help him. The friend said, "Jim, you were in the wrong."

"I know it," Jim said. "If I'd been right, I wouldn't have needed you."

When he died, we lost a wonderful man.

In Dispute of P. Q. Assertion in the
Baltimore Commercial Transcript on
June 9 And 11, 1838, Concerning the
Birth of the Bowie Knife

The Planters' Advocate, August 24, 1838

The first Bowie knife was made by myself in the parish of Avoyelles, in this state, as a hunting knife, for which purpose, exclusively, it was used for many years. The length of the knife was nine and one-quarter inches, its width one and a half inches, single edge and blade not curved; so the "Correspondent" is as incorrect in his description as in his account of the original of the "Bowie-Knife." The Baltimore correspondent must have been greatly misinformed respecting the manner in which Col. James Bowie first became possessed of this knife, or he must possess a very fertile imagination. The whole of his statement on this point is false.

The following are the facts:

Col. James Bowie had been shot by an individual with whom he was at variance; and as I presumed that a second attempt would be made by the same person to take his life, I gave him the knife to be used as occasion might require, as a defensive weapon. Some time afterwards (and the only time the knife was ever used for any purpose other than that for which it was intended, or originally destined) it was resorted to by Col. James Bowie in a chance medley, or rough fight, between himself and certain other individuals with whom he was then inimical, and the knife was then used only as a de-

Lucy Leigh Bowie

One day while Rezin was thrusting his knife into a ferocious bull, the animal lunged in such a way as to draw the blade through his hand, making a very severe wound. It was after he had his hand dressed that Rezin called for his plantation blacksmith, Jesse Clift. With a pencil, he traced on paper a blade some ten inches long and two inches broad at its widest part, the handle to be strong and well protected from the blade by guards. He then gave Clift a large file of the best quality steel and instructed him to make a knife out of it. The knife was very serviceable in hunting, and Rezin prized it so highly he kept it locked in his desk when he was not wearing it.

fensive weapon—and not till he had been shot down; it was then the means of saving his life. The improvement in its fabrication, and the state of perfection which it has since acquired from experienced cutlers, was not brought about through my agency. I would here assert also, that neither Col. James Bowie nor myself at any period in our lives, ever had a duel with any person soever.

Rezin Bowie
Iberville, Louisiana

John Lattimore

John Lattimore was the son of Dr. William Lattimore, a respected planter who lived below Natchez. He had a large plantation with hundreds of slaves and represented his district as a territorial delegate in Congress from Mississippi.—A. J. S.

Know Mr. Bowie? I should smile! He saved my hide when Bloody Jack Sturdivant fleeced me down in Natchez back in '29. My, my. I haven't thought of that in years. Not in years. I kept it from Daddy for years, thinking that he never knew how stupid his boy had been when he sent me to Natchez to sell our cotton crop that year. 'Twas the year he died that Daddy told me he had heard all about it from Sam Wells. He never brought it up to me because he figured I'd learned my lesson and I did return with the money from the crop and all and that was all that counted. He did send Mr. Bowie an emerald stickpin as a way of saying thanks when Mr. Bowie was recovering from wounds in one of our cabins along the Trace, following his canebrake fight. But I'm getting ahead of myself. Things like that happen to old men and it's been nigh on seventy years or so since that happened and my memory's like a rusted bucket full of tiny holes: little things slip away now and then.

But I do remember that day. Yessir. August 13, it was. I remember everything about it. Hot. Hotter than usual for that time of year and so muggy that sweat just puddled around your trouser line and the niggers took to holding up in the shade of the warehouses down on the wharf every chance they got and no overseer said much to them about it. That kind of heat where you just gasp for every breath, thick and heavy.

I got a good price for our cotton—a little over ten thousand dollars: we had a *good* crop that year; lost none to weevils—and was heading back up the bluff after tucking the money into a money belt I had on beneath my shirt. Josiah, my slave, stayed close by my left shoulder. Those were bad days, then, bad days. Natchez-Under-the Hill—we called it "Natchez-Under"—stood on a kind of shelf out from this bluff. Above it, the respectable people lived, although I wonder just how respectable those folks were: most of them owned a tavern or brothel on the flats under the hill.

Yet, Natchez-Under had an appeal for a reckless youth and I was no different from others who visited that place. My, my. I remember some good times down there what with Madame Aivoges and her emerald green eyes and red hair as bright as a flame that made a man feel all warm and weak inside. And Annie Christmas—stood six-foot in her lace net stocking feet. A big woman, full of love for the keelboaters who came down the river and boys like me in off the plantation, cocky as hell with spurs aching to be sharpened.

A lot of medleys were played down there between keelboaters and planters' sons. Those keelboaters were tough ones, quick with a knife. And there wasn't any quicker than Bloody Jack Sturdivant. Or meaner, for that fact. Rumor had it that he did a little counterfeiting upriver around Illinois someplace in a place called Cave-in-Rock. It wasn't so much a cave as caves go, but it was enough. A lot of men are buried up there in the woods and limestone pits around that cave. John A. Murrell and Sturdivant stayed there a time or two. Some say Murrell, one of Sturdivant's confederates who passed that bogus money around, was the bad one and he was bad enough, but that Bloody Jack, well, he'd just as life carve on you like a Christmas goose as give you the time of day. And of course, that was what drew the young people to him, willing sheep for fleecing. He got away with a lot, too, as he was good friends with Col. Robert Crain, Judge Crain, he was then: crooked as a cheap cigar.

One of Sturdivant's runners saw that cash change hands in the Cotton House. I didn't know he was a runner at the time—just thought he was a friendly sort who was out for a good time, like me, before heading back up the Trace before dark. Nobody rode that Trace after dark unless they were trouble or looking for it. We called it the Devil's Backbone. It ran from Natchez upriver clear to Nashville. An evil road, thick laced with wild grapevines and trees festooned with Spanish moss. Where it cut through the canebrakes the cane stood ten, maybe twelve foot high and so thick you couldn't see nothing but the trail in front of you. Worst place was at the Devil's Punchbowl: a depression four or five hundred feet wide and so thickly grown that you could barely see your hand before your face. Something strange about that place, too. A compass never worked in it. Just sort of spun around in circles. A lot of people disappear there. Swallowed up.

I felt a tap on my shoulder about a block after leaving the wharf and heard Josiah tell someone to back away. I looked around and saw this thin, sallow-faced man about my age dressed in a bottle-green coat glaring up at Josiah's shiny black face.

"You givin' me orders, nigger?" he said, kind of arrogant like. Black-haired and black-eyed he was. "I don't care whose nigger you are, you try those uppity ways with me and I'll have you arrested."

"Not gettin' uppity, suh," Josiah said. But he stood his ground. "Yo' just keeps yo' distance from young Massuh less'n he says diffrnt."

"That's all right, Josiah," I said, stepping between them. "I apologize, sir. Josiah was just doing what he was told."

"No offense, then," he said, smiling. Like a shark, I know,

now. But then, he seemed friendly enough. "I was just wondering if you could direct me to a place called the Christmas House? It comes highly recommended."

"Of course," I said, laughing. "But it's only noon. It won't open until five or six."

His face fell at that and he shook his head, sighing. "Well, I guess I'll just have to give it a miss. I sort of thought that it would be a way to kill a little time before I head back home. I'm Phillipe Cabanal, by the way."

"John Lattimore," I answered, taking his hand, clammy and limp like an old dishtowel. "Perhaps I can buy you a drink?"

And that was the mistake I made. Good runners like the kind Sturdivant used had a way about them that made you take charge of the evening affairs. Handy trait it was, too, for if you went to the sheriff after getting fleeced, why they could always say it was your fault.

Josiah tried to keep me from going, but I told him to wait outside for me while I went into Sturdivant's place. We started drinking Sugar Tits—dark, Barbadoes rum steeped in raw cane sugar. I don't know how many drinks we had together or even who suggested a game of cards, but suddenly I was sitting at a table in that smoke-filled, evilly-run place and across from me was Bloody Jack himself. He didn't look like the villain I had heard so many stories about. Broad-shouldered, he was, with thick, black hair carefully oiled and combed down, and eyes as black as an abyss. He dressed neatly, with an old-fashioned, long linen scarf around his neck in place of a tie or cravat and a long, black Bolivar coat. Oh, he was fancy, make no mistake about that. Just the sort of man who would appeal to a young rooster.

It didn't take long before I had run through all the money I had with me. The next thing I remember, someone threw me out the door of the tavern. Josiah helped me up from the mud and brushed me clean while I leaned drunkenly against the building.

"Keep your mouth shut and go home!" someone ordered—I think it was Cabanal, but I can't be sure anymore. "Else you'll be floating down the river to that fancy plantation of yours!"

Well, I started to sober up from all those Sugar Tits real quick when I realized what had happened. Josiah didn't say anything to me, but I could see the disappointment in his eyes and the way his lips sort of turned down at the corners.

He helped me stagger up the bluff. Fog had settled in pretty thick, so I jumped out of my skin when someone gripped my elbow and said, "John Lattimore! Doctor Will Lattimore's boy! You've shot up some since I saw you, and I guess you can't blame me for not knowing you with all that mud on your face! What happened to you?"

I tried to jerk away, but he had a grip that made me yelp. Then, I heard Josiah call him "Mastuh Bowie" and I knew him. I suppose I should have known him anyway, had it not been so foggy. Not many men were as tall as him—well over six foot—and he had this red-gold hair that seemed to shine in the dark.

I told him what had happened. I'm afraid I got a lump in my throat and had to turn away to keep from crying when I realized that I had betrayed Daddy's trust. Jim stood silent for a long minute, then sighed and gave a queer sort of laugh.

"Come on," he said. "Show me where this happened." His voice was soft and, well, musical, I guess. He always seemed to sing his words more than say them. Until he got mad, that is, then his voice sort of tightened up. You remember when you were a kid and dragged your fingernails over a slate board in school? Like that. Made your flesh goosepimple.

I didn't want to take him back to Sturdivant's place—I

guess he had three of them, now that I think about it—but Josiah spoke pretty sharply to me: "Mastuh John, yo' better do like Mistuh Jim tells yo'. Yo' made 'nough fool outta yo'self an' now yo' taks what 'elp yo' kin git."

I really didn't like a nigger talking to me like that, but Josiah had been with me a long time. Daddy had kind of assigned him to me when I was young and he had wiped my nose and dragged me out of more than one scrape while I was making a fool out of myself growing up. I knew if I sassed him and Daddy heard about it, well, I would have a tongue-lashing from Daddy that would make a horsewhip feel comfortable.

"All right," I said, kind of surly like. "Come on. I don't relish this one damn bit, though."

We stumbled back down that bluff. Leastways, I stumbled while Josiah and Mr. Bowie kept me from falling on my face in the mud and making a bigger fool of myself. At last, we came to the tavern—I think it was called Grady's Tavern although Sturdivant owned it—and I hesitated before the door.

"What's wrong?" Mr. Bowie asked.

"They said they would kill me if I came back," I said.

"Do you want to walk away from this?" Mr. Bowie asked. "Your choice. We can leave, now. Or, we can go back in and try to recover your money."

"How?" I said hotly. "I don't have a damn penny left."

"I'll stake you," he said, and grinned, his smile reckless. "What do you say? You were game enough to enter once before tonight. You stick with me, boy, and we'll get your money back. I know any game in Sturdivant's dens is crooked, and I've handled his kind before. Come on! Want to try it again?"

"Why not?" I said, suddenly remembering how I was manhandled out of the tavern.

"Good lad," he laughed, and threw open the door and

walked in. He had to bow his head a bit beneath the low doorframe. The room was as thick with cigar smoke as the fog outside. Voices trailed off at our entrance. I noticed Mother Slappert's girls, who had been hanging about, trying to pick up tricks, were gone.

"I told you not to come back, boy," a tough said. He straightened from where he lounged against the wall and swaggered over to us. "Now, you gonna leave, or do I feed your guts to the catfish?"

"He's with me," Mr. Bowie said.

"And who might you be?" the tough said. "His mammy?"

A low laugh tittered around from those near us. One man, however, rose, leaving his drink on the table, and started for the door.

"Where you going?" someone called.

"Out of here," he said. He nodded at us. "Good night, Mr. Bowie," he said.

Mr. Bowie nodded, and the man left, closing the door behind him. The tough straightened, but he still had to look up at Mr. Bowie.

"Jim Bowie?" he asked. Mr. Bowie nodded. "I've heard about you."

"That puts you up on me," Mr. Bowie said. "I've never heard about you."

Laughter sprung up around us and someone grabbed the tough by the arm and pulled him away. "Come on, Bojee," someone said. "Sit down and shut up before you get yourself in real trouble."

"Which table were you at?" Mr. Bowie asked me. I pointed and he nodded and crossed over to it. I followed along beside him, conscious of the eyes upon us and promising the good Lord that if he'd only help me get out of there alive I'd never go under the bluff again.

We stopped in front of the table and Sturdivant looked up at me, smiling. "Back so soon?" he asked. Then, his eyes flickered over to Mr. Bowie and the smile sort of froze on his face. "Evening, Jim. Been a while since you've been down here."

"Don't have much call to do so, Jack," Mr. Bowie said.

"You after another horse?" Sturdivant said. Mr. Bowie had bought this racehorse from him—Steel Duke, or something like that—and raced it against Major Norris Wright's Kerry Dancer . . . no, I lie: Kerry Isle. A lot of problems came out of that.

"No," Mr. Bowie said calmly. "I'm just seeing how the other half lives."

"And what might that other half be, Jim?" Sturdivant said.

Mr. Bowie shrugged. "People like you, Jack," he said.

Sturdivant didn't like it, but decided not to push it any further. He looked back at me. "Well? You going to sit in? Table stakes, you remember."

My face began to burn from embarrassment. I started to tell him that I didn't have any money and he damn well knew it when Mr. Bowie quietly pressed a wallet on me.

"Go ahead," he said. "Maybe your luck has changed."

I sat down and played for about twenty minutes or so. My luck hadn't changed; the stack of money slowly dwindled in front of me. At last, Mr. Bowie clasped me on the shoulder, saying: "Lattimore, why don't you let me sit in a while for you. Maybe I can shift Lady Luck in your favor."

Sturdivant leaned back in his chair, staring coolly at him. "I don't believe you were invited, Bowie."

I stood up and Mr. Bowie slid into my chair, smiling across the table at Sturdivant. "Sure I was, Jack. Remember what you said when I bought Steel Duke? You told me to step around any time."

"This isn't that time," Sturdivant said.

"It's any time," Mr. Bowie answered. "Your deal, I believe?" He glanced around at me. "Why don't you get us each a drink? Monongahela and not that black rum. Make sure the bottle's unopened, too."

A low murmur rose at the insinuation. Sturdivant wanted to say more, but changed his mind and riffled the deck, slipping the cards from one hand to the other. He dealt and Mr. Bowie won, and the game continued for about an hour with Mr. Bowie breaking about even at the table. They were playing bluff with jacks and nines wild. Suddenly Mr. Bowie laughed.

"Come on, Jack! Surely you can do better than that!" he said.

"What?" Sturdivant said.

Bowie reached out and pushed some cards away with a forefinger, not turning them up. "Those are the wilds ones: jacks and nines. Or I'm a liar."

It got awfully quiet in the taproom. Sturdivant went pale like swamp mist and leaned away from the table. His hand slipped under his jacket. "You better explain yourself, Bowie," he said.

Bowie flipped over the cards; jacks and nines. "I just did, Jack." He rose and scooped the money up, dropping it into his hat.

"Here, now!" Sturdivant protested. "You can't do that, Bowie. You must be drunk! Put that money back on the table."

"Sturdivant," Bowie said, and his voice sounded like those fingernails coming across a slateboard. "One of your runners brought this boy in a few hours ago to be robbed. Now, Dr. Lattimore is a personal friend of mine, and I won't see his boy robbed. I took enough from the table to repay what he's lost. That's all."

Sturdivant shook his head. Dozens of eyes watched him, glowing redly in that smoke-filled room like rat's eyes. He couldn't let that challenge go and still be Bloody Jack. He'd already killed half-a-dozen men, five with a pistol and one with a dagger, and burned down a couple of homes that belonged to a couple of unlucky ones who ran against Major Wright for sheriff. His reputation was worth more than the money Mr. Bowie had taken. At least, to him it was.

"You can't accuse me of cheating and walk out of here, Bowie," he said. "I can't allow that. I must demand satisfaction."

A small smile lifted Mr. Bowie's lips, but it took a brave man to look into his eyes, which had become dark-gray. "Anything you say, Jack. How?"

Sturdivant took a knife from beneath his Bolivar coat and dropped it onto the table. Mr. Bowie nodded and slipped out of his coat, handing it to me. He took a pistol from a pocket and gave it to me with instructions to shoot anyone who interfered. Then, he drew that knife.

I had heard about that knife and what Mr. Bowie had done with it and maybe it was the stories that made me sick to my stomach. Maybe it was the knife. I turned away, taking deep breaths to calm my lurching gorge. Then, I looked back: it glinted like death. The blade looked discolored, graceful watermarks running its length. The crossguard was of brass with tiny balls at each end and a brass back ran the length of the blade to where it suddenly curved to a point that rose to the middle of the blade. A musky smell like dried blood seemed to rise from it.

"Grady," Sturdivant called. "Draw a circle on the floor. Ten foot?" He looked at Mr. Bowie.

"With left wrists strapped together?" Mr. Bowie said, agreeing.

A shudder ran around the room. Everyone there knew that Bowie had thrown another glove in Sturdivant's face. The gambler nodded and took the linen scarf from his neck and handed it to a dealer who bound their arms together.

"Your call, Jack," Mr. Bowie said. Sturdivant nodded at one of the dealers, who slowly counted to three.

When he cried out the last number, Sturdivant dropped down nearly to the floor on one knee and swept his dagger at Mr. Bowie's belly, but Mr. Bowie jumped back, pulling hard on Sturdivant's arm.

Sturdivant tried to gain his balance, and Mr. Bowie swept in and under his guard, stabbing deeply into Sturdivant's arm. I saw that blade sink into Sturdivant's arm. The flesh turned blue, then I heard the knife grate on bone and the hackles rose on my neck. Sturdivant's dagger fell to the floor as Mr. Bowie pulled the knife out. Blood ran like water. Mr. Bowie cut himself free and took the scarf, wiping the blood from his knife. I still got a piece of that scarf somewheres around here.

"I won't kill you, Jack," Mr. Bowie said quietly. "But remember this: leave my friends alone."

We left after that. Sturdivant sent three toughs after Mr. Bowie a little later along the Trace after he found out that his arm and hand would be worthless for the rest of his life, but Mr. Bowie killed all three.

He accompanied me back up the hill to his lodgings and arranged a room for me and Josiah, telling us that he didn't want us out on the road until morning. He sent my clothes out to be cleaned and ordered a fine meal for us.

When I left the next morning, he gave me all the money I had lost from Daddy's cotton crop along with a note explaining that he had asked me to take dinner with him and time got away from us.

"I suggest that you stay away from Natchez-Under for a while," he said. "That's not a place for gentlemen. Even those looking to have a good time."

I thanked him and rode away. I know Daddy saw through the note, now, but he didn't say anything then except to tell me how lucky I was to have made a friend in Mr. Bowie.

I had a chance to visit with Mr. Bowie off and on again over the next year or two. He was always polite and never mentioned that night again. He didn't have to; I still haven't forgotten the lesson he taught me about trust.

John Sturdivant

John "Bloody Jack" Sturdivant was a counterfeiter and one of the worst rogues on the Mississippi River. He was a member of the Cave-in-Rock gang, among whom was numbered John Murrell, one of the most murderous bandits along the Natchez Trace. Sturdivant killed two men in pistol duels and one with a knife. In addition, he burnt down four houses for political favors. At the time of his famous duel with Bowie, Sturdivant was the most dangerous man on the river and commanded a gang of about thirty cutthroats who ambushed and killed many men along the Trace, smuggled slaves, and stole cotton shipments, whatever would turn a dime.—A. J. S.

Yes, I remember Bowie. How could I forget that sonofabitch? See this arm? Useless! Useless! He cut the leaders with that damn knife of his! Damn near bled to death until Mother Slappert managed to get it stopped. That damn drunken doctor did a half-ass job sewing it up, too.

Damn him!

Spiteful? Hell, yes! What do you expect? I can't even pick up a coffee cup. And when I walk, the damn thing flaps like a goose wing. You want to try and make love with a goose wing? Or a living? I'm seventy years old now, and I tell you that if Bowie could come back I'd cut his throat for him. I'd wait until he was drunk and asleep, then cut his throat.

I've outlived my time. For a man like me to live past fifty is vulgar, immoral. Those venerable old men, those silver-haired and reverend seniors, have lived a full life, a life of their own choosing. Bowie robbed me of that! Of life! What is life with only mere existence? No thrill, no chase?

I make no apology for the life I led; it was the life I chose. But Bowie . . .

It began with a race horse I won in a card game—not a very good wager, I admit, for a horse like that is of little use to me. I was not born to the purple, nor could I gain it. That was a closed door to me. It was the winter of my discontent and I had been rudely stamped by the circumstances of my birth. Oh, I could strut before a wanton ambling nymph, but only a nymph; other women would wipe their shoes upon me if I chose to stoop and I chose never to stoop.

Oh, I had pretensions—who does not in such circumstances?—but little good they did me. I was the one the gentlemen (and their ladies) came to when they lusted after the shadows of life, the secret life of their dark side. At night, they would come to me, slinking down the bluff to the flat, disguising their actions under their veils of self-indulgence.

You know about the dark side, don't you? It is the mark of an adventurer, of people like Bowie who could move at will in both worlds, hiding their darkness beneath the glimmer of fine dress and manners.

But manners and fine dress did nothing for me.

An accident of birth kept me from their light.

Bowie bought the horse and raced him against Wright. Wright's horse wasn't good enough and that heated the bad blood already between them. Most people think that horse race caused all the problems, but there was more to it than that; Wright had bought mortgages Bowie and his friends had on land grants and was threatening to foreclose on them. But it wasn't business; oh no, not business. Bowie was having an affair with a woman Wright wanted. And you want to know the funny part about it all? She was the wife of one of his friends. Wright's friend, I mean. I don't remember her name. Judalon somebody. It really doesn't matter. Bowie was the dog in her kennel and Wright was furious about that.

Yes, the Lattimore boy was cheated in my place. But those people who came there knew they were going to be cheated. They expected it and I made sure that they got their money's worth and something to talk about at their *soirées*. Made them look dangerous, you know. It was part of the thrill of coming down the bluff. My man just picked the wrong one to stiff. But who knew that Lattimore was Bowie's friend? I didn't. And when he made that grandiloquent play in my place, why I had no choice but to challenge him. I had to, you see. Otherwise, Bloody Jack Sturdivant would have been ruined on the river. And there were plenty waiting for me to fall.

I gave him warning. "Jim," I said. "You must be drunk. You know that I can't allow something like that to happen. Put that money back on the table."

I had heard about Bowie's eyes—changing from blue to gray like the river surface before a storm—and when he turned those eyes on me, I felt a coldness clear to the soles of my feet. You've never seen the fires of hell, but once you have, why, you never forget them.

"Sturdivant," he said. "One of your blacklegs brought young Lattimore here and your professional thieves robbed him. Now, I know a young lad needs to be taught lessons, but you weren't even subtle!" He pointed at the table. "You didn't even cleanly shave the cards. Now, his father is a personal friend of mine, and I won't see him robbed. I took enough from the table to pay what you owe him."

I could feel the eyes of the crowd upon me. Rat's eyes, waiting to see me fall so they could gnaw at my guts. I shook my head. "No, Jim. That don't make it. You'll have to fight me before I can let you leave with that money."

"Are you sure you want to do that?" he asked softly, so

softly that I don't think any of the others heard him. My mouth dried up so suddenly that I didn't trust myself to speak. I just nodded. The rest you know. I hate him for what he left me. No, I hate him for more than that: we were alike, the two of us. Yet, he could move about at will above the bluff while I had to be content with living under the bluff.

And he had friends.

Annie Christmas

Annie Christmas, a prostitute, witnessed the fight with Bloody Jack Sturdivant from the small balcony above the main floor. Here, the girls hired "cribs" or small rooms from Mother Slappert to entertain their customers and the vantage point gave them the opportunity to look over the gambling crowd for the "high-roller" who might be willing to part with a dollar or two for fleshly entertainment. Annie was one of the most popular prostitutes in Natchez-Under during that time. A big woman, nearly six foot in height, she was large-hipped with a wasp waist and what many claimed to be the biggest breasts in the town—a major factor in the advertising of her charms that made her a wealthy woman and eventually madam at her own place. A lot of people thought she always had her own place because wherever she was, men called it the Christmas House. Men flocked to her room of business, intrigued at the thought of making love to the Amazon who could drink most men under the table, and many madams vied for her, offering her inducements to come to their houses in hopes that the spillover from the demand for Annie's services would help business with other girls they employed. At the time of Bowie's fight with Bloody Jack Sturdivant, Annie was almost self-employed, giving a token of her wages only to Mother Slappert, who was managing that end of Sturdivant's business.—A. J. S.

I had just finished entertaining a couple of "gents" at a "tea party." The men used to sneak down the bluff when their wives were off at their tea parties and we'd have ourselves a little ménage à trois, you know, two gentlemen and a lady. My, how I remember those times! A lot of the girls didn't like tea parties, but, well, I damn sure didn't avoid them! That was one time when my blood got to singing and my juices would pour out of me. Most people thought the tea parties were for the men who got to craving something different, but I tell you that a working girl needs something different, too. I remember Tom and Sid Albert coming to town and making a game out of it, both of them humping away, trying to outlast the other. Sometimes, we would get to going so strong that the bed would give way and we'd be rolling all over that floor, lights glistening off our naked flesh, sweat rolling, wet nakedness wherever you looked.

Oh. Where was I?

Yes, now I remember. The Alberts were in town, then, and we had just finished a tea party when I heard loud yells and an unholy commotion down below in the tavern. I rose and quickly pulled on a shift to see what was going on. Only other thing I wore was my stockings that I tied with red ribbons, the knots held by little rosettes. When men get their juices stirred by a fight, they become very horny and take to looking to dunk their rod in any quim available. It's a working girl's dream and if she's quick enough and experienced enough, she can bring off half-a-dozen cockchafers at double or even triple price before their blood cools with liberal applications of Monongahela. The cotton and tobacco aristocrats who used to slip down the hill at night to mingle with the mudsill weren't long on holding their liquor, and if a girl didn't catch them early in their cups, she'd spend half the night trying to bring a rod to standing attention. Too much liquor leaves a man cold as a wagon tire. But a fight, well, that just served to make men plumb ramstugonous.

I elbowed my way through the other girls lining up by the balcony railing and plopped my elbows on it and leaned over my forearms, pushing my titties up as high as they would go, knowing that some below would be feeling Johnny move already. I spread my legs so they could get a good look at the possibles and looked down with interest at where someone had drawn a large circle in chalk on the tavern floor. Jack Sturdivant stood on one side of the circle while Jim Bowie stood on the other. My interest peaked and I perched right there, slapping a hand away some horny bastard kept trying to slide up my leg above my stockings.

"Ain't no free feeling here!" I snapped absently.

"Bowie called out Bloody Jack!" someone said hoarsely from behind me.

"Like hell!" another answered. "He caught him with trimmed cards and Jack challenged him."

"Big mistake, that," a third chimed in. "I've seen Bowie in action. Over in New Orleans. Killed a man square there."

"About a million people claimed to see that fight," the second answered. "Wisht I had a dollar for each one."

"You calling me a liar?" the third demanded.

"Shut up," I said, without turning around. "I want to see this." They fell quiet.

Grady (I think that was his name—Jack's flunky bartender) tied their arms together with a silk scarf. My interest began to climb. I'd seen a lot of men hacking away at each other, but this was a new twist. A strange excitement began to build in my stomach. Something about men playing their medleys always made my blood hum and my skin jump around with goose pimples. I leaned further over the balcony to catch every moment of the fight.

Actually, it wasn't much of a fight. Jack took a swipe at Jim who just sorta leaned back on his heels away from it. He jerked Jack off balance, then took a little half-step forward and plunged that knife of his deep into Jack's arm and the fight was over. When Jim stuck him with that knife, why, I came twice right there on the balcony. My legs trembled like I had St. Vitus's Dance or something. Oh, my, I remember that. I remember everything about that night.

I saw him leave with that boy he had rescued and I slipped back to my room and threw a cloak on over my shoulders. I stepped into a pair of slippers and hustled down the back stairs and followed them to the trail that led up the bluff back to the respectable people. I watched Jim say his goodbyes and heard him warn that boy to stay away from Sturdivant's places.

The boy left and I stepped out from the shadows to face Jim. I pulled that cloak back so he could see that I had little on beneath. He smiled, his lips sorta curling up at the corners, and this real mischievous light sparkled from his eyes.

"Hello, Annie," he said. "I didn't expect to see you down here."

"Been a while, Jim," I said. We had been together quite often after Cecelia Wells died just a couple of weeks before she and Jim were to be married. He'd come my way one night after he'd had too much to drink up on the bluff and one thing led to the other. For a while, we ran the danger of becoming pretty steady, but that could be only temporary and both of us knew it. Tonight, though, was something different. Maybe it was because I saw him fighting Bloody Jack at a time when I needed someone like Jim.

"How've you been keeping yourself?" he asked.

I tried to draw a deep breath, but my chest ached and I shuddered and gasped. The grin slipped from his face and he stepped forward, putting his arm around my shoulder to steady me. I came again, my cunny running slick and wet. I grabbed hold of the lapels of his coat and hung on like a drowning person to a stick of wood while I shuddered with the waves of desire washing over me, wetting me.

"Damn," I groaned.

"Annie, what's the matter?" he asked anxiously.

I told him and he laughed and held me close. "Well," he whispered, "maybe we should do something about that."

"Hell, yes," I mumbled. I grabbed his hand and ran, half-dragging him behind me, back to my own rooms. I lived as far back away from the water as I could get. A delusion of respectability, I suppose, but I held my business down at a couple of places on the front and kept my private life back under the shadow of the bluff.

I left Jim by the door while I entered and struck a match and lit a lamp on a small table. Suddenly, I felt nervous. I had never had a man back in my private rooms before Jim. I turned to look at him, half-fearful of what I would see. Would he laugh at my pretensions? I wondered.

He stepped into the room and took a long look around. The room felt shabby. He looked at the wallpaper with tiny rose garlands on it, the lamps with the painted shades, the Hepplewhite tables and newer Hitchcock chairs with heart-shaped chair backs stenciled with tiny rose buds—seemed pretentious to me, now. His eyes paused at the Boston rocker, a spindle-backed chair with cyma-curved arms also stenciled with tiny rose buds, I had placed near a window to get light, and on the small marble-topped table stacked with copies of *Niles' Weekly Register* and *Port Folio*. He walked over to it and picked up the book I was reading at the time, looking at the title. His eyebrows rose, and he turned to me in surprise.

"The Sketch Book of Henry Crayon, Gent. You surprise me, Annie," he said. He opened the book at where I had placed a lace ribbon for a marker and read aloud:

" 'The nation,' continued he, 'is altered; we have almost lost our simple true-hearted peasantry. They have broken asunder from the higher classes, and seem to think their interests are separate. . . .' "

Waves of red crept slowly up my neck. I felt my cheeks growing hot. "Well?" I demanded defensively.

His blue eyes crinkled and he smiled. "I like that."

"Just because a girl . . ." I fumbled for words, embarrassed that he now knew my secret.

"Nice," he said. A gentle smile spread over his face as he looked at me.

I fell in love.

"It ain't much," I started to say, but he stepped close and put his fingers on my lips, shushing me.

"It's all it needs to be," he said softly.

And he leaned down and kissed me. Gentle, at first, then I found myself tearing his clothes off and he picked me up and carried me into my bedroom and we tumbled onto the bed, hugging and kissing. My skin felt like fire.

Big, he was. Bigger than most men. And patient. Teasing. He wasn't a man looking for a woman; he was a lover.

I don't know how many times we fucked that night. I didn't think I would ever get enough of him. Every way possible. We even invented a few ways or, if we didn't, we sure enough improvised a few that neither of us had tried before. At least, I hadn't. And that was my business.

Except tonight, I pleasured myself.

And he let me.

I remember riding him . . .

Ah! Even now, I feel his arms, the rough, red, curly hair on his chest, his hands caressing my buttocks, my legs above my black net stockings, my nipples getting hard and . . . I've had a lot of wild times with a lot of wild men before but nothing like that last night with Jim.

I still make love to him for in my memory, he is always there. I can feel him, taste him, smell him. Always.

I suppose it is because he was always a gentleman. Even when we met on the street, he would treat me like a lady, tipping his hat and saying, "Good afternoon, Miss Annie." Just like I was somebody.

He gave women what they want: the right to men without

the demand of a wedding bed. That is a propriety that is an invention of men to separate their lust from their sense of social standing. A wife makes their lust lawful and others are needed, for that lust must have an outlet to keep the wife as near a virgin as possible, thus keeping her name from being impugned as a dishonorable woman.

What woman wants that?

Believe me when I say that women, too, feel the same lust as men and feel the frailty of the flesh as often as do men. Why, then, are they denied this by a man's sense of what is right and wrong?

Jim never did.

With Jim, a woman felt no shame for desiring him. Rather, it became a religion, a communion, if you will, not only of desire, but the flesh as an altar upon which that desire is sacrificed as many times as one feels the need to be holy.

Jim was my deepest religious experience.

DR. William Lattimore

Dr. William Lattimore was one of the most respected planters from the country below Natchez. At the time of the Sturdivant incident, he had been a territorial representative in the United States Congress from 1803 to 1807 and again from 1813 to 1817. He had a large country seat. He owned hundreds of slaves and was widely in demand not only for his crops, which seemed to be consistently of the highest quality, but also as a gracious guest in palatial antebellum homes.—A. J. S.

For man's everyday needs, it usually is enough to have the ordinary human consciousness, but when that is in a young man who has responsibility for the first time, sometimes common sense has to stand aside for spirit.

That is what happened in '29 when I sent my son to Natchez with our cotton crop to sell. Normally, I would have gone along, but politics held me up. I decided to trust young John to deliver the crop to the Cotton House on the Natchez wharf. I cautioned him about coming straight back with the money and to watch himself carefully. Perhaps I overdid my warning for such things are often tantalizing to young people. When a father tries to protect his son there is a natural resentment and rebellion, for the son feels that the father is treating him as a child and not an equal. Foolhardy, perhaps, but a natural trait.

I knew James Bowie. Knew him well and valued his friendship greatly for he was an honorable man. We did not move in the same social circles, and that is as much my fault as his—we simply did not have the same interests. I did exchange drinks with him on occasion and ate with him many times when our paths crossed. He came to my house on several occasions, but there was still a social strain between us. My friends were not his friends although he could and did visit with all of them at one time or another. Being in land speculation as he was, political friends are good to have.

I heard about John's involvement with Sturdivant the day after it happened when an acquaintance of mine came for lunch. He had been "sporting" with Annie Christmas in Grady's place when Bowie walked in with young John. He was a bit surprised when they went over to the table where Sturdivant and one of his runners were fleecing some keelboaters and began to play. He didn't pay much attention to what happened for a while because he became, ah, somewhat engrossed with Miss Christmas and they had retired to one of the rooms upstairs for somewhat of a nocturnal pursuit. Suddenly, he heard some people shouting angrily and came out to see what was going on. Bowie and Sturdivant were facing each other in a chalked circle. The fight didn't take long, but he remembers Bowie refusing to kill Bloody Jack when he could have, telling the man to leave his friends alone. Then, he left with young John.

I invited him out to our place for dinner, but he sent his man out with an apology. That was just before the sandbar incident. He was sorely wounded there and killed two, maybe three men including Major Wright. No loss for that one!

Wright was one of the most arrogant and underhanded individuals I have ever known! He was not above trying to use his money to influence votes or, well, let us just say he was an entirely unscrupulous individual.

I remember once in '27, I believe it was, when I was a Congressman, Wright tried to compromise me with a couple of young ladies from Madame Shipley's establishment.

He wanted some land that we had set aside for the Creeks
to be put into public domain. But I found out that he and
his friends had already filed on the land and were holding
the titles *in situ*, ready to file as soon as the land was declared open. I told him that under no circumstances would
I bring that up for debate on the floor and not only would I
not sponsor any bill for stealing that land from the Indians,
I would fight any attempt to do so.

He laughed and said that he would be willing to contrib-
ute a substantial amount of money to my campaign if I
would change my mind. I threw him off my place and told
him I would have him horsewhipped if he came anywhere
upon my land.

After Bowie killed him, I sent a couple of my men in to
watch Bowie discreetly while he recuperated from his
wounds. When three of Sturdivant's men ambushed him
down along the Trace, I arranged for him to recover in a
hunting cabin we had down there and put a guard around
the cabin along with a couple of niggers to watch over him
until he recovered.

I saw him once again on a riverboat while he was going
back to Texas after settling a land claim. He fought a duel
there on behalf of a woman. It seems that is really the true
story of Bowie: he was always helping someone even to
risking his life. Friendship and honor meant a lot to him.
We need more men like him. Especially now.

Dr. James Long

Dr. James Long was born in Virginia, but moved at an early age to Tennessee. There he obtained a medical degree and became acquainted with Andrew Jackson. In June 1820, he took a band of seventy-five followers to Nacogdoches and on June 23, 1820, named himself President of the Supreme Council of Texas. Upon his return to Texas, he was captured, taken to Mexico, and never returned, leaving behind a twenty-two-year-old widow and two young children. This is an account of his dealings gathered in a journal he wrote before he left.—A. J. S.

I write this to be left behind as a testimonial in the event I do not return from my journey back into Texas for the purpose of informing those who follow me of my work.

I first met James Bowie in 1817 or '18. I saw him at a fashionable tavern in New Orleans where I had been trying to meet someone who knew Jean Lafitte, the notorious leader of a band of privateers and freebooters who lived near Galves Town in the Republic of Texas.

Bowie was pointed out to me. Little did I know how important he would become to me over these last three years. I remember being struck by his appearance. He seemed to be about my age, in his mid-twenties (although I later discovered that he was only twenty), large, a strongly built man with almost red hair and deeply set gray eyes. He was tanned like an outdoorsman and moved with an economy of motion that bespoke tremendous natural coordination. When I questioned my companion about him, he told me that Bowie was a gentleman with a reputation for having been in some chance medleys. At the time, he was smuggling slaves into the United States from Texas. I became immediately interested in him since slavery was unlawful in Texas, but perfectly legal in Louisiana, though the slaves could not be imported. Mr. Bowie was taking illegal goods from one country and illegally crossing a border with these illegal goods. Sort of thumbing his nose at the law, so to speak. Once in Louisiana, however, the goods again became legal and the people flocked to buy them.

At my suggestion, my companion invited Mr. Bowie to our table. I had thought I would be meeting a crude ruffian, but I became very pleasantly surprised to discover that Mr. Bowie was a complete gentleman of the old school.

I remember a snippet of conversation from that night.

"So, you know Texas, Mr. Bowie," I said.

"No one knows Texas, sir. It is a huge expanse of land. There are swamps, grass, and tree-covered hill country, vast plains and desert. Much of this land is claimed by Indians," he answered.

"What kinds of Indians?" I asked curiously.

"Karankawa cannibals, Tonkawas, Caddos, Kiowa, Comanche, Lipans, and Apache. Mostly, though, there are Wichita, Creeks, and Cherokees who are moving out of their ancient tribal lands. That's a few of the tribes. There are more." He became quite animated during his explanation. "The Comanche and Apache are the strongest. The Karankawas are the most to be feared, however, since they eat the dead. I've had some little set-tos with the Kronks. They claim the land west of Galveston Bay to Corpus Christi Bay. If you go by land, you have to sneak through their country. They're big Indians. Around six-foot, mostly."

He paused to sip at his brandy for a moment or two, then continued with his narrative.

"The Kronks usually go naked. They wear tattoos around their breasts and lower lips. The lip is sometimes pierced by pieces of cane. If this is not enough, they cover themselves in alligator grease and the dirt and smoke from the fire gets into that grease and forms a kind of mud. Sometimes, they paint their faces, half-red, half-black. It makes them as ugly a sight as you would ever want to see.

"The only time you are sure of them is when they are wearing a breechcloth. They wear those when they go to war where they carry a long bow almost as large as themselves.

"When the hunting has been good, they're a peaceful and happy group of cousins. When they are hungry, they'll eat anything. Including humans."

He tapped his fingers nervously on the table in front of him, reflecting moodily, lost in the vision of the past.

"Once I was taking a group through their territory when I was surprised by a small band of three or four. Before I knew it, they had shot a man. Their arrows are made of cane and are about three feet long. It went clean through the man and buried itself in a bank."

Mr. Bowie stopped. The scene swam before my eyes: marsh country with stunted trees, darkness, an arrow whirring though a man—probably a slave, though Bowie had the tact to keep that information to himself. I decided then and there that I needed him for my venture.

"What kind of Indians live near Nacogdoches?" I asked casually around a sip of brandy.

"Caddos live mostly in the eastern part of Texas," he replied.

"Could you get supplies from the United States past those Indians and into Nacogdoches?"

He smiled. "Easily."

I leaned over the table and spoke low, telling him everything. I told him about the political climate in Washington and about how Texas had already been settled by Americans and how we had the duty and the God-given right to unite those Americans with the rest of the country. His eyebrows rose in surprise.

"You want to invade Mexico?" he asked.

"Only Texas," I replied.

"Texas is a part of Mexico," he said patiently.

"But it may secede into the United States," I confided.

"Wouldn't the states have to be consulted? It seems to me that this could bring about a war between the United States and Mexico. Is that something anyone wants?"

A tiny smile played around his lips. A lot of profit could be made from such a war. For a moment, I wondered if there was anything to that, then dismissed my thoughts.

"There are many who would welcome such a war, but Mexico would not fight," I said confidently. "They don't settle Texas because they are too thinly spread and too dissatisfied with their own government."

Bowie reflected upon my words for a moment. "You know, a man will have an old plow sitting in his field unused because he's using a new one. But the minute someone tries to walk off with that old plow, that's the very same minute the man grabs his rifle and protects his property."

My companion and I laughed, treating his response as a joke, but many times I have had occasion to reflect back upon that bit of homespun wisdom. Perhaps I should have heeded it more. A little more preparation and maybe some of my troubles with Texas would have been lessened. Maybe I wouldn't have had to flee. However, that night I knew I had to have Mr. Bowie at my side. I knew that this was a man upon whom I could depend and a man who could help Texas grow.

"Mr. Bowie," I said soothingly, "I want you to be a part of my country. I want you to be involved in the future of Texas."

"Well," he laughed. "I confess that country suits me. And there's plenty of land there for the taking."

"You shall have a million acres," I said impetuously. "I'll start by making you a colonel and after I'm elected President of the Council, I shall make you a member of Congress."

"A pretty picture, General," he said. "I think I might be willing to work with you."

And as quickly as that, Jim Bowie became one of the bulwarks of my new country along with Ben Milam and my brother David.

Mr. Bowie became the purchaser and transport chief. By 1820, I had over three hundred men who needed to be furnished with food, clothes, guns and ammunition.

"Jim," I asked him later after we became more familiar with each other. "What do you think would be our best way of dividing duties?"

"I think I'd be best working outside," he answered. "I've never been one to stay cooped up inside. The support you have in New Orleans won't mean anything unless we can turn it into men and supplies we can get in Nacogdoches."

And that is exactly what we did. Mr. Bowie smuggled in arms, trade goods for my brother to use to placate the Indians, and to establish trade, making us less a threat and more a partner with them. This policy helped make us safe, yet there was always the chance that Mexicans would be coming to take back their state.

Mr. Bowie never lost a cargo and got the best prices in New Orleans. Usually he would start off with his cargo of goods for Nacogdoches, then he would take my order for more arms, powder, shot, or whatever, and travel to Galves Town where he would buy Negro slaves from Jean Lafitte and take them overland to Louisiana.

I had planned to make Lafitte the admiral of the navy, but he betrayed me to the Mexicans. That, however, is a story for later. Right now, I need to finish this about Mr. Bowie.

In the years I knew Mr. Bowie, I never met a braver,

more even-tempered man. His intelligence and high principles were an inspiration to us all. And yet, I have never been able to understand his need to roam through the wilderness.

Mr. Bowie was cultured with a sound foundation in literature, painting, and music. He could and did discuss philosophy and knew the fine principles of logic that allowed him to circumvent argument. And although he would drink a glass of brandy and smoke a fine cigar with his friends, the cigar and brandy meant little to him. His natural exuberance worked to make him friends and although he did drink with them, I have never seen him drunk or accept more than one cigar.

He was a gallant man who never spoke about his affairs with numerous ladies, not even those of a somewhat tarnished reputation, as is the habit among most gentlemen when sharing cigars and brandy after dinner.

Yet he still preferred the wilderness to the drawing rooms of polite society. He worked with his brothers to bring technological advancement to Louisiana, yet he would also disappear at times to smuggle slaves into the country.

He was an extremely complex man, yet never have I known a more compassionate one. He treated his slaves as friends and trusted them almost like family. He seemed to be indifferent to money.

Once, I thought to bring him up on that and mentioned that he seemed to be drawing a reputation as a "blackbirder," one who smuggled Negroes into the United States.

"Yes?" he asked and waited. I felt my face growing red, but plunged on ahead with my probing.

"You are a gentleman, a respected member of our new country . . . and the old," I added.

A bemused smile crossed his face. "That's good to hear," he said casually.

"You are invited to the best homes—which happens to

no other slaver—and do not seem touched by this . . . notoriety. How is this?"

He shook his head. "I don't know about all of that. I'm just doing my best to help the family. I like the challenge of doing something better. I like solving problems and doing it the easiest way I can. When you ask yourself what's over the rise or behind a group of trees, the simplest thing to do is to ride over and look." He paused for a moment, then continued. "And while you're riding, you have time to reflect. Think. Plan."

"But what about the hardships?" I asked.

"Another of man's oldest problems. Survival."

He smiled that smile I knew that signified the subject was closed. But I determined that when I returned to Texas, I would take Mr. Bowie with me as my second-in-command. He is a natural leader, but this I didn't discover until the time we were attacked by wild Indians and Mr. Bowie directed the defense and inspired the men.

Once, a fire broke out in a log fort we had erected for defense. A small town sprouted outside the fort's walls and one night, one of the cabins caught fire and the small settlement was in danger of being burnt to the ground.

I remember looking out over the stumps to the shantytown of small cabins and lean-tos. The air was heavy and the clean smell of the freshly turned earth was lost in the smoke. Black storm clouds changed the colors of the countryside, lending a dark and malevolent vision to it.

A flash of lightning came out of the sky and burst upon the cabin belonging to Merridew East, a newcomer and malcontent who constantly bred sedition among everyone. The flash momentarily blinded me and when my vision cleared, I ran towards the cabin, yelling instructions at my men. East had a woman and her child living with him and already the flames blocked the door, preventing their escape.

Mr. Bowie arrived first, sized up the situation, then seized a log about six feet long and two feet in diameter and rammed it hard against the side of the cabin, driving a hole through it. He danced into the flames, grabbed up the baby in his left arm and the woman with his right, and leaped out of the shanty just as the roof collapsed.

Bowie's heroism was lauded by all. The next morning, he left Nacogdoches. Constant praise of his actions made him extremely uncomfortable.

But I cannot forget the picture I had of him, standing there, a young giant in his buckskins black from smoke and gray from ash, his face reddened from the heat. He looked like a god.

There is no one who would be better for Texas than James Bowie and I intend, upon my return from establishing a republic, to make him my second-in-command.

Reverend C. W. Smith

The Reverend C. W. Smith was the first Methodist minister to preach in Texas. Indeed, he little knew how much danger surrounded him when he went to Texas, where it was against the law to have any faith but Catholicism. It was a serious offense against the laws of the country to visit, trade, or own land without first signing a document that proved you were a Roman Catholic.

James Bowie converted to the faith prior to his marriage with Ursula de Veramendi, though he had probably been raised somewhat in the teachings of the Church since his early years in Louisiana were under Spanish rule.—A. J. S.

I have written in my own journal about my meeting with the famous James Bowie. I always think of this fortuitous circumstance with awe and wonderment and then I thank God for the blessings He has bestowed upon me.

I was sent to minister to the spiritual needs of the men and women of the United States who had departed for Texas.

I am not sure how much information is needed by the average reader of today to understand the conditions of those days. Everything seemed to be in movement. People felt the lure of the West. I felt it myself. In the West, a person could grow as big as his dreams, and I had dreams based on my calling. I felt I could help my fellow man be better through speaking the word of God to him.

It was with great pleasure and excitement that I accepted this post in Texas, even though I hardly knew the hardships of camp life or the dangers of the trail. I felt as though I would be able to speak to the multitudes and help them know the wonders of the Lord. Yes, I was young, but my faith was, as it is, sincere.

I crossed the Mississippi by riverboat. That huge expanse of water had been all that separated me from the wilderness. On the far bank there was a little shanty town erected to help outfit people who were leaving civilization. I later discovered that many of these people were bandits, outlaws, or pirates of the worst sort.

HORS FOR SALE CHEAP read the sign. I smiled to myself as I thought about the wrongly spelled word, and that good feeling prompted me to go in to purchase a mount for the ride into Texas.

A tall, red-haired man dressed in buckskins was talking to a shorter, massively built man wearing a blacksmith's apron. The frontiersman carried a huge rifle, a .50 caliber, I believe, a brace of pistols stuck under his belt, and a huge knife hung from the belt in a polished leather sheath, along with pouches for carrying balls, patches, traveler's rations, and other necessities. The man dressed for the wilderness was arguing with the blacksmith.

I say arguing, but that might give the impression of anger. It was anything but a strong exchange. "Jim," the smithy said in a hurt tone, "don't I get to make some money? I got to make a profit, don't I?"

The backwoodsman replied, "Pete, you trim the newcomers from every boat, and there's a new boat every day and sometimes twice a day." He slapped him lightly on the stomach. "I don't see you losing any inches. I am for Texas and I need good stock at a good price."

"Okay, Jim, your price, but I wouldn't do it for anyone else."

"Not even for this poor parson who you are planning to rob in broad daylight?"

The two men both looked at me, and I must have looked perplexed, because the blacksmith hurried to placate my trepidations. "This here rooster's a friend of mine, and we was haggling over price. It's just a friendly little squabble, you know, among friends."

"Well," I said, "suppose I take the same price and maybe my new friend here will ensure I get good stock." I almost laughed at the man's horrified expression. "If you would be so kind, sir. I also am for Texas."

The big man smiled and then we both laughed out loud, for the blacksmith was grumbling as he slowly walked to the back of his shop, and through the large door to the corral where he kept riding animals.

"Actually, sir, I do know livestock fairly well, but I could not help but join in the banter."

"The name's Jim. I'd be happy to ride to Texas with you."

And with such simplicity, we became friends. He helped me to purchase supplies at a decent price and made sure that I only bought what I needed.

After leaving the little road town, we traveled for several days. My friend Jim was a wonderfully knowledgeable man. He seemed to know everything about the country. He hunted so we were able to conserve supplies, and he also knew what plants were edible and where the good water lay. Even so, he never introduced himself as more than Jim.

The first large town we reached was called Nacogdoches. This town had a history of being American from the time when James Long tried to make Texas a separate country.

The town was a collection of ramshackle buildings amongst stronger, more solidly constructed log cabins, as well as the mud houses of the Mexicans. It had many saloons and *cantinas*, and along with the substantial farmers and landowners were border ruffians.

I begged some space on the porch of a local general store and proceeded to tell all who would listen that I would hold a Methodist service on Sunday.

Sunday came and the crowd was large, men, women and

children filled the street in front of the general store. While many were obviously hardworking citizenry, there were many genuine hardcases enmeshed in the congregation.

It was the first time I ever delivered a service to a crowd of arms-toting outlaws. Indeed, many of the men wore several pistols, knives, and carried long rifles.

Even so, it was my first service in this new land and so I endeavored to do the best I could.

We started with singing, and the songs of praise were beautiful, albeit off-key and containing some flat and sour voices. It was still praise to our Lord.

After the singing it was time for me to give the sermon. I began to speak. From experience, I can say it was not the best choice, but then I was new to the area and I was willing to try and speak about taming the wilderness and God's message.

Unfortunately, I was badgered from the audience. One man in particular—big, burly, black-bearded, bristling with weapons and dressed in grease-stained leather—seemed to know the passage of "be fruitful and multiply," and he tried to shock the women in the audience with his use of God's word.

My companion, Jim, came onto the front platform of the store. He was no longer in hunting clothes, but stood in fine gentleman's raiment and addressed the crowd.

"Please, ladies and gentlemen, and those who don't fit in either category." Jim had a fine speaking voice and while usually it was low and clear, when he needed volume, he had it. "You know who you are."

"Yeah," said the burly rascal. "We know who we are, but who are you?"

Jim acted like he hadn't heard but kept addressing the crowd. "I just rode from Mississippi with this man, and I think he's a good man worth listening to. I plan to see he gets a fair hearing."

A series of catcalls and hooraws arose at this. The sheer volume made me fear for his safety, but the burly man spoke up again.

With his hands on the butts of pistols stuck in a sash at his waist he repeated his question. "I said, who are you, Mister?"

"That's immaterial, but my name's Jim Bowie."

A hush fell over the congregation. The black-bearded man pulled his hands from his pistols as though they were suddenly as hot as hellfire.

"Speak now, Reverend. They'll give you a fair hearing."

And they did. My first sermon in Texas was to the best behaved group of cutthroats I have ever seen, and all because of my friend, the bravo, James Bowie.

I said as I started this tale that I was always awestruck when I thought about it. The Lord sent Jim Bowie to me. I would have never been able to have cowed that crowd, and would have probably lost all credibility as a man of God if Bowie had not verified me. And yet James Bowie—Jim— was known to have gambled, and taken lives in duels.

It made me think, once I started hearing about my friend, about how a reputation can be either a compliment or a detriment to one's life. Jim was a fine gentleman, but his reputation established him as a cold-blooded killer, or at least, an adventurer looking for excitement, and yet I never heard him brag about himself, or his adventures. Always a gentleman, never a braggart. Not too bad an epitaph for Jim Bowie.

Bowie's Decree of Citizenship from Mexico, September 30, 1830

His excellency, the Governor of the State, has been pleased to forward the following decree:

The Governor of the State of Coahuila and Texas to all its inhabitants, Know Ye: That the congress of the said state has decreed the following:

Decree No. 159. The Constitutional Congress of the free, independent and sovereign State of Coahuila and Texas decrees the following:

A letter of citizenship is hereby granted to the foreigner, James Bowie, providing he establishes the wool and cotton mills which he offers to establish in the state.

The Governor of the State will be guided by this decree, and for its compliance therewith he shall have it printed, published and distributed. Issued in the City of Leona Vicario on September 30, 1830. Ramón García Rojas, Congressional Chairman; Mariano García, Congressional Secretary; Vicente Valdez, Congressional Secretary, pro-tem.

Wherefore, I command this decree to be printed, published and circulated, and command proper obedience thereto.

Leona Vicario,
October 5, 1830

Rafael Eca y Múzquis [RUBRIC]
Santiago del Valle, Secretary [RUBRIC]

Father de la Garza's Record of Bowie's Marriage

In the City of San Fernando de Béxar on the 25th day of April, 1821, I, the priest Don Refugio de la Garza, pastor of this city, having performed the investigation prescribed by the Canon Law, published the banns on three consecutive feast days—*"Inter Missarund"*—during the high mass to wit, on the 10th, 17th, and 24th of said month, and having found no canonical impediment even after the lapse of twenty-four hours from the last publication of the banns, I married and blessed at the nuptial mass—*"In Facie Ecclesiae"*—publicly in the Church Don Santiago Bowie, a native of Louisiana of North America, legitimate son of Raymond Bowie and Albina Yons, and Miss Ursula de Veramendi, legitimate daughter of Don Juan Martín Veramendi and Dona Josefa Navarro. Their parents stood as sponsors, and Don José Angel Navarro and Don Juan Francisco as witnesses. In witness whereof I have hereunto affixed my signature.

Refugio de la Garza [RUBRIC]

Caiaphas K. Ham

Caiaphas K. Ham fought with Bowie during Texas's War for Independence. But more than that, he was one of Bowie's few friends who stuck with him through thick and thin when he went into a deep, dark depression following the death of his wife, Ursula, and his two children and tried to drink the world dry. Ham and Bowie were familiar figures on the frontier, sharing hunting adventures, speculations, and the friendly camaraderie that confident men share on the frontier. Ham defended Bowie's reputation more than once when the torn warrior lay defenseless and his enemies licked their lips and moved in for the kill. He was with Bowie at the famous San Saba fight and others.—A. J. S.

More and more people seem to be becoming attracted to Jim. Can't say as how I can blame them. He was sorta like a candle who burned so brightly that he just naturally attracted the moths who wanted to be butterflies. I remember when I first ran across Jim. I was immediately attracted to him, too. Shucks, I guess I'm no different than the others.

About 1828 or sos, I began to notice men and estimate their character. At that time, Col. Bowie was a gentleman of prominence. He already had a reputation for great courage, always ready to defend himself and friends, but never the aggressor. No sir, never.

He was a clever, polite gentleman always attentive to the ladies on all occasions and seemed to entertain a devotion for them which we called chivalrous in those days. Seems to be mostly missing nowadays what with the young men running around so's they almost trample any lady what gets in their path. They could use a few lessons like those Jim taught.

He was a true, constant and generous friend, but you get on his wrong side and he became an open and bitter enemy who didn't go around your back talking about how bad you were. No sir. He'd most likely come right up into your face and tell you very quietly what he thought about you. This habit made him quite a few enemies, but he took his enemies as well as he took his friends. And believe me when I say that one look at him made you understand why he was a foe no one dared to undervalue and many feared.

At times, when unexcited, he had a calm seriousness about him that shadowed his countenance, giving him an assurance of great willpower, unbending firmness of purpose, and unflinching courage. But . . .

Well, when anger stoked him, his face bore the semblance of an enraged lion and a man felt fear deep down in his craw. More than one man puddled his breeches when he saw that look blazing from Jim's face.

It was silver that was Jim's downfall, but, hell, ain't it everybody's? We all got these dreams of getting rich quick instead of laboring for it. I ain't no different. But with Jim, why, it was more like an obsession than anything else.

In Bexar, the Lipan Indians came in from the West to do their trading and paid for their plunder with chunks of silver ore, rich and unsmelted. Damn, but that was a sight! Many had tried to follow them back to their village, but not many returned and if they did, they'd only mumble strange stories about what had happened to set them off their feed.

Jim, though, was different. He didn't try to sneak off behind them. No sir. He came right on up to them, squatting on his heels in the sun on the plaza and talkin' with them like they was the people next door. That's when I met him.

I'd been off with the Lipans and made friends with Fat Rabbit, one of the Lipans. One day, we were off hunting and

Fat Rabbit points to a big hill and says that that hill was plumb filled with silver and we'd go there some day, but we had to be careful 'cause if the others found out what we were up to, they'd cut our throats lickety-split! But, hell, they moved the camp the next day and we never got back down that way as long as I stayed with them.

When I told that story to Jim, tiny lights danced in his eyes. I don't think it was the silver as much as what he'd have to go through to get it. The adventure, you know. That's what it really was that drove Jim to wanting that Lipan silver.

He went to talk with the lieutenant-governor of Bexar, Don Juan Martín de Veramendi, telling him what he wanted to do 'cause Jim was figuring on marrying the don's daughter, Ursula. They all tried to dissuade him from his idea, but Jim had the bit in his teeth and the next spring, he met Xolic, a Lipan chief, in the plaza and made close friends with him. Jim gave Xolic a silver-inlaid rifle and got an invite to go hunting with the tribe.

When he came back, he was all excited 'cause Xolic had taken him to the hill of silver—*lomas plato*—and Jim planned on putting together an expedition and going after it. But Xolic died before he could get us all together and this here Indian whose face always looked like he'd swallowed a green persimmon—*Tres Manos*, Three Hands, they called him 'cause he wore this mummified hand of one of his enemies on a string around his neck—finds Jim and tells him to keep out of Lipan lands or he'd stretch Jim's guts from tree to tree.

Jim damn near settled that man's hash right then and there, but we pulled him out of the plaza and calmed him down. That just made Jim even more determined than ever, and a couple of weeks later, fall of '31 it was, Jim had his expedition: his brother Rezin, Jim Coryell, Dave Buchanan, Bob Armstrong, Jesse Wallace, Matt Doyle, Tom McCaslin, me, Jim's man Black Sam, a Mex called Gonzales and a mulatto boy we all called Charles, and off we went, looking for Jim's hill of silver that had once belonged to a mission of friars the Indians had killed.

We was down by the San Saba River, searching for that silver mine, when we got ourselves surrounded by somewheres up to a couple hundred Injuns, riding like the wind and screaming like a bunch of demons. I never heard a human voice make that sound before and it right made my hair crawl up my neck and disappear under my hat.

"What do you make of them?" Jim asks me.

"Wacos," I replied. "Lot of them, anyways. I can tell by the cut of their scalplock. Most look like Tehuacanas, though that batch over there are your friends the Lipans and that gent in front on the pinto ain't none other but old Tres Manos himself. Reckon we're in for it, gentlemen."

Well, Rezin thought it'd be mighty smart of us if we tried to make some peace with them and he and Buchanan sallied right on out to have a little talk with them. Buchanan said something to them, then one of them Wacos waved a bloody scalp and shouted "How do? How do?" and the next thing I knew bullets were buzzing around us like angry hornets.

Buchanan went down, one ball breaking his leg, and Rezin heft him over his shoulders and took off running back towards us in the trees. About eight Indians came riding out to gut him with their lances, but Jim and me and Coryell and McCaslin came out from the trees and ran out to meet them.

"Don't miss, boys!" Jim yelled. But hell, we had no intention of missing any of them and left four saddles running empty in short notice. That sent the rest of the Indians scampering back to their friends on the ridge.

Well, we got back to the woods and here came Tres Manos on that pinto of his, riding back and forth in front of the Indians, insulting them, trying to work them up to charge us. Jim gets real quiet, and says, "Who's loaded?"

"I am," I says.

"Then shoot that *valiente* on that painted pony and do a fine job of it while you're about it."

Now, that was a pretty piece off, but I stood and rested my rifle in the fork of a black oak, and pulled down on that Indian. At first, I thought I'd missed him, but then he threw his arms up in the air like he was calling on the Almighty, and tumbled off the rump of that paint.

The Indians began to taunt us, but Jim ignored them and directed us into a patch of trees a little thicker'n the ones we were in. He left three of the younger ones with the animals and scattered the rest of us around. We had planned well for that trip. Plenty of lead and powder and I tell you we salted many an Indian there. Five days, we fought them, arrows and bullets flying thicker than hail around us.

I don't know how many times they charged us, but we routed their hides every time. At last, they tried to burn us out, and a couple managed to get in close—three, I think, if I remember right—and my bladder swells to near bursting 'cause I figger there's others around. But Jim yells at us to watch the front and he pulls that terrible blade of his and proceeds to carve all three of them up quickern you can spit and say "some punkins."

I thought to come and give him a hand, but he swore an oath that would make the Lord back off. Black-faced from the smoke, eyes red like fire, blood wet on his breast from where he gutted one of them Indians, he looked like Satan himself had stepped outta the fires of hell. I quick decided the Indians were safer than to cross him and went right back to shooting through the smoke.

Well, we got outta that scrape, thanks be to Jim.

The knife?

Well, I can tell you about that. We had been hunting over

along the border and Jim killed a deer. I helped him dress it out and after gutting it, he lay it aside and helped me lift it up to tie it over the withers of a mule we'd brought along for that purpose.

I reckon we got maybe five, six mile away from there when he suddenly remembered that he forgot to pick it back up. That was the knife his brother Rezin had made for him at his plantation near Avoyelles in Louisiana. Well, we rode back to get it, but it was gone. Never knew what happened to it.

About six months later, Jim rode back to Rapides Parish to settle a little land dispute and went on into Washington, Arkansas, to see this blacksmith he'd heard about named James Black. He'd carved a knife from a piece of soft pine as a model and when he went back through a month later, Black had made him that knife. Gave you chills to look at it. Smelled like dried blood. Heavy blade, like a hatchet. Brass along the back and crossguard to catch another edge. That was a knife meant for killing and nothin else, believe me!

I remember once along the Bravo when a ragged gent asked to share our campfire. We had been hunting and Ol' Jim had stepped into the river in an attempt to get a shot at a fine buck. His foot slipped and he fell in, baptizing himself from head to toe. Well, we decided that the day was near finished anyway and besides, Jim was mighty cold. This was November around '29, I reckon, or thereabouts. Time doesn't matter much once it's passed and it's the story that's important anyway.

Where was I?

Oh, yes.

So, we built a fire in a small oak grove and Jim stripped naked and hung his clothes on branches near it to dry. He wrapped himself in a blanket and was hunkered over the fire, trying to get warm, pouring hot coffee down his gullet to take the chill out of his innards, when this seedy devil and his two boys rode up to the fire and asked to share it. They looked as poor as Job's turkey. The old man wore a tattered wolfskin coat pulled around him and tied with a piece of twine and a pair of duck breeches worn shiny from riding. The brim of his hat looked like a termite had been at it and his face had been a stranger to a razor for about a year. His boys had cold eyes, fish eyes, though neither of them had spent time with a razor. Fuzz curled along their chins and cheeks. I had an all-overish feeling about the sight of them and made a point of sliding two pistols closer to my middle and loosening my knife in its sheath.

"Howdy," the man said gruffly. "I'm Seth Jenkins and these're my boys, Jacob and Esau. Looks like yer alone out here. Wondered if'n you mind we share yer fire?"

Now, Jim was never one to deny a man hospitality. He nodded and gave this pleasant grin at the man and said, "Light and sit a spell. Coffee's on and mores where that came from. I'm Jim and that fellow over there is Caiaphas."

I said my howdy as the man climbed down and tossed the reins of his horse to the youngest of his boys and walked stiffly to the fire. He took a dirty cup from a sack he had slung over his shoulder, ran a grimy finger around the inside of the cup and squatted and poured himself a cup of coffee. I watched the boys, 'cause I knew Jim had that man with him, and I didn't like what I seen. Them two boys tied off their horses, then walked to the fire, splitting so's they could come around us from two directions.

"You fellers look like you's come a long ways," Jenkins said. He blew across his coffee and sipped noisily, ignoring me. I could tell he had placed Jim as being the big toad in the puddle.

"Hunting," Jim said and grinned wryly, gesturing at his wet clothes, acknowledging the corn of his clumsiness. "But fell into the water like a damn fool."

"Happens you don't watch where yuh put yer feet," Jenkins said. "Boys been out here long?"

I knew then that he had placed us as a pair of no-account corn-crackers and had decided to kill us and absquatulate with our plunder. I watched Jim carefully, but he didn't rise to him.

"Nope," he said. "Fact is, we just got here less than a week."

Now, that may not have been the exact truth, but it was close enough. Jenkins took that to mean we had just been out West a short time, but Jim was talkin' about our hunting trip from Bexar. But that Jenkins and his two boys were just too eager for our belongings to give much thought to what Jim was saying. He cast a look over in my direction, sort of measuring me, then gave a little nod of his head, more of a twist, I s'pose, at Jacob and turned back to Jim.

Jacob turned those fish eyes on me and grinned a black-toothed smile. "Pa and usns ain't been but wanderin' round tryin' to find a place to settle," he said.

"That right?" I answered. That younger boy began to sidle off to my blind side like a fierce dog. I kinda turned my shoulder to keep him in sight and he shakes his head and grins at me. I'm thinking that both of them are shy a dipper or two to make a jug when that Jacob tries to bring his rifle down on me. I jerked my pistols from my belt and put a ball through his forehead, but that Esau was a tricky one and ducked down when I turned and fired.

I drew my knife, but he grinned and raised his gun, then I heard something whizz by my ear and a *chunk!* like an axe splitting a log, and Jim's knife split that boy's head like a melon. I turned and looked at him and Jenkins. Jenkins had his knife in his hand and was trying to bring it around to gut Jim, but Jim held it away from him, then curled one of those big arms of his around the man's head, seized his greasy beard, and jerked his arm around like he was flipping a tree outta his way. That man's neck made a dry *pop!* and he went all glassy-eyed and just dropped down at Jim's feet.

Ain't many men strong enough to do that. Or quick enough. Or, for that matter, willin' to look out for their friends 'fore they look out for themselves. But that was Jim's style. He never seemed to put much value upon his life. I remember mentioning something along that line to him once while we was sharing a fire up on the plains and he just gave that deep laugh of his and said:

"Caiaphas, a man can live his life afraid for it or he can live it."

I reckon that's as good a way to follow as any.

Now, I don't mean to be saying that Jim was serious all the time. Nope. Not at all. But there was a bit of seriousness to his funnin' as well.

I remember a time down in San Felipe when me and Jim and Joe Powell were sitting in Peyton's Tavern having a tot when this man rode in with a real comely young woman from over West a spell. Now, the man said he was a minister of the gospel and that he and the young woman wanted to get hitched and were looking for a priest.

That sounds funny, I know, but Mex law was such that no marriage in Coahuila was legal unless it'd been performed by the Catholic Church. If that man and the young woman wanted to get married, why, they just had to find a priest to firm up things for them despite what religion they wanted to follow on their own.

Well, Jim he took a look at that man and frowned and stared down in his cup, muttering as to how he was sure that he had seen that man somewhere before and he didn't have "reverend" affixed before his name at the time. Blamed, though, if he could recall just where it was.

About that time, the man just gave up looking for the priest and allowed as to how he guessed they would have to settle for a "constitutional marriage" instead of a church marriage. I could see right away that that didn't settle well with the young woman. A marriage like that was a weak one, mainly to keep a couple respectable until they could find a priest. All it involved was the two of them standing in front of the *alcalde* and saying that they did what he told them to do and then go off and live like man and wife until a priest could be found. That was pretty hard in those days because most priests like their comfort and not many wanted to live north of Mexico City in the frontier away from the fine wine and parties.

The young woman had just about given in to the man's sweet talking, her eyes shining with what she thought was love and all—most young people are that way, you know; all of them seem to think they know all there's to know about love when they ain't got a Philadelphia lawyer's clue as to what it's all about; they're just all honey-fuggled—when Jim suddenly rears back and says: "Whoa. I remember now where I seen him; over in Arkansas way where he escaped from jail after the sheriff caught him stealing a horse. He left a wife and child behind as I recollect."

"Why, that man's got nothin' but shecoonery on his mind!" I exclaimed, and started to rise when Jim clamped that big hand on my forearm and pinned me to the table, knocking over my draught. I hastily resettled that cup.

"This is how we're gonna play it," he says, leaning across the table and motioning for Joe to join us. He talked real quickly, then stood up and went off to fetch the *alcalde* while I put on my straight face and got up and walked over to their table.

"Beg pardon, ma'am, sir," I says with my hat in my hand. "I couldn't but help hearing . . ."

"What do you want?" the man says, giving me the cold eye.

Well, I almost settled his hash for him right then and

there, his manners being such as they were, but I held on to my temper and just gave him this grin that was all teeth.

"Ain't nothing to me, mister," I says. "But if'n it's the priest you want, why he'll be back in a couple of hours. He's just downriver a bit at some Mex's place what got bit by a rattler and is takin' some time to shuffle off this mortal coil, so to speak," I finished grandly. His eyebrow twitched a bit and I knew that I had scored with that one.

"Really? Oh, John! Isn't that the most wonderful news?" the woman says, her eyes shining like mirrors.

"Why, yes. I guess so," he says, and I can tell that he ain't a bit happy about what I've just told him and he looks at me again and if I had just stepped into a nest of rattlers he wouldn't use a ball to put me out of my misery.

About that time, Jim comes into the tavern with the *alcalde* and the man's eyes light up. "But," he says to the woman, "we could get the hitchin' done right now instead of waiting." And he gets up and goes over to where Jim and the *alcalde* are leaning on the bar having a talk.

"I'm sorry, *señor*" he says. "But I have just received word that the good Father will soon be back. There is no reason now to enter into constitutional bonds."

I could see the tiny muscles working along the man's jaw and I think it's about time I paste him one on the mouth when I catch that warning look from Jim and hold my piece. I turn back to my table to get my cup of brandy when the door opens and who walks in but the priest with the hood pulled far over his head, shuffling like he was carrying the weight of the world upon his shoulders.

"But, see here, *senor*" the *alcalde* continues. "Here is the good Father, now."

Well, the good Father don't speak any English, which perplexes the man, so Jim, he leaps in and offers to do some translating for the couple. The man has this here doubtful look on his face, but the young woman smiles and thanks

Jim greatly for his help and the die is set. The man ain't got a choice if he wants to play a flute over that woman.

Jim has this real lengthy talk with the Father, then tells the man that the *padre* is willing to hear the man's premarital confession which they can do if both step into the room next door. 'Course, Jim has to go, too, but the *padre* swears him to the seal of the confessional to make all things legal.

Now, the man seems real doubtful about all this, but he knows he's been rookered, and he follows them into the next room. Jim pretends to close the door behind them, but leaves it open just enough for us in the tap-room to hear everything going on.

There's another long exchange of Mex-talk and then Jim speaks up loudly and begins to ask some highly embarrassing questions of the man about horse dealing over in Arkansas and his wife and child, and the man, thinking that the door is closed like an oyster shell, gets to sputtering and stammering and finally spills the oats about himself with the *padre* going "ah!" every once in a while and clicking his tongue whenever Jim pauses to do a bit of translating.

I steal a look at the young woman while all this is going on and the blood just leaves them red cheeks, leaving her looking as waxen white and cold as death. Pretty soon, the tears begin flowing and I naturally get up and ask if there's anything I can do to help her.

"Yes," she says, sniffling and wiping her nose on a dainty hanky she takes from her sleeve. "You can take me back to my daddy's place, if you will, sir."

I didn't need a howdy to send me on my way. I gathered that young woman's belongings and took her out of Peyton's place and back home.

When I returned a few hours later, there's Jim and Joe having a tot and toasting themselves. Joe looks up at me and pulls that hood over his face.

"Well, how'd I do?" he asks. "I make a good *padre?"*

We all had a good laugh over that one and for months after, whenever someone did something wrong, Joe would make a cross over them and say, "Bless you, my child!" and send us off laughing again!

St. Louis *Globe-Democrat*,
November 1898

The following article appeared in the St. Louis Globe-Democrat *in November 1898. I quote only a part of it to show one individual's idea of how Bowie came to go on his famous San Saba expedition. I question the reliability of the article since it is allegedly signed by someone who calls himself "Brazos" but I did find a shaft and a rough circle of rocks that appeared to have been deliberately erected as a means of fortification between the Dry Frio and the Frio rivers. I remember my father saying that he heard Bowie give just such a description in Gonzales about 1831. I had no chance to explore further as my men and I were expecting an attack by some Indians we had been trailing and we fortified our camp at that very same spot about a hundred yards from water.—A. J. S.*

. . . By some means James Bowie got possession of a lot of old maps of Western Texas, and upon many of these were marked places that had been abandoned for a hundred years. Nobody knows where he obtained his map, but possibly through relatives of his wife who had been trading for a long time with various Indian tribes of the area, including the Lipan Apaches. We do know, however, that it was not long after his marriage before he began to talk of recruiting an expedition in search for St. Denis's silver mine, and the old house, which, at that period, was in the very heart of the country of the terrible Comanches. At that time, the house was only a little more than a hundred years old, and there was not a white man in Texas who had ever seen it.

Colonel Bowie knew that there was such a place on his old map, and he had heard many stories of the wonderful wealth that St. Denis had gathered in the mountains near the old house and he did not allow many days to pass before he found himself at the head of some twenty-five or thirty adventurers prowling about in the mountains of the Guadalupe, southwest of San Antonio. After searching for more than a week, Bowie himself discovered St. Denis's old log house with St. Denis's name and the date, 1714, carved on a rock beside the foundation.

*The reader will notice a few discrepancies between the
account given by Caiaphas Ham and the report written by
James Bowie for Veramendi and Rezin's writing below.
This, I suggest, is due to the time lapse between them, James
Bowie's being rendered first, Ham's second but a product
that came after many tellings in several saloons, and Rezin's
as an afterthought in an attempt to set the record straight but
only confusing it further by the failing of memory.*—A. J. S.

Their [the Indians'] number being so far greater than ours,
one hundred sixty-four to eleven, it was agreed that I should
be sent out to talk with them, and endeavor to compromise
rather than attempt to fight. I accordingly started with
David Buchanan in company and walked up to within forty
yards of where they had halted, and requested them in their
own tongue to send forward their chief, as I wanted to talk
with him. Their answer was "How do you do! How do you
do!" in English and a discharge of twelve shots at us, one
of which broke Buchanan's leg. I returned their salutation
with the contents of a double-barreled gun and a pistol. I
then took Buchanan upon my shoulder and started back to
the encampment. The Indians then opened a heavy fire upon
us which wounded Buchanan in two more places slightly,
and piercing my hunting shirt in several places without doing me any injury. When the Indians found their shots failed
to bring me down, eight Indians, on foot, took after me, with
tomahawks, and when close upon me, were discovered by
the party who rushed out with rifles, and brought down four

of them, the other four retreating back to the main body. We then returned to our position, and all was still for about five minutes.

We then discovered a hill to the northwest, at the distance of sixty yards, red with Indians, who opened a heavy fire upon us, with loud yells, their chief on horseback urging them in a loud audible voice to the charge, walking his horse, perfectly composed. When we first discovered him, our guns were all empty, with the exception of Mr. Ham's. James Bowie cried out, "Who is loaded?" Mr. Ham answered, "I am." He was then told to shoot that Indian on horseback. He did so and broke his leg and killed his horse. We now discovered him hopping around his horse on one leg with his shield on his arm to keep off the balls. By this time four of our party being reloaded, fired at the same instant, and all the balls took effect through his shield. He fell and was immediately surrounded by six or eight of his tribe who picked him up and bore him off. Several of these were shot by our party. The whole body then retreated back of the hill out of sight with the exception of a few Indians who were running about from tree to tree out of gun shot. They now covered the hill the second time, bringing up their bowmen, who had not been in action before, and commenced a heavy fire with balls and arrows, which we returned with a well-directed aim with our rifles. At this instant another chief appeared on horseback near the spot where the other one fell. The same question of "Who is loaded?" was asked. The answer was "nobody," when little Charlie, the mulatto servant, came running up with Buchanan's rifle which had not been discharged since he was wounded, and handed it to James Bowie, who instantly fired and brought him down from his horse. He was surrounded by six or eight of his tribe, as was the last, and was borne off under our fire.

During the time we were defending ourselves from the

Indians on the hill, some fifteen or twenty of the Caddo tribe had succeeded in getting under the bank of the creek, in our rear, at about forty yards distant, and opened a heavy fire upon us, which wounded Matthew Doyle, the ball entering the left breast and coming out at the back. As soon as he cried out that he was wounded, Thomas McCaslin hastened to the spot, when he fell, and observed, "Where is the Indian that shot Doyle?" He was told by a more experienced hand not to venture there, as from the reports of their guns, they must be riflemen. At that instant, he discovered an Indian, and while in the act of raising his piece, was shot through the center of the body and expired. Robt. Armstrong exclaimed, "Damn the Indian that shot McCaslin; where is he?" He was told not to venture there as they must be riflemen, but on discovering an Indian and while bringing his gun up, was fired at, and part of the stock of his gun cut off, the ball lodging against the barrel. During this time our enemies had formed a complete circle around us, occupying the points of rocks, scattering trees and bushes. The firing then became general from all quarters. Finding our situation too much exposed among the trees, we were obliged to leave them and take to the thickets. The first thing necessary was to dislodge the riflemen from under the bank of the creek, who were within pointblank shot. This we soon succeeded in doing by shooting most of them in the head, as soon as we had the advantage of seeing them, when they could not see us. The road we had cut around the thicket the night previous, gave us now an advantageous situation over that of our enemy, as we had a fair view of them in the prairie, while we were completely hid. We baffled their shots by moving six or eight feet the moment we had fired, as their only mark was the smoke of our guns. They would put twenty balls within the size of a pocket handkerchief when they had seen the smoke. In this manner we fought them two hours, and had one man wounded, James Coryell who was shot through the arm, the ball lodging in the side, first cutting away a small bush which prevented it from penetrating deeper than the size of it. They now discovered that we were not to be dislodged from the thicket, and the uncertainty of killing us at random, they suffering very much from the fire of our rifles, which brought half a dozen down at every round, they determined to resort to stratagem, by putting fire to the dry grass in the prairie for the double purpose of routing us from our position, and under cover of the smoke, to carry away their dead and wounded which lay near us. The wind was now blowing from the west and they placed the fire in that quarter, where it burned down all the grass to the creek, and then bore off to the right and left, leaving around our position a space of about five acres untouched by the fire. Under cover of their smoke they succeeded in carrying off a portion of their dead and wounded. In the meantime our party was engaged in scraping away the dry grass and leaves from our wounded men and baggage to prevent the fire from passing over them; and likewise in piling up rocks and bushes to answer the place of breastworks. They now discovered that they had failed in routing us, as they had anticipated. They then reoccupied the points of rocks and trees in the prairie, and commenced another attack. The firing continued for some time, when the wind suddenly changed to the north and blew very hard. We now discovered our dangerous situation, should the Indians succeed in putting fire to the small spot which we occupied, and kept a strict watch all around. The two servant boys were employed in scraping away dry grass and leaves from around the wounded men. The point from which the wind blew being favorable to fire our position one of the Indians succeeded in crawling down the creek and putting fire to the grass that had not been burned, but before he could retreat back to his party, was killed by Robert Armstrong.

At this time we saw no hope of escape, as the fire was coming down rapidly before the wind, flaming ten feet high, and directly for the spot we occupied. What must be done? We must either be burned up alive or be driven into the prairie among the savages. This encouraged the Indians and made it more awful; their shots and yells rent the air—they, at the same time, firing about twenty shots. As soon as the smoke hid us from their view we collected together and held a consultation as to what was best to be done. Our first impression was that they might charge us under cover of the smoke, as we could make but one effectual fire. The sparks were flying about so quickly that no man could open his powder horn without running the risk of being blown up. However, we finally came to a determination: had they charged us, to give them fire, place our backs together, draw our knives and fight them as long as any of us were alive. The next question was should they charge on us and we retain our position, we must be burned up. It was then decided that each man should take care of himself as well as he could until the fire arrived at the ring around our baggage and wounded men and there it should be smothered with buffalo robes, bear skins, deer skins, and blankets, which after a great deal of exertion, we succeeded in doing. Our thicket being so much burned and scorched that it afforded little or no shelter, we all got into the ring that was made around our wounded men and baggage, and commenced building our breastworks higher, with loose rocks from the inside and dirt dug up with our knives and sticks. During the last fire the Indians had succeeded in removing all their killed and wounded which lay near us. It was now sundown and we had been warmly engaged with the Indians since sunrise, and they seeing us still alive and ready for fight drew off at a distance of a hundred yards and encamped for the night.

The Indians made no further attack but quietly withdrew.

During the day's conflict, we had killed some eighty Indians including the Lipan Chief Tresmanos who gave James such a hard time with threats upon his life. When our two wounded men had recovered sufficiently to travel, we abandoned our rude fortification, destroyed our remaining stores, buried our tools, and took up a line of march afoot for Bexar whereupon we arrived in due time.

Rezin Pleasant Bowie [RUBRIC]

Although called the Battle at San Saba River, the fight James Bowie had with the Comanche Indians while leading a small party in search of the lost silver mines is believed to have taken place on Calf Creek, in McCulloch County. Some, however, believe that the fight took place at Bowie Spring on Celery Creek, a few miles north of Menard. Rezin Bowie also penned an account of the fight that can be found in Yoakum's History of Texas [1885]. The following is Bowie's personal report to Don Juan Martin Veramendi, his father-in-law and vice-governor of the state of Coahuila.—A. J. S.

To the Political Chief of Bexar:

Agreeable to your Lordship's request, I have the honor to report to you the result of my expedition from San Antonio to San Saba. Information received through different channels in relation to that section of country, formerly occupied by Mexican citizens, and now in the hands of several hostile Indians, induced me to get up that expedition, expecting that some benefit might result therefrom, both to the community and to myself. But, as my intentions were known to and approved by your Lordship, I deem it useless to enter into these particulars. I left this city on the second of November last, in company with my brother Rezin Bowie, eight men and a boy. Wishing, with due care, to examine the nature of the country, my progress was quite slow. On the 19th we met two Comanches and one Mexican captive, the last acting as interpreter, at above seven miles northwest of Llano river on the road known as "de la Bandera." The Indians, after having asked several questions in regard to the feelings of the Mexicans toward the Comanches, and receiving an assurance on my part that they were kindly disposed toward all peaceable Indians, told me that their friends were driving to San Antonio several horses that had been stolen at Goliad. I promised them that they would be protected, and they continued on their way to the city to deliver the said horses to their proper owners or to the civil authority. On the following day at sunrise we were overtaken by the captive, who informed us that 124 Tahuacanoes were on our trail, and at the same time showing us the medal this year by his captain from the authority of this city, which was sent us to prove that the messenger was reliable. We were then apprised that the Tahuacanoes had the day before visited the campaign ground of the Comanches, and told them that they were following us to kill us at any cost. Ysayune (such was the name of the Comanche captain) having become informed of the determination of the savages respecting us, tried first to induce them to desist from the prosecution of their intention, insisting that they should not take our lives, and telling them he would "be mad" with them if they went to attack us, but they separated, dissatisfied with each other. Ysayune sent us word that if we would come back he would do all he could to protect us, but that he had only sixteen men under his command, and thought we could defend ourselves from the enemy by taking position on a hill covered with underbrush, which the captive was ordered to show us, adding that the houses on the San Saba were close by. (The houses alluded to were the remains of those belonging to the San Saba Mission that had long been abandoned.) We did not follow the Comanche's advice, thinking that we could reach our destination, as we did, before the enemy could overtake us. But once arrived, we could not find the houses, and the ground upon the San Saba offering no position for protection, we went about three miles north of the river, and there selected a grove wherein to encamp for the night. There was a smaller grove about fifty yards from the one chosen for our encampment, and I caused it to be occupied for the night by three men, so as to prevent the enemy from taking possession of it, and thereby have an advantage over us. However, we passed the night without being disturbed.

On the 21st, at 8 o'clock A.M., we were about to leave our camping ground when we saw a large body of Indians close upon us, and at a distance of about two hundred yards. Several of them shouted in English: "How do you do? How are you, How are you?" We soon knew by their skins that they had among them some Caddoes, and we made signs to them to send a man to inform us of their intentions. Just then we saw that the Indian who was ahead on horseback was holding up a scalp, and forthwith a volley of some ten or twelve gun shots was discharged into our camp, but without effect. At the arrival of the Indians, my brother repaired with two men to the smaller grove which was between us and the Indians, but when I saw that most of them were withdrawing and sheltering themselves behind a hill about one hundred varas northeast of our position, expecting that they would attack us in a body in that direction, I went to tell my brother to come back, and on our return, Mr. Buchanan was shot and had his leg broken. We had scarcely joined our camp when, as I expected, the Indians came from behind the hill to dislodge us, but as the foremost men and among them one who seemed to be their leader, fell, they busied themselves in removing their dead; and to do this they had to come closer and fight sharply, but it was at the cost of more lives on their part. This contest lasted about fifteen minutes; but when they perceived they could not enter our camp, they withdrew, screening themselves behind the hill and surrounding timber, and thence commenced firing on us from every direction. While we were thus engaged fifteen Indians, who from the report of their firing, seemed to be armed with rifles, concealed themselves behind some oaks in a valley about sixty varas to the northwest. These were the severest of our foemen, and they wounded two more of our men and some horses. At about 11 o'clock A.M., seeing they could not dislodge us with their firearms, they set fire to the prairie, hoping thus to burn us or compel us to abandon our camp. So soon as the prairie was on fire they loudly shouted, and expecting their stratagem would be successful, they advanced under protection of the smoke to the position they had first been obliged to abandon; but when the fire reached the valley it died out.

Thinking the siege would be protracted, we employed Gonzales and the boy Charles, in making a breastwork of whatever they could lay their hands upon, such as boughs and our property. From that moment until 4 o'clock P.M. the firing slackened gradually and the Indians withdrew to a considerable distance. But the wind having shifted from the southwest to the northwest, the Indians again fired the prairie, and the conflagration reached our camp, but by dint of hard work in the way of tearing the grass, and by means of our bear skins and blankets, made use of to smother the flames, we succeeded in saving the greater part of our animals and other property. We expected a furious attack of the enemy under cover of the smoke, in order to penetrate our camp, but the greater part of them withdrew to a pond, distance about a half a mile from the battle field, to procure water; and those of them that remained kept up firing and removing their dead. This work on their part went on until about 6:30 P.M. when the battle closed, only one shot being fired by them after 7 o'clock P.M., which was aimed at one of our men who went out to obtain water.

We had agreed to attack the enemy while they were asleep, but when we reflected that we had only six men able to use their arms, and that the wounded would have to remain unprotected, we thought it more advisable to remain in our camp, which we had fortified with stones and timber so as to make it secure against further assault. On the 22nd, at about 5 o'clock A.M., we heard the Indians moving to the northeast, and at daybreak none were to be seen. However, at about 11 o'clock A.M. we observed thirteen of them, who, upon seeing us, withdrew suddenly. Subsequently, in order to intimidate them and impress them with the idea that we were still ready for a fight, we hoisted a flag on a long pole as a sign of war; and for eight days we kept a fire constantly burning, hoping thereby to attract the attention of any friendly Comanches that might be in the neighborhood and procure some animals for the transportation of our wounded and camp property.

On the evening of the 29th, the wounded being somewhat relieved, we began our march for Bexar, and on striking the Perdanales river we observed a large Tahuacanoe trail, and noticed several others between that stream and the Guadalupe river, all seeming to tend in the direction of a smoke that curled upward from some point down the Perdanales. Upon seeing these trails we took a more westerly course, and after having crossed the Guadalupe we saw no more signs of Indians, and ar-

rived here on the 6th inst. My only loss among my men
during the battle was by the fall and death of the foreman of my mechanics, Mr. Thomas McCaslin, from a
bullet that entered below the breast and passed through
the loin. He was one of the most efficient of my comrades in the fight. I had also three wounded, five animals killed and several hurt. We could make no estimate
of the loss of the enemy, but we kept up a continual firing during the day and always had enemies to aim at,
and there were no intervening obstacles to prevent our
shot from having their full effect. We saw twenty-one
men fall dead, and among them, seven on horseback
who seemed to act as chiefs, one of whom was very con-
spicuous by reason of the buffalo horns and other fin-
ery about his head. To his death, I attribute the
discouragement of his followers.

I cannot do less than commend to your Lordship, for
their alacrity in obeying and executing my orders with
spirit and firmness, all those who accompanied me.
Their names are: Robert Armstrong, Thomas McCaslin
(killed), Daniel Buchanan (wounded), James Coryell,
Mateo Dias, Cephas K. Ham, Jesse Wallace, Sr. Gonzales, Charles the boy. God and liberty,

James Bowie [RUBRIC]
Bexar, December 10th, 1831

Col. John S. Ford

Word got back to San Antonio about the fight Bowie's party had with the Indians along the San Saba before they did. Somehow, in the telling, the outcome became twisted and word had arrived that the party had been slaughtered to a man with Bowie's scalp, along with the others, hanging from the tent pole of a savage in the wilderness. The entire city went into mourning with the doorway and windows of the Veramendi Palace being draped in black crepe. Col. John S. Ford summed it up best in his diary when he lamented the loss. Unfortunately, Colonel Ford's diary is not available for public scrutiny, the family refusing to let it out for publication.—A. J. S.

The shades of night had fallen on the city. Sad hearts were bewailing the fate of the adventurous Americans. A party of men, mostly on foot, weary and soiled by travel, entered the streets of the Queen City of the West. Some of the men were recognized. A shout went up; it was repeated; it spread from street to street, from house to house. Stout men quivered with excitement, tears of joy dimmed bright eyes. Fearless men rushed forward to grasp in friendship and admiration, the hands of citizens who had proved themselves heroes in a contest demanding courage, prudence, endurance, and all the noble qualities adorning the soldier and the patriot. "Bowie's party have returned! They have won a glorious victory!" was the cry. Lights blazed from house to house as word traveled from neighbor to neighbor. The people in their heart of hearts decreed them a triumph. And well they deserved it. The pages of history record but few achievements.

Tom Owl

More than one person has a story about Bowie's San Saba fight. Indeed, if everyone who claimed to have been there with Bowie and Ham and the others had indeed been with them, there wouldn't have been a Lipan Apache left anywhere in the entire world. As it was, given the Homestead Act, the Civil War, and the firm belief in Manifest Destiny that permeated the nation, I'm surprised that any Indians survived at all. Some of the Lipans, the wild bulls of the tribe, joined with their cousins, the Mescalero and the Chiricahua, riding with Nana, Loco, even Geronimo. But for the most part, the Lipans tried to avoid war with the white man. They had learned early that as an isolated tribe, the Lipans had little chance against men who "numbered among the stars their numbers." The Lipans were moved from reservation to reservation as the Bureau of Indian Affairs tried to find a home for them. At last, they were settled up around Fort Sill in the Nations. Shortly after that, they appeared to have disappeared, but the truth of the matter was that they realized what had happened to the Cheyenne and Sioux could easily happen to them. They disappeared into the outback, sacrificing their unity within a tribal structure for survival. They became farmers and ranchers, scattering themselves among the other tribes, merging their identity with the wilderness and the land. They became silent, holding meetings more in the manner of family reunions than tribal councils, doing business with the white man casually and quietly. Their tribal honor became sacrificed for survival, for the Lipans, unlike other Indians of the stamp of Rousseau's "noble sauvage," believed the survival of the body was necessary for the survival of the soul. It took a while, but at last I found one: Tom Owl, a boy who had been sent to the Carlisle Indian Barracks in Pennsylvania by the Indian Bureau after diphtheria killed his parents. He replied to my query about the San Saba fight in 1892.—A. J. S.

I supposed it would eventually come down to this. I'm just surprised that it has taken so long for someone to get around to me. There's quite a movement going on now among a few college professors to get the facts right. Or, at least right to their way of thinking. Maybe, however, people are just beginning to rethink their heroes. Maybe people are seeing their heroes now in a tragic sense with feet of clay. Then, of course, there are those who simply cannot understand heroism and want to cut everyone down to their own mediocre size.

Frankly, I've had to give some thought as to whether I was going to write and explain what happened at the fight or not. A literate Indian isn't a healthy thing to be in this day and age, you know. People take great comfort in thinking that we are all pagans, savages, and barbarians. As long as they have something or someone they believe is more miserable than they are, why then they can find some reason to be happy. There's comfort in knowing that you aren't at the bottom of the ladder, you know. And there is something romantic about Indians to some who constantly think we all roam around still hunting buffalo, wearing beads and little else, riding naked across the prairies with feathers dangling from our hair. We can thank James Fenimore Cooper and Ned Buntline for that image. People do not realize that the noble savage really did not exist. He was a myth made up in people's minds to satisfy their own romantic whimsies.

You understand, though, that what I know about San Saba

I have from my relatives. My uncle fought in it. Tres Manos, they called him because he had a mummified hand hanging on a cord around his neck. He was the crazy one of the family, according to my father. From the stories they told about him up in the Choctaw hills, I can understand why everyone pretty much left him alone.

Once one of the Council refused to let Tres Manos go walking with his daughter. That night, my uncle caught one of the man's horses, tied a tumbleweed to its tail, lit the tumbleweed on fire, and sent the horse into the village. Most of the village caught fire from the mad horse and three men were trampled to death when they tried to catch the horse. Another time he took flint chippings from the toolmaker's work place and put them into someone's meal. Cruel, he was. And a bit mad.

So when Bowie, El Cuchillo, they called him, came to our village to hunt with Esteban, the chief, Tres Manos treated him with scorn. One day, according to Father, Tres Manos tried to take El Cuchillo's knife. But Bowie picked him up and threw him among the cooking pots in a fire. Tres Manos's clothes caught on fire and he frantically pulled them off to keep from getting burned. The laughter of the tribe shamed him as he was forced to run naked through the entire village, dogs snapping at his bare heels, hands covering his private parts to keep them from being bitten. The women of the village called him Manoslito thereafter, but only behind his back for as is such with people like him, he could not stand ridicule and men such as this are indeed dangerous men.

But I think the worst day for Tres Manos happened when he and his hunting party cornered a group of Comanches on an oxbow by the river. The way across to the land was a thin sand spit only and the Comanches defended it well against Tres Manos and his men.

Bowie went upstream, stripped, and swam underwater to

the back of the Comanches. When he emerged, dripping from the river, his long hair pasted against his neck, his big knife clutched in one hand, the lone lookout shrieked in terror. Bowie fell upon the Comanches, his knife flashing. Tres Manos took advantage of the confusion and sent his men over the spit and onto the island. Later, they found the marks of Bowie's big knife on seven of the ten Comanches.

That night, the Lipans held a dance to celebrate their victory. But it was Bowie who was singled out for praise by the dancers, not Tres Manos. My father remembered how his eyes smoldered and burned, hot coals of hatred, across the fire at Bowie. Whenever he spoke of this, my father shuddered and said he had seen terrible things, but never the dark fire that he saw that night in the eyes of Tres Manos.

I suppose that is why many men were killed in the Fight of the Broken Trees when Bowie and his men were trapped by Tres Manos and his men near San Saba. Tres Manos had his chance to kill Bowie and would not come away from the fight. He no longer thought with reason, but with passion, and passion never mated well with reason. Time after time, Tres Manos sent men into the trees after Bowie and his men and time after time they were killed or beaten back.

At last, Tres Manos tried to burn them out, but the wind turned and our people were almost destroyed by the fire they set themselves. They were hard-pressed to put it out before it swept the plains, destroying the winter grass. After this, my people began to turn away from Tres Manos and his demands to send them again into the trees. At last, Tres Manos led a party into the trees by himself, and that was his death.

What I know, I know from my father, who did not wish to take part in the fight for El Cuchillo was a friend of the Lipans. But he was afraid for by this time, Tres Manos had made many friends and gained much power. At the time, though he had lost many of those who claimed to be his friends, Tres Manos was still a dangerous man. A madness seemed to have descended upon him. Spittle formed in the corners of his mouth and his eyes rolled in their sockets until the white shone brightly in the daylight. From what my father says, I have little doubt that Tres Manos had been driven mad by his desire to kill Bowie.

My father was there when Tres Manos went into the trees and tried to kill Bowie. El Cuchillo gutted him like a deer. My father forced the others to leave after he saw Tres Manos die.

The fight was a mistake, for the Lipans became laughing horses for their enemies. The Comanches and the People from the West became bolder and bolder, raiding our villages, stealing our horses. My father said that the Fight of the Broken Trees marked the end of our life for from that time on, we could no longer command respect among the other tribes. It did not matter that Comanches and others were with the Lipans that day; the Lipans had been the leaders, thanks to Tres Manos, and so had the responsibility for success or failure. No shame could be placed on those who were not Lipan.

But Bowie must also take a part of the blame for the loss of our respect among the tribes, for we had welcomed him into our village only to be betrayed by him when he searched for the Spanish silver. It was the secret of my people and our strength for with the silver, we could buy respect from the Spaniards and Mexicans. Bowie wronged our people and broke his word to us that he would keep our secret as if he were a Lipan, too. But that, I have learned since being here at Carlisle, is common practice among the white people. They have no truthtellers in their tribe, no honor.

Juan Nepomuceno Seguín

Juan Nepomuceno Seguín deserves much more from history, from Texas, than he receives. He was one of the largest ranchers in Texas, a member of the young lions, a political leader in Bexar, a Texas senator, mayor of San Antonio, a captain of a troop of cavalry he raised himself, commander of a regiment at San Jacinto, and a major influence with the Texas-born Mexicans.

A man of strong convictions, he fought for what he considered right, which is why he fought Santa Anna, but when his political opinions differed from those of newcomers to Texas, mostly from the States, some trumped-up charges were laid against him and he was forced to flee to Mexico. There, Santa Anna imprisoned him.

After the Mexican-American War, Juan Seguín was able to live in Texas, but he was never able to be the political force he had been before the war. He was also a good friend of Jim Bowie.—A. J. S.

I knew Don Jaime well. He was my very good friend. He was one American who did not assume he was better than you simply because of where he was born, and yet he was of good blood himself, *de verdad*.

I do not remember exactly what year it was when first I meet Jaime. It was in Texas, and at an inn. He was traveling across Texas, looking at the land. We struck up a conversation and we were friends from that moment on.

I rode with him when we first became *Los Leoncitos*, "the young lions."

It was in Bexar around 1830, and I was only twenty-four

years old. It was a good time for me, but we were having some trouble with one particular band of Comanche. I was in my office at the Rancho Seguín when my foreman ran in against all etiquette.

"Patrón! El Comanche!"

"Dónde?"

"El Rancho sur."

"Rouse the *vaqueros! Andale!"*

Just then my *mozo* came to the door. "Don Jaime Bowie and several riders are here, *señor.*"

"Good! Show him in."

My rifle and best pistols were on the wall. I removed them and began to check their loads when Don Jaime and Caiaphas Ham entered.

"Con permiso, Don Juan. I have brought my friend with me."

Jaime always spoke very curiously. His voice was very powerful, very deep, but as he spoke, one could hear gentleness in his voice. You would always listen to Jaime for he spoke only when what he had to say he felt was important.

"I am sorry that I do not have time to be a gracious host," I replied. "My *rancho* has been raided by Comanche."

"I had hoped the loaded guns weren't for me or Cap here," he joked, but I could tell by the way he touched the knife at his side that he was interested.

"They attacked my little village on the south ranch. I must ride."

"Besides Caiaphas, Ben McCulloch and five other men are riding with me. We've had a few raids all over Texas, and we thought to raise a company of rangers. We were hoping you might have a few *vaqueros* who would ride with us."

"And not me?"

"I did not want to assume to take you away from your

important work at the ranch. And the politics in Bexar," he added.

"My *segundo* will provide supplies, fresh horses, what you need. I will change and then we will ride," I said.

We rode as fast as we could to my village where we had taken horses to be broken. The wails of the women greeted us as we rode into the village. The Comanche had ridden through the village, robbing the storehouse, killing four *vaqueros*, three women, a child, and taking two other children with them when they left, both boys, one having six, the other five years.

Petra came out to tell me about the Comanches. I had attended her wedding to Fermin, who now lay with the dead inside the church next to the little rock grotto of the Virgen de Guadalupe.

"Juan," Jaime said, coming up to me. "I sent out the Lipan Apache who works for you. If we follow quickly, we might catch up to them, but I'm not sure that is a good idea. They might kill the boys."

"What do you suggest?" I asked.

"Leave the trail to the Apache and ride directly north. We might reach the hills above the Rio Frio before they if we do this," he said.

I shook my head, objecting. "But, we might lose their trail. You are only guessing about what they are planning."

"True," he said. "But I think that is our best way. To surprise them. They will be expecting us to come from behind, not ahead."

And that is what we did. We left the trail the Comanche had taken and rode north to find the trail to the Llano Estacado. We rode hard and late that night, we reached the rocky hills and set up a hidden camp and placed our watchers.

"You think they'll come this way, Jim?" asked Ben McCulloch.

"I expect them sometime early tomorrow afternoon," Jaime answered. "They'll be making a big detour south and west, then swing north to cut across the river. This is the best crossing for miles. They'll be here."

He settled down to the fire and began to sharpen his big knife. I remember that knife. Every time I saw it, I remembered the stories that people whispered about what he had done with it. They were just stories, but in stories there is always some truth and it is the truth that may be there that is frightening.

The next day, we filled our waterskins and hid in the rocks. Jaime was right. The noon sun had just passed when we tasted the dust of the horse herd on the wind coming from the south. I looked to my arms. We were all well armed, Jaime more than the rest of us.

"They'll stop by the river to water the horses," Jaime said softly. "Wait until you hear me fire."

I nodded and he slipped away to tell the others. Sweat stung my eyes and my hands grew slippery upon the rifle, but my mouth became dry. Strange. One would think the hands would become dry, but such is not the way.

I settled the sights of my rifle upon one brave, squat like a toad. I followed him, waiting, waiting for Jaime to give the signal. At first, I thought that they would ride across the river, but the horses stopped and began to mill around, each trying eagerly to get to the water.

Suddenly, Jaime fired. Startled, I pulled the trigger of my rifle. The Comanche I had been aiming at threw up his arms and tumbled backwards off his pony. More shots rang out. I reloaded as fast as I could. I fired again, then stopped as Jaime appeared on the rocks over the Indians. His knife flashed in his hand as he dropped down upon them like a cat.

He slipped among the Indians like a shadow, his knife flickering, the blade now red with blood. One Comanche screamed and ran away, trying to hold himself inside, but he fell before going very far.

The rest of Jaime's men fell upon the Indians. Fearing that I would be missed, I rose and ran down into the cloud of dust. A Comanche suddenly appeared in front of me, his mouth stretched wide, his eyes blazing with fear and hate. He swung a club at me. I ducked and shot him with one of my pistols. A blow upon my back sent me sprawling into the dust. Someone leaped upon me. I smelled grease and sweat and a hand pulled back my hair. Then, I heard a *chunk!* and a groan, and the Indian sprawled over the top of me.

I heaved him off and sat up, trying to peer through the dust. I looked at the Indian: his legs jerked and twitched, his hand trying to hold the blood inside his throat. A lance narrowly missed me. I seized it and rose, looking for the enemy. But then, it was over and the dust settled.

"Are you all right?"

I turned to face Jaime. His shirt had been ripped by a knife and a long scratch ran down his cheek. His eyes shined with excitement.

"Sí," I croaked. I swallowed and tried again. *"Seguro que sí.* And you?"

"Oh yes," he said. He looked around and pointed. I turned to look at Caiaphas Ham, who had pulled the children away into a nest of rocks. "I think we got your horses back, too."

That was the first of the Young Lions, the Rangers.

Uncle Ben Highsmith

Uncle Ben Highsmith was one of the original settlers of Texas. Born in 1817 in Mississippi, he came with his father to Texas in 1823. During his many years, he served with Jim Bowie at the Grass Fight, and with Sam Houston at San Jacinto. As a Texas Ranger, he fought Comanche and Cherokee, and he was with the Rangers during the Mexican War. Few men have shed as much blood for Texas as Uncle Ben—A. J. S.

Jack Sowell asked me to have written down all I know about Jim Bowie. I cant hardly see no more so I have to have somebody else put my story on paper. First, let me say that I knew Jim Bowie from the time I was only a young one.

My first trip with him was in 1830. It was then the first Texas Rangers company was formed. Bowie was known as the Young Lion, and all his rangers kinda went under the same name.

Texas was a state of Mexico at the time and under the official protection of the Mexican government. So their soldiers were supposed to keep Indians and bandits away from the settlements.

It never worked that way, though. Most of them Mexican soldiers werent worth a pig in a poke. They would hole up in a town and nothing short of a general would get them out. Unless they could smell a profit, and then they still had to be sure they outnumbered the enemy by three or five to one.

Maybe I shouldnt blame them too much. They was mostly men out of jail from down south sent up North to get rid of a problem. The government seldom paid them and except for the really good officers, never trained them. So, we had a bunch of sorry convicts dressed up fine and given a bit of authority. The upshot of it all was that we Texians were at the mercy of the heathen hordes. Mostly Comanche, but Kronks and Cherokee, Tonks and Kiowa, even sometimes the Apache attacked us whenever they felt frisky or run low on supplies.

I stop to think here a minute and want to say that there were some good Mexican soldiers. I know, cause I fought them, but most of the soldiers sent to Texas were sent to take advantage of the settlers from the states, and not to fight Indians.

Indians raided as a way of life. If they didnt have enough, they went and took it from somebody else. I guess thats mankinds way, so I wont worry about the right and wrong of it, but I will sure say that mankinds way also provides for defense. Us Texians felt we needed to protect ourselves.

My family first settled on the Colorado River about two miles from the town now called La Grange. It was there in 1829 that I saw firsthand what I was just talking about. The Comanche had always gotten along with the settlement in our neck of the woods, but that year they told the men that when the Comanche moon came theyd be down to raid and if they were still living in the settlement, the Comanche would kill them.

Zaddock Wood and Stephan Cottle packed up their families and moved to Rabbs Mill. Six families stayed close to mine and food got mighty scarce cause nobody wanted to be out farming too long. We were staying with Elliot C. Buckner.

There werent much to it; we could weather it out, but we needed supplies and come spring of 1830, Jim Bowie rode in.

Now Jack says hes been gettin stories from others, so I wont go into long descriptions of Bowie. I will just say he rode in on a fine big horse, not a thoroughbred, but a Morgan, one who could travel the wilderness and keep going. Hed conserve his strength so his rider could always have something when the need rose for fast moving. Jim was wearing buckskins that had a reddish tinge to them so they looked like a sunset. I guess thats foolishness, but its somehow right.

You see, when Bowie came into sight it always seemed like all eyes would turn towards him. It wasnt cause he was a dandy. He took care with his clothes and he always was dressed right for the place he was at, but he werent fussy about them. If they got dirty, hed clean up as well as he was able, and finish the job when he got to someplace he could.

There were several things about Jim. He never bragged. He never swore. He only got angry when someone needed killing and seemed always to fit his surroundings even with these peculiarities. He dint drink much, at least when I first knew him. That changed a little later on, though I think people may have let that part of the story grow so as to knock Jims memory down a peg or two.

Like I said, Jim was always the center of attention, without him ever making a conscious effort to be the center of attention. It was just that something about him always made you strive to be his friend, at least that was the way with the good people. There were some who would see Jim stride into a room and would automatically decide that he was something they could never be and then theyd have to try to make him a little less.

The trouble with that line of thought is that hed show how well he could fight. The man was a holy terror, no doubt of that. Hed fight fist or knife or pistol or rifle but hed match any man and best him.

Well, Jim came riding into our yard that day and he says, "Ben, will you take care of my horse while I see your father?"

He slid down off his horse keeping that big rifle—the one Big Foot Wallace ended up with—and keeping it pointing up friendly like. He looked at me but made no effort to force me to take his reins. You see Jim didnt force anyone. He asked a favor and you just wanted to help him out.

"Sure, Mr. Bowie. Pas inside," I said.

"Now, Ben, cant you call me Jim? Youre full grown or near enough."

I remember feeling like I was a king or something right after he said that. Well, Jim went inside and I stabled his horse and brought his pack into the house. He was talking with Pa about the Indian troubles we were having.

It was a long discussion, but it was decided that the only solution was to go into San Antonio on a trading expedition. Over the next couple of days we gathered up anything worth trading, chose the best horse for riding, and those best for packing goods. We also figured out who would go.

The party was Jim Bowie, W. B. Travis, Ben McCulloch, Winslow Turner, George Kimble, Sam Highsmith and me. This was the birth of the Texas Rangers.

It might not seem to be much to you now, but back then it was a real adventure. Since it was spring, it was raiding time. There were Comanche, those whod run us to our neighbors and kept us hungry, then there was Caddoes and sometime Kronks who were cannibals. The civilized tribes of Cherokee and Creek werent so civilized that sometimes they werent above getting their own from the white man.

On the first night out, I asked, "Jim, can I see your knife?"

"Sure," he replied and pulled it from his side and flipped it through the air to catch it by the point, and then tossed it into the cottonwood tree next to where I was standing. I swear it takes longer to tell than it took to happen.

I pulled that big knife out of the tree and stared at it. I was twelve years old and so couldnt be too anxious, but I still needed to look at this mankiller. It was about a foot long and curved at the front. The blade was heavy and if you looked at it from the point, you could see how the whole blade was formed. Kind of like a wedge or an axe blade, with the thick top covered with brass. It had a big brass guard to protect the hand and the soft brass backstrap could easily catch the steel of someone who he was fighting. The handle was ebony.

I handed it back to him and told him that was some knife. I saw he had another that was about nine inches long which he used for cutting meat and such. The pattern was similar but Jim was always thinking and inventing things.

On the third day we saw faint smoke rising from behind a clump of live oak. "Looks like someones cooking," Sam said. Jim looked a little concerned and said, "Lets ride."

It was a craftsmans cabin. The timber was well dressed and fit well. A little green, which is why it didnt burn completely.

Jim walked his horse around the cabin as I stared at the rich black earth that had been prepared for the crop. Hed not wasted. He cut his trees for the cabin and pulled the stumps so that he could plow the land. The rest of the forest could slowly be cut back as he was able to grow more crops, in the meantime he would have some forest for hunting.

Jim rode to the front door, climbed off his horse with his big rifle ready to fire. One pound of lead only made sixteen bullets for it. It had the kick of a mule and whatever he hit went down and he seldom missed. He had that rifle pointed at the door when he told Ben McCulloch to get down and side him.

Ben did as he was asked. He stood next to the door with his own long rifle cocked and ready to fire. The rest of us checked our loads and kept checking the countryside for hidden Indians.

Jim hit the door with his shoulder and went right on inside. There was no shot so McCulloch went in behind him.

They came out shaking their heads. I had to look, and what I saw has lived with me to this day. The man and his wife had been scalped and mutilated. I wont tell you all they did but it was enough to send me out into the fields to pour my breakfast onto the earth. The first and last time that ever happened.

We buried the couple and Jim said a prayer over them. It didnt take us but an hour to get into the saddle again. We fed and watered the horses and grabbed a bite ourselves. There wasnt any doubt that we wanted to find the raiders and wreak vengeance on them.

"How many you think there are, Jim?" I asked, knowing that hed just become colonel of our regiment of seven riders.

"Tracks were too confusing to say for sure, but it was a small party of ten to fifteen. Nothing we cant handle."

It was just past noon when we decided to take a chance and ride up to the top of a hill. It wasnt as reckless as it sounds cause the hill was covered with timber so careful riding still kept us hid from the Indians.

We could see them at the bottom of the hill. It was a little valley with a creek, meadow, and a stand of trees butting up against another hill. There were thirteen Comanche, two of them young enough to be considered boys, the rest young warriors, say around twenty or just past. They were letting their horses drink in the stream. They werent in any hurry.

Jim pondered the sight for a second. "If none of us miss, we could cut the force in half but the rest would make that stand of trees before we could reload. From those trees, theyd make the hill and be gone before we could finish them. So, we will trap them. Now, heres how we do it."

He grinned at us and said, "Sam, you and Ben get to play hero. Think youre up to it?"

Who wouldnt be. They said sure and Jim said, "If you

ride down this game trail you will hit the far side of that meadow before the Comanche get too far into the trees. Theyll want to take your horses and rifles so theyll chase you if they think they can get them. Now, if you were to ride on this side of the creek and straight down from where were sitting those Indians will sneak up on you."

"And I suppose you fellers will amble on down to the edge of the trees and have some loaded rifles and pistols ready to lend a hand," Sam said. He laughed and him and Ben climbed up on their horses. Well, that was just a bit too much for me.

"What about me?" I asked. "Im part of this group too."

"I need you to mind these horses," Jim said. "Just like those Indians have someone minding theirs. See what I mean?"

"Yes sir," I said, but I was mighty disappointed that I wasnt going along with Sam and Ben as they went on down to act as bait for the trap.

They rode along, joking like they was the only ones in the world until they came to a big lightning struck tree that they could use as a bit of cover. Ben walked his horse over to the log and tied on to it with Sam right behind him. They laid out their pistols and rifles and I would have swore they was getting ready for a little nap if I didnt know different.

Those Indians took a long time to creep up on them, but Ben and Sam got up to walk a little ways away from their guns to make water and those Indians snapped right up that bait like rising trout.

A war whoop made me jump near out of my skin although I was waiting for it. Sam and Ben took off back to their guns and jumped behind the tree. Sam shot a buck carrying a lance in one hand and a buffalo shield in the other. Ben hit another and then they pulled up on their pistols and let go with all four bullets.

Now, them Indians had been counting their shots and after that the Indians decided to come right after them. Thats when our boys opened up on them. Those Indians were so surprised that someone was behind them that they stopped long enough for Ben and Sam to finish reloading their rifles. They fired again and that must have confused them Indians cause some took off one way and some took off another.

None made it to the creek, though, or the trees. Jim and me gathered up the horses while the others hunted down the stray Indians that had gone the other way.

We took them horses to San Antonio and sold them and split the money between us. That was the first time I was in town alone without my Pa and I took advantage of it. Everybody wanted to hear the story and bought us a drink every time we told it. I had it down pretty pat by midnight, I tell you, but my head was swimming from all that whiskey and I found a stable and passed out in the straw there. I had me a fine time.

Well, thats how the Rangers got their start. It became sort of official when a group of the men decided they needed to have some sort of militia and they all elected Jim their colonel.

I was given what they called garrison duty and though I didnt like it, I did it.

On their first outing, Jim and his men ran into some Kiowa. Jim had to wade into them with his big knife flashing and those who saw him said it was like watching a lion. And so people took to call us the Young Lions.

I was fifteen when I ran away from home and fought in the Battle of Velasco. That was where some Texians were unlawfully detained by a man named Bradburn. I was in Mr. Elliot C. Buckners company. Strap Buckner, the giant, was killed leading us in the foray along with several of the company. I fought in many a campaign since then. I was even with Bowie at the Grass Fight.

Oh, I joined the Rangers that were sanctioned by the State and can say I was one of the first then too, but nothing was like those early years riding with Jim Bowie and the Young Lions.

Major Ben C. Truman

Many tales exist about Bowie's duels. So many, in fact, that one is hard-pressed in order to separate the truth from legend. Major Truman interviewed an old steamboatman who allegedly was upon the paddlewheeler Rob Roy *when Bowie came to the aid of a young woman whose husband had become the victim of a fleecing by a pair of riverboat gamblers.*

According to the man Major Truman interviewed, in the summer of 1833 this young gentleman and his new bride made a trip up North in the course of which he apparently gathered a large sum of money for investment back in Natchez. The gamblers managed to entice him into a friendly game of "twenty-card poker," a game played with only the tens through the aces and limited to four players, an advantage for crooked gamblers who can control the timbre of the game by limiting the players.

The young man lost everything and was in the process of trying to hurl himself overboard to spare himself and his bride the shame he would encounter when he reached Natchez, when Jim Bowie stepped in and pulled the young man back from the rail. When the bride tearfully made Bowie aware of the situation, Bowie made them promise to wait in their cabin until he had a chance to set things right.

Bowie entered the gaming room and used an old trick to get himself invited into the game by buying a drink and trying to pay for it with a hundred-dollar bill. The gamblers bit and immediately invited Bowie to their table for a friendly turn of the cards. Bowie played carefully, conserving his money. When the riverboat was near Rodney where

it would take on wood, the gamblers made their move. The
pot quickly built to $100,000. The following tells the end
of the tale.—A. J. S.

Well, I was lucky to be in the saloon at the time and saw
what happened. Whilst the betting was going on the stranger
(we didn't find out later that it was Jim Bowie and I wonder
what would have happened if the others knew his name) had
kept his eye on the dealer and had prevented any changing
of cards. Toward the last he saw a card slipped by the dealer
to the man who had made the blind, when, seizing him by
the wrist with one hand, he drew a murderous looking knife
with the other and forced the gambler to lay his cards on
the table face down. All sprang to their feet and the stranger
quietly said that when that hand was raised and it should
be found to contain six cards, he would kill the owner; telling the other to show his cards, he threw down his own
hand, which consisted of four kings and a ten spot. The baffled gambler, livid with rage and disappointment, swore
that the stranger should fight him, demanding, with an oath,
to know who he was anyway. Quietly, and as if in the presence of ladies, the stranger answered, "James Bowie." At
the sound of that name two of the gamblers quailed, for they
knew that the man who bore that name was a terror to even
the bravest; but the third, who had never heard of "James
Bowie," demanded a duel at once. This was acceded to at
once by Bowie, with a smile; pistols—derringers—were the
weapons selected, the hurricane-roof the place, and the time
at once. Sweeping the whole of the money into his hat,
Bowie went to the room where the unhappy wife sat guarding her husband's uneasy slumbers, and rapping on the
door, he handed her, when she had opened it, the hat and its
contents, telling her that if he did not come back, two thirds
of the money was her husband's and the balance his own.

Ascending to the hurricane-roof the principals were placed one upon the top of each wheel-house. This brought them about twelve yards apart, and each was exposed to the other from the knee up. The pistols were handed to them and the gambler's second gave the word, "one, two, three, fire, stop," uttered at intervals of one second each, and they were allowed to fire at any time between the utterance of the words one and stop. As "one" rang out in the clear morning air both raised their weapons, as "three" was heard the gambler's pistol rang out and before the sound had ceased and whilst the word "fire" was being uttered, Bowie's pistol sounded, and simultaneous with this sound the gambler fell, and giving a convulsive struggle rolled off the wheel-house into the river. Bowie coolly blew the smoke out of his pistol, shut down the pan, and going down into the ladies' cabin obtained his hat and divided the money which it contained into three portions. Two of these he gave to the young wife and the other he kept, as it was his own money. Having awakened her husband, the fond wife showed him the money, and told him all she knew about the affair, not having heard of the duel. When the husband became acquainted with all the facts, his gratitude to his benefactor was deep and lasting. Not desiring to be made a hero of, Bowie, when the boat reached Rodney, went ashore.

Judalon de Bornay

Jim Bowie met Judalon de Bornay on his first trip to New Orleans when he traveled there to find a buyer for the Bowie lumber cut at their sawmill in the bayous. It was quite by accident that Bowie met her brother in a coffeehouse and became fast friends with him, their friendship resulting in an invitation to the de Bornay home. There, Bowie met the petite Judalon, whose flawless ivory skin and large, black eyes entranced him. Had this meeting occurred after Bowie acquired the manners and "polish" by which he charmed business associates and Ursula de Veramendi years later, his future would have undergone a drastic alteration. But Bowie was a backwoodsman and although possessed of charming ways, they were not the social manners of an extremely mannered period. Judalon scorned his advances, putting Bowie in a black, brooding melancholy that resulted in a certain recklessness surfacing that caused the death of a dueling master, a M. Contrecourt, whom Bowie killed in a duel, sword against knife, in a darkened room at St. Sylvan's. That was the birth of Bowie as an adventurer.—A. J. S.

M. James Bowie was a buffoon, an ass who had pretensions that we could not tolerate in Orleans society. I remember well when my brother brought him home, awkward, his feet clumsy, hands callused, and trying to appear a gentleman although he did not know how to wear the lace and Spencer coat that my brother had introduced him to. I smothered my laugh and flirted with him, amusing myself with how far I could tease him.

I overestimated once and remember how M. Bowie seized me, bruising my poor arms with his crude fingers, and held me close.

"Judalon," he breathed. "When shall we marry?"

"Release me!" I commanded him sternly.

His eyes widened in surprise, then he smiled. The oaf thought that I, a de Bornay, was teasing with him. He tried to kiss me. Perhaps he did. Well, he did. Yes. For a moment, I almost weakened in spite of myself, then I remember my station in society and his place and I remember his story about broom-jumping and so I did not wish to jump a broom with him, I pushed him away and struck him across his cheek with my fan.

"Brute!" I said, summoning up the most scorn I could to put in my voice. "Did you think that you would be allowed in this house if it were not for my brother? How dare you take such liberties with me? *Sacre!* I shall have you horse-whipped for this!"

And I stormed out of the sitting room, leaving him standing there with the egg upon his face.

I see M. Bowie only once more and it is then I realize my mistake. I have married with Phillipe Cabanal, a weak man whose gambling ruined us in society, forcing us to move to Natchez. I saw M. Bowie there, true, but he did not, or at least pretended not, to see me. Phillipe and I had moved into a small house at the edge of the bluff in not the most respectable part of town. I could not entertain as Phillipe lost our money at the gaming tables. Then, he went into business with M. John A. Murrell and our fortunes rose dramatically. No longer was I *elle est toujours à court d'argent*.

Soon, we were able to move to a more respectable part of town. Phillipe stayed away from the gaming tables and went into business with M. Murrell, selling cotton and speculating in various cargoes for shipment downriver. I do not pretend to know this business, but I was shocked when suddenly the authorities appear at our door and arrest Phillipe. He was, how you say, *il fut pris la main dans le sac*.

Fortunately, our money had been placed in a bank in New Orleans and it was there that I promptly moved before the scandal of Phillipe coming to trial. I pretended that we had been divorced and as such, I was spared ruination within our society. *Je m'en lave les mains*.

I also became the object of several younger men who saw in me a *relever un défi* and in *moment de défaillance* I allowed them their *conquête*. The theater, the ballet, the music. Ah, it was gay times!

It was at the theater that I saw M. Bowie in the company of M. Forrest. I arranged for my escort to approach them.

"Ah, M. Bowie. It is a pleasure to see you," I said, smiling. I knew how I looked. I had spent hours arranging my hair, my gown, cut low to show my breasts, selecting my jewels.

His eyes grew cold. "Is it, Mme. Cabanal?"

"Ah, but I am now again Mlle. de Bornay," I said roguishly, flirting again with him. "I have left Phillipe."

"He is a fortunate man, indeed, then," M. Bowie said.

My escort stepped forward and impulsively slapped M. Bowie's face. "That is not something one says to a lady!"

"You are right," M. Bowie said. "And I would apologize if it had been a lady I addressed!"

My cheeks burned at his words for I knew that others around me had heard his words. My escort then challenged M. Bowie and M. Bowie arranged for his second to meet Dominique You, a pretender to society, one of Jean Lafitte's men.

They met two days later at The Oaks at the Allard Plantation. I heard about it from the young man's second. My poor darling! He tried to play the gentleman to the end, but I should have told him that M. Bowie was no gentleman.

When the referee counted the paces and reached "ten," my darling executed the most appropriate turn-face, but M. Bowie simply leaned around and casually shot him between the eyes.

"A magnificent shot!" exclaimed the second. "But a barbarian made it!"

That afternoon, M. Bowie appeared at my gate. I received him, dressing myself hurriedly in my most becoming gown. He scarce noticed it as he said, "Judalon, I have now killed at least four men on your account. I have no intention of killing a fifth. Henceforth, keep your distance."

"M. Bowie!" I exclaimed indignantly, but the boor turned and left, leaving me alone in my house on Chartis Street.

I believe my servants told of this encounter for visitors to my *salon* became fewer and fewer and when the tiny wrinkles became more apparent, so did the young men.

I am alone. . . .

José Antonio Navarro

In 1833, an epidemic of Asiatic cholera swept over the land, killing many. In Victoria, many, including the great empresario *Don Martin de León and John Austin, the alcalde of San Felipe, fell victim to the Pale Horseman. Whole families were being wiped out. Bowie decided that his family should visit Monclova, where the Veramendis had a summer home away from the heat of San Antonio. Ursula pleaded with her husband to come along with them, but Bowie had business to take care of before traveling to Monclova. In July, the Veramendis left, Ursula and their two children, her parents, and certain members of the household. What they did not know was that the plague had reached also into Coahuila, into Monclova. In September, Bowie learned about the death of his family from a friend of her uncle, José Antonio Navarro, who had received a letter from the Coahuilan city.—A.J.S.*

Please, my good friend, do a favor for us in this, our hour of grief. Poor Bowie is now a widower, and I wish you would in some way advise him of the sad news.

Strange, is it not, that in wanting to save his family, Bowie sent them away to their certain death for the plague has, so far, apparently missed Bexar, if what I read from your letters is true. Sometimes, I wonder if Bowie sent Ursula and his children away for selfish reasons or if he truly was concerned with their health. I suppose it does not matter anymore. The Pale Horseman has ridden hard over our family. All are gone. All.

I suppose you had better tell Bowie to stay away

from here. He can do no good except find his own death and that will serve no purpose except to make him a martyr that no one will remember.

I do not know if I will see you again, my friend. That is now in the hands of God.

Josè Navarro [RUBRIC]

From the Journal of A. J. Sowell

Why? I have been asked this question many times. Why do I have this obsession about James Bowie? I can't quite answer the question, even when I ask it of myself. Admiration? Perhaps. Any person can be subject to the pride that comes with being friends with someone who has made his mark on history, but I think Sam Houston made me wonder about the man who became a hero. Houston told me stories that firmly established the legend in my malleable mind.

When I first met Sam Houston, in 1860, he was sixty-seven and near the end of his life. I was twelve. Houston was desperately trying to stem the tide approaching as the War Between the States, which would result in our secession from the country we had worked so hard to join.

Father and I were in the Capital on Ranger business and we chanced to enter the plaza near Ranger headquarters. Houston sat whittling under a tree, holding court while he talked to various and sundry individuals who happened to pass. He recognized Father and called him over.

Houston was immense, standing over six feet tall and as massive as a granite cliff. He was loud and exuberant, and spoke of himself in the royal person. "Houston says the Union must remain a union. Our differences must be settled in honest debate in the Congress of the United States, not in the individual state legislatures. You never hear me talk of the rights of Southern states because all states have equal rights." That is one of my favorites.

He looked down at me, his eyes twinkling in his tired and seamed face. "Sowell, who's this little ragtag following you?"

Father smiled. "This is my son, Andrew Jackson." I

wondered why he didn't just say "Jack" like usual. But then, Houston pushed that thought from my mind.

"Houston is pleased to meet you, Andrew Jackson Sowell." He stood and gave a little bow. I stammered something about my name being my uncle's name as well, and Houston laughed, the sound booming around the courtyard.

He threw out a huge paw that swallowed up my young hand. "That's a proud name. Houston is pleased to be your servant."

Of course, I knew the name Sam Houston. Who didn't? What I didn't know at that time was just how close he was to the former president whose Hermitage was only a few miles from my father's Tennessee home and whose name I was carrying in honor of him.

Houston asked about Indian depredations in our neck of the woods, and though Father gave him information, it seemed to me that Houston already knew most of it. Gradually, however, the talk turned away from Indians, scoundrels, and politics, and then Houston talked to me. Almost no one knew more tales of frontier Texas than Houston, and he was having a fine time telling these to me when he noticed I was carrying a Bowie knife my grandfather Asa Sowell had made. He asked to see it, admired it, then started telling me about the man the knife was named after: James Bowie.

Well, I knew Jim Bowie's story, or at least I thought I did. My own kinfolk told me about him, but when Houston spoke about his friend, I could almost see him: a tall man with reddish hair, gray eyes, with shoulders like a young Hercules, a soft-spoken Southern gentleman who became a demon when aroused. But as Houston continued his story, a different Bowie began to emerge. I began to see the man who had strong plans for Texas. I watched Father nodding and smiling as Houston spoke, and those little motions and

twitches, smiles and grimaces, made me realize that the
same man could be seen differently by different people.

As Houston continued with his stories, I became more and
more intrigued by the differences between what he remembered and what I had learned from my own family and
others who had offered a tale or two to my boyish demands.

That night as Father and I retired to our room, I sat at the
little oaken desk and made some notes in a cheap, ruled
notebook that Mother had made me take along on the trip,
demanding that I write something on what had happened
every day in lieu of spending the same time in school. I remember taking the notebook from her thin hands with a
deep sigh about how she was spoiling what was supposed
to be a fun trip by turning it into a school trip. But now, as
I wrote, trying to imitate the rhythm of Houston's speech
and laboriously trying to spell what fell so easily from his
lips, I decided that I would try to find out more about Bowie.

The next day when I found Houston sitting comfortably
under the tulip tree in the middle of the plaza, fragrant whiskey fumes bubbling gently from his lips, I asked him if he
would tell me where I could find out more about Jim Bowie.
He grinned, rumpled my hair, then said, "Why don't you
write Bowie's people? Some of them are still alive, and
they'd probably be more than willing to tell you what you
want to know. Houston can get you started. He still has the
address of Bowie's mother back on Bayou Teche. Now,
Houston reckons she's most likely dead, but there'll be
someone there related to old Jim, more than likely."

Mother helped. Even then, it took me nearly two weeks
to get those letters written. And while they were gone, I fidgeted and squirmed with each mail delivery, fuming about
how long it took the mail to get out of Texas and back.

One day, though, I got a surprise: Bowie's mother was
still alive! There was the proof, a package from Elvie Bowie

filled with letters and documents from both her husband Rezin and her son Rezin. The family portraits that she drew gave me a picture of the young Jim Bowie riding alligators in the swamp, fighting, running slaves, finding adventure wherever he could.

I wrote her another letter, thanking her for the package. She answered again, giving me a little more information. That was the start of a long exchange of letters between us that continued until she died. By then, I had a string of letters going out on a regular basis to people all over Texas and places beyond. But the picture I wanted of the man remained opaque.

It still is.

I was fifteen the year Sam Houston died. Before he died, he helped me see history in a different light. Now, as I try to write about Jim Bowie and the Texas War of Independence, I can see the events that led me to contemplating a discussion of heroes and Jim Bowie. I had been working at collecting stories and letters about Bowie for a few years. Strange, that while I had been told dozens of stories and met Bigfoot Wallace, that remarkable frontiersman who showed me Bowie's rifle and told me stories, I still did not know Jim Bowie. Who was he? A brawler? Gentleman? Patriot? Land swindler? I had no idea.

In 1862, I went to Austin with my uncle and stayed at an inn called The Alamo. Just about everywhere you went in Texas those days you'd find something called The Alamo. Usually a saloon, although there were a few hotels and inns and one sporting house up near Waco named after the old mission, although few had any cottonwood trees around them to warrant the name.

This particular inn was a long, low, adobe and wood structure with a tile roof. Tile roofs had become rather commonplace in Texas by this time as people had civilized themselves right out of the old sod roofs that were home to cockroaches, scorpions, and tarantulas that had a habit of falling into someone's food or bed. Now, I wonder if that might not be one of the reasons we have so many people with bad teeth in Texas: they just got that way from grinding down on the dirt that trickled into their meat and beans.

Anyway, Austin was a new town, mostly mud or grass with a large number of newly constructed buildings stretching down Main Street, most of them still raw lumber. Some had hired old Mexicans to build them something along the lines of haciendas, but a lot of people still bristled whenever they saw anything that could be construed Mexican.

The Alamo in Austin stood a ways away from what you could call the "city proper," I guess. An adobe wall wrapped around a space in front of the building to create a sort of courtyard wide enough for a six-horse team to turn a coach around. A porch had been added onto the building where someone had scattered a bunch of wicker chairs. Double doors led inside to a common room. I remember those doors: someone had spent a lot of time carving a picture of Samson fighting the Philistines into the oak wood.

"Andrew Jackson Sowell."

I turned and looked automatically into the deep shadow at the far end of the porch where a tall, white-haired man with a deeply lined face grinned back at us.

"Hello, Sam," my uncle said, clumping down the boards. He stretched out a hand. "You're looking well's could be expected."

"I am." Houston peered at me, then shook his huge, shaggy head. "Don't tell Houston that this is Houston's little friend from San Antonio a few years back."

"I've grown a mite," I said. I put my hand cautiously in his huge palm: meathooks, we called 'em then.

He laughed and solemnly shook my hand. Uncle Andy hawked and spat out into the thick dust. "Well, why you drinking alone, Sam?" he asked. "There something wrong with the Texicans hereabouts that they ain't buying President-Governor-by-God-Sam-Houston liquor?"

The smile slipped from Houston's face. His lips tightened for a moment, then he let out a huge sigh. "It's this war, A. J.," he said. "Houston didn't think it was necessary. He still doesn't, for that matter, but Texes is still Houston's home and he still believes in her laws—even if they're being passed by fools who bray like Balaam's Ass." He glanced around to see if anyone was listening, then hitched his chair closer to us, lowering his voice. "Now, Houston wouldn't want this to get around, but he became a teeto-taler a few years ago." A heavy eyebrow quirked. "Houston's reputation was damaged a mite by that."

They laughed heartily. I chortled along with them, but I was a bit puzzled as to why old Sam wasn't revered by all Texicans. But I was too young then to see the weaknesses of men who had been caught up in the excitement of war, a last adventure in a time when many had given up the possibility for adventure. Houston had had enough of war in his time to understand its brutishness. He also believed firmly in the sanctity of the Union—especially since we had fought the Texas War for Independence so we could join that Union.

Today, a man like Houston would be laughed at, but Houston was positive that the United States had a destiny to rule everything from one ocean to the next and that internal squabbles between states should be fought out in Congress and not on the battlefield that pit brother against brother, son against father. His highly vocal opinions caused many to belittle him. Maybe that's one of the reasons that he died the next year.

Our business kept us at The Alamo for a few days. It was a great opportunity for me, although I didn't recognize it at the time. Later, I was able to piece together some of Houston's views, and jot down some of his opinions and political maneuverings. I listened to the stories people exchanged with him when they came to sit in the sun with him. I learned quite a bit in those few days about how the Texas government came about. Before that trip, I assumed everyone was a Texas patriot and that they shared the same ideas about Texas. Of course, when you're fifteen, you're positive that you have the right idea about everything and that everyone who doesn't agree with you must be either bullheaded or stayed out in the sun too long until they became hydrophobic. Maybe the reason I thought that way was because I was afraid that if too many disagreed with me, I'd have to reexamine my own thoughts, and what young man wants to do that?

When we were alone, Houston spoke long and in great detail about our history. He knew those men well who formed Texas. Maybe he was trying out his arguments on me before he voiced his opinions to those politicians who had frozen him out. Maybe they should have listened to him, because Houston sought to fulfill a dream while others simply wanted to carve great fortunes out of the Texas wilderness.

I think now that the war for Texas's Independence was a foregone conclusion from the time Santa Anna became emperor of Mexico. In a way, I supposed Santa Anna wasn't entirely wrong in trying to stop Texas from becoming Texas. The great experiment when Mexico opened its borders to people settling from the United States had gotten greatly out of hand. At the time, though, Mexico had a lot of land and too few people to put on it. The Mexicans also had a lot of money problems. It didn't take much, I expect, for Mexico to put two-and-two together and hope for six to realize the profit they could make from selling land to certain land speculators called *empresarios*. I guess they didn't figure, however, that the United States had too many people who wanted land.

Anyway, a Connecticut man, Moses Austin, applied for

land from the Mexican government, but before he could come to Texas with the three hundred families he had recruited, he died of pneumonia. His son, Stephen, took over the old man's dream, though, and led those families to the two hundred thousand acres of promised land that Mexico had set aside for them. It didn't take much for others to see a profit in that, though. Men like Jim Bowie soon figured out that they didn't have to attach themselves to a man like Austin. They could become *empresarios* themselves.

Only ten years after Austin's people settled in Texas, the people from the States outnumbered the Mexicans—a subject that caused great concern to some of the political leaders of Mexico. The result was a new dike of immigration laws to stop the flood of people from the States.

One night, Houston took dinner with us. We sat in the common room, talking for quite some time. I realize now that he was laying a foundation for me to comprehend the personalities involved in the beginning of Texas's fight, but it was the next morning before I started getting the full story.

I woke early and wandered down the stairs to the little plaza. Houston was already awake, sitting under a chinaberry tree, whittling on a piece of jackpine. At first, I thought he was studying the work in his hands, but when I came closer to watch, I saw his hands were moving mechanically, his mind elsewhere.

"Come to sit with an old man, Jack," he said.

"Find me one, and I'll do it," I answered.

He laughed, pleased with my response, and moved over on the bench to make room for me. It didn't take long before we were talking about the War. I guess I steered him in that direction, though, because I wanted to pick his brains a little more about Jim Bowie, but like most adults, Houston took a roundabout way of getting to what I wanted to know. He was a natural tease, though, so maybe that had something to do with it, too.

"Well, Stephen Austin came across the Red River with three hundred families that had given most of their savings to Austin for land that Mexico gave free to Austin," he said. He stopped and reached down beside the bench for a tin cup and took a long swallow. I frowned. I thought Austin had bought the land, but here was Houston telling me different. I mentioned this to him. He shook his shaggy head and smiled.

"Yes," he said. "That's what the Austins would like most people to think. Especially now that they're trying so hard for respectability. Makes them appear rather saintly instead of opportunists. But they weren't saintly, Andy; they were just people who had figured out how to make a little money from nothing. Some would call them land pirates, Houston expects, and maybe they were. They probably had to grease the skids a little, but the Austin fortunes were greatly improved by the sale of their land. Now let's see . . . hmm. Houston was still in the States in 1821 when Austin brought all his people in, but stories from these families say that Austin was always jealous of his position." He winked at me. "Like Houston, but with less cause.

"Being fair, Houston thinks Austin always cared for his people and Texas. He had the respect of the Mexican government and many of the other settlers in Texas."

"I've always heard that Austin was a good leader," I interrupted.

"Well, he thought he was; that's for sure. To a point, he was, too. Until he wrote a letter to the Mexican government that got him arrested, he was always pretty sure his decisions were the correct ones, but two years in a Mexican prison changed a lot of his thinking." He winked and tapped a thick broad forefinger along the side of his nose. I smiled.

"The colony was a good one, wan't it?"

"Austin had good people. Most of them, anyway. He didn't bring down any of the Gone To Texas rascals that came later, but good, hardworking farmers looking to carve a living out of the land here." He peered closely at me. "Ambition is a good thing if it is coupled with a habit of hard work. The success of this country comes from people who want to do better and are willing to go out and sweat over a plow or an ax. Men who are willing to hunt up land and raise cattle and horses."

"That's good, ain't it? Isn't it?" I amended when he frowned.

He nodded. "Well, it made Austin worry about his position. He was their leader, but he was really not cut out to be a leader. He always thought he had to dictate to his people instead of leading them. There's a difference, you see?" I shook my head. He frowned and took another deep swallow from the tin cup. "Well, Andy, it's like this. There's two ways of being a leader and being a success at it. Either corrupt those following you, or make them want you because they believe in what you believe. Austin had doubts, but he couldn't bring himself to express those doubts. He couldn't stand others to see him as a human being," he said. He frowned thoughtfully. "Houston doesn't expect you to understand, but it's hard to let others see you as a human. We all want to look bigger." He laughed. "Maybe we all want to be gods." He shook his head.

"Well, Stephen took over for his father, but he wasn't Moses. He snapped out orders and expected others to jump at them. But Texicans don't hop just because another man hollers 'Frog!' "

He paused for a second, then said, "Jim Bowie had cold, gray eyes. When he looked at you, you just simply had to accommodate him. If he told you to attack hell with a bucket of well water, you'd just naturally do it because you wouldn't want to tell him you couldn't. That made a big difference between Bowie and Austin. People just naturally wanted to follow Bowie. They just naturally shied away from Austin."

"Is that because Bowie corrupted them or made them want to follow him?"

He laughed and took his watch from a vest pocket, opening it. "A good question, Andy. A real good question. But Houston is a little peckish now. Let's go get something to eat."

I waited until we sat down to platters of eggs and ham. He piled his plate high, and took a few bites, chewing thoughtfully.

"Mr. Houston," I said carefully. "What can you tell me about Jim Bowie?"

He continued to chew silently for a long minute and I was afraid he wasn't going to answer. Then, a tiny grin tugged at the corner of his mouth.

"Well, now," he said softly. "That's rather hard to do. The man and this country are one. To understand one, you have to understand the other."

I groaned inwardly. I could see what he was fixing to do. Houston liked nothing better than to lecture to a captive audience. It's something about old men: when their bellies grumble and their corns ache on a regular basis, they like to remember their youth, and Houston seemed as old as the hills.

"Well, now. Let's see." He shoveled a load of ham in his mouth, chewed and swallowed. "A man named Don Augustin Iturbide, a high Spanish officer, used a half million dollars Spain had given him to start a rebellion. He hired two men, a Guerrero and Victoria, to help him set up a national congress in 1822 that elected Iturbide president, admiral of the navy and generalissimo of the army. The next year, Iturbide was named emperor by the peasants, the rabble, and the soldiers. To make it legal, he called another Congress, then surrounded the men with bayonets until they confirmed him emperor, then he dissolved the Congress and sent everybody home.

"But there was another man around them who took a dim view of what happened and in December, General López de Santa Anna revolted. Over the next few years, Mexico existed in a state of chaos until a new constitution was confirmed in 1824. But the funny thing is that once someone can see how powerful a dictator is, why, then, it's just natural to want the same things. Slavery was abolished in 1824, but they also abolished other things, too, like Masonic lodges and such. In 1830, they outlawed immigration.

"War broke out in the south and the government opened up Texas for immigration, hoping to get a fighting force on its frontiers. But when Texans outnumbered the Mexicans, why then Santa Anna just slammed the door shut and wouldn't let any more in."

"I got it," I said. "Some Mexicans gave rights to us and others took them away. Mother told me some of that, but I didn't really get it settled until now."

"Well, that's what happened," he said, pushing his empty plate away from him. He fingered a cigar from a vest, bit the end and spat it on the floor, and lighted it with a lucifer.

"We lost a lot of good men over that," he said softly, rolling the cigar around in his mouth. "Both Americans and Mexicans, Andy. Don't get to thinking that all the Mexicans followed Santa Anna. A lot of Texicans are doing that these days. That kind of thinking's going to cause a lot of problems in the years to come."

I never forgot that prophecy.

Sam Houston

Sam Houston was another giant, not only in stature, but in the things that he accomplished. It is almost impossible to relate in a few lines all his achievements, nor is there space to tell of all his setbacks. He was both military man and politician. Unlike many who carved two separate careers out of a lifetime, Houston actually fought and his own blood was spilt in several encounters with his enemies.

He was governor of Tennessee and Texas, president of the Republic of Texas, and was once seriously considered as a presidential candidate for the United States. He served as a spokesman for the Indians, yet he was also responsible for killing more than most any other man.

Sam Houston also wrote about James Bowie. The two were good friends, possibly drinking companions, but always there was a trust between the two. Houston, who had habits that drove lesser men to distraction, such as referring to himself as "Houston" instead of "I," tried several times to get Bowie promotions during the Texas War for Independence, but Bowie's reputation was considered a hindrance. At least, that was the excuse Houston's political enemies gave when they blocked Bowie's promotion for his colonelcy. And yet everyone used Bowie's abilities to organize and to fight.

Houston and Bowie traveled much together in the early 1830s. They also attended several council meetings, and they must have had similar views on the treatment of Indians, because Bowie was sent on several errands to the tribe.—A. J. S.

Bowie? Well, there's an enigma, a walking contradiction if ever Houston saw one, half-truth and half-fiction. To understand Bowie's role in the birth of Texas, you need to understand something of the politics involved. People like Jim Bowie—and Ben Milam—were speculators, but they were also visionaries. They understood that Texas was the greatest opportunity in the New World for fabulous wealth.

Cotton, cattle, mines, lumber—all of these might be found aplenty in Texas where land was open for settling. All it took was a special person.

The Indians of Texas had never really been conquered. Houston doesn't think they ever will be, for they are like ghosts in the night, now you see them, now you don't. In the 1820s, Mexico decided that it would be best to bring in settlers from other countries to provide a buffer against its villages upon the frontier. Thousands of square miles were opened up for settlement. It was a time when the common man—yes, even the poor man—could get rich beyond his wildest dreams.

As an additional incentive to encourage settlers, Mexico arranged for no tax revenue to be levied against the property. On the surface, it appeared to be an ideal situation for a young man. But what else could Mexico do? None of their own citizens wanted to move north and face the Comanches and other Indians. Mexico then sweetened the pot by inviting the new settlers to become Mexican citizens and embrace the Catholic faith.

In 1824, Mexico established a very democratic constitution that offered the citizens of Mexico a decent form of government. Unfortunately, the presidents of Mexico demonstrated little compunction in upholding that constitution. They did find, however, that the independent, free-minded Americans they had invited into Texas were not as complacent as the *peons* they were used to dealing with in the interior.

James Bowie was riding hard from South Texas to Nacogdoches. I know not the reason, for he did not tell Houston. Though Houston suspects it was because Santa Anna had ordered the arrest of all the members of the Monclova council of which Bowie was one.

James Bowie's horse was lathered. It had been ridden hard and it was showing signs of becoming windbroken.

Houston was staying at an inn. There were several of the men who would become Texas Rangers with him.

James Bowie was asked to go speak to Chief Bowles of the Cherokee. He was told the mission was urgent, and he was willing, but his horse was too tired to go on.

Bowie came up to Houston. He greeted Houston and said, "I need a horse. Can I borrow yours?"

Houston replied in the negative. "I have but one horse, and I need him."

Houston did have a fine thoroughbred horse from Tennessee.

"I'm going to take him," Bowie said and left the room.

Houston turned to Caiaphas Ham. "Do you think it is right to give up my horse to Bowie?"

"Perhaps it would be better under the circumstances," replied the loyal Ham.

"Damn him, let him take the horse," Houston said. Bowie was a friend and why should something as lowly as a horse, even a fine horse, break up a friendship?

Before Houston came down to Texas, Andrew Jackson, President of the United States at the time, asked me to see if Texas could be a viable part of the Union. The United States was like a twenty-year-old in a ten-year-old's trousers; fitting to burst its seams what with the massive settlement of its lands within its self-imposed boundaries.

One of the first people Houston met was Jim Bowie. A great gentleman, Jim could have been the prince of politicians had he only turned his charm into that arena. He was a natural diplomat, intelligent, fearless, with a reputation that scared the living bejesus out of his opponents.

In 1832, Jim was riding high; he had married a beautiful and charming woman at the top of the society ladder and had begun his family. He doted on that family; it meant everything to him, and he worked himself into a lather, riding back and forth between Texas and Arkansas and Louisana, speculating on land with his brothers John and Rezin.

Unfortunately, that speculation was earning him a reputation as an unsavory character. He bought many old Spanish grants and promptly resold them only to have the title claims be challenged in court. Of course, people who knew Jim's reputation were a bit reluctant to file charges against him on the off-chance that he might take offense and they would be facing the business end of a pistol or the edge of his knife.

Houston remembers once when he was in Bexar having the odd drink or two in a little *cantina* and Jim walked in. Houston called his name and Bowie peered through the gloom until he found Houston sitting in the corner. His face brightened and he came down the bar to greet Houston.

"Hello, Sam," he said. He called to the bartender to bring a bottle of Saltillo brandy. We sat and worked our way through many subjects, including politics, as we worked our way through that bottle. Houston asked him if he would be willing to help Texas move up in the world.

"You know," he said softly, his eyes disfocusing into the distance, "I love Texas. Ever since I first came here more than fifteen years ago, I've known the potential that is here. I bought land here; I sold land here; and I sold land to those people I thought would make good citizens. Good citizens make a good state."

Houston looked swiftly around the room, for to talk about statehood at this time in Texas was a bit like tempting a rattlesnake to strike.

"Lower your voice," Houston said. "But Houston agrees with you. Take a look at Tennessee. People thought nothing but riffraff lived there and now one of that riffraff is President of the United States."

"True," Jim said. He took a large swallow of brandy, washing it down in installments. "But at least those people had clear claim to their land titles."

"Ah, now, Jim, that isn't your fault. You know you bought that land fair and square from the people who were on it at the time."

"Tell that to Roane," he said dryly, mentioning the Attorney General who was trying to bring Jim to court.

"It's politics," Houston said, trying to dismiss the situation with a magnanimous wave. "Hell, everybody is getting stung by that damn Roane."

"We need a consul in Mexico City who can speak for us," Jim said, ignoring me. "My father-in-law is an honest man and could do a lot of good for us in Mexico City if we let him."

"What about Hotspurs like that one over there?" Houston said, nodding at a man by the bar who was busily damning the Mexican government.

Jim leaned back in his chair and gave the man his attention. The man looked a month from a bath; his dirty shirt hung outside his frayed trousers. Greasy hair stuck out from under a hat and he scratched constantly at his beard as if lice were nibbling at his chin.

"All we need to do is tell that bastard Veramendi that we don't want his damn government anymore, and throw all them damn greasers back across the Rio Bravo," he said garrulously.

Jim rose and crossed to the man. He leaned up against the bar and eyed him. The man obviously didn't know who Jim was for he ignored him.

"What if Veramendi doesn't want to leave?" he asked mildly.

"Then, we'll cut his black heart out and mail it back to Mexico City," the man guffawed.

"What if his family doesn't want to go?" Jim asked.

Houston could see that someone had whispered Jim's name to the people near the man. A space began to widen around him.

"What the hell?" he said. "We'll send them along the same way."

"What about that Jim Bowie?" Jim asked. "I hear he's not one to be pushed."

Houston leaned back in my chair, watching carefully. Houston was beginning to enjoy the little melodrama opening up in front of me. The man shook his head.

"Jim Bowie? Hell, he's a scoundrel and thief. Look at who he married: a greaser." The man laughed and raised his glass, draining half of it. A thin trickle of raw whiskey ran down into his beard.

Houston doesn't know how far Jim would have played it, but at that time, the door swung open and Caiaphas Ham and Ben McCulloch staggered in. They spotted Jim immediately and called out to him.

"Bowie! Damn you, buy us a drink."

The man turned pale beneath his layers of dirt. His eyes

swung down to Jim's side and registered on the huge knife there. He swallowed, his large Adam's apple moving up and down.

"Jim Bowie," he said. The words were a statement, but Jim answered them anyway.

"Well," he said, squaring his shoulders. "I said my piece and I won't back away from a land thief." He tried to pull his pistol from his pants, but Jim stepped in and hit him once: a short, clean shot that sounded like an axe going into oak, and the man fell backwards, out cold.

Houston decided then and there that Texas needed men like Jim Bowie and if we needed men like him, we sure as hell needed him. Houston spent the rest of the evening and two bottles of whiskey convincing him to join our ranks.

Houston has never regretted that decision.

I was twenty-two when I fought the Wichita Indians as a Texas Ranger, and even though I was raised on the frontier and was almost captured by an Indian when I was only six, I had never seen the kind of violence that occurs when many men fight as in battle. It is not an easy thing to put into words. There was blood and body parts scattered throughout the battleground. Men groan in pain and it is a solemnizing change from the demonic howling that pierced the sound of your heart pounding only moments before.

Your concentration seems so intense in battle that you don't even hear the sound of your gun being discharged. Afterwards, the problem is a different one; then your ears ring in the silence. Of course, all of this has to be put into perspective since at first you are relieved at being alive and so you don't notice anything about the enemy except they are not standing and you are. You want to scream with joy, and some do, but then the shock ends and the pain strikes. Every muscle seems to be bruised, strained, or both. Some men start crying for help, others crawl off to tend themselves, still others wait patiently for someone to come look at them.

You can tell a lot about a man by the way he stoically deals with gashes that go bone deep, or those who complain at the slightest scratch. I guess that is why I have always been fascinated by those men who are willing to go through such trials without a thought of consequences.

Every time I see an article about the Alamo, or Jim Bowie, I save it. Ever since Sam Houston got me interested

in true History instead of stories. I have tried to keep notes
about those things that happened in the early days of Texas,
and in Bowie's case, what happened in Louisiana and
Arkansas.

In 1870 I met a man who called himself Pierre Douchet.
He claimed to have been a member of Jean Lafitte's crew
in Galveston. I clearly remember the day I met this garru-
lous old man. I was twenty-two years old and assigned to a
company of Texas Rangers. This information about Bowie
came to me when I and several of my company rode into a
sleepy little town in August of that year.

It was baking hot outside, somewhere around 100 degrees, and we wanted to cut the dust from our mummified
throats. We saw the cantina and with a whoop descended
on it. We hitched our horses to the rail and sauntered into
the cool darkness. No one who hasn't been horseback in
mid-summer can possibly imagine what we felt when we
stepped into that cool adobe building.

A round-faced Mexican bartender stood behind a plank
bar while a small, weather-beaten, gray-headed old man sat
in one of the chairs. The bartender showed only a hint of a
smile when he asked what we wanted to drink. I ordered a
beer and as I waited, I considered the other man, dressed
in canvas pants and a striped shirt, with a broad leather belt
from which a bone-handled knife hung on his right side.
The old man was complaining about the quality of the
"grog," as he called the whiskey.

"Lafitte would have strapped you over a cannon for
serving such piss to real men," he complained. He looked
at us, his eyes wavering, slightly out of focus.

"Rangers," I said quickly.

The old man grinned, and mumbled to himself.

"What?" Jimmy Jones, our youngest recruit, asked. He
leaned towards the old man. "What did you say?"

"I said that you need real whiskey to face the Indians, not so?"

"You claiming we need barley courage?" Jimmy asked.

"No, no. Just real whiskey. Not this . . ." the old man spluttered as he searched for the right word.

"Here, here," the bartender said hurriedly. He reached beneath the bar and brought out a dusty bottle. "There's no need for trouble, now. Right? Is this not so? There, now. All friends. Right?"

A nervous tic began in his cheek as he handed the bottle to me and gestured that I should take it to the old man. I grinned and crossed the dirt floor and pulled out a chair opposite the old man.

As we drank, I mentioned Bowie's name and, much to my surprise, I discovered that Douchet had been present the night when Bowie fought a duel sitting down and nailed to a log by his britches.

"But," Douchet said, "the fight was not over a slave as has been told. No, no. It was over a woman. Bowie cut his man to ribbons before he kill him. Lafitte was so pleased that he sell Bowie slaves at good price. But," he shook his head, "that man! Lafitte was right to make the quick deal and get rid of him."

"How so?" I asked.

Douchet closed one eye in a slow wink, squinting at me. Finally, he nodded his head and said, "All right. I tell you. He is the only man who frightened me."

"Why?"

"His eyes. Gray, but cold like the sea. He was . . . hmm . . . death."

I put our conversation down to the drink that Douchet had been pouring down his gullet. Later, after he told other stories about Bowie's "blackbirding" days, I wondered why he was so reluctant to talk about Bowie. The man had been dead for many years, by then. How could Bowie have generated so much fear in an old pirate? Was it because of the cruelty that he saw in Bowie when Bowie used his knife to slice up his challenger before killing him? Somehow, I doubted that, for surely the old pirate had seen many other cruel tortures performed by others during his long career. But somehow, there must have been something unusual enough about Bowie to make the old pirate fear him even now.

"No," Douchet said, when I brought the question up to him again. "No, it is really very simple. Too many people try to find hidden meanings behind the man. But men are not hard to understand. Especially Bowie. He was easy to understand. He was Death. That is all. That is enough."

He shrugged and reached for another drink.

*On October 6, 1835, Sam Houston was appointed
Commander-in-Chief of the Nacogdoches Department.
This empowered him to raise troops, organize forces, and
do whatever pertained to the carrying out of his duties in
that office. Soon, news came to the Texans in Bexar that
General Cos was leading four hundred men to confiscate
goods from the citizens, who promptly elected Stephen
F. Austin Commander-in-Chief of the Gonzales forces on
October 19.*

*Stephen Austin was the son of Moses Austin, an empre-
sario who received 200,000 acres to parcel out to three
hundred families. Stephen Austin gathered five hundred
troops and prepared to march on Cos in order to defend
Texas property. One volunteer was James Bowie, who
arrived on a small gray mare with six men from Louisiana,
his famous knife secured in his sash and a rifle slung from
his saddle.*

*On October 22, Bowie and Captain Fannin, who attended
the United States Military Academy at West Point for two
years, were assigned a scouting expedition. They were to
reconnoiter the missions of San Francisco de la Espada
and San José de Miguel de Aguayo and gather supplies for
the army. Juan Seguin, whose ranch was south, had
offered provisions to the army.*

*On October 24, Colonel Bowie asked for more men to
guard the large stretch of road. Though Austin was to refer
to Bowie as Colonel, he never actually gave Bowie a commission, a sore point that was never reconciled. —A. J. S.*

Early morning, 22 October

General Austin has ordered Jim Bowie and myself on a scout. We have three duties to perform: establish friendly contact with Texas Mexicans, send back food for the troops, discover where the Mexicans are keeping their horse herd, and choose a mission that will serve as a fortified position to control the Goliad Road.

Late afternoon

We have just sent a message to General Austin. Colonel Bowie also has suggested we point out a campsite for the army that will be most strategic. Colonel Bowie seems to have a natural aptitude for organization that translates well to command. Although he has not received his command from Austin, his men elected him to that rank when he led a company of rangers against the savages who inhabit the wilder portions of the country in the West.

Tomorrow we head for the missions San José and San Juan.

23 October

We had a hot dusty ride and found little of interest. Little food and less of military importance. I am even more impressed with Bowie. He maintained our pace, yet still looks the gentleman. His command of Spanish and the sheer magnitude of his knowledge of both the land and the people of the area have made the trip much less tedious than otherwise.

24 October

Jim and I are taking our ninety men on a scout. There seems to be a strain between General Austin and Jim. I do not understand why, yet I have been in enough councils now to see the harsh looks between them. Where does that leave me if I must some day have to decide which leader to follow? What happens if I have conflicting orders?

27 October

Jim and I were sent to find a good campsite for the army so that Austin can move into a good defensive position. We found the perfect campsite only one-fourth mile from Mission Concepción.

Bowie has broken our command down into four companies to be commanded by Captains Andrew Briscoe, Robert Coleman, Michael Goheen, and Valentine Bennet. Additionally, he has placed our men in pickets that can provide early warning if the Mexican Army travels up the road from Goliad. It also puts Cós's troops between our troops if he attacks.

We were reminded of our deadly position when we bedded down for the night. A cannon roared in the distance and a cannon ball landed near. Altogether, six huge chunks of iron were fired at us. There is no damage—except to our peace of mind.

29 October

I have just discovered that Jim and I were expected back the same day. Austin has written a document that states any order not followed to the last detail will be grounds for court-martial. It seems as though he is aiming this directly at Jim.

The men are not happy with Austin's proclamation. They believe that during a war there must be some room for initiative. I also believe that some of them suspect that Austin is baiting Jim, and Jim is an extremely popular man with the army.

31 October

Austin has received reinforcements and supplies. We now have almost the same number of men as General Cós. The town of Bexar is surrounded. We have kept our position and Austin has placed troops around the city.

Colonel Bowie has, under his own authority, sent a message to General Cós offering to discuss a peaceful solution to the situation. But he received no answer. Instead, we received orders from Austin to move to a more forward position.

1 November

Austin had received word that two companies of Mexican cavalry were willing to desert if given the opportunity. We are that opportunity. We received no answer.

2 November

Austin has called a council of war to determine a course of action. There were twenty-six officers. The question was whether or not to attack the town since we now had more men and supplies. Major Benjamin Smith was the leader of the group who want an immediate attack. He lost.

Bowie returned to our command. He delivered the decision to his own officers of which there were twenty-one.

I rode with Jim Bowie. Many times. I was a Young Lion, and I was with him on 26 November 1835 when Deaf Smith told Jim about a troop of Mexican cavalry a few miles from where the army was camped.

We attacked the Mexicans and a sharp battle ensued. What I mean is we shot about fifty of them and lost two of our own men. We tried to grab up the horse and find out what kind of supplies they were bringing into San Antonio, which we called "bear" then.

The bundles were filled with grass. Can you imagine that? More'n fifty men killed for a bunch of grass to feed their livestock in the city. There were two battles fought before we could try to take San Antonio, and Jim Bowie won both of them, and it was because he won the grass fight that we were able to take San Antonio.

Andrew J. Sowell,
grandfather to the writer

They voted fourteen to seven in favor of this decision and then voted to join Austin's group north of town.

Bowie took this as a sign of unrest in his leadership, and resigned his command of the division.

Austin accepted gladly.

4 November

Bowie was right. Our troops are down to 450 and morale is poor. Many troops have simply gone home.

22 November

We have been waiting for almost one month. The attack on Bexar has been discussed and postponed so many times it is now impossible to generate enthusiasm for the attack.

26 November

Deaf Smith galloped up to the commander and reported a Mexican cavalry column five miles away. Bowie led a force to scout them.

Col James Bowie, Volunteer Aid:

You will proceed with the first division of Captain Fannin's company and others attached to that division and select the best and most secure position that can be had on the river, as near Bejar as practicable to encamp the army tonight, keeping in view in the selection of this position pasturage and the security of the horses, and the army from night attacks of the enemy.

You will also reconnoiter, so far as time and circumstances will permit, the situation of the outskirts of the town and the approaches to it, whether the houses have been destroyed on the outside, so as to leave every approach exposed to the raking of the cannon.

You will make your report with *as little delay as possible*, so as to give time to the army to march and take up its position before night. Should you be attacked by a large force, send expresses *immediately* with the particulars.

By order P W Grayson, Aid-de-camp

S. F. Austin.

The self-styled Colonel Bowie has asked constantly for more men, first fifty, then one hundred and fifty. It seems that he fancies himself more than just a bravo, but also a full-fledged soldier. I placed him in co-command with Captain Fannin who should be able to keep Bowie in line. I think, though, that he has taken command away from Fannin.

I intend to send a message to Bowie asking for a quick reconnoiter and report of enemy movement to which I will bring the army. I have also written a proclamation that will give me the power to court-martial any man who does not follow my orders.

Bowie's long reconnoiter is splitting my force while Mexican troops constantly move closer.

28 October

Morning found us surrounded by fog filtering out the sun. This, however, did not stop Mexican troop movement which began about 7:30 or 8:00. About three hundred soldiers advanced upon our position. Henry Karnes was standing picket when the Mexican cavalry saw him and fired upon him. The first shot caused him to yell, "The damned rascals have shot out the bottom of my powder horn." Another soldier was hit by a bullet that deflected off his knife. He now has a black and purple imprint of the knife on his side.

Skirmishing lasted about two hours. The Mexican infantry and artillery practically encircled us. Bowie shouted, "Keep under cover, boys, and reserve your fire. We haven't a man to spare."

Excerpt from a Letter to A. J. Sowell from Noah Smithwick

The Texian victory at Conception happened because of Jim Bowie. Jim Bowie was a natural born leader: he never needlessly spent a bullet or imperiled a life. His choice of ground was excellent. He was able to use that riverbank to cover our movement until we were right up on them. We suffered only one killed and one wounded, the enemy lost over 100 close to one-third of their entire force.

Grapeshot and canister rattled in the pecan trees overhead, but we were dug in behind a ditch and the shot did very little damage.

The Mexicans advanced to about three hundred yards, and Bowie calmly commanded, "Call your targets and fire." He then sighted on a sergeant who was overseeing the charging of the cannons. "The fat sergeant—bet you two-bits I'll hit him."

Noah Smithwick took the bet and lost.

Fire became very effective. Mexican soldiers were dropping too regularly for them to maintain their position. Their commander ordered a charge and Bowie ordered Coleman's company to reinforce the point of attack. All the movement was accomplished while staying under the cover of the bank so the men were able to inflict heavy casualties while sustaining few.

Twice and then three times the enemy charged and each time they were seriously damaged. When they withdrew, we crept closer to the cannon.

Only about thirty minutes of this intense battle passed

when Bowie saw the opportunity and charged with his men, crying, "The cannon and victory."

Such is Bowie's charisma that all the Texans yelled the same and leaped up to join him. Bowie was first at the cannon and with another man turned it around and fired upon the fleeing Mexicans.

When I asked him why he did not follow the Mexicans, he said, "Had it been possible to have communicated with you, General Austin, and brought you up earlier, the victory would have been conclusive and Bexar would have been ours before sundown."

Undated Entry in Austin's Journal

Bowie is a hero. He has won the battle of Concepción. But, he has done it by disobeying my orders. Now, my own men are refusing my orders after Bowie complained the fortifications at Bexar were too strong. I have encamped and am now preparing for a siege.

Official Account of the Action of the 28th ult., at the Mission of Conception, near Bejar

Dear Sir,—In conformity with your order of the 27th inst., we proceeded with the division composed of ninety-two men, rank and file, under our joint command, to examine the Missions above Espada, and select the most eligible situation near Bejar, for the encampment of the main army of Texas. After carefully examining that of San José (having previously visited San Juan) we marched to that of Conception, and selected our ground in a bend of the river San Antonio, within about five hundred yards of the old Mission Conception. The face of the plain in our front was nearly level, and the timbered land adjoining it formed two sides of a triangle, both of which were as nearly equal as possible; and, with the exception of two places, a considerable bluff of from six to ten feet sudden fall in our rear, and a bottom of fifty to one hundred yards to the river.

We divided the command into divisions, and occupied each one side of the triangle, for the encampment on the night of the 27th, Captain Fannin's company being under cover of the south side, forming the first division, and Captains Coleman, Goheen, and Bennet's companies (making in all only forty-one, rank and file) occupied the north side, under the immediate command of myself (James Bowie, aide-de-camp).

Thus the men were posted, and lay on their arms during the night of the 27th, having out strong picket guards, and one of seven men in the cupola of the Mission-house, which overlooked the whole country, the horses being all tied up.

The night passed quietly off, without the least alarm; and at dawn of day, every object was obscured by a heavy, dense fog, which entirely prevented our guard, or look-out from the Mission, seeing the approach of the enemy.

At about half an hour by sun, an advanced guard of their cavalry rode upon our line, and fired at a sentinel who had just been relieved, who returned the fire, and caused one platoon to retire; but another charged on him (Henry Karnes), and he discharged a pistol at them, which had the same effect.

The men were called to arms; but were for some time unable to discover their foes, who had entirely surrounded the position, and kept up a constant firing, at a distance, with no other effect than a waste of ammunition on their part. When the fog rose, it was apparent to all that we were surrounded, and a desperate fight was inevitable, all communications with the main army being cut off. Immediate preparation was made, by extending our right flank (first division) to the south, and placing the second division on the left, on the same side, so that they might be enabled to rake the enemy's, should they charge into the angle, and prevent the effects of a cross-fire of our own men; and, at the same time, be in a compact body, contiguous to each other, that either might reinforce the other, at the shortest notice, without crossing the angle, in an exposed and uncovered ground, where certain loss must have resulted. The men, in the mean time, were ordered to clear away bushes and vines, under the hill and along the margin, and at the steepest places to cut steps for foot-hold, in order to afford them space to form and pass, and at suitable places ascend the bluff, discharge their rifles, and fall back to reload. The work was not completed to our wish, before the infantry were seen to advance, with arms trailed, to the right of the first division, and form the line of battle at about two hundred yards distance from the right flank. Five companies of their cavalry supported them, covering our whole front and flanks. Their infantry was also supported by a large force of cavalry.

In this manner, the engagement commenced at about the hour of eight o'clock, A.M., on Wednesday, 28th of October, by the deadly crack of a rifle from the extreme right. The engagement was immediately general. The discharge from the enemy was one continued blaze of fire, whilst that from our lines, was more slowly delivered, but with good aim and deadly effect, each man retiring under cover of the hill and timber, to give place to others, whilst he reloaded. The battle had not lasted more than ten minutes, before a brass double fortified four-pounder was opened on our line with a heavy discharge of grape and canister, at the distance of about eighty yards from the right flank of the first division, and a charge sounded. But the cannon was cleared, as if by magic, and a check put to the charge. The same experiment was resorted to, with like success, three times, the division advancing under the hill at each fire, and thus approximating near the cannon and victory. "The cannon and victory" was truly the war-cry, and they only fired it five times, and it had been three times cleared, and their charge as often broken, before a disorderly and precipitate retreat was sounded, and most readily obeyed, leaving to the victors their cannon. Thus a small detachment of ninety-two men gained a most decisive victory over the main army of the central government, being at least four to one, with only the loss of one brave soldier (Richard Andrews), and none wounded: whilst the enemy suffered in killed and wounded near one hundred, from the best information we can obtain, which is entitled to credit; say sixty-seven killed, among them many promising officers. Not one man of the artillery company escaped unhurt.

No insidious distinction can be drawn between any officer or private, on this occasion. Every man was a soldier, and did his duty, agreeably to the situation and circumstances under which he was placed.

It may not be amiss here to say, that near the close of the engagement another heavy piece of artillery was brought up, and fired thrice, but at a distance; and by a reinforcement of another company of cavalry, aided by six mules, ready harnessed, they got it off. The main army reached us in about one hour after the enemy's retreat. Had it been possible to communicate with you, and brought you up earlier, the victory would have been decisive, and Bejar ours before twelve o'clock.

With sentiments of high consideration, we subscribe ourselves,

Yours, most respectfully,
James Bowie, Aid-de-Camp. [RUBRIC]
J. W. Fannin, Commandant, first division.[RUBRIC]
General S. F. Austin

Death of the Lion

The Texas leadership during the Texas War for Independence was fractured. It is hard to discuss because these men have become heroes to the country and especially to their fellow Texans.

On November 3, 1835, fifty-five delegates from the thirteen municipalities of Texas elected a provisional government. Stephen F. Austin lost by nine votes. He resigned his commission as Commander-in-Chief of the army and was replaced by Sam Houston.

The powers of the provisional government were so poorly defined that no one really knew what the limits were, or for that matter, their jobs. This, then, became a free-for-all with everyone trying to gain power for themselves without really thinking about the responsibility that went with the power they craved.—A.J.S.

Sam Houston

James Bowie came before the government to plead for a battlefield commission. Houston has never heard such a brilliant oratory. Bowie, who never spoke about himself, gave all his qualifications. He spoke of the Battle of Concepción, and the Grass Fight. He explained his tactics and strategy. He described battles with Indians and Bandits.

For one hour there was not one person who could not see Bowie battling the enemies of Texas with intellect as well as great natural fighting ability. Yet, they turned him down. Jim Bowie received no commission.

Captain Fannin, his co-commander, received a colonelcy,

and that boastful bombastic Travis got himself a lieutenant-colonel's rank, but Bowie was only offered thanks.

Houston had no openings himself for field command, but to keep Jim Bowie's talents Houston said, "Jim, Houston can put you on his staff. You'll be a full colonel of Texas and not just a colonel of rangers."

"No thanks, Sam. My brothers have always done the paperwork. I travel . . . I fight . . . I kill." His voice was husky with emotion. "Sam, I've lost my family, my biggest land deal was lost in the courts, and now the thing I want to do most is prove myself. I've never talked about myself, or what I've done. My father told me a gentleman never does. I just did, and they rejected me."

"Jim, if you don't blow the bugle about yourself, no one will ever do it for you . . ." I looked into his eyes, saw the hurt there, and knew that I couldn't let my tendency for showmanship hurt my friend further. "Except maybe Houston. Maybe Houston could talk to them, but that damn Wyatt Hanks, the Chairman of Military Affairs, hates Houston, and will do his best to stop Houston from getting the good men."

"I appreciate Houston's good will. If my friend Sam and his *amigo* Houston would walk over to the tavern, Jim Bowie, he, himself, and I will buy those two big-talking sons of Texas a few drinks."

Bowie turned his head, coughing, his face cording from the effort. He swallowed and grinned. Houston accepted with alacrity. Houston may be a showman and a big talker, but he is most certainly not a fool.

Sam Docker

Sam Docker was a sickly young man who came to Texas for his health on the advice of his doctors. He was one of the secretaries at the Brazos meeting when Bowie pleaded his case for a colonelcy in the Texas Army. Bowie spoke long and eloquently and although no official record of his speech remains, Docker jotted down as much of it as he could. Docker later died of consumption while traveling from Austin to Waco.—A.J.S.

Esteemed sirs. I have never pleaded for justice in my life, preferring, instead, to let justice serve blindfolded to pomp and circumstance. Lately, I have been the recipient of scurrilous speculation in regards to my loyalty to Texas. My detractors have repeatedly used my Mexican citizenship as proof of my loyalty and where my sympathies lie.

Gentlemen, nothing could be further from the truth. I place my record beside any man's in Texas from Stephen Austin's record to any present in this august body. None here can say that James Bowie has led a double life. None here can accuse me of treasonous acts against the state.

I know what some latecomers to Texas have said about James Bowie. Pirate, blackbirder, knife-fighter, adventurer, confidence man, gambler. I do not pretend that my life has been one of piety and passivity. I am cut from the same mold like Achilles and like Achilles I have chosen a short but adventurous life, if the Fates allow choice, to that of more platonic bends.

I do not pretend to be anything more than what I am, and I am what Texas desperately needs at this moment. You may detest the life that I have lived, yet you cannot but recognize the value that such a life has to Texas now. I do not ask for anything that is not in your power to grant: only the rank that will allow me the right to recruit more people like me to make a battalion of men willing to fight for their independence.

Many of you are aware that while you were raising children and crops, I, along with several friends who were wifeless and childless, formed a company of men to keep the frontier safe from attack by the savages. We stood between many a settler and annihilation time and time again.

Many of you are aware of my holdings of which I have oft been accused of turning to profit, yet the same number of you are aware that upon much of that land I have allowed people to settle and work, taking a pittance for the price of the land in exchange for giving them homes.

Many of you are aware that I have fought renegades and given money to help those who have been wiped out by the disasters of God and His horsemen without the slightest hesitation or equivocation whatsoever, knowing only that here was a man in need.

Yes, of this you are aware, yet many of you have also taken sides with those detractors of mine who swish through salons, bearing their honor in words instead of deeds, curling their lips at the mention of my name and repeatedly stating their opinion of my character. I do not choose to answer them with words, but am willing to meet any upon a field of honor.

Here, there appears to be a large gap in time.—A. J. S.

. . . although this body has seen fit to place such honors upon men such as William Travis, whose own character could be held to question and proven by his doctor.

Gentlemen, my blood is in the soil of Texas . . .

A rather lengthy passage here has been rendered unreadable by water.—A. J. S.

I therefore beg of you, sirs, to grant my petition for appointment to the rank of Colonel without pay in order that I may use that rank in the fight for the independence of Texas and freedom. Thank you.

John Henry Brown

We have to turn to John Henry Brown in order to get a feel for the full flavor of Bowie's speech. Brown was one of Bowie's friends who stayed with him through his mourning period following the death of his wife and children. That was a true test of friendship as Bowie's personality changed radically. He became sullen and morose and highly argumentative. Yet Brown, who traveled the Mississippi with Bowie in 1829 and ate and drank with him on several of his adventures, refused to give up on the man he had known. Brown was with Bowie when he made his appeal.—A. J. S.

Stepping inside the railing, hat in hand, with a dignified bow Bowie addressed the council for an hour. He reviewed the salient points of his life, hurled from him with indignation every floating allegation affecting his character as a man of peace and honor, admitted that he was an unlettered man of the Southwest, and his lot had been cast in a day and among a people rendered necessarily, from political and material causes, more or less independent of law, but generous and scornful of every species of meanness and duplicity.

He said that he had cast his lot with Texas for honorable and patriotic purposes; that he had ever neglected his own affairs to serve the country in an hour of danger, had betrayed no man, deceived no man, wronged no man, and had never had a difficulty in the country, unless to protect the weak from the strong and evil-intentioned. That, yielding

> The elected representatives who met to debate the need for a constitution and army for Texas became known as the Consultation and not the Congress in order to distinguish them from that of the United States.

to the dictates of his own heart, he had taken to his bosom as a wife a true and lovely woman of a different race, the daughter of a distinguished "Coahil-Texano"; yet, as a thief in the night, death had invaded his home and taken his wife, his little ones, and his father-in-law; and now, standing alone of all his blood in Texas, all he asked was the privilege of serving it in the field, where his name, so frequently besmirched by double-dealing, unspeakable cowards, might be honorably associated with the brave and true.

Not an indecorous or undignified word fell from his lips—he made not an ungraceful movement or gesture—but stood there before the astonished council, the living exemplification of a natural orator.

He tarried not, but turned immediately and left the chamber, satisfied that he would receive generous consideration, and returned to San Antonio. In that memorable December, 1835, Bowie finally received his Colonel's commission.

There are conflicting stories as to where Bowie was during the storming of Bexar. My grandfather, however, claimed that Bowie was at the battle. None of these are clear enough to add to this account of Bowie's life, but it was true that Austin had sent Bowie to Goliad on the third, two days before the attack.—A. J. S.

Sam Houston

The council is a constant thorn in the side of the army. They have just classified a new term. Military agent is a person given rank in the army by the council. This agent can serve as a battlefield officer, but is not responsible to the military commander-in-chief. How can those fools think this will keep Santa Anna from re-taking Texas?

Proposal from John Grant of Matamoros to the Council of Texas

As is well-known to the council, Santa Anna is a tyrant who has destroyed the Constitution of 1824. In so doing he has left himself and Mexico open to brave-hearted individuals who would free the land and the people of other parts of Mexico.

There is nothing as beautiful, nor as rich as the Coahuila. The spoils that could come from the towns of Nuevo León, Tamaulipas, and San Luis Potosí would greatly enrich the coffers of the new Republic you have begun.

An attack on Matamoros would be the beginning of a financially secure Texas.

From Sam Houston's Diary

After tremendous and futile argument, Houston has been ordered to take Matamoros. Houston cannot refuse any more if he expects any cooperation from the council in the future, and so he must choose an able commander.

The only choice is Jim Bowie. There is no one who can touch him for promptitude and manliness. Above all he is valued by Houston for his forecast, prudence and valor. Houston will draft orders for Bowie and give him his rank.

Houston does hope that his cough has cleared up. Texas cannot afford a sick Jim Bowie.

Bowie never received the letter, or at least received it too late. Frank Johnson led the army toward Matamoros, and Bowie on January 12 was told in no uncertain tones that he was not an officer of the government nor of the army.—A. J. S.

Sam Houston

Houston was telling Bowie of his problems with the Alamo. When Johnson left to attack Mexico, thus turning our rebellion into an outright theft, he stripped the garrison of every blanket, horse, most of the shot and powder, and left eighty sick or wounded to protect the city we spent so much blood to take.

Lieutenant-Colonel Neill has asked for men. Houston told Bowie about this when he found him, trying to staunch his cough with sips of whiskey.

"Houston has no extra men, so he will send orders to Neill to destroy the fortification. That damn Johnson and his raid . . ."

"I'll go, Sam," Bowie said. "Give me a chance to ask for volunteers, and we'll go see what we can do."

On 17 January, Jim Bowie left Goliad with thirty volunteers to deliver orders to destroy the Alamo.

Lieutenant-Colonel Neill

I do not believe that Houston wants to give up the fort without a fight. Though we are short of cannon, men and supplies, we are Texans and we can hold this fort against any force of Mexicans.

> Much speculation has been held about the generous
> benefactor who loaned Bowie the five hundred dol-
> lars. A scrap of a letter from Noah Smithwick to A. J.
> Sowell names the man as Juan Seguín.

James Bonham

We will pass a resolution to Governor Smith. We will hold
the Alamo. James Bowie concurs and will be the second to
sign the resolution.

The men have demanded $500 from the council. Bowie
knows without a doubt that they will not send the money
quickly, if at all, so he will arrange a loan for the sake of
the rebellion.

Citizens and Soldiers of San Antonio de Béxar
to Council, San Felipe

At a large and respectable meeting of the citizens and
soldiers of this place, held this 26th day of January 1836,
to take into consideration the recent movements at San
Felipe, James C. Neill was called to the chair, and H. J.
Williamson appointed secretary. The object of the meeting
having been stated by the chair, on motion of Col. J. B.
Bonham, a committee of seven was appointed to draft a
preamble and resolutions for the consideration of the meet-
ing; whereupon the following were appointed by the chair.
Chairman of Committee J. B. Bonham. James Bowie, G. B.
Jameson, Doctor Pollard, Jesse Badgett, J. W. Seguín, Don
Gasper Flores.

Preamble

Whereas we have been informed from an undoubted messenger that the Executive Council and its President, a subordinate and the auxiliary department of the government, have usurped the right of impeaching the governor who, (if we would imitate the wise institutions of the land of Washington) can only be impeached by a body set forth in the constitution which constitution must have been established by the people through their representatives assembled in general convention. Moreover, the said council and its president, whose powers are defined to aid the governor fulfilling the measures and objects adopted by the general' consultation, have taken it upon themselves to annul the measures of the said general consultation. They are about to open the land offices, which were temporarily closed until a general convention of the people should take place, thereby opening a door to private speculation, at the expense of the men who are serving their country in the field. Moreover the said council have improperly used, and appropriated to their own purposes a FIVE HUNDRED DOLLAR LOAN, from a generous and patriotic citizen of the United States intended to pay the soldiers in the garrison of Bexar. Moreover, that private and designing men are, and have been embarrassing the governor, the legitimate officer of the government, by usurping, contrary to all notions of order and good government, the right of publicly and formally instructing and advising the governor and the people on political, civil and institutional matters subject. Moreover that a particular individual has gone so far as to issue a proclamation on the site of public affairs, and to invite volunteers to join him as the commander of the Matamoros expedition, when that particular individual must have known that General Houston the commander in chief of all the land forces in the service of Texas has been ordered by the government to take command of that expedition. This particular individual is also fully aware, that all officers under the commander in chief are elected by the volunteers themselves, and that therefore there was neither room nor necessity for another appointment by the council. Still in the possession of these facts, he has issued his proclamation, and continues to aid all those who are embarrassing the executive.

Therefore, be it resolved 1st That we will support his excellency Governor Smith in his unyielding and patriotic efforts to fulfill the duties, and to preserve the dignity of his office, while promoting the best interests of the country and people, against all usurpations and the designs of selfish and interested individuals.

Resolved 2nd That all attempts of the president and members of the executive council, to annul the acts of, or to embarrass the officers appointed by the general convention are deemed by this meeting as anarchical assumptions of power to which we will not submit.

Resolved 3rd That we invite a similar expression of sentiment from the army under Gen. Houston, and throughout the country generally.

Resolved 4th That the conduct of the president and members of the Executive Council in relation to the FIVE HUNDRED DOLLAR LOAN, for the liquidation of the claims of the soldiers of Bexar, is in the highest degree criminal and unjust. Yet under treatment however illiberal and ungrateful, we cannot be driven from the Post of Honor and the sacred cause of freedom.

Resolved 5th That we do not recognize the illegal appointments of agents and officers, made by the president and members of the Executive council in relation to the Matamoros Expedition; since their power does not extend further than to take measures and to make appointments for the public service with the sanction of the governor.

Resolved 6th That the Governor Henry Smith will please to accept the gratitude of the army at this Station, for his firmness in the execution of his trust, as well as for his patriotic exertions in our behalf.

Resolved 7th That the Editors of the *Brazoria Gazette*, the *Nacogdoches Telegraph* and the *San Felipe Telegraph* be requested, and they are hereby requested to publish the proceedings of this meeting.

Lieutenant-Colonel Neill

Colonel James Bowie has been of vast help. Since he has been here he has been able to gain supplies and much valuable information from the Mexican populace. They seem to love him. A day does not go by when someone comes to see Don Jaime, and the troop movements of the Mexican army are somehow brought into the conversation.

James Bowie to Governor Henry Smith

BEXAR: Sir: In pursuance of your orders, I proceeded from San Felipe to La Bahia and whilst there employed my whole time in trying to effect the objects of my mission. You are aware that Gen. Houston came to La Bahia soon after I did, this is the reason why I did not make a report to you from that post. The Comdr. in Chf. has before this communicated to you all matters in relation to our military affairs at La Bahia, this makes it wholly unnecessary for me to say any thing on the subject. Whilst at La Bahia General Houston received dispatches from Col. Comdt. Neill that good reasons were entertained that an attack would soon be made by a numerous Mexican army on our important post at Bexar. It was forthwith determined that I should go instantly to Bexar; accordingly I left Gen. Houston and with a few very efficient volunteers came on to this place about 2 weeks since. I was received by Col. Neill with great cordiality, and the men under my command entered at once into active service. All I can say of the soldiers stationed here is complimentary to both their courage and their patience. But it is the truth and your Excellency must know it, that great and just dissatisfaction is felt for the want of a little money to pay the small but necessary expenses of our men. I cannot eulogize the conduct & character of Col. Neill too highly: no other man in the army could have kept men at this post, under the neglect they have experienced. Both he & myself have done all that we could;

we have industriously tried all expedients to raise funds; but hitherto it has been to no purpose. We are still laboring night and day laying up provisions for a siege, encouraging our men, and calling on the government for relief.

Relief at this post in men, money, and provisions is of vital importance and is wanted instantly. So this is the real reason of my letter. The salvation of Texas depends in great measure in keeping Bejar out of the hands of the enemy. It serves as the frontier piquet guard and if it were in the possession of Santa Anna there is no strong hold from which to repel him in his march towards the Sabine. There is no doubt but very large forces are being gathered in several of the towns beyond the Rio Grande, and the late information through Senr. Cassiana & others, worthy of credit, is positive in the fact that 16 hundred or two thousand troops with good officers, well armed and plenty of provisions, were on the point of marching, (the provisions being cooked &c). A detachment of active young men from the volunteers under my command have been sent to the Rio Frio; they returned yesterday without information and we remain yet in doubt whether they intend to attack on this place or go to reenforce Matamoros. It does, however, seem certain that an attack is shortly to be made on this place, and I think it is the general opinion that the enemy will come by land. The citizens of Bexar have behaved well. Colonel Neill and myself have come to the solemn resolution that we will rather die in these ditches than give up this post to the enemy. These citizens deserve our protection and the public safety demands our lives rather than to evacuate this post to the enemy.—again we call aloud for relief; the weakness of our post will at any rate bring the enemy on, some volunteers are expected: Capt Patton with 5 or 6 has come in. But a large reinforcement with provisions is what we need.

James Bowie [RUBRIC]

P.S. I have information just now from a friend whom I believe that the force at the Rio Grande (Presidia) is two thousand complete; he states further that five thousand are a little back and marching on, perhaps the 2 thousand will wait for a junction with the 5 thousand. This information is corroborated with all that we have heard. The informant says that they intend to make a decent on this place in particular, and there is no doubt of it.

Our force is very small, the returns this day to the Comdt. is only one hundred and twenty officers & men. It would be a waste of men to put our brave little band against thousands.

We have no interesting news to communicate. The army have elected two gentlemen to represent the Army & trust they will be received.

James Bowie [RUBRIC]

Enrique Esparza

My mother sold beef, tamales and beans to the Texans. I helped her to carry the earthen jars full of food. It was a heavy task at times. One day I was carrying a jar along the log that made a footbridge over the San Antonio River, I slipped and fell into the deep water. Señor Bowie jumped in and brought me out. I could swim from the time I was four years old. This day I think I struck the log in falling, as I was very bloody. I was very fond of Señor Bowie after this. Señor Bowie had no family. Why? Sra. Veramendi and her two children had died. He was a very sad man.

Andrew J. Sowell (My Grandfather)

I was walking with Jim Bowie one day close to the San Antonio River. Jim was in a curious mood. He was organizing the defense of the Alamo, and there wasn't much of anything to defend with. Jim did have a temper, though he hid it most of the time, and this made it just that much worse when it finally exploded. Kind of like a big old Dutch boiler without a steam release valve.

Because he was thinking so hard, I was just quietly walking with him. We stopped for a moment by the footbridge. One of the little Mexican boys was trying to cross while carrying a big old pot of water.

It was somewhat comical watching this little boy, no mor'n three feet tall, wrestling the pot that was probably two foot or two and a half. Then, he fell. I laughed knowing these boys could swim almost from the time they could walk, but the boy wasn't swimming.

Jim tossed his hat down, ripped off his jacket and hit the water. He found the boy and dragged him out. The boy must have hit his head, cause it was bleeding freely from the scalp as Jim pulled him to shore.

Jim started coughing, but he turned around and hit the river again and dived for that darned pot.

"What are you doing?" I asked him, being a little upset at him being in that cold water a second time.

"The boy'll get in trouble if he don't bring home the pot," Jim said. "His folks work hard, but they don't have much."

"Jim, you've already got a cough. We'd best get you a drink to warm you from the inside out."

And after we got the boy home, that's just what we did.

James Bonham, 17 February 1836

Lt.-Col. Neill has left for a furlough. Lt.-Col. Travis has taken his place. Bowie and Travis argue.

The Private Journal of W. Barret Travis

Bowie is insufferable. The ass believes that his Colonelcy in the Texas Rangers a group formed without any official sanction makes him my superior. When Col Neill left due to an illness in his family, he left me in charge, at which point Bowie, fresh from his bottle, said, "Now hear me, Col Neill, I'm not taking any orders from a 26 year old kid." Several of Bowie's men shouted angrily that they concurred with this at which point I ordered an election, under the impression that any wise individual would not elect to be led by a drunkard and buffoon.

The election has been held, and I have been ousted from my command. This is truly incomprehensible. That drunken knifefighter has done the impossible and stolen my command. But I should not have been surprised. When Colonel Neill left, he made the announcement that "due to illness in my family, I find it necessary to return home. Therefore, I am transferring command of this fort to Lieutenant Colonel Travis." A great silence followed his announcement, then Bowie, fired well with his morning drink, shouted, "Now hear me, Colonel Neill, I'm not taking any orders from a twenty-six year old kid!"

The rest of Bowie's men raised their own voice in indignation. At last, I stepped in and said that a vote had to be taken. My fault. I should have known that the men would prefer the drunken Bowie to me. As he left, Colonel Neill said, "Very well, gentlemen, all regular army troops will be under Lieutenant Colonel Travis, and all volunteers will be under the command of Jim Bowie, except for the Tennessee Volunteers. They will be under Colonel Crockett."

Three commanders. This must be how Rome fell.

I have sent a missive to the council. Bowie in a drunken folly has freed all the prisoners in town. He has threatened the duly constituted law and even threatened to destroy the jail because one prisoner was returned to his incarceration. The council must act and this loudmouthed bully must be removed if I am to save this fortress for Texas.

William B. Travis to His Excellency Henry Smith

BEJAR: I wrote you an official letter last night as Comdt. of this post in the absence of Col Neill & if you had taken the trouble to answer my letter from Burnam's I should not now have been under the necessity of troubling you—My situation is truly awkward & delicate—Col Neill left me in the command—but wishing to give satisfaction to the volunteers here & not wishing to assume any command over them I issued an order for the election of an officer to command them with the exception of one under me. Bowie was elected by two small company's & since his election he has been roaring drunk all the time; has assumed all command & is proceeding in a most disorderly & irregular manner—interfering with private property, releasing prisoners sentenced by court-martial & by the civil court & turning everything topsy turvey—If I did not feel my honor & that of my country compromised I would leave here instantly for some other point with the troops under my command—as I am unwilling to be responsible for the drunken irregularities of any man. I hope you will immediately order some regular troops to this place—as it is more important to occupy this Post than I imagined when I last saw you—It is the key of Texas from the Interior without a footing here the enemy can do nothing against us in the colonies now that our coast is guarded by armed vessels—I do not solicit the command of this post but as Col Neill has applied to the commander in chief to be relieved and is anxious for me to take command, I will do it by your order for a time until an artillery officer can be sent here. The citizens here have every confidence in me, & they have shown every disposition to aid me with all they have—we much need money—can you not send us some? I read your letter to the troops & made a speech & they received it with acclamation—our spies have just returned from the Rio Grande—the enemy is there one thousand strong & is making every preparation to invade us. By the 15th of March I think Texas will be invaded & every preparation should be made to receive them. E. Smith will call on you & give you all the news—so will Mr Williams the Bearer of this—

In conclusion, allow me to beg that you will give me definite orders—immediately—

W. Barret Travis [RUBRIC]

P.S. This is a private letter & is to Nibbs for fear it may fall into bad hands.

The Private Journal of W. Barret Travis

The council will waver, and the difficulty between myself and Bowie will not be resolved. This will cause too many insurmountable problems if the Mexicans attack. We have agreed on a compromise that will give him the volunteers and me the regulars and the cavalry. We will sign orders for the command jointly and so the defense of the Alamo will continue.

Antonio López de Santa Anna

Santa Anna was born in Jalapa, Mexico. He entered the military when be was sixteen and by 1833, twenty-three years later, he was president of Mexico. Once in power, Santa Anna quickly revealed himself to be a despot. When Texas proclaimed itself as a Republic, Santa Anna installed Gomez Pedraza as president to serve until January 1833 when national elections would again be held. He then quickly gathered an army and, placing himself in charge, led it into Texas. Vain and arrogant, he called himself the "Napoleon of the West" and adopted Napoleon's mannerisms and dress. One of Santa Anna's hidden secrets was that he was related to Bowie through marriage. He was, in effect, and according to Mexican custom and law, Bowie's second cousin.—A. J. S.

On the 23rd of this month [February] I occupied this city [San Antonio], after some forced marches from Rio Grande, with General D. Joaquin Ramírez y Sesma's division composed of the permanent battalions of Matamoros and Jiménez, the active battalion of San Luis Potosí, the regiment of Dolores, and eight pieces of artillery.

With the speed in which this meritorious division executed its marches in eighty leagues of road, it was believed that the rebel settlers would not have known of our proximity until we should have been within rifleshot of them; as it was they only had time to hurriedly entrench themselves in Fort Alamo, which they had well fortified, and with a sufficient food supply. My objective had been to surprise them early in the morning of the day before, but a heavy rain prevented it.

Notwithstanding their artillery fire, which they began immediately from the indicated fort, the national troops took possession of this city with the utmost order, which the traitors shall never again occupy; on our part we lost a corporal and a scout, dead, and eight wounded.

When I was quartering the corps of the division a bearer of the flag of truce presented himself with a paper, a copy of which I am enclosing, and becoming indignant of its contents I ordered my nearest aide to answer it.

Fifty rifles of the rebel traitors of the North fell into our hands and I ordered their delivery to the general commissary of the army.

From the moment of my arrival, I was kept busy hostilizing the enemy in its position, so much so that they were not even allowed to raise their heads over the walls, preparing everything for the assault which I had determined would take place when the first brigade arrived. At the time, it was sixty leagues away.

As to the matter of James Bowie, I took great pains to make sure that our relationship did not become known. I had vehemently opposed his marriage into the family, so much so that after the wedding, I received a letter from Ursula's father forbidding me to visit in San Antonio. I was shocked that Señor Veramendi would cast me out of the family in favor of this *gringo* and outraged that I would be forbidden to even visit the city in which they resided.

I dashed off a quick letter to Juan Martín, my cousin by marriage, complaining of this harsh treatment. But he never returned an answer to me.

Yes, I knew Bowie was in the Alamo, and yes, I must admit that I took great pleasure in knowing that I had him within my grasp and that I controlled his destiny.

COMMANDANCY OF BEXAR: We have removed all the men to the Alamo where we make such resistance as is due our honor, and that of the country, until we can get assistance from you, which we expect you to forward immediately. In this extremity, we hope you will send us all the men you can spare promptly. We have one hundred and forty six men, who are determined never to retreat. We have but little provisions, but enough to serve us till you and your men arrive. We deem it unnecessary to repeat to a brave officer, who knows his duty, that we call on him for assistance.

James Bowie to Commander of the Army of Texas [Mexican]

Commander of the Army of Texas:

Because a shot was fired from a cannon of this fort at the time a red flag was raised over the tower, and a little afterward they told me that a part of your army had sounded a parley, which was not heard before the firing of the shot. I wish, Sir, to ascertain if it be true that a parley was called, for which reason I send my second aid, Benito Jameson, under guarantee of a white flag, which I believe will be respected by you and your forces. God and Texas.

Fortress of the Alamo, February 23, 1836

James Bowie

Commander of the volunteers of Bexar to the Commander of the invading forces below Bexar

José Batres to James Bowie

As the Aide-de Camp of his Excellency, the President of the Republic, I reply to you, according to the order of his Excellency, that the Mexican army cannot come to terms under any conditions with rebellious foreigners to whom there is no other recourse left, if they wish to save their lives, than to place themselves immediately at the disposal of the Supreme Government from whom alone they may expect clemency after some considerations are taken up. God and Liberty!

José Batres to James Bowie

General Headquarters of San Antonio de Béxar.

Feb. 23, 1836

Dr. John Sutherland

Dr. Amos Pollard, the doctor in the Alamo, called me in for a consultation on Jim Bowie shortly before Santa Anna got there with his men. Bowie had been coughing up blood for quite some time. He tried to stem it with alcohol, a prodigious amount of alcohol, I must say, but that only gave him temporary relief. When I examined him, Bowie's eyes had a dangerous yellow cast to them of a peculiar nature. I could see that whatever ailed him would not be cured by an ordinary course of treatment. Frankly, I believe Bowie had an advanced case of consumption complicated with pneumonia he contracted after leading some of the volunteers across a river on a raiding party. Whatever it was, I knew he would not last long and I think Bowie knew it, too. He gave me a bitter smile and shook his head, saying, "Never mind. I'll keep the medicine I've got for now. I don't think I'll be needing it long." I have often thought this was a peculiar if ghastly prophecy. I think Bowie knew his end. It would be within the man to have that knowledge. Death was a familiar *compadre* to him.

Andrew J. Sowell

On 21 Feb. Jim and some of the boys were trying to set a cannon. Jim had been getting sicker and sicker. He was coughing and drinking to stop the cough. He shouldn't have been trying to manhandle that cannon into position, but Jim always was pig-headed that way.

The damn breastwork collapsed on Jim. He broke some ribs and his hip. Along with his cough and general weakness from that cold he caught in the river that day he saved the boy, he was no good as an active soldier. We confined him to his bed. Madame Candelaria agreed to do for him until he was well again.

On 2 March I saw Jim Bowie for the last time. I was headed out on a cattle drive. I went into Jim's room. He was burning up with fever, but people kept coming in and out, and Jim was working on pure guts.

Juan Seguín

I, as captain of Cavalry and scouts, went by to see Don Jaime. I was being sent as courier with Bowie's request for more men and supplies. Pero, my horse, was windbroken, and Jaime had a fine horse that was not doing anything important while my friend was sick.

He smiled as he saw me. *"Juan, bien de verte."* The great man was sunken to a shadow.

"I travel with your requests, and my horse is not in the best of shape."

"Take my horse. He needs a good run. Just don't let the Mexican troops take him. He is good for little, but I have grown fond of him." He looked at me for a second and then continued, "I have sent my niece and her family away, Juan."

"Porqué?"

"I don't think I can defend this place. Or them."

He fumbled beside his bed and picked up a knife from among those there and handed it to me. It is a thing of beauty. I no longer carry it, but display it with honor, but then all I could do was blink away the salty tears from my eyes. "Jamie . . ."

"Take it, Juan," he said faintly. "I have not forgotten the loan you made, the five hundred dollars. I regret that I cannot repay you nor honor Texas's debt to you, but . . ." He coughed and I turned away so that I would not see his weakness. When I turned back, there were no more words to be spoken between us. The debt, he knew, had been settled as far as I was concerned. He shook hands, but the strength that was once there was gone. I never saw my good friend again, and as I left his room, I heard the sickening sound of his lungs bursting from him as he coughed so hard his breathing halted and the gasps were so weak I thought he might expire even as I left.

This was not the way I wanted to remember my friend from *Los Leoncitos*.

Joe, Slave of Travis Who Accompanied Travis into the Alamo

Much controversy surrounds Bowie's death. The following is a report given by Joe, who survived the battle, to George C. Childress, the editor of the Nashville Banner. *Childress was present at Washington-on-the-Brazos when Joe delivered his account of the final battle to Houston and his staff. I do not know if Joe could read or write, but I do know that he would not have delivered the following in as florid a style as it appears. That style undoubtedly belongs to Childress. We must also be careful to remember that Childress was an editor and probably took great editorial leeway with the account, honing it to serve his own purposes, whatever they were at the time.—A. J. S.*

Well, sir, the Honorable Davy Crockett died like a hero, surrounded by heaps of the enemy slain. Colonel James Bowie was sick and unable to rise. He was slain in his bed: the enemy allowed him a grave—probably in consideration of his having been married to a Mexican lady, a daughter of the late Governor Veramendi. The enemy had made daily and nightly attacks upon the place for ten days. The garrison was exhausted by incessant watching; at last the enemy made a final assault with 4000 men, half an hour before daylight, on the morning of the 6th instant. It was dark, and the enemy were undiscovered until they were close to the walls, and before the sentinels had aroused the garrison, the enemy had gained possession of a part of the ramparts. The garrison fought like men who knew there was but a brief space left them in which to avenge the wrongs of their coun-

try's possession. When driven from the walls by overwhelming numbers, they retired to the barracks, and fought
hand to hand and man to man until the last man was
slain—no, there was a man yet left; a little man named Warner had secreted himself among the dead bodies, and was
found when the battle was over, and the dead men being removed without the walls of the fort. He asked for quarters;
the soldiers took him to Santa Anna, who ordered him to
be shot. The order was executed, and the body was taken
out and burnt with the heroes who deserve as bright a remembrance as those who died on the pass of Thermopylae.

William Fairfax Gray, later associated with the Fredericks-
burg Arena, *was also present when Joe gave his report.
The following is his account of Joe's narrative.*—A. J. S.

The Garrison was much exhausted by hard labor and incessant watching and fighting for thirteen days. The day and
night previous to the attack, the Mexican bombardment had
been suspended. On Saturday night, March 5, the little Garrison had worked hard, in repairing and strengthening
their position, until a late hour. And when the attack was
made, which was just before daybreak, sentinels and all
were asleep, except the officer of the day who was just starting on his round. There were three picket guards without
the Fort; but they too, it is supposed, were asleep, and were
run upon and bayonetted, for they gave no alarm that was
heard. The first Joe knew of it was the entrance of Adjutant
Baugh, the officer of the day, into Travis' quarters, who
roused him with the cry—"The Mexicans are coming."
They were running at full speed with their scaling ladders,
towards the Fort, and were under the guns, and had their
ladders against the wall before the Garrison were aroused
to resistance. Travis sprung up, and seizing his rifle and
sword, called to Joe to take his gun and follow. He mounted

the wall and called out to his men—"Come on Boys, the Mexicans are upon us, and we'll give them Hell." He immediately fired his rifle—Joe followed his example. The fire was returned by several shots, and Travis fell, wounded, within the wall, on the sloping ground that had recently been thrown up to strengthen the wall. There he sat, unable to rise. Joe, seeing his master fall, and the Mexicans coming near the wall, and thinking with Falstaff that the better part of valor is discretion, ran and ensconced himself in a house, from the loop holes of which he says, he fired on them several times after they had come in.

Here Joe's narrative becomes somewhat interrupted; but Mrs. Dickinson, the wife of Lt. D., who was in the Fort at the time, and is now at San Felipe, has supplied some particulars, which Joe's state of retirement prevented him from knowing with perfect accuracy. The enemy three times applied their scaling ladders to the wall; twice they were beaten back. But numbers and discipline prevailed over valor and desperation. On the third attempt they succeeded, and then they came over "like sheep." As Travis sat wounded, but cheering his men, where he first fell, General Mora, in passing, aimed a blow with his sword to despatch him—Travis rallied his failing strength, struck up the descending weapon, and ran his assailant through the body. This was poor Travis' last effort. Both fell and expired on the spot. The battle now became a complete *melee*. Every man fought "for his own hand," with gun-butts, swords, pistols and knives, as best he could. The handful of Americans, not 150 effective men, retreated to such cover as they had, and continued the battle, until only one man, a little weakly body, named Warner, was left alive. He, and he only, asked for quarter. He was spared by the soldiery; but on being conducted to Santa Anna, he ordered him to be shot, which was promptly done. So that not one white man of that devoted band was left to tell the tale.

Crockett, the kind hearted, brave David Crockett, and a few of the devoted friends who entered the Fort with him, were found lying together, with 21 of the slain enemy around them. Bowie is said to have fired through the door of his room, from his sick bed. He was found dead and mutilated where he had lain. The body of Travis, too, was pierced with many bayonet stabs. The despicable Col. Cós, fleshed his dastard sword in the dead body. Indeed, Joe says, the soldiers continued to stab the fallen Americans, until all possibility of life was extinct. Capt. Barragan was the only Mexican officer who showed any disposition to spare the Americans. He saved Joe, and interceded for poor Warner, but in vain. There were several Negroes and some Mexican women in the Fort. They were all spared. One only of the Negroes was killed—a woman—who was found lying dead between two guns. Joe supposes she ran out in her fright, and was killed by a chance shot. Lieut. Dickinson's child was not killed, as was first reported. The mother and child were both spared and sent home. The wife of Dr. Alsbury and her sister, Miss Navarro, were also spared and restored to their father, who lives in Bejar.

The slain were collected in a pile and burnt.

Susanna Dickinson

Susanna Dickinson was the wife of Almeron Dickinson, who served as an artillery officer at the Alamo. She survived the final battle along with her infant daughter, Angelina. When the Mexican soldiers came over the walls, she fled into Bowie's room for protection, huddled in a corner opposite the door. This is her account sent to me shortly before her death in 1883. Her memory had dimmed somewhat over the years, but is still one of the few accounts we have of Bowie's last hour. I do not know if she actually was in the room with Bowie when the Mexican soldiers broke in, but according to Juana Navarro Alsbury, a niece of Governor Veramendi and a cousin to Bowie's wife, she was. The reader must decide if this account of Mrs. Dickinson is the true one or an earlier one in which she claimed to have been taken prisoner while in the chapel. Frankly, I would believe this to be the true account for Bowie, as sick as he was, had the formidable reputation as a fighter. I believe instinct for survival would have driven Mrs. Dickinson to seek him out for protection when she saw the Alamo being captured and all of its defenders massacred.—A. J. S.

Yes, I remember James Bowie. I remember him well as I remember Travis and Crockett who often performed on the violin for us to take our minds off the siege. Bowie was always a gentleman, even at the end when his sickness often made him feverish and sent him out of his mind. I remember listening to him rave about Ursula, calling out to her from his feverish hell for water. At last, Madame Candelaria was brought in to care for him and that account is best left to her.

I remember when the Mexicans, numbering well into the thousands, poured over the wall to kill the one hundred and eighty-two Texan defenders. My husband rushed into the church where I was staying with our child and exclaimed, "Great God, Sue, the Mexicans are inside our walls! All is lost! If they spare you, save our child!"

Then he took his sword and plunged back into the fray, leaving me with three unarmed gunners, one of them named Walker who spoke to me several times during the siege about his wife and four children.

As the Mexicans drew closer to us, two of the gunners found weapons and charged them, fighting desperately to keep them away from us. I picked up my child and told Walker that I was going to Bowie's room. Walker followed me there. So did Juana Alsbury, her eight-year-old son and thirteen-year-old sister.

Bowie was near death when I burst into his room, crying for his help. I remember a faint smile creased his lips, then he turned and said something to Madame Candelaria, but I no longer remember what that was. I huddled in the corner opposite him with Walker in front of me.

When the Mexicans burst into the room, Bowie killed two of them with his pistols and more with his knife before they killed him. Walker tried to keep them from me, but they caught him up on their bayonets and tossed him around like a sheaf of wheat before an officer came in and, addressing me in English, asked: "Are you Mrs. Dickinson?" I answered "Yes." Then said he, "If you wish to save your life, follow me."

He took me to Santa Anna who questioned me about Bowie and Travis. He took great delight when I told him about Bowie's death, but I could tell he would have liked it better if Bowie would have been taken prisoner. I do not know what ever made him think that Bowie would allow that to happen. That just shows the vanity of the man, I guess.

Antonio López de Santa Anna, March 6, 1836

This is the letter that Santa Anna sent back to Mexico City following the final assault on the Alamo. Perhaps it is only fitting that I include it here in order to throw a little light on the complete contempt that Santa Anna had for Bowie and the rest of the defenders of the Alamo by claiming to have killed more defenders than were actually present and severely lowering his number of casualties. The flag to which he makes reference was the Mexican flag with 1823 outline in charcoal and blacking in the middle of the white band. It was made by Mrs. Dickinson and flew over the Alamo until the bitter end.—A. J. S.

Victory belongs to the army, which at this very moment, 8 o'clock A.M., achieved a complete and glorious triumph that will render its memory imperishable.

As I had stated in my report to Your Excellency of the taking of this city, on the 27th of last month, I awaited the arrival of the 1st Brigade of Infantry to commence active operations against the Fortress of the Alamo. However, the whole Brigade having been delayed beyond my expectation, I ordered that three of its Battalions, viz: the Engineers—Aldama and Toluca—should force their march to join me. These troops, together with the Battalions of Matamoros, Jiménez, and San Luis Potosí, brought the force at my disposal, recruits excluded, up to 1400 Infantry. This force, divided into four columns of attack and a reserve, commenced the attack at 5 o'clock A.M. They met with a stubborn resistance, the combat lasting more than one hour and a half, and the reserve having to be brought into action.

The scene offered by this engagement was extraordinary. The men fought individually, vying with each other in heroism. Twenty-one pieces of artillery, used by the enemy with most perfect accuracy, the brisk fire of musketry, which illuminated the interior of the Fortress and its walls and ditches—could not check our dauntless soldiers, who are entitled to the consideration of the Supreme Government and to the gratitude of the nation.

The Fortress is now in our power, with its artillery, stores, &c. More than 600 corpses of foreigners were buried in the ditches and entrenchments, and a great many who had escaped the bayonet of the infantry, fell in the vicinity under the sabres of the cavalry. I can assure Your Excellency that few are those who bore to their associates the tidings of their disaster.

Among the corpses are those of Bowie and Travis, who styled themselves Colonels, and also that of Crockett, and several leading men, who had entered the Fortress with dispatches from their Convention. We lost 70 men killed and 300 wounded, among whom are 25 officers. The cause for which they fell renders their loss less painful, as it is the duty of the Mexican soldier to die for the defense of the rights of the nation; and all of us were ready for any sacrifice to promote this fond object; nor will we, hereafter, suffer any foreigners, whatever their origin may be, to insult our country and to pollute its soils.

I shall, in due time, send to Your Excellency a circumstantial report of this glorious triumph. Now I have only time to congratulate the nation and the President, *ad interim*, to whom I request you to submit this report.

The bearer takes with him one of the flags of the enemy's

Battalions, captured today. The inspection of it will show plainly the true intentions of the treacherous colonists, and of their abettors, who came from parts of the United States of the North. God and Liberty!

Madame Candelaria

We must turn to one of the most colorful individuals to emerge from the Texas Revolution, a Mexican woman named Madame Candelaria, who attended James Bowie during his illness in the final days at the Alamo, to find the truth of what happened in the tiny room where Bowie was taken on his deathbed prior to the final assault. Although no records exist that establish her presence at the Alamo on the thirteenth day when Santa Anna's troops stormed the mission walls, no records exist that refute it either. No detractor, however, can take away her fierce and compassionate dedication to the cause of freedom.

Madame Candelaria was born on November 30, 1785 in Presidio de Rio Grande and moved with her family to San Antonio de Béxar when she was twenty-five, where she was employed as a servant for the wife of Don Manuel Antonio Cordero y Bustamante, the Spanish governor of Texas from 1805 to 1810. Sometime in the 1830s, she married Candelario Villanueva and became known as Madame Candelaria when she opened a small hotel near Alamo Plaza and quickly earned fame for cooking the best Mexican food in town. Her hotel quickly became the meeting place for many, among them David Crockett, Sam Houston, José Antonio Navarro, Placido Benavides, and William B. Travis.

Madame Candelaria hated the Mexican government and Antonio López de Santa Anna with good cause as Santa Anna had been a lieutenant in Joaquín de Arredondo's army of Spanish royalists at the Battle of Medina in 1813 where her then husband, Silberio Flores y Abrigo, a revolutionary who supported the ideologies of Father Miguel Hidalgo, was killed.

Shortly before Santa Anna's army of three thousand arrived at the Alamo, Madame Candelaria received a letter from Sam Houston, asking her to go to the Alamo to care for his sick friend, James Bowie. Houston was unaware of the extent of Bowie's illness, the symptoms resembling those of pleurisy, tuberculosis, or pneumonia.

Madame Candelaria found Bowie lying upon a narrow cot in a small room in the fort, his body wasted from his fever, his breath rattling in his lungs agonizingly slow. Beside him lay a rifle and two pistols given him by Crockett and upon his belly on top of his blanket, his knife.

She stayed by his side day and night throughout the thirteen-day siege, raising his head for sips of water and bathing his forehead in a vain attempt to bring down the fever. She was with him at the end.—A. J. S.

And then the thunder stopped and the bugle blowing the *degüello* stopped. In the distance I heard a few pops like a children's firecracker. The friar's cell felt cold and clammy and I smelled the sickness of Señor Bowie. His eyes looked brightly at the door, his tongue flickering out to wet his cracked lips.

"Come," he whispered. "Come."

He reached out to pick up his pistols, but they were too heavy for his hands and fell back upon the table beside him. He fell back against the cot, groaning from the effort of raising himself for his pistols. He touched a small portrait of his wife, Ursula, that he kept constantly by his bedside, his fingers running over her face. He lifted it, and gently kissed it.

Suddenly, the door flew open and two Mexican soldiers entered. Señor Bowie lunged and grabbed his pistols and shot them. They fell in the doorway and Señor Bowie cried out in pain and fell back on his cot, the pistols falling to the floor. His hands dropped limply upon his blanket, upon his knife.

"Old friend," he said. A ghost of a smile traced his lips. I wiped his forehead with a cold rag. Señora Alsbury ran across the room, pulled the soldiers into the room, and threw the door shut. Suddenly, a great silence fell and I knew we were the last alive in the mission.

"Old friend," he said again. Had the guns not been silent, I would not have been able to hear his words. He rolled his head, facing the doorway, clutching his knife in his hand. He raised the knife, looking at it. The dim light glittered down the edge of the blade. His hand closed tightly upon the wire-wrapped handle.

"Old friend," he whispered, and I heard the words spoken like the words he spoke to his wife and two children the day before when he did not know he was speaking them.

I heard more Mexican soldiers moving down the hall, doors banging open. His eyes glowed brightly, his lips spreading in a smile.

"Hurry," he gasped. His eyes rolled to me, pleading. "Lift . . . me . . . please . . ."

I put my arm under his shoulders and easily lifted him, so wasted was he by sickness. A gout of blood burst from his lips. I turned to get the cloth and wipe them clean.

"Ah . . . You have come . . . *mi compadre* . . . At last," he said.

I turned back, but we were alone in the room. He fell back against the cot. One long, shuddering breath rattled from his lungs.

And he was dead.

The door burst open again and Mexican soldiers crowded cautiously into the room, looking at Señor Bowie upon the bed. A slight smile still hung upon his lips.

"Es el León," someone whispered.

"Es el Diablo," another said. *"El Cuchillo feral."*

"It is only a dead man," yet a third said. He looked down at the knife still clutched in Señor Bowie's hand. "At least, this will be mine."

He tried to pull it from Señor Bowie's hand, but could not. He swore and propped his rifle between his legs to use both hands. Others crowded into the room, bumping him. He lost his grip and Señor Bowie's hand fell back to the blanket, the knife slicing deeply through the man's hand, nearly severing his thumb.

"Ah!" he screamed. "He lives! He lives!"

The others lifted their rifles with the long bayonets upon the end. I threw myself across Señor Bowie, trying to keep his body from being savaged. A bayonet sliced through my upper arm, another through the flesh of my chin. I bear the scars to this day.

Someone pulled me off Señor Bowie's body and threw me into the corner of the cell. They began stabbing him, lifting him finally from his cot and throwing his body up into the air upon their bayonets. Then, they threw him back upon the cot.

"His wounds," someone breathed. "They do not bleed."

"He is not a man," another said.

"El Diablo!" a hushed voice exclaimed.

Some turned and ran from the room. Others crossed themselves and backed away, staring at the dead one upon the cot.

An officer came into the cell and saw me huddled in the corner. He looked at Señor Bowie and shook his head.

"Animals," he said. He turned to those standing back against the wall. "Bring him out with the others." No one moved. "Bring him!" he shouted.

The soldiers moved timidly forward and carried him from the cell. The officer looked down at me.

"Come with me," he ordered. I rose and walked from the room ahead of him.

All was silent now. I heard the bells of San Fernando ringing. The massacre had ended. One hundred and seventy-six of the bravest men the world ever saw had fallen and not one asked for mercy. I walked out of the cell, and when I stepped on the floor of the Alamo, the blood ran into my shoes.

Epilogue

The story is not quite complete with Madame Candelaria's words. After Bowie's death, an auction was held of his belongings. An inventory revealed a Masonic apron of lambskin valued at $4.00, a pair of "crape" pants valued at 50 cents, a blue cloth coat at 13 cents, a blue cloth jacket at 25 cents, a black cloth dress at $2.00, a cotton hunting dress at $1.50, a pair of blue cloth pants at 12 cents, a "casonet" vest at 25 cents, a woman's apron at 25 cents, a pocket wallet at 6 cents, two pocket books at $1.00, a trunk at 25 cents, a "whipsaw" at $6.00, a cross-cut saw at $4.00, two mill saws at $2.00, and 640 acres of land. The auction brought $90.50.

What happened to the rest of Bowie's property is unknown, but without a doubt, Bowie had been one of the richest men in Texas at the time. Surprisingly, deeds to all his Texas land vanished. Some say that John and Rezin Bowie took them, but more than likely Bowie's enemies finally got a piece of him.

I do not believe the account of Bowie's death as given by Apolinario Saldigna, a young Mexican fifer, who claimed that Bowie was captured and taken out to a Captain who ordered Bowie's tongue cut out and had Bowie thrown still alive on top of the funeral pyre. It was not within the man to be taken alive to be ridiculed by his captors. He had too much honor in his soul to allow that to happen.

And so, we come at last to the end of the story of Jim Bowie, not knowing any more than what we had at the beginning. Perhaps that is the way it should be, for to know too much of a man is to eliminate the legend and discover the earth, the clay, in which his feet are mired. We do not need the common man; we need the legend, and the legend exists only in the enigma of what was Jim Bowie. Yes, it is much better this way, for we can all invent what we need from the man.—A. J. S.